DOROTHY M. RICHARDSON

PILGRIMAGE

with an introduction by Gill Hanscombe

IV

Oberland

Dawn's Left Hand

Clear Horizon

Dimple Hill

March Moonlight

T0351949

VIRAGO

TO
J.H.B.

A *Virago* Book

Published by Virago Press 1979
in association with Mrs Sheena Odle
and Mark Paterson & Associates
This edition published by Virago Press 2002

A CIP catalogue record for this book is available
from the British Library

ISBN 0 86068 113 3

Virago Press
An Imprint of
Little, Brown Book Group
100 Victoria Embankment
London EC4Y 0DY

DOROTHY RICHARDSON

was born in 1873. The third of four daughters of an impoverished gentleman, from the age of seventeen she was obliged to earn her own living, which she did initially as a governess-teacher: first in Hanover, then in north London and finally in a country house. In 1895 her mother committed suicide, the family broke up and Dorothy Richardson began a new life in London as secretary assistant to a Harley Street dentist. During her years in London her friends were the socialist and avant garde intellectuals of the day. She became an intimate of H. G. Wells, who, among others, encouraged her to write. She began in journalism and for the rest of her life she lived as a writer, earning very little. In 1917 she married the young painter, Alan Odle, who died in 1948. For the whole of their married life they lived their winters in Cornwall and their summers in London. Dorothy Richardson's journalism includes scores of essays, reviews, stories, poems and sketches written and published between 1902 and 1949. Her journalism was her livelihood but the writing of PILGRIMAGE was her vocation; this long novel absorbed her artistic energy between 1914 and her death in 1957.

PUBLISHING HISTORY

FIRST EDITIONS:
Pointed Roofs (1915), *Backwater* (1916), *Honeycomb* (1917), *The Tunnel* (Feb 1919), *Interim* (Dec 1919), *Deadlock* (1921), *Revolving Lights* (1923), *The Trap* (1925), *Oberland* (1927), *Dawn's Left Hand* (1931) — all published by Duckworth: *Clear Horizon* (1935) — published by J. M. Dent & Cresset Press

COLLECTED EDITIONS:
Pilgrimage (including *Dimple Hill*), 4 vols, 1938 — J. M. Dent & Cresset Press, London: A. Knopf, New York

Pilgrimage (including *March Moonlight*), 4 vols, 1967 — J. M. Dent, London: A. Knopf, New York

Pilgrimage, 4 vols, 1976 — Popular Library, New York

Pilgrimage, 4 vols, 1979 — Virago, London
   Volume 1: *Pointed Roofs, Backwater, Honeycomb*
   Volume 2: *The Tunnel, Interim*
   Volume 3: *Deadlock, Revolving Lights, The Trap*
   Volume 4: *Oberland, Dawn's Left Hand, Clear Horizon, Dimple Hill, March Moonlight*

CONTENTS

INTRODUCTION

OF THE early twentieth-century English modernists, there is no one who has been more neglected than Dorothy Miller Richardson. There are several reasons for this. First, the style she forged in the writing of *Pointed Roofs*, the first volume of the *Pilgrimage* sequence, was new and difficult, later earning the nomination 'stream-of-consciousness'. *Pointed Roofs* was published in 1915 and was, therefore, the first example of this technique in English, predating both Joyce and Woolf, its more famous exponents. Secondly, the thoughts and feelings of its protagonist, Miriam Henderson, are explicitly feminist, not in the sense of arguing for equal rights and votes for women, but in the more radical sense of insisting on the authority of a woman's experience and world view. Thirdly, *Pointed Roofs* explores Miriam's sympathetic response to German culture and in 1915, when it was first published, this was an unpopular subject which contributed to the establishing of adverse critical reaction. Undaunted, however, by ambivalent response to her work, Richardson persisted in her task of completing the *Pilgrimage* sequence, a task which occupied her, intermittently, for the rest of her life.

Richardson regarded *Pilgrimage* as one novel and its constituent thirteen volumes as chapters. She regarded it, also, as fiction, even though the life of Miriam Henderson so closely resembles her own. The reason for this was that Richardson, after many attempts to write a more conventional novel, resolved finally that she must write about the subject she knew best, which was, she maintained, her own life. This is not to claim that every incident and every character in the novel add up to a photographic reproduction of Richardson's early life; but it is to claim that the genuine impulse of her work derives from the tension between her own life and that of Miriam, her fictional *alter ego*. The whole world of *Pilgrimage* is filtered through Miriam's mind alone; the reader sees what she sees and is never told what any of the other characters sees. Fiction usually means that the author invents or imagines his or her material. Richardson used the real material of her own life for her writing, and she used herself as her central character. The fictional process in *Pilgrimage* consists in how she shaped and organised and interpreted that material. There is, therefore, much in her life and personality to lend interest to her work.

She was born in Abingdon, Berkshire, on 17 May 1873, the third of four daughters. Her father, Charles Richardson, came from a family who had achieved financial success through a grocery business, but Charles longed to give up 'trade' and to become a gentleman. He sold the business and lived off the proceeds for some years. His wife, Mary Taylor, came from East Coker in Somerset, from a family whose name was listed among the gentry in local registers. When she was five years old, Dorothy Richardson was sent for a year to a small private school where she learned to read and spell and where nothing else interested her. When she was six, the family moved to the south coast, near Worthing, owing to her mother's ill health and her father's financial straits. Her school made no impression on her. In Dorothy's eleventh year, her father's investments improved and he moved his family up to London. Her life at this stage included croquet, tennis, boating, skating, dances and music; apart from musical evenings at home, she was introduced to the classics, to Wagner and Chopin and to Gilbert and Sullivan. She was taught by a governess, of whom she later wrote: 'if she could, [she] would have formed us to the almost outmoded pattern of female education: the minimum of knowledge and a smattering of various "accomplishments" . . . for me . . . she was torment unmitigated.' After this, she was sent to Southborough House, whose headmistress was a disciple of Ruskin, where the pupils were encouraged to think for themselves. Here Richardson studied French, German, literature, logic and psychology. At this point, her father, through disastrous speculation, lost the greater part of his resources, which forced Richardson at the age of seventeen, to seek employment as a teacher. Her first appointment, in a German school, later provided the material for *Pointed Roofs*.

After six months Richardson returned to England; two sisters were engaged to be married, the third had a position as a governess and her mother was near to a nervous collapse. In order to be near her mother, she took a post at the Misses Ayre's school in Finsbury Park, North London. Her impressions and experiences here provided the material for her second volume, *Backwater*. In 1893,

Charles Richardson was finally made a bankrupt; his house and possessions were sold and the family moved to a house in Chiswick, generously provided by John Arthur Batchelor, who became the husband of Dorothy's eldest sister Kate. By 1895, Richardson had moved from Finsbury Park to a post in the country as governess to two children, her experience of which is recorded in *Honeycomb*, her third volume. On 29 November 1895, while on holiday at Hastings with Dorothy, Mary Richardson committed suicide by cutting her throat with a kitchen knife.

After this, Richardson wanted a complete break: '. . . longing to escape from the world of women, I gladly accepted a post . . . a secretarial job, offering me the freedom I so desired.' She lived in a Bloomsbury attic on a salary of one pound per week. London became her great adventure. During these years she explored the world lying outside the enclosures of social life, which included writers, religious groups from Catholic to Unitarian and Quaker, political groups from the Conservative Primrose League to the Independent Labour Party and the Russian anarchists, and, through books and lectures, science and philosophy. At this time she found the philosophers 'more deeply exciting than the novelists'. These interests and activities provided the contextual material for her subsequent volumes. From working as a secretary, she gradually branched out into translations and freelance journalism which 'had promised release from routine work that could not engage the essential forces of my being. The small writing-table in my attic became the centre of my life'.

As a result of a series of sketches contributed to *The Saturday Review*, a reviewer urged her to try writing a novel. She later wrote that the suggestion 'both shocked and puzzled me. The material that moved me to write would not fit the framework of any novel I had experienced. I believed myself to be . . . intolerant of the romantic and the realist novel alike. Each . . . left out certain essentials and dramatized life misleadingly. Horizontally . . . Always . . . one was aware of the author and applauding, or deploring, his manipulations.' In 1917, at the age of forty-four, she married Alan Odle, an artist many years younger than herself. The marriage, in spite of misgivings, was a happy one, providing her with 'a new world, the missing link between those already explored'. She died in 1957 at the age of eighty-four.

A niece of Alan Odle's, who knew Dorothy Richardson and Alan Odle can add some human detail to this picture. In middle age, Richardson still had a golden heap of very long hair, piled on the top of her head; she had a 'massive' face, dark brown eyes, a clear skin, and pince-nez balanced on her nose, because she was 'always reading'. She created the impression of being tall, because she was 'so stately'. Alan Odle, in fact over six feet tall, was very thin, with waist-length hair wound around the outside of his head. He never cut his hair and rarely his fingernails, but since he had 'beautifully long elegant fingers', the image he presented was not an unattractive one. He, like Dorothy, had dark brown eyes and an ascetic face. They were very controlled together, extremely calm, always sitting side by side. Dorothy talked the most and late into the night; she seemed never to do 'anything ordinary' and had a voice 'like dark brown velvet'. She spoke very slowly indeed and was 'immensely impressive as a person'. Her life seemed to be arranged 'very very carefully' and she was 'not at all spontaneous in her actions'. She could 'only work on a certain image of herself' which was 'very cerebral'. It was hard for her to deal with ordinary people. Although she and Alan were affectionate with each other, they 'didn't touch'. Dorothy always called him 'sergeant', a joke arising from the fact that after only one day's service in the army, he had been discharged on medical grounds. Dorothy, in contrast to Alan, was 'very plump, with white creamy arms and very beautiful hands'; 'as she spoke she would screw up her eyes and slightly purse her mouth and everyone would listen'.

Charles Richardson often called Dorothy his 'son', as a compensation, it seems, for his lack of a male child. Indeed there is the evidence of Richardson's own recollections, as well as the portrayal in *Pilgrimage* of Miriam's relationship with her father, to reinforce the view that much of the original stimulus of the novel was owed to Dorothy's failure to adjust to the feminine role expected of her by late nineteenth-century middle-class society. But was it a failure? Or might it be seen as a triumph? Miriam's pilgrimage is partly the journey towards the resolution of that question. Because Richardson's father used all the family resources, it was necessary for the four daughters to make their own ways and accordingly, at the age of seventeen, Richardson answered an advertisement for an English student-teacher in a German academy for girls. *Pilgrimage* begins at this point, a point at which, for Miriam, the beginning of economic autonomy corresponds with the beginning of autonomous self-consciousness. From this point until her meeting with Alan Odle, Richardson's life is paralleled by that of her protagonist Miriam. The parallels are numerous and strictly consistent, as Richardson's letters and papers confirm.

Consistent with ordinary reality, also, are the descriptions of London life at the turn of the century. And equally convincing are the detailed accounts of households, lectures, activities and even conversations. The precision of Richardson's memory at some twenty to forty years distance is itself remarkable. It should not be assumed, nevertheless, that she saw her function as a writer in traditional autobiographical terms. On the contrary, she always insisted that her task was truly appropriate to fiction and that *Pilgrimage* should be judged as fiction. The mastery with which the author is able to transform the haphazard impressions of subjective experience into a thematically organised psychological narrative is the extent to which this work of fiction achieves artistic integrity.

Miriam's consciousness is the subject matter of this novel. And it seems to her that the experiences and perceptions of women have been brutally and unreasonably discounted by men. Nor has she any mercy for the majority of women who have, in her judgment, colluded with men in the suborning of their female gifts and attributes. Such women are satirised, caricatured and eventually dismissed. On the other hand, her stance is not topical. She does not become a Suffragette. She does not argue for a recognition of the equality of the sexes. She counts it a disadvantage to be a woman only in the sense that the men who govern society refuse to recognise and to allow women's contributions. In all other respects, she affirms, implicitly and explicitly, the value of her own perceptions and judgments, which by inference Richardson would have us generalise to include an equivalent valuation of all women's experiences. The particular virtues concomitant to such a feminism are the deliberate rejection of female role-playing, an insistence on personal honesty, a passionate independence and a pilgrimage towards self-awareness. Its particular vices are correspondingly stark: an inability to compromise adequately in relationship, a tendency to categorise alternative views as ignorance or obstinacy, a not always healthy flight from confrontation and a constant temptation to egocentricity.

These failings, however, Richardson allows Miriam to demonstrate; she is not content, in her authorial role, to idealise either Miriam's moral powers or her intellectual expertise. The qualities of intelligence Richardson most prized were not abstract rationalism and analytic empiricism, but the ability to perceive relationships between phenomena and the effort to synthesize feeling and reflection. This valuation has important consequences for her fiction, since it leads to a breaking down of the structural divisions we normally impose on experience, for example, the assumption that the external world has a finite integrity which is not influenced by subjective states and the further assumption that the division of time into past, present and future is necessary and meaningful. These major structures are, for her, simply categorisations of space and of time which our culture has developed in order to define for the individual his place in nature and in society. The subjective experience of time becomes the framework within which reality exists and the corresponding task of fiction becomes the conscious bringing into relationship of meaningful moments.

The impact on her style of this effort to delineate a female consciousness was radical. She stretched the unit of the sentence sometimes to the length of a long paragraph; she dispensed with the usual rules of punctuation, often substituting a series of full stops in place of explanation or other detail; she changed from one tense to another within a single paragraph; and she changed from the first person 'I' to the third person 'she' within a single reflection. She omitted details about people and places which readers could justifiably demand to know. Yet her feminist stance is not only evident in her uncompromising adherence to the unfolding of Miriam's consciousness and the forging of a new style. Together with her rejection of the technical conventions of the realist novel went a rejection of the values which the tradition of the English novel had attested. This rejection, however, was not formulated either from the principles of aesthetics or from a general philosophical orientation. It issued primarily from her conviction that the novel was an expression of the vision, fantasies, experiences and goals of men and that only rarely in the history of the novel could a genuine account of the female half of the human condition be found.

In *Pilgrimage*, Miriam often argues with Hypo Wilson about the male bias of the novel and in most of these exchanges the main burden of her argument is that authors seek to aggrandise themselves by constructing elaborate edifices which promise to reveal truths about life but which really reveal truths about the author. Nevertheless, like all radicals, Richardson is ambivalent at heart, recognising that a work of fiction must take its place among its predecessors. Therefore, in her own terms, she is forced to make an assessment of the tradition and to take a theoretical stand on the question of the structure and function of the novel. And because of her conviction that the traditional conventions express an overwhelmingly masculine world view, she must transform those conventions to accommodate Miriam's world view. For Richardson, therefore, words themselves become highly charged with ambivalence. The higher insights are above and beyond language.

There is in *Pilgrimage* a direct connection between Miriam's alienation from male consciousness and her distrust of language. Since style is necessary to a structured use of language, it must be acquired. However, she argues in *Deadlock*, style, because of its 'knowingness', is the property of men and of male writers in particular; men who feel 'the need for phrases'. For Miriam, the trouble with language is that it sets things 'in a mould that was apt to come up again'. The fear of things 'coming up again' can be seen as a fear of commitment, which later prompts the extravagance 'silence is reality'. That may, indeed, be true, but it is an impossible position for a writer to hold. Miriam is compelled, therefore, to rationalise her ambivalence by trying to understand how men use language.

Clearly in a work of such length, which owes less than is usual to previous models, there is bound to be some unevenness in technical control, an inevitability Richardson was fully aware of. In fact she often singled out particular sections of her text as failing to fulfil her intentions; such passages she marked 'I.R.', which stood for 'imperfectly realised'. Even so, *Pilgrimage* is a major contribution to our literature. Richardson's very original vision of female experience, together with her uncompromising experimental style, make the novel an extraordinary testament to the validity of female individuality. It is to be hoped that this first paperback edition of *Pilgrimage* to be published in England points to a new, rich and perceptive understanding of Richardson's achievement.

Gillian E Hanscombe, St Hugh's College, Oxford, 1979

OBERLAND

CHAPTER I

THE sight of a third porter, this time a gentle-looking man carrying a pile of pillows and coming slowly, filled her with hope. But he passed on his way as heedless as the others. It seemed incredible that not one of these men should answer. She wasted a precious moment seeing again the three brutishly preoccupied forms as figures moving in an evil dream. If only she were without the miserable handbags she might run alongside one of these villains, with a tip in an outstretched hand and buy the simple yes or no that was all she needed. But she could not bring herself to abandon her belongings to the mercy of this ill-mannered wilderness where not a soul would care if she wandered helpless until the undiscovered train had moved off into the night. She knew this would not be, and that what she was resenting was not the human selfishness about her, of which she had her own full share, but this turning of her weariness into exhaustion ruining the rest of the journey that already had held suffering enough.

There must be several minutes left of the ten the big clock had marked as she neared the platforms. Recalling its friendly face, she saw also that of the little waiter at the buffet who had tried to persuade her to take wine and murmured too late that there was no extra charge for it, very gently. Rallying the remainder of her strength she dropped her things on the platform with a decisiveness she tried just in vain to scorn, and stood still and looked about amongst the hurrying passengers and saw, passing by and going ahead to the movement of an English stride, the familiar, blessed outlines of a Burberry. Ignoring the near train, the man was crossing a pool of lamplight and making for the dark unlikely platform over the way. She caught up her bags and followed and in a moment was at peace within the semi-darkness of the further platform amongst

people she had seen this morning at Victoria, and the clangorous
station was reduced to an enchanting background for confident
behaviour.

All these people were serene; had come in groups, unscathed,
knowing their way, knowing how to quell the bloused fiends
into helpfulness.   But then, also, the journey to them was
uniform grey, a tiresome business to be got through; not black
and sudden gold.   Yet even they were relieved to find themselves safely through the tangle.   They strode unnecessarily
about, shouted needlessly to each other; expressing travellers'
joy in the English way.

There seemed to be plenty of time, and for a while she
strolled delighting in them, until the sight of an excited weary
child, in a weatherproof that trailed at its heels, marching
sturdily about adream with pride and joy, perfectly caricaturing
the rest of the assembly, made her turn away content to see no
more, to hoist up her baggage and clamber after it into cover,
into the company of her own joy.

Into a compartment whose blinds were snugly drawn upon
soft diffused light falling on the elegance of dove-grey repp and
white lace that had been the surprise and refreshment of this
morning's crowded train, but that now, evening-lit and enclosed, gave the empty carriage the air of a little salon.

Installed here, with fatigue suddenly banished and the large
P.L.M. weaving, within the mesh of the lace, its thrilling
assurance of being launched on long continental distances, it
was easy to forgive the coercion that had imposed the longer
sea-route for its cheapness and the first-class ticket for the
chance of securing solitude on the night journey.

And indeed this steaming off into the night, that just now
had seemed to be the inaccessible goal and end of the journey,
was only the beginning of its longest stretch; but demanding
merely endurance.   With hurry and uncertainty at an end,
there could be nothing to compare with what lay behind;
nothing that could compare with the state of being a helpless
projectile that had spoiled Dieppe and made Paris a nightmare.

Yet Dieppe and Paris and the landscape in between, now
that they were set, by this sudden haven, far away in the past,

were already coming before her eyes transformed, lit by the joy that, hovering all the time in the background, had seen and felt. France, for whose sake at once she had longed to cease being a hurrying traveller robbed right and left of things passing too swiftly, had been seen. Within her now, an irrevocable extension of being, was France.

France that had spoken from its coast the moment she came up from the prison of the battened-down saloon; the moment before the shouting fiends charged up the gangway; spoken from the quay, from the lounging blue-bloused figures, the buildings, the way the frontage of the town met the sky and blended with the air, softly, yet clear in its softness, and with serenity that was vivacious, unlike the stolid English peace.

And later those slender trees along the high bank of a river, the way they had of sailing by, mannered, *coquettish*; awakening affection for the being of France.

And Paris, barely glimpsed and shrouded with the glare of night . . . the emanation even of Paris was peace. An emanation as powerful as that of London, more lively and yet more serene. Serene where gracious buildings presided over the large flaring thoroughfares, serene even in the dreadful by-streets.

And that woman at the station. Black-robed figure, coming diagonally across the clear space yellow in gas-light against the background of barriered platforms, seeming with her swift assured gait, bust first, head reared and a little tilted back on the neck, so insolently feminine, and then, as she swept by, suddenly beautiful; from head to foot all gracefully moving rhythm. *Style*, of course, redeeming ugliness and cruelty. She was the secret of France. France concentrated.

Michael, staying in Paris, said that the French are indescribably evil and their children like monkeys. He had fled eagerly to England. But Michael's perceptions are moral. France, within his framework, falls back into shadow.

The train carrying her through beloved France and away from it to a bourne that had now ceased to be an imagined place, and become an idea, useless, to be lost on arrival as her idea of France had been lost, was so quiet amidst its loud rattling that the whole of it might be asleep. No sound came from the corridor. No one passed. There was nothing but the continuous rattling and the clatter of gear. The world deserting her just when she would have welcomed, for wordless communication of the joy of achievement, the sight and sound of human kind.

Twelve hours away, and now only a promise of daylight and of food, lay Berne. Beyond Berne, somewhere in the far future of to-morrow afternoon, the terminus, the business of finding and bargaining for a sleigh—the last effort.

A muffled figure filled the doorway, entered the carriage, deposited bags. · A middle-aged Frenchman, dark, with sallow cheeks bulging above a little pointed beard. Thinking her asleep, he moved quietly, arranging his belongings with deft, maturely sociable hands. From one of them a ring gleamed in the gaslight. He showed no sign of relief in escaping into silence, no sign of being alone. Conversation radiated from him. Where, on the train, could he have been so recently talking that at this moment he was almost making remarks into his bag?

She closed her eyes, listening to his sounds that sent to a distance the sounds of the train. He had driven away also the outer spaces. The grey and white interior spoke no longer of the strange wide distances of France. He was France, at home in a railway carriage, preparing to sleep until, at the end of a definite short space of hours, the Swiss dawn appeared at the windows. Before he came the night had stretched ahead, timeless.

A moment's stillness, and then a sound like the pumping of nitrous-oxide into a bag. She opened her eyes upon him seated opposite with cheeks distended and eyes strained wide above indeed a bag, held to his lips and limply flopping. Bracing herself to the presence either of a lunatic or a pitiful invalid believing himself unobserved, she watched while slowly the bag swelled up and took, obedient to an effort that seemed about to make his eyeballs start from his head, the shape of a cushion, circular about a flattened centre. Setting it down in the corner corresponding to that where lay her own head, he took off his boots, pulled on slippers and pattered out into the corridor where he became audible struggling with a near ventilator that presently gave and clattered home. Tiptoeing back into the carriage, where already it seemed that the air grew close, he stood under the light, peering upwards with raised arm. A gentle click, and two little veils slid down over the globe and met, leaving the light quenched to a soft glimmer: beautiful, shrouding hard outlines, keeping watch through the night, speaking of night and travel, yet promising day and the end of travel.

But he had not done. He was battling now with the sliding door. It was closing, closed, and the carriage converted into a box almost in darkness and suddenly improper. With a groaning sigh he flung himself down and drew his rug to the margin of the pale disk that was his face and that turned sharply as she rose and passed it to reach the door, and still showed, when the corridor light flowed in through the opened door, a perfect astonishment. His inactivity, while she struggled out with her baggage into the inhospitable corridor, checked the words with which she would have explained her inability to remain sealed for the night in a small box. As she pushed the door to, she thought she heard a sound, a sniggering expletive, mirth at the spectacle of British prudery.

She was alone in the corridor of the sleeping train, in a cold air that reeked of rusting metal and resounded with the clangour of machinery. Exploring in both directions, she found no sign of an attendant, nothing but closely shrouded carriages telling of travellers outstretched and slumbering. Into either of these she felt it impossible to break. There was nothing for it but to abandon the hope of a night's rest and drop to a class whose passengers would be numerous and seated. The train had gathered a speed that flung her from side to side as she went. In two journeys she got her belongings across the metal bridge that swayed above the couplings, and arrived with bruised arms and shoulders in another length of corridor, a duplicate in noise and cold emptiness of the one she had left. Everywhere shrouded carriages. But something had changed, there was something even in the pitiless clangour that seemed to announce a change of class.

The door she pushed open revealed huddled shapes whose dim faces, propped this way and that, were all relaxed in slumber. There was no visible vacant place but, as she hesitated within the emerging reek, a form stirred and sat forward as if to inquire; and when she struggled in with her bags and her apology the carriage came to life in heavily draped movement.

She was seated, shivering in a fog of smells, but at rest, escaped from nightmare voyaging amongst swaying shadows. The familiar world was about her again and she sat blessing the human kindliness of these sleeping forms, blessing the man who had first moved, even though his rousing had proved to be anxiety about the open door which, the moment she was inside, he had closed with the gusty blowings of one who takes refuge from a blizzard.

But the sense of home-coming began presently to fade under the pressure of suffering that promised only to increase. She had long ceased to wonder what made it possible for these people to add wraps and rugs to the thick layers of the stifling atmosphere and remain serene. The effort was no longer possible that had carried her through appearances into a sense of the reality beneath. She saw them now as repellent mysteries, pitiless aliens dowered with an unfathomable faculty for dispensing with air. With each breath the smells that had greeted her, no longer separately apparent, advanced in waves whose predominant flavour was the odour of burnt rubber rising from the grating that ran along the middle of the floor and seemed to sear the soles of her feet. Getting beneath them her rolled rug she abandoned all but the sense of survival and sank into herself, into a coma in which everything but the green-veiled oscillating light was motionless forever. Forever the night would go on and her head turn now this way now that against the harsh upholstery.

The train was slowing, stopping. Its rumbling clatter subsided to a prolonged squeak that ended on a stillness within which sounded, one against the other, the rapid ticking of a watch and a steady rhythmic snore. No one stirred, and for a moment there was nothing but these sounds to witness that life went on. Then faintly, and as if from very far away, she heard the metallic clangours of a large high station and amidst them a thin clarion voice singing out an indistinguishable name. Some large sleeping provincial town signalling its importance; a milestone, marking off hours passed through that need not be braved again. Yet when the train moved on it seemed impossible even to imagine the ending of the night. She had no idea of how long she had sat hemmed and suffering, with nothing in her mind but snatches of song that would not be dismissed, with aching brow and burning eyeballs and a ceaselessly on-coming stupor that would not turn to sleep. And at the next stop, with its echoing clangour and faint clarion voices, she no longer desired somehow to get across the encumbered carriage and taste from a corridor window the sweet fresh air of the railway station so freely breathed by those who were crying in the night.

A numbness had crept into the movement of the train, as though, wearying, it had ceased to clatter and were dropping into a doze. It was moving so quietly that the ticking of the watch again became audible. The wheels under the carriage seemed to be muffled and to labour, pushing heavily forward . . . *Snow*. The journey across France ending on the heights along its eastern edge. Her drugged senses awoke bewailing Paris, gleaming now out of reach far away in the north, challenging with the memory of its glimpsed beauty whatever loveliness might be approaching through the night.

Again outside the stopping train a far-off voice, but this time a jocund sound, ringing echoless in open air. In a moment through a lifted window it became a rousing summons. Blinds went up and, on the huddled forms emerging serene and bright-eyed from their hibernation, a blueish light came in. The opened door admitted crisp sounds close at hand and air, advancing up the carriage.

Upon the platform the air was motionless and yet, walked through, an intensity of movement—movement upon her face of millions of infinitesimal needles, attacking. Mountain air 'like wine,' but this effervescence was solid, holding one up, feeding every nerve.

A little way down the platform she came upon the luggage, a few trunks set side by side on a counter, and saw at once that her portmanteau was not there. Anxiety dogging her steps. But this air, that reached, it seemed, to her very spirit, would not let her feel anxious.

The movements of the people leaving the train were leisurely, promising a long wait. Most of the passengers were the English set free, strolling happily about in fur-coats and creased Burberrys. English voices took possession of the air. Filled it with the sense of the incorrigible English confidence. And upon a table beyond the counter stood rows and rows of steaming cups. Coffee. Café, mon Dieu! Offered casually, the normal beverage of these happy continentals.

The only visible official stood at ease beyond the table answering questions, making no move towards the ranged luggage. He looked very mild, had a little blue-black beard. She thought of long-forgotten Emmerich, the heavy responsible pimpled face of the German official who plunged great hands in amongst her belongings. Perhaps the customs' officers were yet to appear.

Fortified by coffee, she strolled up and made her inquiry in French, but carefully in the slipshod English manner. For a moment her demand seemed to embarrass him. Then, very politely:

'*Vous arrivez, madame?*'

'*De Londres.*'

'*Et vous allez?*'

'*À Oberland.*'

'*Vous n'avez qu'a monter dans le train,*' and hospitably he indicated the train that stood now emptied, and breathing through its open doors. Walking on down the platform she caught, through a door ajar in the background, a glimpse of a truckle bed with coverings thrown back. Here, as they laboured forward through the darkness, the douanier had been sleeping, his station ready-staged for their coming, a farcical half-dozen trunks laid out to represent the belongings of the trainful of passengers. Appearances thus kept up, he was enjoying his role of pleasant host. Tant mieux, tant very much mieux. One could enjoy the fun of being let out into the night.

The solid air began to be intensely cold. But in its cold there was no bitterness and it attained only her face, whose shape it seemed to change. And all about the station were steep walls of starless darkness and overhead in a blue-black sky, stars oddly small and numerous; very sharp and near.

When the train moved on, night settled down once more. Once more there was dim gaslight and jolting shadows. But the air was clearer and only two passengers remained, two women, each in her corner and each in a heavy black cloak. Strangers to each other, with the length of the carriage between them, yet alike, indistinguishable; above each cloak a plump middle-aged face not long emerged from sleep: sheened with the sleep that had left the oily, glinting brown eyes. Presently they began to speak, with the freemasonry of women unobserved, socially off duty. Their voices frugal, dull and flat; the voices of those who have forgotten even the desire to find sympathy, to find anything turned their way with an offering.

They reached details. One of them was on her way home to a place with a tripping gentle name, a fairy keep agleam on a lakeside amidst mountains. To her it was dailiness, life as now she knew it, a hemmed-in loneliness. Visitors came from afar. Found it full of poetry. Saw her perhaps as a part of it, a figure of romance.

When their patient voices ceased they were ghosts. Not even ghosts, for they seemed uncreated, seemed never to have lived and yet to preside over life, fixed in their places, an inexorable commentary. Each sat staring before her into space, patient and isolated, undisguised isolation. To imagine them alert and busied with their families about them made them no less sad. Immovable at the centre of their lives was loneliness, its plaints silenced, its source forgotten or unknown.

Of what use traveller's joy? Frivolous, unfounded, dependent altogether on oblivions.

One of them was rummaging in a heavy sack made of black twill and corded at the neck. Toys, she said, were there— '*pour mes p'tits enfants.*'

'*Ça porte beaucoup de soins, les enfants,*' said the other, and compressed dry lips. The first agreed and they sat back, each in her corner, fallen into silence. Children, to them, seemed to be not persons but a material, an unvarying substance wearily known to them both and to be handled in that deft adjusting way of the French. Satisfied with this mutual judgment on life, made in camera, they relapsed into contemplation, leaving the air weighted with their shared, secretly scornful, secretly impatient resignation.

Yet they were fortunate. Laden with wealth they did not count. It spoke in their complacency. Aspiration asleep. They looked for joy in the wrong place. In this they were humanity, blindly pursuing its way. Their pallid plump faces, so salient, could smile impersonally. Their heads were well-poised above shapely, subdued bodies.

Now that it was empty and the blinds drawn up, the carriage seemed all window, letting in the Swiss morning that was mist opening here and there upon snow still greyed by dawn. Through the one she had just pushed up came life, smoothing away the traces of the night. She lay back in her corner and heard with closed eyes the steady voice of the train. The rattle and clatter of its night-long rush through France seemed to be checked by a sense of achievement, as if now it took its ease, delighting in the coming of day, in the presence of this Switzerland for whose features its was watching through the mist.

Incredible that in this same carriage where now she was at peace in morning light she had sat through a flaming darkness, penned and enduring. Lifting weary eyes she boldly surveyed it, saw the soilure and shabbiness the gaslight had screened, saw a friend, grimed with beneficent toil, and turned once more blissfully towards the window and its view of thin mist and dawn-greyed snow-fields.

The leap of recognition, unknowing between the mountains and herself which was which, made the first sight of them—smooth snow and crinkled rock in unheard-of unimagined tawny light —seem, even at the moment of seeing, already long ago.

They knew, they smiled joyfully at the glad shock they were, sideways gigantically advancing while she passed as over a bridge across which presently there would be no return, seeing and unseeing, seeing again with the first keen vision.

They closed in upon the train, summitless, their bases gliding by, a ceaseless tawny cliff throwing its light into the carriage, almost within touch; receding, making space at its side for sudden blue water, a river accompanying, giving them gentleness who were its mighty edge; broadening, broadening, becoming a wide lake, a stretch of smooth peerless blue with mountains reduced and distant upon its hither side. With the sideways climbing of the train the lake dropped away, down and down until presently she stood up to see it below in the distance, a blue pool amidst its encirclement of mountain and of sky: a picture sliding away, soundlessly, hopelessly demanding its perfect word.

'*Je suis anglaise,*' she murmured as the window came down into place.

'*Je le crois, madame. Mais comment-voulez-vous-mon-dieu-vous-autres-anglais-qu'on-chauffe-les-coupés?*'

She was left to pictures framed and glazed.

Berne was a snowstorm blotting out everything but small white green-shuttered houses standing at angles about the open space between the station and the little restaurant across the way, their strangeness veiled by falling flakes, flakes falling fast on freshly fallen snow that was pitted with large deep-sunken foot-prints.   The electric air of dawn had softened, and as she plunged, following the strides of a row of foot-prints, across to her refuge, it wrapped her about, a pleasant enlivening density, warmed by the snow.   Monstrous snowstorm, adventure, and an excuse for shirking the walk to the Bridge and its view of the Bernese heights.   She was not ready for heights.   This little secret tour, restricted to getting from train to breakfast and back again to the train, gave her, with its charm of familiar activity in a strange place, a sharp first sense of Switzerland that in obediently following the dictated programme she would have missed.   But coming forth, strengthened, once more into the snow she regretted the low walking-shoes that prevented the following up of her glad meeting with the forgotten details of the continental breakfast, its tender-crusted rolls, the small oblongs of unglistening sugar that sweetened the life-giving coffee, by an exploration of the nearer streets.

Presently their talk fell away and the journeying cast again its full spell.   Almost soundlessly the train was labouring along beside a ridge that seemed to be the silent top of the world gliding by, its narrow strip of grey snow-thick sky pierced by the tops of the crooked stakes that were a fence submerged.   From time to time the faint clear sound of a bell, ting-ting, and a neat toy station slid by, half buried in snow.

'I don't dislike those kind of breakfasts myself,' she said and turned her face to the window.   Her well-cut lips had closed unpressing, flowerlike.   Both the girls had the slender delicate fragility of flowers.   And strength.   Refined and gentle, above a strength of which they were unaware.   They were immensely strong or they would not appear undisturbed by their long journeying, would not look so exactly as if they were returning home in an omnibus from an afternoon's shopping in their own Croydon.

They had come so far together that it would seem churlish, with the little terminus welcoming the whole party, to turn away from them. And she liked them, was attached to them as fellow adventurers, fellow survivors of the journey. The falling into the trap of travellers' freemasonry was inevitable: a fatal desire to know the whence and the whither and, before you are aware, you have pooled your enterprise and the new reality is at a distance. But so far it had not come to that. There were no adieux. They had melted away, they and their things, lost in the open while she, forgetful of everything but the blessed cessation, had got herself out of the train.

The station was in a wilderness. High surrounding mountains making it seem that their half-day's going up and still up had brought them out upon a modest lowland. There was no sign from where she stood of any upward track. Sheds, dumped upon a waste of snow beyond which mountains filled the sky and barred the way.

Fierce-looking men in blue gaberdines and slouch hats, lounging about. One of these must be attacked and bargained with for a sleigh. But there were no sleighs to be seen, nothing at all resembling a vehicle, unless indeed one braved the heights in one of those rough shallow frameworks on runners, some piled with hay and some with peeled yellow timbers, neatly lashed. Perhaps a sleigh should be ordered in advance? Perhaps here she met disaster . . .

The man knew her requirements before she spoke and was all hot-eyed eagerness, yet off-hand. Brutish, yet making her phrases, that a London cabby would have received with deference, sound discourteous. In his queer German he agreed to the smaller sum and turned away to expectorate.

The large barn-like restaurant was empty save for a group of people at the far end, forgotten again and again as she sat too happy to swoop the immense distance between herself and anything but the warm brownness of the interior and its strange quality, its intensity of welcoming shelter—sharp contrast with the bleak surrounding snow. Switzerland was here, already surrounding and protecting with an easy practised hand. And there was a generous savouriness . . . She could not recall any lunching on an English journey affording this careless completeness of comfort.

Incompletely sharing these appreciations, her tired and fevered body cowered within the folds of the beneficent fur-coat seeking a somnolence that refused to possess it. Fever kept her mind alert, but circling at a great pace round and round amidst reiterated assertions. Turn and turn about they presented themselves, were flung aside in favour of what waited beyond, and again thrust themselves forward, as if determined, so emphatic they were, not only to share but to steer her adventure. And away behind them, standing still and now forever accessible, were the worlds she had passed through since the sleet drove in her face at Newhaven. And ahead unknown Oberland, summoning her up amongst its peaks.

Hovering vehement above them all, hung the cloud of her pity for those who had never bathed in strangeness—and its dark lining, the selfish congratulation that reminded her how at the beginning of her life, in the face of obstructions, she had so bathed and now under kindly compulsion was again bathing. And again alone. Loneliness, that had long gone from her life, had come back for this sudden voyaging to be her best companion, to shelter strangeness that can be known only in solitude.

In a swift glimpse, caught through the mesh woven by the obstinate circlings of her consciousness, she saw her time in Germany, how perfect in pain and joy, how left complete and bright had been that piece of her life. And in Belgium—in spite of the large party. Yet even the party, though they had taken the edge from many things, had now become a rich part of the whole. But the things that came back most sharply had been seen in solitude: in those times of going out alone on small commissions, the way the long vista of boulevard seemed to sing for joy, the sharp turn, the clean pavé and neat bright little shops; the charcuterie just round the corner, the old pharmacien who had understood and quickly and gravely chloroformed the kitten quite dead; the long walk through the grilling lively Brussels streets to get the circular tickets—little shadow over it of pain at the thought of the frightened man who believed it sinful to go to mass and saw the dull little English Church as light in a pagan darkness; the afternoon alone in the polished old salon while the others were packing for the Ardennes tour, just before the great thunderstorm, bright darkness making everything gleam, the candles melting in the heavy heat, drooping from their sconces, white, and gracious in their oddity, against the dark panelling: rich ancient gloom and gleam and the certainty of the good of mass, of the way, so welcome and so right as an interval in living, it stayed the talkative brain and made the soul sure of itself. That moment in Bruges—after the wrangling at the station, after not wanting to go deliberately to see the Belfry, after feeling forever blank in just this place that was fulfilling all the so different other places, showing itself to be their centre and secret, while aunt Bella bought the prawns and we all stood fuming in the sweltering heat—of being suddenly struck alive, drawn running away from them all down the little brown street—the Belfry and its shadow, all its might and sweetness and surroundedness, safe, before they all came up with their voices and their books.

And oh! that first glimpse that had begun it all, of Brussels in the twilight from the landing window; old peaked houses, grouped irregularly and rising out of greenery, gothic, bringing happy nostalgia. Gothic effects bring nostalgia, have a deep recognizable quality of life. A gothic house is a person, a square house is a thing . . .

In silence and alone; yet most people prefer to see everything in groups, collectively. They never lose themselves in strangeness and wake changed.

That man is cheerfully bearing burdens. Usually in a party there is one who *is* alone. Harassed, yet quietly seeing.

He was smiling, the smile of an old friend. With a sharp effort she pushed her way through, wondering how long she had sat staring at them, to recognition of the Croydon party.

Who else indeed could it be? She gathered herself together and instantly saw in the hidden future not the sunlit mountains of her desire but, for the first time, the people already ensconced at the Alpenstock, demanding awareness and at least the semblance of interest. Sports-people, not only to the manner born—that, though they would not know it, was a tie, a home-tie pulling at her heart—but to the manner dressed, making one feel not merely inadequate but improperly hard-up. But since she was to rest on a balcony? And there was the borrowed fur-coat . . . and the blue gown.

The words sung out by the Croydon father were lost amongst their echoes in the rafters. She heard only the English voice come, as she had come, so far and so laboriously. Her gladly answering words were drowned by the sudden jingling of sleigh-bells at the door near by.

Behind the sturdy horse, whose head-tossings caused the silvery clash of bells, was the sleigh of *The Polish Jew*, brought out of the darkness at the back of the stage and brightly coloured: upon a background of pillar-box red, flourishing gilt scrolls surrounded little landscape scenes painted upon its sides in brilliant deep tones that seemed to spread a warmth and call attention to the warmth within the little carriage sitting compact and low on its runners and billowing with a large fur rug.

As unexpected as the luxurious vehicle was the changed aspect of the driver. Still wearing smock and slouch hat he had now an air of gravity, the air of a young student of theology. And on his face, as he put her into the sleigh, a look of patient responsibility. He packed and arranged with the manner of one handling valuables, silently; the Swiss manner, perhaps, of treating the English, acquired and handed down through long experience of the lavish generosity of these travellers from whom it was useless to expect an intelligible word. But there was contempt too; deep-rooted, patient contempt.

This was luxury. There was warmth under her feet, fur lining upon the back of the seat reinforced by the thickness of

the fur-coat, and all about her the immense fur rug. There
was nothing to fear from the air that presently would be in
movement, driving by and growing colder as the sleigh went
up into the unknown heights. Away ahead, the Croydon party
made a compact black mass between the two horses of their
larger sleigh and the luggage, standing out behind in unwieldy
cubes just above the snow. Their driver was preparing to
start. On all the upward way they would be visible ahead,
stealing its mystery, heralding the hotel at the end.

They were off, gliding swiftly over the snow, gay voices
mingling with the sound of bells, silvery crashings going to the
rhythm of a soundless trit-trot. Every moment her own horse
threw up a spray of tinkles, promising the fairy crashing that
would ring upon the air against the one now rapidly receding.
The mountains frowning under the grey sky and the snowfields
beyond the flattened expanse round the station came to life
listening to the confidently receding bells.

The Croydon party disappeared round a bend and again
there was silence and a mighty inattention. But her man, come
round from lashing on her luggage, was getting into his seat
just as he was, coatless and gathering up the reins with bare
hands.

'Euh!'

The small sound, like a word spoken *sotto voce* to a neighbour, barely broke the stillness, but the sleigh leapt to the pull
of the horse, and glided smoothly off. Its movement was pure
enchantment. No driving on earth could compare to this
skimming along on hard snow to the note of the bells that was
higher than that of those gone on ahead and seemed to challenge them with an overtaking eagerness. Gay and silvery
sweet, it seemed to make a sunlight within the sunless air and
to call up to the crinkled tops of the mountains that were now
so magnificently in movement.

'Euh-euh!'

On they swept through the solidly impinging air. Again the
million needles attacking. In a moment they were round the
bend and in sight of the large sleigh, a moving patch upon the
rising road.

'Euh-euh-euh,' urged the driver laconically, and the little sleigh flew rocking up the slight incline. They were overtaking. The heavier note of the bells ahead joined its slower rhythm to their swift light jinglings. The dark mass of the Croydon party showed four white faces turned to watch.

'You are well off with your fur-coat,' cried the father as her sleigh skimmed by. They had looked a little crouched and enduring. Not knowing the cold she had endured in the past, cold that lay ahead to be endured again, in winters set in a row.

Ringing in her head as she sped upwards along the road narrowing and flanked by massive slopes whose summits had drawn too near to be seen, were the shouted remarks exchanged by the drivers. They had fallen resonantly upon the air and opened within it a vision of the sunlit heights known to these men with the rich deep voices. But there was the hotel . . .

After all, no one was to witness her apprenticeship. And to get up within sight of the summits was worth much suffering. Suffering that would be forgotten. And if these were Oberland men, then there was to be *ski-running* to-morrow. Si-renna, what else could that mean? Patois, rich and soft. Doomed to die. Other words gathered unawares on the way came and placed themselves beside those ringing in her ears. Terminations, turns of sound, upon a new quality of voice. Strong and deep and ringing with a wisdom that brought her a sense of helpless ignorance. The helpless ignorance of town culture.

The thin, penetrating mist promised increasing cold. The driver flung on a cloak, secured at the neck but falling open across his chest and leaving exposed his thinly clad arms and bare hands.

She pulled high the collar of her fur-coat, rimy now at its edges, and her chin ceased to ache and only her eyes and cheekbones felt the thin icy attacking mist that had appeared so suddenly. The cold of a few moments ago, numbing her face, had brought a hint of how one might freeze quietly to death, numbed and as if warmed by an intensity of cold; and that out amongst the mountains it would not be terrible. But this raw mist bringing pain in every bone it touched would send one aching to one's death, crushed to death by a biting increasing pain.

She felt elaborately warm, not caring even now how long might go on this swift progress along a track that still wound through corridors of mountains and still found mountains rising ahead. But night would come, and the great shapes all about her would be wrapped away until they were a darkness in the sky.

If this greying light were the fall of day then certainly the cold would increase. She tried to reckon how far she had travelled eastwards, by how much earlier the sun would set. But south, too, she had come. . . .

The mist was breaking, being broken from above. It dawned upon her that they had been passing impossibly through clouds and were now reaching their fringe. Colour was coming from above, was already here in dark brilliance, thundery. Turning to look down the track she saw distance, cloud masses, light-soaked and gleaming.

And now from just ahead, high in the mist, a sunlit peak looked down.

Long after she had sat erect from her warm ensconcement, the sunlit mountain corridors still seemed to be saying watch, see, if you can believe it, what we can do. And all the time it seemed that they must open out and leave her upon the hither side of enchantment, and still they turned and brought fresh vistas. Sungilt masses beetling variously up into pinnacles that truly cut the sky, high up beyond their high-clambering pinewoods, where their snow was broken by patches of tawny crag. She still longed to glide forever onwards through this gladness of light.

But the bright gold was withdrawing. Presently it stood only upon the higher ridges. The colour was going and the angular shadows, leaving a bleakness of white, leaving the mountains higher in their whiteness. The highest sloped more

swiftly than the others from its lower mass and ended in a long
cone of purest white with a flattened top sharply aslant against
the deepening blue; as if walking up it. It held her eyes, its
solid thickness of snow, the way from its blunted tower it came
broadening down unbroken by crag, radiant white until, far
down, its pinewoods made a gentleness about its base. Up
there on the quiet of its top-most angle it seemed there must be
someone, minutely rejoicing in its line along the sky.

A turn brought peaks whose gold had turned to rose. She
had not eyes enough for seeing. Seeing was not enough.
There was sound, if only one could hear it, in this still, signalling
light.

The last of it was ruby gathered departing upon the topmost
crags, seeming, the moment before it left them, to be deeply
wrought into the crinkled rock.

At a sharp bend, the face of the sideways-lounging driver
came into sight, expressionless.

'*Schön*, *die letzte Glüh*,' he said quietly.

When she had pronounced her '*Wunderschön*,' she sat back
released from intentness, seeing the scene as one who saw it
daily; and noticed then that the colour ebbed from the mountains had melted into the sky. It was this marvel of colour,
turning the sky to molten rainbow, that the driver had meant
as well as the rubied ridges that had kept the sky forgotten.

Just above a collar of snow, that dipped steeply between the
peaks it linked, the sky was a soft greenish purple paling upwards from mauve-green to green whose edges melted imper-
ceptibly into the deepening blue. In a moment they were
turned towards the opposite sky, bold in smoky russet rising to
amber and to saffron-rose expanding upwards; a high radiant
background for its mountain, spread like a banner, not pressed
dense and close with deeps strangely moving, like the little sky
above the collar.

The mountain lights were happiness possessed, sure of
recurrence. But these skies, never to return, begged for
remembrance.

The dry cold deepened, bringing sleep. Drunk, she felt
now, with sleep; dizzy with gazing, and still there was no sign

of the end. They were climbing a narrow track between a smooth high drift, a greying wall of snow, and a precipice sharply falling.

An opening; the floor of a wide valley. Mountains hemming it, exposed from base to summit, moving by as the sleigh sped along the level to where a fenced road led upwards. Up this steep road they went in a slow zigzag that brought the mountains across the way now right now left, and a glimpse ahead, against the sky of a village, angles and peaks of low buildings sharply etched, quenched by snow, crushed between snow and snow, and in their midst the high snow-shrouded cone of a little church; Swiss village, lost in wastes of snow.

At a tremendous pace they jingled along a narrow street of shops and chalets. The street presently opened to a circle about the little church and narrowed again and ended, showing beyond, as the sleigh pulled up at the steps of a portico, rising ground and the beginning of pinewoods.

CHAPTER II

She followed the little servant, who had darted forth to seize her baggage, into a small lounge whose baking warmth recalled the worst of the train journey; seeming—though, since still one breathed, air was there—like an over-heated vacuum.

The brisk little maid, untroubled, was already at the top of a short flight of wide red-carpeted stairs, and making impatient rallying sounds—like one recalling a straying dog. Miriam went gladly to the promise of the upper air. But in going upwards there was no relief.

Glancing, as she passed at the turn of the stairs, at a figure standing in a darkness made by the twilight in the angle of the wall, she found the proprietress receiving her; a thick rigid figure in a clumsy black dress, silent, and with deep-set glinting eyes, hostile and suspicious, stirring a memory of other eyes gazing out like this upon the world, of peasant women at cottage doors in German villages, peering out with evil eyes, but from worn and kindly faces. There was nothing kindly about this woman, and her commonness was almost startling, dreary and meagre and seeming to be of the spirit.

She blamed for the unmitigated impression the fatigue she was silently pleading whilst she searched for the mislaid German phrases in which to explain that she had chosen the cheaper room. She found only the woman's name: Knigge. This was Frau Knigge, at once seeming more human, and obviously waiting for her to speak.

Suddenly, and still unbending from her rigid pose, she made statements in slow rasping English and a flat voice, that came unwillingly and told of vanished interest in life. Life, as she spoke, looked terrible that could make a being so crafty and so cold, that could show to any one on earth as it showed to this woman.

Admitting her identity, seeing herself as she was being seen, Miriam begged for her room, hurrying through her words to

32

hide the thoughts that still they seemed to reveal, and that were changing, as she heard the sound of her own voice, dreadfully, not to consideration for one whose lot had perhaps been too hard to bear, but to a sudden resentment of parleying, in her character as Roman citizen, with this peasant whose remoteness of being was so embarrassing her.

The woman's face lit up with an answering resentment and a mocking contempt for her fluent German. Too late she realized that Roman citizens do not speak German. But the details were settled, the interview was at an end, and the woman's annoyance due perhaps only to the choice of the cheaper room. When she turned to shout instructions to the maid, she became humanity, in movement, moving in twilight that for her too was going on its way towards the light of to-morrow.

When the door was at last blessedly closed upon the narrow room whose first statements miscarried, lost in the discovery that even up here there was no change in the baked dry air, she made for the cool light of the end window but found in its neighbourhood not only no lessening but an increase of the oppressive warmth.

The window was a door giving on to a little balcony whose wooden paling hid the floor of the valley and the bases of the great mountains across the way. The mountains were now bleak white, patched and streaked with black, and as she stood still, gazing at them set there arrested and motionless and holding before her eyes an unthinkable grey bitterness of cold, she found a new quality in her fast closed windows and the exaggerated warmth. Though still oppressive they were triumphant also, speaking a knowledge and a defiance of the uttermost possibilities of cold.

Cold was banished, by day and by night. For a fortnight, taken from the rawest depths of the London winter, there would be no waste of life in mere endurance.

She discovered the source of the stable warmth in an unsightly row of pipes at the side of the large window, bent over like hairpins and scorching to the touch. The concentrated heat revived her weary nerves. At the end of the coil there was

a regulator. Turning it she found the heat of the pipes
diminish and hurriedly reversed the movement and glanced
out at the frozen world and loved the staunch metallic warmth
and the flavour of timber added to it in this room whose walls
and furniture were all of naked wood.

Turning to it in greeting she found it seem less small. It
was small, but made spacious by light. Light came from a
second window that was now calling—a small square beside the
bed with the high astonishing smooth billow of covering oddly
encased in thin sprigged cotton—offering mountains not yet
seen.

The way to it was endless across the short room from whose
four quarters there streamed, as she moved, a joy so deep that
she brought up opposite the window as if on another day of
life, and glanced out carelessly at a distant group of pinnacles
darkening in a twilight that was not grey but lit wanly in its
fading, by snow.

The little servant came in with the promised tea and made,
as she set it upon the little table with the red and white check
cover of remembered German cafés, bent over it in her short-
skirted check dress and squab of sleek flaxen hair, a picture
altogether German. She answered questions gravely, responsibility speaking even in the smile that shone from her plump
toil-sheened young face, telling the story of how she and her
like, permanently toiling, were the price of happiness for
visitors. But this she did not know. She was happy. Liked
being busy and smiling and being smiled at and shutting the
door very carefully.

Some movements of hers had set swinging an electric bulb
hanging by a cord above the little table. Over the head of the
bed there was another. Light and warmth in profusion—in a
cheap room in a modest hotel.

Switching on the light that concentrated on the table and its
loaded little tray and transformed the room to a sitting-room,
'I'm in Switzerland,' she said aloud to the flowered earthenware and bright nickel, and sat down to revel in freedom and
renewal and at once got up again realizing that hurry had gone
from her days, and flung off her blouse and found hot water

set waiting on the washstand and was presently at the table in négligé and again ecstatically telling it her news.

The familiar sound of tea pouring into a cup heightened the surrounding strangeness. In the stillness of the room it was like a voice announcing her installation, and immediately from downstairs there came as if in answer the sound of a piano, crisply and gently touched, seeming not so much to break the stillness as to reveal what lay within it.

She set down her teapot and listened, and for a moment could have believed that the theme was playing itself only in her mind, that it had come back to her because once again she was within the strange happiness of being abroad. Through all the years she had tried in vain to recall it, and now it came, to welcome her, piling joy on joy, setting its seal upon the days ahead and taking her back to her Germany where life had been lived to music that had flowed over its miseries and made its happinesses hardly to be borne.

For an instant she was back in it, passing swiftly from scene to scene of the months in Waldstrasse and coming to rest in a summer's evening: warm light upon the garden, twilight in the saal. Leaving it, she turned to the other scenes, freshly revived, faithfully fulfilling their remembered promise to endure in her for ever, but each one, as she paused in it, changed to the summer's evening she had watched from the darkening saal, the light upon the little high-walled garden, making space and distance with the different ways it fell on trees and grass and clustering shrubs, falling full on the hushed group of girls turned towards it with Fräulein Pfaff in their midst disarmed to equality by the surrounding beauty, making a little darkness in the summer-house where Solomon shone in her white dress. And going back to it now it seemed as though some part of her must have lived continuously there, so that she was everywhere at once, in saal and garden and summer-house and out, beyond the enclosing walls, in the light along the spacious forbidden streets.

She relived the first moment of knowing gladly and without feeling of disloyalty how far a Sommerabend outdoes a summer's evening, how the evening beauty was intensified by the deeps of poetry in the Germans all about her, and remembered her fear lest one of the English should sound an English voice and break the spell. And how presently Clara Bergmann, unasked, had retreated into the shadowy saal and played this ballade and in just this way, the way of slipping it into the stillness.

'*Man soll sich des Lebens freuen, im Berg und Thal. In so was kann sich ein' Engländerin nie hineinleben.*'

Perhaps not, but in that small group of English there had been two who would in spite of homesickness have given anything just to go on, on any terms, existing in Germany.

It is their joy; the joyful rich depth of life in them.

And this ballade was joy. Eternal Sommerabend; and now, to-morrow's Swiss sunlight. Someone there was downstairs to whom it was a known and cherished thing, who was perhaps wise about it, wise in music and able to place it in relation to other compositions.

Its charm she now saw, coming to it afresh and with a deepened recognition, lay partly in the way it opened: not beginning, but continuing something gone before. It was a shape of tones caught from a pattern woven continuously and drawn, with its rhythm ready set, gleaming into sight. The way of the best nocturnes. But with nothing of their pensiveness. It danced in the sky and tiptoed back to earth down the group of little chords that filled the pause, again sprang forth and up and came wreathing down to touch deep lower tones who flung it to and fro. Up again until once more upon downstepping chords it came into the rhythm of its dance.

It was being played from memory, imperfectly, by someone who had the whole clear within him and, in slowing up for the complicated passages, never stumbled or lost the rhythm or ceased to listen. Someone choosing just this fragment of all the music in the world to express his state: joy in being up here in snow and sunlight.

When the gown was on, the creasing was more evident; all but the enlivening strange harmony of embroidered blues and greens and mauves was a criss-cross of sharp lines and shadows.

For the second time the long loud buzzing of the downstairs bell vibrated its summons through the house.

Standing once more before the little mirror that reflected only her head and shoulders she re-created the gown in its perfection of cut, the soft depths of its material that hung and took the light so beautifully.

'Your first Switzerland must be good. I want your first Switzerland to be good.' And then, in place of illuminating hints, that little diagram on the table: of life as a zigzag. Saddening. Perhaps he was right. Then, since the beginning had been so good, all a sharp zig, what now waited downstairs, heralded by the creased dress, was a zag, equally sharp.

The dining-room, low-ceiled and oblong, was large and seemed almost empty. Small tables set away towards a window on the right and only one of them occupied, left clear the large space of floor between the door at which she had come in and a table, filling the length of the far side of the room where beside a gap in the row of diners a servant stood turned towards her with outstretched indicating hand.

No one but the servant had noticed her entry. Voices were sounding, smooth easy tones leaving the air composed, as she slipped into her place in a light that beside the unscreened glare upstairs was mellow, subdued by shades. The voices were a man's across the way—light and kindly, 'varsity, the smiling tone of one who is amiable even in disagreement—and that of the woman on her left, a subdued deep bass. Other voices dropped in, as suave and easy, and clipping and slurring their words in the same way; but rather less poised.

The tone of these people was balm. Sitting with eyes cast down, aware only of the subdued golden light, she recalled her fleeting glimpse of them as she had crossed the room, English in daily evening dress, and was carried back to the little world of Newlands where first she had daily shared the evening festival of diners dressed and suave about a table free of dishes, set with flowers and elegancies beneath a clear and softly shaded light: the world she had sworn never to leave. She remembered a summer morning, the brightness of the light over her breakfast tray and its unopened letters and her vow to remain always surrounded by beauty, always with flowers and fine fabrics, and space and a fresh clean air close about her, playing their part that was so powerful.

And this little wooden Swiss hotel with its baked air and philistine fittings was to provide, thrown in with Switzerland, more than a continuation of Newlands—Newlands seen afresh with experienced eyes.

The clipped, slurred words had no longer the charm of a foreign tongue. Though still they rang upon the air the pre-occupations of the man at the wheel: the sound of 'The Services,' adapted. But clustered in this small space they seemed to be bringing with them another account of their origin, to be showing how they might come about of themselves and vary from group to group, from person to person—with one aim: to avoid disturbing the repose of the features. Expression might be animated or inanimate, but features must remain undisturbed.

Then there is no place for clearly enunciated speech, apart from oratory; platform and pulpit. Anywhere else it is bad form. Bad fawm.

She felt she knew now why perfect speech, delightful in itself, always seemed insincere. Why women with clear musical voices, undulating, and clean enunciation, are always cats; and the corresponding men, ingratiating and charming at first, turn out sooner or later to be charlatans.

The nicest people have bad handwriting and bad delivery.

But all this applied only to English, to Germanics; that was a queer exciting thing, that only these languages had the quality of aggressive disturbance of the speaking face: chin-jerking vowels and aspirates, throat-swelling gutturals . . . force and strength and richness, qualities innumerable and more various than in any other language.

Quelling an impulse to gaze at the speakers lit by discovery, she gazed instead at imagined faces, representative Englishmen, with eyes and brows serene above rapid slipshod speech.

Here, too, of course, was the explanation of the other spontaneous forms of garbling, the extraordinary pulpit speech of self-conscious and incompletely believing parsons, and the mincing speech of the genteel. It explained 'nace.' Nice, correctly spoken, is a convulsion of the lower face—like a dog snapping at a gnat.

She had a sudden vision of the English aspirate, all over the world, puff-puff-puffing like a steam-engine, and was wondering whether it were a waste or a source of energy, when she became acutely aware of being for those about her a fresh item in their grouping.

It was a burden too heavy to be borne. The good Swiss soup had turned her bright fever of fatigue to a drowsiness that made every effort to sit decently upright end in a renewed abject drooping that if only she were alone could be the happy drooping of convalescence from the journey.

Their talk had gone on. It was certain that always they would talk. Archipelagos of talk, avoiding anything that could endanger continuous urbanity.

In the midst of a stifled yawn, the call to a fortnight's continuous urbanity fell upon her like a whip. Dodging the blow, she lolled resistant to the sound of bland voices. An onlooker, appreciative but resistant; that, socially, would be the story of her stay. A docile excursion, even if they should offer it, into this select little world, would come between her and her Switzerland. Refusal clamoured within her and it was only as an afterthought that she realized the impossibility of remaining for a fortnight without opinions.

The next moment, hearing again the interwoven voices as a far-off unison of people sailing secure on smooth accustomed waters, she was bleakly lonely; suppliant. Nothing showed ahead but a return with her fatigue to sustain the silence and emptiness of a strange room. She was about to glance at the woman on her left when the deep bass voice asked her casually if she had had a good journey. Casual camaraderie, as if already they had been talking and were now hiding an established relationship under conventionalities.

The moment she had answered she heard the university voice across the way remark, in the tone of one exchanging notes with a friend after a day's absence, that it was a vile journey, but all right from Berne onwards, and looked up. There he was, almost opposite, Cambridge, and either history

or classics, the pleasant radiance of *Lit. Hum.* all about him, and
turned her way bent a little, as if bowing, and as if waiting for
her acknowledgment—with his smile, apology, introduction
and greeting beaming together from sea-blue eyes set only ever
so little too closely together in a neatly tanned narrowly oval
face—before regaining the upright.

Her soft reply, lost in other sounds, made a long moment
during which, undisturbed by not hearing, he held his attitude
of listening that told her he was glad of her presence.

The close-set eyes meant neither weakness nor deceit. Sec-
tarian eyes, emancipated. But his strength was borrowed.
His mental strength was not original. An uninteresting mind;
also he was a little selfish, with the selfishness of the bachelor
of thirty—but charming.

The party was smaller than she had thought. The odd way
they were all drawn up at one end of the table made them look
numerous. Spread out in the English way they would have
made a solemn dinner-party, with large cold gaps.

Someone asked whether she had come right through, and
in a moment they were all amiably wrangling over the pros and
cons of breaking the journey.

Staring from across the table was a man alone, big oblong
foreigner dwarfing his neighbours, and piteous, not to be looked
at as the others could who fitted the scene; not so much sitting
at table with the rest as set there filling a space. His eyes
had turned towards a nasal voice suddenly prevailing; sombre
brown, wistfully sulking below eyebrows lifted in a wide forehead that stopped unexpectedly soon at a straight fence of hair.
Oblong beard reaching the top of stiff brown coat. Russian,
probably the Chopin player.

'Any one's a fool who passes Parrus without stopping off at
least a few hours.'

A small man at the end of the row, opaque blue eyes in a
peaky face, little peaked beard, neat close-fitting dress clothes.
Incongruous far-travelled guest of little Switzerland.

He was next the window, with the nice man on his right.
Then came the big Russian exactly opposite, and again naïvely
staring across, and beyond him a tall lady in a home-made silk

blouse united by a fichu to the beginning of a dark skirt; coronet of soft, coiled white hair above a firmly padded face with polished skin, pink-flushed, glimmering into the talk, that was now a debate about to-morrow's chances, into which sounded women's voices from the table behind, smooth and clear, but clipped, freemasonish like the others. To the right of the coronetted lady an iron-grey man, her husband, gaunt and worn, with peevishly suffering eyes set towards the door on the far side of the room. Fastidious eyes, full of knowledge, turned away. He was the last in the row and beyond him the table stretched away to the end wall through whose door the servants came and went. His opponents were out of sight beyond the bass-voiced woman on the left, whose effect was so strangely large and small: a face horse-like and delicate and, below her length of face increased by the pyramid of hair above her pointed fringe, a meeting of old lace and good jewellery.

To her own right, the firm insensitive hand, that wore a signet ring and made pellets of its bread, belonged to just the man she had imagined, dark and liverish, but with an unexpectedly flattened profile whose moustache, dropping to sharp points, gave it an expression faintly Chinese; a man domestic but accustomed to expand in unrestricted statement, impatiently in leash to the surrounding equality of exchange. Beyond him his wife, sitting rather eagerly forward, fair and plump, with features grown expressionless in their long service of holding back her thoughts, but, betraying their secret in a brow, creased faintly by straining upwards as if in perpetual incredulity of an ever-present spectacle, and become now the open page of the story the mouth and eyes were not allowed to tell.

At her side a further figure and beyond it the head of the table, unoccupied, leaving the party to be its own host.

The atmosphere incommoding the husband, who at a second glance seemed to call even pathetically for articulate opposition, was that of a successful house-party, its tone set by the only two in sight who were through and through of the authentic brand: the deep-voiced woman and the nice man. The invalid and his wife belonged to that inner circle. But they were a little shadowed by his malady.

It was an atmosphere in which the American and the Russian were ill at ease, one an impatient watchfulness for simpler, more lively behaviour and the other a bored detachment, heavily anchored, not so much by thoughts as by hard clear images left by things seen according to the current formula of whatever group of the European intelligentsia he belonged to.

He was speaking softly through the general conversation to the nice man, with slight deprecating gestures of eyebrows and shoulders, in his eyes a qualified gratitude. The nice man spoke carefully with head turned and bent, seeking his words. French, with English intonation. All these people, however fluently, would talk like that. All of them came from a world that counted mastery of a foreign tongue both wonderful and admirable—but ever so little *infra dig*.

'Won't you come in heah for a bit?'

Drugged as she felt with weariness, she turned joyfully into a room opening in the background of the hall whence the deep bass voice had sounded as she passed. A tiny salon, ugly; maroon and buff in a thick light. Plush sofa, plush cover on the round table in the centre, stiff buff-seated 'drawing-room' chairs; a piano. It was from this dismal little room the Chopin had sounded out into the twilight.

There she was, alone, standing very thin and tall in a good, rather drearily elderly black dress beside a cheerless radiator, one elbow resting on its rim and a slender foot held towards it from beneath the hem of a slightly hitched skirt: an English-woman at a fireside.

'My name's Harcourt, M'zz Harcourt,' she said at once.

Books were set star-wise in small graded piles about the centre of the table, the uppermost carrying upon their covers scrolls and garlands of untarnished gilt. The one she opened revealed short-lined poems set within yet more garlands, appealing; leaves and buds and birds lively and sweet about the jingling verse. Swiss joy in deep quiet valleys guarded by

sunlit mountains. Joy of people living in beauty all their lives;
enclosed. Yet making rooms like this.

But it held the woman at the radiator, knowing England and
her sea, and whose smile looking up she met, watching, indulgent of her détour and, as too eagerly she moved forward,
indulgent also of that. Here, if she would, was a friend, and,
although middle-aged, a contemporary self-confessed by a note
in her voice of impatience over waste of time in preliminaries.

But Mrs Harcourt did not know how nimbly she could move,
might think it strange when presently her voice must betray
that she was already rejoicing—defying the note of warning
that sounded far away within her—in a well-known presence,
singing recklessly to it the song of new joy and life begun anew
that all the way from England had been gathering within her.

The announcement of her own name made the woman again
a stranger, so much was she a stranger to the life belonging to
the name, and brought into sudden prominence the state of
her gown, exposed now in its full length. She recounted the
tragedy and saw Mrs Harcourt's smile change to real concern.

Here they were, alone together, seeming to have leapt rather
than passed through the early stages.

Like love, but unobstructed. A balance of side-by-side,
not of opposition. More open than love, yet as hidden and
wonderful; rising from the same depth.

'Hold it in front of the waydiator. Vat 'll take 'em out a bit.
Such a poo'hy gown.' She moved a little back from the row
of pipes.

Going close to the radiator, Miriam moved into a fathomless
gentleness.

But it was also a demand, so powerful that it was drawing all
her being to a point. All that she had brought with her into
the room would be absorbed and scattered, leaving her robbed
of things not yet fully her own.

The warning voice within was crying aloud now, urging her
not only to escape before the treasures of arrival and of strangeness were lost beyond recovery, but to save also the past, disappeared round the corner, yet not out of sight but drawn
closely together in the distance, a swiftly moving adventure,

lit from point to point by the light in which to-day she had bathed forgetful.

Even a little talk, a little answering of questions, would falsify the past. Set in her own and in this woman's mind in a mould of verbal summarizings, it would hamper and stain the brightness of to-morrow.

She found herself hardening, seeking generalizations that would cool and alienate, and was besieged by memories of women whom she had thus escaped. And of their swift revenge. But this woman was not of those who avenge themselves.

Hesitating before the sound of her own voice, or the other which would sound if this second's silence were prolonged, she was seized by revolt: the determination at all costs to avoid hearing in advance, in idle words above the ceaseless intercourse of their spirits, about Oberland; even from one whose seeing might leave her own untouched.

To open the way for flight she remarked that it must be late.

'About nine. You're dead beat, I can see. Ought to go to bed.'

'Not for worlds,' said Miriam involuntarily.

Mrs Harcourt's face, immediately alight for speech, expressed as she once more took possession of the radiator and looked down at it as into a fire, willingness to stand indefinitely by.

'Every one's gone to bed. Bein' out all day in vis air makes you sleepy at night.'

Remembering that of course she would speak without gaps, Miriam glanced at the possibility of pulling herself together for conversation.

'I been pottering. My ski are at Zurbuchen's bein' repaired.'

'But what a *perfect* Swiss name. Like oak, like well-baked bread.'

To get away now. Sufficient impression of the Alpenstock people perpetually strenuous, living for sport, and, redeeming its angularity, the rich Swiss background: Zurbuchen. But Mrs Harcourt's glance of surprised delight—there was amusement too, she didn't think Swiss names worth considering—

meant that she was entertained, anticipating further entertainment; to which she would not contribute.

'No. I 'm supposed to sit about and rest. Overwork.'

'You won't. Lots of people come out like vat. You 'll soon find resting a baw out heah.'

'Should like a little sleep. I 've had none for two nights.'

'Stop in bed to-morrow. Have your meals up.'

'M'm. . . .'

For a moment Mrs Harcourt waited, silent, not making the movement of departure that would presently bring down the shadow of returning loneliness her words had drawn so near; keeping her leaning pose, her air of being indefinitely available.

The deep bell of her voice dropped from its soft single note to a murmur rising and falling, a low narrative tone, hurrying.

Through the sound, still coming and going in her mind, of the name Mrs Harcourt had so casually spoken, bringing with it the sunlit mountains and the outer air waiting in to-morrow, Miriam heard that the people at the Alpenstock were all right —with the exception of the two sitting at dinner on Mrs Harcourt's left, 'outsiders' of a kind now appearing in Oberland for the first time. Saddened by their exclusion, embarrassed by unconscious flattery, Miriam impulsively asked their name and glowed with a sudden vision of Mrs Corrie, of how she would have embraced this opportunity for wicked mondaine wit. Mrs Harcourt, for a moment obediently reflecting, said she had forgotten it but that it was somefing raver fwightful. Every one else, introduced by name, received a few words of commendation—excepting the Russian and the American. The Russian would be just a foreigner, an unfortunate, but the American surely must be an outsider? Insincerely, as if in agreement with this division of humanity by exclusion, she put in a question, and while Mrs Harcourt pulled up her discourse to say, as if sufficiently, that he was staying only a couple of days and passed on to summon other hotels to the tribunal, she was glad that the Russian had been left untouched. Harry Vereker, fine, a first-class sportsman and altogether nice chap, was already lessened, domesticated, general property in his niceness; but the Russian remained, wistfully alone: attractive.

'. . . hidjus big hotel only just built; all glass and glare. It 'll be the ruin of Oberland. No one 'll come here next year.'

Though still immersed in her theme Mrs Harcourt was aware, when next she glanced to punctuate a statement, if not exactly that instead of the object she offered it was herself and her glance that was being seen—the curious steeliness of its indignation—at least of divided attention, a sudden breach in their collaboration; and immediately she came to the surface, passing without pause to her full bell note, with an inquiry. Hoping to please. But why hoping to please?

This abrupt stowing away of her chosen material might be a simple following of the rules of her world; it suggested also the humouring of a patient by a watchful nurse, and since she had the advantage of not being in the depths of fatigue this perhaps was its explanation; but much more clearly it spoke her years of marriage, of dealing with masculine selfishness. And she was so swift, so repentant of her long, enjoyable excursion, that it was clear she had suffered masculine selfishness gladly. Neither understanding nor condemning. It had not damaged her love and she had suffered bitterly when it was removed.

Suffering was pleading now in her eyes off their guard in this to-and-fro of remarks that was a little shocking: the reverberation of a disaster.

Now that it was clear that her charming behaviour from the first might be explained by the attraction there was for her in a mannish mental hardness, that she sought in its callousness both something it could never give, as well as entertainment, and rest from perpetual feeling, she ceased to be interesting. She herself made it so clear that she had nothing to give. Offering her best help, what in the way of her world would be most useful to one newly arrived, she was yet suppliant; and afraid of failure, haunted by the fear of a failure she did not understand and that was perhaps uniform in her experience.

Miriam found her own voice growing heavy with the embarrassment of her discoveries and her longing to break this so eagerly woven entanglement. Trying again for cooling generalities, she had the sense of pouring words into a void. The gentle presence hovered there, played its part, followed,

answered, but without sharing the effort to swim into the
refreshing tide of impersonality; without seeing the independent
light on the scraps of reality she was being offered.   No wonder
perhaps: they were a little breathless.   She was scenting apology
and retreat.   And did not know that it was retreat not at all
from herself, but from her terrible alacrity and transparence:
the way the whole of her was at once visible.   All her thoughts,
her way of thinking in words, in set phrases gathered from too
enclosed an experience.   Enclosed.   To be with her was enclosure.   The earlier feeling of being encompassed that was
so welcome because it was so womanly, so exactly what a man
needs in its character of kindly confessor and giver of absolution in advance, had lost value before the discovery of this
absence of vistas, this frightful sense of being shut in with
assumptions about life that admit of no question and no
modification.

Again the dead husband intruded; his years of life at this
woman's side, his first adoration of her, and then his weariness,
fury of weariness whose beginnings she felt herself already
tasting, so that for sheer pity she was kept in her place, effusive,
unable to go.

But at the moment of parting Mrs Harcourt became again
that one who had waited, impatient of wasting time in formalities.   Her smile glanced out from the past, revealing the
light upon her earlier days.   It was a greeting for to-morrow
rather than a good night.

Going up to the little bedroom that was now merely a refuge
off-stage, she found it brightly lit in readiness for her coming,
summery bright all over, the light curtains drawn and joining
with the unvarnished wood to make an enclosure that seemed
to emulate the brightness of the Swiss daylight.   The extravagant illumination, the absence of glooms and shadows, recalled
the outdoor scene and something of this afternoon's bliss of
arrival and the joy that had followed it, when music sounded
up through the house, of home-coming from long exile.   Switzerland waited outside—enriched by her successful début—
with its promise that could not fail.   Meanwhile there was
the unfamiliar enchantment of moving comfortably in a warm

bedroom, not having the wealth one brought upstairs instantly dispersed by the attack of cold and gloom. The temperature was lower than before, pleasant, no longer oppressive; and more hospitable than a fire whose glow was saddened by the certainty that in the morning it would be an ashy desolation.

The moment the basket chair received her the downstairs world was about her again; circling, clamorous with the incidents of her passage from lonely exposure to the shelter of Mrs Harcourt's so swiftly offered wing, from beneath which, with its owner assured of the hardness of what it sheltered, she could move freely forth in any direction.

The two Le Mesras—that was her pronunciation of Le Mesurier? Three Chators. Mrs Sneyde and Maud Something at the little table behind . . . Hollebone. Maud Hollebone. The American, leaving. Interest hesitated between Harry Vereker, already a little diminished, and the Russian: the reincarnated, attractive, ultimately unsatisfactory Tansley Street foreigner?

Someone was tapping at the door. She opened it upon Mrs Harcourt offering a small tray, transformed to motherliness by a voluminous dressing-gown.

When she had gone she vanished utterly. There she was, actually in the next room, yet utterly forgettable. And yet she threw across the days ahead a strange deep light.

The steaming chocolate and the little English biscuits disappeared too quickly, leaving hunger.

The french window was made fast by a right-angle handpiece, very stiff, that gave suddenly with a dreadfully audible clang. The door creaked open. Racing the advancing air she was beneath the downy billow before it reached her. It took her fevered face with its battalions of needles, stole up her nostrils to her brain, bore her down into the uttermost depths of sleep.

CHAPTER III

FROM which she awoke in light that seemed for a moment to be beyond the confines of earth. It was as if all her life she had travelled towards this radiance, and was now within it, clear of the past, at an ultimate destination.

How long had it been there, quizzically patient, waiting for her to be aware of it?

It was sound, that had wakened her and ceased now that she was looking and listening; become the inaudible edge of a sound infinitely far away. Brilliant light, urgently describing the outdoor scene. But she was unwilling to stir and break the radiant stillness.

Close at hand a bell buzzed sharply. Another, and then a third far away down the corridor. People ringing their day into existence, free to ring their day into existence when they pleased. She was one of them; and for to-day she would wait awhile, give the bell-ringers time to be up and gone down to breakfast while she kept intact, within this miracle of light, the days ahead that with the sounding of her own bell would be already in process of spending.

But perhaps there was a time-limit for breakfasts?

Screwing round to locate the bell with the minimum of movement, she paused in sheer surprise of well-being. Of the shattering journey there was not a trace. Nor of the morning weariness following social excitements.

Sitting up to search more effectually, she saw the source of her wakening, bright gold upon the mountain tops: a smiling challenge, as if, having put on their morning gold, the mountains watched its effect upon the onlookers.

She was glad to be alone on the scene of last night's dinner-party; to be in the company of the other breakfasters represented only by depleted butter-dishes and gaps in the piles of rolls, and free from the risk of hearing the opening day fretted by voices set going like incantations to exorcize the present as if it had no value, as if the speakers were not living in it but only in yesterday or to-morrow.

And when there came a warning swift clumping of hob-nailed boots across the hall, across the room, she demanded Vereker, oddly certain that even at this late hour still somehow it would contrive to be he.

And there he was, lightly clumping round the table-end to his place, into which he slipped smiling his greeting, boyishly. Not at all in the self-conscious Englishman's manner of getting himself seated when others are already in their places: bent, just before sitting down, forward from the waist and, in that pose—hitching his trousers the while—distributing his greetings, and so letting himself down into his chair either with immediate speech or a simulated air of preoccupation. Vereker flopped and beamed at the same moment, unfeignedly pleased to arrive. Knickerbockers; but that was not the whole difference. He was always unfeignedly pleased to arrive?

He began at once collecting food and spoke with gentle suddenness into a butter-dish:

'I hope you had a good night?'

His talk made a little symphony with his movements which also were conversational, and he looked across each time he spoke, but only on the last word; a swift blue beam. In the morning light he seemed younger—perhaps a champion ski-er at the end of his day is as tired as a hard-worked navvy?—and a certain air of happy gravity and the very fair curly hair shining round its edges from recent splashings, gave him, in his very white, very woolly sweater, something of the look of a newly bathed babe in its matinée jacket—in spite of the stern presence, above the rolled top of his sweater, of an inch of stiff linen collar highly glazed.

He was of a type and of a class, and also, in a way not quite clear, a tempered, thoroughly live human being; something more in him than fine sportsman and nice fellow, giving him weight. Presently she found its marks: a pleat between the brows and, far away within his eyes even when they smiled, a sadness; that sounded too in his cheerful voice, a puzzled, perpetual compassion.

For the world? For himself?

But these back premises were touched with sunlight. Some sense of things he had within him that made him utterly *kind*.

'Isn't it extraordinary,' she said, hoping to hide the fact that she had missed his last remark, 'the way these people leave the lights switched on all the time, everywhere?'

'Cheap electricity,' he said as if in parenthesis, and as if apologetically reminding her of what she already knew— 'Water power. They pay a rate and use as much as they like.'

In all his answers there was this manner of apologizing for giving information. And his talk, even the perfect little story of the local barber and the newspapers, which he told at top pace as if grudging the moment it wasted, was like a shorthand annotation to essential unspoken things, shared interests and opinions taken for granted. Talking with him, she no longer felt as she had done last night either that she was at a private view of an exclusive exhibition, or gathering fresh light on social problems. There was in him something unbounded, that enhanced the light reflected into the room from the sunlit snow. His affectionate allusion to his Cambridge brought to her mind complete in all its parts—together with gratitude for the peace he gave in which things could expand unhindered— her own so sparse possession: her week-ends there with the cousins, their blinkered, comfort-loving academic friends, the strange sense of at once creeping back into security and realizing how far she had come away from it; their kindnesses, their secret hope of settling her for life in their enclosed world, and their vain efforts to mould her to its ways; and then the end, the growing engrossments in London breaking the link that held her to them and to the past they embodied—and Cambridge left, lit by their sweet hospitality, by the light streaming on Sunday afternoons through King's Chapel windows; the Backs in sunlight, and a memory of the halting little chime.

When she told him of the things that Cambridge had left with her, she paused just in time to escape adding to them the gait of the undergraduates: the slovenly stride whose each footfall sent the chin forward with a henlike jerk.

He agreed at once with her choice, but hesitated over the little chime.

'It might have been a new church. I never saw it. But if you had once heard it you *couldn't* forget it.'

It was absurd to be holding to her solitary chime in face of his four years' residence. But it seemed now desperately important to state exactly the quality she had felt and never put into words. She sat listening—aware of him waiting in a sympathetic stillness—to each note as it sounded out into the sky above the town, making it no longer Cambridge but a dream city, subduing the graceless modern bricks and mortar to harmony with the ancient beauty of the colleges—until the whole was a loveliness beneath the evening sky—and presently found herself speaking with reckless enthusiasm.

'*Don't* you remember the four little gentle tuneless phrases, of six and seven notes alternately, one for each quarter, and at the hour sounding one after the other with a little pause between each, seeming to ask you to look at what it saw, at the various life of the town made suddenly wonderful and strange; and the last phrase, beginning with a small high note that tapped the sky, and wandering down to the level and stopping without emphasis, leaving everything at peace and very beautiful?'

'I think I *can't* have heard it,' he said wistfully, and sat contemplative in a little pause during which it occurred to her, becoming aware of the two of them talking on and on into the morning, that it rested with her to wind up the sitting; that he might perhaps, if not quite immediately, yet in intention be waiting for her to rise and spare him the apparent discourtesy of pleading an engagement. Even failing the engagement, they could not sit here for ever, and the convention of his world demanded that she should be the first to go.

She had just time to note, coming from far away within herself, a defiance that would sooner inflict upon him the discomfort of breaking the rule than upon herself the annoyance of moving at its bidding, when he looked across and said with the bowing attitude he had held last night as he spoke and waited for her to become aware of him: 'May I put you up for the ski-club?'

It was, of course, his business to cultivate new people, and, if they seemed suitable, to collect them . . .

She smiled acknowledgment and insincerely pleaded the shortness of her stay. All she could do, short of blurting out her poverty which he seemed not to have perceived.

But a fortnight was, he declared, the ideal time: time to learn and to get on well enough to want to come out again next year; and hurried on to promise a fellow sufferer, a friend coming up, for only a few days, from the south, who would be set immediately to work and on whose account he was committed to-day to trek down to the station.

'We were,' he said, for the first time looking across almost before he spoke, and with the manner now of making a direct important communication, 'at Cambridge together.'

A valued friend, being introduced, recommended, put before himself. Warmth crept into his voice, and lively emphasis —compressed into a small note of distress. That note was his social utmost, for gravity and for joy; recalling Selina Holland —when she was deeply moved: a wailing tone, deprecating, but in his tone was more wistfulness, a suggestion too of anxiety. It had begun when he spoke of Pater's *Renaissance Studies*, but had then merely sounded into the golden light, intensifying it. Now it seemed to flout the light, flout everything but his desire to express the absent friend.

'That was some years ago. Since then he has been a very busy man, saying to this one go and he goeth . . .' He smiled across as if asking her to share the strangeness of his friend's metamorphosis.

'You've not seen him since?'

'Not since he bought his land.'

'He's a landowner,' she said, and fell into sadness.

'He is indeed, on quite a big scale, and a very hardworking one.'

'A farmer,' murmured Miriam, 'that's not so bad.'

'It's very arduous. He is always at his post. Never takes

a holiday. For three winters I 've tried to get him up here for a week.'

'Absolute property in land,' she said to the sunlit snow, 'is a crime.'

Before her, side by side with a vision of Rent as a clutching monster astride upon civilization, was a picture of herself, suddenly hitting out at these pleasant people, all, no doubt, landowners. It was only because the friend had been presented to her in the distance and with, as it were, all his land on his back, that this one article of the Lycurgan faith of which she had no doubt, had at all reared itself in her mind. And as it came, dictating her words while she stood by counting the probable cost and wondering too over the great gulf between one's most cherished opinions about life and one's sense of life as it presents itself piecemeal embodied in people, she heard with relief his unchanged voice:

'Oh, please tell me why.'

And turned to see him flushed, smiling, pardoning her lapse, apologizing for pardoning it, and altogether interested.

'It 's a whole immense subject and I 'm not a specialist. But the theory of Rent has been worked out by those who are, by people sincerely trying to discover where it is that temporarily useful parts of the machinery of civilization have got out of gear and become harmful. No one ought to have to pay for the right to sit down on the earth. No one ought to be so helplessly expropriated that another can buy him and use him up as he would never dream of using up more costly material—horses for instance.'

'You are a socialist?'

Into her answer came the sound of a child's voice in plaintive recitative, approaching from the hall.

'Daphne in trouble,' he said, 'you 'll tell me more, I hope'— and turned his pleading smile to meet people coming in at the door. They clumped to the small table nearer the further window and she caught a sideways glimpse before they sat down: a slender woman with red-gold hair carrying a bunchy little girl whose long legs dangled against her skirt—Mrs Sneyde, the grass-widow, and, making for the far side of the table a big buoyant girlish young woman—uninteresting—the sister-in-law, Maud Hollebone.

The child's 'so bitter, *bitter* cold,' sounded clear through the morning greetings in which she took no part. Her voice was strange, low and clear, and full of a meditative sincerity. Amidst the interchange of talk between Vereker and the two women it prevailed again: a plaintive monologue addressed to the universe.

The grating of a chair and there she was, confronting the talking Vereker, who was on his feet and just about to go. She stood gazing up, with her hands behind her back. A rounded face and head, cleanly revealed by the way the fine silky brown hair was strained back across the skull; bunchy serge dress and stiff white pinafore. Pausing, Vereker looked down at her.

'You going out, Vereker?'

'Not yet.'

'Your friend coming? Not telegraphed or anything?'

'He's coming all right, Daphne. He'll be here to-night. You'll see him in the morning.'

'You'll be writing your letters till you start?'

'I may.'

'Then I'll come and sit in your room till my beecely walk.'

She rapped out her statements — immediately upon his replies, making him sound gentle and slow—from the childish, rounded face that was serenely thinking, full of quick, calm thought. Regardless talk was going forward at the other table to which, her business settled, she briskly returned.

The little wooden hall was like a summer-house that was also a sports pavilion. Against the wall that backed the dining-room stood bamboo chairs uncertain, as if, belonging elsewhere and having been told not to block the gangway by moving into the open, they did not know what they were for. The table to which they belonged stood boldly in the centre and held an ash-tray. Between it and the front door, from above which the antlered head of a chamois gazed down upon the small

scene, the way was clear, but the rest of the floor space was
invaded on all sides by toboggans propped against the wall
or standing clear with boots lying upon them, slender boots
gleaming with polish and fitted with skates that appeared to
be nothing but a single brilliant blade. Against one wall was
a pair of things like oars. Ski? But thought of as attached
to a human foot they seemed impossibly long.

From a hidden region, away beyond the angle of the staircase, came servants' voices, staccato, and abrupt sounds: the
sounds of their morning campaign, giving an air of callous
oblivion to the waiting implements of sport, and quenching,
with the way they had of seeming to urge the residents forth
upon their proper business outdoors, the hesitant invitation
of the chairs.

Beyond the dining-room and this little hall, whose stillness
murmured incessantly of activities, there was no refuge but the
dejected little salon.

Filled with morning light it seemed larger, a little important
and quite self-sufficient, giving out its secret strangeness of a
Swiss room, old; pre-existing English visitors, proof, with its
way of being, set long ago and unaltered, against their travelled
hilarity. The little parlour piano, precious in chosen wood
highly polished, with faded yellow keys and faded silk behind
its trellis, was full of old music, seemed to brood over the
carollings of an ancient simplicity unknown to the modern
piano whose brilliant black-and-white makes it sound in a room
all the time, a ringing accompaniment to the life of to-day.

But into this averted solitude there came to her again the
sense of time pouring from an inexhaustible source: gentle,
marvellous, unutterably *kind*. It came in through the window
whose screened light, filling the small room and halting meditatively there, seemed to wait for song.

Drawing back the flimsy curtain from the window, she found
it a door giving on a covered balcony through whose panes she
saw wan sunless snowfields and, beyond them, slopes, patched
with black pine woods and rising in the distance to a high ridge,
a smooth bulging thickness of snow against deep blue sky.
The dense pine woods thinned as they climbed into small

straggling groups, with here and there a single file of trees, small and sharp-pointed, marching towards the top of the ridge.

Beautiful this sharp etching far-off of keen black pines upon the sunless snow, and strange the clear deep blue of the sky. But mournful; remote and self-sufficient. Switzerland, averted and a little discouraging.

The balcony extended right and left, and a glimpse away to the left of mats hanging out into the open, and a maid pouncing forth upon them with a beater, sent her to the right, where the distance was obscured by a building standing at right angles to the house, a battered barn-like place, unbalconied, but pierced symmetrically by little windows; chalet, warm rich brown, darkened above by its sheltering, steeply jutting roof . . . beautiful. Its kindliness extended all about it, lending a warmth even to the far-off desolate slopes.

A door at her side revealed the dining-room lengthwise and deserted, and then she was round the angle of the house and free of its secret: its face towards the valley that was now a vast splendour of sunlight.

Every day, through these windows that framed the view in strips, this light would be visible in all its changings. Standing at the one that glazed the great mountain whose gold had wakened her, she discovered that the balcony was a veranda, had in front of it a railed-in space set with chairs and tables. In a moment she was out in the open light, upon a shelf, within the landscape that seemed now to be the whole delight of Switzerland outspread before her eyes.

Far away below, cleft along its centre by the irregular black line of its frozen river, was the wide white floor of the valley, measuring the mountains that rose upon its hither side.

Those high, high summits, beetling variously up into the top of the sky, where patches of tawny rock broke through their smooth whiteness against its darkest blue, knew nothing of the world below where their bases went downward in a great whiteness of broadening irregular slopes that presently bore pines in single file upwards advancing from the dense clumps upon the lower ridges, and met in an extended mass along the edge of the valley floor.

Here and there, clear of the pine woods, and looking perilously high and desolate, a single chalet made a triangular warm brown blot upon the dazzling snow.

In this crystal stillness the smallest sound went easily up to the high peaks; to the high pure blue.

Turning to bless the well-placed little hotel, she met a frontage of blank windows, each with its sharply jutting balcony, jaws, dropped beneath the blind stare of the windows set for ever upon a single scene. Hotel; queer uncherished thing. No one to share its life and make it live.

On a near table was a folded newspaper, thin, heavily printed, continental. Switzerland radiant all about her and the Swiss world within her hands—a reprieve from further seeing and a tour, into the daily life of this country whose living went on within a setting that made even advertisements look lyrical.

The simple text was enthralling. For years she had not so delighted in any reading. In the mere fact of the written word, in the building of the sentences, the movement of phrases linking part with part. It was all quite undistinguished, a little crude and hard; demanding, seeming to assume a sunny hardness in mankind. And there was something missing whose absence was a relief, like the absence of heaviness in the air. Everything she had read stood clear in her mind that yet, insufficiently occupied with the narrative and its strange emanations, caught up single words and phrases and went off independently touring, climbing to fresh arrangements and interpretations of familiar thought.

And this miracle of renewal was the work of a single night.

The need for expression grew burdensome in the presence of the empty sun-blistered tables. Perhaps these lively clarities would survive a return journey through the hotel?

Voices sounded up from below, from the invisible roadway. English laughter, of people actively diverting themselves in the winter landscape. Far away within each one was the uncommunicating English spirit, heedless, but not always unaware,

filling its day with habitual, lively-seeming activities. The
laughter sounded insincere; as if defying a gloom it refused
to face.

They passed out of hearing and the vast stillness, restored,
made her look forth: at a scene grown familiar, driving her off
to fresh seeking while it went its way towards the day when
she would see it for the last time, giving her even now, as
she surveyed its irrevocably known beauty, a foretaste of the
nostalgia that must rend her when once more she was down
upon the plains.

But that time was infinitely far away beyond the days during
which she was to live perpetually with this scene that clamoured
now to be communicated in its first freshness.

The writing at top speed of half a dozen letters left arrival
and beginning in the past, the great doorway of the enchant-
ments she had tried to describe safely closed behind her, and
herself going forward within them. With letters to post she
must now go forth, secretly, as it were behind her own back,
into Oberland; into the scene that had seemed full experience
and was but its overture.

The letters were disappointing. Only in one of them had
she escaped expressing yesterday's excited achievements and
set down instead the living joy of to-day. And this for the
one to whom such joy was incredible. But all were warm with
affection newly felt. The long distance not only made people
very dear—in a surprising way it rearranged them. Fore-
most amongst the men was Densley of the warm heart and
wooden head, wildly hailed. His letter, the last and shortest,
wrote itself in one sentence, descriptive, laughing, affectionate.
How it would surprise him. . . .

Life, she told herself as she crossed the hall trying to drown
the kitchen sounds by recalling what had flashed across her
mind as she wrote to Densley, is eternal because joy is. 'Future
life' is a contradiction in terms. The deadly trap of the ad-
jective. *Pourquoi dater?* Even science insists on indestructibility—yet marks for destruction the very thing that enables

it to recognize indestructibility. But it had come nearer and clearer than that.

Fawn-coloured woolly puppies, romping in the thick snow at the side of the steps as though it were grass, huge, as big as lion cubs, with large snub faces, and dense short bushy coats trying to curl, evenly all over their tubby tumbling bodies . . . St Bernards, at home in their snow. They flung themselves at her hands, mumbling her gloves, rolling over with the smallest shove, weak and big and beautiful, and with absurd miniature barkings.

The Alpenstock was at the higher end of the village and from its steps she could see down the narrow street to where the little church and its white-cloaked sugar-loaf spire obscured the view, and away to the right, set clear of the village and each on the crest of a gentle slope, the hotels, four, five, big buildings, not unbeautiful with their peaked roofs and balconies and the brilliance of green shutters on their white faces. And even the largest, Mrs Harcourt's 'hidjus big place' recognizable by its difference, a huge square plaster box, patterned with rows and rows of uniform windows, above whose flat roof a high pole flaunted a flag limp in the motionless air, looked small and harmless, a doll's house dumped casually, lost in the waste of snow.

If these hotels were full, there were in the village more visitors than natives. But where were they? The vast landscape was empty. From its thickly mantled fields came the smell of snow.

Going down the street, she was lost in a maze of fugitive scents within one pervading, and that seemed to compose the very air: the sweet deep smell of burning pine wood. Moving within it, as the crowded little shop windows went by on either hand, were the smells of dried apples and straw and a curious blending of faint odours that revealed themselves—when presently summoning an excuse for the excitement of shopping, at the cost of but a few of the multitude of small coins representing an English sovereign, she gained the inside of the third general store between the hotel and the church—as the familiar smell of mixed groceries; with a difference: clean smells, baked dry. No prevailing odour of moist bacon and mouldering cheese; of spilt paraffin and musty sacking, and things left undisturbed in corners. No dinginess. And though shelves and counter were crowded, every single thing gleamed and displayed itself with an air.

But there were no Swiss biscuits. . Only a double row of the familiar square tins from Reading, triumphantly displayed by the gaunt sallow-faced woman, whose ringing voice was as disconcertingly at variance with her appearance as was her charmed manner with the eager cunning that sat in her eyes. She asked for soap and thè woman set wide the door of an upright glass case in which were invitingly set forth little packets bearing names that in England were household words.

She glanced back at the biscuits. Petit Beurre were after all foreign and brought with them, always, the sight of Dinant and its rock coming into view, ending the squabble about the pronunciation of *grenouille*, as the Meuse steamer rounded the last bend. But catching sight, above the biscuits, of a box of English night-lights, she chose a piece of soap at random and fought, while she responded to the voluble chantings accompanying the packing of her parcel, with the nightmare vision of bedrooms *never* bathed in darkness, of people *never* getting away into the night, people insisting, even in rooms where brilliance can be switched on at will, on the perpetual presence of the teasing little glimmer; people who travel in groups and bring with them so much of their home surroundings that they destroy daily, piecemeal, the sense of being abroad.

Regaining the street in possession of a replica of the tablet she had unpacked last night, she found that the busy midst of the village lay just ahead where the way widened to encircle the little church. Many shops, some of them new-built, with roomy windows, and the lifeless impersonal appearance of successful provincial stores. There were more people here, more women in those heavy black dresses and head-shawls, more bloused and bearded men, crossing the snowy road with

swift slouching stride. A post office, offering universal
hospitality.

Post office: offering universal hospitality more vitally than
the little church. A beggar could perhaps find help in a church
more easily than in a post office. Yet the mere atmosphere of
a post office offered something a church could never give. Even
to enter it and come away without transactions was to have
been in the midst of life. And to handle stamps, and especially
foreign stamps, was to be aware of just those very distances
the post had abolished.

As if from the bright intense sunlight all about her, a ray of
thought had fallen upon the mystery of her passion for soap,
making it so clear in her mind that the little ray, and the lit
images waiting for words, could be put aside in favour of a
strange dingy building breaking the line of shops. Looking like
a warehouse, it had a small battered door, high up, approached
by a flight of steps leading from either side whose meeting
made a little platform before the door. Rough sleds were
drawn up round about the entrance, making it central in the
little open space about the church, the perpetual head-tossings
of the horses filling the bright air with showers of tinkles. It
could hardly be a café; yet two men had just clattered down the
steps flushed and garrulous. Strange dark-looking hostelry,
within which shone the midday sun of these rough men living
in far-away chalets among the snow.

It was not only the appeal of varying shape and colour, or
even of the many perfumes each with its power of evoking
images: the heavy voluptuous scents suggesting brunette ad-
venturesses, Turkish cigarettes, and luxurious idleness; the
elusive and delicate, that could bring spring-time into a winter
bedroom darkened by snow-clouds. The secret of its power
was in the way it pervaded one's best realizations of everyday
life. No wonder Beethoven worked at his themes washing
and re-washing his hands. And even in merely washing with
an empty mind there is a *charm*; though it is an empty charm,
the illusion of beginning, as soon as you have finished, all over
again as a different person. But all great days had soap,
impressing its qualities upon you, during your most intense

moments of anticipation, as a prelude. And the realization of a good day past, coming with the early morning hour, is accompanied by soap. Soap is with you when you are in that state of feeling life at first hand that makes even the best things that can happen important not so much in themselves as in the way they make you conscious of life, and of yourself living. Every day, even those that are called ordinary days, with its miracle of return from sleep, is heralded by soap, summoning its retinue of companion days.

To buy a new cake of soap is to buy a fresh stretch of days. Its little weight, treasure, minutely heavy in the hand, is life, past, present, and future, compactly welded.

The priced goods in the shop-windows were discouragingly high. One window behind whose thick plate glass were set forth just a few things very tastefully arranged, showed no prices at all and had the ominous note of a West End shop. Next door was a windowful that might have been transplanted from Holborn, so much steel was there, such an array of rectangular labels and announcements. Skates and skates and skates. Then a chemist's and an inspiration, though the window showed nothing but a perforated screen and the usual coloured bottles bulging on a shelf above.

The counter was stacked with wares from Wigmore Street. Even the tooth-brushes were those of the new shape devised in Cavendish Square. The chemist was a bald preoccupied man speaking English abruptly. She came away with a jar of Smith's cream, her shopping done and the face of the clock sticking out above the watchmaker's telling her it was nearly noon. The little clock on the church said a quarter past eleven and glancing back at the watchmaker's, now in the rear, she saw the reverse dial of the outstanding clock marking half past eleven. And Switzerland was the land of watchmakers. . . . Her own watch said one o'clock, English time. Then it was noon. But this far world was not three minutes' distance from the Alpenstock. There was still half an hour.

The post office was a sumptuous hall. Little tables stood about invitingly, set with pens and ink. No railed counter; a wooden partition extending to the ceiling; a row of arched pigeon-holes, all closed. Like a railway booking-office on Sunday, between trains—blankly indifferent to the announcement of the presence of a customer made by the clumping of her boots upon the wooden floor. And when presently—having gone the round of the posters, brilliant against the white-washed walls, all so much brighter and so much less bright than reality, all resounding with a single deep charm, bringing assurance of possessing, in one journey and one locality, the being of the whole—she tapped at a little shutter, it flew up impatiently, revealing an affronted young man in a blue cotton overall, glaring reproachfully through spectacles. The stamps handed over, the little door shot back into place with a bang, as if cursing an intruder.

The open spaces called for a first view before the sense of its being no longer morning should have robbed them of intensity. But where the street joined the roadway there was a little shop, full sunlight falling on its window, whose contents were a clustered delight and each separate thing more charming than its neighbour.

Two women approaching along the road preceded by English voices distracted her, for a moment, with the strangeness of their headdress—a sort of cowl. In a moment they passed with dangling clinking skates, and her intention of getting a good view from behind was diverted back to the shop window, by 'tourist-trap' interpolated in a tone meant to be inaudible, in the dissertation of the one holding forth in a voice not unlike Mrs Harcourt's, about a hotel 'packed like a bee-hive and swarming with influenza.'

It was true. The shop was full of Swiss brummagem. She fastened on it the more eagerly. Little expensive cheap things whose charm was beyond price. Small clumsy earthenware, appealingly dumpy, flower-patterned upon a warm creamy background; painted wooden spoons. Little brooches and trinkets innumerable. Cow-bells. Some small thing for everybody and a problem solved at the cost of a few marks.

Turning away, she caught sight of an old woman amazingly wrapped up, peering at her from inside a little booth set down in the snow on the other side of the way. A shelf laden with small things in carved wood protruded in front. She crossed to look at them. Silently, with slow fumbling movements, the old woman displayed her wares. Bears. Bears on ski, on toboggans, bears in every kind of unbearlike attitude. Intricate model chalets, useless and suggesting, imagined in England, nothing but the accumulation of dust. But there was an owl, with owlish dignity, very simply and beautifully carved. Her eyes returned to it, and the old woman put forth an aged freckled hand and grasped its head, which went easily back upon a hinge and left revealed a clean white china inkwell.

'Kipsake,' said the old woman huskily.

'*Danke schön. Ich komme wieder*,' smiled Miriam escaping, followed by hoarse cacklings of praise.

Out upon the roadway fenced between dazzling snowfields, the end of the valley came into sight, new, but faintly reproachful, having waited too long, and complaining now about the lateness of the hour. Certainly it was worthy of a whole self, undistracted. But there was to-morrow, many to-morrows. She had done with the street and the shops, save as a corridor, growing each day more dear, to daily fulfilment of the promise of this prospect whose beauty she was clearly recognizing. And more than its beauty. Its great, great power of assertion, veiled for the moment by distractions, but there. Wonderfully beautiful was the speech and movement of the far-off smooth pure ridge of snow, rising high against the deepest blue of the sky, linking twin peaks.

Some of the near slopes were dotted with people, tiny figurines mitigating the snowfields and the towering mountains: the sounds of English voices ringing out infinitesimal in the wide space, yet filling it. Shutting out the scene, yet intensifying it; bringing gratitude for their presence.

That remained even after the quaint peaked hoods of brilliant white or mauve, the effective skirts and jerseys of a group of women passing in the roadway had rebuked with their colours, clean and sharp against the snow, her tweed that in London had seemed a good choice, and her London felt hat.

But though the clever clothes of these people brought a sense of exile, they were powerless to rouse envy or any desire. Envy was impossible in this air that seemed, so sharp was every outline, to be no longer earth's atmosphere but open space, electric.

Perhaps even this morning there was time to get clear, to be, if only for a few moments, along some side track alone with the landscape, walking lightly clad in midsummer sun through this intensity of winter.

The road was dropping and growing harder. No longer crunching under her feet, the snow, beaten flat, showed here and there dark streaks of ice, and her puttee-bandaged legs, flexible only at the knees, felt like sticks above her feet, lost and helpless in the thick boots that seemed to walk of themselves.

The dropping road took a sharp turn towards the valley, showing ahead a short empty stretch and another sharp turn, revealing it as the winding trail up which she had come last night. On the right it was joined by a long track running steeply down into a wilderness of snow in the midst of whose far distances appeared, high up, a little bridge half hidden amongst pines. The track was dotted with pigmy forms.

'*Ash*-tongue!' A fierce hoarse voice just behind and, joining it, another, clear and ringing: '*Ach*-tooooong.'

Plunging into the roadside drift, she turned in time to see a toboggan bearing upon it a boy prone, face foremost eagerly out-thrust, shoot down the slanting road, take the bend at an angle that just cleared the fence and dart at a terrific pace down the slope towards the wilderness; followed by the girl with the ringing voice, lightly seated, her toboggan throwing her up as it bumped skimming from ridge to ridge down the uneven road. She took the bend smoothly with space to spare and flew on down the slope with lifted chin and streaming hair. Both mad. Children of the reckless English who had discovered the Swiss winter.

This terrific scooting was not the tobogganing of which she had heard in London. Two more figures were coming, giving her excuse to wait, lest they were coming her way, and watch their passing from the drift that was like warm wool, knee-deep. They were women, coming slowly, paddling themselves along with little sticks. They took the bend with ironic

caution and went on down the slope, still furiously stabbing
the snow with their little sticks, their high, peaked cowls making
them look like seated gnomes.

Aware of intense cold invading her feet, she plunged out
into the road and was beating her snow-caked puttees when an
intermittent grinding sound, approaching, brought her upright: an aged couple side by side, white-haired and immensely
muffled, sitting very grave and stern behind the legs protruding
stiffly on either side the heads of their toboggans, and set, from
moment to moment, heels downwards upon the road to check
a possible increase of their slow, triumphant pace. Triumph.
Behind the sternness that defied the onlooker to find their pose
lacking in dignity, was triumph. Young joy; for these who
might well be patrolling, in bath-chairs, the streets of a cathedral
town.

And they left the joyous message: that this sport, since pace
could so easily be controlled, might be tested at once, alone,
without instruction, this very afternoon. A subtle change
came over the landscape, making it less and more; retiring a
little, as who should say: then I am to be henceforth a background, already a mere accessory, it yet challenged her vow, an
intimidating witness.

Along the empty stretch towards the valley, the blazing sun
blotted out the distance so that it was pleasant to turn the next
corner and be going again towards the expanse that ended at
the white high-hung collar. The fresh stretch of gently sloping
road was longer than the one above it, and, walking freely here,
she found that her gait had changed, that she was planking
along in a lounging stride which brought ease to her bandaged
legs and made more manageable her inflexible feet. With a
little practice, walking could be a joy. Walking in this scene,
through this air, was an occupation in itself. And she was
being assailed by the pangs of a piercing hunger. Obtrusive;
insistent as the hunger of childhood.

It would take a little longer to go back. It would be wise to
turn now. At the corner ending this stretch. Suddenly it
seemed immensely important to discover what there was round
the next corner. From the angle of the turning, she could see

the little bridge far away to the right, in profile, with pines stretching along the bank of what it spanned, that showed a little further on as a thin straight line of frozen stream steeply descending to join the serpentine that cut the white floor of the valley. Away to the right of the bridge, straggling leafless trees stood in a curve. Behind them something moved; coming and going across the gaps between their trunks. Skaters.

Then for the girl and boy that reckless rush was just a transit; a means of getting to the rink, as one might go on a bicycle to a tennis court.

A voice greeted her from behind, surprising, in its level familiarity, until the finished phrase revealed the American, to whom, turning to find him standing before her, his toboggan drawn to heel by its rope, she gave the smile, not for him, the lover's smile reviewing, as they passed her in inverse rotation while she made the long unwelcome journey into his world of an American in Europe, her morning's gatherings.

But he had received it, was telling her that already she looked splendid, adding that when folks first came up they looked, seen beside those already there, just gass'ly. And for a moment the miscarriage was painful: to have appeared to drop even below his own level of undiscriminating hail-fellow-well-met. And for a fraction of a second as he stood before her in his correct garb she transformed him into an Englishman condemning her foolish grin—but there was his queer little American smile, that came to her from a whole continent and seemed to demand a large face and form, a little smile dryly sweet, as misdirected as her own and during which they seemed to pour out in unison their independent appreciations, and to recognize and greet in each other, in relation to the English world out here, fellow voyagers in a strange element.

It healed her self-given stripes that were, she reflected as they went on together up the hill, needless, since to him, as an American, her greeting would seem neither naïve nor bourgeois. For all Americans are either undisturbedly naïve and bourgeois or in a state of merely having learned, via Europe, to be neither. And this man, now launched in speech, revealed himself by the way he had of handling his statements, as so far very much what he had always been.

Strange that it was always queer people, floating mysterious and intangible in an alien element, who gathered up, not wanting them, testimonies that came from her of themselves.

All the way back to the Alpenstock he pursued his monologue, information, and in an unbroken flow that by reason of its temperature, its innocence of either personal interest or benevolent intention, left her free to wander. There was in his narrow, unresonant voice only one shape of tone: a discouraged, argumentative rise and fall, very slight, almost on two adjacent notes, colourless; as of one speaking almost unawares at the bidding of an endless uniform perception. She heard it now as statement, now merely as sound, and for a moment as the voice of a friend, while, after informing her that he had done the valley run and climb each morning and taken to-day a last turn to add yet one more layer to his week's sunburn, he remarked that the long zigzag was commonly deserted in the forenoon, folks mostly taking the other track, either to the rink, or further to the made run, or way beyond that to the ski-ing slopes.

When she was clear of the shop and crossing the road with the toboggan slithering meekly behind, the invisible distant slopes seemed lonely, and her plan for getting immediately away to them postponed itself in favour of enjoying for a while the thrilled equilibrium with everything about her that was the gift of the slight pull on the cord she was trying to hold with an air of preoccupied negligence. Turning leisurely back from the short length of street ahead that too soon would show the open country, she came once more into the heart of the village and paid an unnecessary visit to the post office, heard the toboggan pull up against the kerb and knew, as she turned to abandon its cord, that she had tasted the utmost of this new joy, and that when once more the cord was in her hands she must go forth and venture.

Out on the road beyond the village, the pleasant, even slither-ing alternated with little silent weightless runs, that at first made her glance back to see if the toboggan were still there. These little runs, increasing as the road began to slope, came as reminders of its character, assertions of its small willingness for its task, enhancing its charm, calling her to turn and survey, as she went, its entrancing behaviour of a little toboggan.

But presently, and as if grown weary of gentle hints, and feeling the necessity of stating more forcibly the meaning of its presence out here in the glittering stillness, it took a sudden run at her heels. Moving sideways ahead, she reduced it to its proper place in the procession until the distance between them set it once more in motion. Overtaking her, it made a half turn, slid a little way broadside and pulled up, facing her, in a small hollow, indignant. In the mercifully empty yet not altogether unobservant landscape it assumed the proportions of a living thing and seemed to say as she approached: 'You *can't* bring me out here and make a fool of me.' And indeed, even with no one in sight, she could not permit herself to walk down the slope with the toboggan ahead and pulling like a dog.

She might go back, make a detour on the level round about the village, turn the afternoon into a walk, and postpone until to-morrow the adventure for which now she had neither courage nor desire. In choosing the time when there would be fewest people abroad she had forgotten that it was also the lowest point of the day. Even this first day had a lowest point. And belated prudence, reminding her that she had come away to rest, cast a chill over the empty landscape, changing it from reality to a picture of a reality seen long ago. At the sight of it she turned and went a few paces up the gradient and perched and gathered up the length of cord, and life came back into the wastes of snow, the mountains were real again, quiet in the motionless afternoon light, and the absurd little toboggan a foe about to be vanquished.

It slid off at once, took a small hummock askew, righted itself, to a movement made too instinctively to be instructive, and slid onwards gathering pace.

But ecstasy passed too swiftly into awareness of the bend in the road now rushing up to meet her ignorance. Ramming her heels into the snow she recovered too late, with a jolting pang in both ankles and a headlong dive into this morning's drift, a memory of what she should have done and stood up tingling with joy in the midst of the joyous landscape, stilled again, that had flown with her and swooped up as she plunged, and was now receiving her exciting news.

The backward slope invited her to return and go solemnly, braking all the way and testing the half-found secret of steering. But the bend tempted her forward. A single dig on the left when she reached it and she would be round in face of the long run down to the level.

But the dig was too heavy and too soon, and landed her with her feet in the drift and the toboggan swung broadside and all but careering with her backwards along the steepness that lay, when once more she faced it, a headlong peril before the levels leading on and up to the little bridge could come to bring rescue and peace.

Pushing carefully off, sliding with bated breath and uncomfortably rasping heels, down and down, making no experiments and thankful only to feel the track slowly ascending behind her, she remained clenched until only a few yards were left down which with feet up she slithered deliriously and came to rest.

It was done. She had tobogganed herself away from Oberland into the wilderness, the unknown valley waiting now to be explored, with the conquered steed trailing once more meek and unprotesting in the background. The afternoon was hers for happiness until hunger, already beginning its apparently almost continuous onslaught, should make welcome the triumphant climb back to Oberland and tea upon the promontory.

The high bridge that in the distance looked so small and seemed to span smallness was still small, a single sturdy arch; but beneath it dropped a gorge whose spines led down to a torrent, frozen; strange shapes of leaping water arrested, strangely coloured: grey in shadow, black in deep shadow, and here and there, caught by the light, a half-transparent green.

There was a great fellowship of pines clustered on either bank and spreading, beyond the bridge, to a wood that sent out a rising arm blocking the view of the valley and the pass. They made a solitude down here above the silenced waters. The backward view was closed by the perilous slope whose top was now the sky-line, leaving Oberland far away out of sight in another world.

The track through the wood, wide and level for a while, with spired pines marching symmetrically by, narrowed to a winding path that took her in amongst them, into their strange close fellowship that left each one a perfect thing apart. Not lonely, nor, for all the high-bulging smoothness of snow in which it stood, cold. It was their secret, pine-breath, that brought a sense of warm life; and their close-clustered needles. Out on the mountain-sides they looked black and bleak, striving towards the sun until they were stayed by the upper cold. Seen close, they were a happy company bearing light upon the green burnish of their needles and the dull live tints of their rough stems. And very secret; here thought was sheltered as in a quiet room.

Out in the immense landscape, in the down-pouring brilliance of pure light, thought was visible. Transparent to the mountains who took its measure and judged, yet without wounding, and even while they made it seem of no account, a small intricate buzzing in the presence of mighty, simple statement sounding just out of reach within the air, and invited thoughtless submission to their influence as to a final infinite good that would remain when they were no more seen, there was pathos in their magnificence; as if they were glad even of one small observing speck, and displayed gently the death they could deal, and smiled in their terrifying power as over an open secret.

And to walk and walk on and on amongst them, along their sunlit corridors with thought shut off and being changed, coming back refreshed and changed and indifferent, was what most deeply she now wanted of them.

The track climbed a ridge and there, below, were the American's wide snowfields.

Before she was assured by the doffed cap outheld while he made his salutation—the sweeping foreign *coup de chapeau* that was so decisive a politesse compared with the Englishman's meagre small lift; and yet also insolent—she was rejoicing in the certainty that the bearded figure, in spite of the English Norfolk suit and tweed cap, was the big Russian. He alone, at this moment, of all the people in the hotel, would be welcome. Remote, near and friendly as the deepest of her thoughts, and so far away from social conventions and the assumptions behind conventions, as to leave all the loveliness about her unchanged—and yet trailing an absurd little toboggan, smaller, and, in contrast with his height, more ridiculous an appendage than her own. He plunged down the ridge in the English style, by weight and rather clumsily, and in a moment was by her side at the head of the run that went, pure white and evenly flattened, switch-backing away across the field out of sight.

In a slow mournful voice that gave his excellent French a melancholy music, he asked her if she had already tested the run and became, when he had heard the short tale of her adventure, impatiently active. Her toboggan, he said, and raised its fore-part and bent scanning, was too large, too heavy and with runners not quite true. It would be better for the moment to exchange. 'Try, try,' he chanted with the true Russian nonchalance and, abandoning his own, went off down the gentle slope on the discredited mount that now she might blame for her mysterious swerve at the bend.

After the gentle drop, carrying him over the first small rise as if it were not there, he flew ahead gathering swiftness with each drop, away and away until at last he appeared a small upright figure far away on the waste of snow.

The run, compared with what she had already attempted, seemed nothing at all. The drops so slight that once or twice she was stranded on a ridge and obliged to push off afresh. And the light little toboggan, responding to the slightest heel-tap upon the hard-pressed snow, taught her at once the secret of steering. And when at last, full of the joy of fresh conquest, she was pulled up by the loose snow at the end of the run, she was eager only to tramp back and begin again. But, tramping at her side, he tore her triumph to shreds. Silently she tried to imagine the toboggan having its own way uncontrolled for the whole of that sweeping trek, for the two quite steep drops towards the end.

The second time he started her in advance and remained behind shouting, his voice rising to a crescendo at the first steepness: '*Il n'y a pas de danger!*' With an immense effort she restrained her feet and entered paradise.

'*Ça ira, ça ira,*' he admitted smiling when once more they were side by side. They tramped back in silence, under the eyes, as they approached the ridge, of a group newly appeared upon its crest and from which, when they drew near, a voice came down in greeting. She looked up to see the Croydon family, all very trim in sporting garb and carrying skates, gathered in a bunch, at once collectively domestic and singly restive. They smiled eagerly down at her and she read in the father's twinkling gaze that she was providing material for Croydon humour, so distinctly and approvingly was it saying in the Croydon way: 'You've not lost much time,' and so swiftly, having told her in response to her own greeting, that the rink was within five minutes' easy walking, did he turn and disappear with his family in tow down the far side of the ridge.

The third run left her weary and satisfied. Again they were tramping back side by side, and although her experience of Russians had taught her that gratitude was out of place and enthusiasm over simple joys a matter for half-envious contempt, her thankfulness and felicity, involuntarily eloquent, treated him, marching tall and sombre at her side upon feet that in spite of the enormous boots showed themselves slender and shapely terminations of a well-hung frame, as if he had been of her own English stock; let him see the value, to herself, of his kindly gift. All she lived for now, she told him, was to rush, safe-guarded by a properly mastered technique, at the utmost possible speed through this indescribable air, down slopes from which the landscape flew back and up. He smiled down, of course, the half-incredulous smile. Of course bored, giving only part of a dreamy attention to all this raving.

'*C'est bon pour la santé,*' he murmured as she paused.

What did he know of santé, unless, perhaps, he had been in

a Russian prison? He might be a refugee; an anarchist living in Switzerland.

When he, too, turned out to be now returning in search of tea and they were climbing the slope towards Oberland, their toboggans colliding and bumping along as best they might at the ends of cords twisted together round the wrist of his glove-less hand, she remarked by way of relieving a silence he did not seem to think it necessary to break, that the Swiss winter must be less surprisingly beautiful to Russians than to the people of the misty north. He agreed that doubtless this was so and gloomily asked her if she had been in Russia. He agreed with everything she said about his country as seen from a distance, but without interest and, presently, as if to change the subject, declared that he knew nothing of Russia and Russians.

His voice sounded again too soon to give her time to select a nationality that should soften the disappointment of losing him as a Russian, and in a moment he was talking of Italy, and the Italy she knew by so many proxies dead and living was stricken out of her mind, to give place to the unknown Italy who had produced this man, simple and sincere, gloomy and harsh-minded, playing Chopin with all his heart. But when presently she learned that he was a business man on holiday from Milan, her Italy returned to her. He was from a world that everywhere was the same, a world that existed even within Italy.

And at dinner again he sat apart wrapped in his gloom, until again Vereker was rescuing him with speech and he was responding in the withheld, disclaiming Russian way.

A Latin consciousness was, in this group, something far more remote than a Russian would have been, and she wondered what it was that behind Vereker's unchanging manner was making his half of the bridge upon which they met. Music perhaps, if Vereker, with eyes candid and not profound and not deep-set, were musical. She caught a few words. It was the weather. Do Italians discuss the weather? Was Guerini, behind his gratitude in being rescued from isolation, wondering at the Englishman's naïveté? Vereker was not showing off his French. He was being courteous, being himself. No one, except, when he could seize a chance, the American, made any sort of parade. Nor was it that they made a parade of not making a parade. Talk with them was easy because it was quite naturally serene. No emphasis. No controversy. The emergence of even a small difference of opinion produced at once, on both sides, a smiling retreat. Deep in his soul the American must certainly be deploring this baffling urbanity. English correctness and hypocrisy. Here was the original stuff from which the world-wide caricatures were made.

And talk with these people always ended in a light and lively farewell, a manner of dropping things that handed a note of credit for future meetings. A retreat, as from royalty, backwards. A retreat from the royal game of continuous courtesy.

And together with the surprise of discovering—when having departed upstairs she was drawn down to the little salon by the sound of the Chopin ballade—not the Italian but Vereker at the piano in the empty room, was the boon of his composure. Of his being, and continuing to be after she had slipped into the room and reached a chair from which she could just see him in profile, so quietly engrossed. A little strung, as though still the phrases that yesterday he had so carefully recaptured might again elude him; but listening. Led on, and listening, and in the hands of Chopin altogether.

Seated thus exposed he was slender, delicate, musicianly; only the line of his jaw gave him an appearance of strength; and perhaps the close cropping of his hair, so that of what would have been a flamboyant mass only crisp ridges were left, close against a small skull, like Caesar's. His spruceness and neatness made stranger than ever the strange variance between the stiff, magpie black and white of dress clothes, and the depth and colour of music.

He played the whole ballade; sketchily where the technical difficulties came thick and fast, but keeping the shape, never losing the swinging rhythm.

Its concluding phrases were dimmed by the need of finding something to say that should convey her right to say anything at all; but when the last chord stood upon the air, the performance seemed to have been a collaboration before which they now sat equally committed. And when his face came round, its smile was an acknowledgment of this.

For an instant she felt that nothing could fit but a gratefully affectionate salute and then a 'How's old So-and-so in these days?' after the manner of men of his type drifting happily about upon the surfaces of life. And when she said: 'You got the whole of it this time,' it was as if the unexpressed remainder had indeed passed across to him, as if she were the newly arrived friend whose presence somewhere upstairs had made him so radiant during dinner and afterwards sent him to pour out his happiness in the deserted little salon.

'After a fashion,' he said with the little flicker of the eyelids that was his way, from sixth-form or from undergraduate days, of sustaining for further speech the pose of his turned head and smiling face. 'There's no one like him, is there?'

'You were playing last evening, just after I came. For a moment I couldn't believe that ballade was actually here. I heard it long ago, and never since, and I've never been able to recall the theme.'

'I'm *so* glad,' he said with his little note of distress. 'I've been trying for *days* to get it all back.'

For him, too, it came out of a past, and brought that past into this little Swiss room, spread it across whatever was current in his life, showed him himself unchanged. And in that past they had lived in the same world, seen and felt in the same terms the things that are there for ever before life has moved. So far they were kindred. But since then she had been flung out into another world; belonged to the one in which he had gone forward only through an appreciative understanding of its code, of what it was that created its self-operating exclusiveness. He did not yet know that she stood outside the charmed circle, had been only an occasional visitor, and that now, visiting again after years of absence, she was hovering between the desire to mask, and remain within it, and her proper business as a Lycurgan: to make him aware of the worlds outside his own, let him see that his innocent happiness was kept going by his innocent mental oblivion.

And whilst they called up cherished names and collided in

agreement, she wondered what these people who lived in exile from reality could find in their music beyond escape into the self for whom in their state of continuous urbane association there was so little space; and presently became aware of lively peace filling the intervals between their to and fro of words, distracting attention from them, abolishing everything but itself and its sure meaning: so that into this Swiss stillness, of frost without and electricity within, nothing had been present of the Switzerland that had brought them both here, and now suddenly came back, enhanced, a single unbounded impression that came and was gone, that was the face of its life now begun in her as memory.

She read her blissful truancy in his eyes, his recognition of their having fallen apart, but not of its cause, which he thought was perhaps the monotony of their continuous agreement, and was now swiftly seeking a fresh bridge that in an instant, since clearly he intended to prolong the sitting, he would, deferentially flickering his eyelids, take courage to fling.

But into the little pause came the sound of footsteps approaching through the hall, and an intensity of listening that was their common confession of well-being and was filling them with a wealth of eager communication that must now be postponed until to-morrow. But, to-morrow, the college friend would be in possession; there was only this evening, a solitary incident. Perhaps the door would open upon someone who would straightway withdraw, leaving the way open for the waiting conversation. And the college friend had come only for a few days. . . .

But this falling from grace was rebuked by the reminder of Vereker's all-round niceness. He would, of course, retain the intruder. If it were a man there would be three-cornered talk, enlivened by what was being sacrificed to it. But with the opening of the door, as she raised her eyes towards it and caught in passing a glimpse of him upon his music stool, out of action and alone, she saw that dear and nice as he was, had always been, he could not fully engage her, was real to her on a level just short of reaching down to the forces of her nature; was pathetically, or culpably, a stranded man; subsisting.

Guerini: huge, filling the doorway, hesitating for a moment and retreating, quietly closing the door, but not before Vereker, wheeling round on his music-stool, had seen his departing form.

It was his unexpectedness, the having forgotten him so that he came like an apparition, that had sent him away. Even so, a woman of the world would have promptly become a smiling blank and suitably vocal; or withdrawn and expressionless in the manner of a hotel guest only partly in possession of a room now to be partly taken over by another. But she had left her thoughts standing in her face, leaving Vereker, who had turned just too late, to be hostess.

Wheeling back to face her, he was again the gentle companion from the past. In his elegant sunny voice he was recalling their morning's talk, begging at once, with his despairing little frown, for more light on the subject of property in land. It was clear that these things had never come his way. It was after all not his fault that his education had held his eyes closed, that they had since been kept closed by wealth and ease taken for granted. And, in his way, he had kept fine. His adoration for his gods of art and literature was alive and genuine—and he was a sportsman. It was difficult, face to face with his gentle elegance, to remember that he was distinguishing himself in an exacting sport. Repentant of her condemnation, she set forth the steps of the reasoning and the groups of facts, saw him eagerly intent—not upon herself but upon this new picture of life, wrestling step by step with what he saw far off—and presently had the joy of seeing him see how economic problems stood rooted in the holding of land at rent. But he was only one; there were thousands of men, nice men, needing only hints, as blinkered as he.

CHAPTER IV

HURRYING through her dressing to keep the appointment that had not been made and whose certainty in her own mind was challenged in vain by all the probabilities, she opened her door upon the silent corridor; stillness and silence as if every one else in the hotel had been spirited away, leaving clear, within the strange surroundings in which for a while she was set down, the familiar pathway of her life. And, when she reached the dining-room, the sight of them there, side by side at breakfast in the brilliant morning light with no one else in the room save herself approaching, had for a moment the hard unreality of things deliberately arranged. She saw them very clearly, and it was as if neither of them were there; as if they were elsewhere each on his own path from which this tacit meeting was a digression.

But before she was half-way to the table they were rising. Their breakfast over, they were going off into their day. She was too late; her haste was justified of its wisdom. Reaching her place, she murmuring a casual greeting, turned away towards the spaces of her own day opening, beyond this already vanishing small disappointment, as brightly as the light shining in from the sunlit snow.

They halted a moment while Vereker introduced his friend to whose height, as she sat down to the table, she glanced up to meet the intent dark gaze of a man on guard. She was already far away and, in the instant of her hurried astonished return to face for the first and perhaps the last time this man who was challenging her, the eyes were averted and the two men sat down: to freshly broken rolls and steaming cups.

The little self-arranged party was secure in the morning stillness that was the divine invisible host equally dear to all three. Happy in this fulfilment of premonition, she sat silent, delighting in the challenge left, miscarried and superfluous upon the empty air, wickedly delighting in the friend's discomfort in following the dictates of the code forbidding him again to look across until she should have spoken, and confining his large gaze within the range of his small immediate surroundings. Refusing rescue, she busied herself with breakfast, enjoying his large absurdity, free, while he paid the well-deserved penalty of his innocently thwarted attack, to observe to her heart's content.

He sat taking sanctuary with Vereker—who at his sunny best was making conversation, enlarging upon the trials in store—slightly turned towards him and away from the barred vista across which no doubt, before she came in, his large gaze had comfortably extended; responding to Vereker now and again, with thoughtful groans.

Beside Vereker's sunburned fairness he was an oiled bronze; heavy good features, heavy well-knit frame. Lethargic, or just a very tired man on a holiday, bemused by his sudden translation. Superficially he was formidable, 'strong and silent.' His few remarks, thrown into the talk that Vereker kept up while he waited for his two friends to fraternize and admire each other, came forth upon a voice deliberately cultivated since his undergraduate days, a ponderous monotone, the voice of a man infallible, scorning argument, permanently in the right. Its sound was accompanied by a swaying movement from side to side of his body bent forward from the hips: suggesting some big bovine creature making up its mind to charge.

She recalled other meetings with his kind, instant mutual dislike and avoidance. This time there was no escape. She was linked to him by Vereker, obliged by Vereker to tolerate his presence, sit out his portentousness, and be aware, since Vereker found him so very fine, of the qualities hidden within. Courage of course, tenacity, strength to adventure in strange places. Were such things enough to justify this pose of omniscience? With that pose it was for ever impossible to make terms; and if this were not a single occasion, if there were further meetings, there would sooner or later be a crossing of swords. She considered his armoury.

Mentally it was a flimsy array; a set of generalizations, born of the experience that had matured him and become now his whole philosophy, simple and tested, immovable; never suspected of holding good only for the way of living upon which it was based.

The fact of the existence of life had either never entered his head or been left behind in the days before he crystallized. He had now become one of those who say 'our first parents,' and see a happy protégé of an entirely masculine Jehovah duped into age-long misery by the first of the charmers Homage and contempt for women came equally forth from him, the manifest faces of his fundamental ignorance. The feminine world existed for him as something apart from life as he knew it, and to be kept apart. Within that world 'charm' and 'wit' drew him like magnets and he never guessed their source; knew nothing of the hinterlands in the minds of women who assumed masks, put him at his ease, appeared not to criticize. And such women were the sum of his social knowledge. One day he would be a wise old man 'with an eye for a pretty face,' wise with the wisdom that already was cheating him of life.

There was no hope for him. His youth had left him Vereker, his chum whose sunny simplicity had always disarmed him, who did not resent his portentous manner. From women he would have, till old age, flattery for his strength. From his workers nothing but work, and respect for his English justice and honesty. It was inconceivable that any one should ever pierce his armour; the ultimate male density backed by 'means' and 'position.'

His pose had found its bourne in his present position of authority, his state of being bound to present a god-like serenity; and it had become so habitual that even when it was put out of action he could not disencumber himself of it. At this moment, for lack of proper feminine response from across the table, it was actually embarrassing him. To proper feminine response, charming chatter or charming adoring silence, he would pay tribute, the half respectful, half condescending interest of the giant in his hours of ease.

Unable any longer to endure silently, she rode across him

with speech; pictures, for Vereker, of her yesterday's adventure. Lively and shapely, inspired by the passage of wrath. Her voice had a bright hard tone, recognizable as the tone of the lively talker.

She was aware of the friend accepting her as the bright hard mondaine; at once attentive, his pose relaxed so far as to be represented only by the eyebrows left a little lifted and still knitting his deliberately contemplative brow. He was looking, poor dear, at the pictures, enjoying them, their mechanism, their allusions. And she, for a weary empty interval, was being a social success. It was a victory for the friend, a bid for his approval.

Vereker was puzzled, meeting a stranger; a little taken aback. But when, grown weary of the game of brightly arranged exaggerations, she relapsed into simplicity, he recovered at once and again brought forth his ski-club. The friend sat by while one after another the persuasive arguments came forth, smiling with the slightly lifted brow that was now his apology for smiling at all.

And suddenly he was grave, intent as he had been at the first moment; this time towards the door, outside which sounded Daphne's eager breathless voice and ceased in the doorway. Her swift slight footsteps crossed the room and brought her to a standstill just in sight, gazing at the stranger.

He remained grave, darkly gazing. Vereker, half-risen, eager to be off, was looking at him in the manner of a hostess arrested in giving the signal for departure. For a moment the man and the child stared at each other, and then she moved stealthily, rounding the table-end. A light came into his unsmiling face. With a rush she was upon him, mouth set, eyes blazing, clenched fists beating upon his breast.

'*Eaden*,' she panted, 'evil, *evil* Eaden.'

There was no defence, no display of comic fear, no wrist-catching dominance. And when she desisted, and stood back still searching him with grave face a little thrust forward in her eagerly thinking way, he turned more sideways from the table, to attend, while hurriedly, with the air of one having other business on hand and no time to waste, she catechized him.

He answered simply, with just her manner of one cumbered
with affairs and eager nevertheless to contrive meetings; de-
vouring all the time with his eyes the strange hurried little face,
the round wide eyes set upon something seen afar.

They had recognized each other.   To the rest of the party
she was a quaint, precocious child.   This man saw the strange
power and beauty of the spirit shining in those eyes almost
round, almost protruding, and, if there had been in the blue of
them, that toned so gently into the pearly blue surrounding, a
shade more intensity of colour, merely brilliant.

'You *must*,' she said, her lips closing firmly on her ultimatum,
head a little out-thrust, hands behind back.   'You'd better
go now,' with a glance at the group that had gathered round.
She pattered swiftly away to her table in the background.

'Daphnee'll always get what she wants with her nagging,'
said the Skerry youth standing by.

'She will get what she wants with her beaux yeux,' said
Miriam warmly, and saw the little form panting along its ardent
way up through life, seeking and testing and never finding, in
any living soul.

'*Yes*,' groaned Eaden and impatiently sighed away the
wrath in his eyes set upon the departing figure of the youth.
Again they were lit and gentle and as if still gazing upon
Daphne.   He sat for a moment, paying tribute to a suddenly
found agreement, before joining Vereker held up at the door
in the little crowd of newly arriving breakfasters.

It was something like cycling in traffic, only that this scattered
procession making for the rink seemed all one party.   The
achtungs, of those starting on their journey from the top of the
slope rising behind her, rang out like greetings, and the agonized
shrieks coming up from below, as one and another neared the
gap visible now in the distance as an all-too-swiftly approaching
confusion of narrowly avoided disasters, were full of friendly
laughter: the fearless laughter of those experienced in collisions.
For a moment she was tempted to steer into the snow and wait

until the road should be clear. But the sudden sideways swerve of a toboggan just ahead called forth unawares her first *achtung*. It rang, through the moment which somehow manœuvred her clear of the obstacle, most joyously upon the air and hailed her —seeming to be her very life sounding out into the far distances of this paradise, claiming them as long ago it had claimed the far distances surrounding outdoor games—and sent her forward, one of the glad fellowship of reckless tobogganners whom now unashamed she could leave, to go along her chosen way.

Ignoring yells from behind she slowed to pass the gap and its glimpse of the descending track dotted with swiftly gliding humanity, took the sharp bend beyond it, and was out of sight careering down the first slope of the valley run with sky and landscape sweeping upwards, mountains gigantically sweeping upwards to the movement of her downward rush.

The dreaded bends arrived, each too swiftly, with its threat of revealing, upon the smooth length of the next slope, an upward-coming sleigh, or village children steering down at large. Slope after slope showed clear and empty, each steeper than the last, and here and there a patch of ice sent her headlong, sent the landscape racing upwards until her heels could find purchase for a steadying dig and bring back the joy of streaming forward for ever through this moving radiance.

The fencing was growing lower, almost buried in deep snow. A sweeping turn and ahead, at the end of a long smooth slope, the floor of the valley, the end. From a drive of both heels she leaned back and shot forward and flew, feet up, down and down through the crystal air become a rushing wind, until the runners slurred into the soft snow, drove it in wreaths about her, and slowed and stopped dead leaving her thrown forward with the cord slack in her hands, feet down, elbows on knees come up to meet them, a motionless triumphantly throbbing atom of humanity in a stillness that at once kept her as motionless as itself, to listen to its unexpected voice: the clear silvery tinkle, very far away, of water upon rock; some little mountain stream freed to movement by the sun, making its way down into the valley. She listened for a while to the perfect little sound, the way it filled the vast scene, and presently turned to search the snowy levels, longing to locate it and catch a glimpse, defying distance, of the sunlit runnel. The mountains were cliffs upon the hither side, their shoulders and summits invisible until one looked up to find them remote in the ascended sky.

Down here at their feet was *terra firma*, broad levels on either side the windings of the frozen river that was trimmed here and there with bare trees sparse and straggling, their gnarled roots protruding through the snow that bulged its rim. A bird-cry sounded from a tree at the roadside; on silent wings a magpie, brilliant in sunlit black and white, sailed forth and away across the wastes. Birds and the tinkling runnel, the sole inhabitants of this morning solitude.

Whose magic survived the long backward climb and the run down to the rink amidst the sociable echoes of the morning's tumult, survived the knowledge that in the minds of these busy skaters it was merely the bottom of the hill; nothing to do down there, unless you were going on down to the station to meet and sleigh up with someone newly arrived.

Here on their tree-encircled rink they were together all day as in a room. Passing and re-passing each other all day long. Held together by the enchantment of this continuous gliding. Every one seemed to be gliding easily about. Only here and there a beginner shuffled along with outstretched jerking arms and anxious face. It was skating escaped from the niggardly opportunities of England and grown perfect. Long sweeping curves; dreaming eyes seraphic, even the sternest betrayed by the enchantment in their eyes. There were many of these in this English crowd. Many who knew there was absurdity in the picture of grown persons sweeping gravely about for hours on end. Only a great enchantment could keep them in countenance and keep them going on. Envy approached and stared her in the face. But only for a moment. She could skate, rather better than the beginners. In a day or two she could be sweeping enchantedly about. It was a temptation, answered before it presented itself, only presenting itself because it could move more quickly than thought: to be racing about on a sled was a reckless flouting of the prescribed programme, but innocent, begun in forgetfulness. To have come and seen, to sit and stroll about each day just seeing, would have been joy enough.

But when she looked across, from the grey crowded rink with its belt of ragged bare trees, to the mountains standing in full sunlight and filling half the opposite sky, and saw, away above the pine woods ascending beyond the little bridge, the distant high white saddle of the pass with its twin peaks rising on either side—they startled her with their heightened beauty. These enchanted skaters, cooped upon their sunk enclosure, had enlivened the surrounding scene not only by bringing forgetfulness of it, but because she knew the secret of their bliss, had shared long ago the experience that kept them confined here all day.

Gliding, as if for ever; the feeling, coming even with the first uncertain balance, of breaking through into an eternal way of being. In all games it was there, changing the aspect of life, making friends dearer, making even those actually disliked, dear, as long as they were within the rhythm of the game. In dancing it was there. But most strongly that sense of being in an eternal way of living had come with skating in the foggy English frost. And this it must be that kept all these English eagerly and shamelessly fooling about on bladed feet; eternal life.

It might be wrong. Wells might be right. Golf. There must be a secret too in golf. The mighty swipe, the swirl of the landscape about the curving swing of the body, the onward march? All these must count, even if the players think only of the science of the game, only of excelling an opponent. Even in safe and easy games there is an element of eternity, something of the quality there must be in sports that include the thrill of the life-risk. Savage sports. Fitness, the sense of well-being of the healthy animal? But what *is* health? What *is* the sense of well-being?

'We know *nothing*. That at least you must admit: that we walk in darkness.'

'And proclaim ourselves enlightened by awareness of the fact.'

A figure swinging swiftly up the rink, a different movement

cutting across the maze of familiar movements, drawing her eyes to follow it until it was lost and watch until again it came by: clothed in uniform purplish brown, close fitting, a belted jerkin, trousers, slenderly baggy, tapering down into flexibly fitting boots. A strong lissome body that beautifully shaped its clothing and moved in long easy rushes, untroubled by shackled feet.

He was not perhaps doing anything very wonderful, just rushing easily about, in the manner of a native of some land of ice and snow. But he transformed the English skaters to jerking marionettes, clumsily clothed, stiff-jointed. Visibly jointed at neck and waist, at knees and ankles and elbows. Their skating seemed now to be nicely calculated mechanical balancing of jointed limbs, each limb trying to be autonomous, their unity, such as it was, achieved only by methods thought out and carefully acquired. They seemed to be giving exhibitions of style, with minds and bodies precariously in tune. He was style spontaneously alive. His whole soul was in his movements.

She made her way to a near bench under the trees to watch for him. Sitting there with her feet upon the ice, she became one with the skaters, felt their efforts and controls, the demand of the thin hard blade for the perpetual movements of loss and recovery. Not all were English, skating with reservations. Here a little Frenchman, with arms folded on his breast, came by as if dancing, so elegantly pointed were the swinging feet above which gracefully he leaned now forward now back. Effortlessly. In his stroke there was no jerk of a heavy-muscular drive, yet he covered as much ground as the English, and more quickly. Behind him an Englishwoman, with a bird's-wing pointing back along the side of her little seal cap, going perfectly gracefully in smooth slight sweeps; serene.

Near at hand two men practised trick skating, keeping clear the space about them with their whirling limbs. They swept about with eyes intent, and suddenly one or other would twirl, describe a circle with an outflung leg, and recover, with an absurd hop. Clever and difficult no doubt, but so very ugly that it seemed not worth doing. The stout man's hop seemed as though it must smash the ice. Between their dervish whirls they talked. They were arguing. Amiably quarrelling; the occasional hysterical squeal in the voice of the stout man revealing 'politics.' They were at loggerheads over the housekeeping, the lime-lit, well-paid, public housekeeping, 'affairs,' the difficult responsible important business that was 'beyond the powers of women,' that was also 'dirty work for which women were too good'; wrangling. The stout man executed a terrific twirl and brought up facing his opponent who had just spoken. He advanced upon him, bent and sliding, arms dangling low: 'Just *so*,' he chanted amiably and, recovering the upright, presented a face really foolish, a full-moon foolishness, kindly perfection of inability to see further than his good British nose: 'We 're back at what I told Hammond this morning: we *can't afford* to ignore the *Trades Union Secretaries*.' With a swift turn he was off before the other man could respond, skating away beyond their enclosure, smiling his delight, staring ahead, with wise eyes, at nothing at all but the spectacle of his opponent caught out and squashed.

The spectacle of his complacency was profoundly disquieting. He was the typical kindly good-natured John Bull. Gently nurtured, well-educated, 'intelligent,' ready to take any amount of time and trouble in 'getting at facts' and 'thinking things out.' And he was a towering bully. Somewhere within his naïve pugnacity was the guilty consciousness of being more pleased in downing an opponent than concerned for human welfare. There was no peace of certainty in him. He had scored and was flushed with victory. And all over English politics was this perpetual prize-fighting. The power of life and death was in the hands of men playing for victory; for their own side.

Morning and evening, in some hotel, that big man's voice boomed incessantly. Behind it a kindly disposition and a set of fixed ideas. No mind.

'Don't you skeete?'

Making for the bench, bent forward to reach it hands first, was the younger Croydon girl; behind her the other, rallentando, balancing to a standstill.

She had greeted them, ere she was aware, with the utmost enthusiasm. Smiling in their way, a gentle relaxation of the features that left them composed, they stood about her, pleased to see and greet a stranger who was also an old friend, renewing their great adventure. At the same time they were innocently rebuking her outbreak.

In her suburban past she had instinctively avoided their kind, scented a snare in their refined gentility, liked them only for the way, in the distance, going decorously in pretty clothes along tree-lined roadways, they contributed to the brightness of spring. Meeting them out here, representative of England, the middle-class counterparts, in their ardent composure, of the hotel people who so strangely had received her as a relative, she wanted in some way to put forth her claim as one who knew of old their world of villa and garden, their gentle enclosed world.

'It's glorious; we're having a lovely tame,' said the younger, looking away down the rink: an English rose, thoroughly pretty in the characterless English way, shapely sullen little face, frowning under the compulsion of direct statements. Her hair, that in the train had been a neat bun, hung now in a broad golden plait to her waist, where its ends disappeared behind a large black bow like a bird with wings outspread.

And now, with one seated close on each side of her, it was with difficulty that she attended to their talk, so clearly did it exhibit their world as a replica of the one just above it: as a state of perpetual urbane association; conformity to a code in circumstances more restricted, upon a background more uniform, and searched by the light of a public opinion that was sterner than the one prevailing above. All the bourgeois philistine in her came forth to sun itself in their presence, zestfully living their lives, loving their friends and relatives, ignoring every one who lived outside the charmed circle.

One against the other, they joyously relived the short time whose sunburn had so becomingly accentuated their Blair Leighton fairness. Their stories centred round the success or breakdown of the practical jokes that seemed to be the fabric of life at their hotel . . . all the old practical jokes; even apple-pie beds. In and out of these stories went Mr Parry, who was presently pointed out upon the ice; a stout little dark man skating about at random, his movements visibly hampered by the burden of his sociability, his eyes turning, to the detriment of his steering, towards every one he passed in his search for prey.

'He makes us all *roar*; every evening.'

There were others, some whose names and their roles, as assistants or willing victims of the schemes of Mr Parry, seemed sufficiently to describe them, and, as central decoration in the picture, these two girls newly arrived and certainly Mr Parry's most adored recruits, ready trained by a brother in the science of practical joking, yet not hoydenish; demure and sweet and, to his loneliness, the loneliness of an undignified little man, not quite grotesque, and incapable of inspiring romantic affection, figures of romance.

Growing weary of their inexhaustible theme—of waiting for the emergence of some sign of consciousness of the passing moment, a dropping of references backwards or forwards, that would leave them in league together, there as individuals— she pressed them for personal impressions of the adventure in its own right, the movement into strangeness, the being off the chain of accustomed things. They grew vague, lost interest, and fell presently into a silence from which she pulled them by an inquiry about the plait.

In the midst of the story of the plait and just as some people were being pointed out who still thought them three sisters, two with their hair up, and one with a plait who did not appear at dinner, came a longing to escape, the sense of a rendezvous being missed, with the scene and the time of day. But her preparations for flight were stayed by their payment for her interest in the plait. They plied her with questions; presently they were offering to lend her skating-boots, and choosing, from amongst the guests at their hotel, people she would like. They were pitying her, thinking that she must be having a poor time and determined at once that she should do more than just stand upon the edge, sunning herself in the glow of the life they were finding so entrancing.

But her contemplation of the desert that must be, from their point of view, the life of a woman obviously poor and apparently isolated, took her for a moment far away, and when she returned the link between them was snapped. Her silence had embarrassed their habit of rapid give and take. Making vague promises, she took leave, rescued by their immediate reversion to the forms of speech set for such occasions, from holding forth upon the subject of the dead level of happiness existing all over the world independent of circumstances. They would have thought her both pious and insane.

All the afternoon they had been in harmony, strolling and standing about together in the snow until there seemed nothing more to say; and after each run there had been something more to say. Till Italy lost all strangeness but its beauty, and he had seemed a simpler Michael, free from Michael's certainty that every one in the world is marching to annihilation.

And suddenly there was a wall, dividing. No more communication possible; the mountains grown small and bleak and sad and even now, in being alone upon the promontory there was no peace, in all the wide prospect no beauty.

Why was it so much a matter of life and death, for men as for women? Why did each always gather all its forces for the conflict?

If all he said were a part of the light by which he lived, he should have been able to remain calm. But he had not remained calm. He had been first uneasy, then angry, and then sorry for the destruction of their friendship.

'The thing most needed is for men to *recognize* their illusion, to drop, while there is yet time, their newest illusion of life as only process. Leave off trying to fit into their mechanical scheme a being who lives all the time in a world they have never entered. They seem incapable of unthinking the suggestions coming to them from centuries of masculine attempts to represent women only in relation to the world as known to men.'

It was then he was angry.

'How else shall they be represented?'

'They *can't* be represented by men. Because by every word they use men and women mean different things.'

Probably Italian women led men by the nose in the old way, the way of letting them imagine themselves the whole creation. And indeed the problem presently will be: how to save men from collapsing under their loss of prestige. Their awakening, when it comes, will make them pitiful. At present they are surrounded, out in the wôrld, by women who are trying to be as much like them as possible. That will cease when commerce and politics are socialized.

'Art,' 'literature,' systems of thought, religions, all the fine products of masculine leisure that are so lightly called 'immortal.' Who makes them immortal? A few men in each generation who are in the same attitude of spirit as the creators, and loudly claim them as humanity's highest spiritual achievement, condoning, in those who produce them, any failure, any sacrifice of the lives about them to the production of these crumbling monuments. Who has decreed that 'works of art' are humanity's highest achievement?

Daphne, preceded by her hurried voice; followed by her maid carrying a tray. She came swiftly in her manner of a small panting tug, eyes surveying ahead with gaze too wide for detail.

'Put it there; near the lady.'

Hitching herself into a chair, she sighed deeply, but not to attract attention, nor in the manner of a conversational opening. She had, without self-consciousness, the preoccupied air of one who snatches a tiresome necessary meal, grudging the expense of time. Her compact stillness was the stillness of energy momentarily marking time. Her face, distorted by efforts, mouth firmly closed, with a goodly bite of the stout little roll, was busily thinking and talking. Continuous. There was no cessation in her way of being, no dependence, none of the tricks of appeal and demand that make most children so quickly wearisome. Yet she was almost a baby sitting there; a lonely infant, rotund.

IV—* D

Her face came round, so perfectly impersonal in its gravity that Miriam knew the irrepressible smile with which she met it for an affront, felt herself given up to the child's judgment, ready to be snubbed.

For a moment the round eyes surveyed her, deep and clear, a summer sea in shadow, and then, with her head a little butted forward in the way she had of holding it during her breathless sentences, she hurriedly swallowed her mouthful and cried:

'You're *nice*! I didn't know!' Condemnation and approval together. Scarcely daring to breathe, she waited while the child drew near, shouting for her maid, who came grumbling and departed smiling when the tables were drawn side by side.

'That's-my-beecely-German-nurse-I-hate-her.'

'She talks German with you?'

'She talks. I don't listen. She has a beecely voice. Vicky Vereker says she can't helper voice, can't help being a silly stupid, and evil Eaden didn't say anything and Vicky said show him how she speaks.'

'And did you?'

'I should have been *sick*. Evil Eaden's gone ski-ing again. Evil Eaden likes Napoleon and Vicky doesn't; he wouldn't.'

'Why do you like Napoleon so much?'

'Because I like him, because he's the good dear little big one. Everybody is a big silly small one almost.'

Meditating on Napoleon as a pattern for womanhood, Miriam heard the returned ski-ers arrive upon the platform and watched the eager calm little face that was still busily talking, for a sign.

'When I've done my beecely edjacation, when I go back to Indja,' it was saying, looking out with blind eyes across the bright intolerable valley.

Vereker's voice, gently vibrant and sunny, sounded near by, and a deep groan from Eaden just visible, collapsed in one of the small green chairs.

'I've got to go now,' said Daphne, relinquishing her second roll and sliding to the floor. Covering the small space with her little quick-march, she pulled up in front of Eaden and stood surveying, hands behind back, feet a little apart, head thrust forward. Napoleon in a pinafore.

'You 're dead beat, that 's what you are.'

'Daphne, I am. I 'm a broken man. Don't pound me. But you may stroke me if you like.'

On a table at his side stood a large brown bear on ski, his gift to her, bought on his way home from the old woman at the corner and that now they were surveying together. She had approached it with two little eager steps and pulled up just short with her arms at her sides, volubly talking just out of hearing, but to his delight who heard and watched her. Between her sallies she sought his face, to bring him to contemplate and agree. Did it please her? She had not yet handled it. Could anything please her? The giver and the giving were calling forth her best, that moved him and Vereker as men are moved at the sight of life in eager operation, spontaneous as they never seem to be, commanding and leading them. Vereker was amused. Eaden disarmed and delighted, protective of a splendour. Suddenly she seized the bear in her arms and held it while she talked and put it carefully down and looked back at it as she turned with her little quick march to someone calling from the house.

'It 's all right, Daphne.' Eaden's voice eager, free of its drawl, crying out in pity and wrath. He had leapt from his chair and was gathering and fixing together the detached parts, bear and ski and pole, found by Daphne returned, lying as if broken upon the table at his side. She stood speechless, a little forlorn child, red-cheeked and tearful in dismay. A little way off stood the Skerry youth with his grin.

CHAPTER V

WHAT had brought this wakening so near to the edge of night? The mountains were still wan against a cold sky, whitening the morning twilight with their snow.

How long to wait, with sleep gone that left no borderland of drowsiness, until the coming of their gold?

And in a moment she had seen for ever the ruby gleaming impossibly from the topmost peak: stillness of joy held still for breathless watching of the dark ruby, set suddenly like a signal upon the desolate high crag.

It could not last, would soon be plain sunlight.

Already it was swelling, growing brighter, clearing to crimson. In a moment it became a star with piercing rays that spread and slowly tilted over the upper snow a flood of rose.

Each morning this miracle of light had happened before her sleeping eyes. It might not again find her awake. But it had found her awake, carried her away in a moment of pure delight that surely was absolution? And when presently the rose had turned to the familiar gold creeping down to the valley it was more than the gold of yesterday. In watching its birth, she had regained the first day's sense of endless time. To-day was set in advance to the rhythm of endless light.

To-day was an unfathomable loop within the time that remained before the end of Eaden's visit, his short allowance that added, by being set within it, to her own longer portion. His coming had brought the earlier time to an end; made it a past, expanding in the distance. And beyond his far-off departure was a group of days with features yet unseen. Looking back upon that distant past, it seemed impossible that the crest of her first week was not yet reached.

Yet the few days that seemed so many had already fallen into a shape. Morning blessedness of leisure, smiled down

96

upon by the mountains again tawny in their sunlight, witnessed to by every part of the house wandered through; rich sense of strength unspent; joy of mere going out again into the wide scene, into the embrace of the crystal air; the first breath of its piny scent, of the scent of snow, and presently the dry various scents confined within the little street, messengers of strange life being lived close at hand; the morning dive into the baking warmth of the post office, to find, amongst the English vehement at their pigeon-holes, the sharpest sense of being out in the world of the free; then the great event, the wild flight down to the valley's sudden stillness.

The afternoon with Guerini; but, after yesterday, there might be no afternoon with Guerini: freedom instead, for fresh discovery until tea-time, on the promontory, in the midst of unpredictable groupings. Sunset and afterglow, high day moving away without torment or regret; the mountains, turning to a darkness in the sky; telling only of the sure approach of the deep bright world of evening.

The gold-lit evening feast was still momentous, still under the spell of the setting, the silent host who kept the party always new.

And it was in part the setting, the feeling of being out of the world and irresponsible, that last night had kept Eaden a docile listener. He had heard a little of the truth, at least something to balance the misrepresentations of socialism in the Tory press. But he had heard in a dream, outside life. Sitting on the stairs, huge in his meek correctness of evening dress. There was, to be sure, in face of Vereker's determination, nothing else for him to do. But it was with one consent that they had all three subsided on the wide stairs, secure from the intrusions that menaced the little salon.

And it was only for a moment she had sunned herself in the triumph of being claimed, forcibly enthroned, in the sustaining blue gown, upon the red-carpeted stairs with the best of the hotel's male guests a little below on each side of her. After that moment there was only effort, the effort to make things clear, to find convincing answers to Vereker's questions.

And there were no witnesses, only Guerini, coming from the

salon and apologetically past them up the stairs; and the maids, passing to and fro.

There is no evening social centre in this hotel, no large room. That is why these sports-people like it. The day is concentrated within the daylight. The falling away after dinner is a turning towards the next day's work.

That Grindelsteig hotel must be rather fascinating. She thought I shared her disapproval of people 'running up and down balconies and in and out of each other's rooms all night long.' I did. Yet they are only carrying out my principles. . . .

She despises even those who come out for sport, unless all day they are risking life and limb. So fragile and brittle-looking, so Victorian and lacy, yet living for her ski-parties with picked people from the other hotels; going off at dawn, swallowed up until dinner-time and then, straight to bed.

The social promise of the first evening has miscarried. The social centre is the Oberland Ski Club; the rest, a mere putting in of time. I am living on the outskirts, looking for developments in the wrong place; have seen all there will be to see until the end of my stay.

Into the golden sunlight fell the clashing of morning sleigh-bells, describing the outdoor world. Listening to them she felt the vast surroundings, that lately had become a setting owing part of its entrancement to the delightful sense of success in a charming social atmosphere, reasserting themselves in their own right, accusing her of neglect, showing the days winding themselves off to an end that would leave her in possession only of the valley road and the fields beyond the bridge.

The dawn had wakened to remind her. Watching the coming of the light, she had been restored to her first communion with it, back in the time when the people downstairs had seemed superfluity, thrown in with the rest. When all was over they would appear in the distance: bright figures of a momentary widening of her social horizon, unforgotten, but withdrawn into their own element; not going forward into her life as this winter paradise would go forward, brightening her days with the possibility of reunion.

This morning she would break the snare, be a claimant for a

lunch packet, an absentee for the whole day. With the coming
of the far-off afternoon, Guerini, looking down from his
window on to the promontory either to escape or to claim her
company, would find no one there.

Even in terror there was gladness of swift movement that
left her pressed like a niched effigy into the wall of the drift as
the beast pranced by, revealing in its wake a slouching peasant;
clear brilliant eyes brooding amidst unkempt shagginess, pipe
at an angle of jaunty defiance to the steep his heedless tramping
brought so near.

She was honourably plastered with snow, and the precious
package that had leapt and might have hurled itself into the
void was still safely on its string about her neck, but the narrow
rising path, bereft of its secrecy by evidence of homely levels
above of field and farm, was perhaps only a highway for humiliating perils. More cows might be coming round the bend; a
whole herd. There might be—it would harmonize with the
way life always seemed to respond to deliberate activity with a
personal challenge—on this very day the dawn had drawn her
away from beaten tracks, a general turning out of cattle for an
airing; mountain cattle, prancing like colts.

Man and cow were now upon the widening path, approaching
the sloping field with the barn at the end, the cow trotting
swiftly ahead, through the half-buried posts beside the sunken
open gate, and now careering hither and thither about the
meadow with flying tail, the powdery snow flung in wreaths
about its course. It was half mad of course, poor thing, with
the joy of release from one of those noisome steamy sheds whose
reek polluted the air surrounding them and saddened the landscape with reminder of the price of happiness: oblivion of
hidden, helpless suffering.

But in summer-time this air-intoxicated captive would stand
knee-deep in rich pasture; mild. Its colouring was mild, soft
tan and creamy white, in ill-arranged large blots; and with its
short legs, huge bony mass of head and shoulders from which

the spine curved down as if sagging beneath the weight of the
clumsy body, it missed the look of breeding, the even shape
and colouring of lowland cattle.   Its horns, too, had no style,
rose small and sharp from the disproportionate mass of skull.

Almost without warning, so slight in the dense pine wood
was the sound of its muffled gliding, the sled was upon her,
heavy with piled logs and a ruffian perched upon them: slithering headlong, fitting and filling the banked path from side to
side.   Somehow she flung herself upon the root-encumbered
bank, somehow hitched her feet clear of the sled as it rushed
by.   The villain, unmoved and placidly smiling, had not even
shouted.

'No time to shout, no use *shouting*,' she murmured breathless,
smiling at the absurd scene, a treasure now that danger was
past, a glimpse into local reality.   But danger was past only
for the moment.   This pleasant wide path she had mistaken
for a woodland walk winding and mounting safely amidst the
peace of the pine woods was a stern highway, almost a railway;
formed like a railway to the exact dimensions of its traffic.

Intently listening, going swiftly where the sides of the track
were too high for an escaping sprawl, she toiled on and up and
came presently to a gap and a view of the small hut, seated clear
of the pines, high against the pure blue upon the curve of un-
blemished snow, come down now nearly to her level and revealed as a chalet with burnished face, inhabited: above its
chimney the air quivered in the heat of a clear-burning fire.

The hotel lunch, opened upon the trestle table, looked pert,
a stray intruder from the cheap sophisticated world of to-day
into these rich and ancient shadows.   The old woman, but for
her bell-like, mountainy voice, was a gnarled witch moving
amongst them, unattained by the cold light from the small low
windows, that struck so short a way into the warmly varnished
interior.

And it seemed by magic that she produced the marvellous
coffee in whose subtle brewing was a sadness, the sadness of

her lonely permanence above the waste of snow and woods—
old grandmother, a living past, her world disappeared, leaving
only the circling of the seasons about her emptied being.

In this haunting presence, the triumph of distance accomplished, the delicious sense of known worlds waiting far below,
world behind world in a chain whose end was the far-off London she represented here in this high remoteness, could not
perfectly flourish, came in full only when the silence had had
time to fill itself with joy that was too strong to be oppressed
by the departed ancient voice, that was like the echo of a sound
fallen elsewhere.

Again, recalling the far-off morning, a dark barn-like room.
But the woman opened a door at the end of it, led the way
through a passage still darker: another door and she was out
upon the edge of the world, upon a dilapidated little grey
balcony jutting over an abyss. As far as sight could reach were
sunlit mountain-tops range beyond range, till they grew far
and faint.

Faced alone, the scene, after the first moment's blissfully
ranging perception, was saddened in its grandeur through the
absence there of someone else perceiving. Thousands, of
course, had seen it from this perch in the centre of the row of
slummy little balconies. But so splendid was the triumph of
the unexpected mountains ranged and lit that no company,
even exclamatory, could break their onslaught. Alone, there
was too heavy a burden of feeling in the speechless company
of this suddenly revealed magnificence.

The woman coming out with the tea that one day she must
take here accompanied, was brisk about the view: an adjunct,
thrown in gratis with her refreshments which were good and
which presently caused the mountains, turned away from, to be
felt preparing a friendliness; becoming the last, best reward of
her day's accomplishment.

The way home, down and down and across the levels to the
rink and up the little homely slope into Oberland, would be a

jog-trot taken half asleep to the haven of things small and known amidst which she would sit renewed, to-day's long life-time stilled to a happy throbbing of the nerves, a bemused beaming in the midst of friends. Its incidents blurred that would come back one day clearer, more shining than all the rest?

Warned by a growing chill, she turned to face the mountains in farewell and found them lit by the first of the afterglow. Far away in the haze beyond the visible distance a group of slender peaks showed faintly, rose-misted pinnacles of a dream-city from whose spires would presently gleam the rubies of farewell.

CHAPTER VI

THE solitary excursion had made a gap in the sequence of days. Those standing behind it were now far away, and yesterday had failed to bridge the gap and join itself to their serenity. To-day looked shallow and hurried, with short hours beyond it rushing ahead to pause in the sunlight of the ski-fest and then to fly, helter-skelter towards the end.

Eaden's departure was helping time to hurry. In the distance, it had promised to leave things as they were before he came. But now that it was at hand it seemed a sliding away of everything.

There was no depth in the morning light.

She turned to survey the scene on which it fell and saw the early gold stealing faithfully towards the valley. Once Eaden had gone, this thinned-out urgency of time would cease. For every one but Vereker his going was only a removal of something grown familiar; a reminder, soon forgotten, of the movement of time. Slight reminder. He reflected only surfaces and was going away, unchanged, to reflect the surfaces of another shape of life.

Yet last night he had talked. Had been less a passenger unable to take root. It was he who had been the first to subside on the stairs—with a groan for his hard day's work. Perhaps the approach of his known life had given him a moment of clairvoyance, showing its strangeness, the strange fact of its existence.

Last night had been good, was showing now how very good it had been: three friends glad to sit down together and presently talking, each voice transformed, by the approach of the separation that would make it cease to sound, to the strange marvel of a human voice. Everything said had seemed important in its kindliness, and, though there had been no

socialism he had talked at last of his peasants and his ceaseless
fighting with their ancient ways as though he wished to excuse
himself from accepting socialism, to point out its irrelevance
to the life of peasant and soil.

Industrial socialism had bored him. He thought its problems irrelevant, raised by clever doctrinaires who had nothing
to lose. She had failed him by standing too much in one camp.
The proper message for him came from the people who saw
land as the fundamental unit.

Tell him to look away from capital and wages. And read
George. And the Jewish land-laws, never surpassed.

'Good-bye. Please remember that work is an unlimited
quantity.'

Then she remembered that this morning there would be a
meeting at breakfast. He and Vereker would be there together
as on the first morning; with time to spare.

But going into the dining-room she found his departure
already in full swing. He was talking, smiling across at Mrs
Sneyde and Miss Hollebone with the eagerness of one who
finds at the last moment the ice broken and communication
flowing the more easily for having been dammed up and
accumulating.

Sitting down unnoticed except by Vereker, she presently
heard Maud Hollebone, to whom he had scarcely spoken,
arranging, across the width of the room, to hasten her departure.

They were going down to Italy together; as casually as guests,
leaving a party and finding that their way home lies in the same
direction, will share a hansom across London. To travelled
people, a journey to Italy was as simple as crossing London.
Was even a bore, a tiresome experience to be got through as
pleasantly as possible. Behind her manner of sonsy, quietly
boisterous school-girl indifference Maud was pleased, but still
kept her poise, her oblivious independence—of what? On
what, all the time going about with Mrs Sneyde, neglecting all
opportunities for recognizing the existence of the house-party,
aloof without being stand-offish, was she feeding her so
strongly rooted life?

She was pleased, of course, to be carrying off as her escort the imposing oiled bronze, now almost animated as he crossed to the little table to discuss details and stood, a pillar of strength, at the disposal of the two ladies now looking so small and Mrs Sneyde, as she fired remarks at him, so scintillating. She, no doubt, had her ideas and thought it an excellent plan. But the sister already knew too late that it was not. Had felt the project change during his approach with his week's happiness all about him, and realized now that she represented a reprieve, was to be, by keeping Oberland before his eyes during part of his long journeying, an extension of his holiday.

Standing at close quarters, already accustomed to her companionship, he was aware, behind his animation, of sacrificing for the sake of it the precious silent interval between his strenuous idling and the arduous work ahead; was paying the price always paid for tumult half-consciously insincere. The finding of Maud also immersed in the business of departure, and therefore seen in a flash of time as a comrade, had enlivened him as one is enlivened by a greeting without regard to the giver of it. That enlivening glow had already departed and he was left reduced, with its results upon his hands.

It was settled. The elopement arranged and he, with his instructions, moving off to clear her path. Perhaps secretly he was pleased after all. Perhaps his life in the south was not a flight from society and he was glad to be ever so slightly back again in its conspiracy to avoid solitude. Glad to be walking again on those sunny levels where there is never a complete break-off and departure. Never a void. Where even sorrow and suffering are softened by beautiful surroundings.

Their windows, she reflected as Eaden, meeting the Le Mesuriers at the door, was halted for farewells, even their hotel windows, give on to beauty. And they can always move on. And soul-sickness, the suffering of mind so often a result of fatigue and poor food and ugly surroundings, was rare amongst them. They were cheerful and amused. If bored, they shift on and begin again. If bored by the life of society itself, they remain within it and cut figures as cynics.

'It's only fair to warn you,' Maud was crying from her table, 'that I'm a vile fellow-traveller. Hate travelling.'

She rose and wandered to the window behind her table.

'You're going to take away our property?'

Here she was, the unknown Miss Hollebone, close at hand, flopped in a chair, schoolgirlish.

'Rather!'

Here in this warm circle was the old freemasonry of school-fellows, two profiles slightly turned, abrupt remarks, punctuated by jabbings at ink-stained desks, the sense of power and complete difference in relation to a stuffy old world; sudden glances, perfect happiness. Happiness that kept both quite still; hearing, feeling, seeing, in a circle of light suddenly created, making possible only slight swift words in whose echo one forgot which had spoken, which was which.

'What are we to do?' They faced each other to laugh delight.

'Don't know. What we really want is *your* socialism in *our* world. The socialist ways you have in your world without knowing it, because you know no other ways.'

'You don't object to us?'

'Good Lord, no! But just to cultivate you would be to go to sleep as you are all asleep.'

'You a Londoner?'

'Till death us do part.'

'Lucky dog!'

Eaden was at her elbow, to whom she turned with a guarded brightness, slipped back into her own world, into the half-conscious conspiracy of avoidance. Orderly world. A pattern world, life flowing in bright set patterns under a slowly gathering cloud.

Its echoes followed Miriam into the deserted little salon. Through the open door she heard a coming and going in the hall that at this hour should be empty and eloquent of people spread far and wide in the landscape. The bright pattern was flowing into a fresh shape, flowing forward in its way, heedless of clouds, heedless of the rising tide. On the little table was Daphne's bear on ski, immortal.

And now in the hall the sound of her, demanding. Drawn to the door, Miriam saw Vereker taking the stairs two at a time,

immersed in friendship. And Eaden arrested in the middle
of the hall by Daphne up-gazing with white determined face.

'Look at me,' she was saying, and his down-bent face lost
its smile.

'You're not to go,' she said swiftly, in a casual tone, and
then breathlessly, still searching his unmoved face, 'You're
not to go.'

'That's right, Daphne,' cried Vereker pausing on the stairs.
'Make him stay for the Fest, he wants to.'

Eaden watched her while she waited for Vereker's footsteps
to die away, watched her in frowning concentration while her
voice came again, the voice of one who tells another's woe:
'Not for the Fest, but because, if you go away, I shall die.'

Miriam turned swiftly back into the room, but she had seen
the pain in his face, seen him wince. Daphne on her last words
had taken a little impatient step and stood averted with clenched
fists, and now their voices were going together up the stairs,
hers eagerly talking.

She made ready to go out amongst the mountains standing
there in their places as for countless ages they had stood,
desolate, looking down upon nothing.

A door opened at the far end of the corridor, and Vereker's
footsteps came swiftly trotting, went by and paused at a door
further down: Maud Hollebone's, at which now he was urgently
tapping. A few words at the opened door and he had returned.
A moment later came Maud, swishing along at a run: for more
discussion.

Her thoughts turned to the promontory within easy reach.
But it would be absurd to sit about, visibly hung up by the
bustle of events that were not even remotely her events. It
was too late to do the valley run and walk back before
lunch.

'I shall *die*.' Who was comforting Daphne? No one. No
one could. Somewhere outside she was disposed of, walking
with her nurse, uncomforted.

She peered into Daphne's future, into the years waiting ahead, unworthy of her.

Vereker's door opened again, letting out the returning Maud; coming back to go on with her packing, to talk to Mrs Sneyde. The two of them, surrounded by the opulence of wealthy packing, talking, skipping about in talk: family affairs, and in both their minds Maud's journey to Milan with the mild and foolish bronze.

When the footsteps had passed, she went out into the corridor and across the space of sunlight streaming through Mrs Harcourt's door open upon its empty room. Far away in the landscape, with those people from the Kursaal, Mrs Harcourt was forgetfully ski-ing, knowing nothing of all this bustle.

But Maud's door, too, was set wide. Her room deserted, neat and calm as Mrs Harcourt's. . . . Where was Maud?

From the room beyond came Mrs Sneyde, dressed for outdoors, brilliant in green and gold, turning, coming forward with laughter and an outstretched restraining hand, suppressing her laughter to speak in the manner of one continuing a confidential talk; laughter remaining in her eyes that looked, not at the stranger she addressed for the first time, but away down the passage.

'I've just,' she whispered, 'been in their room tyin' up Daphne's finger. Cut it on one of their razors. The poor things were terrified. Had her sittin' on the table with her finger in a glass of water!

'No. It's nothing; but those two great fellows were gibberin' with fright. She's a little demon. Two towels on the floor. One all over chocolate and the other bright with gore. They wanted to fetch old Stick-in-the-mud.'

'What a tragedy for Mr Eaden's last hours.'

'He's not goin'; stayin' for the Fest. Nobody's goin' but the dear Skerrys.'

'Didn't know they were going.'

'Nor nobody else. Till Ma suddenly began about her luggage. Wants to save the sleigh fare. Vereker's arranged it;

the luggage is goin' by the Post and they're toboggannin'; can't you see them? "Whee don't ye see goodbee to Daphnee?" says she to Tammas.'

Cruel, a little cruel.

'They found out a good deal about the peasants.'

'The *peasants*? The village desperadoes? *Is* there anything to find out about them?'

'The lives they lead.'

'Tammas been tryin' to convert them? With his weak eyes? Through his smoked glasses?'

'You know he smashed his glasses?'

'He would.'

'Yes. I heard his mother scolding him on the balcony and he slowly trying to explain; all in that low tone, as if they were conspiring.'

'In an enemy camp. They were like that if you spoke to them. We all tried; but by the time they'd thought and begun to answer, you'd forgotten what you said.'

'I suddenly remembered some glasses I'd been advised to bring. They seemed astonished and suspicious and yet eager. "Try them on, Thomas," she said.'

'Tree them on, Tammas. I hear her.'

'And yesterday he handed them back jammy round the edges. I thought he was tired of them. They said nothing about going. But he told me about the peasants.'

'They had jam teas, on their own, upstairs.'

'Anyhow, they got in touch with the natives.'

'I ain't surprised. Natives themselves.'

'With the people in the chalet behind.'

'Old Methuselah? Not difficult if you smash things. The old boy mended Daphne's watch. Of course she went in to see him do it. Went in jabberin' German which she *won't* talk with Frederika. Was there an hour till I went to fish her out. Couldn't see her, my dear—couldn't see *anything*; smoke, like a fog, couldn't *breathe*. Made her out at last squatting close up to the filthy old villain on his bench. Lost, in the insides of watches. She's goin' to be a watch-maker now.'

'It must be his son.'

'Who must?'

'The one Thomas told me of. A woodcutter. Terrible. In the snow. It's only on snow they can bring the wood down from the higher places. Someone bought a high copse, cheaply, because the higher——'

'Higher you go, the fewer—now I know what that means.'

'The cheaper. Over two hours' climb from here; somewhere across the valley. And the men and sleds must be there by daylight.'

'Poor devils!'

'Yes. And the horses for the climbing must be fed two hours before the start. Sometimes they have to feed them before three in the morning. One lot of men was caught up there by an avalanche, and were there four days before they could be got down.'

'Ai-*eee*; don't tell us.'

'At the best it's dangerous work. They get maimed; lose their lives. All the winter this is going on. We don't read their papers, don't know the people and don't hear of it.'

'Isn't it just as well? *We* can't help it.'

'It ought to be done some other way. Men's lives ought not to be so cheap.'

'How did Tammas get all this learning?'

'Speaks German.'

'Jee-roozlum!'

'And French.'

'And Scotch. And having no one to talk Scotch to, talks to the peasants, about their trees. Daphne *hates* the trees.'

'*Hates* them?'

'Would like to make a big bonfire and burn 'm all up.'

Miriam was silent, searching the green eyes for Daphne.

'Yes, that's Daphne. She's mad about Napoleon. Reads all the books. Has 'm in her room. I have to expound when she gets stuck. Won't say her prayers till we've read a bit of Bony. Won't say "Make me a good girl." Says "Make me a man and a sojer." She and Eaden are as thick as thieves.

He's an angel to her. I've got to be *hoff*. Goin' to the Curseall for lunch. Maud's there. She's goin' south to-morrow with the Chisholmes.'

'Before the Fest?'

'Chisholmes have got to pick up their kid somewhere. Maud's had enough of Switzerland for this year.'

CHAPTER VII

THE clouds were a rebuke; for being spell-bound into imagining this bright paradise inaccessible. The world's weather cannot be arranged as a conversation with one small person. Then how did the rebuke manage to arrive punctually at the serenest moment of self - congratulation? As if someone were watching. . . .

She looked levelly across the sunny landscape and the clouds were out of sight. But there was a movement in the air, a breeze softly at work ousting the motionless Oberland air.

She walked ahead, further and further into the disconcerting change. Everything was changed, the whole scene, reduced to homeliness. She caught herself drooping, took counsel and stiffened into acquiescence—'I might have known. I'm accustomed to this. It removes only what I thought I couldn't give up. Something is left behind that can't be taken away'— and heard at once within the high stillness the familiar sound of life, felt the sense of it flowing warmly in along the old channels, and heard from the past in various tones, amused, impatient, contemptuous: 'You *are* philosophical.' Always a surprise. What did they mean with their 'philosophical'? The alternative was their way of going on cursing, missing everything but the unfavourable surface.

Someone has said that there is nothing meaner than making the best of things.

The clouds made soft patches of shadow upon the higher snow. Beside the angular sharp shadows growing upon the northern slopes they were blemishes, smudgy and vague. But free, able to move and flow while the mountains stood crumbling in their places.

The clouds were beautiful, slowly drifting, leaving torn shreds upon the higher peaks.

Upon the ridge beyond the cloaked silence of the little wood the breeze blew steadily from across the levels—that were strangely empty; no sign of moving specks making for the further ridge. Hurrying along the track, she recalled too late the slightness of the information upon which she had built her idea of the golden scene; the gay throng, herself happily in the midst.

Without a single clear idea of the direction, she had trusted to the bright magic to draw her to itself.

The subtly changed air and the melancholy clouds re-stated themselves, became the prelude to disaster. The increasing wind and the cloud-bank hiding the distant mountains were proclaiming the certainty of punishment well deserved: to wander at a loss and miss the Fest.

She glanced at her afternoon in retrospect: aimless walking in a world fallen into greyness and gloom, into familiarity that was already opening the door to the old friend, at whose heart lived a radiance outdoing the beams shed by anticipation over unknown things.

But all the time the ski-ing which now she was not to see would be going forward, mocking her until she could forget it; until the hours it filled should have passed into others bright enough to melt regret.

Climbing the rise beyond the levels, she was at once climbing up to find the Fest, would plod the landscape until she found it, late, but still in time to share and remember. She reached the crest beyond the rise—there it was: a small shape, like an elongated horseshoe, upon a distant slope. Black dots close-clustered in a strange little shape upon the wastes of snow, defying the wastes of snow.

There was plenty of space. Gaps on each side of the track and even towards the top of the rise, where people were grouped more closely about the comforting, the only festal sign, looking like an altar with its gold-embroidered, red velvet frontal. Nothing could be seen behind its shelf but a small hut upon the levels that extended backwards until the pine woods began with the rising mountain-side.

Where to stand? Up amongst the connoisseurs to see the

start, half-way down with a view of the ski-ers coming, or at the bottom of the row amongst the black-clothed natives standing about in scattered groups in the loose snow.

Choosing a place half-way down, she became one of the gathered crowd of Oberland visitors lining the smoothed and steeply sloping course. They were all there. The black and distant dots had become people in every fashion of sports clothes, standing on skis, sitting on toboggans, stamping about in the snow, walking up and down; and all waiting, all looking betweenwhiles expectantly up the track towards the deserted altar. There was a good deal of talking. Here and there the incessant voices of men who make a hobby of talking. But most of them talked intermittently, in the way of these leisured English who veil their eagerness as they wait, half apologetically and wholly self-consciously, for a show. There, patiently they would wait, good-humoured, not deigning to be disturbed, not suffering anything to disturb their pose of amused independence that looked so like indifference and masked a warmth.

Just across the way was a stout lady in a sealskin coat and curiously different snow-boots. She sat sturdily bunched on her toboggan and they stuck out in front of her, close-fitting, the rubber soles curving sharply to the instep and neatly down again into the shape of a heel. She clasped a camera and her sallow heavy face was drawn into a frown that remained there while she turned towards a voice sounding from over the way:

'. . . and we 'll just be *here* till judgment *day*.'

'I was told,' she answered at large, with face upraised, deep furrows from nose to chin giving strength to her hanging cheeks, 'I was to see sky-jumping, but I see no men on their skys to jump.'

American continuousness held up in Europe, brought to despair by the spectacle of tolerance.

Sunlight had gone, and on the slope of the breeze small snow-flakes drifted down to the snow. For a while it seemed as though the gathering in the white wilderness were there in vain.

From the group of black figures at the top of the rise a deep Swiss voice sang out an English name. Heads were craned forward, but the altar remained empty. The confronted figures were transformed. Each life, risen to gazing eyes, waited in a stillness upon the edge of time.

The knickerbockered, tweed-clad form arrived upon the shelf from nowhere, leaped, knees bent and arms outspread, forward through the air upon the long blades that looked so like thin oars flattened out, came down, arms in upward-straining arches, with a resounding whack upon the slope and slid half-crouching, gaining the upright, fully upright with hooked arms swinging, at full speed to the bottom of the hill, went off in a wide curve and was stopped, swaying, just not falling, in wreaths of whirling snow.

Achievement. Thrilling and chastening. Long ago, some-one had done this difficult thing for the first time, alone, perhaps driven by necessity. Now it was a sport, a deliberate move-ment into eternity, shared by all who looked on. She felt she could watch for ever. Cold had withdrawn from the snow and from the drifting flakes. One after another the figures appeared at the top of the rise and leapt, making the gliding race to the sound of cheers that now broke forth each time the forward rush followed the desperate dive. For those who crashed and rolled, slanting ski and sloping helpless body rolling over and over down the slope, there was comment of laughter silly and cruel. Yet one man sliced his face with a ski-point, and one had lain stunned at the bottom of the slope. . . .

Vereker came at last, looking very young and lightly built, leaping neatly and far, and gliding, easily upright, to the accompaniment of frantic cheering, at a splendid pace down the slope and far on into the loose snow and round in a sweeping curve that encircled a distant sapling and left him up the track half-hidden in a cloud of churned-up facing snow.

He was the best. Length of jump, pace, style. The best of the English. And kind life had led her to him for speech, for the recovery of shared things; and was making now more memories that fitted with the rest.

Ski'd on-lookers were planking sideways up and down the course, flattening it. Snow still fell thinly. The distant mountains were lost in mist. The forgotten scene was utterly desolate. Warmth flowing forth from within made a summer in its midst.

'Tsoor-*boo*-chn!' The strong spell-binding peasant name filled out the ringing cry. Switzerland was coming, bringing its so different life of mountain and pine wood, its hardy strength, perhaps to outdo the English in this brave game.

Here he came, in black against his snow, deep velvety black against the snow, gliding past the little hut with a powerful different gait. It was partly his clothes, the way they seemed all of one piece, closely fitting, without angles. And his size, huge. From the edge of the shelf he leapt high into the air and seemed to stand there against the sky, in a dream. Down he swooped, sailing, dreaming, to the track, rose smoothly from the terrific impact and smoothly went his way.

What could be more beautiful? He was heavy and solid, thickly built. But with his shapely clothing and smooth rhythmic movement he made the English graceless and their clothes deliberately absurd.

All the Swiss, though some were rough and ungainly, moved with that strong and steady grace. But Zurbuchen was the best. It was he who would live in her memory, poised against the sky like a great bird.

'You took photographs?'

'For him,' smiled Vereker with his quizzical affectionate glance. 'To remind him of what he has to do next year. But we'll share them. Yours will remind you that next year you won't be let off.' Eaden remained silent and expressionless.

'They will look strange amongst your cypress groves.'

'They will look passing strange.'

'You will come out again?' She wanted neither to know nor to seem to want to know, but Vereker had left him there for a moment on her hands. She was caught in the social trap. Expected, being a woman, not to walk off alone, but to wait and provide, while she waited, suitable entertainment, some kind of parlour trick. For a moment it seemed as though he would not answer. He was silent and used to stillness, yet embarrassed now by stillness in the presence of a perceiving witness. Another woman would not seem to perceive. Would have given her question the semblance of sincerity.

'No,' he said suddenly. 'If I go away at all next year I shall go east.'

'When you 've 'eard the East a-callin' . . .' She turned to look towards the returning Vereker. Eaden gazed away towards the snowy distances. He was taking his farewell. To-morrow, he would be gone back to his chosen isolation, uninfluenced. Tender-hearted lover of brave souls, of Daphne, and who yet would bring so' little to his love-making. He stood in his heavy silence, heavy man's silence of waiting for recognizable things.

'Yes, that man knew what he was talking about.' Suddenly his friendly beam and a forward approaching step, a turning away, at the first hint of something he had heard before, from his formal preoccupation, preoccupation with a glimpse of the next break in his unknown southern life. She had nothing more to say. Vereker was at hand who had held them at truce together. But now, without Vereker, they were at truce, the only kind of truce he could understand.

For a moment she was aware, far away in the future, of one of whom he was the forerunner, coming into her life for mortal combat.

CHAPTER VIII

IN spite of her contempt for tobogganing she was going warily, slowing up a little at the bends, a gnome in an extinguishing cowl, Mrs Harcourt, carelessly carrying her long past and the short future that so strangely she regarded as indefinite, looking forward, making plans for next winter with eager schoolgirl eyes; carelessly bringing the life she carried about with her down to the valley this afternoon with brusque camaraderie, her day-time manner.

Her company added something to the joy of flying through the backward-flowing landscape. But it was shortening the run and fitting it within reduced surroundings—making it show as it showed to her within her larger scale of movement.

Here already was the steepest bend of the run, with the patch of black ice across its middle. Mrs Harcourt had passed it safely and disappeared. It was past and a group of people came into sight midway down the next slope: two figures, pushing off, and Mrs Harcourt at the side of the track, dismounted, beating her skirt. She had collided, managed to run into them; a collision and a humiliating smash . . .

'Fools! Fooling all over v' place. Had to slam into v' side.'

'A blessing the fence is broken just here.'

'Not their fault I 'm not smashed up. I was yellin' for all I was worth.'

'It 's *really* dangerous when you can't see what 's ahead. Someone said tobogganing accounts for more accidents than any other sport.'

'Don't wonder, with so many idjuts about. Where 's Daphne?'

'Held up, poor little soul. A broken cord, just as they were starting; the maid went in for another.'

'Paw kid. She 'll be too late. No good waiting.'

They mounted and sped off, one behind the other, through a scene that was now the child's vast desolation. In place of joyous flight, selfish, in which Daphne had been forgotten, came now this absurd urgency to arrive. Mrs Harcourt felt it. She was sorry, in her kindliness, for Daphne's disappointment, but saw nothing of the uselessness of arriving without her. Thought of nothing but herself, her determination, her hatred of being beaten. This made a shelter. Under the shelter of Mrs Harcourt's determination to be there because she had said she would be there it was possible to be seen rushing uselessly to the last farewell.

Another bend. Beyond it a sleigh coming up and Mrs Harcourt carefully passing it and the other tobogganers drawn up in the snow. It was safely past. Mrs Harcourt was getting ahead. Going recklessly. Even for her, there was something more in this desperate urgency than the mere determination to arrive.

If she, too, were to arrive it was now or never. Now, at once, in the midst of this winding ice-patched roadway, she must give herself up to what she had learned on the safe snow-fields and never yet dared to try here, until the last clear slope was reached. Lifting her feet to the bar, leaning back to swing free and steer by weight, she let herself go. The joy of flight returned, singing joy of the inaccessible world to which in flight one was translated, bringing forgetfulness of everything but itself. Bend after bend appeared and of itself her body swayed now right now left in unconscious rhythm. The landscape flew by, sideways-upwards, its features indistinguishable. She was movement, increasing, cleaving the backward rushing air.

At the last slope she was level with Mrs Harcourt, safely, triumphantly returned to the known world, passing her, flying down so blissfully that arrival would now be nothing but an end to joy. Flying down towards two small figures standing on the level, turned this way, watching up the incline down which speeded, superfluously, absurdly, just these two women.

'Where's Daphne?' said Eaden in his rich, indolent voice; looking over their heads, staring up the slope.

While Mrs Harcourt's deep bass, still staccato with her anger, told the brief tale, she watched the pain and wrath in his face, strong man's sympathy of pain with this child to whose spirit he gave homage, anger with those who had deserted her. Her useless explanation flickered about him unspoken, silenced by the pain she shared.

'It's no good, old man,' said Vereker gently, watch in hand: 'we must be off.'

Formal hand-shaking. To Mrs Harcourt's padding of sociable remarks he paid no heed, keeping his eyes still above her on the bend at the head of the slope until he turned to tramp off with Vereker, to the sound of Vereker's kindly, sunny voice.

'Paw kid. Eaden was frightfully wroth. Thought we ought to have brought her.'

'I couldn't have dared, down those slopes, on a small single,' said Miriam wearily. But the judge within stood firm. She had not thought of trying.

The now distant men were marching swiftly, reaching the point where the road sloped downwards; had reached it and were settling on their toboggans. A face came round. Miriam looked back up the slope still cruelly empty, and round again to see the men seated, gliding off, lessening. Their caps vanished below the level of the ridge. And now the upward slope held a single small toboggan coming headlong. Daphne had made the run alone.

'How *dare* you let him go?'

Miriam moved forward surprised by her own approach. Her mind was filled with the simple selfish truth. The wrath-blazing eyes saw it, recognized her for what she was, and turned away to the wastes of snow:

'Eaden, my Eaden . . . I shall *never* see him again.' Tears flowed from the wide eyes and swiftly down the face so little convulsed by grief that bent her, standing there with arms sideways out as if to save her from falling, to keep her upright, facing her loss, fists clenched to fight her woe. Of themselves Miriam's arms reached forth to stay the torment.

Incredibly Daphne was clinging, sobbing with hidden face: 'Do you love me—do you love me?' She held her without speaking, silenced while still the broken voice went on, by the sense of being carried forward into a world known only by hearsay and that now was giving forth all about them in the stillness its ethereal sounds—sounds she had sometimes felt within a gentle wind.

Daphne's head was raised and her flushed face busy in eager speech as they went forward together over the snow. When presently she assured her that one day Eaden would come back, the child pulled upon her arm and spoke in a new way of her new love. She spoke no more of Eaden, walking sturdily uphill, eagerly talking, sunned for a while in humble helpless love that soon must be removed.

With Eaden's departure holding Vereker away until to-morrow, and Mrs Harcourt disappeared upstairs with all those who sought sleep and early rising, the hotel was empty, strange again and going its independent way as on the day of her arrival. The presence of Guerini, hidden away in the little salon where daily he had spent his unimaginable evening of a Milan business man on holiday, increased its emptiness, made it as desolate as the world of his thoughts.

He must have learned something in seeing her evening after evening—not in the least goloshy in her blue gown of many colours—seated on the crimson stairs between the two Englishmen, in seeing discussion prevail over personalities; new world for him of men seeking, without sentimental emotion, without polite contempt, conversation with a woman. Had any light dawned in him? Would he show any grace of dawning light?

She went into the little salon and there he was, rising to greet her, with the look of a man penned within an office, the look upon his low Italian brow of worry left over from his daily life. He looked common too, common and ordinary—she wondered now that she could ever have mistaken him for a musician wandered from Russia. But beside the pathetic appeal of his commonness, supporting it, was the appeal of his disarray, his obvious gladness and relief, like Michael coming back after a last, final explanation and dismissal, saying impenitently: 'You whipped me yesterday, to-day you must not whip.' He was extraordinarily like Michael in his belief in the essential irrelevance of anything a woman may say.

It was his last evening in Oberland, and the first time they had found themselves alone together since the afternoons in the snowfields that were now so clearly in his mind as he stood still turning over those hopeless little old Swiss books, but turned towards her as she ensconced herself in the chair from which so long ago she had watched Vereker at the piano. Yet their life together had gone on. The grim little room was full of it.

Again she had that haunting sense of being a collection of persons living in a world of people always single and the same. Mrs Harcourt, she reflected, as she said the books were like faded flowers, was fastidiously selective and always one person, one unfaltering aspect. Vereker, Eaden, all the others. Yet the lives she lived with each one were sharply separated lives, separable parts of herself, incompatible. The life she lived with Guerini, beginning unconsciously that first evening when he had turned upon her throughout dinner his brown stare, hurrying forward during their afternoons in the snow, ending with their quarrel, begun again with the reproachful gaze he had sent across the table on the evening of her truancy, had persisted during the intervening time and was now marching off afresh on its separate way.

It was clear that these close questionings held not only the remains of his surprise over the nature of the things that had separated them, but also his determination to try to see these things as she saw them. They revealed much pondering, not over the things in themselves but over their power with her, and presently it was clear that he meant to see her again. She sat ensconced, considering him, measuring the slow movement of his thoughts, the swiftness of the impressions he was drawing from his attention to every inflection of her voice.

She knew she ought to go, that she was building up, with every moment she stayed in the room, a false relationship. The cordiality of her voice, its dreamy animation, was not for him nor made by him. It told its tale to her alone. His talk of London had taken her thoughts there and she saw it afar, vivid with charmed and charming people. For the first time, she was seeing London as people whose secret had revealed itself during this last two weeks, and was at this moment beginning consistently to live her life there as in future it would be lived, as she had lived it, but unconsciously and only intermittently, during the past year.

This man appealed, she realized it now, from the first to a person who no longer existed, to a loneliness that during the past years had been moving away from her life. It was only in its moving that she had realized its existence. This man saw her still as lonely and resourceless; and also as interesting, something new in his narrow experience. He too was lonely, had an empty life, in the busy business man's way of having an empty life: no centre and a lonely leisure. And he was more than half bent on offering her the chance that so often in the past had been at her elbow, of pretending herself into a single settled existence, a single world, safe. Even now it was a temptation. But it was the Italian background that was the real temptation. As soon as he talked of settling himself in London, he was lessened, and the temptation disappeared. Life as a single conversation in a single place, with the rest of the world going by, might seem possible when thought of in all the newness of Italy. In London it at once fell into proportion and became absurd.

In London was Hypo, held up, at any rate saying he was held up, and not now so much awaiting her decision as taking it for granted. A big shadow, that might turn into sunshine. A gleaming shadow that lost its brightness as she faced it. And, behind it, a world that perhaps took most of its glamour from this uncertain shadow.

CHAPTER IX

IT was an urgent tapping on the wall from Mrs Harcourt's side, and she was speaking as she tapped. With half-opened eyes, Miriam grew aware of darkness, half-darkness of early morning, and listened through the companion darkness within her of the knowledge that this was her last whole day, to this strange clamour from the lady whose nightly presence at her side had been for so long forgotten.

'Look out of ve window!'

Sitting up in bed, she saw hanging in mid-air just outside the window a huge crimson lamp, circular in a blue darkness. Sleepily she cried her thanks and leaped awake to dwell with the strange spectacle, the gently startling picture, in its sudden huge nearness, of the loveliness of space. The little distant moon, enormous and rosy in blue mist, seemed to float in the blue as in blue water, seemed to have floated close in sheer unearthly kindliness, to comfort her thoughts, on this last day, with something new and strange.

The day passed with heartless swiftness, savourless. Full of charms whose spell failed under the coming loss.

CHAPTER X

AND, for the last morning again, a strange surprise. Mountains and valley hidden behind impenetrable mist, and even the nearest objects screened by the thickly falling snow. Alpine winter tremendously at work, holding her fascinated at windows downstairs, upstairs; mighty preparation for the beauty of days she would not see, robbing her of farewell, putting farewell back into yesterday's superficial seeing which had not known it was the last.

But when she was forced to turn away to her packing, she found, within the light of this veiled world that cast within doors a strange dark brilliance, something of the London gloom, and the enjoyment of a concentrated activity that had always been one of the gifts of a London fog. It was as if already she were translated, good-byes said and the journey begun. The hours ahead became a superfluous time, to be spent in a Switzerland whose charm, since London had reached forth and touched her, had fallen into its future place as part of life: an embellishment, a golden joy to which she would return.

And when she saw the guests assembled at lunch in full strength, it was as though, having left them for good, she returned for a moment to find them immersed in a life to which she was a stranger. Confined by the weather, they had produced the pile of letters waiting in the lounge and were now rejoicing in unison over the snowfall. In speech and silence each one revealed himself, but as a dream-revival of someone known long ago; and in the dream it was again as on that first evening when she had sat a listening outsider, fearing and hoping to be drawn in, and again it was Mrs Harcourt who, when her association with these people was seeming to be a vain thing cancelled, drew her in with a question.

The short hour expanded. Once more she was caught into the medium of their social vision, into the radiance that would shine unchanged when she was gone and was the secret of English social life and could, if it were revealed to every human soul, be the steering light of human life throughout the world. These people were the forerunners, free to be almost as nice as they desired.

And then, with the suddenness of a rapid river, her coming freedom flowed in upon her, carrying her outside this pleasant enclosure towards all that could be felt to the full only in solitude amongst things whose being was complete, towards that reality of life that withdrew at the sounding of a human voice.

It was already from a far distance that, alone with her upon the landing, she promised Mrs Harcourt remembrance and letters, said good-bye and saw once more her first diffident eagerness; felt that it was she, withdrawn since the first days, who had yet lived her life with her, transferred something of her being into the gathered memories and would keep them alive, keep the mountain scene in sight near at hand.

Alone in her room, still thinking of Mrs Harcourt, she remembered from *Ships that Pass in the Night* how on the last day all but one person had forgotten the departing guest.

Then in getting up from lunch she had seen them all, unknowing, for the last time—as yesterday the mountains. For all these people hidden away in their rooms, immersed in their own affairs, she was already a figure slid away and forgotten. With the paying of Frau Knigge's bill, her last link with the Alpenstock had been snapped.

But when the coach-horn sounded and she went down into the hall, there they all were, gathering round, seeing her off. Hurriedly, with the door open upon the falling snow and the clashing of sleigh-bells, she clasped for the first time strange and friendly hands, saw, in eyes met full and near, welcome from worlds she had not entered. Beside the door she met Daphne forgotten, who clutched and drew her back into the window-space for desperate clinging, and entreaties sounding lest for this new, slow-witted lover the searching gaze should not be enough.

It was not until she was inside the dark coach and its occupants had thanked heaven she was English and let down a window, that she remembered Vereker. He alone had made no farewell.

The coach pulled up outside the post office and there he stood, in the driving snow, and all the way down the valley she saw them one by one, and saw him standing in greatcoat and woollen helmet, heard his elegant light distressful voice begging her to come out next year.

And brighter now than the setting they had charmed was the glow these people had left in her heart. They had changed the aspect of life, given it the promise of their gentle humanity, given her a frail link with themselves and their kind.

She climbed into a carriage whose four corners were occupied and sat down to the great journeying.

'History repeats itself.'

Looking up, she found all about her the family from Croydon, met the father's quizzical brown eyes.

'Had a farewell kick-up at our place last night. We 're feeling the effects. *You* look very fit. Enjoyed yourself?'

'I 've had a splendid time.'

'You collared the handsomest man in Oberland anyhow—that young giant of a Russian.'

'Italian.'

'Bless my soul! Hear that, Doris?'

'We were up till *fave* this morning,' said Doris.

The train moved off, but only Doris, once more grown-up, with her hair in a staid bun under her English winter hat, turned to watch the station disappear.

'Want to go back, Doris?'

'Ah love,' she breathed devoutly, 'could thou and aye with feete conspire——'

Miriam joined the sister in intoning the rest of the lines.

'Ah Moon——' began Doris, and the brother leaned forward, holding towards her a gloved hand whose thumb protruded through a fraying gap:

'A little job for you in Paris.'

She regarded it undisturbed and turned away the scornful sweetness of her face towards the window and the snowflakes falling thickly upon the shroud of snow.

DAWN'S LEFT HAND

TO
VIOLET

CHAPTER I

HE had said *the* train, as if there were no other. It must be the one great train of the night, the Paris train, that was to be an hour late.

'Confound it!' she said fervently into the darkness in the manner of a travelling Englishman faced with delay that to her was nothing but reprieve; a whole extra hour in Oberland. Of which a fraction must be spent in carrying the news to the group still standing in the lamplight at the far end of the platform; meekly.

She sped along, feeling the sharp air expand once more limitlessly across the snows to which she had said farewell, and began speaking, as soon as they were near enough to hear, in the freemasonish Oberland way of addressing strangers as if they were old friends. They turned their three heads as she reached them on the end of her communication; but absently, as if being interrupted, and showing that they had heard only by turning again towards each other, and that they were not of the Oberland world by consulting in murmurs.

Two small women, shapeless with wraps, and a man rather tall and with a customary importance in his bearing, but standing with the women in an equality of sincere attention towards the discussion.

She waited a moment, not to miss the chance of a belated response, yet when she turned away was glad of their negligence that set her free to attend only to the mountain air.

But her spirit turned out to be already in London, refusing to come back to the enchantment of which it had taken leave and watching, as she went, for the lit opening of the waiting-room, and presently welcoming the sound of following footsteps.

They sat down on the far side of the room, a party of conspirators. Speculating towards her, towards the fact, pathetic

131

or improper, of her sitting there alone at midnight. Probably, since she attacked strangers so freely, improper.

She felt them pitiful, living suspiciously outside the world. of universal urbanity, and turned to the nearer wall-posters, glaring in the half-light, for response to the jovial remarks that rose in her mind: their imagined cheerful sound making perfect the spectacle of the cautiously murmuring group.

The man was crossing the room. Aloof and graceless in a stout top-coat, he demanded whether she were going through to London, and at once went away with her answer, and the murmuring began again.

Contemplating without looking at them and yet unable to escape the spectacle without either closing her eyes or gazing at the floor or ceiling, it seemed to be in the very person of Mr Orly, seated at the lunch-table in the bare-walled basement room at Wimpole Street where the confronted lunchers were, beyond the dishes on the table and the unvarying lights and shadows made by the electric light, the only external refuge for unpreoccupied eyes, that she gazed upwards and mentally emitted his humorously despairing sigh, glancing at the same time sideways-down at herself seated at his right hand and just growing aware of the meaning, for him and from his point of view, of one of his kindly sarcasms, and yet obstinately set against admitting any justification for it, desperately refusing to show any sign of awareness and choosing rather to appear idiotic, and justify his sigh, than to give him the satisfaction of seeing her look 'rather sick.'

She remembered saying to Michael in a voice almost trembling with indignation: 'One *moment* of my consciousness is wider and deeper than his has been in the whole of his life.' And the grave conviction of Michael's 'most-certainly,' made all the more comforting by the way the note of shocked amusement in his voice had suggested that the warmth of her statement was waste of emotion.

And now the statement itself seemed meaningless. Monstrous. It was not true that Mr Orly's consciousness was less deep and wide than hers but simply that like all true Oberlanders he was unconscious of his consciousness. Had been trained away from it. A kind of salvation. But what is the use of an unconscious salvation? Insecure. Depending upon being always surrounded by an unvarying world. . . .

When at last the sounds outside announced the train that would set going again the unsuspicious movement of life, the little group of conspirators followed her on to the platform and she found, turning round from hoisting her things into the rack of her chosen compartment, the smaller woman within the carriage and her friends, taking leave from the platform, audible as New Englanders with quiet, unsmiling voices.

The train started, carrying her and the small woman off together into the long night. In spite of the meagre promise, she found herself back within the warmth of shared life. Flowing through her, it gave eagerness to her hands as they attacked the fastenings of her coat whose removal was part of the prelude to a social evening.

Perhaps the woman did not mean to talk. But even if she were silent, her presence would keep the whole world in the carriage.

She had turned away from the window and its view of the departing platform and now, with head bent to unfasten her neat veil, fell into speech as if her farewells had interrupted a conversation already set going. Miriam hurried her preparations to be seated and at leisure, hearing for the present little more than the quality of the woman's speech, the wide New England vowels that always reminded her of sounds heard long ago, she could not tell where; and being confirmed in her first impression of the group on the platform by the way the inflections of her voice had been subdued, by the life she had led, almost to a monotone. It came forth, without emphasis and without colour, from the world in which she lived, a world that had never been made strange to her by any sort of astonishment over the fact of its being there at all. The very way she took off her wrappings seemed to say that every one had the same clothes, and the same way with their clothes.

She came to the middle of the carriage and sat down under the central light to attack her boots, a small, shrivelled woman all grey; grey cardigan and neat grey skirt, grey hair, sallow thin face and faded eyes, expressionless. A fading life. As she moved about the carriage making her preparations for the night, her movements were lissome but had exactly the same expression as her speech. Wonderful to watch. But she would have laughed, if she could laugh, at the idea of their being wonderful to watch. She was following the set shape of her life with a sort of uninspired gusto that had nothing to do with the unique quality of the passing moment. Did not seem to know that moments were passing and her life passing: her uniformly unsolitary life of the transatlantic spinster, enclosed in uniformity even when she was travelling in Europe.

She finished her discourse with her preparations, and neatly composed herself for sleep on her side of the carriage without good night. The world, hidden under a neat grey rug.

Miriam's attention dropped backwards away from her across the brief conversation to which she now heard her own voice contributing warm eagerness that of course the little grey woman had not found attractive because it was centred, not upon the items, but upon the prospect of getting away behind items. She took refuge with the two left behind at Berne to go on with their enchanting task. Why did not English teachers have a sabbatical year, go abroad and lose themselves in strangeness and come back renewed? Why not every one?

Already the little woman was asleep. She slept through the night and until the early grey began, announcing Paris at hand, and when Miriam moved to raise herself through the worst of her fatigue before the voice should begin, it sounded at once. Easy words speaking her way of being, describing her way of coming from the depths of sleep full-grown at once into her level way of life. Driving away, in advance, the sound of the stillness and the light, the richness of the gold that would follow the morning grey, and all the beauty of remembered Paris. To this woman, Paris would be only Paris, in whatever way she had of perceiving it, not a part of something hidden within herself and suddenly revealed.

She talked undaunted by groans and irrelevant statements, as if reciting: a fluent stream of well-worn words dying unconsidered into each other. Miriam's own voice breaking forth, as movement restored her strength, in staccato English, sounded, in comparison, like song. Urbanity was failing at its first test. She wanted to silence this woman and attend to all that was being driven away. Yet each time she spoke, she knew she was carolling her own advantage of youth and high spirits over one not yet alive, and already too far down life's hill really to live.

They were ready to leave the train now slowly moving through Paris grey in mist. The little spinster was unmoved in becoming surrounded by Paris. Yet only a few months ago she had seen Paris and London for the first time.

'Didn't you find London very small and flat?'

'*Mercy*, no.'

She had spoken almost warmly, and went on to explain that this time she meant to see all over England before going home for her marriage in June. The train stopped. But neither that nor her astounding announcement made any break in her discourse.

Meekly Miriam followed the bride-to-be out into the morning twilight of the great station, where she looked smaller, older. But over herself and her neat belongings played a golden radiance from her far-off destiny.

Paris was breakfast in the station hotel, and a drive to another station and the finding of another train. But again, prevailing over the ceaselessly talking little woman, the charm of it, lying all about her in the busy daylight, challenged the mountains, as it had challenged before she had seen them, and won. And the little woman at her side, intent on her uniform world, was part of the prevailing.

And when they parted in the blackness of Newhaven, she felt bereft. For a moment she stood still in nothingness beneath the sky so strangely large and empty. Just behind it the mountains were hidden. They filled her eyes, but only for an instant, leaving her alone upon the airless lowlands.

CHAPTER II

FOR these three, the time she had spent living out in Oberland a golden life within her life, had been just a fortnight of dark London days leading towards spring. Each morning they had come unenviously downstairs to find again, behind the small disturbances and adjustments that disturbed them so little, their sense of untroubled everlastingness. Helped by the warmth of their clear fire that always looked wide, in spite of the narrow, villa grate.

Its glow brightened the frosty sunlight coming in above the little hedges of dense snowy-white lace set along the lower halves of the windows and giving the heavy curtains each side the small bay their rich warmth.

They were all eager to go on with their experiences, backwards, from last night's story of the return journey, into the life preceding it. At leisure. There it all lay, represented by her presence. Awaiting the time when every one should have been carefully provided. Meantime, the to and fro of needful words, the sight of their morning eyes, fresh and dark in their familiar faces, the long, good moments into which flowed the refreshment of their rich serenity, deepened this morning by their sense of entertainment ahead.

They were eager, not through insufficiency but because of their sufficiency that survived Florrie's hopeless engagement, Grace's wrecked romance and Mrs Philps's large experience of 'trouble,' unchanged.

And yet, she reflected, taking in the new, plain wallpaper upon which their heavily gilt-framed, old-fashioned pictures stuck out with an uneasy prominence, with its narrow, gay frieze of sunlit landscape, they particularly liked 'to march with the times.' But only because within all times, however new, they found what already they possessed, over which time had no power. Yet this morning they were a fortnight older than when she had seen them last, a fortnight nearer death, of which they always spoke with grave horror and dilated eyes.

But she could imagine each one of them recovering at the end, with a secret, unseen smile of surprise, behind the externals that in the deaths of others so horrified them, this unassailable happy serenity of being of which they were so unaware and that made the background of life in their company a single continuous moment troubled only now and again by the remembrance of their unconsciousness of its perfection.

Her experience was passing over to them. They were up amidst the sunlit snows, meeting her friends, realizing them in their direct, changeless way; making allowances for her enthusiasm, yet loving it, welcoming each word and seeming to be waiting for her at every point of her journey through her so different life. As if prepared for each experience in advance, and yet seeming not to see, as they accompanied her into a life that for them was new and strange, how very strange was any life at all.

Perhaps it was just their unquestioning acceptance that made life flow from them so strongly that most of her friends seemed, by comparison, uncreated. In some essential way. In the way the innocent Croydon family and the innocent people at the Alpenstock had made them seem uncreated. And yet these uncreated friends would dispose of these three and of the Croydoners and Alpenstockers in a single generalization. . . .

Wandered too far into the contemplation of incompatibles that was the everlastingly disturbing background of social life, she felt the threads of her discourse slipping away and looked across at the row of little villas on the other side of the road, the unchanging outposts of her life in this secluded room, and found them *changed*. And turned back to the table to finish the picture of the ski-contest with the magical strangeness of the villas before her eyes within the background of the scene she was contemplating. Behind the black-clothed figure of the bird-man, poised, with out-flung arms moulded by close-clinging, soft black sleeves from shoulder to glove, for a second against the sky's brilliant blue above the glistening snow-slope,

was the vision of these little houses, that once had seemed so
sharp in outline, blurred to softness by the English air so that
their edges seemed actually to *waver* upon it.

The excitement of the discovery of their new individuality
broke into her voice, enlivening it as she finished her sketch, so
that the three listeners were the more moved by what they were
seeing; sharing her emotion, without knowing that it arose from
the recognition of the gentle mistiness, even in bright sunlight,
of English outlines.

Strange and delightful that this simple discovery should be
so moving as to seem in itself enough as a result of foreign
travel and should go on, while the general to and fro of remarks
was assailing her attention, wrapping her in a happiness that
thrilled through her voice which was now claiming her attention for its own quality grown strange: sounding the gentle
south of England, the west country, too, perhaps, of her family's
origin, and the large-gardened, uncrowded south-western
suburbs—as so often, before, she had heard it sound here in
the alien north, where voices grated even at their gentlest and
bore, for all occasions, a bared and cutting edge; but without
recognition of its essentials beyond the flattering assurance that
she herself belonged to a superior, more cultivated way of being;
the way of being that amongst the Oberlanders had been all
about her and of which at this moment she was being aware
as clearly as of the misty English villas as it made, on her behalf,
within the inflections of her voice, statements clearer than any
spoken words, enchanting and delighting her as she was
delighted and enchanted by the people she loved, giving her a
thrilling certainty as to the unseen future, shaming her into
the knowledge that in her case they were unjustifiable, that she
had grown level with almost none of them, and yet lending
their quality to every word she spoke.

Returning, she looked forth at strangers still radiating
delight, still sounding their alien voices and making hers sound
in response and again proclaim itself a barrier and yet the vehicle
of her everlasting communion with them; of her prevailing
with them by virtue of the echo within it of the way of being
from which it had come forth.

They were hovering now between their desire for more talk and the pull of the shape of their day. The freshness of the breakfast hour was over, the scene drawing to its end, each member of the party moving away into the depths of her secret, separate existence. Her own claimed her, to the new gay undertone that presently in the open she would hear more clearly.

And going down into town for her delayed luggage she heard it everywhere. In every one about her was hilarity, deep-seated; in every one moving in the open, though not on holiday. It was there even in the worried and the sorrowful, the creator of their worry and their sorrow.

Inside the clangorous great station the secret joy palpitated in the exciting, metal-smelling air like the beating of wings. It emanated even from those who were setting out, deedily, only for suburbs, and reached and transformed every hideous object within their sight.

Joy is eternity. Eternity is joy. In railway stations and in trains people enter perforce their own eternity. So that men, even when faced with disaster, so long as they can move from place to place and get away into eternity, are commonly more cheery than women, though unaware of what it is that makes them so.

In Oberland the eternal being of woman is an escorted procession. Its men are trained to pay homage to the giver of life and the pain-bearer. They seek eternity in the Services, in hobbies, in art or science, games. And never consciously find it. Their bondage to the womanly woman is a life-bondage, to eternity personified.

The jingling hansom was carrying her back to her London, filled with people to whom the golden eternity had been just fourteen 'ordinary' days and who, knowing nothing of the change in her that at present seemed to be everlasting, would endanger and perhaps destroy it. She wished she could hand them, like a certificate, at least her record of social success. They would misinterpret. Amongst them all only Hypo

would understand.   He would say, to demonstrate his insight,
'You 've been flattered, my dear, by kindly people at loose
ends, to the top of your bent.   You 're a little drunk with it
all.   I 'm not objecting to that.   Good for you, good for
everybody, once in a way,' and, having protested, begin his own
subtle, but still quite obvious flattery, for his own ends.   But
he would understand that discovery about oneself is impersonal,
as well as personal, like a discovery in chemistry.

Piecemeal, everything piecemeal.   What Oberland had been,
apart from people, no one would ever know.   Yet its beauty
had entered into her for ever; its golden glow must surely
somehow reveal itself.   It lay even over the nauseating,
forgotten detail of Flaxman's now rapidly approaching.

The cab drew up at the mouth of the court.   At number
two, Perrance filled the doorway, one of the wings of his grime-
stiffened cape brushing the jamb as he slouched through on
his way to his basement.   The unchanged sights of the court
seemed, as she entered it, to re-open the door just slammed by
Perrance, to deny her absence and promise speedy obliteration
of her memories and destruction of her renewed strength.

Together with the reek pouring from the opened door, came
the rebuff of the narrow staircase up which the weedy cabman
might refuse to carry her luggage.   Her mind turned away from
this difficulty.   Beyond it, waiting for her upstairs, was not
the Flaxman life grown unendurable, but renewal and continuation of the golden glow.

Turning from the door to the empty court, she met the blue-
eyed friendly glance of a neat working-man, not a Flaxmanite,
seeming, as he responded without a word to her confident
question and went about her business serenely, as if it were
his own, the first of a procession of friends emerging from
the future.

Selina was out.   But the rooms were filled with the dry,
sweet fragrance of mimosa.   Once, only once, she had told
Selina that the scent of mimosa in a wintry room said, each year,
that life is summers.   Selina had missed her; was offering from
her side of the curtain that for so long had seemed the embodiment of their incompatibility, this tribute to their early days.

A pile of letters. Tributes to Oberland, to Oberland past and her return to London accomplished. But alone up here she had no sense of return. The memories accumulated since she landed were like a transparent film through which clearly she saw all she, had left behind; and felt the spirit of it waiting within her to project itself upon things just ahead, things waiting in this room as she came up the stairs. To open all these letters and drop into communication with the lives they represented would be to divert its course.

Graceless she felt, ungrateful, and could not care. Even Hypo's thin grey envelope failed to bring the usual electric shock. It stood out from the others only because her detailed response to it preceded perusal. With planned cunning, he had chosen this moment for one of his concentrated attacks; the obvious moment; the wrong moment; showing him as he was alone in himself, far-off, irrelevant to personal life. And, except for her annoyance with his planned persistence, she felt him stand, compared with the vast strange promise within, in an equality of indifference with all these others. It was only, she thought, as she sat down to open his letter, with the unlocated being of these people that she desired communication and not at all with the sight and sound of their busy momentary selves.

'Welcome to your London, my dear. I'm more in love with you than ever.'

When she reached the small interwoven capitals forming the signature she felt herself returned from flight, unawares, towards a far distance and felt the strong beating of her heart quieten before a vision of this shapely device, so deftly continuing and completing the design of the written lines, set down, in a kind of sincerity, beneath innumerable documents such as this.

He was 'in love' in his way; once again. But behind the magic words was nothing for her individually, for any one individually. And his brilliance, the mental qualities she had hitherto found so full of charm, had somehow, unaccountably, become overshadowed. She no longer felt the importance of trying to find forms of expression for alternative interpretations of his overpowering collection of facts. She felt at this moment that any interpretation was preferable to his and no plan at all better than even the most workable of plans born of the assumptions science was helplessly forced to make. He was offering a stone, a precious stone; but there might be bread waiting hidden in the world whose approaching distances seemed no longer filled only with queer irregular people who held most others in scorn.

She flicked the card, whose wording he had already forgotten, between thoughtful fingers: momentary purpose and plan, converging upon what she had seemed to be a fortnight ago. Supposing a kindly Philistine, with a fixed world and almost no imagination, were in his place? Impossible. Breathlessly impossible. Philistines or intellectuals . . . is there no alternative? Nobody, nobody. She wanted nobody she already knew. But did she wish him away? Or even averted? Only for a while forgotten. And that he could be, since he was fixed, in his place, far away.

Sure of possessing the immediate future, clear of obstacles and with the golden glow undimmed above it, she turned to the other letters and found amongst them one from Alma which somehow she had passed over. The sight of it drew all the rest together, making them seem like the various flowers of a single bunch and rebuking, as if it were a living presence, her desire to escape from their friendly challenges. She hesitated before submitting herself to the always strange, strong spell of Alma's written words, that already in advance were charming and rousing her with their veiled appeal from someone who was neither quite the Alma she had known in girlhood, nor the Alma who humorously fitted herself into an adopted summary of human existence.

When the torn flap of the envelope revealed the graceful hurrying script, she felt herself set down beyond release within the pattern of the life she had left behind on the far side of eternity. Gay, affectionate greetings sailed, bearing down her protests, across the page. . . .

'And, my very dear, tremendous doings. We're invading your London; next week. We'll do a Wagner, you and me and Hypo.'

Not from the past and representing it, but from the golden future and heightening its glow they came to her as she imagined the impersonal sitting down together, before a large stage made vast by outpouring music, of the three equally reduced to silence and committed to experience whose quality could not be stated in advance.

CHAPTER III

ABOVE the shoulder of the parlourmaid announcing her from the doorway, she saw Densley standing at his table reading a letter, preoccupied, making use of spare seconds. And though not a patient, she felt again, as she had always felt on first entering the subdued light of this quiet room, a weakening of her scepticism before his specialized knowledge, and an uncomfortable sense of the ceaseless procession of stricken men and women, trustfully, one by one, crossing this space of floor between door and chair to learn the worst or, at the best, to be reminded that death is waiting and their span of years at the longest only a small number.

But as the maid withdrew and she came forward, the room whose door closed softly behind her was just the room that held his intimate lonely life. And he was once more only his friendship, an everlasting friend standing there in silhouette against the long window-blind yellowed by the sunlight it was keeping out.

At his best, tall and slender, in profile, with head bent so that the whole of its beautiful line, starting from the base of the neck and abruptly disappearing beneath the rounded edge of vigorously sprouting curls to appear again in the curve of the venerable small bald patch, was clearly visible, embellished by the outstanding close-cropped curls breaking into its shape. Newly cropped, and gleaming in the dim light. Very fresh and neat he looked, furbished up for the spring, very serré in the new grey frock-coat whose tails in an instant would perform their dervish-whirl as he swung round and came with outstretched arms to take her by the shoulders and get in the first words, and smother her response with his avalanche of laughter.

But he remained motionless, though now she had nearly reached the victims' chair. If he were really absorbed, she had read into the carefully casual wording of his summons an eagerness he did not feel. She recalled him hunched over his table, throwing down his pen and coming to meet her half-way across the room; talking into the telephone and murmuring a greeting for her the moment it became his turn to listen. This deliberate postponement of his welcome was new. Pretending to be engrossed in his letter, he was reminding her that her life was but one amongst the many he scanned day by day. And whilst this silent statement checked her eagerness to be congratulated and rejoiced over, he was accumulating advantage that would make his pounce the more effective when it came.

But if he were going to refuse to be a flattering mirror for her joy, this visit would turn into a continuation of a conflict of which she had grown weary. This should be the last time. Never again would she waste her golden leisure in fruitless discussion. This progress across the well-known room was the prelude to farewell. Glancing away from him towards its further space, she became aware of a deep peace and her eyes returned to him. Still holding, as if he were alone, his tranquil pose, he was waiting for her to recognize this peace as the reality beneath their differences.

With a pang of guilt she remembered her impulsive, too-affectionate letter from the Alpenstock promontory. It was on the strength of that letter that he was daring this test. The living peace in the room was like a light that seemed to flow towards them both from the corner that formed a triangle with him where he stood and herself where she stood; or to flow from each of them and meet exactly in the corner towards which at their different angles they both faced.

But there was nothing surprising in that. Any two souls could meet if only sometimes they would be silent together and wait. She ought to have known that his Celtic soul would be aware of this. But it would be unfair to let him travel too far in imagining an atonement that did not exist. Yet even as these thoughts flashed through her mind she was regretting the passing of the strange experience of sharing with him an instant of eternity and, in order ever so little to recall it, she banished thought and resisted the further movement that would bring her too near to be ignored and saw, with her eyes on his quietude, the perspective of their friendship open, claiming its place amongst the memories laid up in this room of the years of her London life.

Saw him again as the unknown Great Man serenely produced by Eleanor Dear from her diminishing stock of 'influenchoo peopoo' . . . summoned and coming, a tall handsome saviour in dress-clothes, to her sick-room at midnight, tired and harassed, gently talking and questioning and writing; ignoring the friend in the corner until suddenly he insulted her and her beloved London night-streets by asking, without troubling to look at her, whether she were equal to going out and ringing up a chemist. And her first visit, as Eleanor's agent, to sound him before she cast her desperate net over Taunton. And, as a single occasion, all the sittings, in this room, over Eleanor's difficulties and the business of rescuing Taunton, secretly, under the shadow of Harley Street, under the threat of death, not lifting until Eleanor was provided for away from the brightness of lives still unthreatened.

And all their meetings and conflicts all over London, since the day she had lectured him, with Veresaief's *Confessions of a Doctor* as text, on the inevitable ignorance of the high priests of Medicine; and all his kindly human sympathy with her Socialists and Anarchists and Suffragists . . . and his belief that their hold on her was only a makeshift. . . .

'Glad to be back, dear-girl?' he murmured thoughtfully.

'I'm not back yet; still much more there than here,' she said, smiting at his preparedness to sit down and state her experience in what he believed to be its right proportions; drawing her out with questions and greeting her answers with head thrown back and mouth wide for his indrawn laughter—its final gasp bringing him forward to smite her knee and make his comments and wait, eyes still filled with laughter, for her to share his mirth at her expense. Not one word of enthusiasm should he have, nor anything that might give him food for amusement.

Still remaining ambushed behind his letter, he flung out, as she advanced, an arm that found and gently shoved her into the confessional chair whence nothing was visible but the tall screen hiding the place of anxious disrobings, his littered table and himself, in profile against the high oblong of screened sunlight . . . swinging round with a single swift movement to face her, seated; long grey-trousered legs elegantly crossed, crease going to the devil . . . spats . . . a *pink* moss-rosebud, a grave, tired face surveying her as though she were a patient, a new patient.

He was quite innocent, tired and London-worn, emerging with grave simplicity from preoccupations that made havoc of his grandeur, accentuated the dreadful rosebud more completely than would the debonair manner that perhaps he had worn an hour ago.

'Whose wedding have you been to?' she asked cruelly, through her pity that condemned as monstrous the demand that he should turn aside from his exacting affairs to pay tribute to her festivity.

Mentally she added silk hat and light gloves and set him amongst guests thronging to the reception, saw him play his part, a lightly, musically moving figure of benevolence; radiating, as she had seen him at Socialist gatherings they had visited together, the kindly humanity most of the Lycurgans possessed only as a dogma with which to bludgeon their opponents.

True democracy, the ruling of everybody by their best selves, was more readily to be found amongst the Oberlanders than amongst professed Socialists? And here, to her hand, was a topic that would represent her experiences, give him the key to them in a way that would rob him, if by chance this present gravity were assumed, of what he was secretly chuckling over in advance, and startle him by putting his own case better than he had done in their many battles, and also, by making it one with hers, demonstrate the truth in both and his own one-sidedness.

'I've been to no wedding, my dear.'

This was the low, pitying tone he used when she failed to

be moved by some specially 'moving' human drama selected from his day's experiences.

He looked away, towards the writing-table, took up a paper-knife and thoughtfully tapped the table's polished edge.

'Then why so glorious?'

She smiled, to cover her failure to approve, but with averted eyes, so that she might no longer see the pink rosebud soften his good looks with its dreadful prettiness. Perhaps it didn't. Perhaps the intolerable effect was produced by apathy, by the weariness he was not trying to conceal; spring weariness after his too arduous winter.

Their voices sounded together and she threw away the beginning of her hopeful topic to attend to his meditative voice —the Celtic shape of its tone, the first two words on one middle note, then one two notes higher with a curve in its course that brought it two notes lower than the opening words, then ding-dong up and down, the last drop curving up at its end as if to redeem statement by giving it the form of courteous question; but to-day the persuasiveness, that always made his words seem spoken from the sure ground of belief, was not there, the end of his sentence fell sadly amongst the bright echoes their many meetings had left in this corner of the room. She heard the slithering discouraged soft fall of the paper-knife upon the table and looked up and found him sitting, with lightly clasped hands, forward in his chair regarding her: calm brow, steady searching eyes, the look of weariness vanished, the rosebud serenely saying that physicians have their lighter moments.

'Ye had a brave time, dear-girl?'

He spoke with grave warmth, inviting confidence. Watching his eyes while she banished from her mind all she had brought with her into the room, she could not find the shadow of a smile; but, even while she refused to afford him material, there he sat, entrenched, solidly representing dispersive generalizations. And to-day he was not waiting for her to withhold or give him his chance to pounce. Turning away his eyes he went on: 'I saw Campbell this morning; he told me ye were back and that he 'd never seen ye look so well.'

Professional interest; but she was not going to be drawn into discussing her health that was restored for evermore since she had seen the light on the mountains.

'Of course,' she said judicially, conveniently recalling an overheard phrase: 'the Swiss winter is marvellous. You go out unable to grasp the meaning of a newspaper column'— she felt her stored wealth shift away, as if assailed, as if threatening to depart—'and after twenty-four hours you can read a stiff treatise and remember each point.'

'Did ye read stiff treatises?'

'No; but I could remember anything I wanted to, and see *into* things.' She threw her raised voice after him as he got up and moved away—feeling herself forgiven, having testified, attempted to testify an incommunicable experience — to the blinded window through whose open upper half now came the sound of a car drawing up at the door: interruption punctually at hand, just as she was back again in that moment on the promontory that had filled everything with light, just as she could, she felt, have answered, even though irrelevantly, all the questions on earth.

With a click the blind had shot up, letting in the yellow London sunlight, and in its dense blaze she stood up to depart, for now the thudding of the engine filled the room, voices shouting it down sounded from the pavement and the steps, and the door-bell buzzed through the hall.

'You are fortunate,' she sang out into the blinding light, into the indifferent ears preoccupied already with the communications of the arriving patient, 'to have a corner house!' and saw the several corridors of gold that broke across the long grey street and felt herself already escaped into its echoey stillness, going, as she had come, unspent, to meet the green mists of the park and find its new crocuses; find the close ranks of mauve and white hiding the grass of that little alley again, stand and look and again feel that cool English freshness as if touching her all over, as if she were unclothed.

'Campbell was right,' he said gently into the stillness restored by the stopping of the engine; 'it's made ye like a red, red rose.'

Her happy blush revealed to her the shape of her body—as

if for her own contemplation, as if her attention were being
called to an unknown possession that yet was neither hers nor
quite herself—glowing with a radiance that was different from
the radiance of the surrounding sunlight; and turning to bend
and gather up the gloves on which she had been sitting she
seemed to journey far away from him and from herself into
the depths of her being and mingle there with an unknown
creature rising to meet and take her nature and transform it to
the semblance of his ideal. And in this semblance, a stranger
to herself and nameless, she came upright with the retrieved
gloves in her hand and turned to face him in the room's sunlight that now seemed the light of open spaces.

'Your patient,' she had said before she was aware, towards
him still standing leisurely in his window-space . . . approaching, saying, swiftly he passed her: 'He's early; he can wait.
Sit down again'—and disappearing into the background whence
he asked, as the everyday door of his bookcase came open with
an insouciant squeak, whether she had ever been to Italy.

'No,' she said and paused, remembering Guerini and his
revelation of an Italy that was not the Italy of her dreams. And
his dogmas, and his amazement in hearing them questioned,
and his anger, dull brown like his clothes, and hers that had
cured her, and his sorrow and belated willingness to look at
alternative interpretations, and his obliteration by Eaden in
whom the same dogmas, being held thoughtlessly, had seemed
so much more monstrous and implacable. And seemed at
this moment not to matter so very much. Neither Guerini's
nor Eaden's nor Densley's nor any man's to matter perhaps at
all, except to themselves. Thought of all together, reverberating over the world in all its languages, they seemed just an
unpleasant noise; like the chattering of those born deaf. Yet
she felt that even now, hearing them, it would be impossible
to content herself, as she had observed so many women do,
with a wise smile. Even now.

But this was flying off, running off with what might be an
illusion. She wished the window-blind back in place that she
might see more clearly, see his face when he left his books
and returned; discover whether his general strangeness to-day

meant that on the strength of her absurd letter he was again minded to risk, was not expecting, a rebuff, and was yet, because he once had had one, proudly nervous and uncertain—and meanwhile she must remain here, balanced between return to her customary life and the way of being she had entered a moment ago and that could be, she now realized with sober astonishment, her chosen way till death—or whether he were simply engrossed in some sad case whose story she would presently hear told in his way of telling: pausing at every turn for signs of sympathy, and yet ready to laugh over her harsh comments. And again she was reminded of Eleanor. And this time the thought of her brought within the sun's streaming light a darkness that centred in herself who a moment ago had felt transparent to endless light. A forgotten, deliberately forgotten darkness disqualifying her to be anything to anybody. . . .

'What has become of Eleanor Dear?'

'When did ye last heere of her, lassie?' The sparing, softly treading tone of his stories of his most dreadful cases: gentle judgment, without reproach.

'Oh, I don't know—ages ago'—her voice was hard, frostily selfish, something for a man to fly from—'when that heroic little Jew took her to Egypt.'

'Then ye 've not heard of her death?'

It was not shock or sadness that kept her silent. Immense, horrible relief in being certain that now the burden of Eleanor would never again return upon her hands. And great wonder, that Eleanor had done her dying. Somewhere, in some unknown room, she had accomplished that tremendous deed. Alone.

'Rodkin took her to Egypt'—he was bringing the comfort of his voice across the room—'first consulting me'—but remained out of sight behind her chair with a book, slowly turning its leaves that went over with a crumpling sound, large, glazed clay-paper leaves; heavy—'and kept her there for something over eighteen months. She got no better. When they returned, she was beyond human aid. His resources were exhausted. We got her into St Aloysius's. The sisters were kind and grew fond of her. My mother visited her daily and was with her when she passed away. I think she was happy at the end.'

Eleanor, forced to cease fighting and accept, lying there hollow-eyed and emaciated, growing weaker and weaker, but still charming; free, while she waited for those halls of Zion all jubilant with song, to charm these new friends . . .

'The little atheist Russian Jew was a better Christian than the English curate.'

'He married her; in Egypt. The bairns have father and name.'

'Lancelot and Lobelia . . . *Rodkin*.' Her voice trembled with laughter. In which he joined, and Eleanor, driving away her fierce authoritative little frown, and with rose-blush and arch affectionate smile, seemed, from heaven, to be joining too. She would. She would accept anything but reproach. Ease had come, though the picture of herself indignantly preaching at Eleanor for wasting Rodkin's substance remained an immovable torment and disgrace. He had laughed his lightly gasping extremity of laughter and yet did not come round to face and share her mirth. But she felt absolved. He knew, better perhaps than any one, he had seen again and again, the worst that was in her—intolerance, hatred, malice . . . no, not malice, something worse, uncharitableness, the things he most deplored—without condemnation. He knew perfectly, from first to last, all of Eleanor's manœuvrings; without condemning them. Small wonder he was the beloved physician.

Her sense of her own being, with its good and bad carelessly unmasked, more at ease in this room than in any other but her own, was expanding beyond this corner she knew so well, taking possession of the unvisited parts of the room brought near by his perambulating voice; feeling its way into the wider spaces within the air that filled its visible limits. But imperfectly, hindered by the direct glare of the sun and the presence of the patient waiting in the next room.

'I asked ye about Italy, because I rather think of going there.' This time his voice, coming from the farthest end of the room, as if he were in that deep recess and looking out of its tall, narrow window, was like the voice of someone giving a cheery morning greeting to someone else suddenly and gladly seen from the midst of busy preoccupation: confident of response, not needing to wait and take note of it. It came nearer than if he were sitting at her side.

'People were going down,' she said, and the distance they had to travel made her words songful—they were meeting across the length of the sad room; he and she, from the far distances of their separate beings, obliterating, with the sounds of their common to-day, the melancholy echoes left within it—'from Oberland. They go, in one day, from the Swiss winter into the Italian spring.'

'I'll go,' he chanted back through the clatter of a dray turning into a neighbouring mews, 'if I go, from Paris, where I'll be attending the Medical Congress the first week in May.'

The dray thundered swiftly over the cobble-stones, spreading a clamour that consumed every other sound.

'Don't ye think,' said his gentlest voice just above her head, 'I'll have earned a holiday?' His arms, linked by the large book, came over and round her, and the book came down opened upon her knees: a double-page picture of Venice, Grand Canal edged by stately buildings, gondolieri gracefully driving swift gondolas along the flat water; moonlight and song. He was crouching at her side, his face out of sight, just level with her own, one arm along the back of the low chair, the other tilting the book inwards from the blinding light.

'Isn't that where people go for their honeymoon?' he murmured thoughtfully, as if considering the picture.

She felt him watching while she waited, gazing through the outspread scene, for words more in harmony than was this arch jocularity with the steady return of the strange new light within her that now streamed forth to join the blinding sunlight, so that she was isolated in a mist of light, far away from him and waiting for the sound of her name.

'Ye still scorn honeymoons.'

He was gone. The light flowed back into herself as she turned and saw him standing tall and upright, elbow on mantel-piece, several feet away, saw his face, sad above the pink rosebud and as nearly stern as in its changeless kindliness it could ever be.

What had he seen while he watched? Her perfect stillness while she contemplated a proposition? And perhaps he was right. The strange vision of the future expanding endlessly in light had held as she gazed into it no personal thought of him and prompted no response.

Gently she approached him, trying in the way she again pleaded for his wretched patient to convey the change produced in her regard by this discovery of him as a source of marvels. But he held her off with casual talk. He now believed, and she grew scarlet and took hasty leave as the thought came, that he had completely surprised her, and that this belated response was a clutching at an opportunity whose quality had been realized while she sat silent. And perhaps he was right in that too. Perhaps the strange glory to which she had responded was born of a selfish rejoicing. Perhaps, watching her, he had read only the signs of a secret, selfish triumph. Missed some essential, unmistakable sign.

Yet gravely and with a meditative enviousness he had said more than once that a husband opens for his wife the gate of a temple into which he may not follow her. And still in that moment of being wrapped in light that could have come only through the opened gate, he had expected her to respond in kind to his sly jocularity? Had closed the gate and left her outcast because she was kept silent and entranced, forgetting his personal presence, seeing only the newness of life into which she was about to step.

Walking on down the street, she turned again towards that strange moment, trying to recall the experience. But it was the visible pageant of marriage that rose before her eyes; so suitably, she felt now, a floral pageant. Wistfully, with new knowledge and interest, she watched the form of the satin-clad bride adream in a vast loneliness of time that was moving with the swiftness of the retreating movement of the years that were leaving her for ever, amidst a bevy of wide-awake, hopeful bridesmaids, vanish into the dark porch of the church whose clamour of bell-notes, falling in cascades into the sunlit air, brightened the light upon the grey buildings; saw the led bride, a lonely representative of humanity, measuring off the last moments of her singleness, reluctantly until the other equally lonely representative came in sight, waiting for her at the altar, and the footsteps of her spirit hurried to be with him.

She heard the two voices sound out from time into eternity, amidst a stillness of flowers; and the triumphant crashing of the Mendelssohn March as the two figures came forth from the vestry door and came down the aisle towards the light falling upon them from the high west window.

It was because life with Densley would hold the light of an in-pouring eternity that she had found herself willing to throw in her lot with his. In Hypo there was no sense of eternity; nor in Michael, except for the race, an endless succession of people made in God's image, all dead or dying.

Yet she was approving the rescue of Densley. Vibrating within her, side by side with resentment, was relief. And as she surveyed the little back street, where now she found herself, in search of food to be consumed in the ten minutes left of her lunch-hour, she felt, with a comfortingly small pang of wistfulness, the decisive hour that had just gone by slide into its place in the past and leave her happily glancing along the shopfronts of this mean little back street.

Teetgen's Teas, she noted, in grimed, gilt lettering above a dark and dingy little shop. . . .

Teetgen's Teas. And behind, two turnings back, was a main thoroughfare. And just ahead was another. And the streets of this particular district arranged themselves in her mind, each stating its name, making a neat map.

And *this* street, still foul and dust-filled, but full now also of the light flooding down upon and the air flowing through the larger streets with which in her mind it was clearly linked, was the place where in the early years she would suddenly find herself lost and helplessly aware of what was waiting for her eyes the moment before it appeared: the grimed gilt lettering that *forced me to gaze into the darkest moment of my life and to remember that I had forfeited my share in humanity for ever and must go quietly and alone until the end.*

And now their power has gone. They can bring back only the memory of a darkness and horror, to which, then, something has happened, begun to happen?

She glanced back over her shoulder at the letters now away behind her and rejoiced in freedom that allowed her to note their peculiarities of size and shape.

From round the next corner came a distant, high, protesting, nasal yell dropping into a long shuddering gurgle: *Punch*. She turned the corner. There they were at the end of the street.

In front of a greengrocer's a few slum children standing in the muddy street, more numerous elders, amongst them a busy doctor, paused for a moment, a teacher, excusing her delight with a sceptical smile, two rapt hospital nurses.

Munching one of the greengrocer's foreign apples, tasting like pineapple, she held up her face towards the mimic theatre high in air, from which joy flowed down upon this little crowd eagerly and voluntarily gathered together.

CHAPTER IV

OBERLAND again; its golden light, and its way of making its outer world conform to its inner. Something of heaven, precarious, but temporarily closing the doors of hell. Shedding its light upon the young man swiftly crossing the lounge alone, a little shifty, burdened with some threat, uneasy in hurrying alone from point to point in the world-wide enclosure.

'Here she is!' Alma's voice, and Alma appearing from along a corridor of greenery, in a filmy West End gown. Arrived, with power and freedom to move and choose and be at ease in the manner of a native, in the world whose outermost fringes she had touched in girlhood. (Coming up, on great occasions, in a hired omnibus, with a party of excited people, all being excessively sociable and slaying, without knowing it, the very occasion as it passed—to the Gaiety.)

And now both of them, two little figures side by side, two little Oberlanders, conforming, dressed in defiance of Lycurgan tweeds and *djibbêhs*.

Their voices, amongst those of the birthright members of the world-wide Oberland sounding from all over the quietly-lit restaurant, were alien. In pitch and intonation. But their minds gave to the corner where they sat the character of a small preserve: of originality within the wide spread of innocent conventionality. Yet they were both under the spell of the innocent conventionality; a little eager in their conformity, rather too consciously at home and at ease.

Giving her time, being so far too busy with correct by-play to notice her silence, to delight in their surprising tribute to Oberland. She had expected them to stand out from this world, unmoved by it and revealing their differently directed vitality. They were quenched. By their own correct clothes and the further garment of their surroundings.

157

Toned up, in the midst of the fatigue left by the day, by the interest of meeting them for the first time in the open, she glanced at Hypo sitting at her side in uniform, cut off from his moorings and launched in the sea of London life, and observed how his dress clothes, while accentuating his commonplace type, deepened the quality of the blue-grey eyes that was himself visible.   Grey of high-power intelligence turned outwards, twinkling blue of sanguine nature at home in delights, hampering the austere grey.

There was no seaward window through which his gaze could escape across the world, and the clear light, replacing the upper twilight created by the Bonnycliff lamp-shades, showed the blue and the grey beams together in full power, dammed up and, so carefully was he not looking about, short-circuiting; embarrassing his mind as the rather small sofa upon which the three of them sat side by side was embarrassing his movements.   Embarrassment from which, in Oberland, she, as his feminine guest, should be helping him to escape.

And again, as in early days at the Alpenstock, while bathing in the light created by the men and women about her, she was in conflict with the convention that kept urbane women alert at the front gates of consciousness to guard the ease of men waiting to be set going on their topics.

Reminded by the suave voices sounding from the level near at hand and, in distant parts of the room, from the upper air into which they rose—assailing her with memories of their rivals, the sounds echoing in the open amongst the Oberland mountains—of the instantaneous flow of words in just this pitch of voice and shape of tone the moment two or more Alpenstockers were gathered together, she cried within herself that it was indecent, and could have sat back and laughed aloud over the tide of masquerading sound, only that the ugly poor word worried her with its negative, insufficient expression of the destructive power of incessant speech.

'Outrageous,' she murmured.

'Right.'   Hypo's voice at her side, clear and mirthful within its huskiness like the blue within the misty grey.   'Caviare's outrageous.   No caviare.'

The waiter was there, the evening begun, its events counting themselves off; only this small half-hour available for being together, with the tension of expectation making its moments shallow.

As if he feared the man might run away, as if to register his awareness, and disapproval, of the way waiters are apt to make off before their '*beneficent* and *necessary*,' but '*tiresome*,' business is properly concluded, and to give warning that on this occasion patience was needed but would be rewarded by entertainment, Hypo kept a hand upheld in the direction of the waiter and crooked towards him a detaining, instructive finger while slowly he deciphered, French syllable by syllable, in the manner of a child learning to read—each syllable equally accented, but offered as if in itself it were someone's most priceless unconscious jest—the items of their feast; half raising his head, after each quotation, in the direction of the waiter for confirmation and permission to bend once more, first drawing breath for the renewed effort, over his '*arduous*,' but '*diverting*,' task. When this small exhibition was over he would drop into talk, but only after a swift collecting glance, achieved in the course of turning in speech towards Alma or herself, at the immediately surrounding and possibly appreciatively witnessing neighbours.

Outrageous, she resumed within, while there was yet time, but found in her mind only a vision of Alma gracefully set towards the little drama, the smile produced for it left forgotten on her face while away within her hidden world she mused alone.

The dismissed waiter passed by, gliding headlong, pushed open a near door that let in a wave of heat, the glare of un-screened light, the sounds of foreign voices shouting orders against the kitchen-clatter, in high-pitched nasal monotone: the world beneath this festive scene, supporting it.

Unconscious Oberlanders, complacently accepting. And all over the world a growing strength, with revengeful eyes set only upon the defects of the qualities that had built the high-walled Lhassa now preserving a perilous mental oblivion.

She listened to their sounds. Subdued buzzing, barking and fluting of English voices; laughter: women's laughter springing delicately, consciously beautiful, from note to note upwards or downwards in the scale, spontaneous croakings of elderly women, graduates in life; men's laughter whuffing out on single notes that seemed to resound from distant places where life is risked and won.

'All these manicured voices,' she said quietly, leaning outwards to catch also Alma's ear, and collided with Hypo's voice and saw him drop his remark half-finished and swiftly turn a hopeful, investigating eye. Alma's laugh tinkled, abruptly accentuated; mirthless. An extinguisher. And whilst Hypo, accepting it, passed it on warmed and disarmed by a flattering, appreciative grin, Miriam saw, deep-drawn for her benefit on Alma's brow—as she turned to select her hors d'œuvre, repeating her sound in order to assert her stewardship of the conversation and keep silent during the instant required for improvising a fresh departure, the initiator of so unsuitable a topic—a pucker of disgust.

'Ears,' said Hypo in his low-comedian manner, eyebrows up in hopeless reflectiveness, hands thrown out in a small gesture of mock despair, 'voices and *ears*.'

'I know. Don't be afraid.'

Sitting back to talk for him alone, she said, as the little dishes came her way and she was obliged to come again into the open, in tones modulated to exclude Alma from all but the sound of their cool engrossment: 'There's something a fortnight old you must hear at once, before it loses its first charm,' and helped herself at random and sat back, unwilling to feast and forget or endanger the bright landscape of thought that here, on neutral territory, she could so much more easily induce him to contemplate than if she were facing him, entrenched and defensive, upon his accustomed background.

'You shall tell me,' he said in the restrained, self-amused manner that would show, at short range, as the prelude to a witticism, 'anything you like,' glowing voice for herself, glance at the waiter to share and steer his awareness in the way it should go: nice gentleman humouring wilful young lady; 'if,' finger up to announce arrival of epigram, 'you'll take an anchovy and an olive.' He was unattained, perhaps unattainable, intent only on keeping the balance between his sense of the occasion as public and at the same time a meeting of lovers.

'You'll have to *listen*.' Alma's lovely eye, as gracefully she bent to the morsel on her fork, came round surveying. 'Anchovy,' said Hypo firmly; 'we're here to consume, each other's minds if we've time before they're dissolved in Wagner, but also olives and things.'

'I want you to repeat something for me.' She turned to her food as the patient waiter passed on and Alma's eye, coming round once more, reassured, took another direction; a happy sense of security closed about her, the certainty that neither his adroitness nor Alma's permanent readiness to create diversions would prevent the launching of her discovery upon its beneficent career.

'Say, being careful to speak slowly, "Too many irons in the fire."'

'Is this a parlour game? You *are* a dear, Miriam.'

'It's the time and the place and the topic, all together. Speak.'

'There's nothing in reason I wouldn't do for you, Miretta, even to saying too many irons in the fire.'

'Too fast. I wanted to beat time to the convulsions.'

'As a prelude to *Wagner* . . .' he began, speaking slowly while he felt for a witticism she intended not to hear.

The people at the near table, centring on the man with pebble-eyes, grey-agate, full of unconscious spiritual awareness, and an innocent wide brow—just left off telling a tale in his cheerful-apologetic voice that could press on through anything and leave no one hurt, though some self-judged and perhaps to see him again in memory as he was at this moment, at future moments of being brought face to face with themselves —were now all babbling at once, like those who having heard music must shield themselves from its influence or hide their inability to enter it, by discussion.

'Every one,' she said, free to speak at ease, 'excepting most of the people here and their like, suffer, when they say those words, seven separate, face-distorting convulsions.'

He was attending. Alma, deafened by the clamour to the

right and aware only of her quietly conversational bearing and, glancing at Hypo, of his attention absented inwards in contemplation of something just offered to his thought, let her eyes rest on Miriam's and sent forth, through the dreamy mildness shining from them because her lips were curved in a smile, the deep magnetic radiance Miriam had found in one of her photographs, a radiation of her inner being he must have known while still they were lovers and it was turned only upon himself who had called it forth, and now saw only when by chance he witnessed the turning of it upon others, in payment for help given in the labours exacted by her perpetual stewardship of his well-being.

Receiving this radiance fully for the first time, Miriam felt she could kneel, with the world's manhood, in homage to the spirit of the womanly woman, yet shared, as the radiance passed, their cramped uneasiness, the fear that makes them flee, once they are committed to the companionship of these women, from the threat of being surrounded and engulfed in insufficiency.

She leaned forward seeking for something to sing out by way of greeting, but Alma met and held her up and sent her back with the intense, crinkled, quizzical little smile that was her rallying-call for attention to immediate things. Her sudden immortal beauty had vanished and in its place was one of the many facets of that part of her being that was turned towards outside things: the bright brisk active little person, selfless and strong in endurance behind her fragile austere daintiness, willing to help every one on his way. Approved by both, Miriam sat back, licensed to be happy; and within the enclosed air there came a freshness from the wide spaces through which together they were travelling as they sat.

'Tooo, *men-ny*, *eye-erns*, *in*, the *fy-er*. Incessant chin-wagging. Jaws moving round like grindstones. Toom-ny ahns in'th'fah. Just two small snaps.'

'Labour-saving. I see your point. But it costs beauty.'

'English vowels are ugly to begin with. "I" deserves all its sufferings. The people I am talking about, whose speech

—at least the men's speech—has been shaped at public school and college, turn it into a German "o" modified. And they do the same with the equally ugly English "a." "All that has made England great" becomes with them "öl thöt hös möd England gröht." And they do so not because they recognize that the sound of the vowels is ugly, but for a *much* more fascinating reason. And the genteel *middle* classes turn the ugly "i" into "e" or "a": "refined" becomes "refaned" or "refeened." Also for a fascinating reason which is not the same as the reason of those socially above them. And they, too, jib at "a." "Diana, where is your black hat?" becomes "Di-enna, where is your bleck het?"

'Below these, and for still another fascinating reason, you get "a" turned into "oy" or "ah," "refoined" or "refahnd." The only people who preserve the native hideousness of the English "i" and "a" are the cultured middle classes, academics, and all those who don't care what happens to their faces while they speak so long as their speech is what they imagine to be correct. Respect for beauty is not the cause either of correct English speech or its various manglings, nor of the way English words are accented, nor of the way the English *walk*. Look at the swing of a Highland regiment. Swirling pipes and swaying kilts, and swinging tread that keeps the body always balanced in movement and never with dead flat foot upon the ground. English march music *pounds* its beats like someone hitting out, and if you put Englishmen into kilts the kilts would not swing to the march.'

'Get back to your theme, Miriam. If labour-saving isn't the point, what *is*?'

'There are, of course, people with no ear, or with badly developed speech-organs, speaking horribly, in all classes; but they are not the originators of any of the jargons. And the jargon we are specially considering, the one that is most hated, by those not born to it, because it is upper class and seems supercilious as well as affected, is honest and innocent.'

'Origin, origin.'

'Innocent and most desperately interesting. The other jargons, the middle- and lower-class, are innocent too, but less interesting. The middle-class jargon is *mincing*: originates in a genteel aspiration, a desire to keep the mouth closed. Hence *refaned*, and *nace*, and *nane*. Or, in people with very long noses, *refeened*, and *neece*, and *neene*. The lower-class variations, like the provincial, originate in a hearty revelling in sound, especially in open-mouthed vowels. And when people discuss the possibility of English becoming a world speech, I always wonder which English they have in mind. Speech is the Englishman's only gesture. Hence its heavy accentuation. All the jargons have that. An undergraduate accents his speech exactly as he accents his walk, in jerks.'

'Point, Miriam. What is the origin of the speech you, a professed Socialist, are now found treacherously adoring?'

'I'm not taking *sides* any more. You can't have a middle without edges, right and left. Or edges without a middle.'

'Nonsense. I'm interested in your thread, and have a sneaking sympathy with the way you festoon and tie it in knots. But if you have a point to make, make it. In the straight and narrow way.'

'Narrow; exactly. That's for action. In speech the straight and narrow way is always either a *lie* or an *exhibition*. That is the curse of speech: its inability to express several things simultaneously. All the unexpressed things come round and grin at everything that is said. One day I shall become a Trappist.'

'Wait; a few years. Meanwhile make your point.'

'The point is a technique, born of a spiritual condition. A state of mind, if you prefer. But the condition and the technique are so closely akin that you can actually make discoveries about the state of mind by experimentally adopting the technique. It is, up to a point, of course only up to a point, true, that if you speak in a certain way you will feel correspondingly. Anyhow you can know that the technique was honestly born. And is so born again and again, although it now appears to go ahead in its own right as the manner of a single class, and those who grow up in it, or acquire it at school or college, use it quite naturally.'

'Spiritual condition, state of mind. *Point*, Miriam.'

'Concentration. Imagine yourself in a position of responsibility, a prefect in a public school . . .'

'Heaven forbid.'

'A prefect, obliged to canalize all your forces and have all your wits about you, in order to remain the composed and authoritative representative of a code. You won't spend your strength on elocution, unless you are an aesthete, which is unlikely, since, if you were, you would not also be a prefect. Being a prefect, you will instinctively avoid all sounds that tend to discompose your authoritative and dignified mug. Hence *Ieee left myeee bag at the staytion* becomes *öh löft m'bög at th'stöshn*, and all the rest of it. Ineffable, of course, in a sixth-form boy. But it begins there, and then goes through the services, all over the dominions and colonies, and for a reason probably quite easy to find, is rampant in the Indian Civil. Surroundings perhaps. And in the diplomatic, where graciousness and bonhomie are as important as dignified composure, and authority is not specially called for, I will wager that there is less jargon and more face-convulsion. Humbug, in fact: facial animation, to disarm. People who speak *beautifully*, like those who have beautiful handwriting, are *usually* either humbugs or charlatans. Not that a touch of these is necessarily bad. Or they are Scotch or Irish. Shaw speaks beautifully. But he's never been an English prefect or commanded a battleship, or stood on the terrace of an ancestral home gazing out across an empire. So he can afford to let himself go on musical sounds. And be witty in and out of season. That's all, I think. Just that the apparently deliberate *jargon* of these Romans is, in its origin, both innocent and inevitable. But there is one frightful exception: the way some, only some, of them elaborate one of the a's. When they say, for example, "South Ayahfrica," and call a man a "mayan," they are quite deliberately *drawling*. But perhaps, all things considered, it is pardonable, only, being so noticeable, it is the one fragment of their technique that is usually imitated by outsiders and, in them, can be simply intolerable. For all the rest it is surely better to force speech to pass through your composure and take its chance of damage, rather than to be obediently correct and let it throw you into convulsions. At any rate for men, who can so rarely speak quite spontaneously and beautifully. Flowingly, un-selfconsciously, without any definite tone-shape or technique, ugly and beautiful, of accentuation. That seems to be for women. But that is another whole big question. I only wish to show how unjustly the convention of these Romans is condemned.'

'You 've done it, I think, Miretta, quite triumphantly. But don't waste yourself, your curious perceptiveness and your sensitively discriminating ear, on these clan dialects. Learn languages.'

'But isn't it worth while to realize that these people are darlings and not *poseurs*? . . . *What 's this?*' The savoury-smelling dish had appeared at her elbow slyly, as if it were a trap prepared to take her by surprise while her attention was far away. She stared at the raised roof of sheeny golden-brown crust, fascinated, wondering at her strange sudden apprehensiveness.

'Lark pie, madame.'

Brought back by the sound of her soft, sharp cry from the instant's loss of herself in horrified vision, she found the party broken up; herself set apart struggling with the remains of the emotion that had innocently rebuked their insensibility. Sideways, while she sat controlling her risen tears, she saw Hypo motion the waiter away with what was perhaps the main item of his ordering—she tried in vain to recall what had been served—and keep going, with the manner and gestures of conversational engrossment, the appearance of unbroken continuity; ready to include her as soon as she should have recovered. But for her there was no rescue. She was alone, with them and her Romans to whom they conformed without approval, and the innocent pie that had so horribly reminded her she was off the line of her march.

The *What am I doing here?* that had sounded from time to time during their past association came back on this evening created by that past and yet fitting so perfectly into the present that had seemed to exclude them, and indeed was admitting them only as participators, more favourably circumstanced than herself, in the Oberland life.

But though it sounded insistently, it held now a promise, as if of an appointment made towards which, though all her ways seemed blocked, she was invisibly moving. Always had been moving, driven on in the end, whenever she had for a moment thought herself arrived at her destination, by its warning cry. It had sounded everywhere, almost daily, at Banbury Park at Wimpole Street, at Flaxman's, in the houses of all her friends; everywhere. Except for a while amidst the loveliness of Newlands and, earlier, of Germany, where in the midst of suffering there had been that deep depth of happiness for whose sake she would have gone on enduring for ever.

'Foreign countries,' she said, and felt them both turn a little eagerly, and felt this moment in the restaurant become one with their past together. They were held waiting, attentive to her engrossment in the reality she wanted them to share: the way one's own deep sense of being, so vibrant and so still, is never stronger or more curiously alarming than when it is confirmed by being found existing in foreign, unknown ways of being. The same way set in a different form. A form that in Germany had its voice in music that drew even Fräulein into the magic circle and disarmed her. But they would not share it. There was no way of proving the importance of the individual deep sense of being that for them meant little or nothing. And no means of making them stop their keyed-up mental processes. Shaped by *fashion* . . . well, by *making*, by *men*.

'Of course,' she said, breaking her train of thought and coming into the surface moment, but still so full of widely dispersed feeling that she had no idea what she might be going to say. 'Of course there is actually no such thing as travel. So they say. There is nothing but a *Voyage autour de ma Chambre*, meaning *de tout ce que je suis*, even in a *tour du monde*.'

'We are going to travel, Miriam, *everywhere*. This small planet is a misfit. . . .'

He glanced at her and checked himself, ironically, smiling round over the table where now sweets and coffee and dessert, assembled together, announced the hurried end. He was reminding himself that didactic speculations were the wrong note.

'There's more space within than without,' she said. And he had heard, the first clear statement she had found to assert her world against his own, and refrained and winked at her affectionately from the midst of beginning to be amusing over the hasty winding up of their feast, and presently glanced swiftly again, for his own purpose, genuinely incredulous over her persistent earnestness.

In the dark interior of the cab, part of London's Oberland, linking its sacred spaces, Hypo and Alma became once more fellow-adventurers, reduced to simplicity by the prospect of being submissive items in the community of a London audience. She warmed towards them both, glad of their ignorance of the great moment last week when she had included them in a past that was finished, glad of that common past from which they had reappeared in the guise of fellow-members, more practised than herself but still aspirant, of the world-wide house-party.

Embodying the whole history of her London life, they gave a measure to the occasion that was now falling happily into its place as the first event of the new life begun amongst the sunlit mountains.

For though the being with them emphasized her imprisoning circumstances, it was also strengthening her inward certainty by revealing that the fact-facing and circumstance-facing mood they induced had no longer any power at all over the light shining from the future over her earliest memories: revived in Oberland and now leaping forward regardless of the inter-vening years.

In the midst of Hypo's talk, she smiled towards the visible radiance that was drawing her forward and felt that within some as yet unknown life her being had set in that moment a small deep root.

A passing light flashed on her face and then on his, opposite: far away, the face of a stranger caught approvingly regarding her through the eyes of an old friend. Audibly, through her smile, she sighed her joy in the compact just made with the in-flowing future that already was driving this short evening into the past.

'Miriam in her London is somehow different,' he said,

feeling for a compliment. 'She's . . . pervasively at *home*. You are a Londoner, you know, Miriam, in your *bones*.'

'*Neapolitan* ices,' she said hurriedly, to shake off the discomfort of contemplating his preoccupation with surface environment, 'but it's Covent Garden we're going to. How can I get to Covent Garden when I'm sitting, *avec mes parents*, aged eight, in the front row of the Lyceum dress-circle waiting for the statue of Hermione to come to life, and about to be moved, very deeply, by the sight of a striped Neapolitan ice?'

'Bless'er,' said Alma, converting the dismal interior of the growler into another of the many rooms in which together they had sat and talked.

They were being taken an immense distance along the main gallery, a hopeless distance, nearer and nearer to stage and music. A *box*. Of course.

Who first took the very worst part of the house for seeing and hearing and, by making it the costliest, made it also the most exclusive? The convention arose when theatres were ill-lit and only those near the stage could see the spectacle? And continued now that it was worse than useless? And he was docile to it. 'A box at the opera,' suitable only for those who regarded opera as a social occasion, an after-dinner entertainment of which they were a prominent part, splendid, correct, bored, within the sanctuaries they had hired for the season because it was part of the season's routine.

The first glimpse of the house and curtained stage seemed to prove to her that boxes are not in the theatre at all, but 'in Society.'

And when Alma had been persuaded into the corner commanding the least unfavourable view and she was ensconced in the relative darkness of the opposite corner, her spirit sought in vain for the familiar full power of the play-house, the power that exerted itself independently of what might be presented on the stage. It could be felt in perfection only by those seated centrally, in stalls, not too near; in dress-circle, not too far back; in pit, almost anywhere in the pit; and in gallery so long as the stage was just visible.

Hypo came forward from hanging up his coat in the hinder

darkness, and took his seat between them and the light fell upon the three of them perched side by side upon the face of a cliff, facing the world, facing other cliff-dwellers whose world they had reached. She felt excitedly composed, ensconced and supported, journeying along a wide, easy pathway of life from which there need be no return. This going with them from point to point of a London evening was a sharing of life in a way not possible in their own house, a sharing of experience that committed them to each other for good.

'A box, of course, is marvellous. A lodge in the wilderness. Which is why the French call them *loges*. In their *domestic* way. A temporary *chez-soi*. The English, delighting in separation, call them *boxes*; things shut-in.'

'Privacy, and freedom to come and go without assault and battery.'

'True. But when you visit a picture gallery do you prefer to look at the pictures from one side? Not that one wants to *see* opera. I shall imagine the stage. Sit with my back to it.'

'Don't. The point about this chap's music dramas is that they are music dramas. That is why they are such an admirable solvent. Be advised.'

'There is no possible representation that can compete with the vast scenes his music brings to your mind. I shall see, with the lit stage behind me instead of the Queen's Hall orchestra in front, much bigger scenes than the stage could hold. No one can see and hear to perfection at the same moment. And the wonder of Wagner is that through your ears he makes you see so hugely. All humanity pouring itself into space. A huge, exciting world-party. *Your* musician, by the way. Beethoven and Bach are experiences and adventures of the solitary human soul. In all its moods. Wagner is everybody speaking at once.'

'He's a great chap. He's devised unprecedentedly splendid noises. His fault is a Germanic fault: a weakness for the redemption idea.'

The lights went down as if shocked, blotting out the crowded stalls with a uniform covering of luminous, bluish patches.

'They look like snow under moon-shadows.'

'I *won't* have you away in Switzerland, Miriam,' he murmured while she listened to the magic tinkling of rings and swishing of draperies as the curtains drew apart, and saw the light, from the stage she did not mean to face, fall upon the audience massed below.

But immediately she was aware that she would hamper him by having his face in sight as he leaned forward to look. Having had the last word, without which he could not rest, having fed his indispensable certainty of steering the situation, and having reached both ends by means of an adroit flattery, he was now free to descend into simplicity, impossible, for him, in presence of a witness.

He sat there with his mind on holiday. He had wanted an evening in town, a break with his long, enforced seclusion. Also to catch her in the full after-glow of her successful holiday, and submit her, in the best possible circumstances, to the emotional solvent of music. It had all fitted most admirably and here he was, gladly back in London after his years of seclusion, in correct London clothes, complete with gibus, seated in a box at the opera, between wife and lover elect, with Wagner expressing the world in sound, restoring his confidence in the proportions of the human spirit, rousing and blessing his emotions and the emotions of the young lady at his side. It was all very good, and all well in hand. But he must not be watched, obstructively.

So she turned a little sideways and saw, over her right shoulder, the glow of the stage.

The music swept by on its way to those who were in the direct line of its attack, and left her incompletely attained. Free to think and to be consciously aware of the emotional tinge given to her thoughts by the mere presence of the tide of sound. A solvent, as he had said. But though now she knew why after standing, weary to begin with, for a whole evening listening to orchestral music, she could walk home singing and full of happiness and strength, she could feel no sympathy with the planful tinkering with the hidden shape of things implied in his conscious, deliberate submitting of himself and her to a bath of music. A man's job perhaps. Yet to have a distinct end in view endangers both end and means. To know beforehand where you are going is to be going nowhere. Because it means you are nowhere to begin with. If you know where you are you can go anywhere, and it will be the same place, and good.

Still, his plan was working. But the emotions rising in her as she heard the massed music roll by and saw in her mind's eye the little figures on the stage whose voices boomed or yelled against the orchestral din, now reaching through, now lost in it altogether, were not those he intended. The tremendous ado, by its sheer size and strength, and because through his mistaken technique of sitting in a box it was not having its full chance, was emphasizing for her, in her detached coolness, all that it left unsaid, all that is said by the music of Bach—which would have been quite unsuited to his purpose: stillness, dailiness, the quiet, blissful insight whose price is composure. The deep, quiet sense of *being*—what he called 'turnip-emotion'—was more, even to these protesting people, than all of which they were raving and shrieking. Perfect in itself. Every sound in the world, every protest and cry of agony, every relieving shriek of hysteria, is tribute to the sure knowledge of life's perfection. Otherwise, why *anything*?

Senta's little spinning-song, heard in its setting, flowed forth from this knowledge. It prevailed against the earlier roaring of sea-music and would prevail against the din and fury of life in which she was to be caught. Singing to herself over her wheel, she was truth.

'Is there a good *German* effect?' she asked in his ear.

'Lots of little Miriams in pigtails; *look*,' he answered, and she saw him off guard, simplified, too long ensconced in reactions to capture his usual form at a moment's notice.

Turning to the stage, she saw golden light, the warm gold of stage sunlight, long-haired maidens in full, bright skirts and dark velvet bodices laced across brief triangles of white muslin, Senta at her wheel in the midst: long-haired, a thicker rope of plaited golden hair distinguishing her as the chosen representative of girlish felicity. Singing to herself over her

wheel.   Singing her sunlight and her being and her happiness.
'Tragically brief.' . . . Indestructible.

Back again with Hypo and Alma in their hotel lounge, she
found that the music heard and the few scenes, seen so unsatisfactorily sideways, had yet reached to the depths of her being
and seemed now to assail her, as she sat relaxed and strong,
from the whole of surrounding space.

The cool lager poured down her throat in a single living
stream.

'Bravo, Miriam! Ain't she splendid, Alma? Tossing off
her beer like a man and smoking *con amore*.'

Alma raised a hand to smooth her hair, and dropped the
pearls she had been fingering with the other, to stifle a yawn.

Here, with the many palms giving green light and life to the
little lounge, the evening seemed to begin.   It was time to go,
to drop away and face the walk home, alone, through the chilly
midnight streets . . . that began to cast, as soon as a space
of lamplit stillness lay between her and the scene she had left,
their old, unfailing spell.   Unsharable.   Although, to-night,
the mellow, golden light, falling upon deserted roadway and
silent grey stone building, was deepened by the glow of the
hours from which she had come forth.

CHAPTER V

THE sudden lull seemed to call the attention of these separated groups to something they were missing. Two voices, one at either end of the long room, caught in mid-sentence, combined for a moment their conspicuous sounds, and then fell into silence.

Talkers, frozen in the attitude of conversation, listeners surprised at their task of keeping talkers going, relaxed in relief at the cessation, or, remaining tense, unconsciously revealing their various motives, glanced about the room as if looking for the cause of the interruption.

The gap was filled by the sound of the traffic pouring along the side of the square that was open to the main road. And now into the silence came the deep boom of a distant church clock, expending its warmth through the chilly outer twilight and pervading the room as though the silence were a space prepared for it. As the sixth stroke faded, the sound of the traffic emerged gay and headlong. Evening traffic, heralding the coming of darkness and the bright lights of the London streets.

A few voices had resumed, trying to prolong. But the quality of time had changed. It was no longer afternoon. The evenings of all the people in the room were flowing into their minds. Groups broke up and mingled in the to and fro of departure.

On her way to the door, Miriam was pulled up by the voice of a woman who had turned from a small group standing close at hand, hatless: residents. The voice had an eager, anxious, apologetic sound and gave her exit the air of royalty in procession, graciously halted to accept a petition.

Turning, in the gloom hardly lessened at this end of the long room by the switching on of a distant, shaded light, she saw only a dim outline, a pale oval of face saluting her, obliquely

174

down-tilted above a gown glowing silky rose-red through the dusk in which the forms of the other women showed no colour. Here was 'charm,' some strange grace and charm that was defying the warning voice within. The figure, assuming as she confronted it a fresh attitude of graceful pleading, had now a level face whose eyes were smiling recognition, patiently-reproachfully, a much-tried adorer, who yet was making allowances, for too long an instant being forced to prompt and wait for an answering recognition. Inwardly protesting her extreme unrelatedness to this person moving so elegantly from pose to pose, yet attracted by the unaccountable glow, as if the rose-red gown shone for her in the gloom by its own light, and held by a curious intensity of being in the alien figure, Miriam waited unresponsive.

'You were talking of socialisme,' asid the girl, motionless in a final pose which she seemed to offer as part of her plea, head sideways down-bent as if listening, arms held close to her silken form as if to subdue it to a touch of severity. 'I would like, so much, to hear more of theece.' Very young, but mannered and mature. An intelligent young French girl who would produce very 'rational' criticisms.

Intent on escape, vaguely undertaking to be at the club again quite soon, Miriam received a gracefully-sweeping movement of thanks and withdrawal during which the girl's eyes still held her own, but with the recognizing look withdrawn, as if now she were covering a secret compact with a witness-disarming formality. With the corner of her eye, as she turned away to the open door, Miriam saw her, in the full light now switched on from the hall, move back to the styleless English group from which she had emerged, arms down, white hands a little extended as if to balance the slight swaying movement propelling her, and which the invisible feet followed rather than led.

Down in the street, where immediately the long continuous distances of past and future opened within the air, the little scene slipped into line with the series of momentary encounters staged by the club. The quality of that moment's exchange was complete in itself. Followed up by a definite appointment, it would have robbed this evening light and the evening streets of their power to evoke the continuous moment that was always and everywhere the same. Moving away from it unhampered, she was already losing its features, seeing it as a confirmation of the quality of the long afternoon: the talk with those three implacable women who had responded with such blessed restorative flexible-mindedness while she talked, with the eloquence of the despair that began now to fill her whenever she thought of people in large masses, against the theory of the permanent necessity for a more or less enslaved majority, to which their overheard conversation had made them seem so thoughtlessly docile; the common adventure of the deepening twilight, the sudden silence, the deep-toned bell, the instant of seeing, from within its far sound, the strangeness of human life and its incompleteness.

As she broke in at Flaxman's to dress for Mrs Redfern's evening, the memory of the girl returned as a teasing reminder, in a foreign voice, of a set of ideas that had ceased to move her unless they were attacked by someone holding another set. Waking next morning she found within the air the new spring, the inmost breath of the country springtime of which in her memory there was no trace. It was strange to have no childhood memory of spring: nothing in memory but summer in full blaze, so that even the remembered sight of anemones in woods and of cowslip balls tossed from sister to sister, crushed, giving out their small warm scent, were surrounded not by a spring scent but by summer in full bloom.

Soft deep freshness of spring stirring within the dry, inorganic, beloved London air. This moment will be the best of this year's London spring, unless I manage at last to keep my appointment with primroses. Each spring passes without sight of them, except for that one glimpse which was nothing but a reminder and a promise. All of us going along at sixes and sevens in the east wind. A skimpy cluster of trees at the wayside in the distance. Offering some kind of rescue when it should come near. Coming near enough to be one of the party and to bring a slight change in every one's feelings. Coming alongside. Three women adoring the small clumps pressed flatly against the earth amongst the short grass; sunlit primroses. And those few in the midst, deeper and brighter for being in shadow. While we stood near the trees, the sky was radiant and the cruel wind doomed by the promise of summer. Even the men, who only stood by, were caught and changed, lost for the instant during which they were as nothing to the three women, their hold on their great selves. Afterwards, going on, there were genial voices, relieved, gay voices of women prevailing, keeping warmth in the air.

And here, again, was the air of spring coming in at the thrown-up window with the light. But Sunday light. It was Sunday. Bringing a morning without pressure or hurry. Quietly. Setting all nature's allurements, all allurements, in a beautiful distance. Sunday morning, sweet and still and windless. Bringing its own quality that was independent of all others.

But the scent in the air that had brought memories of flowers was turning out to be the faint scent of soap. Assurance, through the distinctness with which it came from the far side of the room, of having waked from the deepest of deep sleep. From such distant deeps that now, with cool heart and eyes kept closed, and mind recoiled from knowing that the air coming in through the rotten window-frame had passed over the cat-and-garbage-haunted waste between the farther slum and the warren of Flaxman's, every outer thing was distinct, in a life that from the earliest point of memory was the same.

This person who had stood for the first time alone upon the sunlit garden-path between the banks of flowers and watched them, through the pattern made by the bees sailing heavily across from bank to bank at the level of her face, and wondered at them all, flowers and bees and sunlight, at their all being there when nobody was about, and had looked for so long at the bright masses, and now could re-see them with knowledge of their names and ways and of the dark earth underneath, and, still, just as they were in that moment that had neither beginning nor end, this same person was now going, deceitfully, to local, social Lycurgan meetings, frequenting them, since Oberland, only for small delights that were the prelude, the practice-ground for more and more and more. This person, who was about to take a lover, presently, in time, at the right time, was the one who had gazed for ever at the flower-banks, unchanged.

Amongst the joys near at hand, merging into them, was the fun of dressing for these gatherings as for parties in the old days at home, going forth to meet not ideas, but people: to see who was there. To like Mrs Redfern's radiant hostess face, ruddy face, radiant last night above her evening gown, a glinting panoply about her well-built figure advancing across the room to say to a comparative stranger: 'Good girl.' Coming, at the moment of her firm hand-clasp, out of her preoccupations, revealing her desire for more than the distant acquaintance of secretary and group-member. And then, with eyes filming over as though she were going into a trance, announcing, as consciousness forsook her, and as if by way of apology for those so far gathered at her weekly meetings, in the manner of one heralding a Messiah, 'He is *coming*,' and a sigh expressing the end for ever of effort and responsibility, eyes still closed and lips ecstatically smiling. And, moving away with brightly opened eye amongst the increasing guests, her sturdy figure, animated by the twin currents of her emotions as Lycurgan and as hostess, seeming almost willowy as she glided about with her message and presently carried it through the open folding doors to where the earlier arrivals were standing with their coffee-cups, making prevail, over the confused sound of their talking, her blissful voice.

Piteous, harassed hostess, mistress of revels that had seemed all too tame to her burning fancy, blinded now by relief, unaware that she was insulting her guests in making such a to-do over the interloper for whom they were to be merely an admiring congregation. Or perhaps actually, as she had always seemed, delighted with each evening in turn, and now driven to an extremity of delight. But in so ecstatically describing the coming splendour she wrecked it by spreading, amongst the innocent, the wrong kind of anticipation, and by putting the others on their guard.

Going through the little crowd to the far end of the second

room—where the usual gossipings and controversies were in full swing, with the difference that every one was now on the alert, turned towards the coming magnificence that for some was a challenge to their own and for others something to wait for with half-concealed impatience—there came that moment, turning round from securing a coffee at the end table, of being face to face with the tall old woman, flatly serge-clad and lace-collared as she had been on the platform of the Women's Group, stately and venerable, ripe with experience and yet young, still living towards the future; the strange moment of being the short-range object of eyes that always looked at far distances, of feeling isolated with a challenge to accept or find reasons for refusing to interpret life according to whatever principles had given to her tall, upright form the bearing of a prophetess.

As she said: 'Who are you?' in the dry sad voice so different from the one that had rung from the platform, the look of contemplation of wide distances moved from the eyes through which for a moment peeped forth a self-conscious schoolgirl. But that was because I was caught by my awful trick of suddenly being engrossed in a small object—a chain, a belt, or the way, flat affectionate way, a collar lies upon a dress: the individual power of these things and the strange, deceptive way they have of seeming to bestow their own soundness and well-being, even upon a person sick to death. But when I looked away, feeling ashamed and that everything between us was spoiled, the sense of her distance from myself and her attention to some large selfless plan came back.

'You are of the young who call themselves Socialists. But your feet are on the path. Go steadily.'

'I'm a Tory-Anarchist.'

Her eyes looked maternally, bringing a glow of childish satisfaction, a moment's sense of being free from the burden of independence, and immediately of feeling independence robbed of its rigidity, of being an independent person loaded with the jewels of youth and health, walking in the green valley of life far away below this old woman whose tall figure had grown broad and strong in climbing the steep middle years in midday sunlight, till now she had reached to where perhaps feeling fades into thought. And then finding the charm of the party renewed by the brief absence. And gratefully, with the manner of a daughter, taking leave and moving away, just as Englehart came in at the main door. Flaming hair, pale eyes, glinting with resolution. His whole being a torch, peevishly seeking inflammable material, and held up by Mrs. Redfern in the empty middle of the room. Looking down on her from his height as upon something too tiresome even to be disposed of, and she sustaining the blaze with a brave dawning of her most roguish smile, kept back from attaining its fullness by the words with which she told her great news and by her eagerness for his pleased response.

'Is Goldstein here?' Nose-high air of a supercilious camel and, before she could answer, striding departure towards the densest group.

Englehart and Goldstein and Maynard intensively wrangling in the midst of an audience. Rachel, in deep, blended colours and low-falling, heavy beads; looking like a rich and fragile trinket, perpetually breaking in with passionately scornful exclamations.

Mrs Redfern again, saying, just as I had caught Englehart's eye and said 'Tandem's worse than cart-before-horse' and seen his fury: 'My cousin has fallen in love with you. Quite demented.' And off she went, without indicating the cousin, to chant the praises of the Messiah to new arrivals: 'And not only mentally grand. So beautiful. The most beautiful creature in London.'

Miscarried inspirations of a prospective audience too long kept waiting. Rachel's group, the lively group indifferent to the Messiah, broken up and Rachel disappeared. And suddenly restored, close at hand. Eager to talk to one who had no single idea she could recognize as belonging to an intelligible system.

'Hallo, M. H.! How are you? How nice you look! You always do. But specially nice in that gown. Very, very nice. Don't you think so? Don't you like yourself in it very much? Are you alone, or with Michael? Isn't it a queer

gathering? What are you doing so meekly in a corner?'
Pause. Glowering glance round room, and deep flush.

'Really people are incredible. I've just been telling that
little skunk, Mason, he is a liar.'

'Which is Mrs Redfern's cousin?'

'The Octopus? Don't you *know* her? Not a bit like
Bertha Redfern. There she is, just beyond the fascinating
Lena, with St Vincent.'

'St Vincent and St Vitus. Why doesn't she keep still?'

'That intense creature?'

'She's in love with me.'

'The Octopus? And you've never spoken to her? She's
not a lady to adore in silence.'

'She's an aunt. Flirting with new ideas.'

'An *aunt*? That violent being?'

'Short-circuiting in a frivolous world.'

'Short-circuiting! *She?*'

'Who is the old woman in a lace collar and serge dress?
Sitting in the human landscape like a dark rock in a green
meadow. Not blending.'

'Mrs McCrosson. *Strange* being. A *much*-experienced
lady.'

'Not strange at all. She comes up from a deep dive un-
ruffled, and with open eyes. She reminds me, perhaps because
of her age and calm wisdom, of an old woman who cruises
about Bloomsbury looking qualified for a vast abdominal
operation. But her steady, clear eyes keep it all in order.
I go out of my way to pass her and meet them. She knows
me, now, by sight. The odd thing is that she invariably
appears when I am too miserable to go on living. She comes
rolling by, and I am restored.'

Rachel made her usual scientific objections. But listened.
Eyebrows a little up, firm mouth and chin neglected by her
will and slightly drooping together with her whole slender
figure crouched in thought, while I tried to make her admit
that *punctuality* in the coming through of the hidden shape of
things *is* scientific evidence.

Why *mystical*? Why do these scientific people suppose

that something supplying hints, when you are not looking for them, hints that overpower the voices of reason and common sense, is more strange and mysterious than anything else? And a little dangerous and apt to be pathological? One might perhaps die of wonder if one could think hard enough over the fact of there being anything anywhere. And why not? If one could hold on when there comes the feeling that in a moment one will disappear into space . . . But the moment of astonishment passes with the pang it gives and everything for a while is new and strange, as if one had been away on a long visit.

Presently she said that both ways of approach, the inner and the outer, should exist together in the ideal human being. She had a sort of nostalgia. Perhaps scientific people are intellectual saints and martyrs, sacrificed to usefulness.

'Who is Mrs Redfern's latest Messiah?'

'You mean Kingfisher, Arnold Kingfisher? Oh, a *most* brilliant creature and most *incredibly* beautiful.'

And I waited for his arrival, eager to know which kind of adored male he was and forgot him, sitting in that corner of Mrs Redfern's that became nowhere—except at that moment of seeing Redfern cross a clear space of the room driven by a superior force, arms bent, mind in abeyance, head sideways up like a man in a football-scrum—while Rachel, listening, gave added warmth to all I told her of my guilty life; innocently, with her way of finding all well, if life goes pleasantly.

'I knew I should get away from Flaxman's and from Selina. According to you, having decided I must go, I ought to have made a *plan*. I didn't. Feeling myself gone, I began to like the place, and to find Selina less overpowering. It was *she* who made a plan. Suddenly told me she must get nearer her work, and asked me if I'd like to move.'

'You think that was a feeler?'

'Don't know. It's easier to read Selina's thoughts than her feelings. But in the end she betrayed feeling. Suddenly appeared, in the middle of the morning, at Wimpole Street. I sailed into the waiting-room, sailed, so deep was my astonishment, through all the memories laid up for me in the house,

things I had ceased attending to and that would most strongly
have aroused Selina's interest and envy.'

'Beast!'

'. . . envy if she were in the habit of encouraging envy and
were not a Christian stoic—but I 've seen envy touch her, just
prod at her from within and be crushed back by her strong,
Christian-stoical lips and turned into a momentary and perhaps
fortifying sharing of a life that to her has been a gay panorama
available for her contemplation for nearly eighteen months.
You see? Something she can't mould or change, something
independent of her and secretive, of which she does not quite
approve and yet, as you will see, has grown to have an acquired
taste for. Something authentic in a way that does not fit her
scheme of authenticities and therefore attracts her. Appeals
to her charitable broad-mindedness. She is fed and starved
by turns.'

'Vain creature.'

'Not a bit. It has nothing to do with me, and is as much of
a mystery to me as to her.'

'Proceed with your story.'

'Well, here it grows pathetic. At the end of my glorious
promenade from my room to the waiting-room door, I realized
that it had been so glorious because Selina had come uncalled
into the midst of one of my worlds and brought it all clearly
round me from its beginnings, made it magic and new in all
its distances, as it had been at the first and shall be for ever
amen when I get away and it seems to fold up like a scroll.'

'*Are* you going away from that, too?'

'Of course, presently. It is finished, has been finished for
some time, though there 's a large homesick half of me that
wants it to go for ever; as, of course, everything *does*.'

'Nonsense. Proceed.'

'Of course everything is eternal, or it is nothing.'

'Suffering, for instance, oppression, cruelty, lives that are
crushed, ruined, hideous.'

'All that is part of something else. Vicarious suffering is
the only kind that instructs.'

'A *most* convenient theory.'

'You and I are vicarious sufferers, gutter-snipes, poor-law children, underpaid wage-slaves without security or prospects, dancing at the edge of an abyss.'

'True, but you seem to enjoy it.   Go back to your story.'

'The prices of security, especially for women, are a damned sight too tall.   Monstrous.   Unthinkable.   Who wouldn't sooner die than suffocate, even on an altar with incense perpetually rising?'

'Plenty of people, millions, my dear, would choose suffocation, if it is suffocation.   I'm not sure.'

'I am.   All the homes I know are asphyxiating.'

'Cease these wanderings.   Tell me of your Selina.'

'Well, yes.   In that moment outside the door she *was* my Selina, it was as if quite suddenly a large long *life* stood accomplished behind us and there we were, meeting, each with a solid piece of eternity in hand.   Now isn't that sort of thing wonderful, untouchable, whatever may happen afterwards? And all the time I was wondering what could have happened in the hour or so since I left her at Flaxman's.   And knowing it was good.   All of which, stated simply, in a brief poetic lie, would run: "I was pleased to see Selina."   That's somehow plain and powerful.   A man's statement, carrying one sanguinely along the surface of life that is so plain and simple-oh. "Tell me, my dear, exactly what you mean, in a few words." My God!   Ain't they the ultimate limit?   The mere thought of all those men torturing, with their thin logic, the inarticulate women whose deep feelings *must* throw up cascades of words or slay them. . . . Well, with great embarrassment, she told me she wished to stay at Flaxman's and keep on our life together.'

'So you stay?'

'I thought so; I was *thrilled*.   But I heard myself saying, explaining, that I had arranged to join a friend at Tansley Street.   Not a word of truth in it.'

'False creature.'

She meant it, and yet robbed the flight from Selina of its feeling of guilt.   And then she must have sat silent, contemplating beyond my knowledge, according to some chosen system of psychology, for I thought, helped by her presence, her self concentrated on me, of next week, of returning to Mrs Bailey to the old untouched freedom with clear knowledge of what to do with it. Undisturbed space, high above the quiet street, and safely below the old attic with its cruel cold and its sultry stifling heat.

And then Mrs Redfern's party was there again suddenly, a bright scene in a world freshly created, people moving in a room of long ago, recognized one by one, and Rachel, reduced to the scale of the evening, was saying:

'This man's not coming.'

Every one, during the time of waiting, had plunged more or less into far-off spaces from which they had returned refreshed, seeing anew, in the perspectives lit by the promise of the great arrival, the group and its aims. Only those who must always batten externally, on what is going on around them, were weary because nothing seemed to be happening.

And Kingfisher never came. And there was no prize-fight between the purveyors of wit and wisdom, no struggle between opposing counsels of perfection, no dynamic leadership towards a distant aim, but presently a friendly deep sense of life, a sense of current being, shared. A deep power, against which no single assertive individual could prevail, something like a Quaker meeting, after Englehart and his party, already thrown out of their usual form by enforced abdication in favour of the promised Kingfisher, had gone impatiently away. Only Rachel was left to represent the hard edge and she, in the end, admitted the vitalizing quality of the hour.

To-day, being Sunday, will keep intact for several hours this morning sense of spring. Sunday morning stands in eternity and gathers all its fellows from the past. Now that it is here, it is no longer the last Sunday with Selina but an extension of all our Sundays together. Until the late afternoon, when to-morrow will pour in over the surface of the hours.

Across the featureless, blissful moment came a vision of the girl posed, her red gown glowing through the dark, clear for a second and then gone, but in the far distances of the afternoon the thought of her made a barrier beyond which nothing could be seen. Even this last day had already passed out of Selina's hands.

CHAPTER VI

Of course there was no one at the club at this unlikely hour, not even a resident sitting about with an air of being in possession. The well-fed members were resting in their rooms. In this long, empty drawing-room, with morning gone and the afternoon not yet begun, was the end of the world. Life far away, past and done with. The atmosphere of the room, coldly neutral, engulfed feelings and opinions and mocked at the illusions created by mere coming and going. It mocked and weighed and judged. And there was nothing to oppose to it. Nothing to do but stand alone, judged and condemned, here in this corner by the window, giving on to the square whose garden must be yielding a deep sense of spring. Spring going its independent way.

Turning from the window, she faced the open piano, contemplating the alien keys she had never touched and that held the secrets of those who had played upon them and had thwarted the aspirations of those who had strummed. And held the living sound of the music that was now tingling to her finger-tips. In a moment she was back within the strange centre of being she had left on a vain quest, ensconced behind its endless refusal to accept evidence. She stood very still within the stillness it made beneath the glad tumult awakened in her by the returning tide. There was no direct answer to the emptiness about her that still made its assertions. But there was statement. Just sanity reasserting itself after a mild shock? More than that. Her external being, standing here with finger-tips responsive to the challenge of the exposed keys, in no way represented the essential opposition. Yet it was with that consciously reflecting being that she felt the unchanging presence that now joined her in the world it had restored. Everything in the room had a quiet reality, and glancing through the window she saw how the budding trees thrilled in the sunlight.

Through the sound of her soft playing she heard the click of the door. Seemed herself to be outside that door, opening it upon music barely heard from another room and that now, subdued though it was, seemed by comparison with that distant sound to peal out in honour of someone entering in triumph. Holding to her theme, she planned to pass from its nearing end without a break to another that would hold her within this secret world that had opened so unusually from out the lowest point in the afternoon. But the intention gave emphasis to the movements of her hands and presently she was just carefully playing, sharing her music with someone crept cautiously into the room; one or other of the residents now probably hidden in a deep chair and presently to sound its thanks and say it loved music.

It was only because it could be no one else that she recognized this girl crouched on the floor at her side—looking as if she had blossomed from the air—as yesterday's figure in the rose-red gown, again producing the effect of being aware of the impression she made, and contemplating it in the person of the one upon whom it was being directed and also, to-day, offering it as something to be judged, like a 'work of art,' detachedly, upon its merits.

The mealy, turquoise blue of the delicately figured kimono was deep satisfaction, so also were the heavy beads, of curiously blended, opaque deep colours, hanging in a loop whose base, against the girl's knees, was clasped by twining fingers. Smoothly draped sheeny dark hair framed the flower-fresh oval face and heightened the 'jasmine' white of the column of neck. And this unknown loveliness was already radiating affection, patiently awaiting the fruit of a wondering stare; wordlessly, for fear of risking by sound or movement its own full effect.

When Miriam smiled, the girl dropped her beads and reasserted herself with an emphatic movement, defying or insisting or imploring, that left her face upturned as if for easier reading. And then her hands came forward, one ahead of the other, smallish womanish hands, not very expressive, and dropped again to her knees. She was on her feet, had become a figure, fleeing, on soundless feet, down the long room whose social life, flowing back to it as she plunged lightly on slippered feet, with the wings of her kimono fluttering to the swiftness of her movement, through its lights and shadows, was turned to nothing, as if its being as a club-room had waited all along for this transfiguring moment.

Ensconced in a corner of the low settee, she was so retreated into dimness that her mocking little laugh made Miriam, following her down the room, half expect to find her transformed. The eager, coquettish little trill suggested endless tiresomeness. But the girl, somehow aware of the false sound, quenched it with another, a cooing, consoling, deprecating laugh-sound that made together with the first a single communication: in spite of her brave, amazing silence she found it necessary somehow to fill with her image the interval during which she was invisible.

'I 'm not sure I should have recognized you,' said Miriam. At the sound of her own familiar voice a gulf seemed leapt. But of the one who spoke, come from afar to meet this strange girl, she knew nothing. Serenely she took the other corner of the settee, feeling as she sat down that she had embarked in sunlight upon an unknown quest.

With another of her swift movements the girl was on her knees, upright, her face held motionless towards the full light. Again Miriam surveyed. Something had gone. There was thought behind the lovely silent mask, and speech on the way.

'It 's like a peach. Say it, say it.'

'It is,' said Miriam, admiring the girl's open appreciation of her own beauty, at this moment newly created for her in eyes into which she gazed as into a mirror.

'But not so *much*, since Basil.' She waited, eyebrows up and painfully drawn together. Communication was severed. Miriam realized, by its sudden withdrawal, that a moment ago the room had seemed filled with golden light giving an ethereal quality to all its contents. Now they stood distinct in a light that was dark and bitter and cold. Yet this girl was different from the women who at once begin to talk of their personal relationships, and though she felt her face grow weary in anticipation of moving away from their two selves into the story of a life the girl shared with another, which, if it greatly mattered to her, robbed this strange meeting of its chief value, she felt her interest awake behind her suffering.

'It spoils thee corners of thee mouth,' she whispered sadly. 'They are never again so cleare and firm.'

Another sadness, a revelation spreading itself abroad over all humanity, added its bitterness to the surrounding air, but before thought could beat back and find words, the girl said wistfully:

'This makes a difference? You are repelled?'

'No,' she said eagerly. 'It makes no difference,' and within the glow of her admiration for sincerity she felt the lie turn to truth, and added: 'with you.'

'But yes,' she insisted, 'it must make some difference. With all these women here, it would. It divides me from them. They are pewre. I feel a barrier.'

Miriam thought of the residents she knew by sight. The pretty, sour-mouthed one who spent all her leisure at St Alban's, and was always quoting Father Stanton, the too-motherly widow and her hysterical daughter, the small dark woman who darted about and sang snatches of song in a way seeming to express nothing but impatience with every one within sight, the various 'workers' who were either too chatty and cheerful, stoically cheerful, a little mannish, or official and supercilious and thoroughly discontented.

'Without telling them, I cannot get near them. And to Englishwomen one cannot tell these things.'

'But you 've told me.'

A sudden inner laughter glowed from the girl's face, compressing her lips and narrowing her eyes that for a second turned away in contemplation of a private source of amusement, as if some memory or knowledge of hers were being confirmed, and from which she returned fully aware that she held a soaring advantage, but not knowing the depth of repudiation she had aroused, to rival her strange spell, repudiation of the foreign quality of her intelligence, French intelligence with fixed wisdoms and generalizations.

'Yes, you are English, that is the strange thing,' she remarked in a polite, judicial tone, 'and so *different*,' she added, head sideways, with an adoring smile and a low voice thrilling with emotion. Her hands came forward, one before the other, outstretched, very gently approaching, and while Miriam read in the girl's eyes the reflection of her own motionless yielding, the hands moved apart and it was the lovely face that touched her first, suddenly and softly dropped upon her knees that now were gently clasped on either side by the small hands.

Alone with the strange burden, confronting empty space, Miriam supposed she ought to stroke the hair, but was withheld, held, unbreathing, in a quietude of well-being that was careless of her own demand for some outward response. She felt complete as she was, brooding apart in an intensity of being that flowed refreshingly through all her limbs and went from her in a radiance that seemed to exist for herself alone and could not be apparent to the hidden girl.

Who now lifted her face and said, smiling a younger, simpler smile, relieved, gay, with a little flash of the teeth before the lips spoke, like a child who has dared and triumphed: 'I *knew*. You are *more* what I thought, than I thought you were,' and gazed, head thrown back, hands clasped firmly on the deserted knees, and laughed her early, cooing laugh and leapt lightly to her feet and was ensconced once more upon the deep settee.

'Are you living in London or just staying?'

'I do not know if I will stay. There are so many things here that make me not as I would be. After Paris.'

'For example?'

'I could give so many examples. Chiefly it is the way of living, the little things of every day. And there is your Eenglish foode.' She shrugged her shoulders and draped her kimono more closely as if withdrawing from the chill discomforts of life in England; that yet she was living so easily in this quite well-run little club. The shadow her critical tone cast over the background of their meeting, over her London as she knew it, in makeshift poverty of which this girl had no experience, saddened Miriam, forcing her to realize that the wide separation of their circumstances would play its obstructive part as soon as they reached personal details. She herself, her way of living, the lack in it of anything that could charm a fastidious little *grande dame* in the making, would presently be identified with the uncongenial London about to be left to its fate. But 'Basil' was an Englishman?

Yet, though so bravely determined to reveal herself at once and keep nothing back, she clearly disliked direct questions. Or, if not actually disliking them, received them with a cere-monial that made them seem crude, and therefore certainly offensive, to her. First silence and a fresh pose of her whole person, a plastic pose, studied and graceful, and a careful, conscious management of the accompanying facial effects that preceded her answer: a statement, seeming at first irrelevant and presently revealing consistency—so that her talk bore no resemblance, never would bear any resemblance, to the English-woman's well-bred incoherence—and contributing to her effect of being critically aloof from everything but her own power to charm.

Just as Miriam began clearly to realize both how very weary she could grow of the plastic poses and that she herself was not playing the part expected of her, the girl broke off and sank in a graceful heap on the floor, where she sat crouched and once more silently adoring.

Towards tea-time, it was only with an effort that she could remember whither she was bound. Her current life had grown remote and unreal. As empty and turned away and indifferent as the far corners of this club-room, so strangely free, as if deliberately kept free of intruders, for the hour during which she had sat enthroned and talking: being 'drawn out' and set and kept upon a pinnacle and worshipped for wisdom and purity. Seeing herself reflected in the perceptions of this girl, she was unable to deny, in the raw material of her disposition, an unconscious quality of the kind that was being so rapturously ascribed to her. But it was not herself, her whole current self. It belonged to her family and her type, and for this inalienable substratum of her being she could claim no credit. Yet in being apparently all that was visible, and attractive, to this socially experienced and disillusioned and clear-eyed young woman, it seemed to threaten her. She could feel, almost watch it coming forth in response to the demand, thoughtlessly and effortlessly, feel how it kept her sitting perfectly still and yet vibrant and alight from head to feet, patiently representing, authentic. And a patient sadness filled her. For if indeed, as her own ears and the confident rejoicing that greeted every word she spoke seemed to prove, this emerging quality were the very root of her being, then she was committed for life to the role allotted to her by the kneeling girl.

In the end, supplied bit by bit, by hints and responses, sometimes mere exclamations illuminating, by their ecstatic suddenness that which called them forth, with a portrait of herself in all its limitations, as she existed in the mind of the girl, it seemed almost as if this girl had come at just this moment to warn her, to give her the courage of herself as she was, isolated and virginal. Yet, as she stood at last taking leave of her in the centre of the twilit room, facing again her strange beauty gleaming in the space it illuminated, she was glad to be escaping back into the company of people who moved mostly along the surface levels and left her to herself.

CHAPTER VII

WITH so many small movables gone on, the strip of room looked exactly as it had done when the furniture was first brought in, and again, as she went candle in hand down the pathway of green linoleum, she felt with all its first freshness, as in the sacred days before the surrounding neighbourhood stated its misery, the deep, early morning charm radiating from the little polished bureau and its slender brass candlesticks, the long mirror in its dark frame and the moss-green enamel of the toilet set with its pools of light. And especially the long lasting of the early morning charm on that first Sunday morning, before the thunderstorm had brought the poet to his window with waving arms.

She would remember these rooms as early morning light pouring from the high window along the green pathway and reflected, in their different ways, by the bureau, the mirror, and the crockery: the quiet deep bliss of it. Bliss that would remain unchanged and gradually spread its quality even over the shallow months since she had moved her bed away from the night-sounds of the court into the little back room, amongst Selina's battered sitting-room furniture from which there was no escape in looking up at the ancient painted ceiling or out through the small window whose dim, shabby curtains, faded and dusty, seemed to match the dismal waste between it and the opposite slum; and over all the memories of Flaxman's, crowding together, each in turn coming forward with its teasing question and merging again into the crowd with its question unanswered.

And they were going with her into the new, old life, the bureau and the moss-green crockery and the black-framed mirror. Somewhere in her vast house Mrs Bailey would find room for the things they would displace? She had not thought

of that, nor of any tiresome detail, either at Wimpole Street
when Selina made her belated plea and she had improvised
her plan and based it on a lie, or in going round to tell the
delighted Mrs Bailey. Had thought of nothing but going
home to Tansley Street.

She set her candle on the bureau and sat down to find her
list of bills. This was the end of bills and items. In future
there would be nothing but the weekly sum for Mrs Bailey,
passing almost furtively from hand to hand, with a genuine
pretence on both sides that there was between them no relationship of payer and paid. To-morrow, she would be at home.

In place of this large room, divided by the crash curtain—
Selina should have curtain and linoleum and everything else
they held in common—and the small sitting-room and huge
attic, there would be one small, narrow room.

But all round it, in place of the cooping and perpetual con-
frontations of Flaxman life, the high, spacious house whose
every staircase she knew and loved in each of its minutest
differences from its fellows, of shape and colour and texture and
lighting, of everything that makes up the adventure of ascending and descending flights of stairs—absent in Flaxman's from
all but the remote little top flight beyond the reach of the
reek and murk coming up from the basement, absent because
of the close pressure of the lives in the house and in the surrounding slum; lives she was powerless to change or to endure
—and every room, where, extending even into those she had
never entered, richly her own life was stored up.

And the doors with their different voices in shutting or being
slammed-to by the wind. Would she remember Flaxman
door-sounds after she had left? Glancing at the door which
ended the long strip of her half of the room she tried in vain
to remember its sound. Yet, when she first settled in, it must
have impressed itself and played its intimate part in the symphony of sounds belonging to her life with Selina. She tried
for the attic door upstairs and even that refused to return. No
indoor sounds would stay on with her from this house: because
after the first few weeks her senses had never been at home,
had always been a little on the alert, uneasy, half-consciously

watchful for assaults from downstairs and from outside, pressing too closely and difficult to resist.

But the sound of each of the Tansley Street doors came back at once, and some stood out clearly from the others. The dining-room door, quiet, slowly-moving because of its size and weight, closing solidly with a deep wooden sound, slamming, very rarely, with a detonation that went up through the house. The state bedroom behind it, whose door moved discreetly on its hinges over a fairly thickish carpet and shut with a light, wooden sound. The door of the little draughty room at the end of the passage, clapping abruptly to over its thin linoleum with a comfortless metallic rattle of its loose fastening. The upstairs drawing-room's softly, silkily closing door, a well-mannered, muffled sound, as if it were intent on doing its duty in such a way as not to interrupt the social life going on within. And, higher up, the heavy brown doors of the second-floor bedrooms, still with wooden knobs like those below, closing leisurely and importantly, seeming to demand the respect due to the prices of the rooms they guarded; and the rooms above, whose yellow, varnished doors shut lightly and quickly, one with a soft brassy click, very neat and final, one with a sharp rattle of its loose metal knob echoing over the linoleum-covered stairs and landings of the upper floors.

All beloved. For a moment she listened to the prolonged squeak, running cheerfully up the scale and ceasing suddenly as the door stood wide, that was the voice of her old garret. But the breathless midsummer heat and the cruel, hampering cold she had endured there in fireless winters and condoned and explained away and somehow exorcized, so long as they had been the inevitable prices of survival, came forward now to condemn the room that was no longer hers and she turned with joy and gratitude to hear the light, high sound, shut away, scarcely audible, of the remote door of the small strip of room beyond the turn of the stairs as they wound up to the attics. Heard it close, unbelievably, behind her and leave her ensconced, high above the quiet street. In the house, but not, too much, of it. Supported and screened by the presence of the many rooms that made the large house; each one occupied by strangers who soon, just because she need establish with them no exacting personal relationship, would be richly and deeply her housemates, sharing the independent life of this particular house, its situation within London's magic circle, its early mornings, its evenings and nights, all bathed in the quietude of the comely street and blessed by the neighbourhood of the green squares at its either end.

Freedom.

Freedom for thought, when it made its sudden visits, to expand unhampered by the awful suggestions coming from the Flaxman surroundings. To sit down unobserved, and endlessly free from interruption, at this little bureau that now could fulfil the promise for which it was bought.

She became aware of her framed mirror on the wall behind her, reflecting, in its narrow length, her form seated in the shadowy candle-light she was so soon to leave for the cheerful blaze of gas, or the steady companionship of the reading-lamp that at Flaxmans' she had hardly used at all, and half turned to look into it and exchange over her shoulder a smile of congratulation with her reflected image.

The glass was not clear. Across her face, that should have shown in the reflected candle-light, was some kind of cloudy blur. Holding up the candle she found lettering, large and twirly, thickly outlined as if made with chalk or moist putty, moving with a downward slope across the centre of the strip of glass. Mystified—for who in the wide world could have had access to her room, or, achieving it, should be moved to deface her mirror in a manner suggesting it was for sale?—and disturbed by the unaccountable presence that had been silently witnessing, unpardonably mocking, it seemed to her as she pushed away the chair and stood aside to let the candle-light fall upon the strange apparition, her private rejoicings.

'*I love you*,' it said.

With the feeling of coming down and down from a far-away upper distance, a physical sensation of rhythmic descent down and down, her consciousness arrived in the moment and paused, looking out through the eyes of her body at the shadowy semblance left in the room: the figure of the girl secretly and swiftly coming and going, in outdoor garb, cloak or loose coat, something swaying and flowing with her movements, un-Englishly.

She must have discovered the address at the club, come round here on an impulse, and immediately encountered Selina. Selina, in her old dressing-gown and with a candle guttering in her battered candlestick, peering out into the darkness, a little suspicious of the foreign voice and the poses and the extraordinary request that must have followed their brief conversation. Or perhaps already dressed for her evening lecture, and therefore feeling relatively sporting and dare-devil and, at once won over, preceding her upstairs and admitting her for a moment to this room, alone, probably lighting for her this very candle, and coming in to blow it out again after she had shown her downstairs.

With a swift blush, while she assured herself that in the dim light she would not have observed it, she wondered whether Selina had seen the writing on the mirror.

CHAPTER VIII

SPARROWS were tweeting on the leads outside the office, and the servants had carried all the house-plants out into the lightly pittering rain. There was gold on the rain-wet leads and then grey for a while as again the rain fell, until once more its lessening drops were sunned to gold and ceased. The fresh smell of damp earth came in at the open door.

To-morrow morning, at dawn, if I happen—The bell of the wall-telephone sounded from its corner to which she went, away from her table within the freshness of the outer air and the radiance of morning light streaming in through the open door, across the short diagonal into the room's outer world, into the lesser light warmed by the yellow-gold wall-paper, into the flavourless, dry, house-air, and into sight, through the glass of the opposite door, of the stately perspective of staircase and high, shadowy hall and high archway nowadays austere, clear of Mrs Orly's striped oriental curtains with their unspeakable, pathetic, unforgettable tie-backs of transverse stripes, and the forehall leading along past the seated manservant to the dark wings of the closed door gloomily asheen beneath its clouded fanlight—with only the beginning of a friendly movement of her mind towards patients in their wealthy homes, and to this useful link between them and the house extending above and below her perched room, and lately more than ever beloved because with no release in sight she yet seemed already to be living in it in retrospect.

So that it was herself and not quite herself who lifted the receiver and looked down the long staircase up and down which she had run so many thousands of times, each time, even when fatigue or summer heat retarded her steps, with an emotion independent of that aroused by whatever made the journey necessary, sometimes so strong as temporarily to make

198

her forget her errand, sometimes reduced by a particular urgency almost to nothing, but always arriving the moment she started and continuing—making the experience of being on the stairs with the wide eloquent spaces above and below and all about her set in motion by movement, and the beings of the many inmates, and even her own being, momentarily further than usual from her mind and therefore in clearer focus, something distinct from the rest of her life in the house—until she arrived at her destination with a sense of return to a world from which she seemed to have been absent for much longer than the time required for the journey.

Pretty Mrs Ffoljambe on a visit . . . the year Persimmon won the Derby . . . held up, by a patient being interviewed in the hall, and dancing with impatience on this landing that to her was nothing but a stage on the journey from her bed-room down through the professional part of the house to the cheerful den far away beyond the back of the hall through which her arrived, gay friends had just charged in a silence as un-natural as her own.

Glad to escape from her, and her universe where women were judged by their looks and men by their incomes, I whispered, with simulated gallantry, I'll hurl myself downstairs and find out for you. Thanks hawfully, she said, but don't break a limb.

Into the receiver came the voice of Mrs Orly. Her telephone voice: thin and hurried, its usual note of anxious solicitude increased by her incurable impatience with the mechanism, and whispering, as if still she were living here in the house and conveying, through the hall speaking-tube, some urgent message to her husband in his surgery. Her whole self came through, the image of her in hurried speech, the sallow little face worried and frowning, the sweet, radiant eyes a little clouded.

Intent upon the little figure on tiptoe at the wall-telephone fixed in the roomy hall at a level arranged for the convenience of her tall, unreflecting menfolk, Miriam had missed the meaning of the first words, but the anxious voice went on and she felt all the warmth of her being gather itself to sound in her reply to the flustered little phrases.

And when she returned to her table, the vision of the evening, glowing so pleasantly from the midst of next week, owed the whole of its charm to the certainty of the pervasive little presence and the perfect incoherence that so often in the past had provoked her to be unkind.

Whilst going on with her work she saw the vast ex-studio in the Orlys' Hampstead retreat approached, after dinner (during which hearing 'all about Oberland' would have been a few questions colliding with each other across the table and answered at cross-purposes to the accompaniment of family wrangling that held no core of bitterness, and then a little of Mr and Mrs Orly's reminiscences and, filling the spaces between the different consciousnesses moving towards each other and failing to meet, the beauty of Switzerland, lingering in the mind of each one), through the fern-lined, high glass corridor, looking at first gloomy because of its size and the way, above the shaded, standard lamps, the darkness went up towards the cold sheen of the glass roof, and presently becoming a continuation of the old den, though here the Orly voices caught up and echoing in the enormous room sounded less assured, and all they stood for much more remote, than on the old background.

And some time during the evening, since the scholarly aunt is to be there and will want to hear about Reich's last lecture, ideas will creep in:

'The great unassailed inland empires slumbering in superstition, producing grotesque art and no thought. The Aegean islanders, always on the *qui vive*, fighting for their lives, producing Homer. Spreading westwards: Greece. The little Hebrews on their strip of coast, living dramatically, producing a great literature. The Romans a military camp, spreading and conquering, making Empire and Law. Their spiritual descendants the island English, sailors, soldiers, merchants, and, presently, the world's greatest poet. And now asleep in prosperity while in the midst of Europe rises a brutal menace.'

His last words: 'Ladies and gentlemen, I am a Hungarian patriot. Germany prepares for war. Europe knows it. Before this century is ten years old, England will know it. Perchance too late. If I can open your eyes, I shall not have lived in vain. You, and you alone, can save Europe, can save my native land who will receive, on the morning war is declared, a post card bidding it cease to exist.'

If I can put all that *clearly* before their eyes, there will be silence for a moment and Mrs. Orly's voice will sound into the midst of the workings of their various minds, asking a question about Reich, compelling even a European situation to behave, to serve the purposes of kindly living.

Mr. Orly will quote *Anglo-Saxon Supremacy*, and sigh gustily and look about for his African tobacco-pouch, to carry off his embarrassment over his own emotion. And Mr. Leyton will intone 'My house and thy house are half the world's goods' and will remark that if the old boy turns out to be right, the Boer War has taught us we're a C3 nation just about in time; and cross his legs and look stern and capable.

And the walls will have grown transparent to gloomy threats and the high roof ceased to be a shelter. Until Mr Orly sings *Gunga Din* and *My Snowy-breasted Pearl* and their house becomes itself again.

But long before that, *to-morrow morning, at dawn, if I happen to wake, I shall breathe the freshness of morning from a Tansley Street window.*

From within the deep distances enclosed by the railings of the squares, the life-breath of the trees would steal towards her from either end of the street.

Here, going on with her work in the sane morning light, with rain-damp earthy scents streaming in from the potted mould of the house-plants, she felt the heart's ease of going home with a deeper rapture than in yesterday's excited twilight; felt an actual melting and streaming away from below her heart of the oppression that must have been gathering there through all the time at Flaxman's.

Whatever else awaited her at Tansley Street, these moments waited there. And daily moments of return to a solitude that whenever she crossed the threshold of her empty room ceased to be solitude.

The gentle burr of Mr Hancock's summoning bell took her

eyes to the clock as she rose to answer it. Mr Cleeke, narrow head, narrow, cold voice, narrowly specialized mind, must still be here. Going upstairs she heard in her mind the refined, undulating, deliberately challenging voice of Mrs Cleeke. Like so many of the wives of professional husbands, she seemed to be both her husband's guardian and a masked being who betrayed, by the emphasis of her statements, how little of her inward self was behind what she said. An eager, busy, well-dressed ghost, fearful of anything that seemed to threaten the ideas he represented. Wearing her husband's attainments as a personal decoration, she was really indifferent to the system within which she spent her outward life, aware of a world where it had no importance, perhaps taking refuge in it when she was alone. She might say briskly: 'One must be alone at times' . . . or, 'I'm quite *fond* of my own society, occasionally.' But the solitude this kind of woman suggested would be populous with humorous, common-sense reflections on life and humanity. Never quite at home in solitude, she and her kind missed the essential both in society and in solitude: the coming to life of the surrounding air, the awareness that within it is a life-breath; in-pouring. Not one of these women would be passionately shocked by the intruder who comes in vocally, assuming there is no one in the room but its visible occupant, or by the person who looks anxiously from one to another of a momentarily silent gathering, in wait for the next move.

Crossing the room to reach her corner, she felt the glow of agreement coming from the window-space where Mr Hancock stood beside his cabinet mixing amalgam with the remains of his most delighted smile wavering below the calm, obstinate brow and Mr Threele at ease in the chair facing the stained glass window's flitting brown butterflies with the remains of his *quod erat* half-smile still creasing his clever face.

'And the sooner the general public can be made to realize it the better,' said Mr Hancock gravely, with a final forceful sweep of the spatula, and turned to pack the patient's mouth with absorbents.

Dreadnoughts.

Can it be true that my assignation with to-morrow's dawn owes its security to Dreadnoughts?

After the dawn, if Mag and Jan were still at Kenneth Street, the first Sunday morning in the old house, the part beginning just after breakfast and probably finding her feeling she had never gone away . . .

The Flaxman time would roll up and vanish, for there would be nothing to recall it. She and Selina had left no mark on each other, exchanged no thoughts, no confidences, not even small gifts . . .

Perrance. Perrance's alabaster finger, packed in her luggage, impossible to abandon or give away, a reminding, undesired tribute to what in his mistaken eyes she stood for, something bred in her, remaining, friend and enemy by turns. Selina had seen and been won by it at first and then lost sight of it because she called out the self that was opposed to all its standards.

The strange girl had seen it and nothing else at all. Had insisted on it. And left it a message . . . at *Flaxman's.* Am-a-bel, calling herself by her own name, as if at once insisting on her smallness and pathos, in a great world, and her equality to all its forces, had triumphed, without knowing what she was doing, over the impossibility of breaking in at Flaxman's and, unless she should suddenly disappear, would for ever represent it, the whole of it complete in all its details, lying behind the small glimpse she was now carrying about as part of her knowledge of her new friend.

Perhaps she would disappear. Go back to Paris as she had hinted. There was no link between her and Tansley Street. And need be none for many days. . . .

'The fact is, we've been asleep.'

'The British bull-dog, eh, snoring in his comfy kennel?'

'Exactly. A little wider, please.'

After to-night, after more or less publicly settling in, it would be as though she had never been away and to-morrow morning — thanks to Dreadnoughts? — she would hear the familiar house-sounds and, although the toneless echo of St Pancras bells would no longer thud in her chimney—drawing her seeking glance, when she was too preoccupied to remember she could not *see* the sounds, towards its small black aperture that after each thump held a fumbling rumour as if something were moving visibly in the sooty cavity—in that fourth-floor room she would hear them as clearly as before: those first, new, clear, morning notes swinging one by one steadily down the scale and again and again and again until presently she forgot them, ceased to pay attention to the single sounds while still aware of their presence in the increased quality of the light in the room, and presently was reminded that the bells were still at their task by the sudden dead stop, announcing the hymn-tune that broke into the stillness with such appealing lack of confidence, tapping out its bell-notes slowly and carefully, like an untrained musician picking out a tune with one finger; each note sweetly, gently, touching the Sunday morning air, and at the end of the last line the uncertain upward dab at a top note never fully reached, left standing high in the air, perfectly, satisfyingly flat, for too brief a second, so that all one's being, in order not to miss its perfection, in order just to accompany and catch it before its profane comment was covered by the urgent crashing of the final cascades, had to become an attentive ear.

And all the other street-sounds. The pealing voice of the newspaper boy would still come up from far enough below to describe to her mind's eye the height of the confronting rows of quiet grey balconied houses and, with the briefness of its stay, accompanied by the painty crackling open of large front doors, low-toned words clearly audible, calling up a picture of boy and buyer pleasantly in league, and the quiet satisfied wooden flump of each leisurely closed door, to tell of its perfect length between tree-filled square and tree-filled square.

Revelling in every single, blessed sound indoors and out and then, for a moment, undecided between one and another of the many ways of spending the vast morning. No need to unpack. Mrs Bailey would only smile, indulgently, if her luggage hung about for weeks, for ever. Oh, *home*.

If Mag and Jan were still at Kenneth Street, whatever she should decide to do would be done in an interval that would owe part of its secure endlessness to the state of mind brought about by the forgettable certainty of going to them in the afternoon, without going outside the surrounding presence of Central London. That was the change, the only change there would be, that Mag and Jan had gone away outside. And it was not essential. Perhaps it was good.

For those old Sundays with them were left perfect, an everlasting possession. In spite of the curious occasional flaw: the way the girls agreed, amidst all their complete differences, in a half-mocking, *humorous* indulgence for all she tried to express to them. Intolerable, sometimes terrifying: the presence of a secret, magnanimous mockery, that included themselves, included everything and everybody, and was sustained by a sort of taunting attitude towards life that was perfectly inexplicable. But on the whole those Sundays were perfection. Perfect at their time, so that often she and they, though Jan not so much, being older, and more lugubrious about the future and old age, had wished and said they wished, and without damaging the moment, that for ever they could go on living the lives they then were living.

Certain days stood warmly in her heart, gathering about them all the others that would need a special effort to call up, and all of one quality that amid innumerable variations had *never* varied: the three of them, their clearly defined differences, origins, characters, beliefs, and a fourth, something that was there in the room and that depended upon their being together, and being together at the heart of London and immensely at leisure, without past or future. So that anecdotes, stories of the past, and speculations as to what might lie ahead—happening only when, for some reason, one or other of them was not quite there, or was withdrawn into some private preoccupation—drove it away.

Some of these Sundays, some of the best, had been bought at shameful prices: lies that had yet brought no punishment, but the reward of increased eagerness on the part of the friends she had ruthlessly failed at the last moment.

One stood out from the rest with the guiltiest prelude: the going to look in on them on that grilling August Saturday, leaving her bag ready packed for the long-promised week-end with the Pernes at Banbury Park that had been an enchanting prospect ever since the arrival of Miss Deborah's unexpected affectionate letter breaking the years of silence since Miss Haddie's death. And all the more charming because Miss Haddie would not be there deliberately representing Church Christianity and doing her reproachful best so openly to be a good influence, and failing because of her sad, soured immaturity, her *fear*, and cold dark jealousy. Only sunny Miss Deborah and frivolous Miss Jenny and Wordsworth House empty of north London girls. And Miss Haddie's death far enough away for them to be their gay, profane little off-duty selves: little Christian gentlewomen of the last century, mighty without knowing it, and heavenly company.

And as the visit approached, it had become not only their charming idea but also escape for two nights from the stifling attic, and all through the morning languor after a sleepless night she had had before her eyes their cool suburban sitting-room, its open windows letting in the jingle-jingle, plock-plock, of the soulless north London trams that would sound, as she sat with them about the little tea-table and its old silver and fragile porcelain, the Gobelin screen somewhere near, and listened to their delicate chirrupings and chucklings, somehow less incongruous than on that first afternoon so many years ago.

It was midday. The girls both just back from their respective offices, blissful, amidst the disorder of settling down for the week-end. Jan cooking, in a crape dressing-gown, her head contradicting her body, boyishly intellectual with its short sculptured hair. Mag in knickers and camisole, her west-country, Celtic hair a cloud about her face and neck, cleaning all her shoes set in a row. Chanting voices that did not cease when she came in. And both faces flushed and perspiring in the fearful London heat and the extra heat, the savoury heat of their cooking. And a sudden home-sickness for them and for their sweltering little rooms seeming, at that moment, more attractive, and, because of the deep release they brought to her spirit, *cooler*, than any garden could be. There seemed a special importance, that had grown stronger, turned into something that could not be missed, when Mag began laying her spells:

'Trains, week-ends, what *are* they? I *ask* you, *what?*' Yet preoccupied, utterly, blissfully preoccupied. Wanting not so much that I should stay, as that by not going away I should preserve a familiar pattern.

'Having shown yourself, you *can't* leave us. Jan! Can she leave us? *Est-ce qu'elle peut uns verlassen?*'

'*Nein! Bestimmt! In Gottes Rath.*'

'*Ewigkeit, Amen.*' And then, the shoes finished, as she went busily from room to room so that her voice sounded from various distances, its chanting carelessness proclaiming her indifference, but with such intoxicating *attractiveness*, because it revealed her soul's eye set upon her week-end, its succession of moments and events as they appeared, secretly, to her alone and sent their joy into her voice as she moved about in their setting, sharing it with Jan, who saw it with the eye of one born and bred in another country, always to some extent as foreign, as something she had achieved, but that yet remained outside herself:

'We insist, child, on you, or your hat. Go, if you must. But your hat. Stays here. We will suspend it. By its velvet strings. To the mantelpiece. In front of the archdeacon. We will regard'—and here she had stood near at hand, exultantly radiating her charm, through warm west-country eyes and smiling lips, and her easily flowing affection, so sunny, having for its nearest objects her army of sisters and brothers, all safely at a distance and yet securely to be met on holidays she could, without discomfort, just manage to afford; and the half-critical indulgence that was beginning to be her settled attitude, in agreement with Jan, some kind of formula that fitted their scheme of things—'its transparent, silky crinoline. Its roses. With their help. And *torrents* of trrr-anspiration. We 'll enduah.'

Jan, having come in from the kitchen to stand at her side, with her so different, German smile, blondly radiant, denied by the little twist of her closely held lips expressing her bitter comment on life, held always in reserve and implacable:

'*I.* Shall *wear* the hat.'

And they had stood like a tribunal. And reluctantly, taking leave not so much of them personally as of the condensation of their common London life in all its retrospects and perspectives, specially, it seemed at that moment, represented by this torrid week-end she might have shared with them, she had privately decided, while mentally they left her and again took possession of their goods, the security of their isolation together for the immense interval between one week's work and another, that she must hold to her going. But in moving out to the landing and the sight of the descending stairs, the banishment from this innermost depth of the rich deeps of London seemed not only unendurable, but foolish and needless. As if to go, however morally and stoically, was to commit an outrage she would regret to the end of her days. Her thoughts, for a moment, had touched the waiting Pernes and brought a pang of guilt that was nothing beside the deep, everyday joy that poured back when Mag, coming from her room, said quietly, simply, with a touch of anxious pleading making her voice undulate:

'You 're *not* going, Miriam ? *Don't* go.'

'Of *course* I 'm not going.'

'She 's not going, Jan.' Mag had turned her head towards the kitchen without removing her gaze, but in her level tone was triumph and malicious amusement, tempting me to say it was not entirely on their account I was staying, and in her smile a delighted anticipation of Jan's horrified amazement. Jan had almost tiptoed out from the kitchen and murmured, when she arrived, with her crooked smile reduced to its least shadow:

'Not ? *Really* not ?' And their sense of the enormity had come from them in waves.

'No. I don't want to go away. I don't want to wander out into bleak black blank north London. You can't imagine, even on a tropical day, how *cold* it is.' She had carried their thoughts away, driven them away, from the personal aspects, made them enthusiastically see the necessity, and it was Jan who suggested the telegram. And there was an interval, before it was sent, every one separate again, and chanting, and blissful. And over that afternoon and evening had lain the deepest spell they had known together, for her and for Mag at any rate, and their happiness and the presence of the exaggerated weather had distracted Jan, insulated her for a while somewhere quite near the unchanging present.

The twilight had come to them all, coming home from Slater's, a shared, oh, surely that must have been a fully shared event and marvel; immense summer twilight, heavenly refreshment, sky swept clear of its blaze of light and heat, grown high and visible and kind; buildings and people larger and more kindly than by day. Such an immense turning of day, personal, making to everybody a vast communication, deepening into dusk as we walked abreast, three little figures with dusk-white faces and dusk-dark garments, causelessly exulting, towards the morning which came at once, for I slept a rich sweet sleep that paid no heed to the sultry oven atmosphere of my room.

And that Sunday morning for the first time I went round to them before breakfast out into the early summer morning, into all my summer mornings right back to that morning when I first noticed a shadow lying on the *wrong side* of a gable. Across the silent early freshness of the square, feeling the remains of night and dawn in the deep scent and colour of its leaves, drinking its strange rich lonely air that seemed in the heart of London to come from a paradise as deep as any to be found in distant country lanes and woods. It sent a breath of its pure freshness down the little asleep brown street and on to their doorstep, till I forgot it and thought only of them, and in a moment, having found them and yesterday still going on and holding us together, I was out again; and now, the longest part of that day that seems so vast a stretch is the moment of being out again on those steps, going down them, with all the on-coming hours in my heart and their little milk-jug in my hand for ever; for the whole of that summer that seemed then to approach from earth and sky and, as if it were a conscious being, to greet me coming down the steps in my rose-hat with loosely tied strings, and, as I paused in delight, to claim me as part of its pageant; so that in that moment my sense of summer was perfect and I knew it was what I had stayed in London to meet.

The saliva-tube ceased its busy gurgling. Gave out its little click of glass on glass as Mr Hancock bent across and hitched it over the rim of the spittoon. 'Now rinse, please.' He was at the far side of the chair filling the tumbler as the patient came upright mopping his lips, returning to his cold world and his cold use of its words. An emotional groan, facetious tribute to his gagged endurance; a reflective sniff: prelude to speech; but already Mr Hancock, appointment-book in hand, had begun the dismissal. In a moment she would be alone with him in that world of silent or speechful communion that was so powerful still to set her other worlds at a distance. His least word, and Mr Threele had left his thoughts flowing and himself conversational, would evoke the whole of it and break the current of her thoughts.

The speaking-tube clicked, and he came quickly back from his leave-taking across the room to answer it and would perhaps have the next patient sent up at once . . . ?

'Yes?' he inquired, abstractedly listening into the tube and, in reply to the answer, 'Yes,' again, informatively. It was not the patient; a partner with a question, perhaps wanting him for a consultation, or one of the mechanics needing instructions or wanting him in the workshop. The second question was lighting his face with the glimmer of a smile, and she slowed her gathering-up of instruments to make a silence for talk that might last long enough to see the bracket cleared and herself escaped until the patient should be in the chair.

'Thank you.' He turned to face her with his full, delighted beam: 'Lord Wilderham to see you,' he said and paused for a moment, enjoying his role, and moved away to his writing-table with a deliberate air of abdication and withdrawal, enjoying the little comedy.

She had smiled her response to it while their eyes had met and she had taken the unexpected Lord Wilderham and his unknown needs under her wing, and was free now to go off at once for her excursion into the far-off world represented by his name. So far off and unrelated to her own and yet so deeply loved for its floods of golden light, the various rich beauty of its backgrounds and the fresh deeps of high surrounding air that blessed its innocent inhabitants unnoticed, that she seemed to hold a place in it by natural right, and to touch it for a moment just now was an extension rather than a disturbance of her blissful state. She went down to the waiting-room, feeling her spirit's joy the fuller for her errand, flowing more freely through her limbs and to the tips of her toes that scarcely felt the ground beneath them as they skimmed along the hall.

Lord Wilderham rose from a chair in the window-space beyond the table where held-up patients sat trying to read. In a moment she was at his side and as sharply aware, while they exchanged greetings, of his agitation and distress as if they had been her own, and stood poised, accepting and receiving and longing to remove them, glad to radiate the deep peace that to-day was so fully at her command; till the pleasant, woeful, bloodshot blue eyes moved from hers to glance towards the room's silent occupants.

The opening of the door, upon a released patient greeting, and immediately greeted by, someone risen from the table, made a solitude for them in the retreat where they were sharing his eloquent misery.

Through his staccato incoherencies—as he stood shamed and suppliant, and sociable down to the very movement of his eyelashes, and looking so much as if he had come straight from a racecourse that her mind's eye saw the diagonal from shoulder to hip of the strap of his binoculars and upon his head the grey topper that would complete his dress, and the gay rose in his buttonhole—she saw his pleasant life, saw its coming weeks, the best and brightest of the spring season, broken up by appointments to sit every few days for an indefinite time enduring discomfort and sometimes acute pain, and facing the intimate reminder that the body doesn't last, facing and feeling the certainty of death.

This man would risk his life in the hunting field, in wild and lonely distant parts of the earth, but the slow elaborate torments of modern dental surgery had broken his spirit. But not his courtesy. Half of his distress was over the enormity of breaking appointments. His decision to endure for the present no more root-dressings and preparations for crowns, no more long, long, tap-tap-tapping in of gold fillings, was desperate and bought at the price of genuine moral discomfort.

'What *are* we to say to Hancock?'

She sent him away reassured, with all his appointments safely cancelled and perfect understanding and forgiveness faithfully promised; but as through the open front door she saw him spring into his jaunty, holland-blinded private hansom—and in spirit felt his relief as it bowled gaily off down the street through the spring sunlight towards the world of flowered balconies and high grey houses beautiful within: all at their best moment, the spring flowers in house-rooms and club-rooms giving out, with their scents, the essence in advance of the weeks to come right down to Ascot and Goodwood and Cowes, seen in perspective by all the genuinely participant *habitués*, and of these he certainly was one, as a single continuous collaborated jollification, the annual festival, centring in London and London's summer robbed by wealth of its discomforts, of the entire Oberland house-party—he was no longer just one of the social elect, but also a pathetic fugitive. Behind the merrily jingling hansom ran the shadow of death. Easily forgotten in the midst of the secure profane gaiety of wealthy social life, where it is possible even for weaklings and the timid to lose and identify themselves with the group and draw from it daily a dose of vicarious strength; but always there.

He had fled from cessation, and the sense, brought by those moments in the chair when publicly, in one's own hearing and that of another, one's hardest tissues, mysteriously stricken, are ground away, of bodily failure and ultimate dissolution. From the witnessed, audible destruction that brings it so closely home. Neglected teeth may be uncomfortable, sometimes agonizing. But they are a personal secret, easily forgotten in the long intervals.

Everybody, nearly every single person in the western world, except some of the middle European rye-bread-eating peasantries, ravaged to some extent by dental caries. And still doctors scarcely ever looked at patients' mouths. And even dentists seemed to feel that all would be well if only the public and the medical profession could be awakened to the necessity for wholesale, regular dental treatment for everybody . . . school clinics. Enlightened practical common-sense people, hygienists, and public health enthusiasts, pioneers, talking glibly and calmly about the great future, once they were set going, of school dental clinics, never hearing in the very word the cold metallic click of instruments, never imagining the second-rate men who would accept these poorly paid jobs and handle the scared children. And even if they were all the equals of Mr Hancock and everybody were skilfully and gently treated. What then? It would make no difference to the truth: death attacking western civilization by the teeth.

Civilization, she told herself going slowly upstairs, and the helpless, wild, unconscious shriek of a patient coming round from nitrous oxide in a downstairs surgery seemed to her the voice of the western world in its death-throes, depends upon the stability of molars. No longer stable. That is why dentistry, the despised and rejected amongst the healing arts, is a revelation where medicine is a blind. Medicine chases symptoms, checks one disease and sees another increase. Total result: nil. Dental surgery treats symptoms that remain in place and do not change their form. Is therefore in a position to recognize that treatment *does not cure*. Civilization. Disease. And treatment growing all the time more and more elaborate. Nightmare: increasing armies of doctors trained, and in honour bound, even if they themselves, to say nothing of the helplessly onlooking relatives, are revolted by the processes, to 'keep life going to the last possible moment by every available means,' and the fearful array, for ever increasing, of drugs and appliances that can drag the dying back to consciousness and torment.

The ancient crack, where London grime had collected, in the jamb of the glass door of her room confirmed her gloomy reflections and challenged the skylit brightness upon which the door opened. But in vain, in vain. The sweet fresh air from the opposite open door flowed into her nostrils. Her

being went forth to meet it. Here, within the air, far within
this breath of life with the sun on its spring moisture, was rescue
from all the gloom in the world. Flight, like Lord Wilderham's? He to his daily Oberland, she to her morning air?
No. There was an answer, a personal answer and assurance
somewhere within the deeps of this living air: not all the black
evidence of human history could prevail against it. In light
and darkness it was there. It was a touch. It conveyed the
touch of a living, conscious being.

The silent light, sharply signalling amongst the mountains,
had been a message; but this low, sweet English air was an
embrace.

The coming end of to-day's morning tapped stealthily on
her mind and began to spread its influence. Just enough time
in hand for all that remained to be done. With a deep sigh
that brought to her eyes a smile of salutation, she sat down
at her table and gathered together the scattered letters and
cheques and felt time at once resume its deep, morning quality,
and turned to greet Hawkins come quietly in from the basement workshop for the mechanics' wages with the morning in
his eyes. The sunlight would now be striking in through the
barred basement skylight. Above the horrid gold coins, they
met in silent agreement and exchanged their differently worded
tributes, and parted with the cunning smiles of conspirators
enriching their secret by leaving it unspoken.

A glance at her clock showed its hands met on noon and,
propped against its side, a letter come by the mid-morning
post and placed carefully there, clear of the table's litter, by
Eve, addressed to herself. In a strange hand. Queer staccato
pen-strokes, sloping at various angles, with disjointed curves
set between: *Amabel*.

A mass of small sheets, covered, without margins. Strange
pattern of curves and straight strokes rapidly set down. Each
separately. Gaps not only between each letter but also between the straight and the curved part of a single letter. Letters
and words to be put together by the eye as it went along.

She reckoned the cost of reading the whole: the sacrifice of
part of a Saturday afternoon to work that after this invasion of

her unprepared consciousness might go at a dragging pace. Glancing through the pages she found some, in a larger and still more hurried hand, where no single word showed its meaning directly. Between each letter of each word was as much space as between the words they were supposed to compose. Yet each was expressive, before its meaning appeared. Each letter, carelessly dashed down, under pressure of feeling, was a picture, framed in the surrounding space.

When meanings were discovered, they sounded; as if spoken.

It was this strange, direct, as if spoken communication, punctuated only by dashes sloped at various angles like the sharp, forcible uprights of the script, and seeming to be the pauses of a voice in speech, that was making the reading of this letter so new an experience. From its enchantment part of her mind was still held aloof by its strangeness, inquiring, considering. Her eye, not yet accustomed, kept pausing over the expressiveness of the new words attaching themselves to those already read, moving as well as sounding while they came, set together by her eye, to their proper meaning.

Alive. These written words were alive in a way no others she had met had been alive. Instead of calling her attention to the way the pen was held, to the many expressivenesses of a given handwriting, apart from what it was being used to express, instead of bringing as did the majority of letters, especially those written by men, a picture of the writer seated and thoughtfully using a medium of communication, recognizing its limitations and remaining docile within them so that the letter itself seemed quite as much to express the impossibility as the possibility of exchange by means of the written word, it called her directly to the girl herself, making her, and not the letter, the medium of expression. Each word, each letter, was Amabel, was one of the many poses of her body, upright as a plant is upright, elegant as a decorative plant, supporting its embellishing curves just as the clean uprights of the letters supported the curves that belonged to them.

And these word-making letters so swiftly flung on to the marginless page, substituting their individual shape for the letter-shape that she now realized had a limiting effect upon what was expressed therein, were seeming to explain and justify the poses: to show them for so long already habitual in this girl's young life that although they pleased her and were to her the movements of a dance, they expressed her without hindrance. She admired as she took them, called attention to them. Impersonally, as she called herself by name.

'Isn't—E-g-y-p-t—a beautiful word?'

Beautiful? If it were, she was tried in the balance and found wanting. Amabel stood turned away from her, posed in contemplation of something she could not see, so that for her own contemplation only the pose remained.

French. The Frenchwoman, judging, selecting for approval and, by her pose, holding both herself and any one contemplating her in reverence before what she perceived: person, thing, idea. According to some standard that for her was infallible, Amabel collected, as she went along through life.

But this letter, moving breathlessly, staccato, was more English than French. Without her spoken accent, now that she was turned away and her voice no longer heard, it was English altogether.

Egypt. Neither the sound nor the sight of the word was lovely. Written, with its three differently tailed letters properly joined, it was unmanageable: the tails competed. In the whole written language surely no word was more difficult to beautify. The opening sound uglier even than 'cheese,' the pouting spit of the conclusion: hopeless.

Yet she singled it out, pausing before it, offering it. Mystery.

Returning, from scribbling in various styles of handwriting the difficult combination, she gazed once more at the word on the page and saw that as written by the girl it was not a word at all. It was a picture, a hieroglyph, each letter lovely in itself. Beautiful, yes, and suggesting all its associations more powerfully than did the sight of the word written closely.

Written as she wrote it, it was expressive exactly as her script was expressive: a balance of angles and curves. Like the words traced on the mirror. It was their expression, which was Amabel's, as much as what they had said, that had so moved her.

'Forgive—I watched you—in your little English clothes—
go across the square—oh, my lady—my little—you terrified
my heart—I hold it out to you—my terrified heart—in my two
hands——'

Real. Reality vibrating behind this effort to drive feeling
through words. The girl's reality appealing to her own, seeing
and feeling it ahead of her own seeings or feelings that yet
responded, acknowledged as she emerged from her reading,
in herself and the girl, with them when they were together,
somehow between them in the mysterious interplay of their
two beings, the reality she had known for so long alone, brought
out into life.

The phrase scrawled beneath the signature gradually grew
clear: 'I wrote, with your *soap*!'

Alarmed by this almost terrifying resourcefulness, Miriam
put the letter aside and turned to her work.

To-morrow morning, if I happen to wake . . .

But now to-morrow morning and all the visible circumstances
of her life had retreated to inaccessible distance, leaving her
isolated with this girl.

Suddenly, punctually isolated, as once she had been with
Eleanor, and, again this time, just as everything about her
had become a continuous blossoming.

CHAPTER IX

AGAIN the side-door of a small restaurant in a narrow street. Again a dingy waiter leading the way up an ill-lit staircase. Again the conflict between her desire to be a sympathetic presence and her resentment of his ignorance of her perfect awareness of the conflict in him, between his bourgeois scruples and his secret, newcomer's delight in what he had called his 'slum.' Again a distracting preoccupation with the world-wide vision of harpy disreputability offering facilities to the well-to-do. And again, more clearly than all, her whole being set against the plan that last week had perfectly foiled itself without instructing him . . .

Coercion. The unpardonable crime.

Unless he should realize that, and make a convincing recantation, he would wreck this occasion as he had wrecked all the others.

It was his worst fault?

The thought occurred to her, coming as if from outside her mind and gleaming for an instant in the murky darkness, that presently she might discreetly discuss this subject with him. He might listen in the way he sometimes had done when suddenly and irrelevantly she said something with all the force of her nature. And this particular certainty was perhaps her strongest social certainty.

Philosophizing: Well, it was what she most wanted, to remove a barrier of which he was aware without understanding its nature. It would be difficult, almost impossible, in a half-lit, shamefaced room. Perhaps the same room. Whose features, in memory, had already attained a kind of beauty.

But to-night the journey ended in a brightly lit sitting-room with table laid. And instantly the evening was endless. They were alone, in endless time.

Piling her outdoor things upon a sheeny shamefaced arm-chair in a dark corner near a window through the slats of whose dilapidated Venetian blinds came the bluish light of a street lamp, she felt the remains of the day's preoccupations fall away and strength return, flowing in from the promise of leisure, making her hope she was less tired than she felt. Far away from him and from her surroundings her spirit seemed to flee, demanding peace, and to-night, at no matter what cost in apparent idiocy or ill-humour, she *would* reach that central peace; go farther and farther into the heart of her being and be there, as if alone, tranquilly, until fully possessed by that something within her that was more than herself. If not, if she remained outside it, if he succeeded in making her pretend, though he never knew she was pretending, to be an inhabitant of his world, then again they would squabble and part.

As they both came forward into the central light and he rounded off the tuneless humming that had accompanied his disrobing and had been meant to signal self-possession, with a cheerful cadenza on a tone increased in fullness like that of an opera orchestra while the hero enters, and still said no word, she felt time and space open out between them, infinitely available: the gift of last week's evening, of their first evening of being alone and inaccessible.

And paused in deep gratitude to life and to him, just short of the lit table, and turned away to the mirror with her hands to her hair as though arranging it. Immediately his humming broke forth anew; this time to answer her silent abstraction, to tell her they were *both* tranquilly at home and at leisure.

Gazing into the depths of the mirror's fly-blown damp-mottled reflection of a dark curtain screening a door in the opposite wall, she was aware of herself there in the picture, lit from behind, obstructing the light that presently again would lie across the mirror when she turned to join the party: him, and herself representing to him a set of memories amongst other sets of memories. A set covering about ten years of his life, covering the period that had seen him emerge from obscurity to celebrity in his world that was so alien to her own.

In and out of every year of his ascent her life had been woven.

She had been a witness, and was now a kind of compendium for him of it all, one of his supports, one of those who through having known the beginnings, through representing them every time she appeared, brought to him a realization of his achievements.

He was two people. A man achieving, becoming, driving forward to unpredictable becomings, delighting in the process, devoting himself, compelling himself, whom so frankly he criticized and so genuinely deplored, to a ceaseless becoming, ceaseless assimilating of anything that promised to serve the interests of a ceaseless becoming for life as he saw it. And also a man seeming uncreated, without any existence worth the name.

If presently he should ask, really wishing, impersonally, to hear of movements, of any kind of accomplishment: 'Well, what have you been up to since last week?' and she should answer, as a hundred times she had answered: 'Living,' he would emit the little chuckle, half amusement at what he considered an evasion and half disapproval of the spectacle of a life spent, as lately he had so often said, 'in agreeable loafing that leads nowhere.'

But then he would say also, in moods of reflective impersonal contemplation: 'You 've taken your freedom, Miriam, won it in the teeth of difficulties in a way that compels my admiration. You 've lived, you still live, you know, only just above the poverty line, and it hasn't bashed you.' And so many other descriptive commentaries, recognizable, impersonal classifications of all sorts. And yet she remained, felt, unknown to him. And whatever selves he might reveal to her, selves he hinted at, none of which she had any desire to become, she must remain unknown. For so dismally, in every one, he saw only what they were becoming or might become, and of the essential individual knew, and wanted to know, nothing at all.

The dreary young waiter came in with the soup and once more the room asserted its character and Hypo, sharply aware of him, began at once to edit his ideas of the occasion by his manner of supervising his arrangements with a half-friendly, half-patronizing approval, and succeeded only in making the

mournful young man strain yet higher the eyebrows permanently a little lifted by the disappointing difference between the
realities of his life in London and his dreams thereof in his
far-away continental home.

He shuffled away and the room recovered: the fly-blown
mirror, the faded artificial flowers, the obtrusive sofa, were
redeemed by the table's circle of golden light, now populous
and become one with all the circles of golden light within
which she had sat down to feast.

Taking her place, she felt more than the usual familiar sense
of everlastingness that came forward in her at the moment of
sitting down to table with beloved people, and stayed until the
breaking forth of conversation drove it into the background.
Here it was, blissfully beating its wings in the disgraceful room
and coming this time not only from the past but from past
and future alike; for ever.

She held to it, savouring its strange new quality, its power of
so intensifying the radiance in which they sat, that everything
beyond it was a darkness obliterating the walls of the room,
extending back and back, right along the receding years of
their intermittent friendship.

Called by his unusual silence to glance across the separating
inches, she saw that he was being grave, apparently quietly
abstracted. Honestly, quite honestly and sincerely he was
playing up to her, venturing unarmed into the desert shared
life became for him whenever deliberate, incessant gaiety was
in abeyance, whose destructive power he yet knew as well as
he knew its joys.

Robbed of the subtle curves drawn about them by his watchful readiness for witty improvisation or facetious retort, robbed
of the authoritative complacency they wore during his ceaseless social occupation of definition and commentary at every
turn of every occasion, his features were homely, reverted to
his very homely type, the raw material of his personal appearance. Only his brow, the side of it left free from limply
forward-falling wisps of hair, asserted independence, above his
momentarily invisible eyes; thought-moulded, moulded by
the theories and thoughts that built up his mental life.

She was at once charmed and touched by this surely painful experiment, the result of his willingness to try to meet her on her own ground, or at any rate her own terms; for the ground she lived on he believed to be merely a mistaken self-importance.

Turning away her eyes from the strange spectacle of him abdicated and docile, she became aware of the thoughts behind his experiment. He was curious as to what use she would make of the offered leadership, and at the same time sceptical, willing to give her time, at any rate time enough to prove to herself as well as to him that her silence was what he believed all feminine silence to be: a vacuous waiting.

His patience, unless she could almost hypnotize him by the intensity of her concentration, would give out. Long before she could attain. Well, let it give out.

Scarcely breathing, she dropped, aware at once by the way the now familiar objects of the room fused to a unity, as if seen from a distance, that she would remember them for ever, down and down, sure now, if she could hold out, of attaining at last in his presence for the first time, save now and again by accident, to possession of that self within herself who was more than her momentary self, and again and again, intermittently and unreliably, had charmed them both.

Almost arrived, almost down in the innermost sphere of happy solitude, drawing the first deep breath of its fresher air that was like air coming across the sea at night, air breathed above the waters of a bubbling spring, she was halted by the watchfulness of a swift glance, a ray immediately withdrawn.

In answer to her awareness, having first made sure of it, made sure her eyes would turn his way, he raised his spoon and flourished it in a neat little spiral above his plate, with eyes downcast, lips pouched, and eyebrows pathetically up in would-be childish appeal: a small pantomime suggesting that they should get on with their soup.

He was confessing his vow of silence, making game of it, revealing above his half-mocking, half-interested, sceptical submissiveness, his ceaseless mind presiding, its wide shallow definitions and interpretations all neatly in place.

With a flash of insight that freed her for ever, she felt, of jealousy of his relationships past, present, and future, she saw how very slight, how restricted and perpetually baffled must always be the communication between him and anything that bore the name of woman. Saw the price each one had paid with whom he had been intimate either in love or friendship, in being obliged to shut off, in order to meet him in his world, his shaped world, rationalized according to whatever scheme of thought was appealing to him at the moment, three-fourths of their being.

What could any one of them be for him beyond the fact that they were providers of what he regarded as vitalizing physical contacts, but sounding-boards for his ideas; admirers, supporters? Either they were disciples, holding on to and living in the light of one or other of the mutually contradictory interpretations of life perpetually evolved by men, all of them right and all wrong, and were therefore not women at all, but the 'intelligent emancipated creatures' for whom he expressed so much admiration while fighting shy of them in his leisure hours because of their awful consistency and conscientiousness or because, as Jan said, 'a rush of brains to the head usually made them rather plain in the face,' or they played up whenever they were with him, trotted briskly about on his maps and diagrams, and lived for the rest of their time in their own deep world.

All this she felt to-night with the strength of two. Amabel was with her, young Amabel, with her mature experience of men, who had confirmed what hitherto she had thought might be inexperience, or a personal peculiarity: her certainty that between men and women there can be no direct communication.

There was no place in his universe for women who did not either sincerely, blindly, follow, or play up and make him believe they were following. All the others were merely pleasant or unpleasant biological material. Those who opposed: misguided creatures who must not be allowed to obstruct. The majority played up: for the sake of his society, his charm, the charm of enjoying and watching him enjoy the pranks of his lightning-swift intelligence. The temptation was great.

She knew she had not always resisted it.

Poor little man. Isolated without knowing the cause of his isolation. Representing, as he sat there, all his isolated fellowmen.

No, there was no room for jealousy of the association of any woman with any man; only perhaps of their privileges and some of their experiences.

People can meet only in God? The shape—she took her spoon and began on her soup, swiftly, rhythmically, seeing upon the tablecloth in front of her the shape—a triangle. Woman and man at either end of the base, the apex: God.

'Grace,' she said, feeling now quite free, as if in solitude, to entertain herself with her own thoughts. 'That is why people say Grace. At least, one of the reasons.'

'Grace . . .' he began, provisionally, in the rather high-pitched tone that meant he was focusing something for which he had no prepared formula; but very gently so that he might, if she wished, be considered not to have spoken.

'Grace,' she breathed, as if speaking to herself: 'Grace, even if followed by *Snooks* . . . any one bearing such a name, called by it every day, must be influenced.'

With 'Gracie' and 'Grice' sounding hideously in her ears as she reflected that the name, as spoken in English, was a bad example of what she might have wanted to express if her new interest in words as a factor in environment had really been brought into play, she felt his eyes turned upon her and away again as he bent, believing her engrossed, to his filled spoon, without attempting to interpose, by means of some characteristic sally, his bugle-call to some recognizable form of mental activity.

This was marvellous. As now and again in the past, but then only in the midst of distracting conflict, she felt her spirit expand freely in the room and gather to itself, in the immensity of leisure provided by each succeeding second, all that belonged to the occasion.

So prominent in the backward vista that it seemed now to be offering itself as a substitute for the one now surrounding them, the scene of their early conflicts and of the beginning of the false-true relationship now established between them came clearly before her inward eye: the room shaped like a one-armed signpost, the long, cushioned seat in the window looking out to sea, every detail of the room's contents that had flouted her in moments of despair over the absence of words to frame the truths that balanced his and refused to fit into his patterns.

She felt again the delight of the moment of facing silently, alone with him, the sea's distant misty blue behind the nearer blue brilliance of delphiniums and saw again the window-framed loveliness deepen as quite gravely and simply he implored her to remain, for the whole morning dependably there, supporting. Again felt that morning immediately become endless. It did not matter that his consciousness had forgotten all this. Actually, it was the moment preceding this present one. Interruption had fallen upon it. Upon all the opportunities he had made, it had punctually fallen.

But now interruption was banished.

'This is very nice and domestic. You are having your first share of domesticity, Miretta.'

She looked across the few inches of space that separated them as across a gulf on the hither side of which he sat awaiting response to his adroit attempt to steer her thoughts, and met his eyes and saw re-enthroned in them the comedic sprite that gave him ceaseless entertainment and would not let him live.

Having given her the chance of steering the conversation and waited, according to his own reckoning, for dark ages, in vain, he now resumed his usual role in any shared experience: conductor, perpetually defining.

It was true. This *was* perhaps her share of domestic life. Perhaps all she had felt on sitting down to table was the result of a plunge into that zone of experience, now irrevocable and to be bearing fruit for ever.

'Been flying, almost desperately, from domesticity, all m'life.'

'Yes. . . . *Yes*. Lucky Miriam. Sailing free. You *are* lucky, you know. Not domesticity, then. Isolation; in space. But that unfortunate young man 'll be coming in again. Don't go too far into space before we 've done with him.'

'Women carry all the domesticity they need about with them. That is why they can get along alone so much better than men.'

That had launched him; and to the now quite strange sound of his voice, as new and strange as it had been the first time she heard it, she comfortably went on thinking; reminding herself of the many wives in whose eyes she had surprised private meditation going its way behind an appearance of close attention to a familiar voice.

Half turned towards his talk, eating her soup as though her listening supplied her present animation, she considered the strangeness, the perversity of his perpetual denial of the being far away within himself who believed all she wanted him to believe and knew all she wanted him to know. The one who had written the phrase of which his words had just reminded her.

No cunning, no kind of clever calculation could have worked the miracle of that letter. So complete that she had forgotten it, although without it she would not have been here to-night. But it was not until now that she saw it as proof of all he denied.

It was scientific evidence, surely more interesting and valuable, if less directly profitable, than the kind of evidence by which he set such store, and to this, the fact that it was *scientific* evidence she held eagerly, the whole of her mind seeming to be vocal at once above the sounds made by the waiter returned and who now was a friend, one of the strange human family, being and knowing, behind all the surface appearances and comings and goings. Ignoring them both, she prepared to communicate, with all these voices that were speaking at once within her, each presenting a different aspect of what she wanted to say and leaving her to choose the one that would best secure his attention.

But when they were once more alone she felt careless, defiant of any careful presentation. To whatever she might say, he would give an attention that for this evening at least was centred on herself. The beating within her of what seemed at once life and light, was making her breath come unsteadily and her voice shook a little as she said:

'It was in the middle of the morning,' and then steadied, for

its sound, so personal and yet so strange, the thin small thread
of sound, however smooth and pleasant and musical, going
out into space to represent—in a manner that left with every
word so much denied and so little so partially stated—one
person to another, was warning her that the evidence, if it
were to convince, must be given in his language of 'honest fact.'

"There had been,' she went on, looking straight ahead and
filling out her tone to carry herself past any obstructive witticism of word or manner he might find necessary for the decoration of his retirement from discourse, 'a letter from a friend
by the first post. Various letters, of course, from various
friends. But just that one letter standing out from the rest.
It doesn't matter why it stood out. The reasons may be good,
bad, indifferent, anything you like.' His eyes moved from her
face; his thoughts, while the point of her discourse remained
uncertain, had touched the subject's possibilities and his set
of generalizations about it—including the one, a little hampering her discourse, about the feminine habit of writing long,
personal letters that so easily degenerated into a pleasant
waste of time—and, with these ready to hand, had dropped
away.

'The point is that there could not possibly be another of
these very special letters, which in any case always came by the
first post, until the next day. Came a rat-tat. I *do* dislike
that form, don't you? *Came* this and that; even in poetry.
Perhaps because "came" is such a poor sound. Won't bear the
weight of suspense. . . . Now *kahm*——' Reverie advanced
upon her, suggesting the interest to be found in considering
the relative powers of English and German words. He
cherished Saxon English for its sanguine force and rich earthi-
ness, but did not know how continuously vivid was German,
with its unaltered, ancient pictoriality, every other word
describing an action or an object so as to bring it before
the eyes; even the terminology of philosophy being directly
descriptive.

'Proceed, Miriam.'

'*Kahm*, then, the eleven o'clock rat-tat, which I hear every
day unmoved and which, as I have explained, on this particular

day could not be bringing me anything, brought me to my feet in a way that no other rat-tat has ever done in the whole of my life. With my heart beating, and telling me much more plainly than speech could do that there was, down there in the letter-box, only one letter, instead of the usual posse of business letters and circulars, and that it was for *me*.'

'Yes. One has these curious premonitions, in certain moods. Certain states of heightened perception. One is exalted and luminous.'

He knew, then, and accepted this kind of experience, had perhaps gone through it himself, and yet remained incurious. She could tell him no more. Even if he were different, believing in an unseen world and an unseen power in communication with every single soul, even if he could suddenly be turned into a believer and her own man and partner, she could not tell, in words, what had happened in the moment of reading. He was in the midst of truth, surrounded by it as she knew it to be, but not willing to attend to its intimations. So the sacred moment was apart in her own personal and private life, though it was he who had found the words to describe its cause.

'Art, sex, and religion; one and the same,' she said briskly, 'but that doesn't matter. What matters——'

'Tell me, was that letter from me? Nice Miriam; *your* letters are exactly like yourself. Was it?'

'That doesn't matter. The shock, coming from outside, inside, life-as-it-seems-to-be was in having, as it were, read the letter before it came and reacted to it when my rational mind *knew* it couldn't be there.'

And the letter was *not*, in a sense, from him.

'There's no outside that is not——'

'Yes. There *is*. We can move, see, hear, feel somehow beyond our immediate selves. We can. We do.'

And now again the waiter came in, creating diversions with his presence and more food and again departed, leaving Hypo talking of discoveries that would supply scientific explanations for a set of phenomena not at present understood.

She smiled and stretched cool limbs full of strength that an hour ago were so fevered with weariness and, in the deep silence flowing in from the past over the sound of his words and all the words that ever would be used to convey thoughts about life, she demanded of herself whether she cared for him in the smallest degree or for any one or anything so much as the certainty of being in communion with something always there, something in which and through which people could meet and whose absence, felt with people who did not acknowledge it, made life at once impossible, made it a death worse than any dying.

'Religious people in general are in some way unsatisfactory. Not fully alive. Exclusive. Irreligious people are unsatisfactory in another way. Defiant.'

A violin, squeaking and scraping in the street below, making his answer inaudible because it was taking all her attention. Its halting sounds, the uncertain notes scraped out into the air of the gloomy street, were addressing themselves to what was always waiting, just within reach, just beyond the always breaking, always disappearing fragments of every kind of life . . . *Eve's little aria.* Playing itself, appealingly, into her heart. Hearing it now, not in Eve's rendering, nor in that of the decrepit musician down there, but in its own perfection, which now she was realizing for the first time, she was smitten by its meditative beauty and by the power with which it called her to herself. It was his enemy. It asserted, quietly, confidently, and, in coming to her at this moment out of the far past and showing it remaining in herself more deeply than the raw new years that had succeeded it and were still formless and void, as if gently chiding her while it overwhelmed her with its tenderness, all that he denied.

'Gluck,' she breathed, bending her head to listen.

'Glook, dear Miriam,' he said swiftly, and raised his glass.

And she remembered how years ago, when first hovering between relief and admiration for the mental freedom of the Wilson atmosphere, and uncertainty as to the liberties Hypo had taken with the shape of social life, she had told Eve, in a letter written from the Brooms' villa, from the midst of all the old beliefs, that she felt, in not renouncing the friendship of a divorced, remarried man, she was selling her soul to the devil. And how Eve had written imploring her to give him up.

And now she was surrounded by people all of whom Eve would see as 'living in sin.' And was about to join their ranks.

Raising her hand to keep him from further speech, she listened with all her strength and moved as she listened away and away, not back into the past, but forward, it seemed, into a future that belonged to it and drew her to itself, to where by nature she belonged.

Crashing across what now seemed to be Eve's own voice and brought a picture of her as she used to stand, gently waiting, without words, when her feelings had been hurt, came the sound of a heavy vehicle along the narrow street.

'You *are* a dear, Miriam,' he said in his most delighted voice. 'I wish I had your power of complete enthusiasm at a moment's notice. You *do* enjoy life, you know.'

'That is one of the loveliest little shapes of music, of its kind, there can be.'

There ought to be homage. There was a woman, not this thinking self who talked with men in their own language, but one whose words could be spoken only from the heart's knowledge, waiting to be born in her.

Now here, really, was a point for him: men want recognition of their work, to help them to believe in themselves. They want limelight and approval, even if they are only hanging a picture, crookedly, in order to bring them confirmation of the worth of what they do. Unless in some form they get it, all but the very few—the stoic philosophical ones who are apt to have a crooked smile, and a pipe in one corner of it, and not much of an opinion of humanity, but a sort of blasphemous, unconsciously destructive, blind, kindly *tolerance*—are miserable. Women, then, want recognition of themselves, of what they are and represent, before they can come fully to birth. Homage for what they are and represent.

He was incapable of homage. Or had given all he had and grown sceptical and dead about it. Left it somewhere. But without a touch of it she could not come fully to birth for him. In that sense all women *are* Undine. Only through a man's recognition can they come to their full stature. But so are men, in their different way. It was his constricted, biological way of seeing sex that kept him blind. Beauty, even, was to him beauty by contrast with Neanderthal man . . .

'The trouble with Miretta is that one can't take liberties with a philosopher.'

She smiled from far away, from where if only he knew and could have patience just to look at what she saw and fully submit himself to its truth, see and feel its truth, she could travel towards him. But at least this evening he was serene, not annoyed both with himself and with her as in last week's dimly lit room where yet in memory he seemed so much nearer to her than in this golden light. This evening he knew that the barrier was not of her own deliberate placing.

'Now with others than Miretta'—flattery—'one just takes them in one's arms and immediately there is no barrier.'

'Not because I am different. Because there is a psychological barrier. We've not talked enough.'

'Talking comes afterwards, believe me.'

He dropped a kiss on her shoulder.

'You *are* a pretty creature, Miriam. I wish you could see yourself.'

With the eyes of Amabel, and with her own eyes opened by Amabel, she saw the long honey-coloured ropes of hair framing the face that Amabel found beautiful in its 'Flemish Madonna' type, falling across her shoulders and along her body where the last foot of their length, red-gold, gleamed marvellously against the rose-tinted velvety gleaming of her flesh. Saw the lines and curves of her limbs, their balance and harmony. Impersonally beautiful and inspiring. To him each detail was 'pretty,' and the whole an object of desire.

With an impersonal sacredness they appeared before her, less imaginable as objects of desire than when swathed, as in public they had been all her life.

This mutual nakedness was appeasing rather than stimulating. And austere, as if it were a first step in some arduous discipline.

His body was not beautiful. She could find nothing to adore, no ground for response to his lightly spoken tribute. The manly structure, the smooth, satiny sheen in place of her own velvety glow was interesting as partner and foil, but not desirable. It had no power to stir her as often she had been stirred by the sudden sight of him walking down a garden or entering a room. With the familiar clothes, something of his essential self seemed to have departed.

Leaving him pathetic.

The impulse seemed reckless. But when she had leaned forward and clasped him, the warm contact drove away the idea that she might be both humiliating and annoying him and brought a flood of solicitude and suggested a strange action. And as gently she rocked him to and fro the words that came to her lips were so unsuitable that even while she murmured 'My little babe, just born,' she blushed for them, and steeled herself for his comment.

Letting him go, she found his arms about her in their turn and herself, surprised and not able with sufficient swiftness to contract her expanded being that still seemed to encompass him, rocked unsatisfactorily to and fro while his voice, low and shy and with the inappropriate unwelcome charm in it of the ineffectual gestures of a child learning a game, echoed the unsuitable words.

She leaned back surveying him with downcast eyes, dismayed to feel in him the single, simple, lonely helplessness of the human soul from which his certainties, though they seemed blind, had made her imagine him exempt, and wanting now only to restore him as swiftly as possible to his own world, even at the price of pretending she believed in it. With this determination came a sudden easy certainty of being able to rescue his evening from any sense of failure and disappointment.

Looking up at him with a plan in her mind that in his present state of simplicity did not seem impossible, she met his voice:

'Lost lady. Your reputation's in shreds, Miriam, virginal though you be.'

'Yes. Come and have coffee at my Donizetti's. Open till midnight. One of those little Italian-Swiss places where everything is fried in the same fat.'

She had risked the chances of the suggestion by apologizing for it. With an ingenious piece of flattery he would bring the occasion to an end and get away to his own world, with a formula for his evening that would satisfy every test he was likely to apply to it.

'We 'll have a hansom,' he said, making for his piled clothes, with the little creak in his voice that was there only when he was on the way to something that promised entertainment. 'A hansom,' he repeated with comforting ineptitude, 'evade the east wind.'

Reflected in the mirror she saw as if it were elsewhere and invisible, save by an effort of imagination she did not wish to make, the spectacle of him in conflict with garments and drew her eyes back to her own image just in time to see before it was shadowed by the influence of the haste that was needed if she were to be ready in time to escape the embarrassment of his misguided observation, how radiant it was in the promise of side-by-side companionship.

'We always have an east wind. It 's a portent.'

'We 'll elude it. I deplore your superstitions, Miriam, and adore your shamelessness in adhering to them. If I don't look out I shall end by adoring the superstitions.'

As they took their places in a vacant corner, without losing any of the joy that had possessed her when the absurd plan suggested itself, she saw the miserable little interior through his eyes. But the sight of his face wearing the curves it had only when everything was going very well, made her carelessly happy and sent her mind on a private tour all round the well-known space, reviving the memories stored up in it. Her early solitude. Eleanor, blissful here in brief immeasurable intervals between difficulty and difficulty. Michael, in conflict and in truce. Selina, courteously enduring a unique experience, restraining her withering disapproval until the moment before they left. She lost without regret the meaning of the words coming from his side of the table and was prevented from turning to inquire by the sight of little Donizetti bringing his plump, short person as quickly as possible down the narrow gangway, turning sideways where projecting chairs impeded his advance, with china-blue eyes coldly inspecting Hypo from a distance and remaining keen and stern when he arrived and turned them upon herself, and only sending forth the kindly ray of the smile that smoothed away the lines drawn by disapproval on his well-padded brow when she gave her order, in a voice expressing for him and for herself so much more than her delight in this single occasion that when she turned back to Hypo she knew that already he must have come into possession of some of the wealth accumulated here.

But though for the moment he was incredibly sitting at ease and happy here in her world and her life, he would presently need distractions. Forcing herself to ignore the fact that she had on her hands a man accustomed to be 'animated' and to meet 'animation,' she at once recovered the depth of her surroundings, from which she found herself glancing at the picture that was the result of trying on Amabel the effect of her own belief in the impossibility of association between men and women: Amabel at breakfast with Basil in his shooting-box, sitting there in morning light, lovely in her blue kimono, fresh and amusing and delightful and apparently amused and delighted, and Basil, opposite, believing that the behaviour and the talk with which she was filling the gap, to him the enchanting behaviour and the delightful talk and laughter of an amazingly intelligent child-woman, was spontaneous and as pleasing to herself as to him; having no idea of the difficulty, the sheer hard work of holding herself in his world and keeping him at his ease even for an hour.

She stole yet another flash of time to contemplate the alternatives that would confront her in looking across at him as if about to speak: 'pally' conversational remarks, the small talk, in their own coinage, for men only, of the woman who has abdicated, fancies she has become a friend and not only is, but looks, a satellite; the sprightly, amusing, half-cynical, social-revelation kind of talk, adapted to male blindness in social life and vastly entertaining them in their unoccupied moments, and giving women the reputation for scandal-mongering from which most men are free only by reason of their social blindness and incapacity; the man-to-man, generalized talk that must go forward in a language each of whose terms leaps a gap and goes confidently forward and finally leaves both them, and the women who contrive without reservations to adopt their mentality and their methods, in a desert of agnosticism.

In conning over his experience of these varieties of interchange, she grew self-conscious, aware of having slipped too far away, and sadly anticipated that in the second about to follow the one that was flashing by, he would, assuming the blankness of her mind, be amiably embarking upon one of his entertaining, life-darkening improvisations.

'The padrone,' she said dryly, despairingly, 'is always suspicious of my men friends,' and looked up. He was preparing for nothing. For several seconds he had sat contented, apparently thoughtless. With a face a little fuller than when they had come in, he looked at her encouragingly.

'He slew Michael one night with a look. I had been here alone, writing a letter in pencil, and Donizetti most charmingly brought me a stamp. When Michael came in, I told him about the stamp and, horribly, when we were paying our bill, he growled, "And thee *stahmp*?" Donizetti, the Swiss part of him, grew scarlet, and the Italian part sent a stiletto through Michael's heart, but I had gasped "Oh, *no*," just in time, and he turned his back on Michael and smiled his dimpled smile and took leave. He escorts me to tables and to the door in the most courtly fashion. And never talks. That is the comfort of him. I 've never heard him speak. Except to give orders down the lift, in Italian.'

While she went on to tell him the story of her first breaking in at Donizetti's, swiftly because other communications were crowding that would interest him, being impersonal, less and more than this one she was being able to tell so vividly because she had never told it before and felt now so full of life, he listened without any of his usual critical detachment.

'You 've got to switch over into journalism, Miriam. You 're wasting yourself. It 's risky, but you 're a courageous creature. You 've thrown up jobs and taken your chance. Achieved freedom. Most women would have been unthinkably battered by the life you 've led.'

'Oh, no. You don't know Mag and Jan. You *want* to think women are being bashed in industry. And there's no *courage* in the way I have thrown up jobs. Evasion—your favourite word—of responsibility. I don't want to go on earning my living as I do at Wimpole Street. The personal interest has gone out of it——'

'Hancock's married.'

'Just so. But I like his wife when her particular brand of trained intelligence, so much more painful in a woman than in a man, your kind, the kind that is unquestioningly obedient to the latest dicta of science, is in abeyance. But she is open-minded, much more open-minded than you are.' The smile was for her bad taste in abusing a pleasant occasion with unpleasant lies. 'She has no respect for, or at least is very wary of, the high priests of Harley Street. She would like to build the same kind of world as you would like to build. Run by electricity. But she would build it on dancing as much as on science. And by the way, here's an example, perfect, of the kind of blindness a thoroughly trained, scientific mind falls into. There are, you know, "mews" in Wimpole Street, mostly let to poor people because few of the doctors have carriages and some, of course, now, have cars. Well, when first she dawned as a Wimpole Street wife, she visited the mews belonging to the house. Wasn't that nice of her? And called on me in the office to tell me about it. Sat down and began, and went off into one of the queer little attacks of laughter with which she prefaces an amusing communication and that screw up her face as if she were in acute pain. Mental, critical laughter. So I knew I was not going to be able to agree. Because her kind of criticism and your kind of criticism of people who live in a different world is bound to be negligible. So I was free to be tormented by the spectacle of two worlds in collision. Dreadful, she found these poor people, and repeated *Dreadful*, screwing up her face like someone who is being agonized by a discordant sound, but really thoroughly enjoying herself. What she found dreadful was that in their awful, hopeless circumstances they were *trusting in Providence*. "Sitting still and trusting in *Providence*," she wailed, and again had an enjoyable agony. She has helped them without seeing that their trust was thereby justified.'

She had looked away, feeling that she would be beyond her depth if he objected with one of his witty sarcasms, and feeling at the same time a most desperate, unaccountable need to flout all evidence in this particular direction. But her mind whisked off and listened again to Amabel glowingly speaking of asking God to tea, not to consult Him but to share with Him her joy that could be expressed only in radiance and song . . ✓ and came back just in time to break across whatever it was he was saying—with the manner he used when responding, resignedly, to obstinate blindness, eyes fixed on a distant object at which he was not looking, lips compressed, narrowing his voice—with a remark that seemed to come to her out of the surrounding air:

'I know what you mean. Earthquakes. Famine. Hideous wholesale accidents. And what Englehart calls with such gusto "Industrial Maladjustments," all those things that make humanity look so helpless and make all you people call for a combined effort of human intelligence. Which may be all right. But death doesn't matter. And what I mean about these perhaps not highly intelligent people who trust in Providence is that they would go under still trusting: "Though Thou slay me" . . .'

'The personal interest,' she pursued hurriedly, reflecting that she could not tell what she really believed beyond the deep necessity for flouting evidence, 'is largely gone and the life does not use me. But every other way of living I can think of takes away something essential. Any kind of responsible work would. It may be wrong to evade responsibility. But I must. That's why I can't write for the *New Universe*. Even if, as you say, I could, and they would have me. It would mean taking sides.'

'You'll have to, in the end. Even Miretta can't browse all over the field for ever. It's committing yourself you're afraid of. Taking definite steps. You'll miss things. And live to regret it.'

'How can one miss things?'

'Mere existence isn't life.'

'Why *mere*?   Most people have too much life and too little realization.   Realization takes time and solitude.   They have neither.'

'You can't go through life feeling your pulse.'

'I'm not one of those people who boast that outsiders see most of the game.   I hate that.   And it isn't true.   What is true is that certain outsiders, I don't say I'm one of them, see *all* the game.   I believe that.   People who have never, in your sense, plunged into life.'

'Ee-yes.   Books.   Almost everything can be got from books.   Plus imagination.   I believe it's true of lots of women, it may be true of you, that homoeopathic doses of life are enough.   But have at least your homoeopathic dose.   You've had London.   Enormously.   But it'll end by wearing you down.   You want a *green solitude*.   An infant.   Then you'd be able to write a book.'

Tree-trunks, in woodland variety, standing in light dimmed by their full-leaved branches, came before her inward eye, and the London fever in her blood longed for the touch of the moist, deep air called up by his words.   And even as she thought of a little house whose little garden should lead down into a wood, she fled from it, finding it so full of his influence that there was no space wherein her own spirit could make its home.   But the words settled in her mind, the promise of a bourne to which she could see no possible path.

'No economics,' she said in answer to the secondary threat embodied in his offer.   'Whatever I do, no economics.   They shut things off.'

'Right.   No economics.   Unless temporarily.'   His smile, infected with amusement and with triumph, was directed down the length of the restaurant as if addressed confidentially to a humanity wiser and more experienced than herself.

And still the words, put together with his genius for putting the right words together, went on drawing into her mind remembered moments in cool gardens and shadowy woods that were all of one quality, so that many backgrounds were competing to represent it.

' . . . flat in town . . . leisure to write . . . country-house visits for holidays . . .' passed unsuccessfully across her preoccupation, each in turn emptied of reality by the over-shadowing influence that had driven her from the green solitude.

'Middles. You've masses of material for Middles. Criticism. You could do that on your head. Presently *novel*.'

The writing of a novel suggested only a pleasant, exciting, flattering way of filling a period of leisure and thereby creating more leisure. That was what it had seemed to be to all the writers she had met at the Wilsons'; and Michael had cried out against the modern way of regarding letters as a source of wealth.

And Hypo's emphasis suggested that the hideous, irritating, meaningless word *novvle* represented the end and aim of a writer's existence. Yet about them all, even those who left her stupefied with admiring joy, was a dreadful enclosure.

She saw Raskolnikov on the stone staircase of the tenement house being more than he knew himself to be and somehow redeemed *before* the awful deed one shared without wanting to prevent, in contrast to all the people in James who knew so much and yet did not know.

'Even as you read about Waymarsh and his "sombre glow" and his "attitude of prolonged impermanence" as he sits on the edge of the bed talking to Strether, and revel in all the ways James uses to reveal the process of civilizing Chad, you are distracted from your utter joy by fury over all he is unaware of. And even Conrad. The self-satisfied, complacent, know-all condescendingness of their handling of their material. Wells seems to have more awareness. But all his books are witty exploitations of ideas. The torment of *all* novels is what is left out. The moment you are aware of it, there is torment in them. Bang, bang, bang, on they go, these men's books, like an L.C.C. tram, yet unable to make you forget them, the authors, for a moment. It worries me to think of novels. And yet I'm thrilled to the marrow when I hear of a new novelist. *Clayhanger*, though I've not read it.'

'He's a realist. Documenting. You'd like Bennett. Perhaps

the novel's not your form. Women ought to be good novelists. But they write best about their own experiences. Love-affairs and so forth. They lack creative imagination.'

'Ah, imagination. Lies.'

'Try a novel of ideas. Philosophical. There's George Eliot.'

'Writes like a man.'

'Just so. Lewes. Be a feminine George Eliot. Try your hand.'

He was setting out the contents of the cruet as if they were pieces in a game—a lifetime might be well spent in annotating the male novelists, filling out the vast oblivions in them, especially in the painfully comic or the painfully tragic and in the satirists—and now moved them towards her with the air of a demonstrator intent on directing a blank and wavering feminine consciousness:

'*Middles*. *Criticism*, which you'd do as other women do fancy-work. *Infant*. NOVEL.'

His voice was dropped to the very low tone it took when he discussed what he liked to believe were improprieties.

But her interest had disappeared so completely that she went off in search of it. And at once found Amabel, sitting in judgment on her evening, horrified, laughing till her eyes were filled with tears.

'I'm preoccupied,' she said. 'Perpetually, just now, with one person.'

'Unfortunate for me,' he said, unmoved. 'Is this Amabel?'

'It's treasure, beyond your power of diagnosis. Beyond any one's power.'

She looked at Amabel through his eyes. And saw almost everything in her escape them. Her poses and mannerisms, that were second nature, he would amusedly accept as so many biological contrivances. And if he thought her 'pretty'— sacrilege, even in thought, to apply to Amabel this belittling expression that at this moment I see as part of his deliberate refusal to take any kind of womanhood seriously, and is not condoned by his protesting that neither does he take himself seriously—would play up to her as he does, as I have seen him do, with women who 'exploit' themselves; subtly conveying at the same time, to the simple female he saw behind the manœuvres, that he knew what she was about and that she was doing it rather well. But perhaps he would not even think her pretty.

'Do you understand those people, I suppose there are thousands, to whom country life without a carriage is misery? For me, the country is woods and certain kinds of fields. In light. A memory, for nearly all my holidays have been at the sea. But woods, like the German woods, and the Lake District, and the Yorkshire moors, and all the country I 've seen, always in company of people, mostly of people who pull up, wistfully, before a "fine view," have given me a homesickness. It may be that the person who insists on carriages, sees country life as country houses, wants me to feel that no country life could come up to the life we are having together in London.'

'Amabel?'

'On one side it is, I 've just realized, a sort of continuation of Oberland. She belongs to those people. Has a host of brothers in the Services. Titled relatives. All that sort of thing. But she 's broken away. Couldn't endure the life. Imagine a girl who used to climb down out of her bedroom window to go and swim in the lake by moonlight . . .'

'Alone?'

'Of course alone. Imagine her flying downstairs in the morning, so headlong that she couldn't stop, and crashed through the glass door of the vestibule. In the afternoon the door was mended. The next morning she crashed through again.'

'Excessive.'

'When she was sixteen, there is a demure photograph. She was engaged for a while; to a curate. She won't wait to speak of him. And I 'm not curious, only desperately interested, always, in her view of people, and I think I can see him and the way he grew smaller and smaller, until she could scarcely see him. Anyhow she made her people—all of whom she describes, by means of anecdotes, as if they were her contemporaries, so that you see them as they are, devoid of the wrappings of age and dignity; you see all round them and know exactly how they think and why they act as they do. It's rather terrible—made them send her to Paris, to study art. In speaking of Frenchwomen her voice grows devout and, because she is more Celtic than English, being partly Irish and partly Welsh, and has no sense of nationality, she became French. In manner and bearing. Her disapproval of English people is both Irish and French. In any social difficulty the Frenchwoman comes to the front. But intimately, she is Irish. Yet her brogue is as inaccurate as her French. No ear. But a strong sense of rhythm.'

'What is she doing now?'

Life with Amabel, in which she was more deeply immersed than in any shared living that had fallen to her lot, passed before her inward eye defying her to select any feature that more than any other would convey to him a sense of the quality pervading every moment of it.

Even the desire to convey seemed a kind of treachery to Amabel. Yet over everything that might pass between them the spirit of Amabel would hover, distracting, demanding statement. There was in the whole of her previous experience, that with all its restrictions of poverty and circumstance had seemed to him so rich and varied and in many respects so enviable, nothing that could compare with what Amabel had brought. Nothing could be better. No sharing, not even the shared being of a man and a woman, which she sometimes envied and sometimes deplored, could be deeper or more wonderful than this being together, alternating between intense awareness of the beloved person and delight in every aspect, every word and movement, and a solitude distinguishable from the deepest, coolest, most renewing moments of lonely solitude only in the enhancement it reaped by being shared.

If by some wordless magic she could convey to him the quality of that moment, coming in the midst of a conversation lasting for the whole of a Sunday morning from the time of wakening and seeing with the same eyes at the same moment, through the large uncurtained window, the wet grey roofs across the way—the Sunday following the evening at Mrs

Bellamy's gathering, where we were separated and mingling in various groups and observing the drama as one person after another 'took the floor' and expressed views, and suddenly met and were both filled with the same longing, to get away and lie side by side in the darkness describing and talking it all over until sleep should come without any interval of going off into the seclusion of our separate minds—and had been broken into by the shared events of our picnic lunch on the floor, and afterwards had gone on further and further from its origin until Amabel had sought out, to illustrate the world as it had shown itself to her in childhood, that little book of verses with coloured prints, lovely, deep in colour and simple in design, and as I looked at it, while she hunted· for another, I leaned my head back and for a few seconds was asleep for the first time in broad daylight, and woke so utterly refreshed that I said without thinking: 'This is the birthday of the world,' and, while she flew to fling herself down at my knees, I was back in the moment of seeing for the first time those flower-beds and banks of flowers blazing in the morning sunlight, that smelt of the flowers and was one with them and me and the big bees crossing the path, low, on a level with my face. And I told her of it and that it must have been somewhere near my third birthday, and her falling tears of joy and sympathy promised that never again should there be in my blood an unconquerable fever.

'She's very wary and a little scornful of all my people. Of all those I hand out. Wary of souls. Thinks the soul secondary. Coloured. Almost visible. Almost *fat*. The spirit is form. Original form. God. But really I think it's respectable, middle-class people she finds so laughable and intolerable. I think it must be. When I talk to her about my friends and my sisters and their husbands, though she was thrilled by Harriett's Canadian life, taking in "roomers," and her life in Cuba, riding about and growing pineapples, she is at once on the defensive. It may be that when I am trying to *describe* anything in return for all she has told me, she is bored by my *style*, because it becomes an imitation of hers—which I admire but which is a method of expression that does

not belong to what I want to convey and so conveys nothing at
all. You see she has been talking all her life and has all her
formulas ready-made at the tip of her tongue, and I 've been
silent nearly all my life, and when she looks at me as if she
wanted to say "What are all those people to me?" pats her hair
and hides her eyes with her lashes as if to conceal, or reveal,
her lack of interest, and tightly folds her lips together as if
keeping back something she won't let herself say, she is really
suffering from my insincerity.'

'What is her way of describing people?'

'But now and again I can strike her note by what at the
time seems a kind of inspiration, but really is the result of
being with her. For instance, it occurred to me to convey the
idea of somebody by saying on the spur of the moment that
the story of David and Bathsheba was the only scandal he
knew. She loved that. We both did. Had to stifle the yells
objected to by the woman in the room above mine, who finds
it trying enough that we talk from after dinner until the small
hours.'

'That was bright of you, Miriam.'

'Not at all. He is that kind of man, and I saw him, for a
moment, in her terms. I can't see my bourgeoisie, from whom
I have fled and fly, in any terms. But don't imagine she is
merely witty. She can be, if she wishes to. But has several
ways of repenting it. And buffoonery, which I love and excel
in, shocks her beyond words. So I usually refrain. When
I break out because I must, she watches me with affectionate
indulgence. She is witty with her man. Because it is the
only way of amusing him and filling the intervals. Tells him
tales, amusing tales throwing light on people, enlarging his
sense of people.'

'Scheherazade.'

'Incongruities amuse her. She can make them amuse me,
but has to wait for me to see the point and I can't, yet, for long,
or with any real satisfaction, keep my eye on that way of looking
at things. I am distracted by attending to her technique, and
by the sense that there is something about all these people
that is independent of her and outside her knowledge, some-

thing they can't express either to her or to themselves and that
I share and yet, when I am with her, I feel it is something we
ought to shake off and I know that for them as well as for me
the memory of her will be a challenge they can never get behind.'

'Is she pretty?'

'She denies it. It's useless to ask me. Her sense of
incongruity is well fed because every one in the house loves
her and confides in her. She brings it all to me. Without
any sense of betraying them, and simply because she loves to
watch people living and to share the spectacle. But it's only
incidentally that they and their affairs entertain us. She will
come in hysterical over some incident or other and presently
describe, giving every one the same voice. She can't imitate.
But usually . . .'

He had made a remark seeming to come from far away, and
inaudible because she was deafened by the shame of the
realization that in a moment she would have been telling him
of their silences, trying to tell him of those moments when they
were suddenly intensely aware of each other and the flow
of their wordless communion, making the smallest possible
movements of the head now this way now that, holding each
pose with their eyes wide on each other, expressionless, like
birds in a thicket intently watching and listening; but without
bird-anxiety.

'It has just occurred to me that birds, sitting side by side
with their sideways eyes, are *seeing* each other. Er—well . . .
she describes her own people racily, in a rather nice class-
dialect. Not either of those that keep the muscles of the face
almost unmoved. The one that turns "er" into "ah": matah,
patah, Africah, opening the mouth. Not *A*ya-fr'ca, with the
teeth closed.'

'How does she make all these boarding-house people love
her?'

'By loving them. She has the most real rare love for the
essential human being. Even for the people she sees through.
And a deep, unusual respect and solicitude. For what to you
is nothing or next to nothing: the personal life in everybody.
She must already have more individuals, more personal lives,

clear and vivid in her consciousness, than most people have muddled and dull in their consciousness in a whole lifetime. Like a confessor. She, too, confesses everything, the most impossible things. That's why I love her; for her courage.'

'You make me jealous. You've never been moved about me.'

'Oh, I have. But it is so utterly different. There's a barrier. Less with some men than with most. But always there. Amabel agrees. Is always uneasy, even when blissfully happy, with her man.'

'Men and women are incompatible. It's one of life's little difficulties. How does she account for her uneasiness?'

'She has a kind of affection for it. Regards the colossal unawareness of a man as an amiable defect. But she agrees, although she finds it also screamingly funny, that the way all down the ages men have labelled their sexual impulses "woman" is quite monstrous. We spent an evening and half a night thinking out a world in which men should be properly educated. Very stern, detached priestesses for youth. Stern artists.'

'No priests?'

'They were a difficulty. Which in the end we left. The dedicated priestesses would, of course, have to acquire their own education and experience. They would have to be specialists and not specialists, something more easy of achievement for women than for men.'

'Have you told her about me?'

'I've hinted at you. She demurs. Hesitates. Not through jealousy. But although she has a horror of *les pieds jaunes des vieilles filles* she won't admit that I'm qualifying to join that army. Thinks I don't need experience and should make a good thing of being an invalid on a sofa for the rest of my life, talking and being talked to.'

'That's great nonsense. She's surrounding you too much. What you want is to take hold of life as she has done. Things won't *come* to you.'

'But they do. Over and over again, just as I've learned to

be happy with nothing, they have come.   Given me something I wanted and disappeared.'

'You have shoved them away.'

'To get back.'

Approaching the house that now was nothing but a casket for Amabel, her thoughts returned to him gone away with a shadowy idea of Amabel's quality and a definite picture of two young women engrossed in one of those mysterious sudden intimacies that precede the serious affairs of life and end, 'at the touch of reality,' as swiftly as they had begun.   She had told him nothing of Amabel seriously investigating Socialism, taking it in her stride, approving, accepting.   Going to suffrage meetings, being converted by the lacy, delicate old-fashioned ladyhood of Mrs Despard to militancy, writing at once to her people, of their immediate stoppage of her allowance and her weeks of work as Mrs Bailey's drudge, from six in the morning to nine at night, of the rescuing brother, and the way she now lived in her room with her books and her Empire china on almost nothing but bread and milk.

The story would have fired him.   But it seemed secondary to what she had tried to tell.

CHAPTER X

'WE don't want you to go, dearest. We'll be dwedfully lonely when you're gone.'

The golden evening had not lasted long enough to attain the distances of the room that came in sight as she rose unsteadily from her chair by the fireside. They looked cold and morning-like, left with this morning's influence upon them, away in the time before her arrival; waiting for to-morrow.

Hypo got up with the light little hoisting movement that landed him poised in readiness to turn in any direction.

'Yes,' he said, belatedly extending a judicial finger: 'Susan's right. Wisdom's the only way with colds, Miretta. You've been no end good. And if we're not firm *now*, you'll go on outdoing yourself until the smaller hours, and wake shattered. We don't want you to wake shattered.'

Moving backwards towards the door with her eyes on the two who together made all she was leaving, she saw rising in her mind's eye behind them and this room they had made, their other rooms, their earlier selves, back and back, a single clear pattern of endeavour and achievement. Never before in their close presence had their past presented itself for contemplation. It was bringing sadness into this small farewell, giving it a kind of finality. She had rounded the angle and reached the door and they had come forward from the room's centre that now was out of sight, and were leaning side by side over the back of the settee, seeing her off, turned towards her with their mystery, a circle drawn about them and their life of linked experience that none could enter.

'Good night then, darlings,' she said lightly. Sleep thickened her voice. Solitude, pouncing upon her from the empty lounge, brought to-night no promise of to-morrow.

'That's the right sound for to-night, Miriam. It's that wise whisky. You'll be snoring in a trice.'

And to-night the bright fire warming the fresh air of her room was not a mere afterthought of the one downstairs. Its sprouting flames claimed attention like a host welcoming a guest arrived for the evening. And the familiar room seemed strange, newly seen, refusing to be focused without inspection. She moved from part to part, half expecting a hitherto un-noticed door that would open upon an unknown scene. Fore-most in her mind was the shapely little blaze to which in a moment she turned back. The many-clawed flames dancing upon the black upper surfaces of the lumps whose undersides were mingled in the fiery central mass, jigging, shuddering, as if trying to wrench themselves free and escape up the chimney, were like *holly leaves.*

Within the small pang of delight in the recognition of the nature of a superficial resemblance she had noted a thousand times without finding a name for it, was disquietude. In some subtle way, whose fruits were uncertain, she was different from the one who in the past had ignored the flames escaping up-wards to concentrate upon the glowing interior: its caverns and its molten distances.

But since the early days there had not been many open fires burning freely, offering themselves in quietude, for contem-plation. In Hanover, the porcelain stoves. At Banbury Park, slow fires carefully banked. At Newlands, and in the houses of friends, large fires that were an inseparable part of the ceaseless magic behind the coming and going of events and moods. At Wimpole Street, no coal fires save the one in Mr Hancock's room whose genial glow seemed to emanate from and call attention to his kindly presence. . . .

The thought of fires at home recalled little but the remem-bered comfort of winter warmth.

Alone in the doorway of a downstairs room, with the dark hall and the endless staircase behind her, she stood looking into heaven. On the hearth, within the glow of a wide flame-less fire whose radiance came out into the twilight unhampered by the high guard standing like a fence all round the nursery fire and keeping it far away, stood a copper kettle, quiet and bright and beautiful, telling, more plainly than a voice could speak, of the world surrounding the uncertainties of nursery life, kind and careful and peaceful and full of love and forgiveness, now, when no one was there, and making her know that this was what it really was when every one was there.

Farther on, again from the doorway of an empty room, but from the known midst of the heaven of downstairs life, from the midst of joyous confident possession of the beloved house and garden, one other fire: wide and clear behind polished brass bars, radiant rose and gold against the pure cream and turquoise of the tiles, whereon, just inside the marble rim of the hearth, in the combined rapturous light thrown back by the high walls with their pale delicately blended ivory and blue, of fire and the chandelier's bright blaze softened by globes of patterned amber and rose and primrose, and the festal beams of the candles shining down from the high, mirrored girandoles, the square-shouldered bottle of chartreuse stood warming its green mystery.

Only these two; glowing eternally.

From the undesired effort of recalling more than these spontaneous offerings of memory, that promised if she lingered with them to recall in perfect fullness the years lying beyond the barrier raised by the horror that had wrenched her life in twain, her mind slipped back to the holly leaves, remarking that unawares, in the recent past, she had rounded an unseen corner, grown observant and therefore detached. Even here, in this house. To-night, for the first time, her separate existence was consciously prevailing against its glamour, reaching forward away from it to something that would set it in the past.

The gift of the third reprieve that for this evening at least had restored to her the self that since his near approach had almost slept in his presence. A self unhappy, yet full of a strange inexhaustible joy that at this moment was celebrating the foiling of her enterprise.

Yet who could know, who could say? These foilings might be challenges to determination, perversity of fate to be overcome. *No.*

Who could know, who could say?

To regard them as the work of 'chance' would be to ignore their strange punctuality, seeming like blessed evidence of purpose at work. But to follow these hints at all costs, would be to become definitely religious. And to what system of religion could she definitely belong? Everywhere was darkness and challenge. Right and wrong, pointing now this way and now that, offered no help.

The brush, rhythmically moving through the length of her hair from the warm roots to where the ends spread outwards away from it and crackled in the air, worked on in the void that already had driven the evening far away. Glancing for reassurance into the mirror lit softly from above by a frosted bulb, she met eyes that were not those she knew when, coming suddenly upon them in solitude, she caught, just before recognition and the direct gaze, a distant, serene preoccupation like that of a stranger passing in the street. These eyes were caught still glowing with the radiance of social happiness that in a moment vanished to give place to the troubled gaze of one considering a single thought now beating up from the fullness of these recent years that had seemed to bury all that went before: what would life amount to if these links were severed?

Amabel. But Amabel will move on. And remain with me for ever, a test, presiding over my life with others. She stands permanently in my view of life, embodying the changes she has made, the doors she has opened, the vitality she has added to my imagination of every kind of person on earth. And stands, too, insisting on marking the boundary, where she falls short and is in awe of me: of my 'wisdom' and, strangely, the strangest of all her ascriptions, of my 'gift of speech.'

She adores people. Turns them inside out, changes them and moves on, to other people. Basil's friend, already, having seen some of her letters to Basil, is at her feet. An old, distinguished man, running all his life in a single, distinguished groove. And now, at the end of it, confiding, confessing, facing judgment on his lifelong unconscious mental and moral blindness, judgment that emanated from her of itself.

Above her affectations and poses. Above her lies which she admits, and yet claims truthfulness. And is truthful.

Truthful English people are untruthful because they don't know themselves, self-conscious because they don't know themselves. And don't love as Amabel loves. Yet there is something they know and share all the time even in their most formal relationships. A deep, common understanding existing at the heart of English hypocrisy that makes it a relief to turn from her to people who fall so far below her native standards. A deep quality that comforts.

It had been present at home, a tolerant, liberal atmosphere in a conservative home, unrecognized until it was left behind. In the English girls in Hanover, in the Pernes, unconsciously prevailing over the horde of raw girls from 'Olloway, 'Ighbury, 'Ackney, 'Arringay and 'Ornsey, English too, but seeming of a different race from those who lived on the southern side, with its soft-sounding names . . . Sydenham . . . Wimbledon . . . Richmond . . .

In the Corries. In the Orlys and Mr Hancock and the majority of their patients. In all kinds of Oberlanders . . . of all classes?

And all the others, the German girls and the north-country Brooms, Irish Julia Doyle, the Tansley Street people and Michael and radical Mag and cynical Jan, had been adventures outside the world where that deep quality persisted.

But the old-world people, newly-dear since Oberland, can be lived with only at the cost of pretending to think as they do. Not to think, but to live entirely in reference to tradition and code. Sooner or later, they discover that you belong mentally elsewhere as well as to them, and you become an object of suspicion.

And the anarchists and Lycurgans bring sooner or later the feeling of living in a void.

Yet if the links with them were cut, there was no life ahead.

Only the lonely joy that comes and goes.

The air was growing still. The fire had died down. Marking an end. Taking the evening away while still it stood on the horizon.

The little bed was chill, and when the light went out the darkness glowed a feverish red.

All my life, since the beginning, I've left things standing on the horizon.

The two big Eckersleys, Selwyn and Mark, great big men out in life—yet they must have been in their early twenties, not much older than Sarah and Eve—big and kind, going gently about and talking in deep voices, gently, surrounded by the darkness of their unknown lives, playing card-games with Sarah and Eve in the drawing-room on Boxing Day. Trying to think of things to say to the children, Miriam and Harriett. When Selwyn asked me if I'd taken part in the church decorations, it was because I felt while I stared at him that his idea of church had nothing to do with my experiences of All Saints', that nobody who had not been to All Saints' and heard Harry Dancey play the organ, knew anything about church; that I saw, for ever, Harriett and me, the year before, pushing the wheelbarrow to the church-room full of sooty, bitter-smelling evergreens, and said 'I'm going to,' and realized, as soon as I'd spoken, that Christmas was over, and glared at him and saw him blush and wonder if the child was an idiot, and went on speaking to him, in my mind, to get past the awful shame, telling him he shouldn't suddenly speak because he thought he ought to say something to his host's smaller daughters, and that the time he thought it might please me to be asked about was *still there*. But it wasn't and, when I realized that, I felt hopelessly guilty and sad. And yet comforted by *knowing* that I rejoiced in things, even when I took no part, more deeply than the others. So much, that though I missed them when they came I still rejoiced and imagined I hadn't missed them.

Mother would give me the invitations to children's parties to answer and tell me to answer them and I would read 'requests the pleasure of the company of' beautifully printed on a glazed card, and 'Dancing 8–12' again and again and go off into dreams, and only remember to answer when the day before the party suddenly arrived; and all the while the party itself stood in my mind, left there, in exactly the same place on the horizon as when I had first contemplated it. I put things on the horizon and leave them there.

'Quite so, Miriam,' he would say, and ultimately turn away. But he doesn't yet know, to the full, all the discrepancies. I do. I am the guilty party, because I know them and keep them from him. Let him think I fully believe in his and Alma's new social order. Does Alma fully believe it? Did she license us against his personal beliefs? On principle?

Warmth crept into her limbs. Through the darkness that now was cool and black she watched again the strangeness of this afternoon's sea-shallows encroaching upon lying snow. The sight of it had stemmed his discourse and, in that moment of side-by-side pause and observation, there had seemed to be a future of side-by-side. It was only in being physically or mentally confronted that the barriers rose. Agreement of mind or body would be treachery and disaster. Not to any person, but to something of which he was unaware. To join forces with him and appear fully to accept his point of view for the sake of the experience and the enhancement of personal life it would bring, would be treachery . . . to him and to life?

I'm a free-lover. Of course I'm a free-lover. But not his. On the horizon.

Yet in that moment by the sea, after his voice had sounded his affectionate delight and approval of the unusual spectacle, there had been a feeling of innocence that could face the spheres. For a long moment they had stood, watching the way each fan-shaped shallow spread slowly forward and ate with its bubbled edge a little farther into the snow than the last.

There had been something else. The sudden thought, during that moment when he had forgotten both himself and her, of Alma, of the innumerable sharings they must have had of things come upon suddenly, in walks, in travelling together. Of Alma's capacity for pulling up, silently, and going forth in adoration and presently, very gently, paying just the right tribute.

Perhaps long-married people, in the midst of their course, cannot see things together. . . . Was that what he meant when he said Alma's no good for a walk?

Married people cannot walk together. Or only very few. The man always seems to be straining away. Sideways-a-little-ahead. So that he can see his surroundings and escape into them from the ceaseless reminder of his mirror?

She called up married faces seen when a party of walkers were arrested and silenced for a moment by a beautiful spectacle. The sounding of the voice of either of the pair would bring to the face of the other, who for a moment had escaped into the joy given by beauty, the expression of one suddenly jerked back into himself.

But he and Alma are not deeply domesticated. They deliberately set themselves to live independently as well as together.

In a moment he was talking again, pleased and enlivened. Listening to the happiness in his voice, catching at his jests, ignoring what they held of misrepresentation and unfairness, I experienced him as so often I have seen him experienced by passing guests too much under the spell to be aware, until afterwards, of their own repudiations, or dissembling them in order to go on being amused, and I wondered, alone for a second with my sea and my sky limitless, as they were before I had heard them scientifically defined, whether, if the future should bring times of unbroken association, I could sustain, as all those about him now invariably appear to do, the only role that would ensure the persistence, in his voice, of self-confident happiness.

. . . *Rievaulx*. The roadway gone. Green turf and trees and space and the party scattering. Drawn forward and separated, gladly escaping from each other yet more together than when they had been walking along the road. Rounding the bend above the valley, expectant. Rievaulx suddenly there below us, on the floor of the green valley. Heart-melting love and gratitude, even before I had walked on alone along the level made in the rising ground round about it, like a promenade, at just the right distance for seeing this left message, and seeing at different angles the oblong of crumbling stone, arch beside arch, in each of its different perfections, towards those who long ago had expressed in this perfection their own perfect certainties and their enduring joy, and to those, in whom deep down these certainties and this joy were still persisting, who had brought me to see it and, though they lingered at the far end, instead of rambling worshipfully round, and saw it only in one perspective, as if the first shock of its silent beauty were enough, had for ever seen it and would testify, if only in the tones of their voices when they spoke its name, to what they had seen.

After the too-long walk, grey sky, heavy August trees, deepening indifference to an abbey that must be visited and would be exhibited by Edmund, offered with an air of proprietorship. Extremity of endurance. At last the turning away from the dusty road, the end in sight, late afternoon stealing upon us, bringing back the sense of an abiding presence in people and in things, bringing the promised wealth of to-morrow to support to-day's returning wealth, and setting, with the coming of the grass and the end of the sound of trudging footsteps, every one deep in holiday. Voices, linking the party come to life in the remote stillness that made each familiar figure again miraculous; attractive, going softly forward over the grass.

Rievaulx brought forgetfulness and a harvest of happiness. So that the party who had seen, and then wandered away to seek a farmhouse tea, was not the party setting out from the inn to see Rievaulx.

. . . Sound of the edge of a dream crashing in the night-dark curtained room.

At whose farther end a pale glimmer came in from the little top window with its curtain drawn back. Blotted out, as she watched it, by a darkness, a figure close at hand.

'I'm not here,' she said, searching the dreamy void for something beyond mere indignation over this adroit arrival.

'It's a wicked night. I perish with cold. You've a window wide open.'

The dark obstruction became a moving shape. With a soft flop the flourished toga reached the floor.

Alienated by exasperation with the deliberate trickery, drawn by solicitude for his exposure to the cruelty of the night, she held out draperies.

It was uncanny, but more absorbing than the unwelcome adventure of her body, to be thus hovering outside and above it in a darkness that obliterated the room and was too vast to be contained by it. An immense, fathomless black darkness through which, after an instant's sudden descent into her clenched and rigid form, she was now travelling alone on and on, without thought or memory or any emotion save the strangeness of this journeying.

Whose end came in a light that seemed the pale light of dawn. She was up at the high, glimmering window, saw clearly its painted woodwork and the small blemishes upon the pane against which she was pressed; through which, had it been open, she felt she could have escaped into the light that had called her thither.

His relaxed form was nothing to her. A mass of obstructive clay from which the spirit had departed on its way to its own bourne. Its journey, foolishly undertaken through her fault in hiding, failing to communicate their essential unrelatedness, had been through a familiar pleasure into restful nothingness that presumably would bear the fruit he sought therefrom.

The robed figure stood over her like a short doctor: flattering, warning, trying to edit her mind. His words brought into the room the feeling of broad daylight and if now she could leap back into life, get a dressing-gown, revive the fire and play his game by launching into a discussion of possible features for *The Cosmic Rushlight*, he would be launched at once in his lately chosen role of emotional detachment and free of the uncertainty that was dictating his series of tests.

For a moment, unable to determine whether her impulse was heroic saintliness or base betrayal and self-interest, she hung over the possibility. But anything that conversation might produce would be less interesting than that strange journeying whose memory clamoured to have him gone.

He was going, gathering up his toga with the movement of departure. Impossible that he would go, taking away with him, without even being aware of its presence, the soft light surrounding them by which she could see the outlines of his movements.

'I 'm not here,' she said abruptly as he bent towards her, and the sound of her voice went past him out into the dark spaces and left her more separated from him than in the unshared journeying.

'You 'll come back,' he said, standing upright. 'Don't, Miretta'—the word-seeking tone of every day, with its note of protesting exposition—'*don't* attach importance to these inevitable preliminaries.'

She listened for the closing of the door. It made no sound. Yet his silent coming had wakened her like the crash of thunder.

And the return of solitude and dense night darkness within which the glimmer from the far-off high window was no longer visible, banished her preoccupation with the interior reality of her adventure and left her at the mercy of the judgment on her behaviour since like thunder his coming had awakened her, now being flung at her by consciousness. Scornful, reasonable, unanswerable.

Fully consenting to the judgment, and the acid commentaries, turning back to the betrayed and banished past and forward to a horizon swept blank and featureless, she awaited the welling of appropriate emotion. But the power she felt the presented facts ought to wield, and might possibly yet attain, failed to emerge from them. Within her was something that stood apart, unpossessed. From far away below the colloquy, from where still it sheltered in the void to which it had withdrawn and whence it had set forth alone upon its strange journeying, her spirit was making its own statement, profanely asserting the unattained being that was promising, however, faintly, to be presently the surer for this survival. Joining forces with it, using her will to banish the lingering images, she felt herself sink towards sleep.

Drawing back the curtain from the open lattice, she found in the outside scene no escape from the lifelessness of the room. The garden, sunlit beyond the shadow of the house, the blue sea behind the daffodils screening the edge of the downward slope; expressionless.

The world was changed. And perhaps this repellent bleakness was the truth lying beneath the bright surface she had mistaken for reality.

Seeking refuge in imagined, distant scenes, she found their faces wan, and glanced with dismay along the endless years to be lived out in a dead world. But even dismay failed her, remained cold and lifeless, like the features of the room.

At the edge of her circle of vision as she stood before the mirror with arms raised to her head and eyes intent upon the shaping of her hair, birds appeared, three moving specks far off in the farther corner of the scene framed by the open window. Without shifting her gaze she saw them as they came forward downwards towards the centre of the sky. In the form of an elongated triangle they flashed by near at hand and disappeared beyond the window's nearer rim. And the sight of them as they passed had smitten through her as though she were transparent and left her thrilled from head to foot with the sense of having shared their swift and silent flight.

And as surprising and as new as this vivid experience was the way she had taken it: noting it in passing and, while exultantly her consciousness declared that last night's lonely journey through uninhabited darkness had carried her into a way of being that would find its own responses in this dead-seeming world, going on doing her hair.

As breakfast proceeded, it seemed certain his preoccupation was not assumed. In his eyes, directly facing the morning light pouring in through the wide windows, was meditation, fusing the grey and the blue and giving them the characteristic blind gaze, caught by Ritch in the portrait, showing only a single luminously gleaming point focused upon the invisible distance wherein his thoughts were at work.

In a way that kept him all the more sharply aware of his immediate surroundings: of Alma intent on preserving the occasion from complete silence by intermittent gay monologue to which he responded, without drawing in his distant gaze more often than was made necessary by attention to his

breakfast, with brief appreciative flippancy, just enough to keep
things going short of launching into table-talk; and of herself
who could not be counted upon to follow even the most unmistakable clue, and had the socially inconvenient habit of
going off on long journeys and leaving her thoughts in her
face.

She stood at the window regarding the expressionless sea,
listening to the after-breakfast sounds: the whoof of the swing-
door off the lounge, the banging of distant doors as the maids
swiftly accomplished their upstairs work in the brief interval
allowed for disturbances.

Alma came in and, as they talked, she heard his voice go
cheerfully humming through the lounge, and the closing of
the study door.

It was now or never for the cheery greeting he did not
deserve. Departing to his morning without even the usual
inquiry as to how hers was to be spent, he deserved, on emerging
later, to find her meanwhile returned to town. But this morning's strange, rich harvest belonged in a sense to him, and
demanded some kind of expressiveness. A handshake, a small
solo dance in the window-space before the morning's separation.

Alma was going, obstructive, down the room . . . through
the lounge . . . into the study. . . .

With her eyes on the inaccessible interior whence he might
yet come forth before settling down for the morning, or which
yet, if Alma did not stay too long, might be the scene of the
dance now urgent in all her limbs and whose moment was
already passing, she ran up the short flight of stairs and halted
to look out through its landing window upon the neglected
backward view: houses, grey seaside villas climbing the hill,
a small, ancient omnibus ascending so slowly that it scarcely
seemed to move; but moving, alive.

In a moment she heard rising towards her, its repellent
message a little muted by the closed door, the sound heard
rapturously on so many summer mornings: music . . . a
Beethoven allegro being wound off clear and note-perfect.
The prelude to work.

Coming downstairs, she saw Alma emerge from the study

and make for the servants' quarters, radiant with the certainty of a good day launched.

Aware of the futility of her action, she pulled up at a book-shelf and stood surveying the tightly packed volumes. More than ever remote and unreal were the suggestions emanating from the titles of the unread books, and for the hundredth time she wondered what it was that made so many people appear to cherish them more than anything on earth and to be unaware as they sat outside life, reading them, of the revealing aura about their persons.

Choosing a volume whose fine binding and clear letterpress set well within the wide margins of its almost square pages gave it a comforting companionable air, she carried it off and sat down with it in a window-seat and at once became aware of herself sitting there, prominent in a room she had no desire to occupy; putting in time. She could scarcely believe it was herself who this morning, ages ago, had been up with the birds in their sky.

The memory brought her to her feet. The decorative book, abandoned in the corner, because there was no time to restore it to its place, would be a lying testimony to an interest that had never existed.

But out in the lounge she was again held up by the barriers standing right and left within this haunted house.

On her way upstairs she breathed wider air, felt in advance the influence coming from her room of things stored there that knew her in another life. With the touch of the door-knob upon her hand came a vision of garments whose fabric and tone and make would utterly transform her and that somehow before the spring had fully come and gone she would acquire. One gown, at least, would be possible, the room announced now that she was within it: a *Viola* gown, with a yet more strange and subtle combination of colours in its embroideries than the Persian blue and green and mauve. . . .

Viola, Miss Green and Miss Jones, would let her have it, only too gladly, for gradual payments. . . . *Afraid to wake in the night because at once their hearts were beating with anxiety.*

All over England there must be people living like that. Working anxiously all day and afraid to wake at night. To be happy in the clothes they made, and not to share their perpetual anxiety, is unfair. . . .

At lunch, Alma was still radiant. Her thrilled and smiling voice, the glow that made her carefully chosen clothes seem to have assembled upon her by happy chance, her talk, leaping deftly from point to point—all these were sure testimonies to the goodness of his day.

He sat at ease, a neatly plump Silenus with intelligent brow, played upon by Alma's happy radiance. Basking, jesting to laugh and produce laughter. And, all the time, blissfully preoccupied with the sense of work well and easily done, with work ahead ?

The sound of the opening door.

Through the window, she watched the old, lost enchantment flow back into sea and sky and garden.

'Dearest'—it was Alma, advancing swiftly down the room —'the dressmaker's arrived with her bag of tools. You'll be happy, playing alone, until tea-time ?'

Alma knew where he was, what he was doing, was quite innocently playing the part of kind hostess providing alternatives for the central entertainment.

'I'm going out,' she said, thankful, as the beating of her heart shook her voice, for Alma's experience of her varying moods, and adding—for after all it might be she who was about to play truant and he might presently be searching the house for her, cheerfully expecting the usual walk—'if Hypo won't think me unsociable.'

Alma halted, as if at a loss, as if puzzled. After *years* of visits and afternoon walks . . .

'Oh,' she said, almost fiercely, in a tone lower and deeper than that of her daily voice and coming from the depths of a self persisting from early days but taught by life to keep out of sight, '*he* won't notice.' And turned away. A gust of bitterness, sadness . . . and she was gone, as if herself fleeing before it, without another word.

He was not at work. Ostentatiously, he was making this

gesture of withdrawal. Had not even given Alma a cue for one of her tactful misrepresentations.

Methodically, deliberately, he was leaving her to herself. To demonstrate a principle: elimination of the personal. She might consider herself either the victim or the honoured partner in this demonstration for whose sake he was leaving her equally cut off from the resources of her far-away London life and from the life down here that he well knew was centred, throughout its brevity, upon himself.

Her anger ranged out over the world which was too small to contain it, out into space, vainly seeking relief.

To let it wear itself out unexpressed would be humiliation, in her person, not of herself alone, but also of something quite impersonal, sternly and indignantly demanding vengeance.

But the desire for vengeance was not in full possession, or she would now be facing him. . . . He would go on playing his part: would rise, with a cheerful impersonal greeting, describe his employment, inquire her plans. She would confront his pose until it passed from simulated concentration to simulated protest against her failure to recognize the compliment he was paying. And would presently embark on his theme: the right, intelligent way of managing life's incompatibilities. He would become affectionate, with reservations. Repulsed, he would really wish her away, would yearn for Alma and his screened inaccessibility. And would not be capable of knowing that it was something far beyond sympathetic affection that she was desiring. Something as detached and impersonal as even he could wish: a sharing. But a sharing of intimations he refused to recognize.

He was an alien. To Alma, to any woman ever born he was an alien.

That was why last night she had voyaged away alone through the living darkness, and why at this moment her desire to face him with judgment that knew itself to come from life's infallible centre, was imperfectly possessing her, half-heartedly struggling with her sense of being already far away out there in the landscape.

Yet when she shut behind her the garden door and greeted

in spite of herself the air coming from over the sea, her wrath turned upon the craven feet retreating from its object.

Out of sight, wandering down the terraces, she felt anger loosen its hold. It was not anger that was noting the pitiful heads of the ranged spring flowers, swaying in the wind.

In dismay she gazed at their brief moment, their nothingness. . . . The old, immeasurable depth of the seasons had departed from her being. She could see now, in one glance, the whole year, years, circling. And the house, invisible away behind her, meeting her imagination as it recoiled from the revelation of the flowers, had lost its solidity, become a frail and porous structure crumbling upon the plot of earth it mapped into rooms to shelter a few briefly living people.

Half-way through the jungle leading to the fence and its gate, with the sea vanished but audibly approaching, she found her thoughts turning backward with a relieving gentleness. . . . He is a sensual doctrinaire. Torn between his senses and his ideas. *Really* trying to make his liveliest senses serve his doctrines. People are nothing to him but the foolish hope of an impossible unanimity at the service of his plan. Therefore he demands stoical disregard of the personal. All his women play up to this. . . . Pretend to accept his idea of them as subsidiary. Prevent his recognition of them as a different order of consciousness. He is as fatal to the feminine consciousness as it would be, if it were articulate, to his plan. To the element in his plan which regards what is as worthless, in comparison with the future as he imagines it, not seeing that in its turn it will come under the same ban for those who care for nothing but 'progress.'

Here was the roadway. For the first time she was walking along it alone, disguised as a Bonnycliffer out for a constitutional, unsupported, unable at a moment's notice, to take root in this world that she knew by everlasting experience was supplying, even in a single afternoon, accommodation for roots.

The bay opened with sound: the invisible edge of the sea beating upon the beach, trying in its remembered way to bring summer to her mind; bringing only the sense of the to and fro of its tides from coast to coast.

Into the sea's sound came another, rapidly approaching: the jingle of the coast-tram. Tinkling local sound, a reminder, coming faintly from the distance through the windows of the house on the cliff, of villa-life going on down below. But this afternoon, heard in solitude at close quarters, it hailed her from Hanover, from north London, from within the self that was unknown to those in the house on the cliff, and to whom it offered the blessed refuge of its universal hospitality.

Through the sliding door she escaped into the welcome of reflected light, into an inner world that changed the aspect of everything about her. When the tram moved off, the scenes framed by the windows grew beautiful in movement. The framing and the movement created them, gave them a life that was not the life of wild nature only. They lost their new pathos. Watching them, she was out in eternity, gliding along, adding this hour to the strange sum of her central being that now, with the remainder of the afternoon accounted for by the coast-ride and the return, looked with indifference upon the evening coming almost too soon and, although rich with a deep intensity of golden light, seeming secondary. A superfluity she could forgo without loss.

It seemed as if daylight rather than night were standing outside the drawn curtains. Yet everything was as usual. The room, the two figures, the golden light. But between them and herself was this strange numbness, complete, impossible to break, wrapping her like a cloak, pressing upon and isolating her in bleak daylight.

Time passed by, bringing no change in her condition, no lessening and no increase of this extraordinary numbness. Every sound and word and movement, even her own words and movements were coming to her as if from a distance and failing to reach her isolation. The warm richness of evening was an illusion, slain. This was normality. She must learn to endure it. To endure endless evenings stripped of evening glamour.

For the first time she was seeing herself as she had seen countless women in the past, wondering over their aridity of mind and spirit. Now she understood them, was sharing the cold clarity of their vision. Sharing their desire for an occupation for empty hands, for something to justify the space they occupied in the room and supply a screen for their thoughts and an escape from the pressure of life swept clear of the illusion of friends and festivities; of life whose end shows clearly beyond an unvarying succession of evenings spent in knitting away the hours that led to sleep and the next day.

'Would Miriam like, should we all like, a toon, to finish the evening?'

Looking up to follow his spectral movement across to the shelves where the records were stacked up that belonged to the old life, she saw, between his retreating form and herself, Alma beaming a sleepy-eyed benediction upon a good day. For a moment she felt as if some word of theirs might break the power that held her. But they were too far off; alien.

He had switched on the light and stood clear within it, signalling to her with his look of delighted guilt. Playing his foolish game.

'Something quite short, I think.'

He came back down the room, casket in hand.

'Have a parting cigarette, Miretta.'

The room was shut out by the darkness of his figure bent towards her, warm and near. She took the proffered cigarette and as the light flared between them and lit his flushed and guilty face, to which her eyes had turned only for curious investigation, she saw again the strange darkness of last night's voyaging. He moved away and with an icy shudder her numbness passed from her, leaving her alive, ready to plunge into the beginning of an endless golden evening; too late. Again she was paying the price of his methodical calculations.

All the places she had known came unsummoned before her mind's eye with an intimate new warmth of welcome, each equally near and accessible and equally remote; so far away that several could be focused at once, pictured for a moment in their places before they moved and mingled in a confusion of impressions all joyously claiming the same quality: a freshly plumbed interest that promised to have increased when again she should drop back into them in an interval such as was being provided by the journey. That brought her to London without any sense of transition from one place to another.

Pulling up face to face with her hansom was one that had come from the opposite direction. Its occupant leapt forth as she leapt forth and they stood within a yard or two of each other paying their respective fares and together ascended the wide steps of number fifty-two. Last week she would have been tiresomely interested in him, disapproving or approving. Standing, if he were acceptable, in a momentary wordless communion with him, posing if he were preposterous in either of the many ways men had of being preposterous, in direct opposition to his shallow ideas. To-day he was revelation. Without even wishing to observe, she felt him there pursuing the shape of his life that held no unshared mystery, wishing her well as she wished him well. Disadvantage had fallen from her and burden, leaving a calm delightful sense of power. Lightly she stepped across the threshold and found the familiar scene unreproachful; shrunk in all its proportions. Immediate things had lost their hold. Going through the hall, she was obliged forcibly to call her mind to them, to draw it back from where it had roved while she has stood upon the steps comfortably ignoring the revealing young man, away down the street, down through her London, her beloved territory, without let or hindrance. And instead of creeping to her accustomed place half wondering whether it were her duty to explain and risk disgrace, she was full of inward song and wishing for congratulations.

CLEAR HORIZON

TO
S. S. KOTELIANSKY

CHAPTER I

BETWEEN herself and all that was waiting to flow in and settle upon this window-lit end of the long empty room, was the sense of missing Lionel Cholmley. She realized his quality now more sharply than when he had been in the house, and felt his influence like a dropped mantle it would be very pleasant to assume if there were any possible way of making it fit. She was almost yearning for him. Almost willing to sacrifice breakfast-time solitude for the sake of his presence. Every one lingered in this room for a while, after leaving the house. Faintly. But his gentle image was clear and strong. There he sat, on his first evening, at the far end of the table at Mrs Bailey's right hand. Slightly beaky nose pressing ahead into life, uncogitative; rather prominent, expressionless china-blue eyes; round cherub head, closely fitted with soft, fine curls not too closely cropped, gleaming satiny-gold in the gas-light. Looking well-bred, a suddenly arrived oasis of quality. Mr Pewtress had been nearly opposite, between ancient, dilapidated Miss Reid waiting for a chance of describing toll-gate Bloomsbury, and sour Miss Elliot glancing about for material for sarcasm, mopping his moustache after his soup, looking relieved, his brow free from the little pleat of suppressed irascibility always inhabiting it at meal-times, looking almost hopeful in the cheering presence of a newcomer who might perhaps be counted upon to rescue his own conversational sallies from their daily fate of being swamped by the wandering eddies of feminine table-talk. Clearing his throat, by way of announcing his intention to speak, he had remarked towards Lionel, deferentially, but a little too loudly, upon the interesting difference between the spelling and the pronunciation of *Cholmondeley*. And Lionel, after the slightest hesitation and preliminary working of the facial muscles that promises a

271

stutter, said smoothly, in his unexpectedly deep voice, husky, with the glow of a kindly smile in it, 'There's no *onde* in my name; but it's pronounced Marchbanks all the same.'   And flushed when he realized that his little jest was standing on the silent air, homeless.   And his eyes met mine and rested upon them for a moment, gratefully renewing and deepening the smile that had disappeared before the shock of his guilt.   And he went on talking, to bring his topic round to common ground.

And that same evening the whole party, drawn by his power of making every one feel significant, had assembled upstairs in the drawing-room.   And he, not knowing that this assembly was unusual, and unaware of being its vital centre, sat in a corner telling me of his ambition: to disseminate poetry, either to live by disseminating poetry, or to sweep a crossing. And I asked what he thought of Clifford Harrison, and whether he agreed that a musical accompaniment, although in advance it seemed to promise a division of one's attention, actually had the reverse effect, helping, with its unaccentuated flow, to focus and vitalize the images evoked by a poem.   And while he was enthusiastically agreeing, I thought of Hypo's definition of music as a solvent and was about to work off on him an interpretation that had just occurred to me, to say that music favoured the reception of poetry partly by causing the shapeless mental faculties that deal with things, to abdicate in favour of the faculty that has the sense of form and sees things in relationship.   And I heard myself speaking before I began, rather precisely and pedantically, and was glad to be prevented from saying my say by the realization that his voice was sounding in a silent room, in a horrible silence filled with the dying echoes of undesired topics and vibrating with the bitterness of permanent animosities.   And when I asked him to recite, it was not because I wanted to hear a poem, but because his pleasant voice would clear the air.   And he stood up and said into the silence, croakily, his face and voice glowing with the half-smile of his angelic effrontery, so that what he said was like a gentle punch upon the spirit of the hearer, 'Shall I say a short poem?'   And instead of going to face down the room from the hearthrug, or to pose within the curve of the near-by grand piano, he remained in his place and said his poem as if he were a momentary spokesman, like a vocal testifier in a religious gathering, and, although the poem was heroic, his voice was only a little fuller and more resonant than usual, and quite free from recitational 'effects.' So that the poem prevailed and every one saw and felt something of what the poet saw and felt. And after a short pause he said a short pathetic piece, meditatively, without pathos, leaving it to make its own appeal. Because of his way of saying his poems, abdicating, making himself a medium and setting the poems quietly in the midst of his hearers, as if they were the common property of the group, every one could receive them, directly, unimpeded by the embarrassment involved in the relationship between drawing-room performer and drawing-room audience. When his poem was finished, he was immediately talking again, engrossed, and not in the least working off superfluous emotion.

In his gentle composure and sensitive awareness he is something like the ideal Quaker. Living in reference to a Presence. But a presence as to which he makes no profession. His relationship to life is urbane. Unifying sound, rather than unifying silence, is the medium of his social life. So that conversation with him is like an aside, secondary interchange between actors at moments when they are not prominently engaged with the ceaseless drama in which every one takes part. Festive interchange. He greets everything with a festoon. And lessens burdens because he *really* travels in sympathy as far as he can see into every life that comes his way. And the steady operation of his sympathy controls every word he speaks even when he is witty, and, when he is grave, one word or another will break on a mirthful little croak.

'Perhaps if you will have a small piece taken from the back of your nose, *you* will be able to sleep with closed windows.' A smile all the while and a croak on every word. One for me, and my pedantic lecture; given charmingly, disarmingly. I had forgotten him in the interval, yet I felt really pleased to see him back from his operation, with the pleasant little croak unimpaired. And to see him suddenly appear at early breakfast.

Though he brought the world into the room. When he came in, and I saw him for the first time alone with one person, I thought I should discover the individual behind his unfailing sociability and felt a momentary deep interest in what he might turn out to be; what less and what more than his usual seeming. But although he said good morning quietly, and did not at once begin to talk, the way he took his place, and helped himself to toast and speared a pat of butter, was social. Even at that hour of a perfect, still, spring morning he was turned only towards humanity, keeping human lives in the room, the sight and sound and movement of them, and references to the past and references to the future.

Having paid him tribute while pouring out her tea and getting back to the window-end of the long empty breakfast-table, she bade farewell to Lionel Cholmley and watched him for a moment, going his way through life, contributing, wherever he went, his qualities of strength and gentleness, gentle strength, strong gentleness. A missionary from Oberland, poor, obliged to live by selling the family pearls.

He was gone. Her mind, returned to self-consciousness, would throw up no more images of him without a deliberate effort of memory which, if made with this returned surface consciousness, would add nothing to what had accumulated unawares and become a permanent possession, to be deepened and filled out all along the way. And he, himself, would not wish to stay merely to contemplate a spring morning. She turned, holding back her thoughts, holding her faculties in suspension, with eyes downcast so that no detail encountered on the way should disturb her meeting with the light. . . . The door was opening, was admitting Sissie Bailey coming in with food and greetings and, just as she seemed about to depart, moving, drawn by the brilliance of the light reflected into this end of the room from the sunlit house-fronts across the way, to the nearer window, where she stood with her back to the indoor scene, looking out. Silently. Seizing a moment of tranquil solitude in the presence of one from whom she had ceased to expect entertainment, before returning to the busy basement. Face to face with the brightness of the spring morning, she was seeing what it brought to her mind. Hampton Court Gardens in mid-June, seen once in her early girlhood? The green alleys surrounding her convent-school in the Ardennes? These visions, stored up, dimly returned to her in moments such as this? But they were now far away. They had been faithless and unfruitful. There was nothing ahead with which they could link themselves. If indeed they returned at all, they brought no light to her face. Perhaps they could not completely appear when she looked from this window. Even if, on spring and summer mornings, they rose in her mind, they would be driven back by the nature of her familiarity with the spectacle before her eyes, which for her was so much more and so much less than a stately old street, serenely beautiful in the morning light. She saw those façades, known to her since childhood, with intimate, critical knowledge of their condition and their needs. And saw through them into what lay behind, with a mind grown experienced in relationship to the interior being of a large old-fashioned house, to its ceaseless demands and the prices to be paid, in labour and in thought, on behalf of its peculiarities and imperfections. So that for her, an old house was little more than an everlastingly exacting invalid. And her general expressionlessness was the façade of her detailed, intricate inner preoccupation with experiences that remained, for the world with which she dealt, unknown and without repute, a permanent secret behind her cheerless good cheer. Which also it fed, enabling her to face her world, serene in the knowledge of the worth of her labours.

Watching her, Miriam realized, with a pang of loss, how much Sissie had changed. During her own absence at Flaxman's she had grown from an elderly schoolgirl into a young housekeeper, able to command not only respect but also fear, from all the men and women in the house to whom her ceaseless occupations were the mysteries whereby their lives were sustained. A curious, guilty fear, the fear of those whose exemptions are bought at the price of the continuous, unvarying labour of others. Sissie had attained power.

The morning light was harsh upon her graceless shape, upon her young face that already wore a look of age and responsibility,

visible in the slight permanent lift of the eyebrows and the
suggestion of tension about the compressed lips. But apart
from the evidence they supplied of mental preoccupations and
control, her features had gone their way without her knowledge
and were set in an expression of half sulky, half mystified
resentment. In repose. In moments such as this. And for
the eyes of those who did not know and did not care for her.
Including, strangely, even Amabel, who drew every one like a
magnet, brought every one to life, and yet must have failed with
Sissie. For at some time or other she had certainly tried to
capture her. And it was this failure that explained her relentless diagnosis of Sissie's way of being. A more English
Amabel would have been aware of Sissie from the first and
would not have left letters about all over her room, and every
box and drawer and cupboard unlocked. But discoveries
alone would not have alienated a Sissie burdened with the guilt
of spying. And Sissie was not one to make direct use of knowledge to which she had no right; or to be shocked by any one's
private affairs, so long as they were private. She kept her
knowledge to herself, using it to fill out her entirely objective
vision. But Amabel had no private affairs. And being in and
out of rooms all day, Sissie would have seen her casting spells
over newly arrived boarders whom, with the capitulation of all
the others stored up to her credit, to say nothing of her wealth
of outside interests, she might reasonably, from Sissie's point
of view, have been expected to leave alone at least until they
had time to look round.

Perhaps a shocked Sissie had even seen her exchanging kisses
with Captain Norton—between two trills of laughter, the first
encouraging and chiding and maternally consoling in advance,
the second girlishly ecstatic—on the day after his arrival, and
been the more horrified because he was a chance, temporary
lodger and not present at meals. She might have been somewhere about on the next evening when, hearing him pass on
his way upstairs, Amabel, to prove to me the truth of her tale,
called to him through my open door and went out, tinkling and
choking with suppressed laughter, half amusement over my
incredulity and half joyous anticipation, and was silently

gathered up and kissed, and came back dreamy for an instant after her spiritual excursion in the darkness, and then almost weeping with mirth over the kind of man he was: so frightfully *English*, talking at top speed, and as if all his remarks were contributions to an argument, and looking all the time the picture of an injured seraph, brows up, blue eyes wide. Mad on *parrots*. A little taken aback, at first, by her unconventionality, a little shocked too and revealing, 'for the flick of a bee's wing,' the life he had led between whiles, 'poor lamb.' And finally enthusiastic, finding her 'extremely unique' and talking to her about parrots.

'You 've reformed him,' I said, 'someone will reap the benefit.' And she smiled, and for a moment seemed to be looking wistfully along his future. I half-envied the courage that enabled her to gather life-giving endearments as simply and as easily as others will hail a fellow-creature on a bright morning, go out of their way for the sake of the hailing, if the morning be very bright.

But to Sissie she will have seemed the enemy. An artful, fast young lady beside whom, men being what they are, a decent girl stands no chance.

So whenever it was that Amabel had first turned her propitiating ray upon Sissie, though it was probably unexpected, in the course of a conversation with someone else, just a reference to her, an inquiry for her opinion, so framed as to convey the gracious obeisance that was her unvarying salutation to any one who appeared to be standing off, she had nevertheless found Sissie prepared, had received a disdainful retort and met, or probably only seen, half-turned in her direction, cold blue eyes whose haughty gaze, like that of royalty in Academy portraits, saw nothing that was within their circle of vision. Exactly the rebuff that Amabel herself might bestow upon someone whose offensiveness called aloud for strong measures; only that she, unable to be other than radiant, would not gaze coldly into space, but, while administering her reproof, would slightly bow, her face inclined sideways as if to evade, and then raised, ignoring the offender, devoutly towards the nearest innocence; person or thing.

Amabel had mentioned Sissie only that once—mercifully she is now making off, with that bustling, fussy gait that seems deliberately to create disturbance and make a proper to-do of the business of getting herself to the door, and is certainly ungraceful and yet, for me, is redeemed by the way it seems hilariously to celebrate things in general, just as they are, to fly the flag of life and keep going in face of no matter what catastrophes—only that once, and, for a moment, seeming so to illuminate and explain her that I, wounded and surprised though I was on behalf of the Sissie I have known so long and uncritically liked, found nothing to say. And felt, and feel, mean. But she is right as well as wrong in describing her, with contemptuous unwilling lips and bated breath, as an awful example of the woman who hasn't. Yet she is more wrong than right. There is something she does not see. Sissie's puzzled sulkiness with life for failing to fulfil its promises does not dim her cheery sanity, nor the rays shining from her dense blue eyes when she exchanges nothings with people she is fond of. Amabel is too rational and logical, too French to understand what happens during these exchanges. Impossible to make her see Sissie's life from within.

With her eyes upon the vision of Sissie pounding along through the years, incessantly busy and interested, making, for herself, fewer and fewer claims and defiantly defending those of all the people she liked, Miriam said farewell to her and to the discomfort of being unable to find for her any approved place in Amabel's scheme of life, and turned to meet the spring.

She had left, at a remembered moment in the recent past, some portion of her spirit waiting for this instant of serene and powerful realization of the being of spring, mid-spring with its beginnings still near enough to be recalled. And had feared that this year it might fail to come. And now that it was here it opened before her so spaciously, and with such serene assurance of its eternity, that she paused on her way to its centre to look at what had recently accumulated in her life that at this moment was so far away and so clearly lit by the penetrating radiance into which she was being drawn.

The first thing to emerge was the moment with Michael at the concert, a revelation of him that would remain with her always. Just behind it, standing alone in a chain of kindred experiences because it was so solidly linked to earth, was the strange moment of being up in the rejoicing sky. For two, three seconds?

She remembered how her eye had met that of the little manageress edging sideways along the narrow gangway, with a coffee for the man at the next table held high and clear of heads in one hand and, dangling from the other, the usual limp, crumpled table-swab, and it was as if, during that interchanged glance, the stout little woman contemplated, in her kindly, all-embracing, matter-of-fact way, the whole panorama of one's recent life as it lay spread out in one's consciousness.

And it was then that the wordless thought had come like an arrow aimed from a height downwards into her heart and, before her awakened mind, dropping its preoccupation, could reach the words that already were sounding within it, in the quiet tone of someone offering a suggestion and ready to wait while it was surveyed, she was within that lifting tide of emotion.

With a single up-swinging movement, she was clear of earth and hanging, suspended and motionless, high in the sky, looking, away to the right, into a far-off pearly-blue distance, that held her eyes, seeming to be in motion within itself: an intense crystalline vibration that seemed to be aware of being enchantedly observed, and even to be amused and to be saying, 'Yes, this is my reality.'

She was moving, or the sky about her was moving. Masses of pinnacled clouds rose between her and the clear distance and, just as she felt herself sinking, her spirit seemed to be up amongst their high, rejoicing summits. And then the little manageress was setting down the coffee upon the near table, her head turned, while still her fingers held the rim of the saucer, in the direction of her next destination, towards which her kind tired eyes were sending their quizzical smile.

Joy, that up there had seemed everywhere, pulsed now, confined, within her, holding away thoughts, holding away everything but itself.

'I 've been up amongst the rejoicing cloud-tops,' she wrote and sat back and sipped her coffee.

His little figure appeared in her mind's eye, not, as usual, alone in his study or grouped and talking, spreading the half-truths of his gospel, but walking quietly along in space, not threshing the air with his arms as he went, and not wearing his walking look of defiant confidence and determination. Walking along unarmed and exposed, turned, so to speak, inside out. And it was to this solitary unrelated figure that her joyous message went forth. He would understand and approve the bare statement of fact without explanation or commentary. He would become once more the friend who, years ago, as she knelt on the hearthrug in his study, within the deep rosy glow of an autumn fire, pouring out her thoughts and forgetting the listener, had suddenly laid his hand gently upon her head and said—what was it he said that had so much moved her and had brought, for a moment, an unfamiliar sense of unity with humanity? She could remember only the wide, rosy glow of the fire receiving in its companionable depths the poured-forth words that seemed to be a long-prepared forward movement of her whole being.

This solitary figure her scribbled lines would pull up. For a moment her news would engage his attention to the exclusion of everything else; for just a moment, before his mind extended a verbal tentacle to grasp the miracle and set it within the pattern of doomed and disappearing things of which his world was made. He would be simple and whole, dumb before the mystery, held back from his inaccessible and equally doomed and passing 'future' by a present eternity. He would be fully there, sharing, apart from her and one with her, as he had seemed to be on the day he announced friendship between them: 'large, manly, *exploring* friendship, full of ruthlessness; untidy, probably as choppy and squally, dear Miriam, as the old sea is to-day.' And as he had seemed to be on that after-noon in the study, a discovered extension of herself, available for companionship, enriching the companionship she had had with herself since the beginning, by his stored knowledge and his unused, self-repudiated personality. This had seemed so serenely certain that she had poured out her own version of some of the thoughts he had given her and gone on, with a sense of exploration; forgetting until, pausing, she had felt his hand on her head. She clearly recalled feeling alone and independent of him and yet supported by his unusual silence and then, presently, a lonely, impersonal joy in whatever it was she had tried to make clear, whatever it was that had brought that adventuring forth, from her heart's depth, of love and devotion that glowed like the rosy fire and seemed at once the inmost essence of her being and yet not herself; but something that through her, and in unaccustomed words, was addressing the self she knew, making her both speaker and listener, making her, to herself, as strange and as mysterious as, in the shaded lamplight, was the darkness behind the glowing fire.

And at the end of her journeying meditation had come the shock of the unspeakably gentle touch. All her life she would remember it, the way its light pressure, bringing her fire-warmed hair closely against her head, rested a moment. Thought had vanished with the reminder that it was she who had been heard speaking and he who had been quietly with her as she spoke; and the flood of her voyaging love had turned and enveloped for a moment his invisible being, and the few words he gently spoke had filled her with joy in believing that in spite of his ceaseless denials he saw and felt a reality that thought could neither touch nor express. Had the joy and the belief survived for even that one evening?

Of course he would immediately socialize the news in his consciousness and respond to it with a suitable formula, embodying a momentary pang of genuine emotion, but brief and concise, tinged with feeling but carefully free from any sort of expansiveness, carefully earnest and carefully casual—'My dear, I'm no end glad and proud'—and then would immediately sketch unacceptable plans and arrange a meeting for talk; and forthwith banish the circumstance to its proper place amongst his multitudinous preoccupations.

What she had just set down, he would take for metaphor. Up in the clouds. Seventh heaven. Any attempt to prove that it was not, would bring forth his utmost dreariness. He would light up and exhibit his private amusement with the tooth-revealing smile that the scraggy moustache made so unpleasantly fauve, and say rather professorially that the prospect of having a child had given her a great emotional moment, very much to her credit as showing her to be a properly constituted female, to be followed in due course by a return to the world of hard fact.

But it was the world of hard fact she had just visited. Feeling there, in the very midst of joy and wonder, not surprise but an everyday steadiness and clarity beyond anything she had yet experienced. The 'great emotional moments' must lie ahead; perhaps all the way along life. It was their quality, stating itself in advance, that had produced the strange experience? And even he, if it were stated in plain terms by someone he could willingly believe, could not maintain that it was illusion.

She turned back to her adventure in the sky. What was it about those vibrating particles of light that had made them seem so familiar and reassuring? Why had they brought, at some point in that endless brief moment, the certainty that ages hence they would once more be there, only all about her instead of far away? The certainty that this strange experience was just a passing glimpse? They were, she reflected, something like the crystals upon the crust of moonlit snow. But these, by comparison, were large and coarse, motionless and dead. There were no ways of stating the strange blissful intensity of these vibrating particles. Nor their curious intentness. And even if there were, even if she could set down the whole spectacle from first to last exactly as it had appeared, everything would be left out. The rapture and the rapturous certainty. Joy, wonder, recognition. No excitement, because no barrier. There must somehow be *sober* intoxication. Movement that is perfect rest.

There were no words which would prove to him that this experience was as real as the crowded roadways converging within her sight as she looked through the window, as real as the calm grey church across the way and the group of poplars presiding over the cab-shelter. When her eyes reached their high plumes, feathering upwards towards the wide scarf of cloud screening the sky of her adventure, she knew she must not even try to tell him. To insist, against sceptical opposition, would be to lose, fruitlessly, something of the essence of the experience. Just these revealing, misleading words. And then silence, indefinitely. An indefinite space for realization, free of the time-moving distractions of *plans*.

Before her eyes could come far enough round to be met, Amabel's laughter leapt forth and ceased abruptly because she was so eager to speak.

'Yes, I know, I know!' she cried in the high tone of her laughter. 'One feels one ought to dance out one's child in the market-place!' But she, too, had taken 'up in the clouds' metaphorically, and it seemed impossible to insist, even with her. A strange, *glad* reluctance, this time, a sort of happy fear, seemed to prevent.

'Yes, with bands playing and flags flying and people cheering. It's true. Every one can endure more easily with the support of moral limelight than they can shut up in a corner with one person. Think of it, a smart, certificated young woman who cuts any amount of ice with the doctor who employs her if she can manage without him up to the last minute. She can't give the help a man could, either physical or moral, because she doesn't supply the natural right kind of sympathetic opposition, the help and support the old-fashioned family doctor gave before the profession grew bored with obstetrics and invented, made themselves believe, perhaps actually *do* believe, poor, crammed uneducated creatures, that it is just a mechanical process and nothing more, the convenient phrase: "Leave it to nature." Those old family doctors, Mrs Philps told me, used to be as tired as the mother when it was all over. Anyway no one ought to be shut in and left to fight alone, unless they really wish it. It's a wrong idea. False decency. And when people say, "Not a bit of it, look at the beasts, their secrecy in all these matters and the way they creep away to die," they forget that all beasts, so long as they are helpless and *visible*, are in danger, either from other beasts, or from us.

That is why they creep away. They daren't be caught off guard. Domesticated animals don't creep away. And they don't want to be left alone, either when they suffer or when they die.'

'I know,' said Amabel. But she had not been listening. 'I once said something like that to matah.' She had listened to the first part.

'What did your mater say?'

'Matah said: "That's all very fine, my dear, but wait till your time comes. Wait till you *know* a child is on the way!"'

The other immortal moment had been preluded by Michael's telegram. Reading its familiar words, she had failed for the first time to be disturbed by them, and wondered over her failure. It pulled her up in the midst of the square, and the high buildings surrounding it shut her in with a question: with what to give to any one, or to be to any one, was she going so zestfully forward in her life, if she was failing Michael? For it was she and not he who, in the unbearable pain of the last parting, had suggested that in case of need he should call upon her for help. Contemplating his life amongst strangers on the other side of London, she had known in advance exactly how and why this need would arise.

Again and again he had summoned her: for help in his pathetically absurd entanglements with people he attracted and entirely failed to read; for advice about his preposterous, ill-fated engagement, his unworkable plans conceived in the queer high light and cold darkness of rational calculation and perishing catastrophically the moment they were submitted to the smallest glow of imaginative foresight, whose application never failed to start his mind on an unwilling tour amongst the unconsidered, insurmountable difficulties. A tour dreadful to witness, and from which he would return momentarily illuminated and downcast, and more than a little ashamed. And each time she had hoped that on the next occasion he would himself make the necessary imaginative effort. And with each fresh telegram had had to realize afresh his amazing, persistent helplessness; and to know, in terms of real distress, that whatever hurt him must hurt her also while life lasted.

Yet to-day she was feeling no pain. Because she had read the message coming across the square in the first of the spring sunshine whose radiance was assuring her that somehow all was well? Re-reading the wire, she searched her heart for solicitude, turning her eyes aside to conjure up the image of Michael in trouble, and saw instead the way the eastern light shone through the small leaves on the bole of a tree across the road, and immediately felt Amabel at her side, and walked on, leaving Michael forgotten, until presently he again intruded with his demand, and again she refused to be involved.

And then, as though it had prepared itself while she was refusing to take thought, there passed before her inward vision a picture of herself performing, upon an invisible background, the rite of introduction between Michael and Amabel. It slid away. Joyously she recalled it, supplying time and place, colour and sound and living warmth. And it stood there before her, solving the mystery of her present failure to suffer on Michael's behalf, filling so completely the horizon of her immediate future that it seemed to offer, the moment it should become the reality into which she had the power of translating it, a vista ahead swept clean of all impediments. She hurried on, as if the swiftness of her steps could hasten fulfilment.

But her shocked consciousness pulled her up in the midst of relief, insisting that she should drive away the subtly attractive picture while it stood clear in her mind, and use·its suspicious fruit, the aroused state of her whole being, to discover its secret origin and thereby judge its worth. Isolated with possible motives, she found herself in a maze whose partitions were mirrors.

Yet even if it were true that her real desire was to perform in person the social miracle of introducing one life to another, without consideration of the inclinations of either person concerned, even if it were true that she desired only to show off Michael and to show off Amabel, again without consideration, even if it were true that there was not the remotest chance of help coming from Amabel to Michael and that therefore it was she herself, and not Michael, who was the pathetic fragment, so cut off and resourceless as to delight in the mere reproduction of social rituals and the illusory sense of power and of importance to be attained therefrom, it was now impossible to imagine the occasion as not taking place. Something far away below any single, particular motive she could search out, had made the decision, was refusing to attend to this conscious conflict and was already regarding the event as current, even as past and accomplished. This complete, independent response, whose motives were either undiscoverable or non-existent, might be good or bad, but was irrevocable.

There were those two concert tickets for next Sunday afternoon. Michael should come early to Tansley Street, be introduced to Amabel, and then go on to the concert and say his say in the interval. All these happenings would distribute his dark mood and make it easier to handle.

Amabel downstairs at dinner, ignoring every one but me, both of us using the social occasion to heighten our sense of being together, making it impossible for any one to break into the circle where we sit surrounded and alone. So strongly enclosed that not one of those with whom at other times she talked and flirted could mistake the centre of her interest. Bad manners. But how resist the enchantment? Why should all these people resent our silence in our magic enclosure?

Amabel at Lycurgan meetings and soirées, posed, an inquiring, deeply smiling satellite, towards one and another of the men who at the moment happened to be expounding their views. Deep interest in views, deep reverence for ability to express them, deeper reverence, behind it, for everything that seemed to promise change in the social structure. All these emotions came to life, embodied in Amabel posed and listening. Yet always in the end she would break into one of her little trilling laughs. Strange, ambiguous applause. Approval, and criticism. And sometimes she would turn away from a talking group to which, devoutly glowing, she had seemed for a while to be giving all her attention, and drop a tinkle of laughter into space, or into some convenient inanimate receptacle, as if only the flexible air or a decorative, patiently enduring bowl or vase could accommodate all she felt.

Queer fish she had found all these people, even while respecting them and all they stood for. Queer, all of them, except that one man, the thin, tall, white-faced wisp of a man at the Arts Group Nietzsche lecture, an outsider drawn by the subject, standing up during the discussion, standing silent, with working features, for an appalling interval, and then slowly stammering out his simple words, annihilating the suave pseudo-Nietzsche on the platform. During his agonized effort, Amabel had clutched her arm: 'Mira! He's *real*!'

For these Amabels was now substituted another. Amabel meeting a man for the first time. Amabel handling a newly-met man. Amabel in her kimono, a string of heavy, low-hanging beads correcting its informality, sitting crouched on a footstool on the hearthrug, hiding the dismally empty bedroom grate, her Empire coffee-set ranged along the wooden mantel-shelf above her head; she and her chosen china redeeming the room's ugliness like a lit and decorated altar a dark unlovely church. In response to Michael's little stories, told out one after another across the space between Amabel and the uncomfortable small bedroom chair upon which he sat hunched, radiating west-European culture from his fine brow and rich Jewish beauty from the depths of his being, she gave out her little rills of laughter.

She might be finding Michael, too, a queer fish. Within the laughter with which she greeted each of his little tales was hidden her extremity of amusement over his conception of entertaining a lady freshly met. But a caress also, the caress she would bestow upon a charming child. And, at moments when, shielded by Michael's engrossment in his narrative, she would lift a hand to her hair and reveal, on her sideways-tilted face, eyebrows faintly raised and lips ever so little compressed by ironic endurance, a veiled message of all-understanding patronage of the friend about whom she had heard so much.

Already the light had left Michael's eyes and the colour was fading from his voice. Between his intelligent brow and shapely beard his face was the face of a child, clouded and

expressionless with oncoming sleep. Sagging on his comfortless chair, he broke a phrase with a sigh that was almost a yawn.
The heavy white lids came down over his eyes and for a moment
his face, with its slumbering vitality, at once venerable and
insolent, was like a death-mask, a Jewish death-mask. Poor
darling, working so hard at an unanticipated task, exercising,
at this dead time of the afternoon, his one social gift. But
though apparently sinking into lassitude, regardless of the havoc
it worked with his appearance and with the delicate fabric of a
social grouping, he was certainly, behind this abject façade,
cunningly arranging some little plan. At the end of the story
he was telling, he would at once reveal his determination to
escape. Amabel was to see him at his worst.

Aware that only the wildest bacchanalia of laughter would
suffice to relieve Amabel of the emotions she was about to
experience, Miriam abandoned him. For it was now certain
that he could not be kept there for the afternoon. As if his
escape were already achieved, she savoured in advance the
scene following his departure: Amabel's tense face regarding
her, mirth held back, so that for a moment they might share a
perfection of silent incredulity. A mutual, dumb, entranced
contemplation of enormity, enhanced by their simultaneous
vision of the neatly-escaped criminal waiting downstairs; a
vision that would recur during Amabel's rapturous abandonment.

'You will doubtless have anticipated,' he was saying, and,
looking across, Miriam caught the crafty gleam in the eyes that
were blinking sleepily towards Amabel, 'the end of this story.
And in any case I have perhaps told you enough stories and
should not weesh to bore you.' He was on his feet with the
last word, standing before herself, with head, bird-like, on one
side. She exactly anticipated the small, high tone, very gentle,
and the guilty schoolboy smile with which he said: 'Miriam-
shall-we-not-at-once-go-to-this-concert, for which, already'
(and he drew out his jewelled watch), 'we must be very late?'
And almost without waiting for an answer he turned to Amabel,
moving across the room with his easy dignity, his Eastern beauty
once more fully blossoming, dominating his pathetically

ill-chosen clothes. A modest, proud ambassador of his race, going through the ceremonial of farewell, bowing before, during, and after his deep-voiced murmurings; three formal obeisances, two over her hand, the final one, after her hand was released, leaving his head half-turned towards his line of retreat, away from Amabel at her loveliest, without having had any talk with her, almost without having heard her voice.

Amabel had concentrated on her poses and her rills of laughter. Perhaps this was her invariable way with any sort of man, to begin with. Poses to focus attention on her beauty, rills of laughter given forth from each attitude in turn. But all this eloquence had played about Michael unperceived. And she herself, having purposely allowed Amabel to dawn on him without preliminary description and then stood aside to await the result, had presently been too guiltily aware of having staged an absurdity and left it to look after itself, to do anything beyond throwing in a word now and again in the hope of heading off an anecdote. Left unchecked, he had handled the situation after his manner, slaying the occasion before it was fully alive. And now, his duty accomplished, he stood disgracefully before her, bending, hands on knees, face outstretched, eyes quizzically gazing, and voice, though gentle and deprecating, booming as if to recall one from a distance: 'Shall we not GO?'

Turning back into the room from dispatching him to wait for her downstairs, she closed the door to give Amabel free range.

But Amabel was not waiting for her. Gone off alone, she stood at the far-off window, gazing out, very tall, posed against the upright of the window-frame, in her long, flowing robe. Remote. Withdrawn as though deliberately she had placed the length of the room between herself and the scene that had taken place at its other end, and intended not only to ignore but to obliterate it by another, for themselves alone, there by the window, that would carry them forward together as if Michael had never been brought in. Judgment, upon Michael, and upon any one who had found him worth a second thought. Having thus expressed herself, if they had been going to spend the afternoon together, she would for a while, only for a little while, in order to drive her judgment home, give it continuous expression in her gestures: a withdrawal of the eyes when one was speaking, an apparent absent-mindedness, an abrupt movement, ostensibly to adjust a curtain or open or close a window. And suddenly would abandon it and give forth the full force of her charm, leaving Michael placed, a far-off temporary aberration of one to whom all things were permitted.

But to-day there was no time for the little drama of criticism. There was only a moment or two. Reaching the window she stood at Amabel's side, looked down into the garden, and tried, by driving away every image save that of the tall tree whose small new leaves, blurred by mist, seemed rather to have condensed upon it than to have sprouted from within its sooty twigs, to turn Michael's visit into an already forgotten parenthesis in their communion.

But Amabel was not with her. Glancing, she found her bent profile meditative. She was not looking into the garden. The downward tilt of her face gave the curve of her cheek a slight fullness and emphasized the roundness of her chin. Michael ought to have seen her thus. And have heard the small, quiet, childlike voice, in which, after a moment's contemplation, she would state a thought. The stillness held his presence there, dividing them. And with his presence, his unknown trouble, making Miriam feel she ought to be impatient to be gone. But Amabel had something to express. And this valuable something, even if it related to a perfectly mistaken view of him, might throw a helpful light. In a moment, she would speak. Having decided on her comment, she was collecting herself to present it effectively. Disguised, perhaps, not recognizable as a comment. Yet avenging, or justifying herself. Something that would put the responsibility for her unpleasant new experience—for Michael had not only failed to burn incense, he had not even displayed the smallest awareness of an altar upon which incense should be burned— in its right place. Either that; or this deep quietude might be the prelude to one of her wordless little exhibitions of meek protest. But it was beginning to seem like refusal to speak, so that she might have the full force of her nature gathered to meet whatever one tried to say, and to dispose of it in one or other of her ways of acknowledging the presence, in another, of a well-deserved embarrassment; and Michael and his visit would remain for ever unmentionable between them.

'Mira!'

The quiet word, and the pause which followed it, revealing Amabel about to think aloud, made Miriam's heart beat anxiously, reproaching her for all she had caused these two to endure in order that she herself might have the satisfaction of bringing about a social occasion. But even now, with the crime committed and its results on her hands, she found herself resenting, since there was only a moment in which to reassert the self Amabel had invented for her, Amabel's quiet departure from intimacy into one of her thought-excursions whose result would be a statement whose full meaning would elude and leave her to go away imprisoned within it, imprisoned by Amabel and teased by the memory of the Irish laughter that would break over her abrupt English winding-up and departure.

Defiant of this uncomfortable fate, she moved impatiently away into the room.

'You MUST marry him!'

For a moment while the room swayed about her, she found herself, deserted by Amabel now standing reproachfully protective at Michael's side, so close to the impossible destiny that it seemed as though her narrow escape of years ago had never taken place. Amabel was right. Amabel knew, now that she had seen Michael, that it ought not to have taken place. Saw, with the whole force of her generous nature, the cruelty of deserting Michael. Saw it so clearly that she was ready, in order to secure safety and happiness for him, to sacrifice the life together here at a moment's notice. She had already sacrificed it. Judged, condemned, and set it aside. Within it, henceforth, if indeed it should continue, was isolation. Isolation with Amabel's judgment.

The room steadied about her, but it seemed to be with the last of her strength that she forced herself to laughter that left her drained and shuddering with cold, and stood in the air a dreadful sound, telling of her hardness, her implacable, cold determination.

Amabel echoed her laughter gaily. But this laughter revoked nothing of her judgment. It stated nothing but herself, though within it, within this particular gay laugh, statement rather than one of her many kinds of commentary or of emotional expression, was contained her everlasting attribution to others of the width and generosity of her own nature. Taking it for granted, she believed it to exist even below the most pitifully constricted surfaces. This laughter gave no comfort. It gave only time, a breathing space during which thought could operate. And here indeed was thought, a tide flowing freely from an immovable deep certainty which for Amabel had no existence. This certainty stood between them, marking, now that it had been brought out into the open by a deliberate tampering with the movement of life, a fundamental separation. And there was no one alive who could decide, in this strange difference, where lay right and wrong. Why should it be right to have no sense of nationality? Why should it be wrong to feel this sense as something whose violation would be a base betrayal? Much more than that. Something that could not be. Not merely difficult and sacrificial and yet possible. Simply impossible. With her unlocated, half-foreign being, Amabel could see nothing of the impossibility of spending one's life in Jewry.

Re-reading the statements hammered into shape long ago in her contests with Michael, and now recovered and crowding into her consciousness, she felt embarrassment give way to lonely sadness. The sadness she had so often felt in trying to put before Amabel the two sides of a problem for which there was no solution save in terms of temperament; a solution that left it still tainting the air. Here, clear in her mind, was a mass of communication for an admiring, patiently listening Amabel. Not all Amabel's generosity, not even her absence of national consciousness, could prevail against it if it could be stated in the terms which interchange with Amabel would inspire her to discover. They would reach a mysterious inexorable certainty. But even if there were time, the conflict with Amabel would be, in its own particular way, worse than had been the conflict with Michael. And useless.

Driven back into dreary self-possession by memories of that early suffering, when she had had herself as well as Michael to contend with, she looked easily across at Amabel. And found her facing down the room with the expression she wore when admitting an absurdity, smile hovering, eyes veiled pending restatement. But she remained silent, holding condemnation horribly suspended there between them, waiting, with this semblance of an apology, for some defence she could proceed to demolish, waiting to know its nature before taking a fresh pose.

And now she was about to speak, without any meeting of eyes, looking into space, tenderly, as if what she were going to say were to be addressed to someone waiting and listening a few feet from where she stood, or to herself, or the universe called in as an invisible third, as if her words would have no recognizable bearing upon what was dividing them. Yet she was well aware of the suspense her deliberate preliminary silence was creating as a frame for the ultimatum.

'He's wonderful,' she breathed, 'and so beautiful.' And still she did not turn. She had paid her tribute meditatively, and as if he were her own discovery; as if she were defending him from someone incapable of seeing him as she had seen while pretending to listen to his little tales; as if she and she alone were qualified to estimate his worth, with the recognition of which, standing averted there by her window, she was set apart, unable, while she still dwelt on it, to face one who was incompletely appreciative.

Watching her thus, Miriam felt her own spirit leap to the touch of an incredible hope, and as her inward eye took in the vista of a future from which she was excluded and into which the rich present flowed and was lost, she found words on her lips, arrived before she could consider them, the abrupt destination of a journey that in every direction of lightning-swift thought and feeling seemed interminable and yet was so rapid that she spoke almost into the echo of Amabel's words:

'Then marry him, my dear, yourself.'

'I would!   I would to-morrow!' cried Amabel and gathered up her kimono and began to dance.   Not in her usual gliding, mannered style, but childishly pirouetting in the room's clear space.   Light-heartedly *dancing* towards the impasse of marriage with Michael.   Sophisticated, cultivated, coming from a way of life and of being of which Michael, who read no fiction and had no social imagination, had not the slightest inkling. Ready, for Michael's sake, to bury all that she was in Jewish orthodoxy, to disguise herself for life.   And for Michael too, such a marriage, on the religious side, would be more complex than either of those he had already contemplated.   Still . . . with his horror of assimilated Jewesses . . .

At the end of a wild whirl, Amabel stopped dead.   'I'd love his children,' she declared breathlessly, to the universe, or to herself, for now she was ensconced, oblivious, at the very centre of her own being.   And as the flying draperies came flatly to rest against her lightly poised form, she whispered to herself: 'I can see their beady eyes.'

'Beady,' echoed Miriam, 'yes, beady,' and herself thrilled to the pictured future from which she was shut out.   Amabel, Michael, and their children, on some unpredictable background. Their grouped beauty would have the power of lighting up any imaginable interior.   Swiftly she took leave of Amabel incredibly newly found, incredibly newly lost.   Michael's possible saviour.   It was a good-bye that was unlike any salutation that had ever passed between them.   An almost casual good-bye to Amabel left standing still too much adream to come forward for the shared farewell that was both retrospect and anticipation, Amabel grateful for a swift departure from the scene upon which had emerged between them a possibility that hung by so much less than a thread.

With careful carelessness, lest, by an instant's loss of poise, she should presently close the door upon the newly opened perspective, Miriam made her way downstairs to the unsuspecting Michael.

Seeing him, as she turned the last corner, hung up, enduring, without either his newspaper or his bag of grapes, propped against the marble slab with one heel hooked to the rail underneath it while she approached with her incommunicable message not only of salvation but of a salvation on a scale magnificently beyond anything she herself could ever have offered, it seemed that an eternity must pass before this amazing message could be made to address him from within his own consciousness, and she dreaded the burden of the immediate irrelevant hours and of those others which must follow them. For now, indeed, she must keep her hand on Michael.

The buzz of conversation filling the hall, though for a moment the sound had been welcome, was more oppressive, now that she was seated in the midst of it, than the silent glare of the staircase and the long corridor. Though composed of a multitude of voices, it was a single, rhythmic, continuous sound: beastlike. It was the voice of some great primitive beast, deeply excited by the surrounding glow, and sending forth, towards the brighter glow upon the distant platform, through its vast maw, ceaselessly opening and shutting, the response of its aroused, confused perception, half challenge, half salute.

Hundreds of times in the past, she had been in the midst of this sound, without noticing its peculiar quality. But never before on a Sunday. Transferring it, in imagination, to a week-day, she found its character changed. Therefore the chill, observant detachment coming upon her as they entered the hall from the street and that still was with her in spite of her promising experiment, meant only that her being was in revolt against this flouting of Sunday's rich quietude, the closing of its long vistas. For although the storm-dark sky had brought on the lights before their time, so that it seemed to be evening, and Sunday, turning towards the new week, no longer quite Sunday, there was enough pale light coming in to mark the time of day.

The gathered orchestra was tuning up. Through the shapeless vast continuous voice of the beast sounded the abrupt assertions of the instruments preparing for the controlled statement that presently would sound out across the hall.

Subdued preliminary rat-tat and rumble, cheerful tootings, the
warm blare of a trombone, reedy flutings and liquid flutings,
the intimate voice of a violin, two pure solo notes breaking
through the confusion of sound with a promise cancelled by an
experimental flourish, were followed by a stillness before which
the universal voice was dying down, leaving only single voices
here and there, very audible and individual.

But the presence of the conductor was having no effect upon
this curious numbness that made everything so remote and
indifferent. Without raising her eyes from the darkness across
the chair-back in front of her, certain that if they were to turn
to the familiar spectacle of the distant platform they would find
its glamour gone, she pictured him standing motionless against
a rising background of orchestra, his white face stern between
the gentleness of soot-black beard and soot-black wavy crest
with plume, so far, in place, confronting his audience with his
silent demand for silence.

As the scattered sounds began to fall away, something within
her rose to repel this strange, cold trance which now she recognized as a continuance of the deadness that had fallen upon her
on that second evening at Bonnycliff, as if for good. It had
been driven away by the return to London and to Amabel, the
beginning of spring and the moment up in the clouds, and was
now asserting itself as central and permanent, and sternly suggesting that the whole of the past had been a long journey in a
world of illusion. Supposing this were true, supposing this
cold contemplation of reality stripped of its glamour were all
that remained, there was still space in consciousness, far away
behind this benumbed surface, where dwelt whatever it was
that now came forward, not so much to give battle as to invite
her to gather herself away from this immovable new condition
and watch, from a distance, unattained, the behaviour of the
newly discovered world.

To prove to herself that she could ignore the metamorphosis,
act independently while it went its way to no matter what final
annihilation of every known aspect of her external world, she
lifted her eyes to turn towards Michael with an appearance of
sociability and to murmur something, anything, the first thing

that should occur to her, and became aware that her lips were set and her eyebrows faintly lifted above eyes that had left the shadow and had not yet travelled far enough in his direction to call him into communication and were now drawn to a space that opened before her in the air between herself and her surroundings, while the enterprise that had started them on their journey was being arrested by a faint stirring, far away below the bleakness produced by the icy touch of external reality, of interest and wonder.

Even now, with life stripped bare before her and all its charm departed, wonder, with its question, was still persisting. It seemed to call upon her for acceptance, for courage not so much to steel herself against the withdrawal of the old familiar magnetic stream as to push on, in spite of its withdrawal, to the discovery of some new way of being.

Leaving Michael undisturbed by a remark that in any case must be almost inaudibly murmured and would bring a response by no means inaudible, she turned her eyes at last upon the surrounding scene: the sea of humanity gathered in a darkness which all the importance of cunningly arranged illumination was powerless to disperse; the distant platform foliage-fringed, the grey, grimed boards of its unoccupied portions, which to-day she noticed for the first time, pallid beneath the lights clustered above, whose radiance, falling upon the white-breasted beetles of the orchestra, was broken by a mosaic of harsh shadows.

The tap-tap of the conductor's baton, falling into the stillness, startled her with its peremptory demand for attention and its urgent indifference to her need. But though there was no gathering of the forces of her being in response to the music now advancing upon her and of which she was aware only as a shape of tones, indifferently noting their pattern, the alternating prominence of the various groups of instruments and the varieties of tempo and rhythm, its presence was a relief. The process of following the pattern brought the movement of time once more into realizable being and, while she travelled along it, even to the accompaniment of music stripped to its bones and robbed of its penetrating power by this chill preoccupation with its form alone, she hoped that the fragment of courage with which, just now, she had urged herself forward, might be gathering force.

But the movement of time, because she was consciously passing along the surface of its moments as one by one they were measured off in sound that no longer held for her any time-expanding depth, was intolerably slow. And so shallow, that presently it was tormenting her with the certainty that else-where, far away in some remote region of consciousness, her authentic being was plunged in a timeless reality within which, if only she could discover the way, she might yet rejoin it and feel the barrier between herself and the music drop away. But the way was barred. And the barrier was not like any of the accountable barriers she had known in the past. It was not any abnormal state of tension. It was as if some inexorable force were holding her here on this chill promontory of con-sciousness, while within the progressive mesh of interwoven sounds dark chasms opened.

The increase of this sense of unfathomable darkness peril-ously bridged by sound that had, since it was strange to her, the quality of an infernal improvisation, brought, after a time, the fear of some sudden horrible hallucination, or the break-down, unawares, of those forces whereby she was automatically conforming to the ordinances of the visible world. Once more she raised her eyes to glance, for reassurance, at Michael seated at her side. But before they could reach him, a single flute-phrase, emerging unaccompanied, dropped into her heart.

Oblivious of the continuing music, she repeated in her mind the little phrase that had spread coolness within her, refreshing as sipped water from a spring. A decorative fragment, separ-able, a mere nothing in the composition, it had yet come forth in the manner of an independent statement by an intruder awaiting his opportunity and thrusting in, between beat and beat of the larger rhythm, his rapturous message, abrupt and yet serenely confident, like the sudden brief song of a bird after dark; and so clear that it seemed as though, if she should turn her eyes, she would see it left suspended in the air in front of the orchestra, a small festoon of sound made visible.

No longer a pattern whose development she watched with indifference, the music now assailing her seemed to have borrowed from the rapturous intruder both depth and glow; and confidence in an inaccessible joy. But she knew the change was in herself; that the little parenthesis, coming punctually as she turned to seek help from Michael who could not give it, had attained her because in that movement she had gone part of the way towards the changeless central zone of her being. The little phrase had caught her on the way.

But from within the human atmosphere all about her came the suggestion that this retreat into the centre of her eternal profanity, if indeed she should ever reach it again, was an evasion whose price she would live to regret. Again and again it had filled her memory with wreckage. She admitted the wreckage, but insisted at the same time upon the ultimate departure of regret, the way sooner or later it merged into the joy of a secret companionship restored; a companionship that again and again, setting aside the evidence of common sense, and then the evidence of feeling, had turned her away from entanglements by threatening to depart, and had always brought, after the wrenching and the wreckage, moments of joy that made the intermittent miseries, so rational and so passionate and so brief, a small price to pay.

With a sense of battle waged, though still all about her, much nearer than the protesting people, was the chill darkness that yet might prove to be the reality for which she was bound, she drew back and back and caught a glimpse, through an opening inward eye, of a gap in a low hedge, between two dewy lawns, through which she could see the features of some forgotten scene, the last of a fading twilight upon the gloomy leaves of dark, clustered bushes and, further off, its friendly glimmer upon massive tree-trunks, and wondered, as the scene vanished, why the realization of a garden as a gatherer of growing darkness should be so deeply satisfying, and why these shadowy shrubs and trees should move her to imagine them as they would be in morning light. And why it was that only garden scenes, and never open country, and never the interiors of buildings, returned of themselves without associative link or deliberate effort of memory.

Driving through her question came the realization that the 'green solitude' recommended by Hypo and spurned because every imagined leaf and grass-blade had looked so dreary when thought of in the presence of his outlook on life, might yet be hers perforce. His adroitly chosen words now offered their meaning, free from the shadow of his oblivions. For him such a solitude might be just one of the amenities of civilized life, very pleasant and refreshing and sometimes unspeakably beautiful, pathetically beautiful, a symbol of man's sporadic attempts at control of wild nature, in a chaotic world hurtling to its death through empty space.

Presenting itself independently of his vision, it opened its welcoming depths. Inexhaustible. Within it, alone, free from the chill isolation that had returned to her spirit this afternoon, she would somehow sustain, somehow make terms with what must surely be the profoundest solitude known to human kind. Twilight, trees and flowers, the first inhabitants of a future into which, until this moment, she had cast no investigating glance.

All this week, since the moment up in the clouds, she had lived suspended in a dream to which no thought could penetrate. Here, shut away from life's ceaselessly swarming incidents, her mind was moving forward to meet the future and picture its encroaching power, its threat to every stable item in her existence, to life itself.

With these thoughts, plunged grim and astringent into her relaxed being, came the impulse to confide in Michael, and, with this impulse, fear, driving the blood from her cheeks. To tell him would be to tell herself, to see herself committed, not only to the agonized breaking-up of her physical being, but to the incalculable regrouping of all the facets of her life. Glancing at him, she was arrested by his serene beauty. Yet this serenity might be only apparent. Rich Hebrew beauty in repose. From brow to beardpoint, courteous attention, serene. But already, if she could see his eyes, she might read in them weariness of a 'so-prolonged music,' and if she could see into his mind she might find therein the pattern of a chess problem. Swiftly recalling her glance, she subdued her risen smile to an uncontrollable beam that presently became the expression of her thankfulness that the grimmest features of the possible future should first have presented themselves while she was shut away at so many removes from the life of every day. In the vast remove of Sunday; back, within this spacious neutral enclosure, in the past with Michael, who had so punctually returned to be with her at this moment; lifted, by the stimulus of the slightly poisoned air, at least into the illusion of floating free from all attachments. She had regarded them, had already faced them provisionally. For the first and last time. For when they next presented themselves they would be changed. Some of their power would have dissolved. Or perhaps they might be even more powerful?

'*What* is it?' His too-audible whisper revealed him turned towards her, smiling his response to her half-smile; released from boredom and anxious to share her imagined mirth.

Her voice, murmuring within the sonorous farewell of the finale, a reminder that the interval was due, seemed to be speaking the end of a sentence that was begun in the past, and to convey, simply by being audible, all she had to tell him. And when the music ceased and he repeated his inquiry, in the midst of the first crackles of outbreaking applause, strange and sad, a division between them, was the fact that he was as far as ever from the sense of her wordless communication. And the words she now dropped casually into the space between their seated forms seemed a repetition of news about an acquaintance in whom neither of them was particularly interested and passed beyond him and became a stentorian announcement to the whole world, carrying away from her a secret that was received with indifference, flung back and left with her, an overwhelming reality.

His silence drew her eyes to his face, turned her way but not regarding her, regarding only what she had told him, silently and therefore with deep emotion. For nothing less could bar, for him, the way to speech. In a moment he would turn and pay tribute, from the depth of his Jewish being to the central fact, for him the fact of facts; and to herself as its privileged, consecrated victim. What else could he do? What had it to do with him, or with any man on earth? But emotional tribute, respectful, impersonal, racial tribute from him who had never failed to put the whole of his mental and moral power at the service of every situation she had encountered during their long friendship, would leave her more isolated with her share of grim reality than the indifference of the surrounding world.

Through the buzz of conversation and the stir of people leaving their places, came his questions, gently, in his gentlest tones, one by one, steadily. But though his face was calm his clasped hands trembled and he still looked gravely ahead, away from her. People passing out broke into the to and fro of question and answer. But he knew, now, all that there was to know. Even his natural curiosity had been satisfied. And when once more they were alone and the empty seats on either side gave them fuller freedom, she was seized with a longing to cancel their interchange, somehow to escape from its cheerlessness.

'Enough of my affairs,' she said and tried to find comfort in listening to her own voice as if it were that of someone else, someone free and unattained. 'Tell me what it was you wanted to consult me about.'

'After what you have told me,' he said, trying by slow speech to control the trembling of his voice, 'that which I would have said is less than nothing. I have even partly forgotten. I must however tell you,' his dark eyes came half round, grave and judicial, 'that I think in all circumstances it is of the greatest improbability. But if it should be true . . . Oh, Miriam, now, at last, marry me. As brother. At once.'

He had not looked her way. He had set his low-toned outcry there before them both and left it, as a contribution to her private counsels, and mercifully had not seen how, even while this revelation of the essential Michael struck at her heart, the muscles of her lips were uncontrollably twisted by amusement over his failure to recognize that the refuge he offered from what indeed might be a temporary embarrassment as well as a triumphant social gesture, was a permanent prison; over his assumption that she might be scared into flight, disguised as a Jewess, from the open road, down into Judaea. But now, at once, whilst still his outcry lingered on the air, she must somehow make him aware of the silent tribute of her kneeling spirit.

She began to speak of friendship, gently, meditatively, an invitation to think aloud in the manner of their converse long ago, quoting, without acknowledgment, Alma's suggestion that the best investments for later years are friendships made in youth. Contemplating the theme in order to find phrases, she discovered the reason for her instinctive recoil from Alma's theory and remembered feeling the same repulsion when Jan had said that no one need be without friends in a world where there was always someone at hand to cultivate, and when Hypo, talking of the jolly adventure of living, proclaimed that in order to be interesting one must be interested. He meant, of course, mutual flattery alternating with mutual fault-finding. But the objection to them all was the same, the strange motive: friends as a kind of fur coat.

What she was saying about friendship being filled out by every experience of friends separated by circumstance, about every meeting being therefore richer than the last, although it brought a false note into her voice because she was certain that this could apply only to those who were facing the same kind of universe, was finding welcome. Perhaps it was true, in the long run, of all human relationships. So long as they were not compulsory. Drawing a releasing breath, she dropped her topic and felt the division in her mind close up at the summons of something pressing forward, tingling pleasantly through her nerves, waiting to be communicated with the whole force of her being. What was it? Thought presented Amabel, and during the second spent in banishing this unwary suggestion and its countless company of images, the inner tide receded, dying down to a faint, decreasing pulsation.

In the hope of clearing a pathway for this obstructed urgency, she embarked, since speech must not cease, upon a series of inconsequent remarks, compelling his collaboration in keeping going this effortless inanity while the field of her

consciousness fell silent and empty. To be filled, as the
moments flowed through this motionless centre, only by an
awareness of the interval between the two parts of the concert
as a loop in time, one of those occasions that bring with peculiar vividness the sense of identity, persistent, unchanging,
personal identity, and return, in memory, inexhaustible.
Surely he was sharing something of this sense? Feeling how,
in this moment of poise, while they submitted themselves to
the ritual of inanity, the rhythmic beat of life made itself felt
not only physically, but spiritually, imposing its unbounded
certainty, making little of the temporary darkness of events,
the knots and entanglements of life and growth through which
it passed?

But when she glanced she saw upon his face only a gleefully
beaming recognition of the manœuvre with which, in the old
days, in good moods, she had sometimes evaded conversation.
The beam was so vivid, so much like the joyous irradiation of
his student days, that it called from her an uncontrollable
answering beam, gleeful, dangerous, unkind. Quenching it
she prepared to improvise a tiresome, precise topic, turning
away a grave face as she began at random with the idea of music
as a solvent, in the formal tone of one about to launch a challenging generalization. Fortunately, like most men, he had no
ear for artificiality of tone. The tones of his own voice did
not fall into any one of the stereotyped shapes within which
most Englishmen are wont to hide their varying embarrassments.

But his attention was merely marking time, waiting until
her gratuitous generalizations should have run their course.
It was too late, the damage was done. The moment she ceased
talking to herself, she would have to face his reproach. Sooner
or later. Though now she was reaping the reward of her self-
imposed contemplation, finding in her theme the beginnings of
so much interest that she turned with a store of impersonal
strength, its rewarding gift, to ask him to agree that heated
conferences should be automatically held up (as, in monastic
life, are useful occupations) while the gathered members
closed their eyes and listened to the meditations of Beethoven

or of Bach. A group of people squeezing by, one by one, to regain their seats, broke into her inquiry. Assuming, for their benefit, an expression of judicial gravity, he felt for her hand. Unable to repulse, unable to welcome the seeking hand, she looked away beyond him, as if oblivious of his manœuvre, seeking help, and was prompted to use the full force of the pang, always to be hers in seeing him suffer, to enhance the simulation of interest with which she would pretend to discover, far away amongst the audience, an old friend known to them both—and saw a straggler belonging to the returning party, a voluminous lady now moving in from the gangway, and thankfully rose to her feet. Michael, too, was compelled to rise.

Lifted by this compulsory movement into the free flow of air from a near doorway, she felt tensions relax and drain deliciously away, leaving her receptive to the intimate communications of the rescuer, now squeezing apologetically by: two-thirds of the way through a life that had been a ceaseless stream of events set in a ceaseless stream of inadequate commentary without and within. The motionless unchanging centre of her consciousness, bowed beneath the weight of incommunicable experience, announced its claims without achieving freedom from its hunger. Yet it was on behalf of those belonging to her, and not on her own behalf, that she was determined, as the life-moulded, available edge of her bent, conversational profile almost audibly announced, to sustain the ceaseless flow of events, the ceaseless exchange of unsatisfactory comments; haunted meanwhile, in the depths of her solitude, by the presence of youth still waiting within, while bodily youth mysteriously decayed, and by the gathering, upon her person, of cumbrous flesh. Unable either to impose and make it comely, or to check its outrageous advance.

Settled once more in her place, refreshed by pure air and by the lingering presence of the lonely, middle-aged girl who had just gone by, she was aware of Michael only as an embodied commentary on what was in her mind, and could hear the indignant inflections of his protesting voice: 'Simply an elderly woman who has played her part. Why should she be dissatisfied?' Swiftly withdrawing from this old battle-ground, she collided with the subject of the mysterious urgency to communicate, when Amabel had emerged in answer to her thought's vain effort to seize it, standing now clear in the fore-front of her mind: the journey through extended darkness that had been the central reality of her Bonnycliff experience.

Here at last was priceless material for interchange. Its impersonality would soothe him, and she was eager to know how he would regard it.

'What a waste of time it is to try to discover what is on the tip of your tongue.'

'Possibly, in certain instances. I cannot say.'

'It puts a barrier across the path of what is trying to emerge.'

'What you call barrier may be some sort of aphasia.'

'Which is the result of being strung up.'

'Possibly. But without effort there can be no mental process. And this state of having no mental process is frequently good. One cannot afford these efforts on all occa-sions. More: it is good deliberately to encourage absence of thought, to conserve the forces for when they shall be needed. In Holy Russia, for example, amongst the intelligentsia who are driven to live, by reason of deprivation of political freedom, entirely in abstractive life, it would be most-good.'

'M'm. But I mean it requires more effort to control thought than to let it go on talking. For instance . . .'

As soon as she reached her story, he attended, in the way he had followed the Hibbert lectures, with an eager, watchful interest, his sceptical mind in wait for a flaw. Quietly pre-senting point after point, she made him realize that the strange journey had extended further than the length of the small room and had yet brought her to the window high in the wall, actually and not imaginatively, because she had seen, as she hovered there, the unknown detail of the woodwork and the pale glimmer, beyond the window, of moonlight or of dawn, and known she could go no further because the window was closed. And told him how, as the flood-like darkness through which she had driven, face downwards, as if swimming, had expanded before her, sadness had turned to wonder as the thought came that here was the confirmation of her conviction of the inner vastness of space. And that this was less wonderful than the moment up at the little window and the certainty that it was possible to float also in the outer vastness. Drawing a swift breath, to speak again before he should have time to break in, she explained that there was nothing uncanny in the experience, that during the whole of it she had felt its quiet reality.

Out on the further side of her story she grew conscious of her voice as she insisted on this aspect, the scientific aspect that could be perceived and measured, expressed in words and handed about. But the burden of its incommunicable essence was with her still. And even the surface detail might seem to him evidence only of illusion, explicable in terms of psychological theory, and the story, once told, never convincingly to be repeated, would have been told in vain. Life would flow over it, draw over it veil upon veil until it was forgotten even by herself. For it had not, in its hour, proclaimed itself as something to be for ever effortlessly remembered. It had stood aside, just now, when she had told him all the rest.

He was sitting hunched forward over his clasped hands, head raised, eyes set unseeing on the far distance, below furrowed brow. Resting, perhaps. Simulation of interest while he wandered elsewhere, waiting for cessation? But to whom else could she have confided this lonely experience? Not to Amabel, for Amabel must not know of a loneliness she would interpret as failure. The moment up in the clouds had been a triumphant social moment, belonging to all the world, but not to any one likely to remain in her life. Yet though she had told her tale in vain, reward was here, if she could remember to return in thought to what she had just discovered, and find out exactly what kind of experience it is that returns of itself, effortlessly. Glancing up while she made her mental note, she saw the orchestra returning and heard, at her side, Michael's voice gravely agreeing as to the inner expansibility of space. 'In this single point I see nothing impossible and it may be also possible to achieve a certain expansion of the consciousness at certain moments. But it grows very warm in here again.

We must talk of this elsewhere. You shall tell me once more
this remarkable experience.'

   She was glad to fall in with his suggestion of escaping before
the music began again. But when hand in hand they turned
into Portland Place and she felt streaming towards her, through
the saffron haze that closed its long vista, the magnetic power
of the tree-filled park where so much of their years together
was stored up, she clasped his hand more firmly, pulling on
it to change their pace from the easy stroll favourable to
reminiscence, to the steady forward march of friends towards a
separate future, and broke the silence, within which the current
of their thoughts, stimulated by the shared adventure of emergence into fresh air and golden light, had inevitably turned
backwards, by asking him what he thought of Amabel; conversationally, and with a touch of the rallying briskness they
both disliked, so that he should believe the question asked
merely because between them speech was better than silence.
But while her conspiratorial eyes searched the distance and
her whole being held its breath and became a listening ear,
she felt, tingling through her hand, the thrill of the pain
he suffered in believing her to be deliberately dissociating
him from this moment of life renewed in escape from
enclosure.
   'She laughs too much.'
   'She is young.'
   'That is no reason. She is not a *child*. Tell me rather of
your sister in Canada.'
   'Harriett? Left Canada ages ago. Went to Cuba and grew
pineapples, and they all learnt to ride. I think they liked the
life there and never heard why it came to an end. Harry hardly
ever writes. And her letters are just a sort of shorthand, and
exclamations. She feels details are useless because the life is
so utterly unlike anything we know. So she thinks, not allowing for imagination. Says the Americans are *really* different.
Like another race. They 're in New Orleans now. She keeps
the family by running an apartment house, which she describes
in one sentence: "Eighteen roomers, my hat, can you see

them?" Well, I can. But not the rooms, nor the town, nor the weather, nor the look of the countryside, if any.'

'That is bad. And the little Elspeth, who is your godchild?'

'Dreadful. I've done nothing for her since I held her at the font, feeling so proud of the loveliness of her little sleeping form that I realized something of the frantic pride of parents. I tried writing to her after she began to go to school. In her answer, in pure American, she wrote elevator in two words: "ella vater," and the shock of hearing her speak American, and of realizing that she would grow up into an American girl, prevented my writing again. They all seem so far away. And yet no further than Sarah and Bennett in their suburb. In another universe.'

'That is a gross exaggeration, believe me.'

'We all have different sets of realities.'

'That, believe me, is impossible.'

And again, demanding no price for truant contemplation, the heavenly morning received her. Turning, in the fullness of her recently restored freedom, towards the light as towards the contemplative gaze of a lover, she felt its silent stream flood her untenanted being and looked up, and recovered, in swift sequence, and with a more smiting intensity than when she had first come upon them, the earlier gifts of this interrupted spring: the dense little battalions, along the park's green alley, between tall leafless trees, of new, cold crocus-cups, glossy with living varnish, golden-yellow, transparent mauve, pure frosty white, white with satiny purple stripings; the upper rim of each petal so sharp that it seemed to be cutting for itself a place in the dense, chill air; each flower a little upright figure and a song, proclaiming winter's end. Then tree-buds in the square seen suddenly, glistening, through softly showering rain. Then the green haze of small leaves: each leaf translucent in the morning and, at night, under the London lamplight, an opaque, exciting, viridian artificiality. And it was with power borrowed from this early light, and from the chance of stillness as perfect as its own, that these memories were smiting through her. No sound in house or street. Away in the square, the small song of a bird, measuring the height there of unimpeded air. And within this light and this stillness was the reality that disappeared in the din of the drama. Yet almost no one seemed to desire the stillness in which alone it could be breathed and felt.

The door, opening. Being slowly opened by someone holding the loose handle to prevent its rattling. *Amabel*—moved to come downstairs at this unlikely hour—coming, amazingly, as if summoned, to share this perfect moment. With scarcely a sound she is gliding down the length of the other side of the room, to reach the window-space and silently blossom, just within the line of my vision when I turn my eyes from the window. Amabel *knows* immortal moments. . . . They draw her. And she knows how surely life clears a space for them a few seconds. But it is enough.

She remained gazing into the open—for it was possible that Amabel, reaching the end of the table, would whisk herself across the window-space and land, crouching, at one's side and, for a moment, look out towards the light. Into whose brightness had come a deeper warmth, while the house-fronts across the way had an air of confidence, as if sure of healing for the sadness hidden behind their experienced walls; from the sense of which, in general, one's thoughts sheered selfishly away, courting forgetfulness. Yet the inhabitants of these houses were doomed to pass their days without meeting Amabel. Without being able to raise their eyes and find her where she had paused, exactly opposite, beautifully posed in the full light. She had brought herself, and not any special tribute, to this heavenly morning, though of course she was joyously aware of it and of herself as its particularly favoured guest.

Drawn thither by the rising within her of a contemplative smile born of a vision of Amabel upstairs, alight with her plan —dressing with swift tiptoe movements, arms raised, arms extended in graceful flourishing gestures, each one of which served, besides its own purpose, that of luxuriously stretching the whole of her elastic muscles, each flourish a rapturous greeting of the day, until at last she stood for a fraction of a second before her mirror, not to seek its help, but gaily to survey, and triumphantly to salute, herself poised in readiness to depart and dawn, head upflung as a preliminary to the assumption of the graceful tilt, shoulders thrown back, leaving balanced the curves of the body confined by arms straightly downstretched so that the hands, palms downwards and turned a little outwards from the wrists, assumed the appearance of small paddles with which she propelled her lightly balanced form, in the delicately swaying movements her feet seemed to follow rather than lead—Miriam's gaze shifted from the window and found an Amabel transformed.

In place of the chic French morning frock of chequered cotton, with lace tuckers at neck and sleeves, those at the sleeves frilling gaily out just above the elbow, was a filmy gown of English design, pleated where it should have lain flat, disguising, instead of following, contours, and having loose sleeves that began by destroying the curve of the shoulder and ended, destroying the curve of the arm, just below the elbow. Rising from this transforming gown, the firm pillar of her neck supported a face whose pure oval, usually outlined by the silky dark curtains, was broken by the emergence of a small cliff of white brow. From her grave face, turning slowly this way and that to show itself at all angles, shone an expression of serene enlightenment.

'Marvellous, Amabel.'

Amabel's gay trill, directed towards the window, ended on a meditative coo, revealing her nimble wits seeking, unobtrusively, conversational material that would serve to employ her deep excitement without sacrifice of the delight of being entrancedly observed.

'I did it for you,' she said with her eyes on the opposite wall, and tilted her face, suggesting other toilettes, and drew her lips delicately back, partly revealing both even rows of teeth in a 'mischievous' smile, and then, as if remembering, grew very grave, held her head steadily upright like an Englishwoman, and assumed an expression perfectly conveying the brooding, provisional graciousness of the kind of Englishwoman who is always alert to ignore everything to which this graciousness does not apply. They gazed at each other, while still she held this pose, rejoicing together over an achieved masterpiece.

'It's sweet of you, Amabel; because of course it makes you look years older. And perfectly lovely. You know it's rum, and not at all rum when you come to think of it, because I see now why I always wanted you to have a forehead; which I knew would also suit you.'

Amabel turned towards this promising opening with a movement almost too eager for her dress and bearing, and at once corrected it by falling into a graciously attentive pose: floppy-sleeved elbows on table, chin propped, a little sideways, on hands laid flatly one above the other, eyes and lips set, to match the intelligent brow, in an expression of approving expectancy.

'You see . . .' but indeed she was listening as well as contemplating her own metamorphosis; for her spirit, chuckling its recognition of their unvarying opening for serious remarks, almost broke up the stillness of her face. 'Women's faces misrepresent them. No one really knows, of course, who starts fashions, though heaps of them must originate in blemishes or old age. (Dog-collars, for instance, to hide scars, and mittens to disguise shrivelling hands which give away even an enamelled face.) But whoever started fringes ought to spend eternity hunting for a packet of Hinde's curlers. But it's not only the misery of the fringed, not only the incalculable nervous cost of curled fringes for straight-haired people in a damp climate, but the results of never having the brow properly aired, and of never seeing it, or having it seen, without a sort of horror. Of course every one knows Frenchwomen are intelligent and that the eighteenth century was the beginning of a period that was very stimulating to the intelligence. But allowing for the exciting time they lived in, can you think, remembering their portraits, of any women more radiantly intelligent and enlightened-looking than those eighteenth - century Frenchwomen with mountains of powdered hair above expanses of white brow? They were intelligent, and a woman who has a furze-bush to her eyebrows may be intelligent. But the point is that they *looked* intelligent, and this fact must have influenced them, as well as their friends the philosophers. The spectacle of themselves, met in mirrors, must have influenced them. To-day, the average man (almost any sort of man with a more or less decent forehead, and particularly those who early begin to lose their hair), surveying himself in the glass, perceives, whether or no he is conscious of it, at least the appearance of intelligence, a luminous bluff, quietly presiding over the various kinds of sound and fury below; while the average woman confronts a thicket, whose effect is to concentrate attention upon the lower part of the face, leaving the serene heaven of the brow in darkness. The fringe, as a factor in environment. A whole library could be written.'

Amabel's admiring agreement left them tantalizingly hand in hand, at this unavailable time of day, at the opening of hours of contemplative interchange that properly belonged to the far-away evening. Already it was nearly nine. Twenty heavenly minutes had passed since she sat down to breakfast and now she must rise and feel the day seize and begin to devour her; while Amabel, also getting to her feet, leisurely, without compulsion, was turning to salute the same day with outstretched arms . . . and revealing, seen thus in profile, upon the lovely little cliff of brow, just before it met, without any weakening curve, the soft ridge of her hair, the slightest little bombe, wise and childlike.

'Listen to me, Babinka. You are to wear your hair like that when we meet Hypo. You must.'

She slowly turned and stood, meditative, hesitating, finger to lower lip, eyes rounded in childish dismay. But there was no time, no *time* for a scene of this kind.

'Promise; don't forget.'

The sense of urgency reached her. 'Mira,' she said swiftly, dropping her childish pose for one of embarrassed girlhood, smiling face averted, eyes downcast; 'this occasion is *not* going to be easy for your Babinka.'

'Why on earth, Amabel?'

'In the first place,' and now she spoke slowly, strolling gracefully along the window-space, 'he is a very great man.'

Her profile showed her brow lifted a little anxiously above eyes down-gazing as if in dismay at the recognition in her path of an uncanny obstacle which refused to be set aside. 'In the second place, I like not at all my impression of him from what you have told me, and from these books into which I have looked. In the third place, I do not know what is the best pose to take with this kind of Englishman.'

'Why pose for him?'

'For every one, one must have some kind of pose. For men, particularly, or one would too greatly embarrass them.'

'But if you dislike him, why trouble whether or no you happen to embarrass him?'

'Because it is to myself that I owe not to embarrass.'

'M'm. I know. But just for this one evening, Babinka, don't be French—by the way, he'll see through any sort of pose.'

'That I do not mind. If the pose is good.'

'If you must have a pose, don't be French. Be Irish if you like, but not too much. And *don't* be in awe. Except in the sense that everybody ought to be in awe of everybody, it's simply fantastic, do believe me, for *you* to be in awe of Hypo. And you and me together. Think. We'll take the evening in our stride, as a parenthesis. You see? We shall be there and not quite there; just looking in, on a play.'

'Ah,' she smiled, but wistfully and gazing ahead, not looking this way, privately contemplative, looking *wise*—'if this were possible.'

'Amabel, you're simply horrifying me. *You*. If it's not possible for us to be altogether *there*, and quite elsewhere at the same time, we'll put it off.' Her face came round now, dim, with the light behind, but vivid, tense with the effort of holding back the pulsation of emotions at strife within her. 'It would be monstrous for either of us to be under the spell of the occasion. There isn't any occasion and it hasn't any spell. He wrote, and on a post card by the way, note that: "We must meet and talk, bring your Amabel." But as there's now no need to meet and talk, and as by this time he will have had my letter explaining that there is nothing for him and me to discuss, and no plans to be made and no green solitude, thank heaven, needed, and as, even if there were, we could hardly discuss in your presence'—Amabel's trill broke out and she slowly advanced, tiptoe, hands stretched downwards, paddling her through the thin indoor air, face outstretched for a kiss—'we can easily put him off, unless we feel we can make it into a meeting between the representatives of two countries, incomparable and incompatible. But if we can't represent our own country——'

'We *will*,' squealed Amabel gently, sinking to her knees, gazing adoringly upwards for a moment and then turning away her head, her face tense again and staring into space as if a desperate resolution stood there visible. 'Your Babinka is still a little frightened.'

'Get up, Amabel, I simply must go this moment. But remember, you need not have any plan or take any line. It will just be *us*. And the intelligent eye, blinkered in advance with unsound generalizations about "these intense, over-personal feminine friendships," and the clumsy masculine machinery of observation, working in this case like a hidden camera with a very visible and very gleaming lens, will both find themselves at fault.'

And still she hesitated, disquietingly, standing still, with bent head, her inward eye considering her many aspects, grouped for her inspection and each, in turn, being set aside.

'In any case, Amabel, after what I have told him about you, which of course you don't know, do, please, to please me, let him have the shock of your bumpy forehead.'

But though Amabel's laughter, genuine, but leaving uncertain which of many possible images had evoked it, carried them as far as the steps, her engrossment with her problem was still perceptible, coming between them, set between them until next Thursday should have come and gone.

CHAPTER II

'I SEE. You go to all these serious-minded meetings and lectures as young men go to music-halls; only that your mirth has to be inaudible.'

'Until we get home.'

'Until you get home, yes . . .' His lowered eyelids, giving to the fleshily curving smile the expression of the more sensuous representations of Buddha, prophesied the redeeming grey-blue beam that in a fraction of a second would accompany the jest being sought behind those closed shutters—'You bottle it up, carry it home. And then uncork and let fly. Well, I'm glad *someone* is getting entertainment out of Lycurgan meetings. But, you know, you don't *know* how fortunate you are, you modern young women with your latchkeys and your freedoms. You've no *idea* how fortunate you are.'

Here, if one could tie him down and make him listen, was an outlet into their own world, far away from the formal life of men, yet animating it. Both she and Amabel, as seen by him, had run away from certain kinds of enclosure. But there was no question, there, of good or ill *fortune*. No deliberate calculation, either. Just refusal. His picture of what they had run away from would be as ill-realized as his vision of their destination. He ought to be made to pause over the fact that he still found, on their behalf, strangeness and newness in just the things that for them had long been matters of course, had been matters of course ever since the first rapture of escape.

It suddenly occurred to her that perhaps much of his talk was to be explained by the fact that he had never known that rapture. Had always been shut in and still, in spite of his apparent freedom, was enclosed and enmeshed? If this fact were flung at him, he would freely admit it, with an air of tragic hilarity, while overtly denying it, with a conspiratorial smile

316

to emphasize his relatively large liberties, in order to use the admission as a point of departure for fresh insistence upon their neglected opportunities, while, hovering high above the useless to and fro, would hang the question, sometimes accepted by Amabel and sometimes wistfully denied, as to whether men, however fitted up with incomes and latchkeys and mobility, can ever know freedom—unless they are tramps.

But he had moved on, possibly after a second's investigatory pause during which he would have collected evidence from facial expressions, and was launched on the new social world, the world he everlastingly canvassed and discussed and yet lived in so partially, conforming all the time, most carefully, to the world upon which she and Amabel had turned their backs.

Ceaselessly unwinding itself, hurrying along the level set by his uniform reading of occasions, this unique evening that was to have compelled him to recognize the existence of an alternative attitude towards reality, was to be no more than a wearisome repetition of fruitless experience, its familiar features more than ever vivid in the light shed by Amabel's presence, its pace increased by the weariness which kept one far away, obediently letting it follow the shape of Hypo's unvarying technique and pile up for him his unvarying false impressions.

Into the rising tide of discomfort flowed the stream of Amabel's silent communications: her delighted capitulation to his charm, the charm of the grey-blue glance and of the swiftness of the mental processes reflected within it; her amazement over his method, so acute that one could almost hear her trills of horrified laughter; her shame and disappointment, made endurable to herself by a seasoning of malicious glee, over one's failure to handle him, over the flagrant absence of any opposition, to him and his world, of themselves and their world, the serene selves and the rich deep world that were to have confronted him, even though only indirectly, with the full force of their combined beings. And here one sat, divorced from her, weary and alone, not only allowing oneself to be led by the nose, but actually encouraging his collection, in cheap, comic pictures, of the externals of their existence.

And yet this attitude of his, insolent when seen through Amabel's eyes, represented nothing more than his refusal to take people as seriously as they took themselves, and his determination to see life in terms of certain kinds of activity.

Enlivened by excursion, her mind moved rapidly from picture to picture thrown up during an interval of whose brevity she was fully aware, although, now that she returned upon her last articulate thought, the silence about her seemed to be waiting. 'Which self?' she said aloud, and then remembered that she had not spoken and drew from the air the echo of his last remark and said hurriedly: 'Sometimes we bring back treasures,' and raised her eyes and saw Amabel turn her head aside and caught, beaming from her smiling profile towards the darkening window, the benediction she would have received fully if they had been alone.

'What do you do with them?'

Turning, she encountered his eyes on their way from Amabel's averted profile, visible to him only as the unrevealing angle of a jaw, and saw their searching beams become, for her own benefit, an amused smile—intended as a commentary upon the observed manœuvre and at once veiled by a swift dropping of the eyelids, as if for an irresistible savouring of private wisdom, and then returned transformed by a direct gaze, simulating hopeful interest above the deepened wreathings of the Buddha smile.

Coldly, she said: 'We consider them, sometimes into the small hours.'

'Ideas, facts, points of view——' she heard him begin, in an ingratiating tone carefully permitted to vibrate sufficiently to register mirth renewed by the accusation of sacrilege. But her attention was divided between the suppression of the desire for some impossible demolition of the occasion and the spectacle of Amabel returned, her face a little self-consciously meditative, the remainder of her emotion in process of being disposed of by a slight drawing together of the brows. Or was this slight frown the outward sign, at last emerged, of an endurance that had been at work almost from the beginning of the evening? Endurance, amongst other things, of being, as a lovely spectacle, more or less, if not entirely, ignored? And now if she were to raise her eyes and see one's question, would she avenge herself by dropping them, with the little lift of the eyebrows that meant: 'We are not amused'?

Although, according to his acquired code, the arrival of coffee must not be allowed to make any break in his discourse, he did not miss the opportunity it afforded for a parenthetic staging of the small burlesque that was his chosen device for dealing with sudden demands for unusual activity: the investigating glance, dismayed recognition of the necessity for action, a hesitant gesture, suggesting uncertainty as to the exact method of procedure, followed by capitulation in the form of neat swift movements whose supposed banality a subdued smile, as of private hilarity in finding himself possessed of the appropriate technique, was intended to redeem.

'. . . impelled to inquire—Black for Miriam? Black for Miss Amabel? Yes. Austere black for everybody—earnestly to inquire when, if at all, do you sleep? You, Miriam, *ought* to sleep.'

Surprised and stung by the sudden, public discrimination, by its implied featuring of Amabel's youthful immunity and its repudiation of the envy and admiration he had so often expressed in regard to her own independence of sleep and food, she forced herself to concentrate upon his question—already, as it fell, bringing release from the burden of endurance and, in the interval between it and its unexpected sequel, dissolving her mind's fixed image of the room in a series of distant views competing for her attention—in order, by responding to that alone, by making him realize something of the enchantment rising in face of a query that for him was just a way of being charming, she might also make him, and perhaps even Amabel, believe that she had not taken in his concluding words. But while she prepared to respond—keeping her hold upon the material from whose outspread wealth was emanating a disarming joy that must not be allowed to prevent her adoption, for this occasion, of his own manner of address, eyes gazing ahead, guarded from distracting contacts, in order the better to contemplate and the more tellingly to present the subject

of his discourse—a sudden intruding realization of the advantage shared by him at this moment with all who, in sitting at
the end rather than the side of a table, have the longer vista
for the impersonal gaze, had taken her eyes on an involuntary
tour, during which, meeting his own, they encountered the
reinforcement, by a would-be authoritative glance, of the remark that had just left his lips. Composing her features to a
mask, as if her mind, browsing far away, were not merely
unattained but also quite unaware of no matter what message
coming from without, she carried off the look she had received
and read, clearly revealed within its blue-grey depths, the full,
absurd explanation of this tiresome evening, while taking in,
from the vast distance wherein, now, she was indeed ensconced,
the way Hypo's momentarily pointed, personal gaze restored
itself to beaming sociability and turned, with what remained
of its energy, a trifle too eagerly, in the manner of the Englishman who, believing himself to have scored a point, wishes
both to hide his satisfaction and to evade a retort, upon Amabel
who now, as far as he would be able to see, was delighting in
the role of onlooker and suggesting—by leaning a little across
the narrow table and radiating, this time for his benefit, a
half-amused and endlessly patient veneration—that one had
something to say and should be encouraged to say it.

  And now she must speak. But the revelation of the motive
of the gathering had raised a barrier between herself and
whatever it was she would have said. It could be regained
only at the price of falling into a state of being whose external
aspect would look like the torpor of imbecility and, since they
were not alone and he could therefore not openly attempt, by
means of satire or with a show of mock despair, to shock her
back to the surface where nothing could occur but the futile
conflict with his formulae, he would turn, with the smile
with which he was wont at once to claim a victory and to
invite the witness thereof immediately to collaborate in a fresh
departure, altogether towards.Amabel. But since the occasion
had originated in his careless misreading of her second note and
must therefore end in embarrassing explanations, one might
as well abandon it at once and get away, regardless of havoc,

into whatever it was that had seemed so good. Let them wait. Let the whole evening, as far as it concerned herself, crash irretrievably and leave her quite alone. Let them turn, despairing of one's thick, apparently interminable silence, entirely to each other.

Sleep. 'You, Miriam,' ran his message, 'booked for maternity, must stand aside, while the rest of us, leaving you alone in a corner, carry on our lives.' But before that, while the evening, its origin unexplained, was still only a disappointment and farce: 'When do you *sleep* ?' This time, instead of luminous perspectives, the remembered words brought only a thought already shared with Amabel and whose restatement would become just one of those opinions people carry hugged about them like cloaks, and suddenly fling down, remaining, if they are in the presence of those who hug, with equal tenacity, other opinions, defensive and nervously on the alert, behind a mask of indifference, while their statement, taken up and presented afresh from a different angle, is bereft of its axiomatic, independent air. But at least it would indicate preoccupation, separate Amabel from him and bring her in as a collaborator.

'It doesn't,' she said cheerfully, into the midst of the beginning of their interchange, 'require a surgical operation to rouse you when you wake, soon and suddenly, from the marvellous little sleep you have if you have been awake until dawn. You realize sleep, instead of taking it for granted, because, before dropping into it, you had got out to where sleep is, to where you see more clearly than in daylight.'

That was not so clear as the way she and Amabel had agreed to put it last week: 'Real sleep is being fully awake.' And no responsive wave was coming across the table. Looking up, she found her, though still in the same attitude, withdrawn. Downcast eyes revealed, above the smile left useless and embarrassed upon her lips, some kind of disapproval which could not be registered without destroying her pose, or which had already been registered, and seen only by him, been meant to be seen only by him, before the eyelids dropped behind which she was now savouring not only the emotions attendant upon having made her mark, but those also of being, or allowing him for her own purposes to suppose she was, in league with him.

'Sleep,' he said, withdrawing from Amabel an investigatory eye, 'is—we don't know *what* it is.   We only know that whilst we're at it our little thought-mechanism, poor dear, is unhooked and lying about in bits.   Very good for it, so long as it's been busy while it was hooked up.   But sleeping only at dawn, however charming, is not a habit to be *cultivated*.   And life, Miriam,' his eyes came round, 'is a *series* of surgical operations.'

She remained aware, as she seized and fled away with this last, incredible sample of the treatment she had escaped, of his voice beginning again, keeping going, in the way of voices all over the world, the semblance of interchange beneath which the real communications of the evening had flowed, silently and irretrievably to and fro; of its rather excessively cordial and interested tone, at once betraying and disposing of the satisfaction he had experienced in describing her to herself as reduced to her proper status, set aside to become an increasingly uncomfortable and finally agonized biological contrivance whose functioning, in his view, was the sole justification for her continued existence.

She began to consider the possibility of reminding Amabel of an imaginary engagement, breaking up the sitting and thus making him a present of the remainder of the evening.

'But *certainly*?' Amabel was replying to something he had said, in the interrogative tone which she used to rebuke a superfluous inquiry.   He was trying to draw her out.   Imagining she wished, just as if she were a shy English girl, to be coaxed by questions into believing herself to be interesting.   Confused by an unfamiliar type of opposition, he had lost hold of his usual conversational technique, his way of asking questions by making statements and embroidering them until he was interrupted, and had asked her something point-blank. And she had responded, with her head at its most graceful angle and a smile that still lingered and, in a moment, below the eyelids that were lowered to conceal a conflict of emotions, must either turn into one of those tuneful little laughs, a private recitative that left the hearer in doubt as to its origin, the laughter Michael had objected to without troubling about origins, or become the accompaniment of further speech. All the evening she had been on guard, in unfamiliar territory, with nothing to do but look after her poses. With no chance, excepting just that once, a few moments ago, of emotional release.

'All you young women,' came Hypo's summarizing voice, deliberately glowing, deliberately familiar, 'in a long, eloquent, traffic-confounding crocodile of a procession. Yes.'

So he had begun at once on the suffrage, and had remembered being told, weeks ago, about Amabel's passion for the campaign.

'Not *all* pink,' she said, breaking in incisively, and saw his hand pause for a fraction of a second on its way to the ash-tray and his attention gather to test the nature of this ebullition from one who, rebuked and reminded, should now properly be engaged in salutary, dismayed realizations, leaving the way clear for him to test the quality of this young woman who was probably destined to share the 'green solitude,' to socialize it, keep it impersonal and unexacting during his occasional visits and, possibly, one day herself supply incidental romantic interest. 'There will be mothers and aunts, don't forget, and even grandmothers. A real army. With banners. Amabel is going to carry a banner.' Lifting her elbows to the table so that her left hand, with cigarette between its extended fingers, should interpose and hide them from each other, she quenched the husky, opening words of his swift response with the sound of her own voice, full and free: 'Tell him your impressions of Mrs Despard, Amabel.'

'No,' he said, and the meditative downward curve of his tone was still able to create suspense, even though she knew him to be intent on avoiding solitude for himself and, for her, the opportunity of contemplating, at leisure, the evening's revelations just as they stood at this moment, unmodified. As funny, as truly comic as the story of the man who woke from sleep, recognized his own station slowly moving off, leaped from the train, fell, scattering over the platform, amongst the waiting passengers, an armful of books and then saw the train come quietly to a standstill, was the revelation of the needless-ness of his tactics, from the summoning of the meeting to the moment, just gone by, when a hansom appeared from nowhere at the kerb and Amabel, just as she was prepared fully to blossom, though still, to all appearances, remaining gracefully upright upon her stalk and refraining from bending in the direction of either of her neighbours, was unceremoniously dismissed. He would, of course, be unaware of the base temptation assailing her during this last item of the exhibition, for him so satisfying, of his power of dealing with the situation he believed to exist: to avoid, when presently they met again, telling Amabel the truth, to let her imagine that this dismissal was the elimination of an undesired third, the achievement of a lover's solitude rather than a temporary removal of one who promised protection and possible entertainment in the retreat whose provision was now to be discussed.

For him, nothing but his sense of her responsibility in writing to him in what he took to be parables, mitigated the absurdity of his headlong strategy. But far more threatening to the well-being of any further association would be his sense of her being now in possession of a sample of his attitude, either real, or deliberately assumed for her benefit, towards the lover he had believed booked for maternity. For he must know, even he, with his determination to keep sex in its place, while admitting that he did not know what this place ought to be, to keep it impersonal, because he feared personalities, must certainly know that nothing could excuse the flaunting of bogies in the face of a postulant mother. Whatever he really believed, or was training himself to believe, he was confronted now, in this dismal, regardless street, with an evening in ruins and herself as a witness of enormities. Yet, though a moment ago she had felt that nothing he could devise in the way of a fresh departure could shift her determination to dismiss him and, by leaving him to dispose of its remainder as best he might, to repudiate the whole evening—here, already competing with her purpose, was interest in what he might be going to propose.

'*No*—let's go to earth round the corner, in your Donizetti's, and drown our disappointment in a cup of their execrable coffee. For I am disappointed, you know, quite acutely. You had lifted me up into a tremendous exaltation. Miriam, you see, is allusive in a way my more direct, less flexible masculine intelligence doesn't always follow; and when you said you had come down from the clouds, I thought you meant you were experiencing the normal human reaction after a great moment, not that you had been mistaken, but that . . .'

Long before he had finished speaking, her elbow was cupped in his hand and they had turned and were walking side by side up the street and, now that they were no longer confronted, the roar of the traffic almost obliterated his words, relieving her of the need for response and likely to keep them wordless and separate until they were within the doors of the forlorn little retreat whose name, as well as its exact locality, he had so astonishingly remembered. Doubtless his mind was still at work and a plan already encircled this fragment of a wasted evening. But the taut web of events was broken and they were alone together within a gap in its ceaselessly moving pattern.

Eternity opened, irradiating the street whose lights and shadows and surrounding darknesses always seemed more harsh and bitter than those of any other London street she knew, and bringing suddenly back, to flow into the evening-end, only the harmonies of their long association. Within the uproar of the traffic echoed the characteristic haunting little melody of his voice, sounding its pathetic notes of determination and of hope: small and compact, diminutively sturdy, like himself. But it was only in moments such as these, only when making simple statements simply, that it seemed his very self. And although 'normal human reaction,' containing more than one questionable technicality, could not be called a simple statement, coming from him it was just an innocent comment leading to a full stop; and 'great moment' admitted the existence of timeless experience independent of evolutionary development. So

long as he remained silent, she could believe him conscious of
all that he denied, aware, as perhaps indeed, with his mind off
duty, he really was aware, of the element within the vast stillness pouring in through the ceaseless roar of London, not themselves and yet in communion with them and, itself, the medium
of their temporary unity, and to remain when they were within
the little backwater in the evolutionary process whose frosted
glass doors were now just round the corner and in a moment
would be opening to admit them.

Images competing to represent the presence whose invariable
price was some sort of stillness, jostled each other'in her mind
as they exchanged the uneasy northerly direction for the comfort of going westward along the Euston Road, along the
northern boundary of her London world.

Escaped from the resounding corridor; feeling away behind
her the open garden spaces right and left of St Pancras Church;
and, away ahead, the park and the tree-filled crescent lining
the Marylebone Road; moving in the direction where the unchanged air already seemed easier to breathe, she realized her
fatigue. Each part of the day had produced continuous,
exhausting demands and she could see, as they turned into
Donizetti's and made their way to the marble-topped table in
the corner, again offering the invitation of its emptiness exactly
as it had done last year when she had contrived to help him to
save his unusual situation, nothing at all with which to fill the
space that for him was a desert into which she had led him
by her inconvenient lack of directness. For although it was
he who had chosen this retreat, she felt, once within it and
on her own territory, responsible for his well-being and
therefore under the necessity of immediately producing
audible communications.

'If you had walked with me a little further north,' she began,
and felt the topic, the only one immediately available, become
as comfortably at home as she was herself and as desirably
remote from the science-beaten highways of his imagination.
It expanded in her mind as she spoke. She would state, in
clear terms, bearing down his ironically beaming scepticism,
the invariable uneasiness she felt in going north, express,

parenthetically, her regret in being therefore deprived of
Scotland (a contribution in his own vein), and then, if, after a
diplomatic compliment for her curious sensibility, he should
begin with his rational objections and interpretations, cover the
sacred tracks and amuse him with an account of Selina Holland's economical week in Edinburgh: 'a beautiful city one
really ought to see,' of her solution of the problem of luggage
and cabs by wearing 'two toilettes, one above the other, not in
the least inconvenient when travelling by night,' and be prepared, if he were not sufficiently impressed by this example of
feminine ingenuity, to humble herself by confessing that if the
necessary three pounds had been at her disposal she would
admiringly have followed Selina's example, wearing three
dresses and going to an inevitable temporary death in the north
for the sake of seeing Selina's 'city set on a hill.' But their
voices collided.

'I've quite an unreasonable liking for this dreadful little
haunt of yours, Miriam. It's almost the irreducible minimum
in little haunts, isn't it? But Miriam, I'm coming to believe,
has a *way* with irreducible minima.'

'If you get hold of the end of a string . . .'

'I see your point, and I hesitate'—his plump, neat hands
were clasped before him on the table and his sightless, enter-
tainment-seeking and, for the moment, entirely blue eyes were
moving from point to point, searchlights, operated from a
centre whose range, however far it might extend, was constricted by the sacred, unquestioned dogmas ruling his intelligence, he was devoting the surface of his attention to steering
clear of offence, of boring and being bored; steering his way
towards making one pleased with oneself and therefore with
him—'between concluding that you don't want to risk electro-
cution—one must, you know, keep one's metaphors up to date
—and wondering whether, against one's principles, one has to
invent, for Miriam, a special category.'

'Everybody is a special category.'

'Even for an inexorable individualist, isn't that a little——'

'Excessive? Not more than the individuality of individuals.
Within society. Within socialism, if you like. But socialism,

I believe now, is not something that has to be made to come, but is here, particularly in aristocratic England, as plain as a pikestaff. But it's a secret society, with unwritten laws that can't be taught. Inside these laws, the individual is freer and more individual than anywhere else.'

'Socialism won't come of itself. It has to be written about and talked about—everywhere. Now the Lycurgan, if you like, is trying to be a secret society. That's what we've got to bust up.'

'But it couldn't be written about unless it existed. And talking about it makes people suspicious. And makes one begin to doubt. Anything that can be put into propositions is suspect. The only thing that isn't suspect is individuality.' His swift glance towards the next table revealed his everlasting awareness of neighbours-as-audience, and his search, even here, for a sympathetic witness of his tolerant endurance of a young person's foolish remarks, or for escape into some interesting aspect of his surroundings. His glance shifted to a point further down the narrow, crowded little corridor, rested for a moment and returned lit by the kindly beam that is to be seen shining charitably from the eyes of the one, of a party of two, who sees a third bearing down upon them and wishes to appear, to the approaching onlooker who is not yet within hearing, as the easily dominant partner in a friendly contest.

'You shall be the individual individualist, Miriam,' he said, sitting back and addressing, with a smilingly indulgent air of finality and in a tone slightly above his earlier, conspiratorial undertone, partly herself and partly the centre of the widened space between them, whence his eyes, provisionally halted there, turned now, and as if he had just become aware of him, towards little Donizetti; the arrived, temporary third member of the party, standing drawing himself sturdily upright from a barely perceptible courteous inclination—not leaning forward with paternal solicitude, hands upon the table-end to support his stout frame while she murmured her small order, to which he would listen as if it were something that was to call out the utmost resources of his establishment—his air of readiness to serve them sternly mitigated by the expression of reproachful, anxious suspicion with which he was wont to regard any male appearing in her company. It was joy, as always in the presence of an escort upon whom his scrutinizing eyes could be trusted to remain fixed during the whole of the brief interview, to gaze affectionately at this friend who, when first she had dared to venture alone, driven by cold and hunger, into the mystery of a London restaurant just before midnight, had rescued her from embarrassment and fed and cherished her.

Returning from watching him as he plodded sturdily down the narrow aisle, she caught upon herself Hypo's privately investigating glance and read therein his summary of her absence: that she had fallen into a trap, awaiting the socially servile and the empty-minded alike, had reacted to a small interruption, not only with an easily distracted attention but also physically, turning and looking, something which, according to his acquired code, one doesn't do.

'Donizetti's a darling,' she said fiercely, working off the wrathful misery consuming her at the spectacle of the irrevocable ill-breeding of the two of them in dividing up their personalities sur le champ, and making private notes in the course of what ought to be an act of homage. 'One reason why I love this place which in so many ways is both devastating and heart-breaking, is because I never have to deal with cheap waiters with lost-soul faces. Because Donizetti always serves me himself, rushing up and waving them away if they approach, they have left off coming my way. That's why we had to wait so long. He must have been a peasant, it suddenly occurs to me.'

While he listened to her hurried words, without apparently finding in their course anything that could be taken up and used at all effectively, his amiability grew a little weary, its expression hovering perilously on the verge of fatuity when her welcome departure from what he was regarding less as a tribute to Donizetti than as a rather boastful confidence, came to his rescue.

'More probably, you know, the son of a small Ticino inn-keeper, trying his luck over here.'

'A peasant, because men of that stratum when saluting or

conversing with a 'lady and gentleman,' always, if you notice, apparently ignore the lady. It's manners. Not, of course, in sophisticated circles, not if they have come to be urban policemen or waiters in smart restaurants, who are all attention to Madame, while taking their orders from Monsieur.'

'M'yes. You're an observant creature, Miriam.'

'No one less. Say, speaking your dialect, which of course may be applicable, that I'm too egoistic, too self-centred to be observant. But can any one really know what they have really observed until they look back? And if one hasn't a trained mind, methodically observant, one sees only what moves one, rather than what confirms, or fails to confirm, some provisional prejudice with a grand name.'

Coffee arrived while he was stating his determination not to be drawn by glancing, his amused smile held firmly in the place of president, from point to point about the room, and was served by a woebegone young lost soul whose weary, plaintive 'haff-an'-haff' still echoed in her mind as Hypo, having sipped his coffee and set it down, inquired with an almost passionate emphasis why she was not dyspeptic.

'You *ought* to be dyspeptic, living as you do, still only just above the poverty line, you know, and feeding casually for years on end. Yet you remain unravaged and, apparently, unresentful. You queer one's criticisms.'

'I don't really resent, even when something happens to remind me of the things I seem to be missing, if any one *can* really miss things—I mean I still believe that things come to people. Whenever I am reminded of things I should like, playing games, dancing, having access to music and plays, I feel that if I were to make efforts to get these things the incidental prices would rob me of what I want more. Fighting and clutching destroys things before you get them; or destroys you. Perhaps it's my lack of imagination. Low-pressure mentality, as you once politely explained.'

'That was excessive. You've come on no end. You are one of those who develop slowly. I admire that.'

'I don't know. There are so many directions one can move in. You see, there are so many societies. Each with its secret. And whenever *one*, whatever it calls itself—because, mind you, even the different social classes are secret societies— seems likely, or is said to be seeming likely, to get everything into its own hands, I feel, no matter how much I admire it, that something is going wrong. And since, except in spirit, one cannot join all the societies with equal enthusiasm, one cannot whole-heartedly join any. Because all are partial, and to try to identify oneself with one is immediately to be reminded, even reproached, by the rightness of the others. Besides, the people inside the societies suspect you unless you appear to despise the other societies. Which in a way you *must* do if you are going to *do* anything. You must believe that you, or your group, are absolutely right and that everybody else is walking in darkness. That is what makes life so fearfully difficult if you have got out of your first environment and the point of view that belonged to it. I'm willing to be electrocuted. But only altogether, not partially. Only by something that can draw me along without reservations.'

'I believe you capable of devotion, Miriam. It's one of your attractions. But you evade. And you're a perfectionist, like most young people. But all this admirable young loyalty and singleness of purpose must attach itself somewhere, or fizzle wastefully out.'

'It is the same with people. Men or women. No man, or woman, can ever engage the whole of my interest who believes, as you believe and, of course, George Calvin Shaw flashing his fire-blue eyes, that my one driving-force, the sole and shapely end of my existence is the formation within myself of another human being, and so on ad infinitum. You may call the proceeding by any name you like, choose whatever metaphor you prefer to describe it—and the metaphor you choose will represent you more accurately than any photograph. It may be a marvellous incidental result of being born a woman and may unify a person with life and let her into its secrets—I can believe that now, the wisdom and insight and serene independent power it might bring. But it is neither the beginning nor the end of feminine being. It wasn't for my Devon-border grandmother, who produced twenty-two children. *Yes*, and listen:

She was an old lady when I first met her. I *really* only met
her once. I was going upstairs, always in any case an amazing
adventure. But listen. On the half-landing was this new
granny. Up till then, a grandmother had chiefly meant a tall
thin someone who had spent, and was still spending, a rather
bony existence looking all the time into the abyss of hell and
hoping, by strict righteousness in all her dealings, to avoid it;
and yet able to twinkle, sometimes seeming to try to twinkle
me into the narrow path, perhaps because she thought this
the best way of dealing with worldly church-folk. But the
new granny, very plump indeed, and pretty, and whose 'weeds'
made little bouncing movements—instead of dolefully hanging,
like Grandma Henderson's—as she moved lightly about, was
all twinkle. Seeing her only with other people, I had noticed
only that and her voice, which always seemed to be laughing,
as if at some huge joke of which all the time she was aware
and wanting to bring home to those about her; and yet knowing
that this was impossible and not worrying about the impossibility and still unable not to go on twinkling all the time. I
know it might be said that this was the result of her enormous
wealth: her fifteen sons scattered all over the world. It wasn't.
When I came face to face with her on the half-landing, alone
with her for the first time and so near as to be almost touching
her, we looked at each other. She made no movement towards
me and said no word. She was facing downstairs, with her
back to the light that came from the high landing window and
shone into my eyes'—he was losing interest, had just glanced,
still preserving, but only on his lips and almost invisible behind
the untidy frill of his moustache, the smile with which in public
he simulated the appearance of the interested, provisionally
critical listener, at a party of Cockneys audible behind her
across the way. But the interest of her story, with its testimony, unnoticed as such until this moment, to a truth renewing itself at intervals all along the years, made her careless of
his boredom—'so that in getting on to the landing and feeling
her silence and her stillness, I had to peer at her to see what
was there, what this new granny was when she was alone.
And we stood, I seven years old and she sixty-five, though I

didn't know this at the time, looking at each other. And I saw that I was looking at someone exactly my own age. And it delighted me so much to see someone thinking and feeling exactly as I did, and beaming the fact at me and waiting for me to take it in, and being no older at the end of life than I was myself, that I went on upstairs, knowing, after the look that had reached me through her smile, that there was no need to speak, and feeling eager to experience what I should have called, if I had had the words, the enrichment that had overtaken my lonely world through this recognition of identity.'

'There's a link, there's sufficient space for an easy, comfortable link between grandparents and grandchildren. A grandson is a renewal; in a new, unprecedented world. That's why, Miriam, one should have grandchildren and, meanwhile, prepare a world for them to live in.'

'Yes, I know; and I can see that new world in all sorts of ways. But it must also be the same world, to be real to me. It's finding the *same* world in another person that moves you to your roots. The same world in two people, in twenty people, in a nation. It makes you feel that you exist and can *go on*. Your sense of the world and of the astonishingness of there being anything anywhere, let alone what there seems to be turning out to be, is confirmed when you find the same world and the same accepted astonishment in someone else . . .' 'Wherever two or three are gathered together'—by anything whatsoever —there, in the midst of them, is something that is themselves and more than themselves. Why not? Why do you object?

Looking up and away from the vision of Amabel, unexpectedly, at some distant point in an excursion of thinking aloud, breaking in with rapturous assent, she met once more, in his eyes, his mind paused for a moment upon some diagram in his patterned thought, and felt again how wasteful for them both was this fruitless conflict. Yet although there seemed to be a sort of guilt attached to the dragging in, from other contexts, of material arising in a world he did not recognize, it seemed also less evil than agreeing, or pretending to be persuaded into agreeing and so becoming a caricature of himself, and in the end, loathsome, even for him.

'What we 've got to go on to isn't in the least, thank heaven, the same world. Life, especially speeded up, modern life, if we 're to get anything *done*, doesn't, dear Miriam, admit of intensive explorations of the depths of personalities. I doubt if it ever did, even in the spacious days when quite simple people got much more of a show than any one can get to-day. People used to sit confronted, in a world which appeared to be standing still, and make romantic journeys into each other. That sort of attitude lingers and dies hard. But to-day we are on the move, we 've got to be on the move, or things will run away with us. We 're engaged in a race with catastrophe. We can win. But only in getting abreast and running ahead.'

'Running where?'

'Away from the wrong sort of life-illusion, Miriam. If we don't, any one who chooses to look can see, plainly, what is upon us.'

He was stern now, his lips compressed and eyes fixed on a distant point, as if to refuse; to dismiss any further, tiresome questioning of the self-evident.

'As plain as the nose on my face.' And away, out there, the lovely, strange, unconscious life of London went on, holding the secret of the fellowship of its inhabitants. If these should achieve communal consciousness, it would never be the kind he represented and seemed to think the world might be coerced, by himself and his followers, into acquiring. It would be something more like Amabel's kind of consciousness.

'Amabel wants a new world, but she likes people, most people, just as they are.'

'Your Amabel 's a pretty person. Women *ought* to be reformers. Keeping the peace and making the world habitable is eminently their job. But they 're held up by a fatal tendency to concentrate upon persons. Hallo!'

Darkness and cessation, everywhere but above their table and the lit doorway, abruptly announcing midnight and the end, had surprised from him this sudden cry that brought to her—as she heard sound through each of its two notes, one above the other and the last cheerily up-curving in the manner of an expansive greeting, not only his boyish delight in seeing mechanisms obedient to the will of man, but also his glad welcome for the soundless call coming from without—only an enclosing vision of the grey and empty street.

The revealing cry echoed in her mind as she stood alone for a moment between the frosted doors and heard, in the tone of his good night to Donizetti, the genial affability, whose glow when a train is at last about to move, warms the farewells of a securely departing traveller.

The eager availability with which, humming a little tune, he had turned, once the street was reached, towards the future —towards the wealth of interests awaiting him and which seemed to her to hover, vividly bright and alluring, in every quarter of the invisible sky save the one hanging above the region towards which she was bound—betrayed itself in the sound of his voice as he inquired, putting into his question a carefully measured portion of his good cheer, the way to her lodgings.

'I live nowhere,' she said, planted, half-confronting him, with her eyes on the distance whose hoarse murmurings feebly competed with the near, enfolding sound of his voice, weak and husky, yet dominating the interminable depths of the darkness, 'I live *here*. So, good night.'

'Nonsense, Mirissima. We'll walk together.'

In silence they crossed the top of the street they had walked up in a far-off era of this graceless evening. Every step of their way was known to her and was filled with a life that in this midnight hour, transformed by his presence into a darkened gap between day and day, seemed to stand just out of her reach, pleading in vain for recognition and continuance. Counter to it, kept clear by his nearness, ran the stream of her life with him, restored, now that it was so conclusively ended, in clear perspective from its beginning and, surely, remembered by him in so far as his cherished future, for ever beginning, for ever playing him false, allowed him an occasional retrospective glance.

Looking back as they came within the influence of the high trees whose tops disappeared into the upper darkness, she paused upon a memory of one of their earliest agreements, an impersonal unanimity holding them both, in that far-off moment, upright within a fragment of eternity and now substituting, in her mind, for the silence within which, marching side by side, they were so far apart, the sound of the remembered theme. They were now well within the region of the tall trees lining the stretch of pavement, a hundred yards or so as seen with his eyes, but in reality an illimitable space wherein there always came upon whatever was engrossing her as daily she passed this way to and fro, a subtle influence, modifying it, setting it a little aside and toning down its urgency. Even at night, with the trees colourless and only half visible save where lamplight fell upon their dark stems and lit their lower leafage to an unnatural green, the powerful magic came forth that separated this region from the world of the streets. Surely he must be aware of it, must feel it streaming towards him through the stillness whereinto were projected his ponderings, or the pangs of his endurance, whipped up by the promises surrounding him, of the tailing-off of a wasted evening. Under its influence, that was giving her strength to throw, across the interminable distance now separating them, a bridge upon which, as soon as he had recognized it, they might meet and greet one another, he could not fail to respond.

But when the little theme began to go forth upon the air, it sounded rather like one of his nondescript hummed tunes, bereft, in her hands, of its confident purposefulness. As it grew, taking its own shape and recalling how, poised, as she had been when first she heard it, in undefined happiness, it had set a cool hand upon her heart and freed her spirit to wing joyfully forth beyond the confines of familiar life, she felt that her singing not only failed to reach him but, by suggesting a spacious untimed wandering, was increasing his impatience in being carried out of his way.

'Where *are* your lodgings, Miriam?'

Standing still once more, and aware of him brought to a pause in the open, where the trees no longer stood above them and the high blue light of the nearest standard lamp fell coldly from the middle of the roadway upon the desecrated pavement, she braced herself against the truth of their relationship, the essential separation and mutual dislike of their two ways of being, remembering how in earlier days he had mysteriously insisted that a relationship can be 'built up.'

'Good-bye,' she said and turned and swiftly crossed the wide, empty roadway, feeling as she reached the far, opposite pavement, which still was just within the circle of her London homeland, strength to walk, holding back thought, on and on within her own neighbourhood until, stilled by the familiar presences of its tall grey buildings, and the trees detachedly inhabiting its quiet squares, the inward tumult should subside and leave her to become once more aware of her own path, cool and solid beneath her feet; so that when presently she encountered Amabel, the events of the long evening, if, by that time, in her own mind, they were already irrelevant and far away, might be left, by mutual consent, shelved and untouched until they should come forth to fulfil, one by one, their proper role as lively illustrations for the points of intensive colloquies.

CHAPTER III

REGRET for what she had sacrificed in leaving her place at the corner of the Tansley Street balcony to come to the Nursery, was giving way to the desire to identify the quality of this little man from the north. It was already obvious that every one present, and several, she knew, had come anticipating endurance, was captivated in one way or another, and when his second question fell into a stillness whose depth revealed attention, she roused herself to consider the nature of the influence so steadily imposing itself.

This compact little man, his features dim in the on-coming twilight whose soft radiance poured in on the shabby office from the wide high window behind him, came from the north. And though the emanating quality might turn out to be rooted in someone else's thought, carefully grasped and ably presented, there was something in it that was personal, coming from the man himself. Something that set him apart from all the London Lycurgans she had heard so far. The discovery was cheering. For others might visit the Nursery from remote places, bringing unexpected goods, perhaps as valuable as those provided by the Big Men. Perhaps even more valuable.

Taking her pleasantly by surprise, a wave of affection, accumulated unawares during the meetings held in this gloomy room, rose within her and flowed not only backwards over the eventful evenings supplied by the well-known figures, but also forward to embrace the less exciting occasions lying ahead. For these little meetings, she now realized, held a charm peculiar to themselves, independent of the fare provided from behind the table and entirely lacking in the large gatherings of the Lycurgan proper, though Wells condemned even these large meetings for their too local, too enclosed and domestic atmosphere. Seeking the origin of this charm, felt, she was convinced, even by the most superior members—though it would be disastrous to suggest its existence to any one of them— she concluded that it arose partly from the smallness of the gathering and partly from the provisional nature of the surroundings, giving to each meeting the character of a chance encounter, on neutral territory, of people who hitherto have met only amongst others, upon backgrounds soaked with personality and tradition, and who now, poised in a vacuum and reduced to their native simplicity, must conspire to reach an understanding. Even Shaw, shooting up upon the chairman's last word, Jack-in-the-box, magical, electric amidst the shadows of this battered room, had presented his beliefs with a grave simplicity; so that they were more formidable than when they came, festooned with his disarming wit, from the Lycurgan platform. And if the test, so nobly encountered by them all, of appearing bereft of the stimulus of their familiar background, public, limelit, crowded, reduced the big Lycurgans to simplicity, it also left the little audience fully exposed to the operations of the speaker by eliminating the sense, never quite absent from an adult Lycurgan meeting, of being present at a show.

Each of these distinctions, as it presented itself, had a familiar face, recognized as having been glanced at, hurriedly, from the midst of preoccupations, and banished lest its contemplation obscure, even for a moment, the design being offered by a great Lycurgan mind. Only now, only in the presence of this substitute for a god, who was revealing the quality of a small gathering of ordinary mortals just as it had been revealed at the local meeting when Mrs Redfern's Messiah failed to arrive, did they group and present themselves as a whole. For in a sense those earlier Nursery meetings, addressed by the Leaders, each distilling, for the benefit of the gathered infants, his own particular blend of the essences of Lycurgan socialism, had been shows, however modest. Fragments of the great show and, as isolated fragments, revealing here, more clearly than amidst the distractions and rivalries of Sussex Hall, the divergencies of the several minds, leaving one in possession of neatly sorted samples of socialism, disquietingly irreconcilable.

But this nobody from the industrial north radiated a quiet confidence. He was as self-contained as the saffron-robed old Hindu whose high-pitched, fluting voice, sad, seeming to echo through him from the vastness of space, had for a moment reduced the seething ranks of the Lycurgans to a unanimous handful: 'We are an ancient shivilization. We are ruled—by a bureau-crashy. Worsh than that—by a foreign bureau-crashy. Worsh than that—by a bureau-crashy that is always shanging.' And the cosmos reflected in the personality behind his acquired specialist knowledge, unlike that of Shaw or of Wells, or even of Sydney Olivier, though his at least had depth as well as surface, and stillness within its movement, was probably habitable. For he handled his argument as if it were self-existent and the property of every one, rather than a cunning device and a reproach to every one who had failed to discover it. His points emerged of themselves, unspoken yet almost audible in the silence following the rounding off of each of his statements—delivered in a pleasantly meditative undertone—by a question aimed, upon a livelier note, directly at his audience.

The stirrings and whisperings invading her attention from the back row into which had slipped, a moment ago, several late arrivals, were heightening her sense of his way of being, a way that seemed itself a fulfilment of what he was pleading for, and a settlement of the teasing problem by transforming it, in the part of her consciousness it ceaselessly occupied, into a matter of temperament. His temperament was socialism in being. Conscious where the Oberlanders were unconscious, he saw the whole world, just as they saw their small, enclosed Lhassa, as a society. And, just as they did, regarded its unwritten laws as the only sacred laws. Therefore he was a reformer, bent on changing only the unsacred, secondary laws, the written rules of the club whose only justification was the well-being of the members; whereas the Lycurgan intellectuals, some looking at life only through the telescopes and microscopes of scientific research, and others through the stained-glass windows of the various schools of psychology, were competing with each other in a game of social betterment that had suddenly become a scrimmage in which rules were no longer respected.

Turning to discover the source of the increasing stir in the back row, and in turning, aware of herself as an object exposed to the quiet radiance flowing from the speaker, she saw, in a swift series of dissolving views penetrated by this same radiance, her own career as a member of the Lycurgan; saw herself not only drawn hither and thither attentive to mind after mind in her search for an acceptable doctrine, not only, when temporarily impressed, using borrowed opinions as weapons, but finally using the Lycurgan spectacle as a continuous entertainment and feeling that if it were dowered with the unifying something whose presence she had felt at smaller gatherings, it would cease to be interesting. Yet she had had moments of passionate conviction, and upon these she could look back without feeling that the society would be better off without herself and those like her who were eagerly looking for arguments wherewith to floor all comers and who would immediately be driven off by the prospect of doing, year in and year out, some small, obscure task dictated by the chosen exponent. She saw the interior of the stuffy little room in the East End where she had spent the whole of a day's holiday joyfully folding circulars, sustained only by the presence of other workers, an occasional cup of cocoa, and the excitement provided by the coming and going, with the latest news, of other Lycurgans who also were working for Webb. And recalled an evening's canvassing during which she had felt willing to make almost any sacrifice if she could be certain that soon the suspicious people in the mean tenements would find themselves belonging to a vast world-wide society, rather than on guard against everything and everybody; and the strange moment of hungry affection for all the people she had visited, friends and enemies alike, whom she had seen while they talked with her, or in their way of getting rid of her, as they were to themselves, in isolation, apart from the dense atmosphere of family life and from the world in which they struggled so bitterly to maintain themselves.

And nothing short of conviction could have urged her, lying

in bed with a high temperature, to get up and go down through
an east wind to vote at the decisive meeting; only to discover
that even amongst these emancipated intellectuals fair play
was not a matter of course. Hope lost its foundations with the
spectacle of the Leaders deserting their guns and denying their
principles in their frantic attempts to destroy each other. The
one calm person on the platform, the only one who made
any attempt to restrain the combatants, was a woman.

And yet, she reflected, turning fully round, women are
refused the suffrage because they are supposed to be ruled by
their emotions. Her eyes reached the centre of the disturbance
at the back of the room, from whose dimmer twilight shone out,
distinguishing them from their neighbours, the glowing eyes
and flushed cheeks of three young women whose expressions,
different and alike, each revealed a restive, vain desire to escape,
from emotions rioting within and excited neighbours besieging
from without, back into a vanished clear vista at whose end
had gleamed a bright indefinite goal. She remembered with
a pang of dismay that the march of the militants on the House
of Commons had been fixed for to-night and realized, in the
midst of the warm flush rising to her own cheeks with the
thought of the prison cells awaiting these girls to-morrow, that
at this moment Amabel, certainly amongst the arrested, would
be waiting for her at home in a far more abounding state of
exaltation than either of these could attain, one of whom was
betraying, by a forced smile directed at random, and by a
continual insufficient compression and recompression of her
tremulous lips, that she was scared as well as excited, while
her companion on her right, responding to an eagerly whispering neighbour, glanced about collecting incense, and the one
on her left, drawing back from a whispered conversation with
someone turned towards her from the row in front, was now
gazing fixedly at the lecturer in a vain attempt to suggest that
being arrested was all in the day's work.

'This cannot come about of itself. It can be brought about.
But only by means of concerted effort. Do we feel such an
effort to be worth while?'

For the first time, his voice was tinged with emotion. Was

there to be a rising tide? A few more tracts of quiet statement, each ending with a challenge more insistent than the
last, and then a rousing appeal for activity, and the familiar
experience of finding one's interest shifted from the theme to
the spectacle of a speaker in full blast, and finally the vision,
arriving at the end of so many Lycurgan meetings, of the entire
assembly dispersing to stand on soap boxes at street corners
and the sense, in the midst of one's admiration, of something
lacking in them all. Which Amabel had shared, or she would
not so delightedly have agreed that the Lycurgans were a
Primrose League without a primrose—though she had said
afterwards, looking away and speaking very gently, as if to
herself, so as to exclude from what she said any element of
retort or even of criticism: 'Most of those they are fighting for
haven't any primroses,' following up the English jest, because
at the moment she was not with someone who needed to be
flattered all the time, with a typical movement of her own mind,
irrelevant to the issue but so sincere that one refrained from
insisting, also irrelevantly, that most of those who were fighting
were fighting against something incompletely defined rather
than for anything at all.

Amabel's socialism was out-and-out. She stood for the
poor and outcast, not because they were poor but because
they were people, belonging to the club. She would have no
objection to a stockbroker on account of his calling. But why
was she a suffragist? During the whole of their earlier time
together she had upheld the Frenchwoman's point of view.
On one occasion she had expressed 'affection' for the old-
fashioned feminine disabilities and declared herself horrified
by the efforts of the Lycurgan Women's Group to get at the
truth about these celebrated handicaps, though certain of their
discoveries had impressed her. But she believed in exploiting
feminine charm and feminine weakness, believed in controlling
and managing men by means of masked flattery, scorned most
Englishwomen as being caricatures of men, and pitied those
who either lacked, or did not know how to use, feminine
weapons.

To the accompaniment of the little man's now relatively

animated discourse, whence now and again an emphasized
word or phrase dropped into her musing a reminder, like the
sounds coming from round about them in the house when she
and Amabel sat talking their way along a promontory of thought,
or silently contemplating a scene or person one of them had
set up for inspection, that life was going busily on its way, she
considered the ranged fragments that were all she knew of
Amabel's relation to the movement.

It was she herself who had offered her tickets for a meeting,
rejoicing in having something to offer, and feeling that she
might be entertained and feeling at the same time a shamed
sense of her own lack of interest in a meeting composed entirely
of women. Amabel had glanced at the tickets, with the little
moue that meant both amusement and disdain, and had laid
them aside and immediately become animated and charming
in the manner of one who wishes to cover the traces of a
blunder or, by flinging blossoms on its grave, to indicate where
it lies. But she must have gone to that meeting, though she
never mentioned it. For, soon after, she was an active member
of the society. Perhaps one's responses were too slight to call
forth any connected account of her experiences at the many
meetings she must have attended before she became one of
the banner-bearers in the great afternoon procession. Once
she had described Mrs Despard with devout adoration until
one could see her; see her silky white hair and the delicate mesh
of her old lace and could recognize the characteristic quality
of the English gentlewoman of her period, the disciplined moral
strength concealed behind the gentle façade, within the fragile
network of nerves and the delicate structure of bones and sinews,
and supporting her now that she compelled herself, in old age,
to break through the conventions of a lifetime and fight for a
cause seen, in the light shed by her long experience, as necessary
to the civilization of which she was a representative.

And Amabel had said one night, suddenly, that she wished
Israel Zangwill, who really was a peach, would leave off being
facetious. Both these items had made their appearance
irrelevantly, at the far end of long conversations, revealing
her ensconced within the events of which they were salient,

detachable fragments. But she never tried to draw one in, until the big procession made numbers desirable.

Either she regards me as disqualified for any kind of mêlée, or she wishes to keep me as an onlooker at the drama of her own adventure. Of course she is worthy of an audience, if only because she so readily becomes one herself, so long as the show has her approval. What she so rejoicingly exploits is not only herself, but what she impersonally represents; moving, in all her exploitations, from self to selflessness. Willingly dedicated? She is what a man can never fully be: the meeting place of heaven and earth. Is that why men delighting in limelight and mirroring audiences are always a little absurd?

Lovely she was, worthy of throngs of spectators, swinging gracefully, steadily along in bright sunlight, the rhythm of her march unimpeded by the heavy pole of the wide banner whose other pole must have been carried by someone walking with the same steady rhythmical swing; at whom I never looked, seeing only Amabel, just ahead of me, a single figure worthy to stand as a symbol of the whole procession, gravely jubilant, modestly proud. She seemed to invite all the world to march with her, to help and be helped. Certain in the way a man so rarely is certain, whole where he is divided, strong where he is weak. Deeply ensconced within her being, and therefore radiant. And it was she, and others here and there in the procession, particularly those the general public was not prepared for, matronly, middle-aged, and obviously gentlewomen, who gave it the quality that shamed into so blessed a silence the pavement-scoffers and the gutter-wits; and who were so deliberately ignored by those of the newspaper men who still went on with their misrepresentations to support the policy of their employers. And it was the sight of Amabel and these others that brought so many male pedestrians to the point of overcoming their British self-consciousness and stepping into the roadway to march alongside.

Since then, Amabel has said nothing of the progress of events until she told me of to-night's march.

Someone switched on the light, an apparition, banishing the June gloaming, driving the expanded being of every one back upon itself and revealing the face of the lecturer. It was deeply lined by some sort of endurance, and something in the modelling of the rather narrow skull, something about the expression of the whole head seemed to cry aloud the limits of the man's imagination and to classify him with those who adopt, and devote a lifetime to expounding, a doctrine thought out but not thought through, and therefore doomed from the outset. But his state of being sociably at home and at ease and available, in the midst of a self that had become identified with a belief without losing its pleasant individuality, had the power of freeing, within his hearers, the contemplative spirit, and moving them to assemble for its operation their accumulated experience, modified, so long as it was examined in his presence, by the influence of his personality. Even those who were interested in following his discourse from point to point must feel the reflective process going on within, a troubled accompaniment to his serene expressiveness; and the few authoritative intellectuals who by this time had approvingly or scornfully identified his school, must be discomfited by the self-effacing simplicity of his address, his failure to use an opportunity for display.

He was something like that outsider who had come to take the Three Hours service at All Saints'.

The incident had sprung forth unsummoned from its hiding-place in the past where all these years it had awaited the niche prepared for it partly by yesterday's evening on the balcony, which had taken her unawares back into the time when going to church, even at the risk of being upset by the parson, was still a weekly joy, and partly by the influence of this man whose spirit was an innocent reproach to feigned interest. Just as for this last hour she had sat unparticipating and yet glad to be present, so, on that far-off day, she had sat and knelt and stood, singing, without experiencing any emotion that in the opinion of a sound churchman would have justified her presence. But not without uneasiness. The gladness she was now remembering had arrived during the moment after the unknown parson suddenly broke off his discourse to appeal, in his everyday voice, quietly, to his congregation, to every member of it, to cease attending to him as soon as anything he said should rouse a response, or a train of thought, and to spend the remainder of the time in private meditation.

And because this man knew all about the difficulty of occasions, how most of them are ruined by being belaboured in advance and insisted upon during their progress, she had listened to him for a while. But must soon have left off listening. For there was no further memory of him. Another's self-effacing honesty had recalled him and there he stood, a comfort and a reproach.

Recalled by this central figure, the whole of that far-off midday stood clear. She was walking across the common to church, alone between those who had started early and those who were going to be late, feeling strong and tireless and full of the inexhaustible strange joy that had come with this six-teenth year and that sometimes seemed to assert its indepen-dence, both of Ted and of the ever-increasing troubles at home. To-day as she walked, suitably clad in her oldest clothes, quietly through the noon stillness under a rainless grey sky, it seemed to have the power of banishing for ever all that came between her and what she wanted to be whenever she reached down to the centre of her being. And then, half-way between home and church, as she watched the flower-dotted grass move by on either side of the small pathway, she felt an encroaching radiance, felt herself now, more deeply than she would on the way home from church with the others, the enchanted guest of spring and summer. They were advancing upon her, bringing hours upon hours of happiness, moments of breathless joy whether or no she were worthy, whether or no she succeeded in being as good as she pined to be. And as the grey church drew near, bringing her walk to an end, she had realized for the first time, with a shock of surprise and a desire to drive the thought away, how powerfully the future flows into the present and how, on entering an experience, one is already beyond it, so that most occasions are imperfect because no one is really quite within them, save before and afterwards; and then only at the price of solitude.

Sitting far back in the church with the soberly dressed

forms of the scattered congregation in front of her, all more than usually at home and in touch with each other within this special occasion which drew only those who really wanted to come, she had felt for a moment the warm sense of belonging. For she, too, had wanted to come. But these people were gathered to feel sad and she tried in vain to experience sadness, being aware only of the welcome unusual deep quietude and of the lovely colour of the drapery over the altar frontal, pure violet deep and fresh, glowing in the sunless grey light, drawing the eyes into its depths, foretelling the Easter blossoming of this same scene into flowers and sunlight. And even the Good Friday hymns, beautiful in their sadness, moving slowly in minor key over only a few tones and semitones, and the punctuating of the intervals of silence by the Words from the Cross brought only a sense of pathos from which, Easter having happened for good and all, joy could not be excluded.

And she had sat unlistening, aware only of the flowing away of the occasion, and stood singing, lost in the eternity which singing brings, and knelt, taking down with her amongst the enclosed odours of dusty hassocks, old books, and the scent, against her face, of warmed kid gloves, the profane joy against which it was useless to strive.

And just as on that day the quiet, exceptional little parson had made her realize that she would never be able completely to experience the emotions of orthodox Christianity, so, this evening, it was a modest and sincere little Socialist who had confirmed her growing conviction of being unable to experience the emotions that kept Lycurgan socialism on its feet. Throughout his discourse, as her mind wandered about on its own territory, she had had the sense of being confined by him, within the room where the others were building up a clear relationship with the world and using their minds as repositories for facts supporting the theory they had accepted in regard to it, in a private confessional wherein at last she was fully perceiving herself disqualified.

The rising of the chairman to open the discussion set her free to banish herself without offence and hurry home empty-handed to become, for the rest of the evening, Amabel's admiring audience. But when she emerged from the secrecy of the ancient by-way into the lamplit clarity of Fleet Street, where only an occasional upper window teasingly represented, with its oblong of yellow light, the vociferous competition to define and to impose definitions, she desired only rest.

Watching the stout morocco-bound volume disappear into Amabel's handbag, she pictured her sitting in her quiet prison cell undisturbedly reading the whole of *The Ring and the Book*, with all her needs supplied and honour and glory piling up against her release, and felt almost envious.

'Yes,' and again Amabel shook off the invading influence of to-morrow. 'Yes! Mira, it was truly rather wonderful as well as really funny.' This time she had only partly turned away from the centre round which her thoughts were collecting, and two manners of presenting what she was about to impart, one gleefully meditative and the other gravely romantic, competed together in her voice and bearing. 'She and I rolled out of the meeting . . . led the way . . . arm-in-arm, down the street.' Her eyes appealed for mirth, delighted mirth over an intense clear vision of the defiant law-breaker, the smasher of outrageous barriers, to set enhancingly beside the one she knew was also immortal, the picture of Babinka poised on the edge of her bed in pale delphinium-blue kimono, retrospectively rapturous.

'The two policemen appeared from nowhere, took our outside arms in their great paws, and there we were!'

'Arrested.'

'I politely asked my bobby if I was arrested. "That's right, miss," he said!' Cascade of laughter, not quite so trillingly triumphant as it must have been when she provisionally told the story to the Baileys downstairs. A little broken, devitalized now that the adventure was over and had once been recounted, by a growing apprehension of its uncontrollably approaching results.

'He's a peach,' she went on, meditatively. 'Told me his

wife belonged to the militants and we'd win if we kept on making trouble!' Smiling into space, she wistfully recalled, in the remoteness of the quiet, familiar room, a great moment irrevocably gone by, and turned her head and sent a sweeping glance across her domain. In a moment her eyes would return and the to and fro of their voices would resume the task of reviving each detail of the adventure while still it was fresh in her mind. Meanwhile for an instant, Amabel was alone, in her presence, for the first time. For this investigating glance was not the one which meant that she could not wait while one took in something she had said, nor the one which meant that she had lost interest and retired on to some presently-to-be-communicated item of her store of experience. It was a genuine investigating search for a reminder, amongst her scattered belongings, of something she might have forgotten.

Watching her thus, temporarily removed, Miriam felt the blood rising to her cheeks before the shock of discovery. Deep down in her heart was the unmistakable stirring of a tide of relief, and her eyelids, as soon as she became aware of it and of how, to-morrow, its cool waves would invade and heal her, had dropped their screen, and fear, lest Amabel's returned glance should have read upon her features something of the embarrassing revelation, brought her to her feet and improvised swift statements, spoken aloud as if she were thinking on Amabel's behalf, but just half a tone too high and a shade too emphatically, about the detail of getting to Vine Street police court at nine in the morning.

Even when the door swept open, revealing Amabel cloaked and hatted, not coming in, waiting, a silent summons, upright and motionless, her bag in one hand and the other upon the door-knob, Miriam remained alone, deep in her renewed solitude, and her hands, though now become conscious of what they were doing, could not at once cease their lingering, adjusting movements amongst the things on her dressing-table, begun automatically while she stood, ready to go but unwilling, hastily and inattentively and as if the movement of external events could close its reopened avenue, to leave the little roomful of morning light restored to her in its original peace and freshness at the heart of the universe. Her continued movements, of whose exasperating effect, suggesting mis-timed, meditative preoccupation, she was uncomfortably aware, were yet sustaining; for now they had become, since she was caught in the act of making them, the reinforcement of her unspoken response to Amabel's silent assertion, conveyed by her manner of waiting, a taut patience ready to snap but also ready to pass into forgiveness if not tried too far, that the placid ripples of a quiet existence must allow themselves to be swept into the tide of her world-changing drama.

It was a tug-of-war wherein she felt herself pulling on both sides, but Amabel, to-day for the first time, was pulling on one side alone, and awareness of this new feature in their intercourse kept her for yet another instant serenely engaged in making leisurely little movements; for too long.

'Mira! *Not* this *morning*!'

As if she—who, while Amabel floated about at leisure, with the whole day before her to fill as she pleased, just managed, with the little store of strength drawn from a few hours of troubled sleep, to get away to work leaving everything in confusion—stood every morning tiresomely adjusting the objects on her dressing-table. It was a statement of opinion, a criticism hitherto kept in the background.

Down, down, down the long staircase, with Amabel, better known and more beloved than any one on earth, a stranger and hostile, a young girl in a cloak, going, breakfastless and sick with excitement, to pay for effectively stating the desire and the right of women to help in the world's housekeeping.

CHAPTER IV

SOME kind of calculation is at work, a sort of spiritual metronome, imperceptible save when something goes wrong. It operates, too, upon sentences. A syllable too many or a syllable too few brings discomfort, forcing one to make an alteration; even if the words already written are satisfactory. Perhaps every one has a definite thought-rhythm and speech-rhythm, which cannot be violated without producing self-consciousness and discomfort?

The whole process is strange. Strange and secret, always the same, always a mystery and an absence from which one returns to find life a little further on.

When the new volume arrives in its parcel, one has to endure the pang of farewell to current life that comes at the moment of going away on a visit. Everything in one's surroundings becomes attractive and precious. In their midst, threatening like a packet of explosive, lies the new book. The next moment, everything is obliterated by the stream of suggestions flowing from the read title, bringing the desire immediately to note down the various possible methods of approach busily competing for choice. To open the book is to begin life anew, with eternity in hand. But very soon, perhaps with its opening phrase, invariably during the course of the first half-page, one is aware of the author, self-described in his turns of phrase and his use of epithet and metaphor, and, for a while, oblivious of the underlying meaning in the interest of tracing the portrait, and therefore reluctant to read carefully and to write about the substance of the book rather than to paint a portrait of the author and leave his produce to be inferred. Presently there comes a weary sense of the mass of prose extending beyond this opening display, and the turning of leaves and reading of passages here and there; the appearance of alien elements, of quotations and gleanings of facts; at last the rising of a crowd of problems, at the centre of which stands the spectre of one's own ignorance. Nothing to hold to but a half-accepted doctrine: that the reviewer should treat a book as a universe, crediting each author with a certain uniqueness and originality rather than seeking, or devising, relationships and derivations.

Then the careful reading from beginning to end, sometimes forgetfulness of one's enterprise in the interest of the text, and sometimes increase of panic to the point of deciding to return the book and, nearly always, whether one feels capable or disqualified, reluctance to spend any more time on it, to sacrifice an indefinite portion of one's brief leisure shut up and turned away from life.

And then the strangest of the experiences—the way, if one feels sure of one's opinion, one meets, in the interval between reading and writing, a clear and convincing expression of an alternative point of view, so that when one comes to write one must either include it and indicate its limitations, which are not always obvious, or leave it silently presiding, undisposed of. Just as strange is the way one meets, after enduring days of being tormented by some special difficulty, in a conversation, or in a book or newspaper, something that clears it up; just in time. And, if there is no special difficulty, but only un-certainty as to method, keeping one uneasy when one is alone, and absent-minded when with others, one wakes one morning seeing exactly what to do and with phrases, ready-made for the turning-points of the argument, saying themselves in one's mind; again, just in time.

And yet, each time, one passes through the same miseries, forgetting.

She gathered up the scattered sheets. They seemed alive, warm, almost breathing within her hands. She felt sure, and knew that to-morrow also she would feel sure, that the idea of reviewing this particular book in the form of what now ap-peared to be a kind of short story, bringing it down into life and illustrating its operation there, was good. Perhaps this was a turning-point, leaving panic behind. In future she would read each book calmly, ignore the difficulties encountered on the way, set it confidently aside and wait for the 'subliminal consciousness' to throw up an idea. But even as this pleasant prospect presented itself she suspected it of being too smooth and easy and wistfully feared that some disturbing price must each time be paid, that only through engrossment and effort could the path be cut through which a solution would emerge.

But at least, henceforward, there would be each time a different solution, a fresh, delightful, though arduous adventure, worth having and paying for in time sacrificed and leaving, when it was over, something alive within her hands, with a being and substance of its own that owed nothing to her but faithful attention. And never again need she take the easy way out that, a few months ago, had seemed difficult enough: catalogue statements, 'is . . . is . . . is . . .' helped out by paraphrases of the preface or the conclusion.

Repeating her laboriously acquired creed, 'Beware of verbs "to be" and "to have" and of "which"; begin article with adverb; pile up modifications in front of verb to avoid anti-climax; keep gist of sentence till end'; she became aware of the sudden coolness of the air against her forehead, drawing her attention to the faint happy dew of release broken forth there, and lifting her eyes towards the outer night and the familiar, supporting cliff of house-fronts across the way, whose tops, now that she was no longer in her attic, she could not see. Its upper windows shone dark, or sheeny-blue where gleamed the reflected light of street lamps. Most of the french windows along the balconies were sociable golden oblongs, lace-screened. And that upper window, away to the left on a level with her own, was again lit and uncurtained. The solitary was still there, had doubtless been sitting there at work every evening since he came home from Flaxman's. But after those first evenings before Amabel had settled in the house, the whole of her consciousness had flowed, as soon as her work was done, backwards towards Amabel's room down the passage.

And now all the forgotten wealth of this shut-in, skyless prospect was her own again as it had been on that first evening when her little bureau had been brought in and set down in the window-space and Mrs Bailey had cheerily agreed to banish the bedroom crockery to make room for her own moss-green set. To-night, it was as if the intervening loop of time had closed up and vanished, as completely as the time with Selina had closed up and vanished, when she escaped from Flaxman's. But the second loop was weighed down with stored wealth, inexhaustible, an income for life, and beyond.

There was still something pressing for notice, laying a numbing finger upon the recalling of Amabel who, with her departure, had vanished so utterly. Something that had touched her mind when first she looked up, before her eyes had noted details. Looking within, she saw the skyless cliff, grey in fading light, heard Mrs Bailey's departing voice, warm and kindly with the pleasure of her return, took in the perfect position of the ramshackle little old gas-bracket, just above and behind her left shoulder as she stood close to the bureau absorbing the sudden stillness and the sense of solitude and enclosure; nothing visible through the window but the stationary cliff. No changing sky, no distracting roadway, and inside, all her belongings gathered within the narrow strip of room, surrounded by other rooms and part of another London cliff. This evening of freedom renewed was joined without a break to that first magic evening, whose promise it had fulfilled.

Her thoughts moved on to the moment of waking on the first morning in this room, richly at home, deep in the sense of Sunday leisure and the sense of people all about her in the house, but not impinging; the gradual realization of the freshness of the air pouring in from the squares, in place of the foul reek of the cat- and garbage-haunted waste ground at the back of Flaxman's and, presently, as she lay steeped in bliss, the attack on her nostrils from within the house: not the mingling of stale odours perpetually rising through the confined dust-laden air of the Flaxman tenements, but, stealing up from Mrs Bailey's vast, cheerful kitchen and carrying through key-holes and the creaks of doors its invitation to breakfast, the savoury smell of frying rashers.

The tuneful booming of St Pancras clock called her back to listen and brought before her eyes the tree-filled space across which it reached the stately old streets. Eleven. And her article must be posted in the morning. Copied before breakfast, with morning clarity to discover ill-knit passages. But it lay there, alive, with its mysterious separate being. The editor would approve. Hypo would approve. 'Bright of you, Miriam,' he would say.

Not until the door stood open did she ask herself whither, so eagerly, she was hurrying. Before her lay the passage, in economical darkness. Ahead, behind its closed door, Amabel's room, silent and empty.

CHAPTER V

STILL without a word, the wardress pulled out for her the chair
that was set at the end of the long bare table nearest the
entrance, stalked away, and disappeared through a door and
along a passage opening just beyond the far end of the table,
at which stood another chair. There, presumably, Amabel
was to sit, smiling, a triumphant prisoner. But it would not
be easy to converse across the long, drab waste. This was the
prison salon, its social side, a bleak space furnished entirely
with this table, running almost its whole length, and the two
kitchen chairs, and giving on to the courtyard through which
she had come. There was nothing here, and had been nothing,
since that low archway at the entrance, wherein one could find
refuge, nothing anywhere but stern angles and, to-day, cloud-
dimmed daylight. A challenging atmosphere, isolating and
throwing one, bereft of support, back on oneself. The street,
left less than two minutes ago, might have been a hundred
miles away; the archway, the blunt beauty of its low curve, in
another world. But it was the woman, much more than the
surroundings, who had effected the translation.

Her atmosphere was totally unlike that produced by other
women in uniform, servants or hospital nurses, who always
suggest a distinction between themselves and their office, an
unbroken consciousness of a personal life going on behind their
appearance of permanent availability. This woman seemed
undivided, as if she had been born in prison uniform and
had never done anything but stalk about, a gaunt marionette
and, like a marionette, because of its finality, because of the
absence of anything to appeal to, a more horribly moving
spectre than is a living being. No appeal. That, her mechanical non-humanity, was what made this woman so
perfect a representative of prison life.

Stone walls do not a prison make; but this woman could make a prison anywhere.

Reappearing, she slowly advanced, pacing rigidly, mechanically, along the side of the table nearest to the courtyard whose grey light upon her face revealed an expression of watchful cunning, gleaming from her cold eyes and drawing her thin lips into a kind of smile. Half-way down, she stopped and looked towards the little corridor, along which advanced another figure, again a procession of one, but moving still more slowly, as if sleep-walking, eyes wide on vacancy, or as if drugged, or mad.

Two paces, and the figure emerged from the passage and, reaching the chair, placed a white hand upon its back and swung with a single graceful movement——

It was Amabel! Unrecognizable in the large ill-made dress of chequered cotton, her hair hidden beneath a clumsy cap of the same material, set, as if to accentuate pathos, a little dismally askew, but now, since the gaze of the eyes beneath it, in becoming direct, had moved from incredulous amazement into a mingling of reproach and scorn, taking the part of an ironic commentator.

But why all this drama? And *why*, in the presence of the wardress, this tragic, martyred air? It was not only the prison dress, it was also partly her desire to make an impressive entry in the character of a prisoner that had made her unrecognizable. After all, she was in a sense a hostess and oneself a visitor expecting to be welcomed. But the entry she had devised apparently precluded speech.

'I didn't recognize you,' said Miriam, angrily aware, as she spoke, of hanging herself in the proffered rope, impatiently waiting for Amabel to cut her remorsefully down.

'No,' breathed Amabel tonelessly, and glanced apprehensively at the wardress, now standing a little averted. Assumed apprehensiveness, deliberately calculated to add to one's embarrassment by suggesting that at the first sign of spontaneous interchange the marionette would turn and annihilate the two of them. A series of remarks passed through Miriam's mind, each unsuited to the occasion as Amabel wished it to appear, each revealing herself as insufficiently impressed. She remained silent, watching Amabel's face for a change of tactics.

'It was kind of you to come,' said Amabel, isolating each word by a little pause, as if speech were a difficult, long-forgotten art.

'I wanted to come,' said Miriam, wondering with the available edge of her mind what kind of truth lay behind her words, whether she had wanted most to see Amabel or, most, to achieve the experience of visiting an imprisoned suffragist; while the rest of her mind remained tethered and turning round and round in the effort to decide whether after all Amabel was staging her drama wholly for her benefit, or whether it was part of a week-old campaign against the inhumanity of the wardress.

'I shall see you again before long,' she added lamely, acutely aware of the difficulty of projecting emotion across the long waste of table, and saw Amabel register, by a perfectly normal glance of disapproval directed away from their colloquy, sideways towards the observant, long-suffering universe, impatience with her failure to play a suitable part.

Which of them had laughed first? It was impossible, in the midst of this swift to and fro of Tansley Street items, to remember. And it was really hostess and guest who were now separating, facing each other, across this exaggerated precautionary distance, grimacing at each other while the wardress, who had turned and beckoned, moved to the open door. But even as Amabel kissed her hand and smiled her smile, her bearing resumed its former tragic dignity and she turned and crossed the small space between her chair and the door, where she became, on passing the rigidly motionless form of the wardress—whose look of cunning watchfulness was now inturned, leaving her eyes sightless and herself unapproachable—a forbearing suppliant, head bowed and eyes down-gazing, as if patiently waiting until it should please the tormentor to relent and respond.

CHAPTER VI

'Dst Miretta,

'I don't perhaps catch your drift. But I think you 're mistaken and I don't share your opinion of yourself. The real difference between us is that while you think in order to live, I live in order to think.

'Yrs,   H.'

Trying again to recall the drift of her letter, she succeeded little better than she had done this morning, remembering only that the mood dictating it had been the result of his unexpected little note whose contents had revealed him glancing, from the glowing midst of a pause in a stretch of satisfactory work, out across his world and immediately discerning herself, temporarily prominent amongst those who stood, when not actively engaged in the tasks so mercifully keeping them out of the way until they were wanted, turned towards him in admiration and support. Within that 'exalted and luminous moment,' he had been moved to knit up the broken mesh of their relationship by selecting her for the role of reflector of his joy in achievement. Sanguine and kindly, her superior in kindliness and in freedom from vindictiveness, impersonally friendly and reluctant quite to lose her, he had sent a greeting during a mood wherein he felt at peace with all mankind.

That he should assume this information to be a sufficient gift of himself, enough to feed her interest and to hold her turned his way, was largely her own fault. For although from time to time, under the spell of his writing, she felt that from him alone was coming a clear, vital statement of mankind's immediate affairs and that all human activities should cease while he said his say, she was haunted, even in the midst of the miracles of illumination worked by the theories guiding his perceptions, by the insufficiency of these theories to encompass reality; and found herself growing, whenever the spell was broken and criticism awakened by the sudden intrusion and zestful exploitation of some new-minted textbook term, increasingly impatient of the scientific metaphors tyrannizing unquestioned within so much of his statement. Therefore the thought of him immersed in work brought now a sort of anxiety, a sense of a vast number of people being overcome by his magic and misled, ignoring the gaps in his scheme of salvation—which, naïvely, under pressure from without, he would sometimes attempt to fill with concessions whose very phrasing betrayed at once his lack of interest in what was in question and his desire somehow, anyhow, to convert to his plan those who remained so obstinately and, for him, so mysteriously, indifferent to it — and believing themselves satisfied with a picture of humanity travelling, a procession of dying invalids, towards the ultimate extinction of all that is, or, at best, towards a larger, better-equipped death-chamber, an abode which he so amazingly failed to see would be, for those inhabiting it, as much a matter of course as that in which their ancestors had suffered and been extinguished.

It was her fault. She had played him false, had kept in the background the completeness of her intermittent repudiation of his views, for the sake of his companionship, for the sake, too, of retaining her share in the gaieties of his prosperous life. But here an element entered against which she was powerless: the love of backgrounds, the cause of endless deceptions and the basis of an absurd conviction—that these backgrounds belonged more to herself than to the people who created them. Yet, even here, was mystery and uncertainty. For these backgrounds, thought of without the people to whom they belonged, faded and died. And this would seem to mean that places, after all, were people.

Vanity, too, had helped. If it were vanity to hope that she herself might be instrumental in changing his views. Yet she knew that she would gladly sacrifice his companionship and all that depended therefrom for the certainty of seeing his world of ceaseless 'becoming' exchanged for one wherein should be included also the fact of 'being,' the overwhelming, smiling hint, proof against all possible tests, provided by the mere existence of anything, anywhere.

Recalling herself from this unfailing mental pasture, she turned to him again. Within his limits, he was innocent and whole. He saw his 'job,' and gave to it his whole strength. No one else, considering the human spectacle, saw so clearly as he and in so many directions or on so large a scale what was going on. No one else had a greater measure of intellectual force. But Newman had predicted the force and brilliance of the modern mind and called it Antichrist. Chesterton believed that clear thought was incomplete thought. It was certainly cheerless thought. Beginning nowhere, it ended in a void.

Being versus becoming. Becoming versus being. Look after the being and the becoming will look after itself. Look after the becoming and the being will look after itself? Not so certain. Therefore it is certain that becoming depends upon being. Man carries his bourne within himself and is there already, or he would not even know that he exists.

Why, instead of writing whatever it was she had written, had she not sent just a statement of that sort, upon a post card? He would have dismissed it as 'cloudy'; and, meeting him, she would have no words ready with which to confound the silencing formulae he carried about, like small change, and could put his hand upon at will. But anything would have been better than responding, to his zestful sketch of himself, so thoroughly in the masculine tradition, and which any 'sensible' woman would indulgently accept and cherish, with something that had been dictated by a compensating complacent vision of herself as the Intimate Friend of a Great Man; but without the justification so amply supporting his complacency, without a single characteristic to qualify her for the role, or a sufficient background of hard-won culture to justify a claim to it. His rebuke, though addressed to a non-existent person, the meekly admiring follower he desired rather than an opponent facing the other way, was well earned. But his manner of administering it, insufferable.

Even this morning astonishment had preceded wrath, and now, after a day's forgetfulness, repudiation of deliberate formal offensiveness still called aloud for suitable action. She regretted having kept the note for even a single day instead of casting it forth at once, posting it back on her way to work, so that he might have received it by this evening's delivery at Bonnycliff. It was too late, now, to reach him even to-morrow morning. But it must be banished before the depths of night should present it in the morning as a long-harboured possession. To-night it was still new, an aggressor, material for prompt destruction. But not to be honoured so far. He should destroy it himself and should be told to do so in a manner leaving no doubt as to her opinion. A simple return would have left her reaction uncertain.

With a pang of relief, she welcomed the arrival of a phrase and wrote serenely, sideways across the wide space left below the compact lines in the centre of the card: 'I have no waste paper basket. Yours, I know, is capacious. M.'

Returning from post, she found her room flooded with the first radiance of afterglow and filled with rain-washed air promising the fragrant freshness of night in the neighbourhood of trees, and bringing a vision of early morning, waiting beyond the deep brief space of darkness. Both darkness and early morning once more peace-filled. Once more her room held quietude secure, and the old in-pouring influence that could so rarely and so precariously be shared. Here, in the midst of it, everything seemed immeasurably far off and even thought seemed to exist and to express itself in another world, into which she could move, or refrain from moving. Her being sank, perceptibly, back and back into a centre wherein it was held poised and sensitive to every sound and scent, and to the play of light on any and every object in the room. Turning gently in the midst of her recovered wealth, in the companionship that brought, even with movement, a deepening stillness, she saw upon the end wall the subdued reflection of London light, signalling the vast quiet movement of light about the world. It held a secret for whose full revelation she felt she could wait for ever, knowing that it would come.

Was it just the posting of that letter together with the presence of this perfection of clear light after rain that had so vividly restored her sense of the sufficiency of life at first hand?

Turning back to face the window, upon a deep breath at whose end she knew she would be invaded by an army of practical demands calling for the attention she could at this moment joyously give, she found, advancing ahead of all other claims, the remembrance of the little store of letters. As if, before she could begin upon the arrears of sorting and mending and tidying, so long forgotten and now promising delight, she must rid her room of an alien presence.

Why not send them all back?

'Beyond space and time.' Springing before her mind's eye in their place upon the written page, the words no longer had power to move her as they had done on that morning when the unexpected letter had announced its arrival with the sound of the postman's knock, and the hammer-blow upon the door had struck to the centre of her being and sent her on flying feet down the stairs and across the hall to the letter-box, and back to the room with the letter in her hands at whose address she had not even glanced, knowing it was for herself. But they reminded her that indeed she had been transported beyond time and space, that her being, at the moment of reading, had become an unknown timeless being, released from all boundaries, wide as the world and wider, yet still herself. And when her breathing was even again and her surroundings motionless, she had turned to him in boundless gratitude.

And now she found herself regarding the experience as overwhelming evidence for direct, unmediated communication. Before this particular and quite unexpected letter had arrived, she had heard from him a hundred times and now and again been deeply moved as she read. On this occasion, some part of her had read the letter as it lay in the box and she had experienced in advance the emotions it aroused, the transfiguring twofold emotion of belief in his love and joy in the admission, at last, of a faith akin to her own. But now it seemed likely that this admission, which she had taken for the expression of a conviction persisting, in spite of his facetious protests, deep down in his consciousness, was merely a figure of speech.

Hitherto, this one letter had irradiated all the rest, both those preceding it, appreciative responses to her own and written, gravely, almost in her own style, and those that followed: brief impersonal notes, sent to bridge intervals between their talks. Now, it seemed possible that this central letter might have been devised to meet her case, might be the culmination of a carefully graduated series.

'Writers,' he had said, ages ago, 'have an immense pull when it comes to love-making. They are articulate and can put their goods alluringly in the window.' She remembered repeating this to Mr Hancock and the way, looking back along a past which she knew held a broken romance, he had said with the note of respect for his subject that throughout her association with him had been balm for the wounds inflicted by the modern scientific intellectuals: 'They are very fortunate.' It was on this occasion, just before the announcement of his engagement, that she had said, aware of him still standing conversationally near, on a sudden impulse and without looking at him: 'First love is not necessarily the best.' That, too, was a quotation, though he did not know it and answered simply and sincerely in his unofficial voice, the voice that still encircled and held her, while it sounded, in a world whose values were unchanging: 'I hope that may be so.' Sad; uncertain and sad in the midst of his grave, deep happiness.

And now she was for ever excluded from that world, and the world she had entered was closing against her and the one she had inhabited with Amabel was breaking up. Ahead, nothing was visible. Joining company with this sense of the isolation of her personal life came a deep, disturbing apprehension, imperfectly realized when the pain of parting with Hypo had fallen upon her in the midst of the ceaseless events of life with Amabel. Pain had been numbed, and loss set aside by the cultivation of the idea that what was lost had never been worth having. But even after she had suggested this final judgment to Amabel by saying, suddenly and irrelevantly from the midst of a communion wherein she had felt that the admission, overdue, would enhance their unity, 'He is just a collector of virginities,' and Amabel, applauding the formula, had expressed at the same time, in voice and manner, genuine surprise over what she regarded as slowness in arriving at the self-evident, his presence had remained, haunting the outskirts of her consciousness, and now, picturing him as for ever turned away, she was invaded by a kind of spiritual panic.

Yet, even in the midst of it, she could not regret returning that last letter. To her dying day she would stand by that repudiation. But the others she would presently destroy herself. They, at least, were worth destroying.

Had Amabel, always more interested and curious and less contemptuous of him than she professed to be, really read those letters when she dropped and broke the bog-oak casket? The suspicion, temporarily forgotten, had dawned and hovered, neither accepted nor rejected, at that vanished moment, now so vividly returned, when, relating the incident, Amabel had wound up by regretting that it should have happened to 'this particular magpie-hoard.' The apt expression, although disconcertingly revealing an opinion privately cherished, and produced only under the urgency of events, had distracted her attention from the disaster and so powerfully reinforced Amabel's presence, its way of filling the room and bringing with it, like a tapestry screening all that had existed before she came, the whole of their shared experience, that the broken casket, become an obstruction to the movement of the evening, had been put away, and forgotten.

But now the event itself, no longer obscured by Amabel's handling, came forth with a startling question: How had the casket been broken? How, in the first place, had it at all come into her possession?

She had appeared at the door, in the evening, the moment one had come in, holding the casket in her hands. Looking contrite, she had explained, hurriedly and breathlessly and without pausing for comment or response—her way of disposing of matters that entailed a momentary breaking of their interchange — that she had managed somehow to drop it, and then had come her striking comment: that she would rather have damaged anything than *this particular magpie-hoard*. Was that her way of confessing that she had examined the contents of the box, as indeed she must have done?

But how had it been broken? Supposing her coming in, curious, and taking it up from where it used to stand on the top of the bureau, how could she drop its solid little form? And, if she did, would that be enough to break it?

Where was the casket?

A search revealed it lying hidden in the bamboo wardrobe behind things fallen from their hooks. For the first time, she examined the break. It extended, below the hinges and determined by the outline of the carving, in an irregular curve across the back. It would be possible, by holding the two parts as far from each other as they would go, to shake out the letters. The double lock, though loose, was still secure.

She faced an inconceivable conclusion. True. Untrue. Her own mean suspicion. Again she looked at the box. It was old. It had held grannie's bog-oak bracelets, chain, and brooch more than half a century ago, and might be older than that. But it was strong and sound. Along the break the wood was firm and clean. A fall, since the contents weighed next to nothing, could not break any part of it.

It had reached the floor from a height, violently. It had been deliberately and forcibly flung down?

While the imagined picture held her eyes, she felt, striking through her uncertainty and bearing down her anger, its heroic appeal, the appeal of Amabel's determination to drive through veils and secrecies. She put the casket away, trying for forgetfulness. But the little box, itself, reproached her. Mended, of course, it could be, and the break would not even show.

She felt Amabel watching, indulgent, as with a child, but essentially amused and contemptuous. She was so easily moved to solicitude. Like Sarah. But, unlike Sarah, her solicitude was for people only, and not also for the things they held dear. Sarah cherished the beloved belongings of others more than her own and would deny herself in order to restore or replace them. Amabel was a tornado, sweeping oneself off one's feet and one's possessions from their niches.

Perhaps, in the end, things, like beloved backgrounds, are people. But individual objects hold the power of moving one deeply and immediately and always in the same way. There is no variableness with them, neither shadow of turning. People move one variously and intermittently and, in direct confrontation, there is nearly always a barrier. In things, even in perfectly 'ordinary and commonplace' things, life is embodied. The sudden sight of a sun-faded garment can arouse from where they lie stored in oneself, sleeping memories, the lovely essences of a summer holiday, free from all that at the moment seemed to come between oneself and the possibility of passionate apprehension. After an interval, only after an interval—showing that there is within oneself something that ceaselessly contemplates 'forgotten' things—a fragment of stone, even a photograph, has the power of making one enter a kingdom one hardly knew one possessed. Whose riches increase, even though they are inanimate. But, if greatly loved, are they inanimate? They are destructible. Perhaps the secret is there. People cannot be destroyed. Things can. From the moment they come into being, they are at the mercy of accident.

With Amabel present, casting her strong spell, my hold on things was loosened. They retired. Perhaps to their right place. 'Set your affections on things above, not on things of the earth . . . for we brought nothing into this world, and it is certain we can carry nothing out.' Catholic Amabel, without taking thought, is one of those who represent what lies behind Paul's eager moralizings. Yet she worships beauty, every sort of beauty, with a hushed devoutness. And surely beauty is a thing 'above'?

She is a sort of vengeance on restricted affection, a consuming fire for 'treasures,' selecting for destruction amongst my few possessions, only cherished things. The little scissors, fine and sharp, pathetically precious as having been Michael's botany scissors in his student days, borrowed and somehow swept away amongst Amabel's carelessly handled belongings. The Liberty brooch, its subtle green and blue enamels gleaming out from the pewter-coloured metal, radiating always the same joy. 'Lovely. Isn't it lovely?' Looking gravely at it, she had agreed. And when its pin came off, she had gathered up the brooch with the swift, maternal solicitude of one taking a broken doll from the hands of a weeping child, to keep and get it mended. Where is it now? If I live to be two hundred, I shall grieve whenever I think of it. And the moss-green ewer, a daily joy. That destruction, almost witnessed, brought me anger. Impatient anger over the needlessness of the headlong plunging, up the stairs, in a foot-impeding kimono, with the filled jug. Slap-dash, as Mrs Bailey had said, resentfully taking up the drenched stair-carpet. But Amabel went to no one with her cut and bleeding hand, dealt with it alone in her room, coming back only to have the little bandage tied and be forgiven.

Headlong. Urgent to know. Urgent to rescue and help.

It is easier to imagine her at large in the universe than in her home of which I know so little. In her letter, just those two pictures: of herself and the cousin, supporting each other in coming down to breakfast in kimonos; sitting, in the midst of garden beauty, stitching 'for dear life' at the cousin's trousseau. As long as they live, they will remember those sittings in the June garden. And it will be when they are thus alone that Amabel will tell her prison stories. In open sunlight, surrounded by sunlit flowers, or in a shadowy summerhouse whence with sheltered eyes they can look out across garden distances. The cousin will ask questions, dispute points and break up the record, weaving into it fragments of her own affairs and remembering it, in the way of busy, talkative people, scrappily and inaccurately.

Told as Amabel, listened to silently and believingly, had told it, it became experience and, in retrospect, increasingly a personal experience. Looked at now, coolly and critically, most of it remained obviously true. It was certainly true that someone had fainted in the Black Maria, after a foodless, exciting day in the stifling police court, and had had to 'stay fainted' until she came round. And certainly 'the worst' occurred in the inevitably verminous reception room where, still foodless and untended, they all remained, with only just space to stand, for hours. A Black Hole of Calcutta. But prisons are not accustomed to receive, on a single occasion, an army of criminals. They were not, perhaps, kept waiting until nearly midnight, but they must have had to wait at least until the resentful, contemptuous wardresses, their number not increased to deal with this influx of tiresome females who had 'no business' to be there making extra work, had finished their usual duties and were free to attend to them. It was true, too, that they were weighed in their chemises and, on their departure in their outdoor clothes, in order to prove that they had put on weight. No one could have invented that. Also that they were bathed in dubious water, and had had their clean heads washed, before getting at last to their cells and the grey cocoa.

'Enter the chaplain,' the unfortunate male who had to pray for Parliament to the accompaniment of giggles from the lady prisoners, and call, on each one of them. His hearty '*Good* morning!' Amabel's freezing grande dame bow. Silence, the poor man's pastoral urbanity glissading down the ice-wall of her detachment. His eyes searching the bare cell for a topic, discovering the big red volume, the one visible link between them and the world they both knew. Taking it up, fluting: 'Ah . . . Robert *Browning* . . . a little *beyond* me, I fear.'

Did Amabel glance in his direction when she murmured: 'So I should have supposed'?

Towards the end of the fortnight, hearing her wardress, in the corridor, speak kindly to a *cat*, she wept.

CHAPTER VII

THERE he stood, unchanged. On each day of the long interval he had been seen by an endless series of in-coming patients, standing thus, at his best, tall and slender in profile against the window whose light fell upon his benevolently handsome head, bent and thoughtful, suggesting the stored knowledge and experience awaiting the anxious inquirer; concentrated meanwhile upon the letter in his hand. As the door went wide and the parlourmaid stood aside for her to pass, the quiet joy of finding the well-known picture unaltered and the effective pose still able to arouse, as well as admiration, a secret mirth, was dimmed by regret for a lost refuge. The past she was vainly approaching lay as far away as her former self, inaccessible behind the transforming events of fifteen months.

While before her within the well-known room there opened unexpectedly a strange, uncharted region beyond which he stood, for the first time a little formidable and challenging, she reminded herself that she was here not on her own account but as Sarah's representative. Sarah's need alone had brought her back and, even supposing him still to have a right to her confidence, this visit was not a suitable occasion for confession and the regretful, unstinted absolution with which it would be met. For Sarah's sake she had ignored the barrier raised for ever by their last, decisive meeting. For Sarah's sake, she must carry through the interview, treat with him on a fresh footing, as a relative calling on a physician, impersonally.

But as the parlourmaid receded and the door, moving back over the thick carpet, clicked gently to, she found herself enfolded by the familiar stillness, spacious and deep and, apparently, even to-day, even in the face of their division, to last until at some point during her transit from door to chair he saw fit to swing suddenly round. But on this occasion, Sarah's

occasion, he could hardly greet her with his old device of mirth
repressed and waiting for her first word before breaking into
the voiceless laughter which was his chosen defence.   Standing
there with Sarah's fate in his hands, he would reveal himself
in a new light.   She would see him as he was seen by the
relatives of patients gravely ill.   Indeed, he was already so
revealing himself.   For although she had now passed the
point in the journey at which, usually, he came to life, he still
retained not only his air of professional gravity, but also his
motionless pose, letter in hand.   She found her breath coming
quickly and the weight on her heart, lifted a little since she had
written to him, pressed down again, darkening the room and
showing her the near objects isolated in a sad individuality.
Just ahead stood the chair, the seat of the condemned, soaked
with memories.

'I've seen your sister.'

The meditatively murmured words were addressed to the
letter in his hands and, still, he did not look up or turn her way.
Instead, dropping the letter, he moved swiftly to the mantelpiece upon which were ranged, exactly in their old positions,
the dreadful little framed female faces looking reproachfully
or soulfully forth from between their heavy cascades of waved
hair, and said, in the same low tone, into a jar standing at the
far corner: 'Did you hear from her?'

Compelling her quivering nerves to sustain the interval
before knowledge should fall upon them, she told him she had
been away for the week-end and, with the sounding of her
voice, felt herself in company with all who in this room had
spoken cool-sounding phrases while waiting for judgment
from which there was no appeal.   Upon her last word he
swung round.   With outstretched hand, for the first time only
one hand, he took her own and steered her into the patients'
chair with a steady withholding grasp which might be either a
call to endurance or a relic of the embarrassment of their last
meeting, and was seated, fully facing her, professional, knees
crossed, elbows propped, met finger-tips making of his hands
a little hutch.

'I went to see her,' he began, his eyes searching the various distances of the room, in the even, leisurely, rather high-pitched narrative tone that seemed to summon, for the purpose of linking to it the incident he was about to record, the whole of human history, and that always in the past had turned her imagination upon the spectacle of social life as he appeared to see it: whole, all in one piece yet graded, in classes and professions sacredly distinct from each other and united, for him, by mutual respect and an unquestioned common aim. But to-day his assembled humanity was a vast dim background upon which appeared the figure of Sarah, sick and suffering and cut off from access to first-class advice and first-class treatment, save amidst the inevitably detestable conditions of a hospital ward, and now, at last, after years of puzzled advice and heroic endurance, set suddenly within the full beam of medical enlightenment. And when, after the characteristic little pause always punctuating the Celtic sing-song of his narrations, he brought out 'on *Saturday*,' as if even the days of the week called for respectful emphasis of their individuality, she saw lifted from that distant figure its heaviest shadow, the shadow of tragedy that might have been averted.

'I was there,' he said gentle, 'for an hour or more.' Again, the careful, witness-box pause. But if a case is hopeless, an hour is not required? Not a whole hour of the time of an overworked physician?

'We went into everything and, I think'—his hands separated and one of them, followed by his averted gaze, moved to the writing-table, and the tips of the outstretched fingers came to rest, pressed down upon its edge, momentarily clearing the circle of her attention of everything but a single thought: that any doctor worthy of the title, in pronouncing an opinion, flinging, across the dark gulf between effect and cause, the bridge of a fragmentary creed, becomes self-conscious, embarrassed, pleasantly, by the presence of a witness of the exploit and, unpleasantly, by his own sense of insecurity—'we've found the way out.'

In the stupor of relief that fell upon her, relaxing the taut network of her nerves and leaving her seated as of old, infinitely at ease and at home within the friendly enclosure, she waited

for his facts, the 'medical facts' she had for so long scornfully
regarded as misreadings of evidence isolated from the context
of reality, inertly going their way until another group of facts,
equally isolated from reality, brought about a fresh misreading.
But the facts she was now to hear, drawn from the realm of
Sarah's being and regarded from the point of view of Sarah
who, in spite of her experiences, still unconsciously endowed
all specialists with omniscience, would carry conviction borrowed from the hope that Sarah's faith might introduce a
power that would carry all before it.

Without looking her way, still with his eyes upon a distant
point, he had risen as if to seek something, but actually, she
realized a moment later—returning from a solitary excursion
into bitter self-reproof for not having long ago thought of
consulting him on Sarah's behalf—to drop, from the midst
of apparently trivial preoccupations intended to minimize its
impact, the most alarming of his communications.

For how could nursing-home and operation be afforded?
She felt her face grow drawn and the teasing and nowadays
so easily provoked little fever patches of fatigue burn again
upon her cheek-bones as her thoughts turned to Bennett and
the difficult years since the rescue of his floundering brother,
and Densley's voice went on, carrying its messages into her
mind more directly from its place in a near corner of the not
too large room than if he had spoken, confronting her, across
the narrow space lying between them a moment ago. But
when for an instant it paused and the words 'serious operation,
radical, a cure if it succeeds,' were beating to and fro with the
beating of her heart, she wanted him close, eye to eye, to read
his thoughts and *know*. But she had no strength to rise.

His hand came down upon her shoulder and gently pressed.
'She has a hundred-to-one chance, my dear. If she were
my nearest relative, I'd send her to it with an easy mind. She
has a sound constitution, a sound nature, and the fact that she
has endured all she has gone through and remained as I found
her, speaks volumes for her character. I *admire* that sister
of yours, my dear.'

Coming into view, he let himself down into his chair and

faced her, with his smile, radiant, quizzical. He had said his professional say, administered the grim, spiritual purge and the tonic, and would now deal, cheerily, with immediate necessities.

'Yes,' she said, calling home the thoughts that a moment ago were pouring into the empty space ahead of her and now lay tangled in her mind. 'So do I. We are utterly different, belonging to different sides of the family.'

With his mouth open for his voiceless laughter, he was relapsing into a mood easily to be afforded by his unthreatened security, handing out a challenge to aggression in her own style, to tramplings on his logic and regardless excursions into ways of thought running counter to his own; as if, with Sarah's affairs happily settled, nothing remained but an opportunity to resume.

'I told you they were frightfully poor,' she said, and listened hopelessly, pictured the world of nursing homes, most of them cheaply run dens of extortion, speculative investments exploiting the worst fears and the most desperate human necessities—uncomforted by the idea of Densley as a blessed mediator, tempering the gale of expenses all along the way. For, however tempered, they would be beyond Bennett's already overstrained means.

'Have ye heard,' he said lightly, as if about to change the subject, 'of the Florence Nightingale Homes?'

And again he was on his feet and speaking from a distance. 'There's one in the street here. Your sister's room is booked. She'll have the services of one of the best of the few men qualified to undertake this operation. I shall be her medical attendant and the total inclusive cost, my dear, will be one guinea a week.'

Remaining hidden in the background, he was aware of her reviewing him afresh, seeing him as a worker of incredible miracles, and was savouring to the full, in this room that had been the scene of so many conflicts and drawn battles, the moment she needed for recovery from the stupefying blow. But in an instant and before the welter of her emotions could be made to subside and leave a clear channel for the heart's ease that could not fail somehow to express itself, he was returning to his chair, speaking as he came.

'Tell me, *why* did your good brother-in-law give up medicine?'

He really wanted to know, was really interested in every human soul he met. With Sarah's affair settled and nothing more to be said about it, he was now, having, as always, appointments waiting one behind the other, dismissing it from his mind and, wishing her away, using this hang-over, left in his mind as an item of interest, to wind up the occasion. Standing up, still faint and weak, she looked at the far-off landscape of Bennett's arduous life and saw there feature upon feature that would appeal to him, call forth his admiration and his refusal, even in the face of so much apparently wasted effort, to admit any shadow of failure. But the impossibility of launching out into all that, even of handing over a significant item, while still his own wonder-working remained untouched between them, kept her dumb until she looked across and found him waiting, with twinkling eye and mouth half open, only to meet her glance and then await her answering smile, before going off into the silent, gasping laughter that showed him still relishing her amazement over his thoughtful conjuring. He did not rise and there she stood, alone, glad of the sudden, convenient flush upon her cheeks as an equivalent for what she knew he would now allow her to say.

'Bennett?' she brought out, clutching at Amabel's manner of conveying 'Do you really want to know?—well, if you *do*——' and saw him settle his shoulders in his chair, elegantly, not in weariness, but as if at the beginning of a sitting; and again, as during that half-hour after she had left this room, for good, more than a year ago, she regretted, seeing it from the point of view of daily personal intercourse, the life she might have shared with him. For, to-day, it stood clear in her mind as he saw it: no professions or assurances, deeds rather than words, and their results to be recognized in conspiratorial laughter.

'His career,' she said, refraining from accepting his tacit invitation to stroll about the room, 'was shattered by a ne'er-do-well relative.'

'He'd have made a good medico.' Light, as he spoke, fell upon the distant picture of Bennett plodding sedulously along his encumbered way. Just the handing out of the fact and its reception by one who *felt* the lives of others, seemed irrationally to lighten both Bennett's burdens and the task of contemplating them. What an outpouring, item by item, might she not have known, in association with Densley, of all the hidden miseries so pressing upon her, whenever her thoughts turned to her family, that she had grown hardened to avoidance of the spectacle and, lately, it now crushingly occurred to her, had even forgotten her old aspiration: to make money, and help right and left.

'He began late, you see, first having to provide the where-withal for his training and then, in the midst of it, was obliged —felt himself obliged—to rescue his relative by parting with his capital. Of course since then things have been difficult. He started a small, precarious business in the City, and married, when our crash came, the girl he would never have aspired to unless the crash had come.'

'He married well, my dear. The right girl. A man happy in his home life can face the world.'

'He married, poor dear, the whole family.'

Silence. Was he, with his exceptional capacity for interest in people he had never seen, examining this item, away there in his chair, with a view to further questions, or recognizing that only an elaborate narrative, for which there was no time, could fill it out?

'It must be late. I'll go home and read my week-end letters . . . Sarah's letter,' she finished gently, and felt, piercing through the glow of her gratitude, the chill of returned apprehension on behalf of Sarah: 'a hundred-to-one *chance*.'

Springing lightly to his feet, 'There's one more thing I'd like to ask you,' he said, looking round the room. 'How have you managed to get so pulled down?'

Although the sitting was surely now over, the unexpectedly invading urgency that had prompted her to respond in detail to his questionings was still unsatisfied. There was still something, just out of reach, waiting to be apprehended. And when he began yet again and seemed now to be going leisurely towards the expression of his borrowed dogma as to the evils, for women, of intellectual pursuits, she assumed a listening attitude, hunted swiftly for what had occurred to her since last they discussed the subject, found, rising to the surface of her mind, the useful indictment of the limitations of abstract reasoning, and the glowing certainty that the deranging and dehumanizing of women by uncritical acceptance of masculine systems of thought, rather than being evidence against feminine capacity for thought, is a demand for feminine thinking, and retired to the background of her being, where, she found, like a third person looking on and listening while she talked, some part of herself had been piecing things together and was now eager to discuss the situation, so unexpectedly created, with herself alone. But Densley's voice, emerging from its meditative sing-song, interrupted the colloquy, from which she turned with a vision of Oberland before her eyes, to find him saying, in the despairing tone of one contemplating a vexatious unalterable phenomenon: '*spend* themselves so recklessly!'

'You would rather they posed, elegantly, on pedestals, breathing incense; in the intervals between agonies.'

'Western women. Take the Japanese Butterfly; and consider the splendid sons the little lady produces.'

Proof even against the shock of this amazing blindness, the wordless colloquy that had thrown up the suggestion of Oberland—useless, since it would mean waiting for the winter—still went on. But now it was pulling her up, marking time, keeping her watchful for something yet to emerge, and she felt relieved as well as annoyed in perceiving his inattention while she reminded him of the stern ethical training ruling the life of the Butterfly and, possibly, the root of her charm.

'What,' he said, gravely and simply, 'are you going to do to get the better of this seriously run-down condition?'

She felt trapped. Knocking at the door of her mind, his gravely spoken words released and confirmed her intermittent conviction of being vaguely ill and getting, progressively, a little worse.

'I know,' he pursued quietly, 'it's useless to suggest that you should cease burning the candle at both ends as well as in the middle.'

She now realized that she had told him, borne away by the relief of telling, too much as well as too little. With Amabel away and half the night no longer spent in talk that had often been renewed at dawn, with easy, empty August not far off and holiday waiting in September, life had become more manageable and had, again, beneath it, enriched by all that had happened, its earlier inward depth. The state Densley was considering was the result of the past year and could now gradually improve.

'But in one way or another, my dear girl, you ought to pull up.'

Controlling face and voice against the onslaught of the emotions raised by a vision forming itself within, impossible to realize, yet dictating, as a move in its favour, that she should make him say, unenlightened, the whole of his say and give a definite verdict, she asked him what he proposed, what he would suggest if he were advising a patient regardless of circumstances, and waited guiltily; breathlessly watching this unconscious assistant who was to put the weight of an opinion in which she could not quite believe at the service of a scheme. that could not be realized and that yet was sending through her wave upon wave of healing joy and making this grim, dim enclosure, from which he, poor dear, could not escape, the gateway to paradise.

'Well, my dear, I should say, in the first place, rest; and secondly, rest; and, in conclusion, *rest*.'

'I thought you were a *churchman*!' Her intoxicated laughter carried her on to her next question, which already she had answered, so that his reply seemed like an echo:

'Six months, at least, and the first part of the time to be spent resting, though not necessarily in bed.' Her feeling of guilt vanished. No one but an invalid could be told to lie up for weeks on end. Thanks to Sarah's need, she had unexpectedly and innocently become a patient provided with a diagnosis, and a prescription that in the eyes of both the worlds to whom explanation was due would be a passport to freedom.

'I see, a rest-cure,' she said judicially, to cover the sacred tracks and keep his thought-reading at bay. 'And only the other day I read somewhere that that big neurologist, I forget his name, the one who is always sending people to rest-cures, had himself broken down and gone into a nursing-home to take his own cure.'

'And don't ye think he's a wise man?'

'Well, I mean if a neurologist can't keep himself right, what is the value of his neurology? And if his science is unsound, why should one believe in the treatment based upon it?'

Resisting the flood of his inevitable laughter, her thoughts went their way, beating against the last barrier, and leaped, rushing ahead into the open even as they leaped, and stood still upon the blessed fact of her hoard, the thirty pounds saved towards her old age years ago at Mag's instigation and systematically forgotten until it had faded from her mind.

'Despise the profession, dear, if ye must. The question is, can they spare you? Could it be managed?' Meaning, can you afford it, you poor waif?

But the really strange thing, after all, was not that she had suddenly become an invalid under sentence in spite of herself, but that it had never before occurred to her that well or ill she had within her hands the means of freedom.

'I shall go away,' she said, 'but I don't promise to rest.'

His upflung hands came down upon her shoulders and held her exposed to his laughter and to the malicious, searching beam of his eyes wherein she read his discovery of her strategy.

'Thank you,' she said, as he set her free, 'and now I really *will* go.'

Not only gay and strong, but oddly tall she felt and, certainly, for his eyes, bonny, going to the door with his arm round her shoulders and his kind voice in her ears:

'Bless you, my dear; my dear, dear girl. Come and report yourself when you get back.'

CHAPTER VIII

Now Lorna, come all the way up through the house to offer tea, framed in the doorway, all smiling friendliness as she took in the reason for refusal, seemed to be within the secret, sharing it. There must be some unvarying reason for the way servants, not only those one knows and likes, not only those rather carefully selected, as have been all of the long series appearing in this house, but just any servants, anywhere, seem to keep things intact. And more. While I was saying those few words to Lorna, everything remained with me, not only undisturbed, but perceptibly enhanced by her presence. Perhaps it is because one speaks to them directly, in language calling up the 'everyday' things that hold being rather than thought. With others, one must use words embodying special references, prejudices, ways of thought, a hundred and one hidden powers amongst which communications must be steered across to someone who remains, however well known, several times removed. But it is only to women-servants that this applies, and only to those amongst them who are aristocrats, unresentful of service because of their unconscious, mystical respect for life. Unconsciously respectful to their mysterious selves, and to others, so long as they are treated courteously, so long as there is no kind of spiritual gaucherie to shock them into administering reproof in the form of a deliberately respectful *manner*.

Wise, they are. It is much easier to understand why Wisdom, Sophia, is a feminine figure when one thinks of old-fashioned servants than when one thinks of modern women, assimilating, against time, masculine culture, and busying themselves therein and losing, in this alien land, so much more than they gain. With these bustling, companionable, 'emancipated' creatures ('no nonsense about them') men wander in a grey desert of agnosticism, secretly pining for mystery, for Gioconda. That explains the men who marry their cooks and, also, why somebody, some Latin sage, said that the only chance of equality in marriage is to marry an inferior. Meaning in culture, so that he may in one direction retain the sense of superiority without which he seems to wilt. Yet humanist culture, which so many of the nicer, though rather selfish and self-indulgent kind of men find so infinitely beguiling as to become devout, and even ecstatic, in referring to it, may be assimilated by women, at the price of discovering themselves depicted therein only as they appear from the masculine point of view, without so much loss of identity as they suffer in assimilating 'scientific' culture. But when they go under to it, they lose much more than do humanist men, who at the worst are unconsciously sustained and protected from birth to death by women who have not gone under. For male humanists, particularly scholars, are either unmarried, and therefore cherished by servants, or they marry women who will look after them rather than revel in the classics.

As she looked up from the half-written letter to shift the trend of her thoughts, her mind's eyes was caught by three figures emerging from the long line of servants who had ministered in the house during the ten years now, in spite of their distant perspectives, outspread before her in a single brief span.

Mrs Orly's wheezy old Eliza, who used so much to admire my menu-cards, living in the half-dark kitchen, never leaving the house in which old age had come upon her, stumping slowly down in the morning from the high attic to the basement, toiling back up the many stairs at night; gaunt and green-faced and looking like a death's-head that day she told me she had walked across to the Park on a bank holiday, held on to the railings feeling as queer as a cockatoo, and decided never to go out again. Mrs Orly's pretty Janet, busily forgetful of her fair prettiness, somehow restrained from exploiting it, perhaps by being one of a large family of boys and girls, a chastening environment from the beginning (yet in the large Cressy family, all the girls, their mother conniving, were bound together in a conspiracy to exploit good looks), perhaps by a natural well-born proud modesty, somehow fostered in her home-life; always ready, whatever she might be doing and however tired she might obviously be—eyebrows lifted a little enduringly, corners of her pretty mouth a little drooping—to attend, welcoming a demand with confiding blue-eyed gaze, and to help, swiftly; getting wet through on a holiday excursion, drenched to the skin in her bright, best clothes, stricken down into fever and pain, passing into the certainty of death, passing through death, at twenty.

Just like her in swift, willing helpfulness was Mrs Orly's tall, dark Belinda. But less sure of life's essential goodness, going about her work with puzzled, protruding eyes, that remained puzzled even when she smiled, and slow, long-fingered, disdainful pouncings—as if one never knew quite how badly inanimate things might be expected to behave—and bringing to mind, when portion by portion she cautiously got herself to her knees, the movements of a camel; always hampered in her speech by the need of making her lips meet over protruding teeth, always contemplative, as if regarding a spectacle that never varied; until the outbreak. She was a misfit in domestic service, should have been a grenadier, or a countess. Going through the hall to answer the door, she was a procession, capped and aproned, humanity in disdainful movement, in haughty right and left contemplation of a world that at any moment might have the bad manners to go up in flames.

Of course, when she went down with surgery messages for the workshop, Reynolds looked up at her with his permanently adoring, pious young bachelor smile, and matched her refined, withholding stateliness with his courtly manners and flowery speech. Made her hopefully begin to be arch. Scared, in the end, into being less yearning and courtly, he perhaps even left off looking up from his bench when she came in, perhaps left someone else to receive the messages and take, without ceremony, the cases from her hands. To her hurt dignity and stricken heart, the note, inquiring whether she had offended him, had seemed an inspiration of providence and had brought timid joy and palpitating hope. And then, like a thunderbolt, exposure. Cruel, unthinkable exposure to the whole house-hold. Even while she waited for the sun to shine again, he must have been sneaking upstairs to Mr Orly. And the next day, Mr Orly expected me to be *amused* by his murmured story, and by his description of himself and Mr Leyton, helped by the sturdy Emma, late in the evening, somehow getting Belinda, in wild hysterics, up the long staircase to her room. And part of me was. I grinned, I suppose, because Belinda was so large. But her tortured cries go up to heaven, for ever. Perhaps she has made herself a dignified life somewhere. With fastidious maiden ladies, an enclosed group, disdainfully contemptuous of the world.

And later, Eve. For years, balm. An inexhaustible reservoir of blessedness. Coming gently into the room, taking her time, as though aware that otherwise something would be destroyed, instinctively aware of the density of invisible life within a room that holds a human being; and so selflessly objective that one felt her to be an embodiment, an always freshly lovely and innocently reminding embodiment of one's best aspirations, and every moment in her presence retained the reality underlying the thin criss-cross pattern of events. She brought comfort for bad moments, substituting, for what-ever might be making torment, the unconscious gentle tyranny of her image and the sense of her untroubled being; and, to good moments, so great an enhancement that one could share them with her in a beam she would receive and reflect, hovering for a moment before announcing her errand. So that her brief visit, when quietly she vanished, had been either a blessed interlude leaving one restored, or a punctual confirmation of lonely joy.

Of course she had to pass on, going away into marriage. 'Did you see poor Eve? No, you were away when she was here during Ellen's holiday. Poor girl, you 'd hardly recognize her. Worn out. Her good looks quite gone.' In a year.

Shifting her gaze, she saw, set out on the leads invisible behind the closed door, Mrs Orly's melancholy aspidistras being washed free of house-dust by softly falling autumn rain and gathering, as affectionately she gazed at them, scene upon scene from the depths of the years before the retirement of the Orlys and the disappearance of the den and her passage-room downstairs, before the closing upon her of the home-life of the house with the arrival of the Camerons and the transforming changes that had left only Mr Hancock's room as an untouched storehouse of the past. If she were to rise and glance through the door's glass panes, she would behold only Mrs Cameron's brilliantly flowering pot-plants standing in midsummer sunlight, representing the shallows of recent years.

It was as if, in allowing so much time to get to Sarah's nursing home and in deciding, on the way, to turn aside for the odd experience of breaking in at Wimpole Street on a Sunday afternoon, she had known that in the silent, emptied house these receding perspectives would draw near, lit by the radiance falling upon everything since she had left Densley's consulting-room to go forth into freedom. The intervening weeks had been an intensive preparation for their bright approach. Carefully, effortlessly, blissfully, during the free intervals of the crowded days, and in many zestfully consecrated extra hours, chaos had been reduced to order, each finished task a further step towards the blessedly empty future, and an increase of the sense of ease and power that had given her the measure of the burden of arrears daily oppressing her during the years while the practice had been reaching its present proportions, although her earlier intermittent conviction of insufficiency had long since given way to the constantly comforting realization of being a trusted pillar of support.

This sense of ease and power might have been hers all along, if she had been content to live, as so many working women whose paths had crossed her own were living all the time: entirely concentrated on the daily task, refusing to be carried away right and left, spending their leisure in rest and preparation for the next day. These strictly ordered lives held serenity and stored power. But they also seemed to imply a drab, matter-of-fact attitude towards life. The world these women lived in, and the passing events of their daily lives, held no deep charm, or, if charm there were, they revealed no sense of being aware of it. From time to time, in the ceaseless whirl

of her days in this populous house, she had envied them their
cut - and - dried employments and their half - contemptuous
realism, but now, looking back, she could imagine no kind of
ordered existence for which she would exchange the uncalcu-
lating years, now triumphantly finished. Perhaps a little too
triumphantly to be in keeping with the whole record. For
these cupboards unreproachfully full of neatly ranged, freshly-
labelled bottles, these drawers of stored materials newly sorted
and listed, the multitude of charts and the many accounts, not
only in order, but so annotated and tabulated that her successor
would relievedly find herself supplied with a course of training,
were not representative of herself. They were the work of a
superhumanly deedy female and could be lived up to only by
an equally deedy female who, if indeed she did live up to them,
would lead a dreary life.

Ten years. One long moment of attention, more or less
strained, day and night, since the day she sat, dressed in mourn-
ing, reluctantly and distastefully considering the proffered
employment, on one of the high-backed velvet chairs in Mr
Orly's surgery, wondering over the heaviness of the indoor
London light, still further dimmed by the stained glass of the
lower half of the large window, and drawn, while she hesitated,
by the depth and spaciousness of the house as revealed by the
stately waiting-room and the view from the large hall; already
immersed therein before the interview was at an end which had
revealed the fine, divergent qualities of her two would-be
employers.

Consulting the clock whose face for so long had brought the
time of day to her mind in swiftly moving, steroscopic scenes
and was now only the measurer of the indifferent hours before
time should cease, she found it was already a little past the time
for admitting Sunday visitors to the nursing home. Grace
Broom's letter must wait and her plan could still remain in
the air.

On the hall table amongst the letters waiting for to-morrow,
she found one for herself.

Alma. As the envelope came open, she recalled from where
it lay, far-off and forgotten, Hypo's offer to lend his own secre-

tary for six months to Mr Hancock while she reclined, following
the sun, all over the Bonnycliff garden. The indifference she
had felt towards this invitation that a year ago would have
seemed to offer an eternity in paradise and now seemed like a
sentence of imprisonment, had perhaps prevented her response
from fully expressing the gratitude smiting through her when
she received his incredible message, gratitude for thought on her
behalf, for swift imaginative sympathy.

'Dearest,
'If you really won't come here for your six months, at least
let us see you before you go. Say next week-end.'

Was this invitation from them both, equally, or chiefly from
him? For the first time, the question seemed indifferent.

CHAPTER IX

APPROACHING Sarah's room, she heard, emerging from the endless silence into which, for herself, she had supposed it fallen, the voice of Nan Babington, and paused to savour the unexpected sound. Sarah's property. Sarah's quality, alone, had drawn Nan into their circle. Up went the voice, in a phrase that was like a fragment of a lilting song, and paused, on the top note. After all these years, during which the peculiar individuality of Nan's speaking-voice had remained a gathered treasure undefined, the secret of its charm stood clear: Nan set all her words to music. The little phrase, swiftly ascending in a sunny major key, sounded, with the words inaudible, like a brief, decorative, musical exercise. She would gladly have lingered for a while outside the closed door, listening, testing her discovery. But now Sarah was speaking; almost inaudibly.

Inundated, as she went forward, by a flood of memories, she saw, floating free of the rest, vivid pictures of Nan, surprising her, since, when they were before her eyes, she had not taken note of them, by their prominence and the clarity of their detail: her tall form, approaching elegantly along the Upper Richmond Road, very upright in a tailor-made of a subtle shade of green, so clear at this moment before her eyes that she could have matched it in a shop. For a moment she watched her coming, defying the leafless, chill winter's morning, bringing with her the summer that had passed, the one that was to come. But the other picture was intruding, calling her to look for the first time upon a masterpiece hanging unnoticed in a remote gallery of her memory.

Nan's lovely, slenderly rounded figure, outlined, in smoothly-clinging, snow-white, sheenless muslin, throwing up the satiny gloss of her dark piled hair, against the misted green of the conservatory door as she stood, at the elbow of some forgotten accompanist seated at the grand piano, her head lifted for song, tilted a little upon the pillar of her lovely throat from which flowed so easily—through lips preserving undisturbed upon her face, by never quite closing for labials, the expression of a carolling angel—the clear, pure, Garcia-trained voice, slightly swaying her to its own movement. 'Sing, maiden, sing. Mouths were made for si-i-ing-ing.' A picture of Nan paying a call, seated, talking. Still very upright, still swaying a little to the rhythms of her voice, all deliberately colourful inflections and brief melodious outcries, falling effortlessly from the full flexible lips perpetually disciplined, by Nan herself, to smiling curves, the curves of a happy smile coming from within, from some kind of enchanted contemplation, and sending through her eyes its deep, continuous beam. 'Any one who chooses, my dear, can have a mouth with what you call curly corners.' It was Sarah, lying ill in there and being tunefully visited, who had collected and revealed the facts that had made Nan seem all artifice. The facts about the curly mouth and, when she had come upon Nan enchantedly hemming a sheet on a grey morning, after the tennis season was over and before anything else had begun, the facts about the becomingness of a mass of white needlework flowing downward from crossed knees above which the head of the sempstress, blessed by the light falling upon it from the window and reflected upward from the white mass upon her knee to illuminate her face, is gracefully bent. And the facts about the opportunity yielded, on dull days, by long sittings at needlework, for training the face to remain radiant in composure. Stern secrets of charm, akin to those of Densley's Butterfly, but less disinterested. Had Garcia taught them all? Taught life as radiant song?

And Sarah's illness had produced this meeting, to which, confidently opening the door, she went forward, feeling herself already set upon the path of redemption from Nan's disapproval by her own delighted recognition of treasures gathered unawares and for ever laid up to Nan's account, and found not only Nan but Estelle also, seated at the far side of the bed. Between them, a little flushed and weary, lay Sarah, deprived by Sunday of the needlework that would have occupied hands unused to idleness, and would have carried off the excitement of a social occasion bereft, for her imagination, since she alone was its centre, of any compensation for the trouble taken by her visitors in coming so far.   This was the old Sarah, emerged from the desperate struggle that had found her unself-conscious, spiritually strong and agile; growing well and, once more, rigid and shy.   Miriam wished that the Babingtons could have seen her before the operation, serene, at leisure, escaped from incessant demands, escaped, under compulsion, into the first real holiday of her married life and seeing, from her bed in this quiet room, the world that hitherto had shown itself chiefly an antagonist in her struggle for the welfare of her family, for the first time as an item of interest; so that she had demanded, in place of the happily ending novels, so far her only means of escape into a restful forgetfulness, books of travel.

'It's Miriam,' she said croakily, still almost in the voice of Grandma Henderson and, strangely, since she knew and, with her innocent frankness, had always admitted, the Babingtons' general disapproval of oneself, with a note of relief; as if her labours as a hostess were now at an end.

It was so long since she had moved in Barnes circles that she could not be sure whether this simultaneous rising of the Babingtons was, simply, for the purpose of greeting her or, solemnly, to fulfil the law forbidding callers to overlap.   Shaking hands, she felt the radiation, as in turn each sister smiled and looked her up and down, of a deep, almost deferential interest, and immediately suspected Sarah.   Thankful for anything to set before her visitors, she had prepared them for this meeting by little staccato announcements wherein one would have appeared, without any supporting data, as something altogether out of the common; so that instead of being Mirry Henderson returned to pay a belated tribute, one must now be a discomfited witness of Sarah's disappointment in perceiving their failure to be impressed.

'She looks very *raiediant*,' chirped Estelle, with her remembered, mysterious vestige of a Cockney accent, pulling her little coat to rights, head bent, lips pursed and chin indrawn for easier downward-frowning investigation. Sarah's voice broke in upon the idea that Nan, too, might once have spoken thus and have been cured, by Garcia.

'She's had a nervous breakdown,' said Sarah in the manner of one defensively displaying the points of a proud possession to those suspected of unwillingness to appreciate it, and then, unable to wait for the first point to get home: 'She's going away. For six months. Sit down, girls, you needn't go yet. Sit down, Mim.'

Pulling up a chair to face all three, as the two resumed their seats, Estelle just subsiding, Nan distributing songful little phrases as she made a preliminary careful adjustment of her long skirt and the back of her neat little open coat before letting herself down to sit beaming upon the world, Miriam remembered having told Sarah who, also, had not seen her before her transformation by the mere prospect of release, that Densley had said her nervous machinery was out of gear and that therefore she supposed she had what they called a nervous breakdown; for which there was never anything to show. It had served as an answer to Sarah's anxious questions and had evidently impressed her and in some way modified her idea that nerves were mostly nothing, or just ill-temper. But it had not occurred to her that it would be necessary to produce, for others, reasons for her flight. And to the Babingtons, well versed in every kind of illness, it might seem a ludicrous claim. Relieved to see their faces grow sympathetically grave and interested, she decided that whatever a nervous breakdown might or might not be, it would henceforth serve as a useful answer to demands for specific information.

'Sarah's nice medicine-man is yours, too, Mirry, I hear,' said Estelle, in her remembered way of glancing about as she spoke, as if looking for something, so that one never knew to whom she might be speaking until, with her last word, she sent a direct glance through her twinkling glasses. Seen now, after the long interval, this manner told its story. Estelle lived alone, excluded from direct participation; looking on.

'Nan and Estelle are *charmed* with Dr Densley, Mim.'

Ah! *Here* was the topic, the source of the deferential interest.

Sarah had been showing her off, in the way best calculated to
appeal.   She could hear her saying, in response to the Babingtons' ardent approval: 'He 's a *great* friend of Mim's,' and
even going on to tell them of Densley's plan for a quiet dinner
together before she left London, communicated when Sarah
had first spoken of him with a delight reducing one to seventeen
years, and to the ways of the old life together when one's status
went up or down according to the presence or absence of an
attentive young man.   But when could Nan and Estelle have
seen him?

Brought back by Sarah's voice, she found herself returned
from regarding Nan and Estelle, alternately, in the character
of persons uncritically enthusiastic in regard to Densley, and
flushed as it occurred to her that this habit, revealed to her by
Hypo, of thinking about people in their presence and leaving
her thoughts in her face, must have been one of the many things
the Babingtons had disliked in her.

'Rushed in, just now,' Sarah was saying; 'I told him yesterday you might be coming.   But he couldn't stay.'   Sarah's
eyes, as she cunningly dropped this flattering item with a
perfect imitation of a woman of the world boredly summarizing
details, were downcast upon her clasped hands while she
relished to the utmost what was for her an overwhelming
triumph for the clan Henderson in the presence of the Babington clan, regarded in the past as having all that life could offer
except the large house and garden which had been, at the worst
of times, though then all unrealized, the Henderson asset.

'He 's a nice creature,' she said, and hesitated, herself again
translated into the past and sharing to the full Sarah's fond
pride in the younger sister exhibited as destined to be a queen
in Harley Street, before the eagerly interested eyes of the two
who considered, as would any of their neighbours, the wife of
a general practitioner in the suburbs as very well placed indeed,
and wondering whether Sarah's disappointment in learning
that she was mistaken' would be greater than her satisfaction if
she should see, sharing the wonderful vision with the Babingtons, a sister who had chosen not to marry into Harley Street.

But this vision would be founded on a half-truth.   She

looked up therefore, with a non-committal smile, and accepted perforce the character of heroine of romance, warmly greeted by Nan in the manner with which she demanded, her singing face all joyously alight:

'And where is she taking herself off to?'

'I don't know.'

Into the astonished outcries coming from each side of the bed and taking her deeply back into the brightest days at home, into days whose joy had been too perfect to be dimmed by the perpetual overhanging shadow of disaster, came Sarah's voice, as nearly, as her state would permit, the clarion voice with which, childlike, she would announce the good fortune of others:

'Nan and Estelle are going to Strath—— What is it, Nan?'

'Peffer, darling. Zoozie *says*, it's rather chilly, at the moment, in the chambres à coucher.'

'You must have hot-water bottles,' proclaimed Sarah, not that her thoughts were engaged with obstacles to perfect comfort, but because, while her imagination went recklessly to work upon the social and domestic glories of a holiday in a Scotch hydro, she automatically grasped, in order to keep flying the bright flag of this entrancing topic, what was obviously a familiar fragment of the Babington household creed.

Miriam suggested, with genuine apprehension, imagining, added to the indefinable psychic chill of any area north of central London, a definite physical chill, that perhaps hot-water bottles might not be available.

'My *dear*!' cried Nan, with an expression as near to contempt as was compatible with the preservation of the smiling curves, 'they will accompany us. In our portmanteaux. I should never *dreeem*'—there, again, was the high, clear, forward note, the upper end of the little festoon, opening the face, beaming through the eyes, as she rose and stood, for a moment upright, triumphantly blossoming, and then bowed, in the manner of one receiving an ovation—'never, never *dreeem* of going away without Mademoiselle H.W.B. Darling, we must go. Your dragon said only twenty minutes.'

'We always take our hot-water bottles,' murmured Estelle, rising and shaking herself, engaged, behind downcast eyes once more occupied with her garments, in quiet retrospective and anticipatory enjoyment of the perfect comfort of the circumstances within which, since she was not expected to shine, she could observe and thoroughly enjoy the surrounding dramas. And be a good friend to the actors, Miriam went on to reflect, seeing outwelling kindliness transform her rather hard little face as Estelle turned towards Sarah, and thinking of Freda, and the untiring hard-working loyalty of these two friends without whom she would never have had the opportunities which had carried her to her bourne.

Returning to Sarah, engrossed with the spectacle of the sisters still going the round of their year, still leading, within an unchanged mental and moral enclosure, the lives they had led since they left school, she already could not remember whether she had stood, reduced, when alone with them, to childhood, silently contemplating the retiring figures that had appeared so bright and salient and socially powerful upon the margin of her own and Harriett's profane, unsocial existences, and even now, as they disappeared round the bend of the stairs, represented a goodly heritage she and her sisters had been fated to forgo. A heritage keeping them cheerfully unaware of the passage of time, unaware, apparently, even of their advanced years. For Estelle, older even than Sarah, was almost old.

While she sat listening to the plans for Sarah's home-coming, all dictated by an ungenerous necessity, and helplessly noted the return, as Sarah talked, of the little pleat between her brows that during her convalescence had altogether vanished, she felt her own exhaustion return upon her, the fevered weakness that for so long had made every task an unbearable challenge and had given to the busy spectacle of life the quality of a nightmare. But to-day it was almost welcome. It proved that the mere prospect of escape had not cured her and it removed from the new cabin-trunk and the many other purchases she had incredulously made, still hardly able to believe they could be for herself, the shadow of reproach through which, each time she saw them, she had to pass on her way to the heart of their rich promise.

By the time she had convinced Sarah of her independence, telling her of the forgotten hoard in Mag's wonderful insurance company, although the lingering presence of the Babingtons assailed her with a faint nostalgic desire for shelter and security, her strength was returning and, with it, pity for all the confined lives about her. For Sarah's, thwarting at every turn her generous nature. For those of the Babingtons, who saw nothing of the world outside their small enclosure. For all those she was leaving in fixed, immovable circumstances. But what, even for those who were nearest to her, could she do? And why, contemplating the rich void towards which blissfully she was moving, leaving Sarah to return to a life in which, after all, there was no possibility of joining her, should she feel a kind of truant?

CHAPTER X

STILL he stood, entrenched on the hearthrug, with his hands behind his back and the light from the brilliant sky making plain every detail of his face and very blue the eyes fixed—save when he posed a question and they came to life falling upon her from a distance as she roamed about, or at close range when she halted before him—with sightless, contemplative gaze upon the quiet blue sea. And still he was holding something in reserve behind the amused comments and questionings wherewith he encouraged her anecdotes.

'It makes me feel like a sort of visitor. But I can't tell you how uncanny it is to see the new secretary doing my jobs. It alters them, makes them almost unrecognizable and at the same time gives them a sort of dignity I never knew they could possess, although, for her, they are lifeless, just a series of elaborate processes that have come into her hands. She doesn't know the history, you see, either of a probe or of a patient. When she reads a letter from Mrs Smith, asking for an appointment, it is just something to be attended to, a detail in a ceaseless series of details. It doesn't bring before her mind, and in amongst her emotions, the whole of the Smith family going through their lives, about which, you know, in one way or another, we get to know a great deal. She doesn't, for example, wonder whether again, just as the first guests for a dinner-party were ringing at the front door, Mrs Smith, awaiting them in the drawing-room, sneezed her denture into the midst of the glowing fire. Not that she would be likely, of course, to repeat such an achievement.'

'You know, Miretta, if you really *are* going away, you ought to write the first dental novel. Or there 's a good short story in your Mrs Smith's adventure—which, by the way, must be unique in the history of mankind.'

'Yes. But it isn't only that she hasn't the history of the practice, laden with human documents, in her mind. These people don't *mean* anything to her. It is not only that each patient is tested and revealed before one's eyes from the moment of being let in at the front door to the moment of departing thence. The mere sight of a family account, with an ancestral address at the head which in itself is part of the history of the English spirit, or with a series of addresses, crossed out, one below the other, and of branching accounts, as children marry and set up for themselves; or of spinster and bachelor accounts, proceeding from elaborate filling operations to extractions and the final double denture, crowd up your mind with life because all these people are known to you. They all talk in the chair and reveal not only their histories but themselves from almost every point of view.'

'Angles of vision. Yes. You know, you've been extraordinarily lucky. You've had an extraordinarily rich life in that Wimpole Street of yours. You have in your hands material for a novel, a dental novel, a human novel and, as a background, a complete period, a period of unprecedented expansion in all sorts of directions. You've seen the growth of dentistry from a form of crude torture to a highly elaborate and scientific and almost painless process. And in your outer world you've seen an almost ceaseless transformation, from the beginning of the safety bicycle to the arrival of the motor car and the aeroplane. With the coming of flying, that period is ended and another begins. You ought to document your period.'

'Poor soul. She takes up the telephone receiver as if it might explode in her hands and, instead of being immediately in touch with someone she knows, speaks, timidly, to a stranger.'

'You've been a great chucker-up, I admire that. But I'm not sure that you're being wise this time, Miriam. What are you going to *do* ?'

Whence this strange prophecy? Nothing she had written or said could have suggested that she was going away for good. Even in her own mind the idea had risen only in the form of a question to be answered in the distant future, at the end of her reprieve that seemed endless.

'Nothing. I'm going away.'

'Where?'

'I don't know.'

What could it matter, to him? Why this protesting attitude, and the many questions keeping her restively held up, keeping something in reserve which, amazingly, she did not wish to hear?

'I'm simply going away, right away.' Pulling up in face of him she saw, in his silent smile, his reading of her momentary satisfaction in including him in a general repudiation.

'Don't chuck your friends, Miriam. We *are* still friends, by the way? You'll still hold me up, be interested in my work?' For a moment he watched her thoughts. 'Don't,' with a deepening smile, 'chuck your friends. A *friend* advises you.'

Here was his quiet message. Smiting through the detachment that had kept her feeling she was watching the scene from afar, unable to be present within it, it brought her back for an instant into this roomful of memories and took her eyes away from his face to find space and depth for their tribute to the past. But when they returned and she saw, still quizzically regarding her, his smile—which, it only now occurred to her, was the only smile he had and must therefore serve, as best it could, all his purposes—helplessly expressing his view of human beings, each one, wise or foolish, noble, base, or simply pathetic, a momentary puppet on the way to extinction, she could only go on watching him wait for a response that could not come because from him and from his words reality had departed and he seemed, standing there smilingly sustaining her silent contemplation, distinguishable from the many figures she was leaving behind, each, with the exception of Amabel, moving in a fixed orbit, only by the range and power of his imagination.

Footsteps, rustling a frilly dress, sounded within the far-off invisible doorway.

'Susan! She's chucking us! Chucking everything and everybody.'

As Alma drew near, bringing a little scene whose every movement would be a shadow of the one now ended, she felt, hearing his version of her statements and silences, as if he had taken her by the hand and set her beyond recall upon the invisible path.

CHAPTER XI

'How is your sister?'

'Getting on splendidly. Both doctor and surgeon are delighted.'

'Oh . . . *Oh*. I'm glad to hear that.'

Although Brenton, with an anxious face, and a wax model held gingerly by a lifted corner of his long apron, was now almost dancing with impatience outside the open door and Mr Hancock was just about to turn to him, she was moved, in order to amuse him, and herself to enjoy its implied criticism of orthodoxy, to tell him the story of the biscuits and thus remain, for yet another moment, encircled by the glow of his kindliness, in the midst of the busy activities of the practice, by whose orderly turmoil surrounded they had so often taken counsel together.

'As a matter of fact, she has no right to be,' she said, in the smiling, swift, narrative undertone with which, in his surgery, while a patient mounted the stairs, they would exchange notes on the day's occurrences, and thrilled to see him turn back with anticipatory smile, deepening as she swiftly outlined the scene, between Sarah, beginning to recover from her relapse, and both desperate and sceptical under the imposed starvation, and Mrs Bailey, moved by sheer goodness of heart to visit her lodger's sick sister.

When it came to the smuggling of the biscuits—'Oswego, you know, one of Peek Frean's finest inspirations'—the lines of his face relaxed into gravity and it was only in response to her combative insistence on the proven harmlessness of Sarah's rebellion, only as a retrospective salutation of their many drawn battles, that his smile returned and became his characteristic, conversational laugh: the abrupt 'have it as you like' lift of the chin and the breath thrice sharply indrawn between the smiling teeth.

'I'll be back in a moment. Don't forget that ten pounds.'

Making a note for the new secretary, returned refreshed and rather more confident from her first week-end, but still bewilderedly seeking her balance amidst incessant, overlapping claims, she opened the safe and helped herself to the superfluous funds, feeling as she did so a pang of remorse. For he certainly supposed her to be returning at the far-off end of the six months. Yet, while his half-jocular insistence on her acceptance of the holiday salary, not yet nearly due, had given her an opportunity of indicating the uncertainty of her return, she could not take it, could not, even for him, lay a finger on the unknown future.

She must stand therefore, in the midst of her empty room, a remorseful millionaire, and feel this last proof of his imaginative kindliness renew from their deep roots her earliest impressions of him, and her sense, when he came, with quickly spoken reassurances, to the rescue of Mr Orly's gruff embarrassed attempts, forced upon him by his situation as senior partner, to gather in his mind and convey to her some idea of her manifold duties, of being not only at home and at rest, but of moving back, led by the accents of his voice, into the life left behind in the Berkshire from which they had both come forth.

And when he returned and again with an approving glance took in her wide unpractical straw hat and the successful scabious-blue pinafore-dress, with its soft lace top and sleeves, that she had known he would approve, she felt as they shook hands and he wished her good luck, that although this was the end, his good wishes, still more to her than those of any one in the world, would somehow follow and bless her wayfaring.

DIMPLE HILL

CHAPTER I

WHY pounce upon the cathedral? There it stood, amidst its town, awaiting them, three little people about to join the millions over whom in its long life it had cast its shelter and its spell. In strolling about, they would come upon it, see it from various points of view, gradually wear down the barrier between it and themselves, and presently, either together or alone, venture within its doors. But for Florence and Grace there would be no venturing. Boldly, all eyes, they would march in, and immediately begin to poke about amongst its vitals. Privately she decided for going alone, sloping secretly in and seeing and feeling it, as far as her intermittent scepticism allowed, in the way of the ascetic young man, the sight of whom, sitting in the railway carriage aloof and meditative over his missal, had reminded her that they were bound for a cathedral town.

In that moment, abandoning Florence and Grace and the mood of gay unity in which they had all set out upon the suddenly improvised week, of holiday for them and, for herself, the easily spared extension of her few days' visit, she had entered the gateway of her six months' freedom. The task of keeping them entertained lost both its charm and its importance. They became the symbols of all she was leaving, and when, as silently she gazed at the journeying landscape, that group of flaming poppies had darted by, she had commented on them in a phrase addressed to the consciousness of the young man, bringing his eyes across the carriage and, with them, a vision of the cathedral within whose twilit interior lived a stillness akin to that wherein spirits recognize each other, as she and the young man had recognized each other; although, in order that the recognition might take place, she had precipitately assumed a vestment to which she had no right.

But as the tide of her opposition flowed across the breakfast-table towards Florence now withdrawn into silence, and Grace

who had made the suggestion and was awaiting agreement, she
recognized it for annoyance with their remembered technique
in the handling of excursions.   Exactly as on this first morning
the town's most prominent feature was rousing them to headlong activity, so on that far-off day whose frustrations could
still torment her, they had been moved immediately to toil,
through fierce noonday heat, to the church on the high hill,
thereby setting at an impossible distance the little valley by the
sea that the enchanting toy railway had brought so conveniently
near, and whence, serenely, in the cool of the late afternoon,
they might have climbed to the church and surveyed its famous
brasses with eyes already satisfied.

Because the suggestion had caught her unprepared, just as
the charm of the little railway, winding, like an erratic tram-
line, at the level of the road, in and out of the scattered hamlets,
made way for the charm of the little valley, visible, as they
alighted, in the near distance with a sailless windmill on its
ridge and, at its feet, the sea not yet hazed by the sun, she had
failed not only to state but even to assemble in her own enchanted consciousness the objections to their plan for ruining
the day.   But when, in the late afternoon, the baked little
town still enclosed them and the green valley, unexplored and
to be forever regretted, mocked them from afar, it was Florence
who had bemoaned their failure to take refuge there with the
lunch-basket whose contents had been consumed, in the silence
of exhaustion, amongst the roasted tombstones.   And Florence,
to-day, would offer no resistance to a planless wandering.

But when, in the hope of making it acceptable to both, she
groaned, with the force of an annoyance they would not perceive, and with the expansiveness that never failed to arouse
their hope of entertainment, a tribute to the length of days
ahead, thus identifying her visibly blissful state with the prospect of spending seven days in their company, the figure of
Grace on holiday, miraculously seated at breakfast in strange
lodgings and yet placidly moored within her accustomed enclosure, became a summary that removed all desire to influence
her movements.

There she sat, dutifully pondering her morning's adventure,

radiating the serenity born of her unreflective acceptance of all the orthodoxies, and fostered by a security that supported her belief in the indefinite persistence of her enclosed world. And this it was, just this serene, unquestioning security, so clearly revealed by the unaccustomed surroundings as the basis of her existence, that had made the Banbury Park villa, ever since her suppliant affection had first drawn one hither, so deeply restorative. On countless week-end visits, on Christmas Eves, and at Easter and Whitsun holidays, reaching their remote doorstep with what had seemed the last of one's strength, one had punctually felt, hearing the tick-tock of footsteps approaching along the tiled passage and seeing the door open upon one or other of them, or upon all three come eagerly out to welcome, the beginnings of renewal and the ability to share, if only for the first evening, as a beatific convalescent, the family relish, rich and racy, of the ritual of daily life and its recurrent rewards that brought, to each moment of the day and into each corner of the rather dark small house, the radiance of festival achieved or imminent.

So complete on each occasion was the transference from weariness and lonely responsibility to surroundedness and irresponsible ease, that with the resounding slam of the little front door, accompanied by the metallic, evocative rattle of its empty letter-box, her daily life became a past upon which no future opened. To return, towards the end of the visit, and to offer, seen afar in clear focus, with its tints refreshed and its features newly attractive, in the midst of some too-prolonged excursion amidst incidents brought forth for her inspection from where they lay recorded in terms she could not accept, as if in answer to her need for escape from a stereotyped universe, a sudden incredible refuge.

So that her response, when the eagerly mingled voices died away and the enclosed Sunday twilight vibrated with the demand for it, radiated joy whose source remained unsuspected; and the small shock of her voice, bringing into the room the present whence she had been looking into their past, abruptly restored to them the sense of their surroundings and of the rapidly fading light, calling for movement and for the zestful

introduction of the evening portion of the long, shared day.
But in the moment before the globes of patterned, tinted gas-
light drove the afternoon into the past, the dim radiance from
outdoors, since now she was seeing it from the centre to which
she had returned, no longer filtered in upon endurance but
signalled, bringing joy, from its own vast distances; and when
she and Grace were left alone, all that she had told in response
to gently eager questioning, was lit, for herself as well as for
Grace, by an unquenchable radiance.

No one else, sitting there at the table, could embody so long
a stretch of the past. All the years from Wordsworth House
days onwards lay embalmed in the treasure-house of Grace's
faithful memory. Inseparable, too, from the sight of her, a
visible background of dissolving views freed from their an-
chorage in space and time, was Grace's home, in the stateliest
of whose upper rooms the whole of one's life, as known to
oneself, was stored up.

Other guest-rooms, in houses sheltering a ceaseless conflict
of ideas, so that nothing within them seemed quite real and no
one currently alive, reverberated, when one reached them at
the end of swiftly passing evenings, with various kinds of sound
and fury or with the echoes of a keyed-up gaiety to be continued on the morrow. So that whatever was contemplated in
the upstairs solitude, whether the world at large or one's own
life within it, looked both dreary and meaningless.

But in the stately, old-fashioned spare room at Banbury
Park, itself a retreat from the superficially dynamic world of
external change and new ideas, even down to the way it owed
its deep refreshingness to continuous zestful housewifery and
the gleam on its furniture to methodical hand-polishing, one
had seen one's life from afar, whether with quiet or with
fevered mind, as part of a continuous reality whose challenge
came, directly, to oneself and whose hidden meaning, just
because at times it was so unbearably disturbing, was secure
and was what at other times made each distant detail suddenly
miraculous. From no other spare room could she have seen
the world as it had opened before her in that first moment of
realized freedom. With no other companions could she have

remained, throughout the days preceding this setting forth, with all her surface being sound asleep and her essential self looking forth upon its own, so long withheld and now at last accessible.

Sitting there unchanged, the always gentle recipient of her being, Grace innocently reproached her for ever having felt that the descent upon Banbury Park would be a ludicrously humiliating end to the weeks of anticipation during which her departure had remained, alluringly featureless, upon the horizon. The eager invitation, taking her by surprise in the midst of her preparations, had reminded her of the necessity of selecting a destination. But long before her shopping was finished and the glossy new cabin-trunk and hat-box, incredible symbols of freedom, were beginning to fill up, she had realized that in no other spot on earth could she so deeply savour the bouquet of her release. Arriving on their doorstep late at night, she had been too weary to feel the bliss of escape. But when in the morning, as she stood, ready to go downstairs, before the wide mirror in which hitherto had been reflected her image entangled with a thousand undetachable associations, she saw only her solitary self, there had come that all-transfiguring moment during which in the depth of her being she had parted company with that self, masquerading under various guises, with whom she had gone about ever since leaving home, and joined company with the self she had known long ago.

The little rose-buds of the Limoges ware on the dressing-table came vividly to life, for ever memorable. Strong and cool, with a strength that welled up unobstructed from the roots of her being, and a coolness that was one with the morning freshness of the little garden towards which the Limoges roses had turned her eyes, she had swung to the tips of her toes, as if to come level with the being within her outrunning all her faculties to greet the illimitable life ahead. And as she went downstairs, the thought returned that had so often beaten gladly to and fro while her release was delayed from day to day by the need to leave everything in order and the timid new secretary more or less launched upon her hazardous career: it was still only July. Never, since childhood, had she known freedom in July.

'All right, Grace,' she said, no longer feeling them jailers about to march her methodically round and round a prison yard, but rather embodiments of the past, prolongers of the anticipation of the ocean of beatitude wherein, at the end of this short week, she would be ready to plunge; alone. 'You shall go and examine the inside of the cathedral and I will stand about outside, and stare.'

Florence's accepting giggle reminded her how easily the two of them could be kept entertained and how, while day by day they were occupied with their objects of interest, she would be able to wander, near at hand, alone. It took her eyes across the table, at that moment richly irradiated by a shaft of sunlight, town sunlight, densely golden, to meet those of Florence and find there the penetrating gaze she had so often encountered in turning suddenly toward her from the midst of some lively to and fro of narrative and response at the Banbury Park dinner-table. But to-day, instead of sinking back into her dark eyes the moment Florence knew it to be observed, it remained, transforming the occasion, making it as deep and as interminable as itself.

'I could spend a year staring,' she quoted automatically, and for a moment took refuge in Kenneth Street, years ago, with Mag and Jan, in whose presence the words had first been put together. Returning from this vain flight, she found Florence's gaze, veiled now by a scorn so lively as to lift a corner of her delicate mouth, still fixed upon her. 'Couldn't *you*?' she demanded, unable to banish from the insincerely ingratiating tone the tremor of self-consciousness.

'I've never thought about it,' said Florence. Huskily, with dropped eyelids, and cheeks flooded with scarlet: shame, of self-betrayal, or for one's attempt to escape a challenge.

'I'm never going to think any more,' said Miriam, and felt the words become true as she spoke them, and saw in the far distance the sunlit scene, approaching. But between her and her bourne, obstinately barring the way, stood the figure of Florence, the one figure, of all those set intimately near her in the past, from whom she had been held away by a barrier she had no desire to shift. Incredulously inquiring of the form

seated across the way, ensconced as if forever, or at least until
its challenge should have been met, in a strange room grown
suddenly, leeringly familiar, Miriam found the eyes once more
upon her, unchanged, as if they had never left her face.

'You never worry about anything, do you, Miriam?'
Florence's judgment, accumulated during the years and at
last, and only because, for the first time, one was not her guest,
coming easefully forth; to remain, unless now it could be dis-
lodged or in some way transformed, a marginal note, set by a
disinterested observer forever against one's own version of
one's record at Banbury Park. Stung into defence, Miriam
turned from Florence's disturbingly half-true picture of herself
as a fickle, insincere, easy-going creature evading all issues, to
that of the kind of young woman Florence would approve:
mature, calculating, making terms with circumstance, planning
to outwit it, playing for security. Facing back to Florence's
demand for worry, she hit out:

'There's nothing, really, to worry about. I mean to worry
about *completely*, or we should all be mad.'

Florence was pulled up, puzzled. A little ashamed of her
attack, a little frightened and ready to believe one's profanity
accountable by something she did not understand and ought,
perhaps, to respect.

'Well, let's go, Miriam darling. It's past ten, already.'

Stretching her arms, punching, with closed fists, right and
left into the unresisting air, she let Grace's phrase, for her so
meaningless with its accent on the passage of time, go to and
fro in her mind, erasing the features of the strange collision
with an unknown Florence.

'Come along, my sweet,' murmured Grace, at her side now,
urgent and responsible.

'Had we any napkin rings?' she inquired, to gain a moment
for greeting, in solitude whatever lay ahead of this week of
small comings and goings.

'Here's yours, Miriam.' Florence spoke hurriedly and was
handing the veined and shiny bone ring with grave, eager
glance, as if it were valuable property she delighted to find and
restore. 'Ought we to take umbrellas?' On the last word

her voice was again husky, but this time with the huskiness of her irritable breathing apparatus, stirred by mirth unsure of itself but ready, if encouraged, to break forth into the asthmatic laughter that would fill her eyes with tears.

'Is Florence *quite* insane?' demanded Miriam, glaring into space and listening, her guilty heart throbbing its tribute to a Florence content to be puzzled, willing to withdraw her condemnation and credit it to her own insufficiency, for the laughter belonging to the ancient jest brought forth as a peace-offering.

CHAPTER II

THE little old woman, murmuring an almost inaudible good morning, set down what she had brought, and turned away without having once raised her eyes above the level of the table.

The greeting Miriam had intended to smile across the room the moment the expressionless face should turn her way was left unspent, and pity, rising as the dismal figure turned away towards the door, gave way, the moment the door was closed, to a gleeful self-congratulation. The impression received during the first queer interview, as she stood on the door-step shouting her few questions and responses, was blessedly confirmed. Like the ancient thick-walled house, whose air of quiet contemplation she shared, the old woman had turned her back upon the world. Speaking as if for years speech had been unfamiliar, yet serenely, without either the emphasis or the anxious or resentful accents of the deaf, she had seemed to offer, as her contribution to the world she faced at her front door, her own serenity. Her low, effortless monotone, her avoidance of all but the necessary minimum of interchange, had invited one to be as remote as herself. Her affliction would be a cloak, a protection from indoor exposure, the only exposure it is usually impossible to evade. She was a guardian, making perfect this arrival into solitude.

With her disappearance humanity vanished, leaving no echo within the room, making no break between to-day and last night's darkness in whose unfathomable depths she had lain thankfully awake—no sound but the intermittent breathing of the wind in the wide chimney, the slight stirring of the window-curtains, as if, to call her attention to the stillness, ghostly fingers gently touched them — until the sudden coming of unsummoned sleep and the morning's soft grey radiance.

Sitting down to breakfast, she looked out at last across the desolate scene invisible last night, so powerfully drawing her to itself when first she had come upon it, standing with the girls at the turning of the road from the village, that immediately she had put it away, saying no word, hoping they did not find it worth comment, turning aside and saying hurriedly that if the old grey house took lodgers she would go and stay in it, and seeing again, set for ever indelibly within, the sudden view of the house and its background of mud-flats and grey sky.

'Oh, Miriam dear, would you? It looks so dreary!'

'Grey, yes, I'm English.' And she had looked at them, finding them small and far away, seeking words to keep things going, to distract their attention from her sudden absence, the completeness with which in that moment the week had come to an end and she had left their company. 'So is O'Hara. Isn't she?' For Florence, though as little able as Grace to understand a passion for this grey scene, would gladly do her utmost towards convincing herself of its perfection. And now, singled out because her penetration was the more to be dreaded, she flushed with deep pleasure and drew near, her eyes full of that half-shy, half-envious supplication that always seemed to say: 'If only you would recognize it, I am far more attractive than Grace.'

Returned from their first glance at the scene as it showed from the house which before had been part of it and now, itself only a window, left it empty, a vast expanse ending in a wedge-shaped ridge low against the low sky, her eyes sped once more across the flats, now beginning to disappear beneath slow sea-water, and reached the misty ridge and found trees there, looking across at her from their far distance so intently that she was moved to set down the thin little old spoon raised to crack the shell of the egg whose surface, in the unimpeded light, wore so soft a bloom. Last week's room, where she and the girls had sat at breakfast feeling themselves ensconced so far away from the world, was in a city deep and dark, filled with human darkness.

'Trees,' she said, aloud.

Secret tears surprised her, welling spontaneously up from where for so long they must have been waiting to flow forth, and now finding their course obstructed by the smile risen to greet their message: for the first time since childhood she was alone with summer trees. There they were, at hand day and night for as long as she chose, no longer held off by the wistfulness with which she had gazed in the company of others, imploring them to yield their secret, known long ago. With the sea, she had kept her old self-losing intimacy. And with stars, and the depths of the sky. But all these were impersonal. And the trees of London, even while, surrounded by streets, they preserved their secret being, were a little social and sophisticated. But these trees across the way, alone and silent like the woodlands she had passed through with parties whose talking voices kept their own world about them, looked into the depths of her, the unchanged depths awaiting them since childhood.

Moving the things upon the table to make room for her elbows, she looked across again and found the trees further off and a little averted; suggesting that she should finish her meal and join them in the open.

The need to escape from the rain-sodden grassy levels about the house carried her to the only refuge in sight, a muddy lane hiding all she had come out to see. Once within it, she hesitated, tempted to turn back, retire to the house and the window-framed view, and wait for the afternoon and the ebb of the tide. Here, in the lane, she had the illusion of being in suburbia with all the world at hand. Away behind, there could well be the ragged edges of building plots and, at the lane's end, a sophisticated village with a good service of buses to town. The birdless, flowerless hedges looked cowed; outskirt hedges accustomed to traffic and unable, in its intervals, to recover their wealth and assert their ancient power.

No country scene could be more unlike the destination she had pictured herself reaching, by some unpondered route, immediately on leaving town. All these weeks it had accompanied her, filling every background, richly reflected into the inner twilight of her being: vast echoing woodlands, their green

alleys and sunlit clearings traversed by streams with flowery
banks and, in between, green open country, unfenced and uninhabited, beneath high blue skies. Still, it was a lane, with its
own little quality, however surrounded. The short stretch
left behind lay now between her and all that her eyes had made
her own. Ahead, an indefinite length of the tame corridor
asserted its strangeness and independence, bringing self-
consciousness, embarrassing her gait by drawing her attention
to its surprising weakness, of which, in strolling about with
the girls, she had been unaware.

And now, this chastening realization was transforming the
dull indifferent lane to an actively benevolent hospice. Feeling
like a phantom, needing all her strength to keep upright and
progressing amongst the gentle, powerful presences all about
her, in the mud, a healing salve beneath her feet of mingled
earth and rain, in the dismal hedges, drenched and dulled by
the same rain, giving a rank, sweet fragrance to the air beneath
a grey sky pressing so low as to be visible without an upward
glance, she smiled a wan secret greeting towards these kindly
witnesses of her disarray and set herself to her task, the only
task now demanded of her, to press forward through the soft,
dense south-coast air that was a tangible substance, in-pouring,
presently to steady her footsteps and bring poise to her body.

There would be barely time to cross the flats and get back
again before the in-coming tide should sweep over the little
causeway. To-morrow, the causeway would be clear only in
the morning. And the morning belonged to the lane and to
the anticipation of walking, in the afternoon, in the face of the
wind across the vacated floor of the sea, whose return belonged
to the evening and the sound of its bells to the night.

For this afternoon, what tryst could one make? To go,
leaving the edge of the world, up the road to the village, would
be to move away from enchantment. Away up there, amongst
the cottages, with the sea left behind, the air would be thin and
dry. There would be people. Village people, circling unaware. She remembered the ancient churchyard, where

Florence had remarked that every one in the parish lived to be ninety. But to prowl there would be to step back into last week, the other side of eternity. To go anywhere, yet, away from this corner where strength had begun to return, would be to leave that strength behind.

To-day the sheen upon the buttercups was dry; their own live varnish. And the grass, though still, under the low grey sky, a dull deep green, was polished and dry. Dry enough to sit upon, for the sand had drawn away the rain, making available this handy small slope dotted with flowers and out of sight of all but the sea and the ridge. Summery, like the lane this morning, dried and recovering its frilliness, preparing for people who were looking forward to August. Already belonging, together with the tree-trimmed ridge and the silky emerald weed on the mud-flats at low tide, to summer visitors. This magic angle at the edge of the world, seeming at first so desolate and so unknown, a solitude indefinitely available, was a cherished spot, busily ripening for those who knew it well.

August visitors, still held afar by a space of endless days and nights. Before they could arrive, she would be away within the wooded distances of her first vision, with August only at its beginning and, behind it, still inconceivably far away, September that for years had been the whole of summer, its glad beginning and its mournful end. And, behind September, untold months.

Only to-day had the possibility of reading in the open suggested itself. Looking back, she could recall no outdoor reading, save in the Bonnycliff garden, with people always at hand or imminent, and the echoes of conversation just past, and the certainty of more conversation just ahead, preventing all-forgetful absorption. But with infinite hours available, not a moment need be lost.

Opening the book at random, she heard the voice of Michael, and saw his face, lifted, its grave eyes fixed on hers to hold her attention: 'You will, I assure you, find here not only a most-admirable stating of the thinkings of your Emerson, but also a most-clear presentation of the world-view depending therefrom. Believe me it is a good book. You will see. The fellow has even something of Spinoza.'

Remaining for years untouched, it had been packed only because her intention of reading it, still faintly alive, had been roused from its lethargy by the prospect of leisure. Everything coming from Michael had been good; even the alien unacceptables. 'Your great Buckle, the first to make a really thought-filled and perceptive history of civilization. You shall immediately read this author. It is indeed most-strange that in your country he is relatively unknown; and good that your Grant Richards should have the inspiration to publish at minimum buying-cost these most-nice little pocket volumes.' ... 'Yes, I can possibly agree in a manner that, being English, the English themselves have no great *need* of this man. But every Russian student knows him. More perhaps than any other one man save Tolstoy, is he the bible of the Russian intelligentsia, creating revolutionaries by showing that only in those countries which have escaped from religious and political despotisms has civilization been able to develop.' Mill's *Influence of Women*, proclaiming women as the sustainers and preservers of inductive reasoning. Tolstoy? Shedding darkness as well as light. Sad, shadowed sunlight, Turgenieff. Perfection. But enclosed, as all great novelists seem to be, in a world of people. People related only to each other. Human drama, in a resounding box. Or under a silent sky.

Something was pressing eagerly up beneath the realization of being blessedly free to keep the printed page awaiting full attention for as long as she liked: Raskolnikov. Boxed in, but differently. Travelling every moment deeper and deeper into darkness; but a strange Russian darkness, irradiated. Dostoievski does not *judge* his characters? Whatever, wherever, they are, one feels light somehow present in and about them; irradiating. *Schuld und Sühne*. German translations are in general very faithful and good, Michael had said. *Guilt and Redemption*, much more Dostoievski's meaning than *Crime and Punishment*, suggesting a handbook of jurisprudence.

Again the book slipped askew, drawing her attention to the

grassy slope, this afternoon's gift, already strange and remote and needing fresh recognition, upon which the small book lay between her propped elbows. Rolling over, she sat up, seeing again the world that had vanished in the middle of the chapter with Michael bringing up the rear, bowing as he made way for his book, smiling as he swept round to depart on the end of his bow, his most courtly, ambassadorial smile, with a triumphant what-did-I-tell-you in his eyes and at the up-curving corners of his Jewish mouth.

Hypo had implied that the prestige of these last-century figures was at once enviable and beyond their deserts.

'But Emerson saw *everything*. The outside, as well as the inside things you don't believe in.'

'Saw life steadily and saw it whole,' he said instantly, with his jest-greeting grin. 'Yes, life in those spacious days stood still enough to be looked at, comfortably, from solidly upholstered arm-chairs. Everything was known and nothing was ever going to happen any more. The stillness, dear Miriam, was so deep that a book appeared almost *audibly*. There was no end of space for it to expand in and it did its own publicity, multiplying itself across the literate regions of the globe. All these chaps, you know, your Arnolds and Emersons and Carlyles, all the prominent men in that stagnant old world, had no *end* of a show. There they sat, a few figures, enthroned and impregnable; voicing profundities. No one will ever get such a show again.'

The spaciousness, he felt, had been unfairly squandered on the wrong people. For him, their profundities, going the round uncensored by science, were nothing more than complacent, luxurious flatulence, disguised in leisurely, elegant phraseology.

But was Emerson ever consciously a great man? He could lose himself watching the grass grow, and would never have called delight in the mere fact of existence 'a turnip emotion.' He saw that commerce was dishonest and calculating, but accepted the market-place as well as the shrine, while Hypo detested the one and suspected the other. But Emerson, with a private income and a mystical consciousness, remained unperturbed.

A stately house, within the serene immensity of New England, and all his needs supplied, he was for ever free, once he had decided that the sacraments were a gracious ceremonial and retired upon a life of cultured contemplation, to read and meditate and exchange long, leisurely letters with other meditators all over the world. A slender, but not an austere figure, arm-chaired, behind whose rather hawk-like profile sat the determination to exclude all but accredited invaders and remain, thought in hand, aloof from even his nearest relatives. Detached, in order to be able to focus. Rising, moving across the room to a cliff of books, taking down a volume, reading, with held-in eagerness, a swiftly discovered passage, replacing the book and turning again towards the well-known chair, his place on the invisible battle-field, pausing on the way, window-lit, to gaze nowhere, with thin, flexible lips firmly set, below keen eyes smiling delighted welcome for a thought-link forming itself within the serenely tumultuous mind.

Did he keep it in one place, or did he move from room to room the book wherein he set down, under appropriate headings, the crystallizations of his thought the moment they appeared, until there stood, ready to hand, the material of the essays?

Hypo would approve that cunning little trick. 'Put that down, Miriam. Don't forget. One of the most important, perhaps, next to clear thinking, *the* most important of the permanent responsibilities of the writer is the business of catching himself at his best. Nothing, *nothing*, should be allowed to stand in the way of that. Exalted and luminous moments may occur unexpectedly. But you'll find, if you keep an eye on yourself, that certain circumstances are particularly favourable to the precipitation of felicitous phrases. The meditative moments before sleep, for example, or on waking, after a good night. Then there are the valuable precipitates one finds in one's mind on waking in the small hours. Always have pad and pen at hand, to catch these things as they fall. Talking can be creative, too. Lots of good things are struck off in talk. After-tea talk, for example. That's why writers retire suddenly to their studies.'

Yet Mrs Boole finds harmful, both to the giver and to the recipient, the direct expression, whether in speech or in writing, of a deeply moving thought; believes one should allow it to pass into one's being and there work itself out.

'Ah yes, my dear,' pater had said immediately, 'Emerson is for the young. Now when I was a young man of thirty . . .'
Because I was trying to imagine what it must be to look back on thirty as youth, his repudiation sank into me without resistance, and I forgot to remind myself that he still, after a lifetime as a physicist, believes in direct intuitive perception. How can't there be direct perception of ultimate reality? How could we perceive even ourselves, if we did not somehow precede what we are?

Turning back to the early pages to discover the author's name, she became aware of her surroundings and of herself once more peering forgetfully into a book, seeking light amongst recorded thoughts. Yet those bringing her the greatest happiness, the most blissfully reassuring confirmations, had been found in the books of men who, professing thought and its expression to be secondary activities, had nevertheless spent their lives thinking and setting down their thoughts. Precipitating doctrine. If they really believed what they so marvellously expressed, would they go on turning out elegant books?
Returning to her chapter, once more indifferent as to the author's name, she read, glancingly, from phrase to phrase, losing threads when quotations from the essays brought back the surroundings wherein they had become inhabitants of her consciousness; and presently found the page clearer, the text blacker, and looked up to see the sky grown high. Behind the thinned clouds, a radiance waited to break through. For how long had she sat here, travelling again all over Emerson's world, finding again its reassurances, the stronger for being given back to her in phrases that were more directly powerful than Emerson's, although dependent upon his inspiration, because they were less mannered, and free from the haunting

shadow lying over the page the moment one returned to it from a pause filled with the eager movement of delighted recognition: of sadness, nostalgia for an essential something missing from Emerson's scheme, whose absence left one alone with serenely burning intellectual luminosities in a universe whose centre was for ever invisible and inaccessible. Listening within its silence, one heard only his poetic voice, moving from pitch to pitch, persuasively, logically, almost relentlessly optimistic.

A familiar quotation, one that for years she had carried about like an amulet and in the conflict of ideas had long since forgotten, appeared upon the page in a context that had not prepared her for its coming. Before she could place it or recall the conclusion towards which it had always been a point of departure, it had struck down through her and vanished, leaving only the shock it had brought, a physical shock passing through her body, carrying with it all she knew and was, so that she found herself looking up to take astonished counsel with her forgotten surroundings and discovering, upon the upper foliage of a group of trees in the dense mass at the far end of the ridge, a patch of bright colour in a golden light so vivid that for a moment she seemed to discern, as if they were quite near, each of the varnished leaves. Risen to her feet, she found the radiant patch more distant and less bright, a small splash of brilliant colour such as she had seen a thousand times before, picked out from a spread of dark tree-tops by a ray of haze-screened, shadowless sunlight. But the rapture that had seized and filled her emptied being at the first sight of it still throbbed to and fro between herself and that far point upon the ridge, and still she felt the sudden challenge of that near, clear vision, like a signal calling for response; and like a smile, of amusement over her surprise.

'I know,' she heard herself exclaim towards the outspread scene whose grey light could no longer deceive. 'At last I *know*! I have seen the smile of God. Sly smile.' Urging with tremulously apologetic fingers the book that with such faithful punctuality had served its turn, out of sight into a convenient pocket, she saw upon the jocund, sympathetically listening grass-blades at her feet a vestige of the vanished radiance and looked thence into her mind and found there, bathed in its full light, the far-off forgotten world from which she had fled and, with a last glance at the sunlit trees, turned to run and seek it there.

Joy checked and held her as she flew up the rising ground, stilled for a moment her craving for the sight of a human form, turned her running to a dance, swung her arms skywards to wave to the rhythm of her dance and pull upon the very air that it might lift her.

Scarcely touched, the upturned faces of the many flowers took no harm.

Approaching the solitary house, she went quietly. Between her and the luminous human multitude welcoming her from far, familiar surroundings grown as new and as strange as was every step of this oft-trodden little pathway, between her and her man, the unknown sharer of the transfigured earthly life, quietly going his way amongst those distant friends, there waited in the battered old house, as within a shrine, the first of the new, heaven-lit humanity, a part of her own being, confidently approaching its end.

'Yes, he's doing well, my grandson. He''s in the cathedral choir.'

The remembered, bustling life of the sleepy old town, clamorous in its market-place and narrow, resounding streets, invading the small, quiet room, robbed it of its ancient peace. But when again Miriam turned to consult the old lady's eyes she found in their depths a warmth that was not all pride in the satisfactory grandson, and the room's deep peace returned as she exchanged with Mrs Peebles a shy, appreciative smile.

With everything on the table, and the tea by this time thoroughly infused, the old lady was feeling it was time for her to disappear. But before she went, moving soundlessly with her remote, sleep-walking air, she bent to give the tea-cosy a small, adjusting pat; a silent sign, a tribute to their meeting.

Just having stood there, without any *manner* for the old lady, remaining relaxed as if alone, rather than keyed up to sustain

an invasion, had been enough.   The moment she had come in
with her laden tray and found one standing unarmed and
available, though not even looking her way, Mrs Peebles had
known the barriers were down.

During the second rustling subsidence of the congregation,
she sought relief from her uneasy solitude in the memory of
her one visit to a Quaker meeting, recalling the sense of release
and of home-coming in the unanimous unembarrassed stillness, her longing, as she had sat breathing in the vitalizing atmosphere produced by these people gathered together to submit
themselves communally.to the influence ruling their individual
lives, to exchange her status of visitor from another world for
that of one born amongst them.   Perhaps it was the completeness of that one experience that had made her so easily forget
it and fail to seek a renewal.

During the reading of the first lesson, she recalled her regret
when at last one after another of the gathered Friends had
broken into speech, remembering particularly a dapper little
man who had delivered a lecturette on natural science and an
old man who had prayed, simply, in broken phrases that seemed
to carry away into the presence of a healing sympathizer, the
woes of all the world, and how his voice had suddenly acquired
volume until it was howling, into the ear of a far-distant
Deity, Old Testament descriptions of Jehovah.

And it was the absence, here in church, of intervals of stillness that was preventing the sense of unity and home-coming.

Meeting, as she came through the porch only a few moments
after it had occurred to her to seek the church, the familiar
dense mustiness coming forth to blend with the outer air, she
had been back for a moment in her childhood's glad sense of
two interdependent worlds, each discoverable at the heart of
the other.   But when she stood at the aisle corner of the pew
into which she had been shown, she felt even weaker and more
exposed than in first confronting the silent presences in the
little lane, and had wondered with the available edge of her
mind whether this feebleness were the result of the shock of

immersion in a remembered world and the discovery that this immersion was of the body only, while her spirit sought in vain here for a home for the joy of yesterday; gasping, almost, for breath in the heavy atmosphere wherein these subdued people were going through their performances, under the leadership of the parson, an automaton with an assumed voice and accent, and a mind tethered elsewhere.

During the sermon, her mind flew, seeking, amongst the recognizable types whose faces and bearings had impressed themselves during her first swift survey. Tranquil, unquestioning 'church people,' finding within the strongholds of their orthodoxy both comfort and peace. Most of them loved the grey old church, the casket of their religion, whence one day they would depart for the last time bound for a heaven where still would be heard the language of the English Bible and Collects, the music of Purcell and Hopkins, Barnby and Smart, and the singing of hymns, Ancient and Modern. She felt nothing of her old desire to smash their complacency, to make them realize the unfoundedness of most of their assumptions and the instability of the privileges they took for granted. Only a blind longing for admission into the changeless centre of their enclosed world, the dwelling-place of the urbanity that made the sons of these people, scattered all over the earth, the pioneers of a world-club in a manner unattainable by the angry social reformers.

CHAPTER III

THE worlds from which one after another she had retreated, gathered round her redeemed from bondage to time and place, each, now, offering a brimming cup her unsteady hands had been unable to hold, each showing as a most desirable dwelling-place. And this desirability was not quite what Lucie Duclaux had meant when she had said, sitting in her lean grey cloak, with her narrow feet on the kettle and her lace-trimmed toque aslant above her rational eyes, that she could now live anywhere and with anybody; meaning she believed herself to have mastered the art of managing people and steering clear of open collisions. The desire to commit oneself came from the sense of having, at last, an available identity.

And even now, though she could imagine herself built into Fräulein Pfaff's school, tolerantly collaborating with her in handling successive drafts of girls from prosperous English families and, in the end, taking over the school herself; or staying deedily on with the Pernes and becoming, at last, approximately, a modern Perne; or even staying with the Corries until she had learned their world and become a flexible part of it; and finding, in any one of these careers, each moment full to the brim; and though yesterday she had been able wistfully to imagine herself, at fifty, a serene, stout Mrs Michael with grown children and a husband equally stout and serene, it was an immense relief to watch Michael move away at last beyond recall.

This first batch of letters must have lain for days in those lodgings before going on to Banbury Park to be forwarded together with the rest. Sorting them according to their dates, she read them once more and saw, hovering in the background of the scenes they evoked, the figure of Amabel's elder brother, the immediate progenitor of the little drama, unconscious both of his handiwork and of his symbolic significance. There he stood, far away in the unimaginable distances of India, tall and handsome, wealthy and secure, watching the London life of the babe who had toddled at his side in a sun-bonnet during the last of his Oxford vacs; amiably tolerating her foolishness in taking up with 'the shrieking sisterhood,' regarding it as the sowing of a harmless oat whose growth would be cut off for good and all when, at the end of his next leave, he carried the adored small girl, now his proudest and most cherished possession, back with him to Simla. Taking her part meanwhile. Coming to the rescue when the rest of the family, going up in flames with one accord, made her penniless and ordered her home, with the modest allowance that had made possible her full, rich life at Tansley Street. Until he heard she had achieved Holloway. Then the horrible change, justifying Hypo on the subject of the conventions: 'Don't forget, Miriam, that Mrs Grundy is a man. Always has been. Every father, every brother, every husband, every man born upon this unhappy planet, is a potential Mrs Grundy.' And leaving Amabel in the hands of her family, a beggar sentenced to imprisonment, with a generous dress allowance, either at home or in Simla, until she should marry.

With a borrowed railway fare, she had fled back to London. And found this queer, new tea-shop on the very first day.

'You see your Amabel, rather scared, but oh, believe me, thumping with happiness, her nose to the window-pane. The shop was empty, meaning, I know now, that the waitresses were doing the morning jobs in the kitchen part. Behind the counter, a woman watching a kitten, *on* the counter, lapping milk as if she, I mean the woman, who had her elbows amongst the buns and rather gorgeous red hair, never did and never would have anything much else to do. I tilted my hat at a better angle, the little one you like, with the one rose that you said brought to life my check frock, yes, the blue and white one with the little frills—you see me?—took a deep breath and swam in. "Good morning. Do you happen to want a waitress?" Mira, even with my deep breath I was breathless, with a sort of unexpected horror. A *really* awful moment to get to the other side of. She said "I might!" My dear, she's Irish, and before we'd done talking I was one of her waitresses, we found. It's in the Strand. They have another in Piccadilly. Quite new, and rather like that place in Baker Street your Mr Hancock found so embarrassing to sit still and be waited on by ladies in. But rather less refeened. No palms. Striped, satiny wall-paper and tub-chairs. She's a lady. Her crockery needs to be seen to be believed. And so are most of the waitresses. And thank God there's not an atom of that lady-pluckily - gone - into - business - and - isn't - it - fun - and - don't-I-do-it-charmingly atmosphere. We are, I tell you, *chic*. Remote, therefore, as well as *gai*. We wear lilac gingham and high heels. Before the lunch rush, if you can believe, we have —whiskies and sodas. I'm the youngest as well as the newest and they make me wait on Mr Raphael Phayre, who comes here regularly, almost every day. They all detest him and, considering his books, he is really rather a remarkable old bird. Brings various ladies. One day, he was accompanied only by a satin slipper, which he posed, on the table, while he had his tea. One can't exactly mother him, nor, quite, laugh at him. There's something venerable. Pathétique. He told me, rather charmingly, I might have sat to Rossetti if I'd been born a few decades earlier: "His loss, my dear young lady, his abominable loss."'

The thought of her there irradiated the Strand, enriching its daylight and bringing meadow coolness into its fevered commercial atmosphere. And even into Flaxman's. . . . 'Mrs Bailey was sweet when I gave up my room. Refused to let me pay for my weeks away, and would have let me have your old garret. But Flaxman's is cheaper. Top attic, five bob, in the next house to your old rooms. Yeats is still opposite. A landlady quite mad, but a darling. Has a herd of gawky fowls in the back yard, all with names. Occasionally there's an egg, but most of them are bald and doddering. She keeps them till they die of old age. I am *chez moi, sous les toits et le ciel*. I adore it. I've put geraniums on the sill.'

And in that far-away, troublous London, the abode, for oneself, of so many frayed, loose ends, at this moment and for ever Michael was safely within Amabel's all-penetrating radiance. Did he realize, would he in a lifetime learn to realize, even half of his amazing good fortune? 'Miriam, even now is it too late? To sit with you for an hour, to hold your hand and see your eyes, is more to me than a lifetime with this charming girl.' For the present he believed this and suffered in believing. The Russian in him believed it, knew, in spite of his Jewish philosophy, something of the unfathomable depths in each individual, unique and irreplaceable, making it forever impossible to substitute one person for another, or to lose the life existing between two who have experienced prolonged association. And the Jew in him so far saw Amabel only as charmingly qualified to fulfil what he still regarded as the larger aspect, the only continuing aspect of himself, his destiny as a part of his 'race,' the abstraction he and his like so strangely conceived as alive, immortal, sacred, and at the same time as consisting of dead and dying particles with no depth of life in them, mere husks. 'The whole, Miriam, is greater than the parts.' That had sounded unanswerable. But now I see the catch in the metaphor. Too late to make it clear to Michael. Amabel, indirectly, without reasoning, will shake his rationalism.

Are all the blind alleys and insufficiencies of masculine thought created by their way of thinking in propositions, using inapplicable metaphors? 'See these silent wonderful.' Are all coherent words, in varying measure, evidence of failure?

Very rationally, presenting himself at the evocative door with, poor darling, that defiantly songful expression looking out at one from the student photographs and still inhabiting his face whenever he braced himself to a difficult undertaking, he sought out Mrs Bailey to demand the heedlessly, cruelly, uncommunicated address, of which Mrs Bailey, too, was still in ignorance. Standing there at a loss, disappointed by a Mrs Bailey both amiable and regretful and, secretly, devoured by a wide-branching curiosity, he recalled Amabel, held his ground, made his further inquiry, and, probably that very evening, paraded pathetically outside the tea-shop at closing-time; a lonely little figure in the frock-coat and silk hat of his precarious City importance, his portfolio of legal documents under his arm; caftan and silk cap, praying - shawl and phylactery assembling themselves for any imaginative observer about the form whose expression and outline had grown, during his years of independence, so consciously Hebrew.

And when at last Amabel emerged, probably with two or three others, blossoming into the weary dust-laden July-afternoon Strand, and certainly laughing in the way he had found, during that one encounter, so inconsequent and so irritating, and suddenly silent and dumbfounded, calling up all her controls to grasp and handle the situation, he surely will have begun by saying, hat in hand and features working beneath the pressure of his embarrassment: 'Good afternoon. You will most-certainly be surprised to see me,' and will immediately have gone on to announce into the depths of her uncomprehended, all-accepting, heaven-thanking smile, whose inward wild rejoicing encircled the earth: 'I came to ask you how is Miriam and where is she, do you know? Pairhaps I shall walk with you to your home; yes?'

And Amabel, returned more swiftly than light to the moment that was still at its beginning when she found herself walking up the street at his side, hearing, in the sound of their mingled voices, the echoes of the future, would have held away the weariness so swiftly coming upon him in any conversation failing to reach his central interests, exercising her power to visualize and to interpret with an art so perfect that he would be unaware of it, and would identify the pleasantness of the hour with his relief in getting news of me.

Her joyous blessing lay ready for post, needing only its stamp. Looking out across the harbour with her eyes on the half-remembered village post office, unvisited save by Florence in search of local photographs, she saw the whole district reduced to a single eyeful, set compactly in its place in contiguity to other districts, bereft of depth and of long vistas, of mystery and glamour. While she read the letters, moving from scene to scene, watching the drawing together of the two who had severally supplied her richest experience of human relationship, it had become a site. Even the flower-dotted hillock seemed now to disown and dismiss her. And the London interposed between herself and her surroundings was no longer hers, belonged now to the two who for so long had given it life and of whom at a single stroke she was deprived. Onward they went, hand in hand, smiling, towards a future wherein she had no part.

This was jealousy, showing its mean little face and clutching hands. So late. Only a few months ago, bewailing Michael's inability to perceive Amabel, she had put aside, to preserve it from danger, even the thought of her enchanted hope. Seeing it realized, she grudged the attendant happiness. But even as she felt this jealousy's deep-seeking manipulations, the vision of Amabel alone and unchanged, however surrounded and accompanied, sent it to its death. With an almost audible snap, the last link parted that had held her to the past. Released, she could seek those to whom she belonged. But they made no sign, and the open spaces of her first vision of freedom no longer attracted.

Gathering up the letters, she found them aged, the long-pondered opening scenes of a drama wherein she was to collaborate only as an interested spectator. The last sheet, Michael's second little note, fluttered to the floor and lay, face downward, revealing, upon its unexamined reverse side, a straggling paragraph and, beneath it, what appeared to be an address. Retrieving it to acquaint herself with the latest of his ill-considered schemes, or with the data of some embarrassing demand, she read the hurriedly scribbled words: 'If you are seeking a quiet place for your writing, why should you not go to the family of my fellow-boarder here, which lives only a quite small journey from where you are and is willing for boarders? There is a mother there and a sister, or some sisters, I am not sure, and it is in quite deep country, a sort of farm.' Under the address, three illegible words expressed the wearied collapse of Michael's effort. Would Amabel succeed where she had failed, make him realize how prejudicial to his British career was his impatience of the written word? 'They . . .

are . . . *Greeks*?' Jews, then. Greek Jews, in the heart of the country? The name, prefacing the address, *Roscole*, sounded neither Greek nor Jewish. Ros . . . *corla*. Cornish? 'They are . . . *Quakers!*'

Far away within the cool twilit deeps of her innermost consciousness, she went up a pathway towards a farmhouse within whose doorway stood a little group of grey-clad Quaker women, smiling a gentle welcome. Michael's gift. A little Quaker stronghold at the heart of all she had first come forth to seek. Itself as remote as the deeps of country wherein it was set.

The little plop with which the note to Amabel and Michael fell into the letter-box, should have brought, with its finality, her heart to her finger - tips. But they remained steady, clasped about the letter that was to open the way to the richest depth of shared life imaginable upon earth, and thrilled with joy as they lifted and let it fall.

CHAPTER IV

ALL but one of the passengers got down at the village, taking away into its rain-dulled twilight, with themselves and their packages, dense odours and the sound of heavy breathing. And the slow, wide, richly inflected voices with which they had greeted each other and talked together. Leaving the dim enclosure a haunted place. So much speech come down into, so heartily, yet leaving the far distances of their individual lives, visible in their faces in repose, solitary and unexpressed. Following them imaginatively to their homes brought no relief from the burden of this visible solitude. Villagers. Farm labourers. People seen afresh who had been seen here and there in brief glimpses, long ago. The sound and sight of them was dreadfully, deeply familiar. Never before experienced close at hand. Fear used to come, as well as oppression and sadness, and, even in childhood, a feeling of guilt, at the sight and sound of these people living outside the gates, circling, all their lives, in immovable circumstances over which they had no control. And it was the desire to avoid the sight of them and the problems they suggested, and the challenge they unconsciously flung at the world dependent upon them, that had kept one, during these last weeks, away from village and villagers.

'You never worry about anything.'

Craven fear, of facing what they faced, what gave them, even at their most rubicund and kindliest, the moment they were not speaking, that expression of staring fixedly at something unchanging, relentless, and inexorable. It was worse than the secretly stricken expression of the town worker who realizes himself caught for life in a machine that will yield him, grudgingly, only the minimum. He, at least, has a vicarious amplitude, the support of London all about him, its oblivion-bringing resources and the illusion of stability created by its bustling surfaces.

When the carrier had hauled out the side of bacon propped at the far end of the bus, she moved up and across to the corner that would be nearest to the green hedge and the low fields as soon as they were clear of the village, flitting self-contained within the moment between two lives, swift and invisible upon light, impalpable feet, her spirit already dancing within the nowhere and everywhere whither she was bound, whither days ago she had been translated; so that now, for the first time, life-obstructing speculation and excitement were excluded from the experience of arriving amongst strangers in a strange place. Towards which the bus moved off as she reached her corner and sat revealed, before the eyes of the remaining prisoner, now no longer alongside but visible in his place near the door, as an ignorant excited tourist, peering, when the last of the cottages had vanished, through the low, narrow strip of window as if, in the surrounding fields, there were something to be seen.

Looking across, as the emptied vehicle became a racing chariot, interposing its oblivious impatience and the din of its loosely rattling joints between herself and the jolted hedgerows, she saw, rigid and motionless in the far corner, something strayed from a waxwork show . . . a tailor's mannequin . . . a ventriloquist's dummy—topped by a soft felt hat, with a downy bloom upon its clean unhandled nap, set, rather than worn, upon the head and, like the rest of the unassimilated garments, a size too large. Beneath it, twin bulges of smooth brown hair clasped, with a wig-like closeness, a round, paint-bright face whose wide blue eyes, expressionless, contributed nothing to the fixed smile that heightened the shock of encountering, in place of detached observation, this vacuous intentness.

The orbs came round, still unattained by the curving smile, and projected across the intervening space a gaze so wide and so all-embracing that for a moment she was lost in it, becoming both the instrument and the object of this horrifying glare.

'A nice evening,' she ventured, returning the smile. People like this, one person like this, was to be found in every village, always there, a common possession, unforgettable. He had caught her on the way from solitude to perfect human association, to remind her that country life included the visible, inescapable presence of every kind of affliction.

As if worked by a mechanism, the plump lower lip dropped to reveal the extremity of a tongue, repulsive herald to slow, difficult speech. But the soft 'ath' emerged as smoothly as the sound produced, in response to pressure, by a talking doll, and with just its abrupt, colourless tone. Smiling again, she turned away relieved. Friends with the local idiot, she could now compose herself to arrive in heaven.

The horses slowed for a hill. The steadied hedgerows flowed quietly. Discovering a catch upon the little square of window near her shoulder, she released and pushed the pane as far as it would go and met the outer air. Streaming from the misty rain-soaked meadows, visible whenever a gate passed by, it poured into her being, describing those meadows, miles of them covering the earth in all directions, solitary, averted in the dim light, breathing out secretly, unnoticed, the evening fragrance of all that grew in them; claiming her, not as something added to the rest, but as her known companions, left behind long ago and now returned to and demanding forgetfulness of everything but themselves, for whom, they declared, she had mistaken the strangers at the top of the hill.

If she had heard of the Roscorlas as living in London, would she have sought them out?

The place was not in the least like a farm. A white five-barred gate, fastened back, a sweep encircling a bed of evergreens, grass-bordered, a square plaster house, two-storied, bleak, an enclosed glass porch nakedly protruding, asking, in order that it might blend with the house, a share of the ivy sparsely climbing the left side of the frontage as far as the sill of an upper window.

A small trigger, on the lintel of the outer door, pulled on a wire and jangled a bell not far within.

A tall lean maidservant suggesting Wiggerson; like what Wiggerson might have been in a very godly household fifty years ago. The bony form that dipped, swiftly, as Wiggerson used to dip in eager service amongst the wealth-provided luxuries wherein she had no share, to seize and carry off one's bag, was surmounted, in place of Wiggerson's muslin mob and gallantly flying streamers, by an oblong strip of starch-stiffened cotton lace laid, mat-like, upon the narrow head whose reddish hair, scraped smoothly into a small high bun that tilted the little mat downward from back to front, helped the scant freckles to heighten the pallor of the long lean face. When again this face was visible and the pale blue eyes once more met her own, Miriam received with joy their cold, unseeing gaze. Announcing that Miss Roscorla was out and would be back in time for supper, the servant led the way upstairs, revealing upon brow and lips and thin cheek visible in profile as she rounded the angle of the short flight and was softly lit from above, the unmistakable look of conscious salvation.

It carried Miriam far away beyond the remembered Quaker meeting, wherefrom, indeed, she could recall no face bearing exactly this expression, back to Blewbury and the enigmatic vision of Great-Aunt Stone sitting blind and motionless in the clasp of the graceless parlour chair whose high back had the dreadful shape of a halved cylinder, plaintively querulous with all about her; crippled Aunt Emma on the other side of the fireplace, bent listeningly over her cross-stitch texts, distributing, without looking up, abrupt rallying comments and snappish rebukes; the convulsively talking uncles, coming and going and still, in late middle age, browbeaten and uneasy. And in them all, something that her eight-year-old mind, feeling its way, unhappy in the restricted surroundings, scared by the mysterious illiberality, had dimly recognized as an independent extension of each personal life, glad and free. A secret, new and strange, something not present in her own home, and outwardly expressed by this look shining from the face when in repose, this look of *conscious* salvation; the hall-mark of the chapel.

Encountered in a Quaker household, although in this young woman, now silently departed, it might be merely a youthfully exaggerated imitation of a deportment, it was nevertheless disconcerting.

A Philistine room, furnished without deference to shape and colour and, surprisingly, dominated from the end wall facing the large brass bedstead, by an enormous portrait: a dark, bouncing, handsomely dressed middle-aged woman whose swarthy face, topped by a heavily beribboned lace cap, was bounded on either side by large, low-hanging earrings—wealthy, a member of the mercantile aristocracy—sitting in judgment upon a world of incapables. Surely, not a Quakeress? When the candle was alight, she shone forth from shadows, filling the room with the din and bustle of the visible world. But immediately below her, at the wash-stand within whose rose-pink cake of fresh soap were safely stored the days to come, one escaped. And the dressing-table, set askew across a corner between wash-stand and window, proved also, since the eyes stared across the room and did not follow one about, just outside their line of vision. Nor did they bore one's back as one stood at the window which turned out to be the one reached by the climbing ivy, and gave on a wide, dim expanse ending, very far away, against a brightness along the edge of the dark sky.

Opening to a gentle knock, Miriam found at her door a small stout woman—the mother or the daughter?—from whose dark brown eyes, as she made her explanations and apologies, there shone a smiling radiance so transforming the homely face that she regretted the almost immediate movement into the room, resulting in its unseen transference to inanimate things. But when presently the dumpy, dowdy little figure drew up in front of an opened drawer and, looking within, said gently: 'That is petal-dust, to keep away moth'—immersed, at the end of her busy day, in the contemplation of a cherished, enchanting mystery, desirous of sharing it and, at the same time using its quiet presence as a test of the newly formed relationship—there was visible, upon the bent, candle-lit profile from which Miriam's eyes shifted to gaze at the fine brown powder scattered over the drawer's paper lining, and giving out a faint, dry fragrance that called up a fleeting vision of sunlit flowers moving from their prime to fade and die into the makings of this beneficent dust, something of that same radiance. And while they stood side by side, united in silent appreciation, Miriam felt it enfold and set her adrift upon the borders of the world wherein this woman had her being.

It was the head of a girl, revealing, while its attitude laid bare the line of the neck between hair and low, stiff collar-band, the semblance of childhood; a middle-aged, inexperienced girl, selfless and out-turned, full of objective interest in all about her and attentive, grown, through long practice, permanently attentive to guidance coming from within and productive of that withdrawn, far-listening look that recalled the remembered Quakers.

When they turned together to the room's open space, the temporary cessation of audible interchange had produced, rather than the uneasiness that prompts a search for fresh conversational material, a time-expanding satisfaction and the sense, behind them, of an achieved, indefinitely durable past. It was easy, looking up at the alien flamboyance now confronting them from the wall with its splendour of indifference to things unseen, to make an apprehensive inquiry.

'That is Mrs Joshua Bullingham, the mother of our last pupil, who had this room.'

'Not a Quaker?'

'No, she's not a Friend. A Presbyterian lady.'

'And your servant, who let me in?'

'No. Eliza is a village girl, a Strict Baptist.' She had turned as she spoke, with a smile that was almost a chuckle of glee over one's confessed dismay, and a searching glance that betrayed her surprised interest in learning that one had at once spotted these two outsiders.

CHAPTER V

OUTSIDE her door, launched on the journey from her own world established in the room she had just left, to breakfast downstairs at the centre of the universe, she hesitated, remembering the window opposite the door whose knob was still in her hand. While she had hurtled from point to point, hoping not to be discourteously late for the very early meal, wondering whether the two Roscorlas took it in a silence that would deepen, by enabling it to be shared, the heavenly morning stillness, this window had let in brilliant light telling of a fine day. Last night's silent friends, the ivy-leaves framing the sill, she had remarked again and again in passing to and fro, but of the wide view she had been aware only as a glimpse of flat, rain-silvered pastures sunned to gold.

A whirr, coming up from the hall, followed by a single hammer-blow, woodenly soft and unreverberating, announced the presence there of a grandfather clock and the fact that she was a quarter of an hour late. Abandoning the door-knob, she went along the passage fenced by the balustrade on whose far side, beyond the well of the staircase and the further balustrade, was a door set opposite to the one she was now passing. At the end of the passage, facing the descending staircase, another door and, visible at the far end of the companion passage, in an alcove, a fifth door, shadowy, unreached by the morning radiance falling from the skylight.

Here was the hall with its two-doored glass porch. Doors right and left and, somewhere along the passage to the left, the little room where last night Miss Roscorla had given her supper and talked of the Botinskys, of whom Michael had said so little, revealing a strange, half-malicious amusement over young Paul Botinsky's ignorance. Coming into the country for the first time in his life, how should he recognize its spectacles or plumb its secrets? Why should it be *funny* not to know an ox from a cow? Not to recognize growing corn? But she had revealed also her admiration for the frank simplicity of his request to be allowed to pray each day up in the drawing-room. 'He'd brought his little mat and his shawl,' she said, with affectionate approval. *Up* in the drawing-room. That, then, was the room with the shadowy doorway near her own. In the front of the house, looking out across the wide expanse.

The little room, where last night she had supped, stood open and empty, shut into a green twilight by a high brick wall a few feet from the window, and partly screened by the trunks and feathery down-dipping branches of larch trees. At the angle of the passage an open door showed a wide gravel pathway and more larches, between whose trunks a wooded distance sloped gently to rise again on the horizon in a slanting line upon whose upper end a windmill stood in profile, against the sky. Pure morning air came in and stillness, deep country stillness far from the sound of the sea. Yet sounding, even while, as one paused to look, the stillness seemed complete. Offering if, free from an urgent errand, one should step out into it, small near and distant sounds, clear, measuring the height of the sky, making denser the enclosed stillness of this many-roomed, strangely deserted house. Where, at this spellbound moment, was its life concentrated? To the right, a short passage offered another closed door from behind which, as she approached, a man's voice sounded, deep and leisurely, matching the stillness, shattering its promised peace.

The two men, subsided in their places facing each other at the far end of the table, recovered from the disturbance of their relationship as narrator and listener, created a world apart. Down here, the youth, returned with her cup of tea to his place at her side and now deftly assembling the rest of her meal, shut her off in the clear space created at this end of the room by the absence of Miss Roscorla who evidently had breakfasted at the head of the table to one's right, and of Mrs Roscorla, pre-

sumably taking her meal in her room and represented only by
an empty place across the way.

Taking in, from the doorway, a long low-ceilinged room
apparently full of men, Miriam had smiled ruefully to herself
at the celestial joke. Sold, she was. But innocently. The
power drawing her to this house, the remembered quality of
Quaker women, instead of carrying her forward into the heart
of peace, had led her back into the known world. Surely
Michael must have known of these brothers? At the far side
of the table, well away from her direct line of vision, was the tall
one, dark and curly-haired, with features indistinct—for this
room, too, at that further end, was inhabited by a kind of twilight—who as she came in had risen with an easy, lounging,
broad-shouldered movement from his place opposite the door,
and had said, after greeting and introducing her in a deep,
gently vibrant voice: 'My sister, I expect, will be here shortly.'
Out of sight beyond the youth sat the short fair one who, half
rising from his seat, had given a small rough hand and swiftly
subsided. It was to him alone that the tall brother was
addressing his interrupted narrative, sitting, as she could see
without looking across, sideways, at leisure, cross-legged, his
breakfast finished. Her neighbour, too, with an empty plate
before him, was meditatively sipping the last of his tea. A
familiar surroundedness. After-breakfast leisure, minus the
confronting hostess whose care and forethought made possible
this care-free ease and this standing still of time; as she had
known it on Sunday mornings at Tansley Street when the presiding Baileys had departed downstairs and the women boarders
had vanished to their rooms. Only the men remaining, able
to breathe in peace, each on his own centre in integrated morning mood, the party held together by the ceremonial furnishings
of the table and securely apart by the impermanent nature of
the gathering.

Behind the empty space across the way, a deep-set wide low
window revealed a high-walled garden whose nearest blossoms,
red-gold, standing high, so that they were visible just beyond
the line of the sill, held the light of the invisible sun, filling
the garden and projected by the terminal wall into the low-ceiled

room, making this end of it a chamber of amber light.   A cross-shaped thinning amidst the dense masses and a glimpse of a rose-garlanded trellis, suggested pathways.

While still her eyes dwelt upon the various loveliness gathering this portion of the room, with the bestowal of a reflected brilliance, into its own deep being, she grew aware that the room's other end was also somehow lit from without and turned and saw, outlined against the angle of the wall and what appeared to be a distance-narrowed greenhouse door, the seated form of the elder brother drawn upright, arms extended, powerful large hands, upon whose wrists the frayed sleeve-edges of an old Norfolk jacket lay tired and faded, set by the finger-tips upon the table, ready to hoist the big frame about to rise and depart—already, before she had finished her meal, become, at this moment the gift of those labour-coarsened hands, and while there rose in her as she read the expression of the handsome head, a little shabby and unkempt, benevolent, but saved from mere benevolence by its air of customary pride, the demand that her welfare should be his immediate concern.

'She rode down the middle of the street, with this great mass of hair falling nearly to the saddle.'

The room contracted to its linear measurements.   Every object stood near and clear, lit by a morning light made cold and lifeless by those on whom it fell, absentees, to whom it made no appeal.   The remote peace of this homely room, the message of the golden light shining in from the flower-filled enclosure, were being willingly sacrificed to far-away London, itself bereft of meaning, regarded merely as a show-room for exhibits, and where, quite recently, he had stood, upon some pavement-edge in Regent Street, gazing at the Harlene lady riding by in full view, along a street momentarily clear of traffic, impressed by the mere quantity of her flowing hair, oblivious of the travesty and the pathos defacing the street's restrained dignity; his outward eye beholding an engaging picture, his inward, Godiva.

He had returned.   In a few days' time, or even at this morning's end, he would be once more fully ensconced.

'I know that apparition,' she said conversationally, and felt

herself launched, in relation to the household males, as one of
those women who, during the day's social gatherings, turning
their backs upon their own territory, remain hospitably alert
upon the outer edge of consciousness to welcome the versions
and verdicts of the men-folk, to keep them at ease and in good
conceit of themselves; an arduous, petrifying role, impossible
to sustain.

'That's just what it was.'

The expression of his face, turned to her before he spoke,
avenged her treachery by revealing the most dishonouring of
social animations: the innocent blind satisfaction of the male
who discovers in a woman, newly met, whose ministrations
have not, therefore, become a familiar unregarded sustenance,
a flattering echo of his own imaginings. But while he spoke,
judicially, in the manner of one bestowing prompt reward for
deserving effort, she saw how haggard were the blue-grey eyes;
puzzled, the stricken eyes of one steadily enduring uncomprehended sorrow. For which life occasionally supplied, was at
this moment supplying, a relief whose public expression was
held back by lips so firmly compressed upon his last word as to
lift away from their corners the frayed ends of the lustreless
brown moustache.

This handsome, battered giant was the household referee?
The centre of meal-time talk, uneasy in silence? Even so,
there was a deep difference between him and the average
talkative male, a Quaker difference, perceptible in the weighti-
ness of his simple statement and in his present air of waiting,
with grave eyes still on her face, expecting her to take her time,
to weigh, in her turn, the proffered statement, and keep the
topic, which here at least, would not be regarded either as a
test or as an opportunity for display, unembarrassingly hanging
fire in a stillness, the first available fragment of the deep,
shared stillness wherein she had hoped to plunge immediately
on arriving in the house, and to find broken only by statements
made in a language yet to be learned. But before anything
could arrive in her mind that would sustain the disappointingly
mundane theme, his eyes moved to a point just beyond her and
came to rest there with a smile that opened his lips for speech

which refused to come because words were beyond reach, routed by the objects of his radiant contemplation: an onlooker, and himself caught napping.

Turning, Miriam found Miss Roscorla at her side, come into the room through an unnoticed door set in the alcove to the right of the fireplace and revealing, left open, a dark passage along which distant kitchen sounds sent their peace-shattering message. Though revealed, by her flushed face and slightly dishevelled hair, as bondservant to the tedious indispensable mysteries, Miss Roscorla stood, as if permanently free and available, taking in the disposition of affairs, a little wistfully perhaps, being a sister and sharer of the past rather than a wife and, therefore, to some extent, an alien; but also with pleasure, since she radiated a rich renewal of yesterday's intimate kindliness, standing still for a moment in the midst of her busy life with a mind 'at leisure from itself' and from the affairs that gave to her presence, though her eloquent dark eyes were free of the shadow of preoccupation common to the eyes of housekeepers, something of their odious power to disqualify and to drive away the masculine morning mood and to substitute, for its vast leisurely perspectives, the prospect of immediate activity, already, Miriam observed through the corner of her eye as she stood responding to Miss Roscorla's greetings and inquiries, embodied in the figure of the elder brother, bent forward to gain from the edge of the table, upon which still his hands were resting, purchase for its huge upheaval, and now, upon the would-be decisive 'well' of one aware he should have moved long since, risen to its full height.

Settled in the decrepit deck-chair under the chestnut tree whose huge being made of this corner of the lawn a kind of retreat, its sturdy trunk between her and the backward immensity, its wide branches a roof beneath the towering heights of sky and an irregular crescent of shadow upon the invading sunlight, Miriam felt the crowding impressions of the last twenty-four hours make way for a sense of the stillness fallen, now that she was still, upon her surroundings and their far, various perspectives, all, now that they were removed from sight and could be contemplated without shifting one's gaze from point to point, simultaneously visible as a whole wherein the garden, and the grounds sloping away so abruptly that their end could not be seen from the upper level, showed as an unenclosed part.

This morning's sunlit flats beyond the front garden seemed now a world apart, belonging to the rooms whose windows looked out on them, her own and the unexplored upstairs sitting-room together occupying the width of the frontage that described the house as square until, coming down through it, one discovered the spread of its hinder part, the wing holding the kitchens and the rooms above them, hidden from the front view of the house by that enormous dark-green tree to the right of the façade.

The undisturbed coo-rooing of invisible doves poured into the stillness a rhythmic unvarying pattern of sound.   Busy. Yet suggesting peace.   Secretly inviting her to stay and share, for far longer than the projected fortnight, their care-free protectedness.   Up and down it went, up and down; five gurgling notes encompassing the octave, always with the same omissions and always failing perfectly to reach the upper note, accentuated without a pause and leading the return journey down the scale.   But Densley had suggested altitude.   She recalled his face, its professional gravity banishing the affectionately malicious smile greeting his discovery of her newly dawned determination to exploit, for the sake of its attendant possibilities, the verdict of a science she half despised: 'Not necessarily your beloved Oberland.   Something more easily accessible.   Say Crowborough.'   This retreat, though on an eminence, could not be called high, and Miss Roscorla had referred to the flats in front of the house as 'the marshes.'

From the door in the high-walled stable-yard came forth a man carrying a large boat-shaped basket with a low, curved handle.   His tweed cap pulled aside and down at a snarling, football-crowd angle above a pallid, smoulderingly talkative face, a pink moss-rosebud in the buttonhole of his blue serge suit, he looked more like a shop assistant on holiday than a gardener as he sauntered, meditating, along the garden path to disappear behind the huge sycamore standing at the opposite corner of the lawn where the bank ended that separated it from the downward slope of the estate. Voices sounded from behind the stable wall, low-toned, unhurried, Quaker voices in question and answer, arranging the day's work. Richard Roscorla, Alfred; and the pupil, who now appeared at the gate and made off down the path, going headlong, without attention for the sunlit scene, to his chosen work. Stocky. So colourlessly fair that his hair and face, all of a piece in their tonelessness, faded into the pale tweeds that also were the colour of south-coast sand above the tide-line. His blue eyes, too, had been pale; crafty, dishonest nonconformist eyes, hypocritical; the eyes of the chapel-leading grocer or dairyman who sands the sugar or adds water to the milk. Distinguishable from the shifty Anglican or Roman Catholic eye by the absence from it, and from the mouth beneath, of a guilty malaise. Grown, during the after-breakfast moments while Miss Roscorla was interviewing the higgler, very strange new friends. Eyes inherited from a 'saved' family, looking out upon the world these elders had utterly condemned, with a quiet, steady interest. While she evaded a second encounter with these revealing eyes, his talk had somehow moved forward from courteously eager descriptions of a liner snapped by him in dry-dock, begun the moment Miss Roscorla left the strange young lady on his hands, to his thoughts on marriage; and while she listened, glancing, off-guard with amazement over the reaching forth of this country lad, not long emerged from his co-educational Quaker school, to the idea of experimental marriage for an agreed, limited period, she recognized the embarrassing expression of the eyes, so oddly contradicting the boyish smile, for an inherited spiritual mannerism, and the next moment was half-enviously regarding his cherished school-mates, seen as lately as last week when he and they had returned for the annual festivities: 'She sang *Killarney*. . . .' A side-long, shifty glance and a smile revealing faultless teeth and recalling the confident life-welcoming beam of Dr von Heber.

'And when any one sings *Killarney* really well, you feel there's nothing you wouldn't do for them.' And her mind, hovering wistfully over this co-educational idyll, had tried to imagine itself into the future of these young people growing up all over the provinces, away from London sophistications, although, indeed, they all read newspapers written by and for enclosed Londoners who unconsciously conceived of all humanity as equally enclosed and surrounded. Encountering for the first time provincial confidence—or was it Quaker co-educational confidence?—she had felt, when he told her his home was in Berkshire, like one taking possession of a newly revealed heritage.

He went down the path to his work as if heaven waited in the lower garden. Followed almost at once by Alfred Roscorla trundling a wheelbarrow. A small, slender form. Isolated. A lonely life. In the outdoor light his face, its freckled pallor heightened by the hatless dense thatch of close-cut wavy red hair, showed sad, lined by suffering. But a radiance from within took this suffering in charge and redeemed also his faded tattered garments. Escaped from the hive, come forth alone to meet the day's demands yet looking, with his eyes on an invisible distance, like a sleep-walker, was he aware of the still lingering fragrance of this heavenly morning? Why sadness, on this lit face?

With his disappearance beyond the sycamore and the dying away of the sound of trundling wheels, the scene was silent again. Uninhabited, unwitnessed, lonely beauty. Somewhere away down the far slope, the men were at work, part of the world-wide army ceaselessly toiling through the centuries, without whom secure, smooth-lawned enclosures would never have come into being. Why were some exempt? Why such armies to support the exempted? Why, of these few, almost none worthy of exemption?

Threatened by the approach of the doctrines of Lycurgan socialism, marching upon her embodied in the persons of those she had heard give voice to them, she closed her eyes, hearing once more only the cooing of the invisible doves, seeing the wide lawn, tree-guarded at its corners, overlooked only by the

serene face of the old house that already she could sketch from
memory.   Four upper windows beneath the overhanging eaves,
or five? Drowsily opening her eyes to recapture the detail
of this backward view of the house, now, with its inmates away
down the garden and in the kitchens whose windows gave upon
the hidden stable-yard, given up to her eyeless and deserted,
its perfect self and the completion of this lawn-world that
already, absurdly, she regarded as her own, as being for the
first time perceived and inhabited, she was stricken fully awake.

Standing halted on the far side of the empty lawn, Richard
revealed, before he moved, exactly the leisurely strolling gait
of his approach.   Gun on shoulder, his rough russety tweeds
suggesting autumn woods, what had he to do with these acres
of mild, laborious fruit-growing?

The instant of his setting out, diagonally across the lawn
towards her chair, aware of his surroundings, no longer regarding them with habitual eye, seeing them re-created by the
presence of a stranger, seeing them as she saw them, experiencing their beauty as it had shown when first he beheld them
fourteen years ago, dropped, as he stepped from his sunlight
into the wide shadow of the chestnut, away into the far past.

'Now that's wise of you.'   Had Miss Roscorla told him of
her breakdown? 'Most folks endanger a holiday by doing
too much the first day.'   She had not told him. He regarded
her as a paying guest on a fortnight's holiday and had come
across to talk, to pass the time of day and to renew, in solitude,
a promising acquaintance. Mistakenly. For she had drawn
him at breakfast by a social trick. Not possessing the qualities
he imagined existing behind it, she could neither hold him,
nor pleasantly pass his time. Here he stood, at her disposal,
Quakerishly silent, looking away across the view whose further
reaches would be visible for him above the bank.

'I never saw anything quite like your view,' she said, 'the
way it spreads all round the horizon, and the huge distance
across it to that green rim against the sky.'

'It's quite a way off,' he said meditatively. Adroit, then,
to move on. Abandoning his topic without any bucolic
stammer of the mind, though certainly a trifle shocked, perhaps

pleasantly shocked, in spite of his disappointment in discovering her failure to respond to his challenge in the recognized
way of young ladies talking with 'the opposite sex.' 'Jack
Cade,' he went on, with a shadow of emphasis, and glancing
to fasten her attention as he spoke, 'walked along that ridge
nearly five hundred years ago.'

Henceforth populous, a roadway domesticated within the
world of every day, the desecrated ridge reminded her of her
recent doubt, which, at this moment might be laid to rest.

'It looks high. Much higher than we are here. But perhaps
we are rather low.'

The reputation for feminine intelligence and social capacity,
as he was accustomed to estimate such things, so firmly established by her little display at the breakfast-table as to bring him
hot-foot to her side at the earliest opportunity, lay shattered
and destroyed. He saw her now gauche, as well as stupid.
Nevertheless, whatever should be the outcome of this inane
departure, she would now play fair, would refrain from returning, in order to please him, to his valuable Jack Cade. His
eyes had left the ridge, to make a little tour of the nearer ground.
Always the slight pause. Never, in this new world, a hasty,
or even a swift answer. Conversation within a medium wherein each speaker remained at home in full possession of his
individuality even to its furthest reaches. But of course he
could not know how much turned upon his answer.

'It 's quite a bit higher than we are. We 're three hundred
feet up.'

Not exactly, she told herself, in a hollow, but disappointingly
far too low to come anywhere near Densley's prescription.
But if she should carry out her resolution to abandon London
indefinitely, was she not free to waste opportunity as she chose ?
She listened for the voice of conscience to be drowned beyond
rescue by this other voice.

'From sea-level, not from the centre of the earth.' His
eyes, returned, met hers gravely above compressed lips while
he waited for her response. Summoning a smile, she saw his
features relax and his eyes once more seek the distance.

'We had a young friend of my brother's here not long ago.

A young fellow not much accustomed to country ways. When I told him the height of our hill, he asked: "Up from where?"' M'yes. Again the compression of the lips, controlling the features to gravity and concentrating in the eyes his delight in sharing mirthful reminiscence. 'Ye'd hardly credit it. Of course he wasn't thinking; much. But he was as sober as a judge. The first time he came out here, the ducks were about; some of them on the top of that bank. "Why," he asks, "do they go up there?" I told him I expected it was because they wanted to have a look at the view, and then he inquired didn't they feel the sun on their heads. "I guess they do a bit," I said, "I'll be making them some little straw bonnets like they give the horses in London."'

He paused for her laughter, but with eyes downcast to safe-guard his theme, evidently not yet exhausted.

'I waited a bit, keeping so grave as I could, and then suggested blue ribbons, to look pretty and match the sky.'

His deep chuckle and the cascade of her renewed laughter, for which it was so satisfying a support, came forth simultaneously and ceased together, a duet, unanimous and accomplished, bringing before her eyes as still it sounded upon the leaf-sweet air, their shared possession, the distant immensity, outspread boundless beneath its high, morning sky, upon which again his eyes were resting—seeing it again revitalized?—and whence now they turned to meet her own.

'Too bad,' he murmured, in the deep, caressing bass of repentant solicitude, with a smile in it that shone also from his haggard eyes. Adjusting the sling of his gun, he moved, to glance once more across the distance before taking leave. No, merely to shift his weight from one foot to the other and remain standing there, halted, squandering his morning; but this time unwitnessed, invisible either from the kitchen window or from the lower garden where the workers were scattered.

'You are going to shoot?'

'I may. There's a deal too many rabbits at the farm. Haying was late this year and we've a busy day on the ricks, so I'll not be back till late and I'll get a few, I dare say, when twilight falls.'

In speaking of the farm, he had looked away above her head towards the west, towards this morning's distance, seen from the little doorway and before her eyes had met the splendour of the northern expanse, and seeming so far and so satisfyingly lovely with its slanting rim perfectly accented at the highest point by the profile of the windmill. Recalling her mind, already at work upon the labour of adjustment to his unknown, many-featured world, whose every event had for its stage a widespread ceaseless loveliness, she put her question.

When he had gone, strolling back across the lawn, the leisurely, experienced owner of the Mill Farm, two miles away as the crow flies, but a bit further off by road, its woods and meadows and the many crooked stiles m'sister found so difficult to climb, and had disappeared beyond the larches screening the eastern end of the house and the stillness, broken only by the cooing of doves, once more enfolded her, its quality had changed. No longer stretching out across the world and carrying her gently down towards an unpeopled sleep whence she would awake to renewed, impersonal adoration of her surroundings, its radius was reduced to visible limits, ceasing northwards where Jack Cade, life in hand to fight injustice, forever marched along the road concealed behind the rim of the sleeve whose green draperies hung suspended from the sky-line; ceasing to the west upon the ridge sloping downward from Richard's mill.

Crushing down to its death her lingering sense of the iniquity of spending upon a hillock beside a marsh the months allotted for recovery, she felt time cease. Her stretch of freedom, seeming almost endless when in London she had contemplated and refused to endanger it by clamping down upon it any time-enclosing, time-shortening pattern, expanded now to infinity.

Through the wide gate she came out into the green world that last night had declared itself the triumphant rival of the strangers on the hill-top. Ahead lay the marshes, almost

colourless under the sun and patched with the shadows of
clouds drifting forward from the south, ending away to the right
against a high, enclosing ridge of downs. Turning to walk
down last night's hill, she saw waiting, not far away, a clump
of trees, the first feature, the first companions to greet her in
this renewal of solitude. As the road descended towards them
the marshes and the distant spur of downs vanished behind
the high hedge, leaving her, save for the oncoming trees, alone
with the road. They spread out as they approached, became
a row that presently showed widening spaces between each
trunk and its neighbour. Elms. They passed by, seven,
planted at regular intervals, their witch-arms inharmoniously,
gracelessly dangling; gaunt forms attaining dignity only
because they were tall. How did they come to be there, seven
and no more, an unfinished sketch of one side of an avenue?
Standing methodically apart from each other, professing night
and day to screen a small portion of an oblivious meadow,
casting long morning shadows there and, in the evening, the
same shadows from hedge to hedge across the roadway, they
proclaimed nothing, offered no tree-message, nor any fellowship, either for each other or for the passer-by. Promise un-
fulfilled, sending one's eyes in search of further features, of
some destination that would not disappoint. The vista offered
nothing. With the elms away behind, she was alone with the
densely hedged country road, a high road, well made, free
from cart-ruts, neat and sophisticated. Along which, she
remembered with displeasure, an occasional motor car was
known to pass. Miss Roscorla told her little stories very well,
with quiet gusto. Her description had set the old washer-
woman visibly there, tall and erect upon the crown of the road,
refusing to budge for the advancing 'machine saying brr, brr,
in such an authority manner.'

No movement in the air, no savour. Noon stillness, and
the empty road. Any suburb, exhaling scents from its watered
gardens, would bestow a richer sense of the time of year.

At last a milestone, sunk deep in the earth amidst the long
grass of the roadside, settled there askew, offering its slanting
message, worn faint, though once deeply cut, to yet another of

the thousands passing by during its centuries. Offering it most potently to strangers passing in solitude, to those for whom it was a bourne, sturdy company, the shadow of a wayside domicile. Standing just here at the fork of the road, it suggested more sharply than could the local grass and the short-lived wayside flowers the invisible unfrequented distances, proclaiming the rarity of a human presence with whose aid the traveller might learn his whereabouts.

If the market town and yesterday's railway station were four miles away, she had walked a mile, and the beginning of yesterday's village must be just ahead, a few hundred yards along the unchanging corridor. Just the seven trees and this milestone. No other features. No visible hint of release into the green depths she had come forth to seek. Choosing the alternative road, sentinelled by high trees set close together, she found stately greeting rather than welcome. Avenue dignity enclosed her and a hush, suggesting privacy and the arrival, as soon as she should be round the bend of the road, of a lodge and high gates defending a tree-darkened drive sweeping along to disappear on its way to a stately, hidden mansion.

But round the bend, at the end of the second short stretch of avenue, it was a church that confronted her, filling the vista with its unwelcome challenge. Old, grey, beautifully proportioned, its grey-and-orange-lichened tower further softened by the full leafage of the high, surrounding trees, its façade patterned by black, spiring cypresses well placed amongst the ancient tombstones of its richly green churchyard, it reproached her. Silently it reminded her that the depths of her nature had been subtly moulded long ago by its manifold operations and could never fully belong to the household on the hill.

While she stood held up by this inexorable presence, disappointed of escape along this road to the deeper essence of the countryside suggested by the fragrance of the trees, the answer to its reproach reached her mind in the form of a congregation imagined straggling down this avenue on a Sunday morning. Well-dressed local families, coming as a matter of course, of lifelong habit, not to share in adventure of which they were a living part, not to move into a stillness at whose pulsating heart was to be found the source of their inmost being. Coming 'to church,' to a service wherein no single moment would be without its specified occupation. Villagers, too, dependents, respectful in their Sunday best, meekly occupying the inferior sittings.

The folks on the hill lived all their lives in church. All their doings, whatever happened to them, took place in church. The crumbling old edifice, seen isolated from daily life, became a lovely shell whence life had departed.

A solitary bell-note, clear and sweet, sounded from the tower and stood upon the air sending forth, in wave upon wave across the quiet countryside, its gentle message. Dominating the stillness even while it faded, speaking a quiet assurance.

The midday meal was upon the table, the depleted party assembled an up-hill mile away.

Surprised, she consulted her plate as if the mystery might there become visible. Long ago, before she had learned that food could be a substance indifferently consumed to keep life going, its flavour had had this assaulting power, taken for granted; never bringing this present sense of a beneficent force, impalpably in-flowing, nourishing one's spirit rather than one's body. Yet this meal had been kept for her and should have lost its first fresh savour. Was it that in all the years since leaving home she had lived on food shop-staled rather than fresh from gardens? And that the vital, spiritual goodness of fresh garden food consumed in the houses of friends had gone unperceived because as a visitor one was expected to supply entertainment? Why then had the meals provided by the deaf old lady and consumed in unthreatened solitude, lacked this sacramental quality? Was it the gift of those by whom she was now surrounded, existing in the very air of the room where daily they were gathered together? For a moment, with the first shock of perception, she had indeed felt that even in a potato grown upon their happy land some special virtue must reside. But now, withdrawn into inquiry, she was obliged to recognize, enfolding her more closely than the radiations of their remembered presences, the sense of being incorporated, far from towns and from sea, with the countryside whose life-breath, found and finding, even while she trudged the road vainly seeking admission to green depths, was now mingled with her own.

Here, indeed, was Richard Roscorla's promised rain, driven streaming against the panes by a boisterous wind that buffeted the ivy leaves, keeping them tap-tapping as if to call attention to their plight. The shut window, rain-dulled, hid the outside world. Moist earth-scented air, its sole representative, came in through chinks of the loose frame, enriching the sense of enclosure. In the chimney a gentle moaning. At the window the patter of the distressed ivy leaves. No other sound.

Wealth, not to be finding rain unwelcome. Not to care if it rained for days. To be revelling in the sound of 'awful weather.' Hitherto, rain, or even the threat of it, had been the sworn enemy of holiday, a cruel intruder banishing enchantment, leaving one exposed to awareness of the swift passing of allotted days, the ruthless approach of their impossible end. Last week, down on the coast, it had become for the first time a challenge to adventure. To-day, it was blessed exemption from seeing and doing. Descent, laden with treasure one could afford to forget, down into impersonality where past and future, vanished from their places, lay powerless to nudge and jostle, far away within the depths of a perfect present.

Reading, from this secure ensconcement, was new experience. A passing sense of treachery, to the wellnigh unlettered life downstairs, tried in vain to dim the joy it brought. Conversational joy. Sitting back, after a few moments of this strange, hitherto insufficiently pondered communion, she recalled delight, on the first morning in Oberland, in the text of a local newspaper found on one of the green tables on the newly discovered promontory whence for the first time she had seen the length of the valley, its undulations of diamond-sprent snow, cleft along the low-lying floor by the motionless black serpent of its frozen river, and had turned her back upon the flanks of the great, heavily cloaked mountains across the way, upon their tawny summits, too sharp to lodge the snow, piercing upwards into the high blue, to answer the call of the printed page. Had that joy lasted? It had not been put to the test. She could remember no further reading in Oberland.

That sacred little newspaper lay forever beneath her eyes against the morning-lit, shabby green paint of the little iron-legged table, its leaves so thin and poor that the heavily leaded headings of its little columns seemed set there to give it weight, to prevent its flying away. And it had seemed strange that the Swiss, so industrious, having so much at home, being so self-contained, so unrelated, in their middle-European mountain fastness, to the rest of the world, should fuss with newspapers. No odour of culture, no rich flavour of well-earned decadence anywhere, since leaving Paris behind. Did it exist, even down in the lake towns? Could it, with mountains looking on and pure air everywhere? This doubt gave a strangeness to the discovery of intelligibility in the text, drew my attention for the first time to the miracle of intelligibility, the taken-for-granted, unconsidered revelation lying behind the mere possibility of so arranging words that meaning emerges from their relationship.

And presently I ceased to look for meanings, took a phrase or a single word from its context and let it carry me into fresh contemplation of familiar realities. But the origin of that morning's joy had been sudden arrival in surroundings that made even advertisements read like lyrics. The deep joy of this afternoon is born of establishment not so much in a place as in a moment, the moment that began when I saw the motionless ridge alight and moving and that now I am inhabiting with people who have lived in it all their lives.

Yet the delight of this reading is profane, dependent upon a kind of culture alien to these people. Read downstairs in their company the text would lose much of its savour. Up here, unobstructed, it comes so near as to seem spoken rather than written; spoken by a cheerily booming voice that fills the room; unoppressively. Telling its absurd tale, not quite fantasy in the sense that implies a belief in the dullness of everyday life, but a fantastic intensification of everyday people, it speaks also a creed. But if he really finds everyday realities astonishing, always, in their recurrence, newly astonishing, why must he deliberately introduce these fantastic exaggerations? In order to make people attend, George Taylor said. Attend to what? To his philosophy. The philosophy of astonishingness. The astonishingness of doors opening when you push them. But what is much more astonishing than things behaving after their manner, is that there should be anything anywhere to behave. Why *does* this pass unnoticed?

Poetic philosophy. The horns of elfland faintly blowing, in the mind that yet believes the sound of a tin whistle to be the more moving.

What could more perfectly express unheard woodland sounds; harebells, inaudibly tinkling as they sway? Yet in expressing nature in terms of fantasy, he robs it.

A tap on the door. Who was to discover her, not resting but revelling in a fashion that might be considered equally possible either sociably downstairs, or accessibly in that unexplored sitting-room next door? The door opened, upon a small tray and the red-haired maid, who crossed the end of the room without turning her eyes, and set the tray down upon the dressing-table.

'Miss Roscorla's having a cup and thought you'd like one and said to tell you tea's at six.'

Thanking the departing figure, she sat up to look across. A small cake, too, golden in the grey light, and spiky. A home-made rock-bun. Little unneeded feast, announcing her a member of the household rather than a boarder.

Consuming the golden cake, sipping the tea whose fragrance had met her as she went across the room to fetch the tray, she heard the booming voice of Basil, discoursing in the balloon of the arboreal house-agent, give way to a friendly silence that shared her concentration on the difference between the consuming of very choice food that always produced a nostalgia for the kind of living where the best of everything should be a matter of course, and this homely fare so intimately announcing arrival in the place where one would be.

Tea-time, far away on the horizon throughout the afternoon, became a swiftly approaching reality. With introductions over, this second appearance amongst the gathered party would be the beginning of belonging to its intimate life. Carelessly she would go down, silently merge. The false impression created at the breakfast table, but upon Richard alone, and kept going during the encounter on the lawn, for, manlike, he had been unaware of being the sole speaker, had been carried away to the Mill Farm. This meeting with the others during his absence would leave her ensconced against the next encounter. Seeing her again, he would surrender the young lady of his misled imaginings and would recognize, in place of an enlivener of the hours spent at home, a stranger kindred to the group and ready, even if not fully qualified, to share its vital silences. If in his absence no one should be moved to speak, and, so far, compared with him, they all appeared to be conversationally negative, responders rather than initiators, would the meal run its course, apart from the necessary small courtesies, in silence? Imagining it thus, eager to taste for the first time this perfection of social intercourse, eager to prove that her presence would introduce no disturbing element, she looked at her watch. Already it was ten minutes past the hour. For the second time, on this first day, disgrace. Wondering whether the absence of any sounding summons, bell or gong, were a Quaker custom, she set off on the journey that held her room so eventfully remote from the household's central life, holding back as she went along the upper landing and down the two flights, through the hall and along the dimly lit passage, the assaults of inanimate surroundings.

Rich adventure, after returning the welcoming smile of Miss Roscorla seated behind the tea-urn at the far end of the table, to go silently down the room with lowered eyelids, withheld and self-contained and *therefore*, as on the journey downstairs she had already discovered, in full possession of even the external goods of the present moment: of the room's unseen perspectives, of what lay beyond them, seen in this morning's sunshine and lying now, rain-sodden, in the shadowless purity of the storm-light.

Reaching her place, aware, in the atmosphere about her, of
something of the peace encountered at her one Quaker meeting,
and that the morning meal had failed to renew, she took in the
presence, across the table, of a lace-capped old lady whose fawn-
grey ringlets beautifully framed a pale face surprisingly youthful in its contours and in the luminous beauty of the eyes smiling
into her own.

'You haven't met mother, I think,' said Miss Roscorla, smiling towards the urn her small, plump, work-worn hands were
carefully tilting.   Deepening her smile as Miriam half rose to
make her obeisance, Mrs Roscorla gave her a small nod, a gay
little nod that seemed to tell her she was an old friend and
exempt from formalities, and also clearly expressing pleasure
in occasions for nodding; and then, as if to signify the end of
the audience and the freedom of those concerned in it to welcome the next event, turned her limpid gaze to another quarter
of the table, bringing it back as Miriam apologized to Miss
Roscorla for her unpunctuality, and saying, before her daughter
had time to speak: 'That's no matter, we should have sent
thee a messenger.'   And again her smile shone forth, con-
gratulatory, suggesting a shared sense of gaiety and good
fortune.

Though low in pitch, her voice was neither rumbling, nor
gruff like those of so many old women who, according to the
little man passionately squeaking from the back row at one of
Amabel's suffrage meetings, 'ath thoon ath their pwoper and
only valuable thervith ith fully accomplithed, begin to approathe
the vocal, *and mental*, level of mathculine adolethenth.'—'Of
course, my dear, we pounded him with laughter, but really,
Mira, he was rather a darling, without knowing it.'

The old lady, stirring her tea with downcast eyelids whose
firm moulding recalled the vanished eyes, and with the smile
still alight upon her fragile features, so softly contoured that
they seemed to have been serene throughout her long life, was
awaiting the next departure and would certainly soon speak
again.   But only in response.   Statement or restatement.
Setting the tone.   Presiding.   Already with her brief phrase
she had done so much.   With the subtle modulations of a voice

that turned each word into a phrase, with parentheses.   Representing the family, she had settled the trouble by an even distribution of responsibility, administering each share with a consoling pat on the back, had smiled the incident into its grave, and was now awaiting fresh material.

Whence ?   Was it she alone who produced within the air this faint thrill of expectancy?   Miss Roscorla, having provided the late comer with tea, was cutting into the bun upon her own plate, absently, as if preoccupied, or simulating the mental preoccupation demanded by conversation, in the way of women who create the appearance of paying tribute to what is being said by deliberately assuming a manner suggesting distraction from whatever at the moment they happen to be doing.   The ever so slightly lifted brows, drawing across her forehead that, by comparison with her mother's cliff of brow rising smooth and unwrinkled above the delicately arched eyebrows, seemed so low, almost imperceptible puckerings, might signify nothing more than preoccupation with ceaseless complex housewifery, from which yesterday's encounter in the upstairs room, and particularly the moment of contemplating the petal-dust side by side with a stranger so far not a witness of the incessant daily pressure, must have been a rare holiday.   But she was keeping watch, out-turned, ready, if no one else should speak, to supply what the stranger would expect.   Here, then, was the stranger's grand opportunity, while still Mrs Roscorla's words lingered on the air and the subsequent Quakerly pause had not run out.

Aware, away to her left, of a quietude so dense as to render unlikely any vocal contribution from that quarter, Miriam took leave of the ladies and turned her eyes, since merely to drop them would be to suggest retreat via embarrassment into loneliness and would instantly provoke some kind of rescue, towards the far angle created by the junction of the greenhouse door and the wall of the room, accessible across the empty stretch of table extending away on Mrs Roscorla's right.   Immediately on reaching this refuge she felt upon her face a relaxation of the surface muscles, suggesting herself and her own state of a moment ago as the source of the obstructive little thrill upon the air.   All the more fully, therefore, she received the shock of discovering the secret of the deep stillness of her neighbours to the left, whose territory she now overlooked sufficiently to perceive a magazine lying open upon the table at the far side of the pupil's plate and, propped in front of Alfred Roscorla's, another, whose exposed page displayed an illustration.

Two groups. The outdoor toilers, and the women of the house. In all her experience of family gatherings she had encountered nothing comparable to this conspicuous sexual division, belonging to life on the land. The toilers, returned indoors with doubly emptied being, asked only food, and escape from household enclosure to the world beyond the gates. Which of its aspects were claiming such absorbed attention? The two women, one the recognized president and the other the provider momentarily escaped from multitudinous tasks, were both out-turned and socially available. But separated from half the gathering, whose eloquent absence, permitted and condoned, was yet, in the presence of a stranger, a little embarrassing? Between the two groups, emptiness, wherein the grey light made its own assertion, pouring in over the far-away morning, the vanished afternoon, stating this party's uniqueness, its wealth, running to waste.

The voices of mother and daughter, sounding together, showed her herself as seen by the speakers, staring directly along the space occupied by the readers, a witness of enormity. Recalling her eyes, she projected from them, in order to make them appear all-welcoming instead of half critically observant, an amiably meditative gaze suggesting one absent-minded, slow to take bearings. A look enabling her to turn with the dawning smile of one deeply pleased to find herself where she was, towards Mrs Roscorla in time to see that what she was saying, with eyelids serenely dropped and expression placidly intent,· was apparently addressed to no one in particular.

'Thee's boots to Elphick, Alfred,' emerged clearly into the silence left by her daughter's deferential retreat.

In response to this assault from the feminine end of the table, Alfred raised his face towards the vacancy ahead of him. Seen thus in clear, extended profile, it was startling in its stern purity and gentleness. The thoughtful brow and delicate features

were moulded by dominated suffering, their pallor enhanced
by the soft light's obliteration of their thick powdering of sun-
born freckles. With unseeing gaze, while his reluctant mind
recaptured what had been said and scanned its meaning, he
made his journey into the forgotten present.

'There wasn't,' he said at last, and paused and half-turned
his face, with eyelids lowered, towards the head of the table,
'not a single soul at home.' Lingering for a moment, the
peaceful, blessed moment of Quakerly deliberation, he turned
back and leaned again towards his book.

'*Well*-now,' said Mrs Roscorla, and looked across at Miriam,
and held her eyes with a smile, arch, gleeful, suggesting depths
of entertainment, that must have been hers in girlhood and
that now, though uncontrollably it still expressed her sense of
being good to look at, served to convey her message of universal
congratulation.

'Gone to hospital, I reckon,' murmured Alfred into his page.

'Perhaps they 'd not had their post card.'

The pupil, too, spoke into the page over which he was bent,
but his voice was warmed by a smile that made his cryptic
remark an offer of sociability.

'There 's a young farmer near us here,' explained Miss
Roscorla, turning to Miriam, 'whose uncle, a while back, was
taken ill far from home and carried to hospital.'

Every one sat back to listen. Every face wore a smile,
reminiscent, anticipatory, to be held in check until the arrival
of the end of a well-worn yarn returned with its freshness
restored by the presence of a new hearer. Compelled by
courtesy, but with an evident relish for her task, quietly and
evenly, with something of the deliberate quietude of the practised dry humorist, and at the same time a little diffidently, as
if she were reproducing an effect usually exploited by someone
else, Miss Roscorla proceeded with the narrative whose end was
clearly going to demand evidence of mirthful appreciation.
Distracted from the attention so well earned by the home-made
cake whose smooth even texture, bland and cool in the mouth,
broke without crumbling, so that the raisins, red-brown within
its pale brownish grey, offered a pleasant slight resistance

before mingling their sudden deep flavour with the mild
sweetness of the rest, Miriam listened apprehensively.

'"I lost the card that were for 'ee this morning," said the postman. "'Twere from y'r uncle in hospital. He's doing fine."'

'Imagine,' she said, and flinched at the sound of her own
voice, feeling it break up the newly achieved unity and isolate
her with the men, who alone would fail to detect its insincerity.
'Just *imagine*,' ah, that was better—l'appétit vient en mangeant
—creating an expectant pause, space for the drawing of a breath
and the mind's insensible readjustment; and for an instant
she found herself forgetting what was to be imagined, smiling
forth, at large, her sense of having joined the party. Glancing
across to consult the window, whose light seemed now to be
lifting, she met the smiling gaze of a Mrs Roscorla prepared,
with hands clasped upon the table and face jutted a little forward so that the fluted pillars of her curls, hanging free, exactly
framed it, for imaginative flight in whatever direction might be
indicated. Thus reminded, she recaptured her intention:
'such a thing happening in London!'

'*No*,' said the old lady, without even a vestige of the Quakerly
pause, gleefully snapping her eyelids above a wide smile that
revealed to Miriam's trained eye the excellence of her denture,
'ye can't imagine any such a thing happening in London.'

While silently, and vastly at leisure now that the excursion
was so successfully concluded, they smiled across at each other,
Miriam saw again the sly delight irradiating Miss Roscorla as
she reached the climax of her little tale, heard her own laughter
join the chuckles that had sped its passing, and felt again the
warm downward plunge into a unity that now was offering
itself as a part fulfilment of the hope with which she had come
downstairs.

'Well, I'll have to be moving.'

Flushed and glowing, Miss Roscorla rose and turned to the
window, lingering there a moment and remarking on the beauty
of the light, contemplating it while she gathered herself to
pursue the labours that through all the years had formed a

continuous background for the achievement whose story had
filled the time since the men left the table.   No need, now, with
the sitting broken up, for response, for any inclusive verbal
tribute.   Her listening presence, silent save for an occasional
question, and regarded by both women with a favour increasing
as increasingly she became for them a mirror of the heroic past,
had given them all they asked.

But when her daughter had vanished kitchenwards through
the alcove door, Mrs Roscorla, now a frail form standing, with
her hands on the back of her chair, outlined against the brilliance framed by the window behind her, seemed to await some
sort of continuance.   In the limpid young eyes still contemplating across the width of the table one's unoccupied available
person, there was, as well as approval, an embarrassing childlike expectancy.   There she stood, an immovable obstacle
between oneself and the glowing light, this evening's light
stating its independence of all one had heard, and that had
subtly changed the outdoor scene by drawing across it the
shadow of incessant anxious labour.

'I think,' she said casually, feeling the light win, draw her
irresistibly away from the demands of the old woman, the
lonely witness of a selfishness she was noting with the crafty
intentness of old age, storing it up in a consciousness dependent
now upon supplies from without: 'I 'll go and see what the
garden looks like after the rain.'

'That will be pleasant,' said Mrs Roscorla, still holding, as
if for support, to the back of her chair, 'if thee has thee's boots
on.'   And she nodded, as if in dismissal, but with a smile in
whose depths, away behind simulated approval, lay both
disappointment and reproach.

Escaped at this high cost, reaching solitude and the garden
door, she found her eyes drawn up and up to measure the immense height, above the outspread scene, of pearl-blue sky.
Its grey shroud, cleared away by the wind, lay piled along the
eastern horizon, its bulging protuberances, that for the last
half hour had been projecting their glow into the little walled
garden upon which her eyes had rested as she listened, bright
coppery gold in the light of the hidden sun now sinking, away

to the north, towards the invisible sea. With deep delight she inhaled the pure freshness, the many rich damp scents pouring into her nostrils, noted the softened outlines, the sweet drip-dripping of rain-laden trees and roofs; with newcomer's delight, to which was added a touch of the proprietary satisfaction of a member of the household.

Going along the rain-darkened gravel path, the unknown path, this morning's busy thoroughfare upon the far side of the lawn, deserted now, inviting, she passed the angle of the high bank and reached the broad lower level where stood the many greenhouses. Set there in the evening light, forgotten, trustworthy, though still suggesting toil, they also announced themselves as the makers and keepers of the world whose inhabitant she had so gladly become. Fourteen years ago, long before she had come to London and been shut out from garden summers, this haven was already being made. With their own hands the brothers, country-bred, escaping the London that had broken and cast them forth, were building these houses. Digging their land. In the spring. With summer and autumn stretching away ahead, making the arduous life under this high sky amidst these vast clear distances, in contrast with the life in London, dark with the helpless darkness of small honest enterprise struggling in vain against unscrupulous speculative commerce, seem like a prolonged holiday. Season by season, they had learned the ways of peaches and of grapes, of cucumbers and tomatoes, flowers for market; bees. And to this ripened knowledge, Richard, the haggard, situation-saving hero of all the tales she had heard over the disarrayed tea-table, was adding now the lore of the farmer, complex knowledge of the ways of cattle and of corn.

Apprehensively, not on their account, but for the peace of her own mind, she wondered whether they could ever be fully alive to the gardens about the house, to the original intention with which this place was built? House, large garden, a unity, complete. The wide lawn, sentinelled and shaded on three of its corners, by this morning's shadowy chestnut, the sycamore balancing it across the way, the high larches screening it from the approach to the back of the house and marching, single file,

round into the front garden; the lovely little pleasance beyond
the stable yard. Whether, when socialism came and every one
was a worker, there would be any joy left uncontaminated?
Women, Hypo said, were the great garden-lovers, and indeed
they inhabited gardens, while most men, until old age, only
visited them. Made them, and worked in them; for women.
Men to make, and women to love that which is made. If
Swedenborg is right, the 'uncreativeness' with which men
reproach women is explained and justified.

She remembered shrinking from the mere spectacle of the
family in Barnes who did their own housework, and kept their
garden in order, shrinking from the idea of house and garden
thus inhabited; loved with a horrible difference. Coming to
the tennis-club or to a dance, they came always partly tired,
used up. Like men from offices, they could never be considered fully there. Were there only on leave, and one could
see in their eyes the tethered look of servants. They enjoyed
their outings, a little too obviously and excessively, with the
joy of those temporarily set free, never with the rapture of those
inhabiting unthreatened territory.

To make. To love what is made. If making things is
humanity's highest spiritual achievement, then women *are*
secondary and the question for the Fathers should have been,
not have they souls but have they spirits?   But *is* making,
pictures and bridges, and thumbscrews, humanity's highest
spiritual achievement?

Becoming aware of having wandered back into problems
forever left behind on the hillock by the ridge and that in
this new world were without significance, she recaptured the
question here being asked aloud. The answer was ready,
reassuring. The sensitive creatures by whom she was surrounded were certainly alive to the beauty of their gardens.
A treasured superfluity. Like the proletarian parlour so cruelly
condemned by commonsensical half-wits. A temple undese-
crated by the presence of the implements of toil. Kept always
swept and available. Rarely used, but always operative, a
refreshing harbour for the mind. But not for the body. These
toil-worn Quakers, when their day's work was done, did not

rest. Lifting his brooding face from *The Wonders of the Universe*, murmuring to the pupil, at the end of the gentle sigh with which he closed its pages, 'Well, you and me ought to be getting along to Lodge,' Alfred had had the patiently enduring look of one who refuses to a frail body its petition for rest.

Whence, under a clear high sky, this small sound of falling rain? It came from ahead, from somewhere beyond the greenhouses, an incessant soft pattering. At the end of the wide level, a path led downwards through a wilderness of grass and weeds, until she reached the end of the domain. Thus far, no further. The distance, so vast when seen from above, was narrowed here by the folding together of the valleys, and the ridge, drawn nearer, stood higher in the sky. Just beyond the broken-down fence, the ground fell abruptly; and here, on the edge of the wild, was the secret of the rain. Just within the fence, a row of Dutch poplars, oddly urbane and seeming to squander here their formal beauty, announced, with a ceaseless gentle rattling of their myriads of small leaves, an almost imperceptible breeze. Alone down here on the neglected edge of the property, they lived unnoticed, according to their manner, vocal whenever the air stirred them, sending forth, into even the most flawlessly radiant summer's day, the sound of pattering raindrops.

Clear evening light, stillness; so fully inhabiting the room that one felt, coming in, like one being admitted to a lovely ceremonial.

The moaning chimney was silent, the tapping ivy leaves quiet in their pattern against the window, to which she was drawn by the wide gaze of the light. Pushing up the sash, she leaned out into air rich from its voyage across the drenched levels. Beyond deep green meadows, the distant marshes lay pale, glistening, every hillock and thorn bush and patch of scrub standing sharply out, each in turn asking to be gazed at until it should vanish into the darkness. Here and there, a wide, shallow pool lay silver or silvery blue beneath the high evening blue that on this side of the sky was cloudless to its

edge, its colour thinning as it arched down over the further
distance until, at the rim, where the sun had sunk nearly an
hour ago, it was almost white.   Reaching this far rim, her eyes
found, zigzagging along the middle of its line, a black etching,
minute, sharp-angled.   Buildings, upon the far edge of the
marsh.   On either side, a line, clean and narrow, dark indigo,
impossible, unmistakable; the sea.

During the moment of being on that far-off strand with the
sea stretching endlessly away before her eyes, everything else
had vanished.   Why so eagerly, the moment she had recognized
it, had her spirit flown like a bird from the side of a cliff to that
small distant shore, and why, now that it had returned and
place and time were here once more, these deep, delighted
heart-beats?   Only this morning she had rejoiced in being
ensconced, far from towns and sea, in unbroken verdure.   But
this discovery of the sea's nearness, the certainty of being able
sometimes to see it from afar, seemed now to make perfect
the circle of which this gentle hill-top was the centre, and that
ecstatically eager flight, as towards an unexpected friend discerned amongst a gathering of strangers, was tribute, to perfection suddenly realized?

Her returned spirit, escaped during its absence from the
pressure of some forgotten preoccupation, hovered blissfully
over its immediate territory, descending here and there, noting
the enticing gaps in her knowledge of indoor and outdoor
scenes.   Greeting their promise.   The vast realm already her
own, given over to her by the busy routine ruling the lives of
those about her and kept intact by solitude's freedom to evade
the dreariness of planned exploration, would reveal, portion
by portion, its inexhaustible wealth.

For what bourne was she making, with her hand on the door-
knob?   The outdoor world was darkening to twilight and it
was too early to go down to supper.   But time to change, if
indeed one were going to change.   Here, back again, was the
teasing, forgotten problem with which she had come upstairs.
If there were no changing, save for Sundays, one would feel
conspicuous, worldly, unquakerly.   The stuff dress Miss
Roscorla had worn last night was not the one in which she had

appeared this morning. But she had been out yesterday to the mothers' meeting. In the cabin trunk, still to be unpacked, lay the three new cotton blouses; the old white muslin blouse, and the pale mauve velveteen, mercifully not moulted when she had washed it and now more than ever delicately pale, the ivory silk with the real lace collar; all become new in new surroundings. The tweed she had on, already so experienced and to be, together with its coat and mushroom straw, the daily sharer of outdoor wanderings. Behind these, the dateless embroidered gown of visits and Lycurgan soirées, the pinafore scabious-blue frieze, with its three tops and little square coat and Liberty cartwheel; for Sundays. The Burberry and the thick Heinz chutney. Plenty of good effects, for a fortnight. Few, when thought of as spread over all the months ahead.

Deciding to hoard, she opened the door. There was a bourne close at hand within the realm of this upstairs world: the unexplored sitting-room, seeming so far off on the other side of the well of the staircase, yet whose door, though set further in, was next to her own.

Clearly this was the best sitting-room, the room of state, unfrequented and, in spite of the unexpected piano's sociable air, lonely. Though narrower than her own, it was a good deal longer and also, in spite of its three windows, darker. The light coming from the further of the two that gave on the front garden she found to be obstructed by the central mass of the dark dense tree. Turning to the near corner whither her eyes were drawn as she stood at the window by something gleaming at her from its deepest shade, she found, within a glass case upon a what-not, the skeleton of a bird, bone-white, unimaginably small and fragile, many of the bones no more than threads. Who could have gathered up and set it, intact, upon its little mount, to speak, from within its sheltering frame, its loveliness into the unbeautiful room? Beside it on the whatnot, cupped in serpentine rock, stood an egg the size of a small Spanish melon, its speckled surface coloured like a meerschaum. For all its symbolic expressiveness, dead, while the experienced little skeleton still seemed full of life.

The odd window, between the what-not and the piano set crosswise in the opposite corner, gave upon the little walled garden, and revealed its fourth wall to be a long lean-to green-house, above which were the windows of the wing that helped to darken this room that yet, even in its twilight and cumbered as it was with ungracious furniture, was making no impression of gloom. Taking in the chairs on either side of the fire-place whose mantelpiece supported a number of vases, two of them containing dried grasses, and a clock, silent, surmounted by a mild water-colour landscape, one a masculine chair, capacious, with arms, the other, for the lady of the house, elegantly and uncomfortably narrow and minus indulgent support, both protected by crewel-work antimacassars, the round table between the front windows, a little old writing-table near the end window, velvet-seated drawing-room chairs drawn up here and there against the walls, she left these desolate reminders of a life that no longer flowed through the room and returned to the little bird, so living in his death. Rigid in his glass case, it was he who gave the dark room its light. With the blinds up, even on moonless nights, he would faintly shine, stating immortal beauty.

Thud-*thud*. The footfalls of a cyclist alighting, clearly audible. Was it she who had pushed that window a little up, or had it been open when she came in? The gate clicked, yawned wide on its squeaking hinge, swung to again, latched. The figure whose firm slow footsteps were crunching the gravel to the accompaniment of the ticking of a wheeled bicycle, was hidden by the obstructive branching of the dark tree, and in a moment the sounds were out of hearing round the angle of the house, leaving stillness and a deepened sense of evening. Heavy stillness in the room that seemed now to demand a reason for her visit, confronting her with a past of whose inward depths she knew nothing, and amongst whose inheritors, now assembling downstairs, she must presently intrude her alien presence. Making her way to the door, she felt the room withdrawn, satisfied by her acceptance of banishment, into the peace she had disturbed and heard, equally withdrawn, equally not concerning her, the sound of footsteps in the hall.

'We finished the fourteen acre.'

Richard Roscorla, returned, his day behind him, weariness in his deep, gentle voice, restrained, endured weariness within the warm spread of its tone over the last word. Evening, the falling away at last of toil, the evening gathering. Indeed it was intrusion to claim a place within the intimacy of this engrossed, incessantly occupied family, to force upon it the exertion of paying, even in the smallest coin, tribute to one's presence. This taking of boarders was the sister's welcome contribution to the family budget, the visible extension of the unseen gift of all her waking hours.

But where could he be, speaking so near at hand?

Passing the top of the staircase on her way to her room, she looked down into the hall. There he was, standing, propped by one shoulder, with the unconscious grace of power relaxed, against the grandfather clock, his head inclined towards the upper panel of the door to the left of the entrance.

'Yes; 'twas all done before the rain came.' . . . 'No. The wind's changed. It looks all right for to-morrow. Well, good night, mother.'

Lifted by the wind, the light lace curtains floated towards her as she opened her door. Roscorla curtains, loyally protesting witnesses, subsiding as the door closed, lying passive on either side of the framed landscape towards which she hastened, holding back her selfish exultation until she could lean out and pour it towards the all-accepting innocence of meadows and sky: daily, by nine o'clock, Mrs Roscorla was hidden away for the night in her hall bedroom. This evening's gathering, all the evening gatherings, would lack her presence, her out-turned watchfulness for recognizable signs of life; as she saw life.

She was ready to raise her head. Inexperienced in this form of grace before meat, she raised first her eyes to discover whether the other heads were still bent and found them all, as if with one consent, recovering the upright. As if here, too, as in every human activity there seemed to be, was a concrete spiritual rhythm; so many wing-beats of the out-turned consciousness on its journey towards stillness, a moment's immersion within its pulsating depths, and the return. To a serenity flooding her being and surrounding it, far richer than the same kind of serenity achieved in solitude. It held off the possibility of embarrassment and promised to deal effectually, even though the most tempting opportunity should arise and implore her to seize it, with the desire to make a personal impression.

Now that someone had stretched forth a hand and turned up the lamp, she saw upon each face a radiance recalling the look of a happy lover. She remembered it upon Gerald's. Sometimes upon Bennett's. Every one had emerged from the silence luminous. Given back to themselves renewed, freshly available, they were in no hurry, since still their happiness held them, to break the silence within which it had been born. From herself, too, a measure of this glad radiance must be flowing, proving her no longer an outsider, but one who had come to them already qualified, by kindred experience, for membership of this small unit of the company of believers.

Balm, this home-coming confirmed by the fact that still, beyond the small courtesies belonging to the distribution of food, there was no talking. If she were not with them where they abode, someone, the one most sensitive to atmosphere, aware, within the stillness, of the uneasiness of an alien accustomed to ceaseless vocal accompaniment to the process of feeding, would have come to her rescue. Holding back, evading by a hairbreadth the onset of a complacency making her aware of the probability of its presence permanently menacing this knife-edge balance between two worlds, she turned her eyes to the light upon the centre of the table. The banished gloaming, though standing now apart outside the uncurtained window, was still part of the gathering, holding in its midst, as the leaf-and-petal-scented mist stole invisibly in, both the shared day and to-morrow waiting beyond a shared darkness. But within the depths of the lamplight, moving at the heart of its still radiance, was the core of the shared mystery; far away within the visible being of light.

'There wasn't too full a meeting to-night.'

Hatred of the outrage and forgiveness for the speaker, struggling together, brought her sharply back to herself, the stranger from London admitted to this family circle by her ability to pay a guinea a week. Glancing at Alfred, she found forgiveness easily triumphant. This frail, innocent creature, bent over his supper, serene, preoccupied, as unlistening as if he had not spoken, was the one most worthy to break the silence.

The ancient brass lamp that by daylight would show battered and tarnished, lent to the table something of its own dignity and stateliness. Its golden flood illuminated the seated figures, smoothing their garments, hiding defects, bringing out colour. But its beams fell too low, leaving heads and faces in shadow, as if already partly captured by the coming night. Only the figure of Alfred, the smallest of the party and sitting a little bowed, was clearly visible, wholly the guest of the light that fell full upon the luminous pallor of his face. Richard, upright, loomed gigantic, his face in dark shadow, the light falling directly only upon his tweed-clad breast, heightening its tawny warmth and finding upon it, incongruously small and fragile, a little frond of vetch dangling wearily from a buttonhole and revealing, beneath the arch of a curling tendril, a single tiny bloom.

'It turned out a fine evening, you see.'

Clamped down upon his last word, Richard's lips remained pursed as his grave eyes were raised to meet her own. A falsetto chuckle from Alfred called her eyes away in time to see him bent, shaken by his mirth, still further over his plate, and the pupil turned towards him, showing all his good teeth in a smile of benevolent delight. Consulting the face of Miss Roscorla, she found it down-bent, dreamy, set in smiling curves and turned, now, as if in response to her inquiry, with an expression of girlish adoration upon her brother, whose eyes, awaiting the return of the visitor's, now met them with a penetrating smile, eyebrows ever so little Mephistophelically up. Like Densley's. But what sounded from them was not Densley's triumphantly delighted crow. Something more gentle, palliating mirth, seeming to cherish her slowness.

''Tis a pity more don't come, all the same,' said Alfred sideways smiling, with lowered eyelids, towards the company; forgivingly.

'There was a wonderful sky, after the rain,' Miriam said conversationally, repudiating impeachment, offering, in place of a receipt for it, her desire to share the remembered spectacle of the high pearly blue, dominating, with its serene independence, the coppery masses in retreat along its edge. Addressing Miss Roscorla, obtaining of the mask of her face, its outlines and texture, an impression so sharp and indelible as to tell her it was added forever to her mind's gallery of portraits, she still saw the final warm radiance of Richard's Mephistophelian smile.

'*Wonderful*,' he said immediately, and again his face wore this morning's weighty gravity, and again, screened by muscular contractions, its expression of private satisfaction.

All at once, as if of itself, silence fell and gathered strength. The meal was over, and the talk that had outlasted it and had left in her mind a record, constructed from his brief references and the asides he had sent across the table when anything was said that might puzzle her, of Richard's day at the farm. She saw him interviewing his foreman, the man with only one eye, 'good enough to do the work of three'; working side by side with his labourers who got through more work, more quickly, on the supplied lemonade than others did on their beer, and didn't at all mind the little extra money; wandering in 'the little copse,' which she saw as a lovely little solitude apart from the main mass of the woodlands, quiet, sunless, as to-day it must have been after the morning's work and before the onset of wind and rain, sunlit, all broken light and shadow, lying in darkness, touched by dawn, known in all its states by the visionary, appreciative eyes of the tweed-clad figure strolling thoughtfully, parenthetically.

Two things disturbed: the new artificial fertilizer sent down from town, threatening the fundamental welfare of the land, suggesting the kind of interference with natural processes inspiring gentle George Taylor's outburst against intensive cultivation—'Bad enough that they should poison the land.

But its not only the *land* the fools are poisoning. They know not what they do'—and the punctuation of Richard's homeward ride by dismountings that revealed it a social progress.

The party was ready to break up. The earlier pauses, a little disconcertingly akin to those occurring in the conversation of people gathered together without the link of a unanimous vision, had been brief, throbbing with the almost audible to and fro of thought in pursuit of fresh material for entertainment. But the present silence was serene. In place of the sense of loss oppressing the air when silence descends at last upon a talking group and its members, fallen apart, deprived of the magnetic stream, realize each other as single individuals, lessened and variously pathetic or in some way, for all their charm, offensive, there was a sense of recovery, of return to a common possession, the richer for having been temporarily forgotten. And even now, for this pause, too, must in its way be brief, being the occasion's consummation and having, like the initial voyage into stillness, its own rhythm, there would be no brisk, escape-like departure of any one of the party. Leisurely dispersal would pay tribute to this animated gathering and greet those that lay ahead.

'*Well*'—Miss Roscorla was gathering up her table-napkin.

'Yes,' responded Richard at once, and his tone held the warm approval of one seconding a motion, and he looked into space, as if contemplating there a destination of which he was glad to be reminded, with his hands against the table-edge, about to heave himself to his feet; ready to go, having waited only for this signal. Glad to go.

No one else was moving. Side by side, Alfred and the pupil sat relaxed, the one a figure of weariness happily at ease, the other, buoyant in his stillness, smiling; both serenely keeping their places in the broken group. The sister, once Richard was upright and obscured by the higher shadow, followed with a glance of affectionate pride the tall figure turning, not going away, not making off down the room towards the door of escape into a mysterious freedom; turning, with its characteristic, gracefully halting swing of the body from feet to shoulders, towards the shelf near at hand in the darkened alcove between fireplace and window.

Richer, deeper than had been the surprise and comfort of his return to the seated group, bearing a huge and heavy Bible, old and much worn, protruding, as he held it inclined upon the table against one huge and sunburned hand while with the other he cleared a space for it to lie open, many bunches of leaves with tattered edges, loosened from the thick mass between the battered covers, was this tide risen as she waited while the thin leaves, gently turned, crackled softly in the breathless stillness, for the sound of the deep-toned voice. Or any voice. This it was, this sudden interpolation from some detached part of her surface mind calling to her to notice that this risen fiery tide of longing was for the sound, whence-soever it might come, of the read words, that was bringing such a depth of gladness.

Thirst; created long ago, before she could remember. Assuaged from her earliest years—a bell and a pomegranate, a bell and a pomegranate, round about the hem of Aaron's robe—and, during the years of repudiation of almost every church reader's way of reading, still partly assuaged, and therefore unnoticed. And now awake and crying out, because at last she knew something of what lay behind the forging of the magic text.

The deep, vibrant monotone, simple, childlike, free from unfelt, tiresomely elucidatory expressiveness, leaving the words to speak for themselves, was the very sound of the Old Testament, the wistful sound of Hebrew piety, trustfully patient within a shadow pierced only here and there by a ray of light ahead. It gave the reading a power independent of the meaning of the read words which presently sank away, leaving only the breathing spirit of their inspiration, sending the hearers down and down into depths within themselves, kindred to the depths whence it came, till the emotion creating this scripture became current and the forms seated in the golden lamplight fellows of those who had brought it forth, sharers of its majesty; a heritage bringing both humility and pride.

'The valleys also are covered over with corn; they shout for joy, they also sing.'

The fuller tone, a little raised, the deliberate pause and emphasis, called her up and out and took her eyes across to spy upon the man who so naïvely had chosen just this psalm, the farmer's song of triumph; and upon the man in whose nature resided love for the poetry of that last line. His face was no longer haggard, a strong man's face, joyous, youthfully contoured as he closed the book.

How parched seemed lives whose day went by unpunctuated by the sound of this shared reading. How attractive almost any life of which it was a part.

And how different was this dispersal from what it would have been a little earlier. Every one, now, was ready for it, separated, freed, each a self with its own dignity. Having admitted and communicated all there was to communicate, every one was comfortably silent, ready to go, and lingering a little to relish the quality of this separation. It would be possible, she felt, to stroll away without a word. It would be a tribute.

As silently he returned from replacing the Bible in its dark corner, Richard's face expressed his pleasure. He realized that the occasion had passed its test, given its guarantee.

'If you want a clean boy to-morrow, Rachel Mary, I must have a fresh bit of soap.'

Every one looked affectionately up at Miss Roscorla's boy, who received no answer but the adoring smile she kept for him alone. It made her almost beautiful. She moved now, decisively, to distribute the party, set it on its way towards to-morrow, before retiring at last to her room in the wing beyond the dark staircase.

CHAPTER VI

GENTLY closing the glass door, he disappeared without calling her eyes to follow up the path his departing figure. She was left in full possession of this silent light in whose midst she sat perched upon the little step-ladder. Morning light, no longer sending its signal across the world, but concentrated here in a reached destination; softened and diffused by the hundreds of little panes and by the clustering translucent vine-leaves. The vines now seemed conscious presences, breathing out a delicately penetrating incense, more perceptible than it had been last night; become, with the help of stillness and solitude, an almost audible emanation.

At the end of the long moment that had fulfilled her desire to be alone in this house, set apart from the others by its size and the loveliness of its cultivated inhabitants, she was eager to begin. Lifting from amongst the scattered berries in the trug at her side the sacred weapons, the delicate crutch and the bright destructive scissors, she descended from the perch to whose height, when he had stepped off the ladder and stood at her side smilingly talking away her lack of confidence, she had gone gaily up; just to be there, grapes or no grapes, and had sat crouched, just short of endangering the bloom of the higher bunches, and had looked down and caught his look, appraisal, admiration, naïvely open, startling her into aware-ness of the rarity, for him, of even mildly attractive feminine spectacles; and subtly modified, as he made his little farewell speech, all kindly reassurance, by the gleam of an amusement he clearly imagined her to be sharing. He believed her to have climbed to her perch fully aware that up there she would look both funny and nice.

Setting the trug on the floor, she chose a rung that brought several bunches within easy reach and selected a victim: a

prize bunch, broad-shouldered, beautifully a not quite sym-
metrical triangle, tapering to a central point in a single berry.
Just above, just out of sight unless she looked up to it, was the
bunch he had thinned, his large, skilled hands guiding crutch
and scissors with such astonishing delicacy, working swiftly
until the bulging opulence was reduced to an elegant skeleton
foretelling the final perfection.

Snip! She had begun. The abrupt metallic sound, shattering the stillness her movements had left undisturbed,
announced the presence of an intruder. But she had heard
also the flop of the fallen berry on to the wooden floor and
ruefully pictured the far and wide scatterings to be arduously
collected when her exacting work was done. There was no
idler to hold the trug as she had held it for him. Placed as it
was, it would catch a few of the berries. The rest could be
left for someone else? Someone who might suppose she
imagined them refuse to be swept up and destroyed. But
Richard knew she knew they were not refuse.

In yesterday's twilight, at the end of the long tour, this house
had been going its way towards darkness in a grey-green light,
leaf-thickened. Showing her round, beginning with that
unknown region beyond the hedge to the side of the lawn,
where that row of beehives squatted in the shelter of a screen
of sweet-peas grown so high and so full of tendrilled leaf
and brilliant bloom that their supporting sticks were scarcely
visible, taking her on along through the colony of chicken
coops and foster-mothers, bending from his height to demonstrate with outstretched finger the working of the little flannel-
draped entrance whose cunning deceit gave to her stranded
mind the relief of movement, on past the wide duck-run whence
dropped those far-sloping strawberry beds, across which she
had looked wishing him silent, wishing him away and herself
alone with those flowers newly met . . . *delphiniums*—but if
he had not been there, they would still be nameless—and that
at once had claimed to be a sufficient reward for her travels,
he had kept this house until the last, when, weary of pretending
to listen, and to observe the contents of the many houses, she
was still with those flowers, trying to recall their many blues.

Perhaps this afternoon, far away in the future beyond this depth of morning, might bring, if that side of the garden were clear of workers, a chance of visiting them.

'We called this the Jubilee House,' he had said as he opened the door, 'it having been built in that year,' and she saw the vines and presently discerned the tight clusters of dull green berries, no larger than peas. While she had gazed down the long vista, seeking, in this ultimate spectacle, rest from too much seeing, snuffing the moist warm air, more faintly scented but seeming more subtly alive than that of the other houses, he had gone on talking, telling of Paul Botinsky's amazement in discovering that the black grapes of the London shop-fronts could ever have resembled these small green currants, and then, as if for this stately palace a mere standing inside the doorway were insufficient tribute, had turned to close the door. Taking his hint, she had moved further into the green gloom and looked up through it at the multitude of little darkening panes protecting this concentration of hard-earned loveliness and had seen, flitting behind the leafage in a far corner, the marauder, somehow escaping notice and shut in when the houses had been closed, and now disturbed by unexpected visitors.

That instant wherein she had cried out, gently, lest the wild beast, hearing her, should banish itself before he saw it, was the only one in their tour having depth, the only shared moment. Together they had gone down into it, blended, indistinguishable, she the pioneer's mate sighting the enemy, proud to announce in one word both its presence and her knowledge of its malevolence, he at her side in an equality of pioneer watchfulness.

'That's a *wren*,' he had said, the moment his eyes reached it, and the warmth of affection in his tone had told her, before he explained its beneficence, how welcome was this small, confidently flitting creature to its spacious lodging. But the tremor in his voice took her eyes to his face, to find it flushed and alight, confessing the pride his unsteady tone had betrayed. Pride in the spectacle the presence of the little bird, by taking both pairs of eyes simultaneously and forgetfully down the length of the vista, had brought into full prominence.

Strolling down the aisle, he had begun telling her about the thinning, the intensive labour, nearly a month late this year, and it was then, when she deplored the inevitable waste, that she had heard of Miss Roscorla's green-grape jelly. And at the door, he had halted, looking back, as if reluctant to abandon the storehouse of an achievement brought home to him afresh through the eyes of an onlooker.

Shifting the trug, she snipped again, carefully lifting a heavy stem with the polished crutch, fear, lest the stem should break, bringing for a moment her heart into her throat. As the most obviously superfluous berries fell away, she heard again the gentle meditative words accompanying his deft movements: 'You 've got to imagine,' snip, 'the bunch fully grown,' snip, 'the berries full size,' snip, snip, 'so you know,' snip, 'how much space to clear for each.'

Again and again, with inexperienced eye, she measured her half-depleted bunch. Girth must be preserved as well as width. Then should this undersized little fellow in the middle of the front be saved rather than one of his larger but less prominent neighbours? Would he grow to his full size and fill the space cleared for him if one of them were removed? Richard had made too light of the real difficulties. He should have stayed longer; have let her thin a bunch under his guidance. A view from the side might help. But to crane round would be to risk endangering the bloom of some neighbouring bunch. How had he managed to clear his bunch without moving from his place? By holding the main stem in the crutch and lifting it, *boldly*, this way and that. But even if she could bring herself to risk so much, no kind of lifting and turning would settle the problem of this small girth-making berry. The only thing to be done was to get down from the ladder, shift it and obtain a side view.

Seen from the side, it showed as standing altogether too far out, destroying the frontal curve. Getting back face to face with the bunch, snipping out the little creature so laboriously outwitted, she recognized that the thin little stalk, grown too long in its striving towards the light, would have prevented it, when fully grown, from settling into the curve of the bunch that now, she observed with delight, was beginning to approach the shapely elegance of the one above. The soft light, playing freely through these two skeletons, singled out each berry and, though paling its colour, making it look wan and cold in comparison with those of the unassailed bunches, also gave it importance, individuality. With the triumphant solving of the last problem, her outfit of knowledge was complete. Flowing down into her hands, of which the tools now seemed intelligent extensions, it made her work steady and confident. Too easy.

Surveying her three luminous skeletons, she found them creditable company for the one above. One, its perfect twin, the others longer, narrow-shouldered, differently elegant. The greater part of the morning still lay ahead, a mass of time to be shredded into moments by an unvarying occupation. Although there was nothing more to learn and she had now, as an everlasting possession, the eye of a qualified grape-thinner, each bunch in turn would demand the continuous concentration she had given so eagerly to the first two, and that during the work on that last bunch had been accompanied by the consciousness of spending the very substance of her being. Leaning sideways, she looked down the leaf-screened vista, populating it with the workers at present scattered over the garden, next week's intensive labour in this very house more or less prominent in their minds. Dark figures on ladders, in what for them would be merely a workshop, lacking, because they worked in a group, t'.e deep magic that had drawn her within its doors. But perhaps finding in companionship another magic, small and ceaseless; homoeopathic doses of magic taken unawares, holding off the arrival of weariness?

Measuring with unwilling eyes the proportions of her fourth bunch, she transformed it in a single act of contemplation. If only the condemned berries would fall obediently away. . . . Lifting a shoulder stem, opening the scissors, the handle of whose inner blade had made across the side of her thumb a painful dint, she became aware of increasing light and warmth. If the sun, now nearly overhead, should break through its thinning veil ? Confined in the steamy heat of this serre that had no claim upon her and seemed now to be gathering its forces to expel an intruder, would she be able to endure until a round dozen of bunches should stand translucent, and the morning, which might have been endless, lay sacrificed for labour that now was making time move with a heavy, almost audible tread ?

Setting down her tools and the berry-laden trug in the cool harbour of the little room, she listened to the voice sounding out through the open dining-room door and wondered what could have brought to this house the person it so vividly described: a brisk middle-aged woman brimming with common sense and permanently impatient with the lack of it in almost every one she met. A Cameron voice, developed in a Christian Philistia. Like Mrs Cameron, she had brothers, scattered about the world in positions of responsibility. A professional husband, perhaps promising sons. Had lived all her life in the world as interpreted by men. But there was a difference. The rallying tones of Mrs Cameron's breezy, laughter-filled, Diana-of-the-uplands voice were conscious and deliberate. Within their inflections Mrs Cameron, herself, heard something that reminded her of her favourite heroic poet. The voice of the mysterious visitor was unconscious. Innate. The voice of one accustomed to dominate, unaware of the extent to which she was the product of sunlit, provincial opulence.

It was just dinner-time. But to go immediately upstairs would be to risk missing the intruder. The warned workers had not yet begun trailing in from the garden. Passing her hand over her hair and once again her handkerchief over her flaming face, she went along the passage to investigate, wondering which of the Roscorlas was the victim, regretting the fatigue that was taking the edge from her hope of sharing a carefully concealed enjoyment. Pushing wide the door, she came upon hostess and visitor seated on either side of the near corner of the table already laid for dinner: Miss Roscorla, flushed from her final dealings with the dishes for which the table waited, and a stout lady in a very good tailor-made and a

florid picture-hat, askew, and rather too opulently trimmed
for her rubicund face. A gentlewoman, a provincial Ober-
lander. Yet not quite. Something, undefined, was missing.

Introduced, she gave Miriam a brisk, kid-gloved handshake
and, from wide blue eyes, a glance that stopped just short of
meeting her own, so that she felt free, when she reached her
chair at the far end of the table, to gaze as well as to listen. The
woman had a calm, intelligent brow, suggesting ideas. But the
rest of her face, so imperfectly controlled when compared with
the Roscorla faces, seemed to show these ideas as moving in a
circle from whose centre she was perpetually hitting out with
the whole strength of her being. Shillingfold. One of the
many names dropped by Richard in his account of his ride
home. Perhaps the one that had brought his eyes across the
table with a gleam in them of blended pride and amusement as
he said, in parenthesis, 'one of our leading church ladies.'

'They're not only unseemly. They're misguided. I *want*
a vote. I ought to *have* a vote. My *gardener* has. Why
not *I*?' Sitting back, she crossed her knees, leaned forward
again and fixed Miss Roscorla, who sat there at leisure, as if
for eternity, and pleased, as if enjoying an edification on whose
behalf even the feeding of her household must be indefinitely
postponed, with a gaze that in profile seemed intended to prepare the listener to receive a tremendous impression: 'But
I'm not going to *scream* for it.' And again she sat back,
watching for the effect, in the complacent *that's*-got-you
manner so often, at Lycurgan discussions, reducing Amabel
to almost unmanageable hysteria. And Miss Roscorla,
although for a blessed moment her eyelids flickered and fell
to screen private diversions over the spectacle of Miss Shillingfold emitting shrieks that would so notably outdo the average,
was nevertheless attained. Impressed a little by the rhetoric
and, of course, in agreement with this woman's disapproval of
militancy, but also by something that had a permanent hold.

Withdrawing her eyes, she sat weary, unable to drag herself
away, longing for the woman to be gone, angry with Miss
Roscorla for so meekly suffering the continuance of this
untimely intrusion.

'I must be off,' She was on her feet, about to vanish and leave no trace, and out there, coming down through the little garden on his way to the kitchen, was Alfred, the peaceful light upon his face rebuking one's disarray. But Alfred knew so little of what was at stake, lived enclosed in a too simple universe. 'I've spent the best part of an *hour* trying to instil a *little* common sense into that *unfortunate* Mrs Wheddon. Thriftlessness. *That*'s the secret. With *most* of them.' A bow, a smooth-voiced murmur, she was gone.

The room is free of her. In a moment, the house will be; returned to itself, enclosed, inviolate. She exists only in their minds, not in their lives. Impressed, unresistant, Miss Roscorla is showing her to the door, but will return. And find me still here, rooted in wrath. Unable to move until I have expressed it. Back in my old world, my old rampant self. That *ancient* tag: my gardener, why not I! Sounding so effective when first it began going the round. How many of these peaceful, rational suffragists would face prison, face forcible feeding through a clumsily, agonizingly mutilated nostril? Would I? Have I the right to speak for the militants? For Amabel. Yes. But perhaps Miss Roscorla has gone round to the kitchen. In a few moments every one will be assembled and the incident sliding away, covered by life, unquestioned.

Miss Roscorla came in, came down the room towards one, smiling and rubbing her little hands together, her way of saying 'Well, and how are we getting on after all this time?' Perceiving that something was wrong, she came quite near and stood still, looking up, still with her smile, that now held a question.

'What a voice!' Crude, but earning the reward of a tinkling laugh.

'She's like a drill-sergeant. I mean essentially, without knowing it.' And now the eyes were quizzical, but still kindly, still showing Rachel Mary prepared to listen, even at this ill-chosen moment.

'She's not always quite so vociferous. She can be quiet; when she likes.'

Not always. Suggesting intimacy, frequent meetings, approval.

'Doesn't she *know* that nothing can ever be changed, *no* reform come about, without some kind of unpleasant, enmity-creating agitation? The mild suffragists may keep on asking for votes and having orderly processions world without end. Isn't it the same in private life? If the woman of the house wants anything *done*, she may mention it, to the average man, again and again without result, until she endures the unpleasantness of making herself unpleasant, by using a sharp tone, or by being sarcastic. In politics, even *that* is useless.'

Kicking open the door, the maid appeared with a laden tray. Voices sounded behind her, coming along the passage.

'Friends don't see it quite like that,' said Miss Roscorla, and again looked up with her expressive, waiting smile, still available, with the steaming dishes cooling on the table.

'She's a church worker, I suppose, a cottage visitor.'

'Miss Shillingford's a Friend, a born Friend,' said Miss Roscorla and waited, with her eyes on one's own, like Richard's while he waited for one to see a joke, with a glint of kindly malice in their depths that became, while horror flew along one's tingling nerves, apology, healing, full forgiveness.

Again the shock of their loveliness. Their situation on this piece of rough ground at the edge of the cultivated acres and with a waste patch sloping away behind them to meet the meadows, increased their power of suggestion; the way, in their banishment, they stood for leisure and elegance, and called up a long-lost world whose gardens, taken for granted, never realized as exceptional, were full of lovely growth.

But no other garden flowers, however lovely, imagined as set here in a row, would have quite this look of ultimate beauty. Lovely enough those massed sweet-peas. Enchanting, for a moment. But without the power of making one want to gaze forever, of vanquishing other claims, the claim of the panorama ending on Jack Cade's ridge, and even of Richard's distant farm, so alluring with its gently rising slope and terminal windmill. These moved, changed, were variously expressive. The delphiniums, drawing everything into themselves, made some final, unalterable statement.

It was not their shape. Lupins, though less strong and stately, and now, forever, almost colourless, had just this shape of steeples in the air.

It was their colour, the *many* blues.

Masses of roses, of different shades, make statements one against the other. These make one claim, reinforcing each other. Masses of a single kind of flower, all one tone, however lovely, even the deeper lilac, even laburnum or red hawthorn, presently send one's eyes straying to a neighbouring colour. Marigolds? Fire and food, sending one away nourished and cheered. But these many, contrasted blues keep one's eyes moving from shade to shade, and back again, satisfied. A haze of bluebells in a wood, seen suddenly from afar? Enchantment, a hovering mist, almost a hallucination, impenetrable, without depth. And not blue.

Seeking amongst memories of blue flowers, she came at last upon lobelias, the little clumps of deep, deep blue that in childhood had always made her gaze and gaze and wonder what was their secret, and that now, set once more before her eyes, seemed to hold their own against these proud steeples. She remembered how even when she passed them at a run, late for school and with her heavy satchel thumping at her side, they would exert their small influence from where they sat low upon the earth around the border of the flower-bed at the centre of the sweep, and make urgency seem less pressing.

Imagining lobelias massed here far and wide in front of her, not in their one deep shade, but in all the delphinium colours, she caught her breath. It was colour alone that possessed this strange power.

And it was just that *one*, that deepest but not darkest, that bluest blue. Within it all the others were gathered, so that still one saw it as it passed upwards through speedwell to pure dense mauve-washed turquoise and down to the one approaching black. Returning, from any one of the other shades, to gaze into its central depth, one had the feeling of being on a journey that was both pathway and destination.

CHAPTER VII

CAP awry, soot-smeared apron, arms, and cheek-bone, and, as she turned eagerly away to scurry through the hall, soot, thinned to grey by scrubbing-water, visible around the hem of her short skirt. Ultimate household grime, between which and the rest of the household, someone must for ever stand protective.

'Eliza's a spectacle, I'm afraid,' chuckled Miss Roscorla setting down the tray, 'she's having her Saturday contest with the kitchener.'

Though not wishing, on this unexpected occasion that Miss Roscorla had so deliberately contrived, to think either of Eliza or of the kitchener, one yet had found oneself saying: 'It's queer. Something in servants; though they can't all be alike. I have a sister who can clean *flues*, whatever they may be, in her best gown, with everything ready in the drawing-room for people expected to tea, when her maid is away on holiday.'

'I admire that,' said Miss Roscorla, her decisive tone warmed by an invisible smile that still lit her face as she turned and came across the room with the brimming cup. At ease, and leisurely. Yet not more leisurely than she seemed to be when one came upon her in the midst of kitchen turmoil.

'She sighs, and say she could do *all* the work in *half* the time, and without turning the house upside down.' Neither what Sally had said, nor her way of expressing herself, but carrying on the topic, sounding like the overheard talk of brisk, household women. 'It's nothing,' Sally had said, looking potentially eloquent, but finding, in the hidden reaches of her lonely housewife's mind, only crowding experiences, unanticipated and incommunicable; from imagining which, when drawn towards them by her eloquent silence, one had flinched away, wanting to ignore and forget. And now, to make suitable

486

conversation, one seized and misrepresented her as the user of terse, condemnatory phrases and, in misrepresenting also oneself, threatened the afternoon's treasure, the sense of the sure approach of Sunday that had kept one haunting house and garden, within sight of the cheerfully keyed-up activities of the hired workers and within hearing of the kitchen din.

If it were not too late, for already, everything, indoors and out, seemed debased, if one could fully control the disturbance created by Miss Roscorla's unexpected little invitation, refrain from backward and forward references, a shared sense of the occasion would presently become perceptible.

'Everything points to to-morrow.' What confusion of emotions, if she happened to be looking my way, must Miss Roscorla have read in my face as from the far past that forgotten incident came back to me, luminous at last, and reproachful. The one thing left out from one's recallings of that long-ago week-end at Babington that so surprisingly had brought Mr Hancock cycling across from his distant riverside cottage, ostensibly to visit his long-neglected cousins and really, as they all delightedly believed and tried to make me believe, to meet the secretary he had not only seen that morning, but had travelled down with, and to-morrow would see again. On the Saturday, the day before he came, the little incident must have occurred that now shone out as clearly as the rest.

Down from the spacious house away above the town, full of summer light in the midst of its sunlit garden—'I'm glad to see it all again another year,' Mrs Farmer said as she took me, London-weary, from path to path amongst flowers and bees, the wandering vicarage bees; and all these years she had seen again the coming of spring and summer—taken unwillingly by Beulah, who so repelled me, as soon as the house was left behind, by offering, out of the blue, three attendances at church in one day as evidence of Hilda's growing sanctity, down into the High Street distressful with shop-imprisoned workers, wishing them away, wishing to forget them, round into a mean little side-street, into a small dark house, into a street-darkened room, low-ceiled and stuffy, to stand confronting, in banishment from youth and summer beauty, 'one of our most devoted district visitors,' a small, small-featured, small-minded and very refined elderly woman whose thin lips, while she held out for inspection a limply dangling, freshly ironed lace collarette, had produced the phrase that then had seemed, even in separating day from day, so repulsive, and that now zestfully offered itself as fitting the present occasion, and brought back with it the little woman's smile, risen from the depths of her surviving youth, obliterating the sour lines that in repose made her face so disdainful. Between that moment and this, no distance, no separation. Yet the proffered words, even when thought of as exchanged between people whose minds ran parallel, seemed sacrilege, isolating what they touched, dimming its lustre that not once, during that church-dominated Sunday, had fully appeared. But what now lay ahead was a *Quaker* Sunday, the culmination of days punctuated by moments of silently shared recognition.

Settling herself on the shabby little old sofa, Miss Roscorla put up her feet. Here, in this daily brief afternoon rest in the sanctuary of this apparently quite superfluous little sitting-room, was part of the secret of her endurance from dawn until midnight. At present, inhabited by two, its air dense with misrepresentations, it carried no suggestion of repose. Its furnishings, hitherto unnoticed, became dismally prominent in the light dulled by the presence, too near to the house, of the huge evergreen oak. This morning, when first one had discovered it, it had seemed the deepest, most secret niche in the homestead. Remote, although its door opened on the hall opposite to that of Mrs Roscorla's room; made remote by exactly the obstructive oak that screened it from the outside world and screened one's escape through the french window along the little path skirting the house and leading direct to the little walled garden.

'I think,' said Miss Roscorla, stirring her tea, and the longing to hear what she was about to say ran neck and neck with the desire to arrest her and to laugh, as so often, upon this opening for communication, one had done with Amabel, over a mutual conviction of the inadequacy of speech, 'Eliza rather enjoys making herself look like a sweep.'

And she sent across the room, for oneself alone, her loveliest smile, the one invariably projected from her place at the head of the table, down the length of the dining-room to meet the in-coming Richard, a deep, deep radiance come forth to meet him and not again, so long as he was in the room, fully retiring. This smile was latent in her, in the core of her being, revealing it so irradiated, that this, whenever it was moved, was its inevitable expression. And her words had summoned Eve and a true tale. Eve, tired and triumphant in the horrible little room behind her little shop. Saying, 'I like to let everything get into an appalling state of chaos, and then to attack it and *see* things getting straight. Which you can't if you 're always niggling.' And while I hesitated, taken up with the realization that at last it was possible to think of the dead Eve, Miss Roscorla had gone on; talking of long tramps, the little shaw, the woods beyond the village, the places she had found long ago and wanted to see again. And the sound of her voice deepened the glow of everything she touched and I was sure that if she really did find time to join me on my walks, I should still see everything as I did when alone, as one could with a member of one's own family. And then came that moment that cast a darkness and left me desolate and the homestead chilled and darkened. But even then, when for an instant I tried to realize the Quaker point of view—all days equal, and Sunday distinct only as being the first day in the week—the light began to return; but lay only ahead, leaving the past excluded.

And this morning, gaiety; in each one of them, brimming quietly over. Partly because Sunday brings cessation, and the effort implied in becoming very clean and spruce made them all a little pleased with themselves and relatively frivolous; ready to smile, almost eagerly welcoming excuses for laughter. Consciously, enjoying to the full a permitted licence, they revelled in the irregularity and go-as-you-please of their Sunday morning. Unexpected, so that for the first time one had been the first to appear, save Miss Roscorla who had already breakfasted and vanished, and had helped oneself from the huge pie-dish packed with cold baked herrings and wielded the mighty teapot, feeling a little wan, finding even the reflected sunlight powerless to banish the sense, falling upon one in being alone in this usually populous room, of essential loneliness.

And the alcove door had opened, letting in Miss Roscorla transformed. Fresh and bloomy in a blue alpaca elevated to stateliness by a lace collar and an antique brooch whose dark, luminous stone, set in pale old gold, seemed to hold, like her eyes that shone with a happiness that was something more than the quiet happiness of every day, the light of festival. Yet last night, at eleven, awaiting Alfred not yet returned across the marshes from his selling-round along the coast, and sure to bring a score or more of beach-bought herrings requiring at once to be gutted and washed, she had been pallid with a weariness too great to be banished by a little sleep.

Seeing her thus, one was back in the mystery of Sunday, reminded of Mrs Boole's psychologically sacred seven-day rhythm, her insistence on the necessity of reversing engines once a week that had moved Dora Taylor to spend her Sunday afternoons in reading sentimental stories helped out by chocolate cream. Back in the mystery and persuaded that she had shared one's young Sundays, sure that somehow she intimately knew them and that the interchange of commonplaces enclosed identical experience, so that to look into her eyes was to see perspectives vividly re-created. And when one's own voice, the inalienable, evocative family voice, sounded in the room, these far perspectives, ceasing to belong entirely to the past, came near, became something that was still in process of realization.

And when she had gone, the little garden, withdrawn into itself, unthreatened to-day by even the passing footsteps of a worker, became one with the garden at Babington and the Barnes garden, both of them empty and, as they had always seemed on Sundays, a little aloof. So that even when one went out to watch pater cut the sacred asparagus, before church, or, after church, carefully detaching a few peaches, one saw the whole garden in a single eyeful and from all angles at once, because the part one was in, belonging to itself and seeming to throw one off, sent one's mind gliding over the whole, alighting nowhere. And it was at these times that all the different beauties were most apparent and most deeply bathed in unattainable light. Distance does not *lend* enchantment. It shows where it is. In the thing seen, as well as in the eye of the beholder. And I realized one of the Quaker secrets. Living always remote, drawn away into the depths of the spirit, they see, all the time, freshly. A perpetual Sunday.

'There, dawns no Sabbath, no Sabbath is o'er, Those Sabbath-keepers have one evermore.' Even after Harriett's direct little mind had ridiculed the words whose meaning one had never considered, light shone from this hymn and from its bright little jog-trot tune, a tiptoe quick-march for Fra Angelico angels, and kept it, together with *Light's Abode*, *Jerusalem the Golden*, and *O Paradise*, in a class apart.

And I wanted to get Miss Roscorla back again and tell her I understood why Friends make no separation of days and wondered whether, since only those who are not exploited by others can spend all their days sabbatically, Friends all work together, Friends for Friends, keeping their firms apart, unexploiting and unexploited, engaging only in honest trades? For most workers, especially for those helplessly employed in dishonest enterprises, only Sunday is at all comparable to a game or a dance whose rhythm lets one immediately into an eternal way of being. But only so long as the day keeps people upright and apart, as in a dance or a game; by having an invariable shape, and therefore in all its parts unfathomable depths. And I knew why even in my most agnostic days I felt cheated when spending Sunday with people who skate over its surface improvising means of passing the time, and why solitary Sundays in London, kept in shape by the audible surrounding world, the recurrent church bells and the sound of the traffic unburdened by the ceaseless heavy rumble of commerce, and admitting, between the passage of lightly running wheels and echoing hoof-beats, stillness and distance, held a depth no other day could provide.

And I heard his footsteps coming down the passage, weighty, yet not heavy, suggesting his outdoor gait, its firm, lightly swinging lounge, each footfall provisional, as if prepared, in response to a demand it seemed consciously to anticipate, to remain sympathetically halted. And he came, bringing his wealth, his power of lightening the burden of every occasion, into a room where no occasion was in progress, free to breakfast in an accompanied solitude whose quality was now to be put to the test. But he began to speak as soon as he came into sight rounding the end of the table: 'Well, I see you're early, or I suppose I should say I'm *late*.' A social voice, with a bustling manner in it, not his own. Belonging to, invented by, a type to be met in all the circles of piety. Like that woman, really good and quite certainly booked for heaven, who filled a rather yawning pause by saying you *never* know which moment will be your next. People who delight, during the intervals of compulsory activity, in attributing a make-believe importance to very small actions, addressing themselves by name, asserting, with an irrepressible complacent flounce of body and spirit, their own identity, their certainty of salvation in the next world and, meanwhile, of ability, heaven helping them, to deal with this. Though not of their kind, he had acquired, for emergencies, the witnessed devices of their social behaviour and, in using one of these, felt their presence about him, banishing embarrassing solitude with a young lady.

The little Babington woman, or even Beulah, automatically conforming to the code dictating animation in talking with men, would have entered brightly into the game, would have said, 'My being early is, I assure you, *quite* an accident,' or something of the sort, smiling across and finding his incredibly, abominably changed appearance an improvement upon the week-day shagginess that had vanished together with the tawny Norfolk jacket. And the would-be frivolous back-chat of simple piety, though setting him at his ease, would always leave him solitary. As he wished, and did not wish to be. But I was too stunned by his appearance even to play the game of leading him towards material for anecdote and, while he began on his meal and the weather, prophesying thundery rain-storms, I was taking in, one by one, the items that would make it impossible for Amabel, if indeed she came down only for a Sunday, to re-realize him as tiger, tiger burning bright.

For this Sunday edition of Richard was the shockingly handsome young man of the family album upstairs, the gleaming,
bravura-moustached, sleek-haired calicot endimanché, diminished by age and toil. The ill-cut dark suit alone would not
have accomplished the amazing reduction. But the thinned,
down-plastered hair, flattening the skull and robbing the head
of its dignity, the transformation of the straggling moustache
ends into spear-points extending from side to side of a face
denuded of its gentle stubble and shining with recent soap,
destroyed him beyond redemption.

'Thunder above. That'll be Alfred; hurrying.'

Looking across I found his eyes on mine waiting for them
to share his vision of the frail slight figure hurtling from point
to point, causing the floor tô rock. And I produced an unwilling glimmer, and his smile became a deep-chested chuckle;
delight in sharing. And congratulation. A kindly teacher
applauding a pupil's achievement.

If Amabel could see him thus she would perceive, through
no matter what disguise, the culture in him, its generous depth.

A rumbling, along the road behind, and, in a moment, the
carriage, pulled up at her side with its door already open. The
first drops of the promised shower fell heavily upon her face
as she climbed in, to the sound of Mrs Roscorla's eager welcome: 'That's right, that's right. Now thee's safe, and
thee's pretty hat.' The chariot moved off, the din of its
rattling joints and the downpour on the roof preventing further
hearing and allowing her to escape into entranced contemplation
of the deluge.

'Lovely,' she presently shouted towards them, in the hope
of justifying her preoccupation. Miss Roscorla sat forward
to share, but the old lady, her frail form bent within its burden
of clothing and looking as if it must break beneath the weight
of the heavy veil-hung bonnet, after directing toward the outer
world a single wide-eyed glance, disappointed in her anticipation of something to be seen there that might explain the sudden
outcry, kept upon Miriam's face her searching gaze, embarrassing in its lifelong singleness of vision, its unvarying statement.
So far, apparently she was satisfied. Her habitual half smile

blossomed full whenever her eyes were met, and was accompanied by a decisive little nod that seemed approvingly to pat
the passing moment on the back and at the same time so elo-
quently to plead for acknowledgment of the vision she cherished
with such deep strength of conviction that Miriam presently
felt her prevail, win her competition with the outside scene,
and make it pleasant to sit back and be told from the depths of
the motionless limpid eyes how good life was upon the beaten
tracks, and how well that she had been rescued from foolhardy
adventure, brought home into the coach to be forgiven, rejoiced over, congratulated on being where and what she was.
So that she noticed only when they began to draw up that the
sudden rain had ceased.

With the village away behind, they were in a little lane
leading to open country, drawn up outside the larger of two
adjoining cottages. Labourers' cottages, fronted by tangled
gardens enclosed in battered palings. Huge in his ulster,
Richard was clambering down from the box as she escaped into
the road to look away towards the distant fields, trying to get
past the disappointment of this too-modest substitute for her
imagined rural equivalent of the once-seen London meeting-
house, to keep in mind the Friends gathered inside, the nucleus
of living reality with which in a moment they were to be
merged. Mrs Roscorla was alighting, being carefully helped
out by Richard. As if to meet her, the sun came out, its light
falling full upon her face, radiantly smiling and secretly adream,
the face of a woman delighting in the necessity of being for the
moment central, delighting in her right to exemption and rich
escort; the face of a bride.

Turning, Miriam found the cottages transformed. Against
the deep grey of the retreating storm-cloud, their whitewashed
fronts shone out patterned with green rose leaves and red roses
and with the clean shadows of leaf and bloom.

The door opened to the sound of their arrival, was held
open from within for them to pass. Entering just behind Miss
Roscorla, Miriam found herself, all unprepared and expecting
only a stranger, almost face to face, in the gloom between the
two doors, with the forgotten half-wit of the carrier's omnibus,

the dreadful ventriloquist's dummy. . . . Inescapable, a barrier not to be passed, driving her with his powerfully clear description of it, into the depths of helpless human solitude, bringing horror into the gathering she was about to join and that insisted on reminding her of his existence, of the inevitability of his daily presence somewhere within the radius of this small inhabited area amidst the wastes of downland and meadow. Part of the local household; all of them nightmarishly immovable and unvarying. Out of sight, she had forgotten him. But, for these Quakers, even he was never out of sight?

Guiltily tiptoeing, Miss Roscorla led the way to the last row of chairs to the right of the gangway and stood back for Miriam to pass in first and gladly take the end seat within the shelter of the wall whose windows, rather high up, cast their light chiefly upon the other side of the room; upon the forms seated there in scattered groups, amongst them a little old woman just across the way who for a moment held her eyes, so still she was and so intent, and across the faces of the row of elders confronting the gathering from the raised platform. In their midst, Alfred Roscorla, his lonely early departure explained. Little Alfred . . . was a minister, or an elder; perhaps both. Small and still, with arms folded and head inclined so that his chin rested upon his breast, he sat at ease, at home, perfectly yielded up to the central depths of his being. The pale mask of his face, shining out beneath the fluffy red-gold ridges that softened its deep lines and beautifully completed its shape, had in this place a look of unconscious dignity; telling her that in their pardonable tour of investigation her eyes would not rest upon him again. To his left, sitting very upright, a dapper professional-looking man in dove-grey, whose clear grey eyes gazed through gold-rimmed spectacles down the room above the heads of the congregation, unseeing. On the other side three women, their bonneted heads at varying angles, their eyes closed, already settled in meditation or in prayer.

The clock above the doorway at the far side of the platform, disconcertingly suggesting, with its loud, wooden tick-tock, a farmhouse kitchen, stood at ten minutes past the hour. Meeting had not long begun, there was yet time to join the opening stillness before it should bear fruit. But the little party could not fully subside until Richard, attending to horse and vehicle, should have come in, stealthily admitted by the ventriloquist's dummy whom still, without turning her head, she could see at his post, a rigid form set sideways on the edge of a chair, listening, ready to rise at the sound of a footfall on the garden path. Even a Friends' meeting must have its out-post, scouts on the watch. Was he the permanent door-keeper, given by this Quaker colony not only the sense of being a member of a kindly social group, but also the pride-bestowing importance of office?

Tick-tock, *tick*-tock. Richard was halted somewhere, talk-ing; releasing someone into a momentary freedom from the direct pressure of daily life upon lonely individuality.

Imagining him set down in meeting, inactive and silent, solitary yet not alone, less alone and less protected than in the midst of social life, she was glad to be so far removed from where he would sit, and eager to escape still further, to join the travellers already launched, so that when he arrived she would be unaware of his presence. A last glance carried her eyes to the figure that had drawn them as she took her place, the old woman sitting a little ahead across the gangway, dressed, in spite of the oppressive warmth, in stout black serge and little elbow cape. Her white hair, confined in a coarse black net, lay in a bang across the nape of her neck. Above it stood the wide brim of her flat-crowned circular black straw hat, defying fashion, asserting antique modesty and respectability, yet triumphantly, by the superfluous width of its brim, pro-claiming itself a hat. A village grandmother, bringing herself, her childhood and youth, her lifeful of memories and gathered wisdom, to sit in company and make, youthfully truant from all that on her behalf could be summarized and put into words, her journey towards the centre of being. Intent and lost, knowing the way of escape, the points of departure from deceptive surfaces, she, with her ancient simplicity, rescued this small meeting from the enclosedness it suggested when one remembered that these local people lived always in the white glare of village publicity, carrying about with them from the cradle to the grave their known personal records. More powerfully than her more sophisticated juniors, she represented the world which she had never seen, made this meeting one with the larger meetings and showed them for what they were, always the same; and always new.

Closing her eyes to concentrate upon the labour of retreat into stillness of mind and body, she recognized the iniquity of unpunctuality in attending a Quaker meeting. The room was utterly still. Half-way through the drawing of a deep releasing breath, she was obliged to hamper the automatic movements of her limbs that with one accord were set on rearranging themselves. Stealthily her body straightened to sit upright, her head moved to relax the supporting muscles of the neck and came to rest a little bent. Lifted by a powerful circular movement of her shoulders that before she could restrain it had caused a gentle crackling of starched blouse-sleeves, her arms released themselves, unclasping her hands and setting them, with fingers relaxed, one upon each knee, while her feet, approaching each other, drew in just short of lifting their heels.

Even a beginning of concentration held an irresistible power. The next breath drew itself so deeply that she could prevent its outgoing from becoming a long, audible sigh only by holding and releasing it very gradually. It left her poised between the inner and the outer worlds, still aware of her surroundings and their strangeness and of herself as an alien element brought in by sympathetic understanding of the Quaker enterprise and engaged at last upon a labour whose immediate fruits were making her regret that it had not been, consciously, from the beginning of her life, her chief concern. To remain always centred, operating one's life, operating even its wildest enthusiasms from where everything fell into proportion and clear focus. To remain always in possession of a power that was not one's own, and that yet one's inmost being immediately recognized as its centre.

Already she was aware of a change in her feeling towards

those about her, a beginning of something more than a melting away of resentment towards the characteristics of some of those she had observed as she came into the room, an animosity now reversing itself by a movement of apology towards the women on the platform and the dapper little man of ideas. Feeling now something more than a rationally tolerant indifference, something akin to the beginning of affection, she was free to take leave of them.

Why should it be only Quakers who employed, in public as well as privately, this method of approach to reality? Again, as at the beginning of the meeting she had attended in London and where she had been little more than an interested spectator, she considered the enormity of breaking into sound the moment a congregation is assembled and keeping on, with scarcely an instant's breathing-space, until the end. 'For where two or three are gathered together in my name, there am I—*in the midst of them*': to be immediately assailed by a torrent of words, confessions and protests, part-singing and the recital of poetic prayers, by readings aloud and at last by an address, compiled and delivered by one who may, or who may not ever, have suffered a moment's religious experience.

What prevents the spreading, throughout Christendom, of a practice born of belief in the presence of God; necessarily following on that belief?

Be still and *know*. Still in mind as well as in body. Not meditating, for meditation implies thought. Tranquil, intense concentration that reveals first its own difficulty, the many obstacles, and one's own weakness, and leads presently to contemplation, recognition.

Bidding her mind be still, she felt herself once more at work, in company, upon an all-important enterprise. This time her breathing was steady and regular and the labour of journeying, down through the layers of her surface being, a familiar process. Down and down through a series of circles each wider than the last, each opening with the indrawing of a breath whose outward flow pressed her downwards towards the next, nearer to the living centre. Again thought touched her, comparing this research to a kind of mining operation. For indeed it was not flight. There was resistance from within, at once concrete and buoyant, a help and a hindrance, alternately drawing her forward and threatening, if for an instant her will relaxed, to drive her back amongst the distractions of the small cross-section of the visible world by which she was surrounded. And here, indeed, she was, up in her mind, open-eyed, everything about her very sharp and clear, though the room had darkened to a twilight.

A satiny flexible straw, pale warm fawn shot with dull gold and green and mauve, subtly blended so that where the light caught it all the colours appeared at once and one could see each in turn as predominating; an inexhaustible interweaving of soft brilliancies, deeply satisfying. A sophisticated, rather expensive Regent Street sort of straw, the basis of a hat costing guineas. Small silky flowers, bunched, repeating more definitely the shades of the straw. And then that ill-placed band of cheap satin ribbon, its hot brown colour ruining both flowers and straw. With velvet ribbon of a neutral fawn, dull, shaped close to the straw on its way to join the flowers set on one side only, instead of in uniform bunches on either side, and the hat set at an angle to make of hat and hair and face a continuous design: lovely. A hat to keep itself in memory together with the summer of which it was a part. Quenched by the odious ribbon and standing, rather than set, upon the head, above rigidly crimped hair whose lengths were tightly pinned into a row of transverse sausages, it became a frightful proclamation. Beside it, any faded wreck, stuck on anyhow, would be a thing of beauty.

Moving stealthily in search of relief, her eyes fell upon the head-gear of the old woman across the way. That, too, had proclaimed itself a hat, independent of its wearer. But the little old woman was deeply a part of the gathering. And this other? Why, without knowing her, without even seeing her face, should one feel so certain of her lack of understanding co-operation? There she sat, however complacently conscious of the horror perched with lunatic independence upon her repulsive coiffure, within the fold, at least reverent and conforming, waiting, patiently, for the results of an uncomprehended process?

Reaching down once more into the featureless inner twilight, she found the outdoor world obtruding, assailing her ears with mid-morning chirrupings, the sudden chackle of a scared thrush in flight across the garden, sounds from distant farms and meadows. External contemplation, divorced from sympathetic imagination, had closed the pathway to recovery of the state whence a fresh beginning would be possible. Each effort to be still brought the outdoor world into her mind.

After all, this was her first Sunday. A stranger, unaccustomed to labour here, she might well be allowed to rejoice for a moment in the place itself, to be aware of the little temple as set in a green world, porous to the evocative sounds of its background; to be, for those who intimately knew and could so easily forget it, just this once a delighted emissary? Who was she, that she should expect to find herself all at once in the presence of God?

Truant in the open, she saw, closing her eyes to the surrounding twilight, not the features of the scenes whose memory was the power that had drawn her forth to the gently clamorous sounds, but the corner of an unlocated meadow, rain-drenched and so near that she could perceive, as if she were some small field-beast in their midst, a forest of grass-blades, coarse, rank, July grass, the ribs and filaments of each blade clearly visible. Just grass, the least considered feature of all that had made the joy of a week's wanderings, yet now offering itself as a sufficient representative and a bourne, narrowing to a single clump, to a few large blades bent beneath the weight of their own growth; individual, precious. In every nerve she felt their chill touch. And now the whole of the unknown field lay clear, hedged and sloping, and she was above it, looking down upon a wide stretch of open country, sunlit, showing here and there a nucleus of remembered beauty.

With opened eyes she was observing the deepness of the room's grey light. Another storm-cloud. The hour was ticking itself away and here she sat, an outsider, using this unique depth within the depth of Sunday to exult in the memory of solitary joy and in the certainty of its continuance in the week lying ahead and showing, of its massed hours, only those that she would spend alone.

'*O Lord—foundation and end of our being—bring amongst us the sense of thy presence and of thy love—help us to set aside all that would come between ourselves and thee—that we may merge our wills with thine—and go our way—in confidence—along the path that thou wilt show.*'

The even, meditative, unemotional tone of the man in dovegrey was the tone of Quaker prayer? Again she recalled the old man who had prayed at the London meeting, beginning so beautifully, breathing out, to a lifelong friend, human sadness and aspiration, seeming to carry, in the tones of his gentle life-worn voice, the collected sorrows of the gathering—and then letting that voice fill out and bawl. The man on the platform, cultivated, humane, *spoke*. Quietly, without protestations, to someone very near at hand, implicated in human affairs, ready currently to collaborate with those who held themselves available.

She imagined the brief prayer spoken, as if the speaker were uncertain of its reception, with emphasis upon the leading words, so that they might carry to someone whose attention must be assailed and held; spoken poetically, in a manner revealing the speaker's satisfaction with his own choice of words; intoned, more or less unctuously; recited in church, like a collect, in musical or unmusical monotone, rather swiftly.

What would be the result of this lead from the platform, so comfortingly suggesting that for others, as well as for herself, the meeting had yet to begin? Silence. Wherein the little prayer reverberated. Suppose there should be no further contribution? None was needed. Supported by the kindred spirits amongst whom it was distributed, fulfilled, the prayer should presently disperse the gathering fully armed into its immediate world. There to confront cattle awaiting the terrors of slaughter, leaky mouldering cottages consuming life apace, distant towns where people starved, or died, hopelessly, by inches, of ceaseless exploitation?

And indeed, it was against such things, though so far she

had heard nothing of Quaker vegetarians, that Friends raised
their voices.

'"*For if I build again the things which I destroyed, I make
myself a transgressurr.*"' A burly middle-aged man, outlined
against the further wall in ill-fitting Sunday best, described by.
his clothes and his accent as a farmer or superior farm labourer.
With an almost defiant upward fling of his massive head, he
cleared his throat and proceeded in a deep quiet tone, the more
impressive for the gesture preceding it: '"*for it had been better
for them not to have knawn the way of righteousness than after
they had knawn it to turrn.*" *These two sayings of Paul have been
much in my mind this past week. Tur'ble sayings. Tur'ble
truths. Both found to bear the same meaning. To destroy evil,
the devil's bad building, to keep on at it, not turning away.
That is the will of the Lowerd. Betturr not to knaw that will
than, knawing it, to fall away from trying to carry that will out.*'

That first long silence, inviolate, had shielded and encouraged
active labour. This second interval echoed with the two contrasted voices, one fragile, refined, suggesting the complex
external protections whereon the very life of its owner was
continuously dependent, the other, independent strength. Two
widely separated natures, expressing different features of a
common experience. One, the clear aim, the cost of attaining
it, the other, an ever-present danger. For one morning,
enough? Yet seeming to call for some kind of response,
audible endorsement by the whole meeting as one person.
A hymn? Excluded, though Miss Roscorla had confessed to
hymns at evening meeting, introduced to attract outsiders. A
concession. These morning meetings, the core of Quaker
communal life, could not admit recitations. Yet the Bible
was quoted? Two desires pressed equally. For more voices
to sound into the stillness, for the stillness, already full of
testimony, to remain unbroken until the end of the short hour.

The darkness, increasing since the farmer voiced his sturdy
warning, seemed to press that warning home. And now, upon
the roof, single drops fell heavily, increased, became a deluge.

'Pawin' wi' rain!' A child's voice, clear and confident,
addressing its universe. No whispered rebuke, no movement.

The young parents, whom she had found before the voice
ceased, remained peacefully upright on either side of the
small figure. In craning round, she became aware of her
forgotten neighbour, twinkling towards her own delight.
Proud. Justly proud of the witnessed reception of the babe's
contribution, and of the babe, sustaining, mute and motionless,
the long silences, at home and at ease, qualifying as a Friend.

Far away towards the downs, a low, prolonged cannonade.
'Thunder. *Rumbledumbledumble.*' The crackling of a
cautiously handled paper bag. A biscuit, peacefully crunched.

'*Dear* Luard'—a weak, low-toned, conversationally expostu-
lating voice from the platform, from one of the bonneted
women, ceasing, seeming to have no more to say, seeming, for
an instant that kept Miriam pressing the edge of a sharp heel
into a vulnerable ankle, merely to intend a gentle protest
against the roof-battering torrent. 'Send down thy *blessing*
upon us this morning. Upon us *all.* We have gathered here
to *receive* thy blessing, Luard. . . .' Going on and on, the
thin dry voice gained strength and a little warmth, but still
seemed continuously to expostulate. Listening only to its
inflections which now were suggesting a genteel customer
admonishing a careless tradesman, Miriam wondered how
it could be that upon this woebegone female should have
descended the honour of a place upon the platform. A break
in the voice called her attention. 'Especially, we would
remember the little *chewdren*, Luard.'

Struggling in vain against a fierce loathing, she found herself
isolated with two assailants. On the one hand memories,
rare but vivid, of outlying elders who, in thus distinguishing
herself and Harriett from the surrounding adults, had inspired
only nausea and reaped only contempt, and on the other a sly
voice requesting her to note the difference between the masculine and the feminine contributions, and to admit St Paul
justified in forbidding women to give voice in public.

For the helplessly squirming children, including the boy
whose consciousness, the engrossing biscuit forgotten, would
once more have become an intelligent ear, she could do nothing.
For the insistent voice there was an answer laid up in the

archives of her intermittent feminism.   Searching the records, to the accompaniment of the intolerable intonations, she met resistance coming from within, seeming at first a sense of the unsuitabilïty of the occasion and becoming, while she reminded herself that the occasion, already banished by her own anger, left empty space excellently available for a pressing matter, the misty dawn of a conviction, new and startling and bringing, as it cleared and took shape, a return of the sense of unity with those about her.

I no longer care.

Could this be true?   Summoning the hitherto infallible inspirers of wrath, things read incredulously, opinions, roundly expressed or casually implied, she found that they failed to move her.   Deprived of their old power, lustreless, deflated, they seemed now only the harsh and pitiful echoes of a world from which for ever she had escaped, the world, outside Quakerdom, where still they pursued their poisonous way.

The voice ceased.   Unawares, her eyes flew to the tormentor. There she sat, at the end of the row, leaning back in her chair, weary, exhausted by joyless activity.   A gentle face, reproachful.

Tick-tock.   *Tick*-tock.

Into this third silence had come the lifting of the light, and now its full radiance restored the aspect of the room to what it had been at the beginning of the hour whose end was now at hand.   The outer world reasserted itself, its clear sounds echoing into the height of its sky.   Every one must feel its influence, the sense of emergence, the thinning of the enclosed atmosphere, the dispersal of concentration.   Trying to recall the end of the London meeting, she remembered only the faces of the women who stood talking together, lingering to greet and converse, their look of deep controlled vitality,   In their neighbourhood there was none of the atmosphere of essential isolation spread by even the most sociable church-woman.   Without being dignified, they had a serene dignity. Like Rachel Mary.   Even in this little village meeting, the Quaker social rudiments were represented.   If only on account of these, it was good to be here, to be in the midst of a community that was swayed by them. Even though the only woman to give voice created the impression of being a lonely, sourly puritanical Low Churchwoman.

Would there be another word, to lift the gloom she had left upon the air and that even the returned sunlight had failed to disperse?

'*We thank thee*'—the voice of Alfred Roscorla, hardly above a whisper, seeming to emerge from the stillness rather than to break it—'*for thy nearness—during another week—for thy sure promise—always to be with us—close at hand—in all our difficulties—to give us—whenever we turn to thee—thy peace.*'

'She's a kind soul, she does her best, but usually working a little beyond her strength.'

'She needs a *holiday*,' said Mrs Roscorla, who had been eagerly waiting to speak. 'Too much meetings and visitings.' Having spoken her mind, she turned with a smile that said, 'Let us forget her and enjoy our stroll home in this sunlight after the shower. Life is pleasant, as Mrs Bradley ought to know. I've no patience with her.'

Automatically, hardly realizing what she did, finding her standing alone and frail, swaying a little on her uncertain feet in the road to which she had made her independent way while still the others lingered talking, she had given Mrs Roscorla her arm. To that sudden blind movement, she owed her present position between mother and daughter slowly climbing the endless hill. By the time the far-off house should be reached, a lifetime of revealing association would be left behind. Forever she could have gone on talking to Miss Roscorla, from whom still emanated warm appreciation of her relief in learning that this halting little meeting was merely a tentative offshoot of Quakerdom, a scattering of local people drawn to Friends from church or chapel, drawn, she suspected, in the first place by the quality of the Roscorlas, the personality of Miss Roscorla, operating in her missionary days down here before the farm-life started. By the charm of a voice whose every sound was communication more eloquent than the words it so beautifully transformed.

Each of them had risen to her innocent-sounding allusion to Mrs Bradley, relishing, while the one gently defended and the other zestfully explained her, the presence of a companion sufferer to whom opinions might be confided without risk of leakage. But now, as she passed into silent contemplation of a possible world suddenly fully supplied with Quaker meetings drawing together all who were Quakers unawares, the link on her left was snapped. The slight weight on her arm, alternately, to the irregular rhythm of the tottering footsteps, lifting and pressing, became a warning, powerfully demanding its restoration. Returning to what she had been a moment before, all ears for the responses to her own relief in learning that the dismal woman on the platform had joined Friends from the Plymouth Brethren, she found the warning gone, the link ready to be restored. By further discussion of local people? By making conversation whose deliberate contrivance would come between oneself and this present well-being; this heavenly sense of belonging, of being surrounded and secure?

If she could shake her mind free, topics would spontaneously arise. But effort brought only the realization, upon a tide of joy, that still it was only July. She decided for silence. Soon, the approaching milestone would offer a topic and then, as slowly they climbed the last of the hill, the elms would come into sight and provide material that would branch and grow. They rounded the bend and there, just ahead, lay the milestone and the fork, the turning-point of her first excursion. A vehicle, rumbling along from behind, was almost upon them. An event. The old lady must gently be propelled a little nearer to the grass-fringed roadside. Already Miss Roscorla had dropped behind. Pressing the frail arm to her side, she turned and smiled, while making the necessary sideways movement, freely down into the bonneted face, making the most of the adventure of moving a few steps upon the surface of a shared earth in order to escape the impact of something moving more quickly along the same path.

That's right, said Mrs Roscorla's answering smile, brilliant, almost roguishly expressing her approval and appreciation. A carriage passing and we moving aside. A pleasant adventure. *That's* right. Then, turning her eyes once more to the roadway: '*There* they are,' she said gaily.

Looking ahead, Miriam recognized the family coach and, with a smiting self-reproach, the figure of Richard, the forgotten Richard who, as far as she was concerned, might have spent his morning in another world. Turned full round in his place on the box beside Alfred who was driving, supported by a hand on the rail behind him, he was looking back, unsmiling, at the three walkers. Looking directly forth from the centre of his solitary being, as though unwitnessed and alone. With a pang of apprehension, solicitude on behalf of the man who was being deceived, she saw in his face his reading of all he had seen, in approaching, in going by, and now, as he fronted and focused the group whose centre was the young lady: looking 'a picture' in the scabious-blue gown, its shoulder-straps set firmly upon the creamy lace that rose to her neck and moulded her arms to the wrists, supporting upon one of those lace-clad arms the beloved frail figure. Meeting hers, his eyes moved immediately to his mother and back again to rest upon her own, seeming so near and so engulfing that for an instant nothing else was visible. Released as he turned away, she found herself alighted, on the further side of that irreversible moment, amongst London friends arrived upon the scene incredulous, protesting; powerless. They vanished, driven away by confident glad laughter, leaving her alone with Richard's relatives, needing somehow to employ her swiftly moving breath.

'The clouds seem to have vanished quite away,' she said and heard the tremor in her animated voice and turned to search the face of the chief witness, present with all her faculties serenely about her during that age-long moment. For the second time to-day she saw Miss Roscorla transformed. Upon her cheeks was a rose-red flush, removing the years.

'Yes,' she said evenly, and the pulsating interval brought no message, dropped no hint as to the nature of the onlooker's experience—'the thunder seems to have passed quite off.' She looked, as if inquiringly, away across the meadows beyond the further hedge, and kept her eyes upon them as she walked; collecting herself.

'Alfred 's a good driver. They 'll soon be home.' Serenely, in an unchanged world, the old lady was watching the distant carriage climb the gentle rise.

'Yes,' she responded, 'they haven't far to go,' and knew that her voice, emphatic and insincerely judicial, confessed, to her other companion, her thankfulness for the diversion. Returning, she caught Miss Roscorla's face turned fully round, silently regarding her. Catching at the elms, the promised topic, now mercifully visible in the distance, she launched forth.

'I 'll ask you,' said Miss Roscorla, the moment she rested from the labour of stringing sentences together and driving into them the semblance of an animated interest, 'a question. You 'll notice as we pass them,' and now her voice, relievedly escaping into a neutral topic, might have been one's own, 'that they 're not quite evenly planted. Can you tell me which two are furthest apart?'

Here they were, the desolate trees, suggesting for years past, to Roscorla eyes, only this simple catch.

'I 'm afraid I 'll have to disappoint——'

'Ah, she 's guessed it!' chuckled the old lady, stumbling a little in her eagerness. 'Now isn't that the first person who 's guessed it, Rachel Mary?'

'Well, no. I think just one or two guessed it.'

'Ah, yes. One or two, I expect.'

She seemed to be reading from afar the known features of a dream. The voices, the words, even the small sounds in between of slow footsteps upon the ascending ground, were familiar, as if recited, and recognized as they fell.

Easeful silence while she listened in this dream-world, identified with its players, for the next familiar sound.

'We 'll have to show you,' said Miss Roscorla, and her voice came isolated, from to-day, with quiet confidence and cheeriness, restoring novelty, 'some of our further woods; before the autumn comes.'

She had spoken firmly, from the context of her private speculations.

The open window had filled the room with rich moist air. Wealth, solitary, forgotten, accumulated up here during the eventful evening. Leaning forth, she met the unexpected deep scent of cloves, somehow wandered round from the near corner of the little walled garden. On any of the earlier evenings it would have drawn her spirit forth. To-night it competed in vain with the life of the day.

Leaning further out, she fixed her attention on the scent alone. Its character had changed. No longer a garden scent, it seemed to come from interiors. Sunday interiors decked with flowers severed from their roots, lavishly spending their perfume as they die. Vividly it recalled from the past a single forgotten experience as a stop-gap Sunday-school teacher, the embarrassments of inexperience set to instruct unembarrassed inexperience, in enclosed air that held, prominent amongst its stifling odours, the pungent fragrance of crushed and body-warmed lemon thyme and the oily-sweet aroma of red carnations. And now this same rich scent came from to-day, shut her in with visions of Sunday tea-parties in farm and cottage.

At these flower-scented festivals, every seated figure was touched by a glint of regal individuality, independent, for an hour, of the concerns wherein to-morrow each, grown smaller, would be absorbed.

With triumphant indifference, these images held themselves before her in the outer darkness, declaring themselves, if she should pursue her present path, henceforth inseparable companions of the scent of cloves.

With the curtains drawn and the night shut out, she faced the flood solitude had released. Strangely prominent in the scenes closing in on her, even in those wherein he had played no part, was the figure of Frankie. Challenging the light, accentuating the darkness. And yet it was he who had brought the day's deepest satisfaction.

Every time she had seen him he had been apparition. Sitting in the carrier's omnibus, a punctually placed reminder, forgotten as soon as he was out of sight. In meeting, a hint of the ceaseless presence in village life of things one would rather forget. At the Roscorla tea-table, an affront, a spectre denuding the richest feast of the day. Yet after the pang of acceptance and of realizing that of such, of those not invited elsewhere, would be the Roscorlas' chosen guests, his presence had brought this strange happiness.

Frankie's alien *completeness*, which they, in their kindly, active pity, failed to recognize, was somehow akin to every happy state?

When they all sat down together, restored to each other with Sunday still wielding its full power and the known burdens of each life temporarily lost, their combined wealth, emphasized by the presence of a stranger, magnetized the air. Meeting Frankie in the midst of them, it was easy to find things to say, not directly addressed to him, whose meaning he could apprehend. To feel impelled to say them, even in growing aware, in the presence of a surprised audience unaware of themselves as sources of inspiration, of appearing to be deliberately playing a charming part. Charming the pupil, who sat half turned, glowing towards one's geniality; and Miss Roscorla, who was grateful as well as pleased; and Mrs Roscorla, because the concrete little pictures, reduced to their utmost simplicity, not calling for reflection, dramatized by emphasis on single words, and that yet, helped by vocal modulations that made one listen as if to a voice not one's own, seemed to bring the whole of truth, visitant, into the very air, proclaimed the old lady's central unconscious belief: that every one knows everything worth knowing and is immensely to be congratulated. And Richard . . . pleased and approving, well satisfied to take a holiday from his task of being general entertainer, descending into speech at need, in support of the role that was spontaneously playing itself.

The richest depth of social experience is to be had only in relation to those who, while exercising a poignant appeal, make no demands?

But she knew she could not permanently respond to this appeal. That she would feel, if Frankie were always there, impatience with the obstructed mind, disgust, seeing it in motion, for the shambling body.

And now she could see only Alfred Roscorla, his quiet pale face shining with an unearthly radiance. Alfred it was who had brought Frankie home to tea, enduring, all the way up from adult school and all the way down to evening meeting, his solitary companionship.

Could one even have kept the tea-table conversation somewhere within the restricted circle of Frankie's vision, if the afternoon had been different?

'A pleasant afternoon.' And so perhaps it appeared to Richard as he came strolling down the garden in his Sunday leisure. Nothing had changed, but the whole domain seemed saddened, depressed, lifeless. The effect of what psychologists call 'reaction,' which somehow ought not to be. Even when he reached one's side, things remained sad. Overwhelming in their sadness. 'Pleasant.' So mild, and yet too great a tribute. And too small.

'If you were thinking of taking a walk, you might like to stroll across to the farm.'

Joy and disgust, inextricably mingled. Not the farm. Anywhere but the farm, anything but toil-suggesting spectacles. Coming from him, even the idea seemed a kind of Sabbath-breaking.

'Isn't it a very long way?'

'A tidy step by road, but not far across the fields.'

A useful piece of farmer's lore. But would one remember at such a crisis, and have the courage to crouch in a ditch, if such were handy, and face the bull, looking up at him, until he grew weary, or someone came along?

Another narrow track, a corridor between rustling walls of grey-blue oats, another stretch of wandering single file in easy silence.

The small, squat farmhouse, set amongst its barns and

haystacks and warmly sunlit, yet seeming desolate, incomplete,
with only a foreman living there. Meadows and meadows,
each with a different loveliness, linked by the crazily sloping
stiles. Strength, behind the hand that steadied and steered
at the same time. Long intervals of strolling on and on,
feeling, although he seemed content to walk in silence, that
one ought to be asking intelligent questions and, all the time,
the lovely setting, aloof, each prospect sending with the first
glimpse, its intimate message, its demand to be seen in solitude.

'Yes, it's pretty stuff. Sainfoin.'
'But what a lovely beneficent name! *Holy hay*.'
Spoken gently, affectionately, so that it seemed to caress the
opulently successful meadow, the ancient word, so strange upon
his lips and yet so fitting, unable, even when anglicized, to
lose either its beauty or its descriptive power, broke the spell
of desolation lying, even here where the lovely old windmill
looked straight down upon the valley, over the uninhabited
farm, summoning thither the spirits of those who in early-
Christian Europe had single-heartedly given to this herb its
still-persistent name. But there was tiresome amusement,
the shadow of a grin behind the look of aroused, gratified
awareness, as he turned and gravely met my eyes.
'Is that *so*-now? I never knew it. It's true enough.
Sainfoin makes good fodder.'
And when he had grasped the connection between sain
and wholesome and holy and I asked him to agree that
it was a pity holy had become so specialized and narrowed
down, he spoke swiftly, heartily, as if from deep conviction:
'That's so. There's no sort of doubt about that.'
Walking in high-heeled shoes across the stubble over which
he strolled so easily, feeling at a disadvantage, a hobbling towns-
woman out of place upon the raw surfaces of masculine labour,
I yet felt, the moment he apologized for the crossing that was
to shorten the way, glad to be there rather than anywhere else,
to be realizing the powerful exacting life of cultivated fields,
even though the realization meant that henceforth this lovely
farm, seen from afar, would proclaim the price of its beauty.

'You may find it strange, me being here every day in the week, that I like sometimes to stroll over on a Sunday.'

'The farm has two faces for you, a week-day and a Sunday face? I mean, when there is no one here you can see how lovely it is?'

'*Well*-now, since you 've asked me, I suggested us coming over this way because I certainly think the views hereabout are as pretty as any in the neighbourhood, barring the one from our garden.' Pretty views. Pleasant weather. As if to such things only moderate feelings must be accorded. 'But there 's a queer thing,' slowly, judicially, and looking round to pin my attention. 'Any farmer 'd tell you'—and I saw that it still gives him pride to call himself a farmer—'that Sunday 's the only day you can see the place, take stock and make your plans.'

'Nobody there to distract and remind you of the difficulties of working with hired labour.'

'I guess that 's it.'

And when somehow I was asking him if he 'd come to the farm when, on a Sunday, he felt depressed, meaning that in its lonely uninhabited state it was depressing:

'Well—no. I 'll tell you what I do when I 'm depressed. Something for somebody else. As quick as I can. There 's nothing like it for curing depression.'

And I regretted missing the opportunity of telling him that no labour should be hired, that the payment of wages rather than shares created a wrong relationship. And we reached the sacred little copse, the mystery of its company of trees and of the sunlight striking through, silently, yet making one listen.

'Yes. It 's a pretty little wood. I eat my lunch here when I can command a clear half hour. You can generally find a more or less dry spot. There 's a good deal of pine, as you see, and not much undergrowth.'

The farmhouse and its meadows, the distant woods grown near, the little copse seen in its intimate loveliness, all too near to be felt, sending one in search of a vanished bourne. Everything recedes as you approach, unless you come in solitude, unaccompanied even by memory.

Yet after going back across the fields, forgetful of surroundings, putting together, turn and turn about, competitively,
a map of London and at last agreeing, in the serious voices of
people discussing an invalid, that no one who had once lived
in the country could ever again want London for more than a
brief interval, the walk round the wan and desolate farm became
an achievement, and the last bit of the way, the lane leading
into the road just above the house, had the enchantment of a
sudden plunge from enclosure into air whose scents are almost
tangible.   Every hedgerow flower a promise and an invitation.

And it was the certainty, when we joined the others at tea,
that Richard too felt this sense of achievement, keeping him
poised and, even in his silence, expansive, that made it easy to
talk for Frankie and helplessly to appear, for the second time
to-day, in a charming character-part.

And the third time; at evening meeting. Conspicuous
amongst the stocky Sussex peasantry, two rows ahead across
the gangway, at the near end of the row, Richard seemed nearer,
being visible, than when at morning meeting he had sat alongside, with mother and sister intervening. But also most comfortably far away, cut off from his own party which he could
see only by turning fully round. An impossibility, once
meeting was settled, even for an unprominent Friend. Yet
difficult to banish, not only because he was so visible, but
because of that strange, disquieting remark. If, for him, in a
meeting that does not soon produce spoken words, there is
'nothing to do but sit and think,' he cannot be called a Quaker.
Is just a charming Irishman, fascinating in the way the Irish
mysteriously are, brought up on Quaker tenets and conforming
without understanding what is implied?

Concentration, in the gentle, diffused light of lamps and
afterglow in competition, was easier than in this morning's
livid storm-light. Presently he vanished, from sight and from
memory.

If the hymn-books had not been insufficient for the crowded
meeting, the old lady would have had one to herself and Miss
Roscorla, too, would not have been sharing, head turned in the
direction of her brother, with her neighbour. And if someone

had not selected from the strange collection, apparently compiled from the hymn-books of every denomination, one of the
few Ancient and Modern, Richard, when he looked round,
would have seen me peering for the words in the badly printed
little book.

The decrepit harmonium, incredibly wheezing out the tune
beloved from childhood, sent me back to All Saints' on summer
Sunday evenings when the altar flowers, massed beneath the
neat unwavering flames of the high tapers, drew into one's
mind the bliss of to-morrow, its flowers and sunlight, waiting,
so near at hand. The familiar words returned, no longer a
mere filling, whose meaning remained unnoticed, for the lovely
little tune, but real, winged, bearing one up. So that when
impossibly he turned, the scene was set for him in a way no
cunning contrivance could have bettered. The young woman,
holding the shared book so that the frail old eyes could comfortably follow the words, stood upright in the becoming glow
of a near lamp, singing, from memory, with all her heart;
arresting what might have appeared as a casual sweeping glance
directed towards his people, part of a movement permitted by
the general upheaval of the meeting for song.

And without turning my raised eyes, to which at that moment
everything ahead although unseen was clearly visible, I was
aware, turned to follow his gaze, of the faces of the village girls
in the row behind him, and that of his sister, she also, turned
upon me to inquire. It was only for an instant that his eyes
rested, showing, as clearly as if I were looking directly into
them, a calm grave scrutiny, determined, careless of onlookers.
For an eternity during which everything vanished, leaving us
alone in space.

In eternal life.

Here, amongst the Roscorlas, the sense of everlastingness is
about one all the time. And the sense of indestructible individuality. With any one of them, such a moment would be
possible; though without the marvellous sense of support and
earthly security.

It is true. Such an experience is possible in relation to
Rachel Mary. When we are together, we are conscious mainly

of each other, of something unchanging and trustworthy far
away within the personal depths. Such a moment, with man
or woman, is a spiritual experience, moving body and soul.

What ought I to do? Tell these folks I am not what I seem,
am, from their point of view, a wolf in sheep's clothing?

Richard is not a child. With all his simplicity, he is more
worldly than the others, broken, as Rachel Mary hinted, by
some great unhappiness, capable of a measure of understanding.

CHAPTER VIII

SETTING down the pail with a business-like bang upon the grimed floor of the little summer-house and rolling up her sleeves, Miriam felt herself a companion of Eliza and wondered how far the girl realized the wealth and security of her situation. Year in, year out, amidst scenes of inexhaustible ever-changing loveliness, with no responsibility beyond the creation of cleanliness, she shared the zestful, varied life of the household.

'She's nothing but a slap-cabbage.' Whoever was thus contemptuously disposed of, Miss Roscorla made no comment and the girl, when Miriam reached the interior of the kitchen, was still volubly talking, filling with her voice the room in which she was so fully at home, bustling about, supported by and obviously revelling in the confusion all about her of piled breakfast things, vegetables brought in fresh and dewy from the garden and the preparation, upon one half of the large table, for a tremendous jam-making; delighting, too, in the quiet presence of Miss Roscorla, in pouring forth to her as she worked, in being youth to her middle age and in knowing herself immensely important and valuable.

'I'll get there, soon's we've finished this afternoon, and if they don't like me without me best dress, they can look at something else.' And she vanished, with hurried footsteps, but dancingly, with the poise belonging to consciousness of recognized ability, into the back kitchen.

'I want, Aunt Mary, a pail; and a scrubbing-brush.'

Coming forward to meet Miriam in the middle of the vast kitchen floor, she stood there smiling, at leisure, rubbing her little hands together in the manner of one who says, 'Well, and what can I do for *you*?' as if to shelter their meeting in this very public thoroughfare, by giving to it, in the eyes of witnesses, even if these should be only their surface selves, the air of important business, while she sent forth, standing so near that Miriam felt it enfold her like an embrace, the all-obliterating smile that carried with it herself and her resources.

'You shall have them,' she said, and stood there, at ease and available, ignoring her clamorous surrounds and also, for the moment, the unexpected demand, in favour of this momentary isolation of their two selves, their brief common past and the brightly hovering future gathered so richly together, here, at the busiest centre of the homestead.

Longing to hug her, aware that the time had not yet come, unable to project into her own eyes enough of her inward self to respond to Rachel Mary's fullness of expression, Miriam swung her arms into the air, making of them a broken arch above the little figure.   'What,' she cried, 'ARE you doing ?' And poured down towards the upturned, smiling face the joy irradiating her as she realized the intensification, in standing thus closely confronted, of the promise of to-day and of the memories, heaped in rich confusion upon the background of her consciousness, of the days lived through under this beloved roof.

'All sorts of little odd jobs,' chuckled Miss Roscorla and still held her place.

'There was an earwig,' she began, dropping her arms and watching lively childlike interest dawn in the face before her, and heard heavy, firm footsteps, approach along the garden path towards the door of the back kitchen.

'Ah, well, the earwig can wait,' she said, 'and I 'll come back in a minute for the pail and brush.   I 'm going,' she mouthed voicelessly, under the shelter of Eliza's voice promising Richard his cleaned boots sooner than he would be ready for them, 'to scrub, if you don't mind, the summer-house and sit in it.'

'Don't tire thyself.'

Escaping along the passage, and through the open alcove door, skimming down the sitting-room and out into the green-house within whose moist warm air, faintly flavoured with whitewash, mosquitoes sang and ripening peaches spread their increasing perfume, she still felt upon her burning cheek, fallen there just as Richard appeared framed in the doorway at the kitchen's further end, the affectionate touch of Rachel Mary's toil-roughened finger.

The delight of being a postulant Eliza, triumphant in the kingdom of cleansing wherewith all other things were given, was already losing its power. Her desire to inhabit this remote dilapidated little interior, dawning the moment she had looked in upon its dust-smothered ivy and festoons of spiders' webs, returned in strength to demolish the enterprise of achieving cleanliness for its own sake. There was comfort, shared and happy, in seeing the dust of years move out into the open, into its rightful place, to proceed there, refreshed by dew and rain, once more upon its own adventure. And comfort mingled with solicitude in seeing startled spiders scamper away to weave fresh webs elsewhere. But now that the wooden seat was clean and the webs that hung too near were brushed away, enough was done. The enclosure, habitable, still retained its appearance of untouched security and its peace, dwelling there so long alone and now to have an undisturbing guest.

Making her way up through the house in search of writing materials and the rickety little bedside table upon which presently would fall the garden light coming in through the ivy-draped entrance, she found it suddenly, strangely, aloof, an unknown dwelling-place wherein she was a stranger. A shaft of sunlight falling through the skylight upon the upper landing brought back all that Amabel had drawn from her and shaped and set up and rapturously blessed: a tale told long ago of someone who was not quite herself.

Coming back along the deserted landing, feeling her way step by step down the stairs that were hidden by the projecting table whose tilted top held, precariously slanted, all she needed for the newly acquired workroom, she found herself once more closely besieged, moving thus slowly through the silent, evocative house, by memories of moments wherein the whole of her being had been caught up. Holding them off, helped by the sense of traversing a public highway, she went forward step by step until the hall was reached and, with the sound of distant voices, the full security of public life.

To escape encounter, she carried her burden through the

little hall sitting-room and out across the sheltered space created by the shadow of the huge dark tree. Here memory vanished and her lonely purpose filled all the future. But in the sunlit neutral territory around the unfrequented little summer-house, the past returned with the full power of the independent life given to it by Michael and Amabel.

Until Michael's coming, the moments now once more assailing her had stood, whenever she was alone, motionless upon every horizon, asking questions; provisionally. Without learning of their existence, Michael had made them move, and had begun to answer some of their questions. Bringing to mind workaday London and, with his dingy office clothes and the grime accumulated upon his person during a morning in the city followed by a railway journey, the very odour of London's summer streets, he had startled into active being, during those moments of piloting his pathetically incongruous figure from the meadow-girdled railway station to the carrier's wholesomely dusty little omnibus, her nascent determination to escape at all costs from gloom and grime. His two days of lyrical enthusiasm for his surroundings, which in the course of a single week would have given place to an impatient longing for libraries and a rich provision of newspapers, expressed only the satisfaction of a hunger town life could not satisfy. But his instant appreciation of the Roscorlas—'There is something in this Celtic nature far outdoing the character of simple English types; *most*-subtle in its charm. But still, well, I can still say, with the reservations of which already you know, *good* old Johnny Bull'—was indestructible.

It must have been from her bedroom window in the wing that Rachel Mary had witnessed the little scene she had described so gently after he had gone. Overnight, Michael had cast his spell upon them. Sitting there in their soft lamplight, glowingly beautiful, delighting them with his rich dignity and simplicity. Revealing to them, even while he told his little anecdotes and asked his naïve, direct questions, the reserves of intellectual force speaking independently from brow and eyes. Bringing them fresh experience in his reading of the psalm. Not the pensive, devout recital of an ancient text embodying

permanent truths, but the passionate intoning of a poem, so
that it seemed an improvisation, carrying the tide of the
reader's current emotion.

Looking from her window, early on Sunday morning before
any one was about, Rachel Mary had seen 'Mr Shatov' out on
the dewy lawn alone, believing himself unobserved . . .
dancing. A lonely little Jew, jigging about on her lawn,
solemnly, clumsily, and yet with an appealing grace, the heavy
bulk of his body redeemed by the noble head, face uplifted to
the sky, beard-point extended in the alien Sussex air; rejoicing
before the Lord, with the tablets of the Law invisibly held
within his swaying arms. Was it because she saw me so nearly
weeping that tears rose in her eyes also, behind the glint of
amusement? Did she see his pathos?

Amabel, too, had won her. 'She's a proper Irishwoman;
broad-shouldered, and she knows how to laugh.' Nostalgia,
felt throughout half a lifetime amongst the chill, unresponsive
English? Yet all the time, and although there was so much
space indoors and out to whirl about in and fill with her laughter,
Amabel had seemed confined. Without having been told in
advance of the vastness in every direction of the outdoor scene,
without being asked to admire, she had begun by seeming to
ignore and then had judged it. 'How,' she had murmured
dreamily, 'can any one *exist* in the country without servants
and a carriage?'

In face of the picture she called up, of a country life wherein,
upon a taken-for-granted background of undisturbing and
subservient natural beauty, leisurely people of a single class
have easy access to each other, both bustling Eliza and the
family coach ceased to exist. Beyond that one remark she
made no comment, said no word about the Roscorlas, kept me
ceaselessly in London, living through the events of her last
days in the tea-shop—drawing belated exoneration from knowing that at last she, too, knew what it was to feel broken at the
end of the day's work and, in the morning, still broken, longing
only for cessation and stillness. 'You must have *hated* me, my
dear, when I used to sail in to wake and make you talk at five
o'clock'—hearing of her fate at the hands of her family, even

the adoring Indian brother, foiled of his desire to launch her
in the only world he knew, sitting down within its still high-
walled security to cast her off with a single phrase; really
believing he would rather see her dead than married to a Jew.
And the group at home, made up of his counterparts, their
unconsidered immunity partly resting upon exploitation of the
country wherein he was so prominent a figure, repudiating,
banishing her for life, not because she proposed to change her
religion but because she was placing herself, socially, outside
the pale.

She had recounted it all, had seemed sincerely to regard it,
as a farce playing itself out in the background of the scene
whereon she made her preparations for triumphant emergence
as a Jewish matron.

Just as she was leaving: 'Mira! He's a *darling*! You'll
be utterly happy.'

'Then they don't make you want to fly for your life?'

Laughter, carrying off thought or its absence; carrying off
the excitement of her return to her own centre.

And through the sound of her laughter I looked ahead, to see
and state for her the worst of what I saw.

'You see, Babinka, I make mean calculations. On one
side, I should *live* upon the people occasionally turning up
who more or less think and read—I mean beyond *Mrs
Wiggs of the Cabbage Patch* and Longfellow—and wouldn't
be embarrassed by free discussion of ideas. You see although,
now, I'd sooner confess to a mermaid's tail than to any sort
of mind, I found myself *making* these calculations. You
see? *Now*-then.'

She hesitated, and there rushed into my mind those many
pictures of a Richard she had not seen. Richard tending his
sick mother, and, when I strained my ankle, spending all his
leisure in keeping me entertained, reading Longfellow, playing
spelicans, and winning with the inconceivable delicacy of his
large rough hands, the hands that this morning steered the
earwig down, bit by bit through carefully folded pleats in my
muslin sleeve until it fell upon the ground. Richard wanted
in the village, whenever there was trouble.

'No, Mira. . . . There's only one thing I couldn't stand. My God, those *awful* silences!'

And she glared, reminiscently, and as if into the face of some ultimate horror, into space, standing there on the step of the omnibus, her visit safely over; restored to me, unique, irreplaceable, removing with the *strength* of her repudiation of what most attracted me, my last doubt.

'I'm going to *hit* Mike, as soon as I get back, as *hard* as I can punch.'

And I went back and found Rachel Mary waiting where we had left her, paying tribute, by remaining there unoccupied and by the radiance of her welcome, both to the departed Amabel and to our restoration to each other. It was as though the forty-eight hours had been a week. We knew, now, that the gap was closed, that we had grown, during the long scattering of concentration, nearer to each other. For a moment we were silent. No embarrassment. No need for speech. And when I carolled 'It's so nice to have friends, so nice when they come and so nice when they go,' she tinkled appreciatively. But when I risked telling her the story of the hard punch, feeling as I spoke that she was listening to the sound of my voice addressed to her alone, as well as for the distant sound of Amabel, she spoke eagerly, without weighing her words, glowing with delighted approval that seemed glad to escape: 'She's a proper Irishwoman . . .'

And they stood alone, Rachel Mary and Amabel, so strangely assorted; in league.

Here, amidst the dust-filmed ivy leaves and the odour of damp, decaying wood, was the centre of her life. The rickety little table was one now with its predecessors, the ink-stained table under the attic roof at Tansley Street, first made sacred by the experience of setting marginal commentaries upon Lahitte's bombastic outpourings; and the little proud new bureau at Flaxman's, joy for her eyes from the moment of its installation, new joy each day when morning burnished its brass candlesticks and cast upon its surface reflected pools of light;

and, later, depth, an enveloping presence in whose company alone, with an article for George Taylor being written on the extended flap, she could escape both the unanswerable challenge of the strident court and the pervading presence of Selina, and becoming, when it went back with her to Tansley Street, the permanent reminder amongst easy and fluctuating felicities, of one that remained, so long as its prices were faithfully paid, both secure and unfathomable.

The ancient summer-house, again a visible surrounding, the private property of the Roscorlas, strangers whose ways were not her ways, in whose domain she had pursued, for the whole morning, this alien occupation that had banished them to the ends of the earth, to return now, bearing with them a challenge she had no strength to meet. Soon she must join them, convalescent, too weary to play her established part. Weariness might be explained. Already they had had a writer beneath their roof. But he had been a bird of passage, uninvolved, remaining apart. Finding here, surrounded by purposeful, unimpinging activities, a peaceful, romantic perching place. His preoccupation known in advance, he had not arrived and been accepted in one guise and then suddenly presented himself in another.

And there was nothing, in this mass of hurriedly written pages, to justify the havoc-working confession. They represented a chase, soon grown conscious of its own futility, after something concealed within the impulse that had set her down to write, bringing fatigue and wrath over her failure to materialize it in the narrative whose style was worse than that of the worst books of this kind. These tracts of narrative were somehow false, a sort of throwing of dust that still would be dust even if its grains could be transformed to gold; question-begging, skating along surfaces to a superficial finality, gratuitously, in no matter what tone of voice, offered as a conclusion.

Perhaps if she put it away and forgot it, it might one day be transformable into something alive all over, like the best of the articles for George Taylor, interesting to write and to read apart from the idea being handled, and best in those parts that ran away from the idea and had to be forcibly twisted back until they pointed towards it, or cut down to avoid the emergence of a contradictory idea.

Bob Greville. It was Bob, driving so long ago a little nail into her mind when he said, 'Write the confessions of a modern woman,' meaning a sensational chronicle with an eye, several eyes, upon the interest of sympathetic readers like himself— 'Woman, life's heroine, the dear, exasperating creature'—who really likes to see how life looks from the other side, the women's side, who put me on the wrong track and created all those lifeless pages. Following them up, everything would be left out that is always there, preceding and accompanying and surviving the drama of human relationships; the reality from which people move away as soon as they closely approach and expect each other to be all in all.

CHAPTER IX

ENCOMPASSED by the sound of Rachel Mary's voice, the future lost its power of putting unanswerable questions. In her presence was fullness of joy; in a new silence. Eloquent of her desire, pressing somewhere far away beneath the sense of companionship born of investigation of each other's point of view, to make, if the way should open, the ever-hovering communication, that yet, shining from her face and sounding in every word she spoke, need not be made.

Pausing, Rachel Mary called her attention to a dragon-fly, 'the devil's darning needle,' shuttling from point to point above the sunlit stream. Irradiating the universe.

A noisy old perambulator, pushed by a labouring man, rattled across the end of the lane. Raised by the sound, their two pairs of eyes were watching the aperture. No one else appeared. The man was alone.

'Now that,' said Rachel Mary, 'is a thing you'd never see in Ireland.' Pride sounded in her voice, approval of the ways of the country of her birth. Disapproval of the sight she had just witnessed?

'Irishmen,' asked Miriam, sensing in advance the reply that spread the flat landscape, opening as they approached the mouth of the high-hedged lane, drearily from end to end of the world, 'are contemptuous of women and what are called women's jobs?'

After a more than usually prolonged Quakerly pause, 'I think,' said Rachel Mary, 'there's a little contempt.' Her voice was uncertain, her eyes downcast. She had spoken the truth. Regretfully?

Abandoning the stricken landscape, Miriam departed on a mental tour. Picture after picture emerged from the past, sources of the deposits of convincing statement any one of which, she felt sure, remembering her own release as the light went up, now here, now there, until the pattern of thought stood clear, would appeal to Rachel Mary. But the deposits, so long neglected, had lost their first lustre and become, save for a word here and a phrase there, indecipherable. Home was approaching, clouded over, and there was no time for anecdote and exposition.

'Queer,' she said, catching at the first handy fragment, and aware of her companion's face turned, swiftly, expectantly, and saw, beyond the single projected statement, the way to a small clear line of thought, not the best of the evidence, but able to keep the matter within the safe borders of generalization, 'how men *fear* to lose caste, seem to be nothing, most of them, apart from what they *do*. Perhaps fear accounts for their contempt?'

'Well, I shouldn't exactly call it *fear*.'

'Ignorance?'

'Perhaps sometimes there may be a little ignorance.' She *had* a stop in her mind in regard to masculine assumptions, but in her selfless life had never paused to put it into words.

'Well, you know, nowadays, men are being challenged out of their own mouths, by their own researches. Science is beginning to say that when of the two parents the father is the stronger character, the family will contain more girls than boys. Well, there is your large army of brothers and my little army, four, one died in infancy, of sisters. I don't know, of course, which of your parents was the stronger, but my father, at any rate mentally and nervously, was vastly stronger than my mother. Whose life was saddened by his scepticism. Which frightened her because she had an unbounded respect for his mind and did not realize how much it was formed and led by the sayings of eminent men of the moment. Now listen, Rachel Mary. If science is right in this account of the proportions of the sexes, then, since there are always more male than female births, women carry the palm. Of course science may presently cancel this theory. Meantime there is a fact that points the same way, although it is always, even by scientific people, called inexplicable, or, which is the same thing, a

mysterious provision of nature. In the period succeeding a
war, during which thousands of men are killed, the percentage
of male births goes *up*. Which, if their theory is right, is what
might be expected and not at all mysterious or to be laid to
the account of nature's wisdom. You see? The best men,
especially where there is conscription, what is called the flower
of the nation's manhood, is wiped out, the daughter-producing
party is diminished, and there will be a larger percentage of
sons than ever. You see?'

After a moment's thought, she turned with her adoring smile.
Its departure left her face clouded. One of those rare women,
the salt of the earth, she judged silently. While every century
rings with the voices of men, of all sorts, complacently bellowing
their judgments of women. She was *troubled* by masculine
pretensions, but would sooner die than complain.

'While *we* do' . . . her voice had tailed away, and then,
after a pause, had murmured indifferently, as if they were not
worth naming: 'the little jobs.'

Standing small on the meeting-house platform, her little
muffin hat askew unawares, she had looked so sweet. And so
fierce as she described one by one the horrors of the drunkard's
home, witnessed during her missionary years in London.
'Terrible, isn't it?' Rhetorical pause, and then, still sweetly
fierce, 'But that's not the worst.' Going wherever she was
called, shielded by her little grey cloak and bonnet, she had seen
life 'in the raw.' Had passed through terror. In that moment
of becoming aware, after she had helped the woman through
her dying and closed her eyes, of the human vultures all about
her, waiting. 'Putting up a prayer,' looking round to find,
standing in the doorway, her tallest brother and the policemen
who had fetched him on seeing her enter the alley into which
they ventured only in couples.

And then, her chosen work given up altogether, and *all* her
time given to her brothers. 'My brethren had need of me.'

'You have built your whole life into the lives of your
brothers,' said Miriam meditatively, taking in, bit by bit,
what daily through the years this must have meant, 'and they
are not even aware of it.'

Herself overwhelmed, she looked round at the little figure plodding along at her side, making the ground holy, and saw that Rachel Mary's eyes were full of tears.

In a moment, her self-command regained, she was speaking again: 'I don't think I 've ever told you I 'm fond of music'— then the thunderings of Beethoven, and the gaieties and intensities of the Chopin waltzes and nocturnes, had reached her, sounding down through the open sitting-room window to her kitchen in the wing, as something more than an alien noise? Her voice had been low-toned, confessional, but now, in deploring the leaving of this love untaught and in describing the change in the attitude of Friends that had come too late to affect her own upbringing, she spoke cheerfully in her usual tone.

Recalling the young women met at quarterly meeting, comparing them with Rachel Mary, Miriam wondered. In being submitted to the whole of secular culture, they had lost something that only Puritanism can supply? Brisk and tolerant, entirely out-turned, they seemed without depth; too sure of themselves.

'I 've never had a musical sister-in-law,' said Rachel Mary, and looked away across the hedge on her further side and paused, as though awaiting, to a remark addressed to it alone, an answer from the landscape. 'I have always wanted one,' she added gently.

Soundlessly, in the deep hush created by the low-toned confession, the heights and deeps of the long weeks, showing now as a brief period in Rachel Mary's life, unremarkable and, in their essence, not to be distinguished from any other group of weeks, were swept away. Ahead, vanishing into the far distance, lay an untellable number of days as level as the marshes now come into view beyond the low hedge as they climbed the rise. Directing towards these days her hitherto averted eyes, Rachel Mary had also revealed their bleakness, lit and warmed only by the glow of a confessed alliance; a hidden bond of mutual love and support.

CHAPTER X

MR MAYNE, bringing his deck chair across the lawn. For more talk. To get the whole point of view set up and look at it, quietly and undisturbed. At the argumentative age, yet seeking truth rather than the opportunity to score a point. A Quaker, with a difference. A Quaker intellectual, having a free edge that escaped the circle down here? Yet they all liked him, presenting him a little eagerly, in advance of his arrival, as pitiful with his poor health, and fortunate, therefore, in being well off, and then, proudly and unanimously, as something of a wonder. Coming innocently across the lawn, eager for talk, he knew nothing of the havoc he had wrought.

Trying to remember what had led up to yesterday's fatal remark, she recalled the general pleasantness of the atmosphere during those last moments before she became for them a kind of monster, the satisfaction radiating from all quarters of the table as she talked with the formidable guest; feeling at first glad to be able to help them in the business of entertaining him, and presently a half-impatient interest in his mental equipment.

'The difference between trade and commerce.' Happy ground, since it was the early Quakers, who, while still the ancient chaffering went on, had asked one price and refused to bargain, creating a new world in trade and gaining the trust even of those who would trust nobody. A pleasant moment, bringing the sense of sharing with the descendants of those who had brought it about, the contemplation of a beneficent revolution.

And while he began to consider this difference, sitting with bent head and an air of suspended judgment, and the others, hearing the comparison between trade and commerce for the first time, waited for some kind of elucidation, she had been invaded by thoughts of the Stock Exchange, the 'capture of markets' that meant ruin for those who lost them, and had remembered the glowing face of Philip Wicksteed as he held forth about the iniquity of dealing in money until he had made her know that so as long as any one was starving it was wrong to have even a post office account; a mean little nest-egg.

'Money ought not to be saved.'

Only that. Just an encircling statement for him to think over. And even as she spoke there had dawned at the back of her mind a picture that challenged Wicksteed's caricature.

Ensconced in meditation, Mayne had not noticed the quality of the stillness about the table. Its lively disapproval had reached and wakened her with the force of a blow. Full realization of enormity had come before she looked up to see the flush upon Alfred's pale face, Rachel Mary's discomposure, Richard stern and stormy, with clamped lips. All eyes averted, save those of Mrs Roscorla, whose wide depths, as they gazed across the table, held hatred as well as scorn.

Yet only last night, when, stimulated by the visitor's presence and reunited by his early departure to his room, they had all sat talking together in the little back sitting-room and young Benson, speaking irrelevantly from the midst of his own thoughts, had suddenly said, 'I'd love to see Miss Henderson meet Joseph Judd, I wonder what she'd do,' Rachel Mary had replied triumphantly, in almost ringing tones: 'I'll tell you. She'd look—*straight*overishead.'

Perhaps the damage done by her insane remark was less than she feared.

'I like this tree better than the one in the front garden.'

Under the eye of Alfred making, more slowly than usual, his way down the path, looking across as he went, Mr Mayne unfolded and set up his chair near enough to her own to share the shadow of the chestnut.

'That front one is an evergreen oak, a most queer tree. It sheds its leaves in the summer, making a litter when everything else is more or less tidy.'

Richard's description of the habits of the dark tree, no longer just heightening her objection to it, became a piece of country

lore, part of her reapings during the weeks that had translated
and built her into the life down here and that now appeared as
a wealth of knowledge qualifying her to be, in relation to this
urban young man, a faint shadow of the departed Richard, for
whose absence life had punctually provided compensation,
a brief return to the world whose inhabitants spend their
leisure in discussion.

Departing this morning, unseen, by the early omnibus,
Richard had carried away with him, if indeed, escaping from
home, he should cast any backward glance, the picture of
herself unveiled, innocently revealed by this young man who
now sat so confidently at her side, as a young lady with the
most extree-ordinary ideas. By this time he was already
settled in London, deep in the suburban home of the younger
married brother, deploying his charms, bearing himself in his
light, pleased way, belonging to no one, never coming quite
forth from where he lived and suffered alone.

Bereft of his presence, so all-pervading and so comforting
that even the very worst of the local disasters lost, once they
were confided to him, their first power, the two villages and
the surrounding country became one with their further neighbours, subject to a fatality that no one had the power to redeem,
seen by this young man as a charming bit, amongst many other
charming bits, of Sussex.

'It throws a darkness.'

'Like all evergreens. I don't like them, don't want green
all the year round. Bare trees let in light, besides being in
themselves so lovely.'

'It's a lovely old homestead.'

'"So odious and so dear." Do you read Emerson?' The
quotation, slipped out unawares, brought vividly back the
scene from which it was inseparable: the evening light falling
wide through the window of the little hall sitting-room upon
the figure of Rachel Mary darning socks, lingering, because
the reading held her interest, far beyond the time for preparing
supper. Richard, his cleaned gun propped in the corner
behind him, sitting further from the light, with crossed legs
and Quakerly hands set one upon the other on the topmost

knee, listening, his face in shadow. Lifted, as the page was turned upon this phrase, revealing him at first startled by the strangely mated words and then, as they lanced the blind abscess of his unacknowledged thought, uneasy, stretching forth a hand, as the reading went on, to touch and shift the cleaning rags left upon the corner of the table; carrying off his discomfiture.

'I know some of the essays, but I 've not met that. Does he really put it so?'

'He was probably middle-aged when he wrote that. Youth, desiring only freedom, does not yet know that home is dear. What struck me, when I first encountered it, was the increased power of the contrasted adjectives. Not having for years given any thought to any kind of home and lumping all homes together as prisons, my interest was purely academic. And I imagined that the dear was thrown in with the odious to make an effective statement. It would have greatly surprised me to discover that the Emerson I knew should find home *dear*.'

'I think I don't quite realize Emerson as a person.'

'A poet, and a mystic. Also a man. And fair-haired. That is important. The fair-haired people invented scepticism. Philosophical scepticism. Philosophy of cut-off-from-the-roots *ideas*.'

'*Do* explain a little.' Rather like the intonation of Cambridge Vereker.

'The Westerns.'

'Ah, I see what you mean.'

'Particularist. Vikings. Not the Latins. Whose scepticism is quite different. Formal and jocular. By the way, I 've seen a man, who may be said to have a happy home of which he is the pride, react to "odious and dear." A masculine reaction. Secret. I have shared it, again and again, in the presence of unsuspecting wives.'

'You believe most homes are not happy, most married people that is to say?'

'Even when they are, I am sure they all stand in their own light, in a way that is perfectly preventible. In a single, frightfully important, disregarded detail. Which perhaps may

be the origin of épergnes and other high centrepieces. Have
you ever been made uncomfortable by the efforts of a quite
nice husband to avoid meeting his equally nice wife's eye across
the table, or even to avoid seeing her there? In restaurants,
it is even more striking. The two come in, exhilarated, out
for the evening, both enjoying the sense of escape from home
into the wide world. They sit down, at a small table, confronted, with each other as the sole immediate prospect—
obstructive. Even if they are on the best of terms, you will
see the man glance here and there, anywhere to avoid the sight
of his wife, the compendium of dailiness—you remember
Kipling: "the same, same face of my wife"? If they are not,
the spectacle of the man's angry embarrassment is most painful,
and the woman's efforts to conceal from surrounding humanity
the true state of affairs, quite horrible to contemplate. *Why*,
that is what I ceaselessly want to know, do *all* these people,
either at home or abroad, sit *confronted*? And not only engaged
couples and husbands and wives. Think of the amount of
happiness needlessly destroyed by the construction of our
trains and omnibuses. It is not only because they are comfortable that corner seats are so popular, but because they
afford a partial escape from gimlets. Everywhere, people
should be side by side, facing the spectacle, meeting in it.
Confronted people can't meet more than once, you know.'
   'I think that is true, though I have never put it to myself
in that way.'
   A steady swishing, away behind. Someone cutting the
hedge. She wondered, as their talk moved from point to
point, who was the invisible auditor of this resuscitation of
forgotten interests. In every direction the young man's standards seemed to be aesthetic. These younger Quakers were
more interested in arts and crafts than in ethics?
   Eliza, advancing down the lawn, crying out from a distance.
The carrier, a package, something to pay.
   Left alone, she listened to the swish, swish of the hedge-
cutter, a busy accompaniment to the lazy, ceaseless coo-rooing
of the doves, and heard it cease. A moment later, pushing a
barrow of weeds, Alfred Roscorla came through the gap in the

hedge, turning the barrow as if to cross the lawn immediately in front of her. Why, with the dump behind the duck-run close to where he had been working, take his refuse on such a long tour?

Pulling up just short of her chair, 'It 'll be near dinner-time, I reckon,' he said, dropping the handles. Never before, though she had spent a part of almost every morning beneath the chestnut tree, had he paid her a call.

'Warm work,' she said as he mopped his brow.

'It is that,' said Alfred with his smile, eyes downcast, that seemed never to appear save at his own expense. 'I reckon it 's near dinner-time,' and he glanced up at the sky.

'I wish I could tell the time by the sun. So much nicer than consulting a watch.'

'You can generally tell to near a minute or two.' Returning his handkerchief to its place, he glanced away down the garden. Looking for a topic?

'What a pity all that lovely stuff has to be cut down. The fool's parsley, I mean. I 've been revelling in those great level plates of bloom standing nearly as high as the hedge. Or is it sheep's parsley? I once heard the smallest kind called Queen Elizabeth's lace.'

'That 's a pretty enough name. Cow-parsley, we call this.'

'I like wild flowers better than the garden ones.'

'There 's some do, I know. That 's all very well, if you don't happen to be in business. That 's making seed, that cow-parsley. We can't have it spread all over.'

Pausing, he stood there with downcast eyes. Waiting for the talk to go on. Alfred, who never spoke more than the necessary words. Who knew the deepest truths.

Hanging impatiently about while, half an hour after he had asked her to be ready, he lashed the last pots of geraniums to the rack of the high-piled wagonette. Seeing in advance the enchanted day. The drive through the leafy lanes and out across the sunlit marshes amongst fierce roaming cattle recalling the story of the cyclists riding home from the coast after dark, racing, heads down, ahead of the thundering hoofs. Richard, riding behind, keeping the beasts at bay with his waved bicycle lamp.　And the lore of the lonely Looker in his hut on the far side of the marshes, and his belief that one day the sea would come back to claim its scattered pebbles and cockle-shells. The emergence at last upon the deserted coast road, and the sea; sandwich - munching whilst Trustworthy strolled with loosened rein along past the martello towers squatting amongst clumped sea lavender and yellow horned poppies. Alfred's brief disjointed responses to scattered outpourings. The approach, with world beyond world left behind, of the sophisticated little town. The afternoon alone, while Alfred did his rounds, amidst blissful, pitiful fortnighters on the crowded front, facing the blue and gold of the summer sea. The pier, the sunbaked, dusty front full of glare and noise, seen from the pier, suddenly beautiful in the distance. Tea, flavourless, in one of those smart new tea-shops, all varnish and bright colour. Freshness arriving with the dropping of the sun and the coming of saffron and rose upon the rock pools. Waiting for Alfred in the little gaslit temperance inn on the outskirts. The pleasant security of sitting side by side with him, two sleepy adventurers facing the night coming in through the open door, frugally consuming gritty buns and flour - thickened mauve cocoa while Trustworthy tossed her bag outside. The drive out of the town and along the edge of the marsh-mist and up through it across the marshes where the seated cattle loomed like islets. The deep home lanes, lit by glow-worms. Suddenly remembering, on that first afternoon at the seaside, that one had ceased, ever since escaping from town, not only to smoke, but even to think of smoking. 'Friends don't smoke?' 'Well, there's some do. But you're not *used* the same way if you smoke.' You are no longer a clear, clean vessel?

He had been a witness, lately, of so many conversations, wanted to join, to have his share? Searching his face while she felt for a topic, she saw its muscles contract for his difficult speech and waited, ready to respond, even to the most uninspiring fragment, from depths in herself that Richard could never reach.

'I thought I'd tell you,' he stammered, and hesitated—what could be coming so to break up his half-averted face, that was fixed now in an expression wherein fear and anxiety stood mingled? His eyelids flickered up from eyes that flashed an uneasy half-glance in her direction on their way to the sycamore across the lawn, on which they came to rest as if what he was about to say stood placarded there. 'Our friend Luke Mayne's got a young lady. I thought I'd best tell you.'

'Oh, yes?' she murmured lamely, striking out into the ocean of bewilderment whose waves had closed over her head. If she knew Mayne was engaged, she would refrain from speaking to him, unless others were present? Or was Alfred heroically, yet not without private amusement, warning her not to lose her heart? But in the world where fiongsays are regarded as private property, and also as butts for unconsciously foul facetiousness, a world that perhaps, unawares, was now all about her, was she not set apart as 'walking out' with Richard, and therefore immune from such a danger?

'Well, I was wondering what she'd think, you see,' and he ducked his head as so often she had seen him do before the gales of affectionate family mirth at his expense, and gave vent to the helpless little chuckle with which he was wont to admit the onslaught justified. 'It'll be dinner-time, I'm thinking; I reckon I'd best be off.' Seizing the handles of his barrow, he wheeled it briskly away across the lawn.

What she'd think, if she saw you, an available, unappropriated, and therefore justifiably anxious and hopeful young woman, talking to her young man?

Richard—was a privileged person. To *his* goings-on, though they were to be deprecated, Alfred attached no importance.

With Richard still away, and Luke Mayne no longer at her side, the toil-roughened hands of Alfred and the pupil, seen moving amongst the things on the spread table, had a new beauty. They alone kept her world about her in peace and security.

CHAPTER XI

AT least the ducks should have daily with their mashed meal this well-loved and all too rare addition costing nothing but labour and helping to keep the gardens clear of weeds. Strolling in the deserted domain alight with the glow of sunset, going from point to point in search of the best growths, she gathered the nettle-tops, joyfully, her hands safe in their leather gloves. When she passed their run with her high-piled pannier, the ducks gathered quacking, aware of her burden, eager, dull-eyed for lack of water, the tormenting lack supposed to forward their cruel fattening.

The last ray of the setting sun lay red upon the inside wall of the potting-shed, a living presence.

Passing in masses through the chaff-cutter, the crushed nettles gave forth their odour, delicately potent, prevailing over the familiar odour of shut-in sun-baked straw and dust. This nettle scent was in league with the open, with the ray now fading from the rough grain of the ancient wood. Watching until it was no longer there, she came out from the enclosed shadowy warmth into the clear shadowless light of evening, satisfied.

Rain chores softly down amongst lime leaves. Which bend to its touch. It whips the laurels and rebounds. Or slides swiftly off their varnished surfaces. Amongst beeches it makes a gentle rattling, a sound like the wind in the Dutch poplars. The hiss of strong rain on the full leafage of the wood. Its rich drip, drip, in the silent wood. The rising wind opening the tree-tops, sending down sudden sheets of light; like lightning.

Awake, deep down in the heart of tranquillity, drinking its

freshness like water from a spring brimming up amongst dark green leaves in a deep shadow heightening the colour of the leaves and the silver glint on the bubbling water. A sound, a little wailing voice far away across the marshes, dropping from note to note, five clear notes, and ceasing. This was the sound that brought me up from dreamless sleep? Again the little wailing sound, high and thin and threadlike and very far away. But so clear that it might be coming from the garden or from the deep furrows of the stubble-field beyond the hedge. It has come out of the sea, is wandering along the distant, desolate shore. Nothing between us but the fields and the width of the marshes. There it is again, leaving the shore, roaming along the margin of the marsh, in and out amongst the sedges, plaintive.

It has reached the grey willows huddled along the dykes. Shrill and querulous amongst their slender leaves.

Many voices, approaching, borne on an undertone, shouting and moaning, dying away into lamentations. Reaching the hedgerows, filling them with a deep singing. The evergreen oak quivers under the threatening breath, harplike in all its burdened branches. Stillness.

Tumult, wild from the sea, sweeping headlong, gigantic, seizing the house with a yell, shaking it, sending around it the roaring of fierce flames. Rattling the windows, bellowing down the chimney. Rejoicing in its prey.

The wind, is the best lover.

Things had come so near. Even this dingy old evergreen oak, the least valued of her possessions, was individually beloved. Stretching up her arms to it in the last of the last twilight before his home-coming, she knew that she wished Richard would not return. Everything, since he left, had fallen to a new depth within her. Nothing disturbed this ceaseless communion. And the Sunday in the midst of these uninterrupted days had been the best of the Sundays. Concentration had never been so easy, nor the sense stronger, although that party of visiting Friends had altered the external aspect of morning meeting, of being in touch with fellow labourers.

If an opportunity offers, I must ask Rachel Mary this very evening, whether the impulse to speak is always accompanied by that amazing experience, seeming like a sudden touch upon one's inmost being, electric; discharging all round one just above the waist a zigzag so clearly felt as to call to mind, within the infinitesimal period of its duration, the illustrated advertisements of electric belts. So startling in its nature and so new, bringing the sense of being, for the fraction of a second, oneself the dynamic centre of advancing life, that it delayed the mind's descent into words and brought instead the shamed, thwarted feeling accompanying the missing of a ball at tennis. And the words, when finally they came, were spoken, while still one hesitated, by someone across the gangway. Exactly as Rachel Mary had said when explaining what happened if a Friend suppressed his message.

And it was on that same Sunday, in the midst of the Richard-less party supplemented by the visiting Friends, that I confessed what an eye-opener had been my one experience of a Friends' business meeting and declared that all the world's business should be transacted on similar lines, and Rachel Mary said, when they showed surprise in discovering me an outsider: 'She's a Friend in all but name.'

And at once I felt cooped, and wanted them gone, these Saxon Friends who seemed to miss something the Roscorlas did not miss, and my mind went back for a moment to life as it had been before Richard left. To the currant gathering, out on the slope under the dense, low sky. Not a moment to lose in the race with the storm. The copper glow shone out in the north when the basket was only half full, and then a faint stir and a moment's freshening of the sultry air and then stillness again and the mutual livid stare of earth and sky. The pile of fruit, chill in the leaf-lined trug, growing slowly. Heavy drops tapping the bushes and ceasing. The first pale flicker, making one put down the trug to free a second hand and gather, frantically. Presently a vivid streak, zigzagging, and a crash. The incessant dance of mad daylight all about one. The wheels of the storm rattling across the vault. The joy of finishing, of loading the basket before Richard arrived to race me up to the house where every one was assembled.

Early morning light filtering through the larch trees, lying across the globed peaches gleaming pale, cheek by cheek, gaining colour under the widening stream of day until they shone full as the hothouse sunlight had left them, rose-washed velvet, crimson fading into rose, rose into green, creamy purple blanching to pale primrose. Learning to lift them without pressure, to grade and pack them in their nests of cotton wool.

The auction at Wetherby's. The whole neighbourhood collected in the vast meadow round about Wetherby's extravagant outfit, still as good as new. The effort to forget oneself and one's interests in order to please Richard by being interested in slag-distributors, swath-turners and threshers, rib-rollers and reaper-and-binders. The longing to see and hear them at their work rather than lying there for horrible sale at the hands of the nimble-tongued auctioneer, inflaming acquisitiveness by distributing nips of gin. No one noticing the passage of the clouds, the ripening of the afternoon light; save perhaps those village girls hovering on the outskirts of the moving crowd.

Pride in Richard, everywhere greeted and welcomed, serene and steady where the others were muddled and basely excited. The pleased grin of the auctioneer when he made his only bid and the crowd thickened and drew close and the bids rapped out and up in quick succession. Richard, one foot upon the prize, elbow propped on the bent knee of his gaitered leg, bidding steadily until the new chain-harrow was his own.

CHAPTER XII

MORE than the light of the unscreened kitchen lamp, more than its warmth, filled this corner. With his say said and the mended satchel hanging from his hand, Richard still lingered. She was penned, between his obliterating presence and the figure of Rachel Mary standing close at hand, turned towards the little table busily occupied, but aware; waiting for a voice to sound, her own, or Richard's, gently, acknowledging and expressing, as it broke the silence fallen with one consent upon the three of them, the wealth of this shared embarrassment.

'We shall want any number of nose-bags,' she breathed, addressing the lamplit wall, half-prepared to see it miraculously open before her.

'Thee 'll be tired, Richard, with thee's journey and all.'

Turning she beheld the small figure confronting them, perilously propped against the edge of the larger table. Gone to her room after the supper she had stayed up to share in honour of Richard's return, uneasy, made uneasy by his wandering attention, his silences and random replies, she had come back, ancient and haggard, frail and tottering and determined; to watch and protect.

'We 'll need heaps of nose-bags,' said Richard, so gently that his tone could hardly have carried across the room, and moved nearer, so near that only a few inches divided them as they stood side by side facing the hapless little figure. Flouted. His mother, flouted and defied. Realization, throbbing in the air, keeping every one silent; deepening the golden glow.

'It 's been a very delightful day. I hope it has not tired thee overmuch.'

'Never shall I forget the sight of the blessed Bunny sitting on the ground with his legs solemnly inserted under the table-cloth, making mountain ranges between the plates.'

'It was his first picnic.'

Stretched at full length upon the hearth-rug in Rachel Mary's room with her hands clasped behind her head, Miriam felt the day come into its own with the descent at last of the stillness its crowded hours had failed to provide. Only those two moments alone with Richard. Needed all the time, playing the leading parts from the moment of the belated start until they were all packed into the wagonettes for the return. He had broken away to show her the horsetails, isolating her, standing apart with her, gathering and breaking a jointed stem, murmuring its age-old story, putting the gay little picnic in its place with his picture of this plant in its prime, a vast tree, almost the sole growth in the misty swamps wandered through by prehistoric monsters. And to show her sundew, its single starry bloom shining from the midst of the dark bog.

Trying to rouse herself, to recall, for the conversation Rachel Mary seemed to expect, the day's more impersonal incidents, she found the way barred. Happiness was upon her like a sleep, sharpening her perceptions, depriving her of the power of directing them. The figure of Rachel Mary moved about the room, dreamlike, approaching, receding, unreal and yet intimate, a part of her own being.

Rachel Mary was ready to go downstairs. Must break, now, this long, confessional silence. Was approaching, looking down, shedding upon one's recumbent form her deepest radiance.

Getting to her knees, Miriam spoke, swift breathless words coming as if dictated. 'Let me go,' she said, and her voice surprised her with its passionate pleading, 'send me away before it is too late.'

Bending, Rachel Mary dropped a kiss upon her cheek. 'I like,' she said, 'to see thee in that gown.'

CHAPTER XIII

'*Dew* not for*get* me,
Dew not for*get* me,
Sometaimes think of me *still*.'

The voice of London, wavering drunkenly up from the room below,

'*When* morning breaks,
And the thros-*sul* awakes,
Re-*mem*-ber the *mide* of the *mill*.'

Two voices this time, not quite together, sopranoing yearningly up to the final *dew* of the refrain.

'Wah. They 'll stop presently.'

'I don't mind them, I love them.'

'Mira! My God, how can we leave it all?'

The voices ceased, the house was still. Even the courtyard was now silent. Flaxman's courtyard, transformed by Amabel's presence. The moonlight fell across it uncontaminated, pouring in through the high uncurtained attic casement, patterning the little bed with its bars and with the shadows of Amabel's geraniums and lying white upon her upturned face. The evening had been a song of triumphant reunion. Reaching Donizetti's, whirling confidently in through the frosted door she had compelled herself to enter for the first time all those years ago faint with hunger and rigid with determination, she had seen only the risen figures of Michael and Amabel that presently were seated one on each side of her, hemming her in, delighting in her recovered presence and in a witness for their joy. Sitting thus between them in the dim little resort in the heart of London, she had felt herself more abundantly than in the Twopenny Tube, where every one had looked so pallid and ill-knit, a product of the woodlands and meadows.

'*Whatt* is this strange plant you wear?'

'Honesty.'

'Honesty, Mike! Mira's honesty.'

All the evening they had fêted her.

'You know, Mira, we find Emerson *trite*.'

Her first words, spoken hurriedly, the moment they were alone. So much for your Emerson, and Michael, who used so enormously to admire him, agrees with *me*. In place of your Michael, who has ceased to exist, another has come into being.

At first I was shocked, and too angry to retort, and then, since Amabel must be right, looking quietly back at Emerson, looking at his quality, while she took the parcels from the mad old landlady, for the first time fully in the face, I saw what she meant. Saw him disappear, his scholarly urbanity perpetually checking his poetic insight, keeping within decorous bounds what, unleashed, might have reached out to ecstasy.

And now this outcry calls me down and down to share the agony of the depths whence Amabel watches the disappearance of her world.

'Why can't we stay as we are forever?'

'I know.'

'Let's get away. Get up and go, you and me and all we have.'

'I know.'

Completeness of being. Side by side, silent, with the whole universe between us, within us, in a way no man and woman, be they never so well mated, can ever have. In a few hours, Amabel will be isolated, for life, with an alien consciousness.

Bright morning light, pouring in. Only a few moments ago, moonlit night had looked in upon a death. From the far side of the room the hollow snore of a tin kettle preparing to come to the boil high up in the air above a spirit-lamp on a wooden table. The voice of garret life, quickening every nerve. Too soon. Other voices were speaking upon the edge of one's sleep-cleared mind, demanding to be heard before one moved.

Emerson is luminous. Amiable, reasonable, humanistic; incomplete.

Far away in his own world where last night in talking of him to Amabel, one still had seemed to dwell, Richard stood remote, inaccessible. Inconceivable in the world whither during sleep one had been translated. Reduced to nothing. Indifferent. Apart from his surroundings, Richard is nothing to me?

The snoring of the kettle fell to a soft fierce hiss.

'Is that my breakfast?'

'Mira! Could you have said anything more perfect?' Folded arms pressed against her own arm lying, sleep-lightened, disembodied, outside the coverlet.

'*Mira!* Turn your face to the light. Let me look.' Amusement stood behind the horror in her voice but, behind the amusement, no preoccupations. The old, unappropriated Amabel was there, whole, in the centre of the moment.

'My dear, I *am* sorry. It's only a small one, but I wouldn't have had it happen for a peck of pearls. I hoped you'd escape.'

'Doesn't matter. An adventure.'

'My dear, she told me, poor old thing, just after I got here, that there might be a few. Oh, Mira, I am sorry. It's the mattress. She couldn't afford another. But she *told* me. *God*, I've been happy here!'

Up on her feet again, she was standing in the middle of the floor, looking at the perspectives the room recalled, sharp and clear beneath the shadow of parting. Farewell, farewell to youth. Recklessly she was plunging ahead, parting life's clumped and screening leafage, breaking through. Always and everywhere breaking through, serenely eager, eagerly serene, alive within each moment, alive to its meaning.

Detaching a hanging garment from its nail on the wall, she turned, holding it outspread.

'Look!'

Soft crêpe, pale dove-grey, little billows of white chiffon at neck and sleeves, held curtainwise, barè toes beneath, radiant face above, showing her lifted to a pinnacle of delight. Amabel's wedding gown, miraculously achieved. The right note, in all her incarnations, somehow miraculously achieved.

'Isn't it sweet? From Tony, designed by me. Tony's coming, my dear, to see me married. Can you believe it?'

The smart parson brother, relenting, separating himself
from the family to countenance the marriage, at a registry
office, of the family rebel to a foreign Jew.

For ever we shall be walking together, swinging our sponge-
bags, down the Euston Road in the morning light.
That little chuckle came from the attendant far away down
the deserted corridor. Pallid, inert even at the beginning of
her long day in the steamy heat, she had tolerated, since no one
was there to object to it, the unnecessary din echoing up to the
high roof. The wing of Amabel's bright spirit had brushed
and gained her as it swept by and now, seeing Amabel's sponge
soar up over the high partition, she chuckled her approval.

The large handsome face gleaming from the darkness behind
the bouquet spraying in through the low doorway was proud,
sacerdotal; but not dishonest. *Crack!*
'Oh, Tony, I'm so sorry! I ought to have warned you.'
No need to have made him climb the winding stair. Yet it
was good. The silencing, in his person, of the whole family
before the vision of Amabel, their lovely jewel, unashamed of
the setting to which they had condemned her and that now
was taking his eyes, as he stood for a moment rubbing his
outraged skull, upon an incredulous tour.
The mad old landlady, out on the pavement, out in the sunlight of yet another of her small store of remaining days, all
wild eyes and a curtsy for the grand gentleman and the unexpected coin, but paying tears for Amabel's kiss and the
flower recklessly torn from the bouquet's abundance.
Michael and Amabel side by side at a counter with an
aspidistra at its either end. Facing them from behind the
counter, a man with the manner, at once dignified and ingratiating, of an elderly shopwalker. Tony, large and decorative
in the mean enclosure, embarrassed, knowing, no more than
one did oneself, whether, during the preliminary moments, one
should speak in ordinary tones or, as in church, in subdued
murmurs.

CHAPTER XIV

'TICKETS,' announced the secretary, peering down the hall over the tops of his glasses, 'will be half a crown and two and six.' Realizing his mistake before the general laughter broke forth, he led it and sat down, beaming his delight. The old, cosy, family party atmosphere, so deprecated by Wells.

Now here was the man she had always wanted to hear and had somehow always missed and now was regarding with a detachment not far removed from indifference. No one henceforth could show her the socialist mind, whether scholarly and philosophical, poetic or witty, grown all over with the sweet herbs of kindliness or flaunting the proud red blossoms of righteous indignation, as anything but a desert, offering a fine view of a mirage, a promised land that in its turn would be revealed as desert too.

Nobility sat here, and faithfulness, unremitting, unembittered, side by side with bitterness and the desire for vengeance.

When this man's persuasive eloquence should have spent itself and those who held slightly different or altogether different conceptions of the best route towards the human commonwealth should have fired the bolts they were busily weighting and polishing, only a fragment of this last evening in town would remain to be got through. A touch on her arm, from behind. A protruded hand, holding a folded slip of paper. Turning, she saw only a stranger, his eyes fixed upon the lecturer.

'Are you alone? I have to catch the nine o'clock slip from Charing Cross. Perhaps we might leave together. Hypo.'

Looking round once more, she discovered him two rows away, already preparing to depart.

'I had no business to be there. Was at a loose end after Amabel's wedding. I'm sending in my resignation.'

'Wise Miriam. So am I. Retiring from futility.'

'Not so much futility as blindness. You see them as standing still, marking time. I feel they are marching, in increasing battalions, in the wrong direction.'

'What are you doing with yourself? Where are you hiding? Like you, I went to that old meeting to fill a spare hour. Was groaning under its emptiness, looked up and, behold, Miriam. That, you know, was pleasing.'

Strange that life's secret shape should select, of all people, Hypo to hear her first outpourings on Quakers and Quakerism. Meaningless, for him, the picture she was composing from material brimming in her mind, swiftly, urged by the pressure of the brief moments. Yet he seemed to attend.

Shutting the door of his compartment, leaning forth, elbows on the lowered window, 'I think,' he said, 'I must come down and have a *look* at your Quakers.'

'You wouldn't see them. Coming deliberately down, with a prepared spy-glass, you wouldn't see them.'

The train was moving. Leaning forth, he projected his husky voice: '*What* a silly thing to say, Miriam. What a *damned* silly thing to say.'

'Good-bye!' she cried, and strolled away up the platform, towards the house on the hill brought so near by her talk, and kept near by the evening freshness that had crept even into the enclosed air of this great station. Suppose he had come, bringing his poverty to confront their great wealth? It was to his poverty that something in her discourse had appealed. Could they teach him, could he learn, do anything more down there than be charmingly interested and appreciative, while his mind worked its swift way to an enclosing formula?

CHAPTER XV

NONE of the summer days, no going forth to discover and explore, had brought so deep a pang of love as this sudden finding, within the moist, cool air, of autumn's first breath, hitherto, through all the years, announcing farewell and the return to imprisonment, greeting her, now, as an intimate, and opening, as she met the assaults of its astringent freshness, new depths within her still incredible freedom.

Turning away from the pillar-box in whose keeping lay the record that to-morrow, in her new home—'Of *course*, Babinka, I realize that the best is Michael's ritual reading, with his silk cap on his head. I hear him. And you know I begin to think that in ways the Jews, held up, marking time, are still the best Christians. Socially, already, they are, amongst themselves, the best the world has . . .'—Amabel would be reading, she looked up towards the woods beyond Dimple Hill, every day of whose slow, rich transformation would be securely her own, and found at her side a halted bicycle. Richard, alighting.

'Do you know,' she said, aware of his haggard, friendly, lonely eyes upon her as still she looked away down the vista, scanning, to retain her strength, the beloved features of his recovered rival, 'I've just been realizing that the country comes into its own, looks quite different, somehow relieved, when the summer visitors have cleared away.'

At once, on his response, ask him the time, pleasantly and casually, and make off.

'Ah, yes,' he breathed, unsteadily, still with his eyes on her face. Here they were, side by side, with only his bicycle between, alone for the first time since her return, alone with the burden of their mutual knowledge. Was he expecting her to look at him while he spoke, and read? Did he not know he was invisible, infinitely far away?

'I want to get,' she said, and her voice rang clear and hard, 'as far as I can before tea. D'you know the time?'

Why was he here? Why coming home so early?

'It won't be much past four yet.'

His voice had steadied, but still he stood motionless, gazing down at her. He would stand thus, and talk, no matter what sacred undertaking awaited him, for half an hour, with her, with any one.

'Then I'll go my best-beloved way and watch the bracken beginning to turn. Good-bye.'

'You see, Amabel, you picture it all? The three of them, for certainly the old lady will have talked to Rachel Mary as well as to R., having it out during my absence. Alfred and the pupil stand outside, unaware and unembarrassed. R. M. will not, I think have talked to R. Her embarrassing embarrassment when we are all together means that she has seen R. draw back, as she has often seen him do before; but this time with more pain to herself. She is saddened, as well as ashamed. The old lady, who lives for R. alone, I never really liked and, not being a wise woman of the world, have never courted. Could not have courted, even if it had occurred to me to attempt an estimate of her power over R. Imagine the impressions she collected during my table-talks with Mayne. ʻ. . . Imagine the use she made of them in bringing R. to his right mind.

'I hide my agony, living, when in their company, perpetually on a stage. But there are intervals, during our silences, when everything is as it used to be. You see, Amabel, there is something we all share and that even for me, who am only at the alphabet, is what makes life worth living, the only real culture, the only one that can grow without fading and carry through to the end. But you know this better than I do, and in relation to more people, because you soon run through your personal relationships and want to move on to more people. Me, nothing short of dynamite will shift. And when I think of the life here going on without me, I wince. And they all show me, at every turn, how much, before I go, they want everything to be restored, trying to heal the rupture in advance, even the old lady, having got rid of me, tempering her naïve exhibitions of triumph and delight by singling me out, whenever possible, as the object of her flirtatious girlish flattery. And R. and Rachel Mary by a special kind of niceness, a genuine eagerness to share with me every smallest thing, are actually healing it so perfectly that even while I pine to stay, I pine, in equal measure, to be gone. Perhaps to Oberland. I've written to Mrs Harcourt, who at once tells me of a fearfully reasonable pension kept by an English ex-schoolmam up above the lake of Geneva. She'll be somewhere in the neighbourhood herself, in January. Vereker sends, at regular intervals, reminders. Found a new place last winter in Austria. Kitzbühel. Says it leaves Switzerland in the shade and is known, so far, only to a few.'

MARCH MOONLIGHT

CHAPTER I

My dear, dear Dick,

Behold me in a *chaise-longue* in the shadiest ¬art of the *Lauriers* garden. Not at all a good position for writing, but excellent for enjoyment. There you may picture me now, every morning. I write until Miss Hancock comes in at eleven and reads to me while I needlework.

To whom, so much letter-writing?

At present the book is *Helbeck of Bannisdale*. I know you have many objections to Mrs Ward, but this particular book is very interesting to me personally, because Alan Helbeck is so very like B.V. But now and again it awakens the strain and the sadness I felt during those last days just after you left. You misunderstand when you think this sadness comes from contemplation of his possible death. No, no; it isn't that. Death is all right. Besides, his health is enormously improved. And it seems so sad that now, when he feels himself capable of enjoying life like other men, he can't allow himself to do so because of his religious convictions.

Miriam finds her eyes upon Sally's chestnut tree, whose buds just now seemed so indifferently freed from their fancy dress of April snow to reveal, in this morning's sunlight, their varnished beauty. But they are no longer the buds Sally had looked out upon when she came upstairs holding the little pile of letters and slapped them down, with a gesture of mingled congratulation and protest, upon the bedside table; swiftly withdrawing her hand as though it had been at once charmed and chilled by contact with the evidence of so many unknown ties; putting so much of herself into the small manœuvre that nothing was left for speech; and then at once aware, as I said have you seen the chestnut buds, of the morning quality of this usually shrouded spare room, now full of upper garden light, less screened by the

trees than the light entering her kitchen. For a moment she
stood responsive, on a level with the budding branches that
were invisible from her front bedroom, taking in, in the undisturbing company of someone of her own blood, their full loveliness. Aren't they lovely? I asked. Lovely, she said in her
warmest voice and still looked out on them, her features relaxed,
letting through a radiance. But even while I watched her
restored to girlhood, protest reached her face and her eyes grew
sightless. There ought to be *two* Aprils, she said bitterly.
The month is all house cleaning and the hideous noise of lawn-
mowers. When it is over, another spring has gone.

But now the chestnut tree has joined company, being a
participant of mystery, with those bare larches opposite the
Lauriers balcony where every afternoon I sat talking with
Jean.

What can Jean mean?

She recalls the day of the great tea-party. The sight of Miss
Lonsdale, immediately after breakfast, excitedly inquiring
through the service hatch how much extra butter would be
required. 'Un demi,' Berthe had sung carelessly out from
some remote corner of her kitchen. 'Combien?' called Miss
Lonsdale, inclining her better ear. 'Trrrois quarrts,' came
the sing-song voice quite near, cold and clear and sly, describing
the cunning eyes gloating in advance over the spare quarter
tucked away with the other perquisites in the huge covered
bucket she carried off under our noses as she made her nightly
way out through the lounge. The arrival of the dedicated
afternoon and of the guests: the retired Major, pride and
president of the local English; Mrs Harcourt, bringing the
German professor, rubicund as a farmer, his natural perceptiveness overlaid by a training that made him so klassicimustically
insist on calling the peaks across the way our Greek gods, and
yet, with his booming voice and solemn round eyes, so good to
have in the room representing the sound and sight of Germany;
the two Poncets, eagerly pleased to be there, the daughter, her
prim liveliness outdoing even her mother's, giving, with
obvious delight in an exceptional public, a neat little demonstration of the Swiss style of prune-and-prism behaviour, so

unsuited to her undulating, mountain-bred voice; the handsome stripling son of Miss Lonsdale's landlord, pirouetting elegantly about with the cakes, eyebrows perpetually up, above a smile intended at once to deride and graciously to approve his occupation amongst these valuable, astonishingly ignorant British who came out year after year without acquiring more than the necessary minimum of simple words and, therefore, kept him almost silent. Only once did he emit more than the obligatory politeness, suddenly exclaiming, in a clear light tone into the midst of the professor's disquisition on Chopin's pianoforte miracles: 'C'est tout simplement parcequ'il c'est consacré au piano. Il faut se consacrer.' And when they had all made their farewells and pulled on their snow-boots and departed to become shadowless black figurines upon the deserted snow, and the deep freshness of the cold, advancing into the house like a solid, and the ruby patches still staining the topmost peaks across the valley, reproached Jean and me for an afternoon spent in a room, we closed the door and went back to the little *salon*, feeling that we shocked the robust, pockmarked boards of the empty lounge with the frivolous tap-tap of premature evening shoes, and were greeted, on entering the room, by the quiet *here* they are of the Bishop, so that to the glow of rejoining fellow survivors of a tempest that had left the house party sitting weary and relieved amidst the wreckage, was added the pleasing assurance of being essential parts of the reunion. Just at that moment, the exempted Marlboro' boys, back from their ski-ing, plonked, waking its echoes, through the lounge, and the Bishop's meditatively murmured 'Dear me, someone would appear to be arriving,' completed their mother's joy in their safety. Always, when I think of her, I shall see her as she looked when the sound of their boots was heard, the light on her raised face and the way, after the Bishop had spoken, she looked down, without shifting her pose, towards her clasped hands, to control and hide, from the roomful of people, the love and pride the whole cosmos is too small to contain.

And then it was that Miss Lonsdale, standing tired and dishevelled in the middle of the room, made her little speech: 'Friends. You have all behaved with conspicuous nobility. I thank you for the happiest tea-party the *Lauriers* has ever experienced.' And before anyone could respond she had turned and marched, with her brisk, audience-terminating, schoolmarm step, to the nearest window, to stand looking out and murmuring, as if to herself: 'Oh, I am going to *remember* the winter of '08–'09.'

And while most of us were uncomfortably waiting for some-one else to speak, the Bishop, silent for a moment to give others the chance of seizing an opportunity he imagined all to have desired, sent his grave deliberate voice, a little raised for Miss Lonsdale's defective hearing, across the room: 'We must *not*, my dear Miss Lonsdale, allow you to forget your *own* large part; the happiness, to say nothing of the comfort and wellbeing, we owe to your daily presence amongst us. I may, I think, speak for our whole party. For myself, I can say without hesitation, that the winter '08–'09 will stand in my memory as the happiest I have ever spent.'

Then *what* can Jean mean? What veil, if she were here to be questioned, would she gently withdraw to reveal, to an eye she trusts but sometimes finds blind, the truth she is so swift to perceive?

When the others had departed to their rooms, we ensconced ourselves on the little settee, one at each end, compactly filling it with our feet up and our persons dovetailed, at home together at the end of the long afternoon and at peace, feeling our weari-ness give way to the living joy that always held us the moment we were alone. But this time, facing each other, instead of, as usual, side by side. Each, therefore, a witness of the other's joy, so that for a while we could only smile and drop our eyes before this mutual recognition, face to face, of our joy in each other, and look away into the room as if confiding it to some third presence before returning to smile again. And her only reference to the party was a demand to know what I had been discussing with the professor. And when I told her I had said tame nothings just for the sake of hearing German, she said: 'Dick, I have seen you radiant. You don't *know* what you are like when you are radiant'; as if, for her, this new vision of her friend had been the afternoon's chief gift. That was all.

Until now, she has never voluntarily mentioned the Bishop. When we wept together over the memory of his plaintive inquiry, sent down the table from his vice-presidential seat with the Marlboro' boys to right and left of him, as to *why* a sudden silence should fall upon the table just as the three of them were discussing the awkward topic of *washing*, it was probably I who recalled it. And when I told her he refused to agree that Hugh Benson's *Light Invisible* was a forecast of his going over to Rome, we were certainly considering the wonderful Benson family. And when she took me on tiptoe into the *salon*, to see the special little feast Miss Lonsdale had prepared for the Bishop, obliged that evening to be late, we were tempering our real sympathy for the old lady with a little wicked amusement.

What, as seen by Jean, is wrong with his religious beliefs?

She fully admits his happiness in telling me why, when he went down to Montreux, it fled. A vivid picture, in her last week's letter: 'Unfortunately the dear soul made the mistake of being as easy and confiding with them as he was with us: letting them darn his poor old socks and generally look after him as we did here. But while we surrounded, we also left him free, and respected what you call the so beautifully unassumed and unassuming dignity of his office. *They* cultivate him on the strength of their officious services.'

I see them, those bishop-lionizing women. Yet don't I come near them in being thrilled, that second afternoon of my stay, by a bishop's invitation to join him in a toboggan ride?

But in what courteously guarded terms he will have conveyed to Jean the difference between the two pensions, trusting her instantly translated, eager, perceptive consciousness to fill out the picture? By letter, these rueful confidences. Then it is to him she is so sedulously writing?

'If you remember in the book, Alan Holbeck in Lent and Easter week, how he felt he *must* not let his thoughts stray at those times, you will understand how it was this last Easter. Dickie, he told me—and I know it to be perfectly true—that I am much too tolerant and that it lessens my power as also does my too great allowance for the independence of others and my consequent hesitancy to interfere. The truth is, as he knows, too, I think, that I am quite aware of it all, but I don't really want to change. I feel so sure that love is in itself the supreme power and will in the end conquer all things.'

Jean's carefree wisdom. And he cannot see that she is right. Yet even he can find in her only this one generous fault.

'Gissing says: "I used to judge the worth of a person by his intellectual power and attainments. Now, I think that one has to distinguish between two forms of intelligence, that of the brain and that of the heart, and I have come to regard the second as by far the most important." C'est ça, n'est-ce pas? His sadness, before he left, succeeded in making me sad, too, and consequently, we laughed a great deal, hilariously, all day long, because we did not wish our sadness to appear. On his last day here he said we shall never meet again on this side of the grave—but beyond. And then followed a dissertation on his ideas of a meeting there. Of its happiness and naturalness. He may be right; but I wonder.'

Then it was *Jean*, and not someone remembered from his far-off youth, who shone within his mind when he asked me as silently we toiled, trailing our luges, side by side up the long tracks, that astonishing question.

'The loveliness of this scene,' he began suddenly in his elderly and habitually rather devout low tone within which there lingered, bestowing a touch of colour and warmth, the persuasively protesting cadences of youthful academic controversy, shattering not only my newly found joy in being again amongst the snow-cloaked mountains and the snowfields and the million-needled assault of the crystalline air, but also the silence that I had imagined filled with the ease of immediate good understanding. A good understanding, resulting from our mutual stock-taking during the social gatherings of that first twenty-four hours, ending with his final summing-up, that day, when at lunch I had caught him taking, while Miss Lonsdale dealt with that queer, convulsive young man who was spending his last hours under her roof in trying to persuade her to uproot herself from a Switzerland faced with ruin if Germany should start a war, a snapshot of me, with a flattering lens. I did not then know that already Jean had told him I was more or less of a Quaker, probably just saying, with the restrained twinkle that accompanies her communication of odd facts, she's a *Quakeress*, and that his mind, as he observed me under cover of an assumed air of attention to the impassioned duet, would certainly be at work upon this piece of information.

Still fevered with the sleepless journey, knowing I was once more in Oberland rather than feeling myself there, and still taking in only with my mind the quality of the party into which I had been gathered overnight when they all came, one by one, after tea in the *salon*, to pay a little vicarage call on me, sitting at my side on the low settee that looked out on to a fierce Gumfluh made gentle by their kindness, I was probably staring, while he imagined me far withdrawn from the unquakerly tumult raging round the equally unquakerly theme, blankly into space. And I remember contemplating, from the depths of my twenty-four hours ensconcement in Alpine winter, in its peculiar quality of seeming to be there, freed from turmoil and from change, for ever, and from my still deeper ensconcement in the immortal moment between taking stock of one's surroundings and becoming involved in them, the autumn beauty of Dimple Hill; the fiery blaze of its northernmost woodlands in afternoon sunlight, their misted gleam when a strong south wind drives across them the gigantically stalking wraiths of fine rain; the gentle onset there of what, incredibly, was this same winter. Its first dusk, so different from the thin twilights of spring and from the ripe gloamings that come later and yet, because the memory and the promise and the clear vision of these is contained within it, so deeply moving; and how for a mile I raced it as it trailed, increasing its pace, strengthened by the dense, low-hanging grey that since morning had screened the sun's brief journey, upwards towards the house on the hill, to find there the depths of this dusk, warm in the firelight of the front room whose lamp was still to come; and the December morning singled out from the rest by the small warm scent of violets within in the early mist and, later that same day, the voice of Richard as he said I reckon it would puzzle one of those quaint little contraptions to get *me* over the snow at a pace like that; and presently feeling, although in that moment of new birth his image in my mind seemed little more than a ghost, a fresh surge of resentment towards his eternal, self-protecting facetiousness, and probably revealing, to the Bishop, in my expression, a combined wistfulness and vexation not unnatural in a Quaker overhearing the conversation of potential warriors; and there, full upon me as I shifted my gaze, in search of release from the final object of my contemplations, away from the space these had opened before me in the air between myself and my opposite neighbour, was the mild, deeply speculative eye of this oddly planted ecclesiastic.

'The loveliness of this scene carries one's thoughts to the world beyond our world. Tell me, do you believe that we shall meet there, free from terrestrial barriers, those for whom on earth we have felt a deep affection?'

Fraudulent I felt. Again, as at Dimple Hill, though the blessedly generous and generalized culture of those who here were crediting me with the estate of a fully fledged Christian did not demand of each individual that he should be his own priest and prophet, I felt myself a wolf in sheep's clothing. But also so much taken aback, by the priest's appeal, to a lay-man and a relative stranger, for reassurance in regard to so bright and precious a part of the faith he represented, that in my embarrassment I abruptly said oh yes, keeping my eyes upon the mountains because the answer he sought seemed there so much more fully expressed than in any words I might, upon reflection, have brought forth.

'Thank you. It cannot, I believe, be otherwise.' And in a moment we were at the top of the track and I was envying him, reduced, in the interval, from the height whereon my inex-perience had placed him to the level of average humanity, the gaiters saving him the daily tedious labour of unwinding puttees that nevertheless, whether drying unrolled upon the radiator, demanding, before they could be assumed, to be re-rolled to the compactness of a surgical bandage, or waiting, trim dry bundles firmly wound off the day before, side by side upon a shelf, supplied a ritual within the moments of whose

laborious accomplishment was enfolded the day's deepest
consciousness of a snow-bound world.

It was *Jean*.

Weary, broken by a life methodically devoted to everyone but
himself and also, on principle, to no earthly creature in particular, this prematurely aged mission-priest, unaware of what
awaited him, had made his way across the world to Jean, to a
lover by nature rather than through the reasoned acceptance of
a creed. Jean. Not Miss Sclater, the college-trained Eucken-
reading, Kierkegaard-reading young missionary-in-the-making,
like himself on holiday after a breakdown, and yet dividing her
time between a selfish invalid and the local evangelistic enterprises. Better looking than Jean, an interested, self-effacing
talker and listener, yet no effort of hers could have drawn him as
Jean had drawn him without an effort or a thought. Instantly,
he must have recognized her. Who would not? And
presently found himself in a new life, in the midst of revelation,
in love, for the first time, with all the banked-up force of an
almost perfectly disciplined nature. Joy, shattering and
incredible, and presently torment. Keen enough to drive him
to open his heart to a stranger.

And Jean? One day, incredulously aware. Plunged,
presently, to her own surprise, in emotional response. And
when the barrier made itself felt and, at last, with the help of
his characteristically guarded generalizations, clearly perceived,
unable to grant it the tolerant welcome she so readily extends to
individual peculiarities. Able only to deplore the belief that so
inexorably built it up.

We never directly discussed religion. But when the English
chaplain, losing his head during his furious denunciation of
Christian Science, went so far as to boast of his ignorance of the
writings of the founder, she blushed her shame for him, and
smiled, looking down at her tightly clasped hands, her sympathy
for my hysterical giggle. (Will she remember, will she always
remember, how, deserting for a while the English church to go
the round of the local bethels, we climbed one day up the hill to
the Réformée, arrived late and innocently made our way into
the choir?) And though her interest in my Sussex experiences

led more than once to a discussion of the technique of Quakerism, I recall her only as questioning and listening; never as
giving a verdict. Save perhaps on that one occasion, left for
ever perfect by the sudden appearance on the balcony of my
first sample of the local English, unmistakable in a shabby,
perfect tailor-made, at once eager and composed, middle-aged
and girlish, waving an ear trumpet and to become, as soon as
she had departed, one of two sisters sustaining compulsory
exile, on small means in a small chalet, with the help of daily
excursions undertaken by each sister in solitude with the idea
of gathering material for interchange sufficient to last, if
economically and exhaustively doled out, until again they
should separate on their respective rounds. Advancing down
the balcony, she made straight for a Jean hoisted a little in her
chaise-longue, surrendered to this intruder as to someone eagerly
awaited, perched herself on its base, leaned towards her,
trumpet to ear, considered for a moment Jean's flushed and
eager face and said coquettishly: '*Say* somefing sooving.'
And while I fumed and in vain reproached myself for fuming,
I felt the moment preceding her arrival strike its deep root.

I had been watching Jean, hitherto known only in weekday
guise, ever so little sabbatically withdrawn in the company of
her small Oxford Bible and had been speculating, while carefully she turned its delicately crackling leaves, as to the composition of the local Bible study circle and the nature of its appeal to
her alert, college-trained mind, and presently had become
aware of the beneficent restfulness of our common silence, and
in a moment was desiring interchange on the subject of Sunday,
on its way of standing outside time, divesting active, planful,
out-turned, time-table people of the cutting edge of their power
to disturb, providing a deep retreat whence long perspectives,
lost during the turmoil of the week, again became visible, even
amongst Friends, compelled, by custom, to be sabbatarians
against their principles. And I broke the silence to call her
attention to the Quaker repudiation of the idea of singling out,
as the Lord's Day, any one of the seven, and went on to confess
to a nostalgic longing, when isolated on Sunday with people
who completely disregard it, for the company of even the most

lugubrious of Old Testament sabbatarians, and saw her glowing face turn my way and felt the working of her instinctive knowledge of the superiority, for the purpose of encouraging discourse, of a delighted, appreciative smile directed across the speaker's path and keeping speaker and listener free and firm in their respective solitudes, over an encounter of the eyes and an ardent rejoinder. And felt, too, in that same moment, again the strong deep sense of Sunday uniting and holding us apart, confirming our growing delight in each other by providing, even while we sat side by side, a distant focus; and at the same time enchantedly recognized, saw that I was intended to recognize, as she bent once more zealously over her Bible, both the suspension of her thoughts and the desire for continuance confessed by her smile, so nearly approaching a schoolgirl's grin as to show her eager to recover and to share, from within the shelter of a genuine preoccupation, schoolgirl joy in illicit exchange screened by an apparent pious engrossment in an imposed task.

Inspired by her response, I discovered sturdily flourishing in my consciousness and at once confided to the framed landscape ahead of me, a preference for living, if ever circumstances should compel the choice, with even the most hypocritically sanctimonious pietists, flopping to their knees on every possible occasion, singing many hymns and having a long grace before each meal, rather than with even the most enchanted and enchanting humanists. And again she turned my way, and unawares I abandoned my role and watched her while cautiously, holding back the laughter that had filled her eyes with tears, she murmured so would *I*, and perceived for the first time the strength controlling her sweetness, the power that had drawn me when as a stranger I had observed her at table and wondered why, for all her apparent absorption in making inane conversation for her neighbour, this inconspicuous girl seemed somehow to enliven the whole decorous group, and felt in equal measure a desire for close acquaintance and a fear lest the desire be realized. And now again, in this eternal moment, she was a stranger far removed, and I saw her gently making her way through life, upheld by this mature strength, unconsciously inspiring all those she would meet and draw to her side, to seek and find their own. And as once more, aware of my scrutiny and betraying her awareness by a lingering flicker of the school-girl grin, she bent above her crackling leaves, I longed, bereft and breathless, for the sound of her voice, conning over in my mind its peculiar cadences, neither trained and mannered like Amabel's, nor making, like the deliberating voices of the Roscorlas, each word a statement with parentheses, yet convey-ing, in their gentle, unaggressive movement, her whole self, the tolerance and the wealth of her sympathetic imagination, so that after she had spoken there lingered within the air, rather than the meaning of what she said, its sound; protective. But just as she asked in level, meditative tones 'What is a humanist?' Miss Cadogan and her ear trumpet appeared in the doorway.

We had no premeditated discussions. Apart, we could forget each other: but our serenity in absence owed its power to the quality of our meetings.

Separation from Amabel used to bring both regret and relief. Relief from the incessant applause-demanding drama, regret for failure to emerge unwearied. Meeting her again with strength renewed, one would find her already divorced from the past she so readily discards, involved in fresh excitements that brought the uneasy sense of time rushing ahead and were overshadowed, even while she dramatized them, by the certainty of their imminent doom.

To return to Jean is to find oneself at an unchanging centre. Even when, during some of our silences, we reached, travelling independently, different destinations, and returned then to consultations that left for one or other of us a point of view for ever modified, the ensuing sense of the flowing away of the time at our disposal surprised me by its painlessness. Again and again I recalled my helpless woe when Amabel first hinted her desire for fresh people, her need to pass on, opening a gulf across which I still look back. Still, I can feel the sudden hard indifference of the wall behind us as we sat side by side across my narrow bed and, still, my own surprise at the swift tears flowing, quietly, resignedly, as though for long they had been prepared without my knowledge, for this inevitable moment, and seeming, so swiftly in that instant of silent realization had I moved back into loneliness, the witnessed grief of another. And to this day I do not know whether she desired only to test her power, or whether her response to my tears, her undertaking never to leave me, was native generosity, or just a way of comforting a child.

But the thought of leaving Jean was promise as well as pain, carrying me forward across a future that held no assurance of a fresh meeting and yet promised reunion.

The moment we found ourselves together, time stood still. Our relief and our unspoken delight expressed themselves in smiles, observed rather than exchanged. Every memory of rejoining Jean evokes her flushed face lit by the radiance her downcast lids were powerless to veil; her perfect prelude to speech. The sound of irrepressible joyous laughter flowed through her gravest communications. And our intermittent silences, rather than tension-creating searches for fresh material, were fragments of a shared eternity whence, upon an identical rhythm—since our recovered voices, boxed by the balcony's sloping roof and enclosing balustrade, its fragrant log-stack and the evocative piled instruments of sport and yet escaping to challenge, with their small individual threads of sound, the snow-bound outer stillness, would simultaneously restore these beloved forgotten surroundings—we contemplated whatever had been summoned to stand before us.

Bless her for her ardent agreement as to the charm of a country winter, apart from the long lingering of autumn-coloured leaves and the sight, when they fall, of spring buds much too small to blur the clean beauty of stripped trees, apart from January's April-green mosses and the distant view of June's gold summoned by winter gorse—the way, during the dark months, *all* the doings of the light, half of whose pageant, in the height of summer, must daily be missed, fall well within the waking hours.

And for admitting the townsman's misreading of the consciousness of the yokel. The inability of the civilized, relatively isolated, uneducated and inexperienced town dweller to imagine himself into the situation producing the slow, round-about speech and the guarded, in-turned facial expression he mistakes for stupidity. She sat holding the scales, a little dubious over the implied lack of reverence for civilization. But when I asked her, myself considering it for the first time, to imagine herself spending her life in a village, amongst people all known to her and many of them her relatives; to picture the experience accumulated in the consciousness of a village child, even before school pumps in its supply of easily forgotten irrelevancies; to compare a town life's relatively small *direct* knowledge of the business of birth and death, sudden sickness, insanity, the relentless slow progress of every kind of incurable disease, of infirmity and senility, with the exhaustive knowledge of all these things acquired in a village lifetime; to remember that in 'a sleepy village where nothing happens,' crime and cruelty, kindness and joy and sorrow go their way under the highest white light of publicity known to mankind. And then to imagine falling into a richly experienced, preoccupied village consciousness whose every day brings a fresh event somewhere in the huge family, even the simplest of questions, even a demand for the way to the next village, to the inquirer only an imaginary destination, the momentary halting-place of his will-o'-the-wisp, but for the local man a storehouse of memories and the scene of current events through whose crowding presences, while with vacuous, expert eye he sums the stranger up, he must thrust his way to the desired information, she turned and swiftly kissed me.

I shall never know what she would have said when presently our voices sounded together and mine prevailed because I desired to hide from her the certainty that had dawned at Dimple Hill and increased there. And now, having put into words something of what I had felt about the wealth and the woefulness of village life, I realized how far beneath her I stood in preferring, to its enclosure and its tests and exposures, the more distributed life of the townsman, its exemptions and pro-tected solitudes, I hurried on, holding forth on the universally belauded quality of local work and the tributes paid to village kindliness; making her see that native honesty in craftsmanship, and village sympathy, born of witnessing distress at close quarters rather than merely hearing about it, are not always of sufficient account; making her realize how, in a village, everyone carries about with him his own inalienable record, known to everyone else, and that a bad piece of work, or a lack of active sympathy when need calls, will brand a villager for life. And again she glowed towards me, missing, in the interest of the subject, my flight from judgment.

But the best and, for me, the most searching moment of the afternoon was the sudden perception of what lies behind the 'simple' person's inability to summarize, behind the obvious deep enjoyment, particularly remarkable in women, of the utmost possible elaboration of a narrative, of what is evoked in the speaker's mind, while in torment one waits for the emergent data: 'Well now, let me think. It couldn't have been a *Thursday* because I've been out working every Thursday this month, owing to Mrs Jones being ill and sorry I am though I don't deny the extra bit came in handy with prices going up like they are.' Hopeful question. 'Yes, it *might* have been a Wednesday. I'd set my iron to reheat just as I heard the click of the gate. My big iron, it was, to press Joe's trousers for him to go to the sale. What am I *telling* you?' Pause for enjoyable laughter. 'I must be going silly. Oh, deary me. What I mean to say, now I come to think of it, it couldn't have been so late as Wednesday. I had a great pile of things on the table here ready to iron. I remember that because I thought to myself shall I ever get all them things done *today*? Easter coming, I'd done me curtains too. Tuesday, then, it must have been, because I was telling Joe this morning every Monday this month has been a good drying day, like you often get in March.'

But when we agreed, recalling, as I thought, tortures, how easily, if one set oneself to realize the deep delight of the dancer of the interminable *pas seul* in honour of the joy of life at first hand, and executed, wordlessly, while it lasted, a similar *pas seul* of one's own, the trial might be supported, and with what refreshment one might emerge to greet the finale, I knew, watching Jean's luminous face, that what for me seemed an onerous laudable venture, a possibility I might in time learn to realize, for her, already, in relation to nearly everyone she met, was a commonplace of daily life, a labour to which she had given no name.

And always our contemplations discovered a truth that left us united, so much one person that in the talk following the arrival of an outsider it seemed, when either spoke, as if it were the other, and I would hear, in Jean's voice addressing someone else, myself speaking, and see her lessened, moved away from her centre, a little too out-turned in her responsiveness and with all her faults upon her, and when, in fact, I spoke, would be aware of Jean controlling.

And Miss Lonsdale became aware of this close interchange, and, in spite of herself, jealous. Socially, with her deafness, the neediest and, with her cultivated intelligence, the wealthiest member of the household, she had had, before I came, the largest share of Jean. And steadily Jean kept up the pathetic lip-reading lessons without perceptible progress. Wistfully, arriving on the balcony towards tea time, she would demand, standing between the foot-rests of our *chaises-longues*, and looking from face to face, a share of our thoughts, sending Jean upon a search for something that could be communicated in a few shouted remarks.

It is the puritanism of his Anglo-Catholicism that troubles her . . ?

And I saw nothing. My picture of him was almost himself as he wished, or thought he ought, to be. Serenely immune, I believed him, as well as so gifted with sympathetic imagination as to be living several lives besides his own. Light falls now upon those two small incidents, giving them vivid life: that morning when, coming down to breakfast on the stroke of the hour we had named, Jean defying me to succeed, I found the Bishop unexpectedly late and in his place at the end of the table, and Jean just round its corner instead of in her usual seat and, when Berthe brought in my coffee and set it also near that far end, I murmured towards Jean, through the clatter, 'You see I have kept our appointment.' It was because he might have heard my words that her lie was justified when she rebuked my crudity and cut me to the heart by saying in her clearest tone, 'Oh, I had forgotten it.' I imagined she would have done something of the kind whoever might have been with us, and sat crushed and furious, yet contemplating a perfection of social awareness perhaps to be acquired under her guidance.

But now I see that it was more than Jean's in-born courtesy. Knowing what had happened to him, and herself more deeply involved than her letter admits, she feared even the suggestion that she would sooner breakfast, at the beginning of yet another heavenly day, with me rather than with anyone else.

And the day we all went suddenly, with one accord, to Gruyères. Did anyone particularly want to undertake that tremendous outing? Who suggested it? Miss Lonsdale, urged by her teacher's desire to introduce her party to the things that ought to be seen?

It was arranged on one of those rare occasions finding us all having breakfast about the same time, everyone there beneath her eye and the day, through each window, showing its perfection. The Bishop, who must have come down late, having finished the meal he usually took in solitude, lingered vice-presidentially, urbanely chatty, glad to be there amongst us all. When I came in he must have been paying his tribute to the morning's splendour. 'In *Switzerland*,' he was gently saying, in the dry, plaintive tone that meant a little tale at someone's expense, usually his own, a blessed sound enclosing the leisurely good humour of the English, their refusal to rush or be rushed, 'one may quite *safely* employ such a remark in the service of conversational interchange. Whereas in *Madeira*, as a stranger, deeply impressed, *day* after *day*, by the continuous sunshine and blue sky, I met, when remarking at breakfast upon the fineness of the day, with what seemed to me a singular lack of *response*, and was *puzzled*, if not somewhat *embarrassed*, until I discovered that in Madeira *every* day is a fine day.'

I'd just escaped remarking that in that case the visiting English must be condemned to perpetual silence when I felt, as hastily I swallowed my brick, running round the table amidst the general chirruping, an uneven ripple, and heard the Bishop inquire, voice raised for Miss Lonsdale at the other end: 'And you? You will join us?'

Peering round at us all through her dense glasses, 'I *must*,'

she sighed, 'you give me no choice, dear people, I *must* be in it.'
And she called confidently to Berthe-in-the-kitchen as if she
imagined her a witness of this gratifying scene: 'Alors, Berthe,
dix déjeuners en paquet!' And Berthe, with a despairing
shriek, appeared at the open hatch, all her teeth illuminating the
most beatific of her smiles. And when she dispatched us, her
sing-song blessings ringing out from the doorway to which at
such a far-distant hour we were to return, and the faces of the
scattered party all turned obediently towards her, even that of
the Bishop wore the uncritical glad expectancy of a child on
holiday.

For all of us, even for Rosabel when she is an enlightened old
woman, that day will stand out as the peak of our unity at *Les
Lauriers*, at all time perceptible and, after Gruyères, present in
the very air of an empty room.

It was a Saturday, a day always drawing us more closely
together, with Sunday ahead to bring the formal ease of an
unvarying ritual, a later breakfast, our more stately clothes, our
unanimous church-going; our party collected, within that of all
the local English, in the little plaster church, a nucleus of conviction that the chaplain's woolly haverings could not obscure.
And it was in the depth of the Swiss winter's best, before the
February sun grew strong enough to free, at midday, some
small frozen torrent to tinkle in the stillness out of sight, and to
summon, to the heads of the village children, those weird little
inverted baskets of embroidered, brightly coloured straw.

Rosabel—newly impressive with the strange surroundings
heightening her solid beauty that everywhere attracted eyes
whose owners presently wondered what had drawn them—
restlessly haunting the corridor of the little train in a blind
quest for fuller response than any *Les Lauriers* had afforded
her, and finding, instead, the uninspiring producer of Jean's
little scene: a young man negative almost to vanishing point, of
whom even Rosabel's imagination could not create a figure of
romance and who yet, by appearing unexpectedly, awoke in her
an animation that must have astonished and may have brought
him, since he would not perceive its impersonality, both pride
and fear in equal measure. And Jean, summoned, flew forth

to greet and stay talking with him until at the next toy station he left the train and for a few moments stood visible upon the platform, his wooden bearing and unillumined face revealing the fruitlessness of Jean's effort to make him serve as a partner in an animated conversation. Audible amongst the voices sounding in the enclosure, her gentle outcries, projected from the open carriage door, made her visible: sweetly absurd as she stood in the doorway rapturously savouring her wealth, the far-off cherished home his presence brought so vividly before her and that yet subtracted nothing from the riches of her enchanted exile.

And she came back, with the delight that had shone from her as she went forth heightened upon her flushed and eager face, and I watched her coming down the gangway and revelled in my pride in her and in her controlled and gentle movements as she came to resume her seat at my side and give me, in a single swift look, before she settled down to recount her adventure, the measure of her joy. And she went, not even glancing my way, straight to the Bishop, tucking herself compactly down, hands in muff, against his arm, her face all smiling curves, her eyes, while still they looked reminiscently into space, radiating a perfect satisfaction. And it was he who, after a single, indulgent glance at her profile, looked across at me, smiling, so I thought, his fatherly pride in being singled out as the recipient of her surplus, and his half-mischievous sympathy for my plight in being set aside in favour of an older friend.

I know now what will have been for him that moment in the depths of the untethered day.

Blind, I was, to the drama playing itself out under my nose.

Throughout the winter I believed, and silently at every turn she seemed to confirm my belief that she and I together, because we were together, irradiated our surroundings, she for me, I for her.

From the moment I first saw her sitting opposite to me at table and tried to discover why she was impressing me, Vaud, anticipated as a renewal of Oberland, and becoming Oberland as the train wound upward from the cloud-dimmed lake and the first tawny crag looked down from a gap in the mist, began to become Jean. There, for ever, she sits, her slightly prominent blue eyes apparently quite vacant beneath the arches of her delicate eyebrows that at once attracted me and that help so much to give to her serene brow and to her oval face, whose soft bloom recalls Eve in her teens, surrounded by Eve's brown hair grown silkier and arranged in puffs that would be Japanese save for their irregular massing, something of the look of a conventionalized eighteenth-century portrait.

Landed amongst strangers, their presence the inevitable price of access to joy whose sure approach alone made bearable those last weeks at Dimple Hill, I watched her, from the depth of my weariness, making conversation as though she were giving it the whole of her attention, though now I know that her clear intelligence and her gentle heart were all the time aware of every point within the compass of her surroundings, with the mild, neat-featured young man whose gentle, rather high-pitched voice had the Balliol accent and the apologetically plaintive cadences so often accompanying it, and who, two days later, turned into Jim Davenport quietly and efficiently building a pine-branch fire for our picnic in the snow at the top of the world and, later, in the swiftly descending after-sunset cold, when the off-horse, on the narrowest part of the high path between precipice and mountain face, got a leg outside the long rein and began to plunge, rising from the last, most wildly swinging luge of the tail and somehow getting himself, serenely watchful, along past the row of slithering luges and the rocking sleigh, to the horse's head.

'No, Sally. No one shrieked.'

No one made a sound. Not even old Miss Lonsdale, hilariously conducting her pension on the grand spree, and having, from her seat in the sleigh, the clearest view of what was happening, nor the small wise mother of the Marlboro' boys ('courtesy in youth may be little more than good spirits; if it survives the trials of life, it is *genuine*') sitting beside her amongst the empty picnic baskets, nor Rosabel just behind the sleigh, nor the disdainful girl heading via Cheltenham for Girton, poised elegantly upon her luge with the Marlboro' boys for van and rearguard, nor the tall, jocular young woman heading, via Woodbrooke, for the West African mission-field, whose peaked white helmet rose above the head of the young man on furlough from the C.M.S. who was to get so many quiet snubs from the Bishop for his masculine superiority and sat, blissfully unconscious of Jean's half-amused pity and my impatient scorn, just ahead of us.

Davenport's exploit had made a good sample story for Sally; really holding her attention. To almost everything else she had listened with indifference. Patiently at first, buoyed up by the expectation of hearing at any moment something that would serve as a basis for hope. But always in the end revealing her disappointment in the smile that plainly said, as she bustled away to labours piled up while she had sat listening: this is all very well, but leads nowhere. Jean's first letter, bearing the Swiss postmark, had given her a momentary relief whose departure had been avenged by her impatient reference to the difficulty of distinguishing 'nowadays,' between masculine and feminine hand-writing. 'It's these *modern* women,' she had said with patient contempt, 'who write like men.'

Then all our deep happiness, never confessed, never even alluded to, was nothing more than a background. Lit by glowing rays from an unsuspected source. Yet it had seemed so real, so independent. Renewed every morning, it reached perfection during our afternoons in solitary possession of the balcony. Silent, or endlessly talking. One of the prices of this perfection she taught me: to accept incursions without evasion or resentment. ('Hadst thou stayed, I must have fled.') Jean knows that *nothing* can be clutched or held. Were we ever more fully together than during that evening when we were impelled, after the snowstorm, to escape and creep out into the moonlight? At the very door we were caught by Miss Lonsdale emerging from her hall-bedroom. I could have slain her as she stood, schoolgirlishly hopping while she announced her intention of joining us. And, as we wandered about, for her lyrical outcries, Jean, responding, made her happy. 'A *most* delightful adventure. I thank you, my children.' And, as once more the house door opened to let us in, triumphantly preceded by Miss Lonsdale, Jean, gently pinching my arm, murmured with her little sigh: 'That's *life*, Dickie.'

But once, she rebelled. The day we watched the first avalanches thunder down into the valley, a murky grey cloud of snow and stones and pine branches rolling helplessly over and over. Yet only in face of a needless demand. And with a recklessness, considering our combined poverty, that surprised and enchanted me, Miss Lonsdale, dressed for visiting, confronting us in our *chaises*, looking from one to the other, saying exultantly: 'Now *which*, I wonder, of you two, in my absence and most *charmingly*, will preside this afternoon in the *salon*? I go, unfortunately, by duty bound, *out* to tea.' Instantly, Jean's little cry: 'So do *we*!'

It was the first of our deliberate extravagances, so well repaid; the first time we sat, silent and apparently damned, drinking in the conversation of the gathered English excitedly keeping things up—and watching our beloved E. F. Benson, sitting sternly alone at a little corner table with his back to everyone, making us wonder how he endured hotel evenings, how he passed his time until another morning should set him on the rink to glide about looking, even in his enchantment, a lost soul.

'I am very glad you persuaded Miss Hancock to come out here. We are a great deal together. She repeated to me, this morning, very gravely, you know her unfailing quiet sense of humour, the following:

> "Go to father, she said, when he asked her to wed,
> Now she knew that he knew her father was dead,
> And she knew that he knew the life he had led,
> So she knew that he knew what she meant when she said:
> Go to father."

'So you see, Dick, I can't possibly tell her my naughtiest stories.'

Does Miss Hancock find her, as I promised Mr Hancock, feeling so glad to have something to offer in return for that first gift of Oberland, a host in herself? Does she recognize, as the daily recipient of Jean's being, her great good fortune? Do they wander as we wandered, talking and talking, inevitably meeting an acquaintance, or some half-known resident Britisher, either of whom I would desire to strangle, while Jean patiently and amiably conversed, as if the whole of time were hers and the whole of her sweetness at the service of vacuous conversation-makers? Miss Hancock, she will not find it necessary sharply to rebuke: 'Dicky, one *can't* cut people short and just march away.'

Do they sit talking on the balcony?

One more sheet, closely covered . . . '*Gentian*.' She has nothing more to communicate but the changes in the surrounding scene, now, too late, revealed as neglected, pushed aside on behalf of an illusion. But even if I had held aloof, kept myself free for untrammelled unity, I left too early to discover whether the blue of gentian gives the same sense of an ultimate distinction as do the best of the Dimple Hill delphiniums.

Turning back to read to the end, Miriam welcomed as accompaniment to the undesired excursion, the odour of wood-smoke coming up from some downstairs fire-lighting, sending its fragrance to compete with this painful pother about people, providing, too, a refuge from the pressure of the personalities within the house, a way through; the local gentian, always somewhere discoverable.

In any case, the Swiss gentian, like the famous edelweiss which may be noble but is no more white than the Swiss snow-drop, the disappointing perce-neige, creamy and insipid, may be no more than a spurious blue.

'Dick, I don't say much about our friendship. It is a very precious thing. I am silent before the wonder of it. And before your understanding of everything. Unconsciously now I find myself comparing everyone I meet with you. And they always fail. I hunt and hunt to find another you. I never shall. I share your happy optimism, but haven't learned how to convey it to others as you do by just being *there*.

'Each time I hear from you I feel armed for the fray. You make me laugh. But when you threaten to go about labelled ginger-ale for ladies only, you use the wrong expression. For

me you are like the most refreshing of sea breezes. No, that
won't do. There is nothing to compare with the effect you
have on me. And it works however you are feeling. At this
moment I am lonely. No, I'm not. Looking at your letter, I
hear your voice and am at once under your influence. How I
miss you—when I forget to love the fellow creatures about me.
I feel starving. You won't misunderstand. I am enjoying
every moment.

'The crocuses are coming out. I shall send you the first
gentian. Perhaps next week.'

The door clicked, calling her attention to her flaming cheeks,
moved half open, mercifully came to rest, its handle held by
some one not intending to appear; either one of the children
with a message, or Sally herself come up with something to say.

'I've lit the fire in the drawing-room, in case you feel like
coming down.'

'Oh, that'll be lovely, Sally.' To come down, from the top
of the world to the miracle of a fireside, of any fireside.

'I'll keep the children out of the way.'

'You needn't.' Jean speaking, herself speaking to Jean, to
Sally, to the world flooded by the tide risen within. 'Unless
you fear the remains of my flu.'

Sally was looking at her nails, or away across the landing,
while she listened, taking the moral temperature of this sister
once again returned empty-handed and therefore justifiably
gloomy, and, astonishingly, from what she saw as a field of
infinite possibilities, judging from the warmth of her voice,
restored to her usual mysterious, half-vexatious, half-enviable
confidence in face of a future both empty and menacing.

'No. Really, I'm all right, Sally.' Again Jean speaking,
addressing herself to that far region of Sally's being where,
unknown to her, or forgotten, overlaid by each day's thronging
multiplicities or obscured by beguiling pictures of a 'future'
that would compensate for the not much more than endurable
'present,' the same certainty dwelt secure. 'Only a bit wobbly.'

'Well. We'll see.'

The door closed. Sally's patent shoes creaked hurriedly
across the landing, down the stairs.

'To love everyone about me.' Jean could not speak these, her inmost secrets, if we were to meet again. They can only be written. Or lived. That's why there *must* be churches, and dogmas, to formulate and cherish and pass round the things that cannot be mentioned. Jean lives them, gaily. Lives in a world she sees transfigurable. Already, for her, transfigured. What comes to others only at moments is with her always. . . . Her natural genius. Cultivated.

Somehow she has mastered the art of incessant prayer? Incessant orientation of her spiritual compass toward the love that is the centre and the gaiety of the universe, and the secret, too, of her deep enjoyment of any and every moment. That is why she never flies into rages, and holds me back when I do, laughingly as well as in pleading, because she knows what I am missing. And is the reason, too, for the quality of her outward responses. Even her swiftest pities are always a little shy, as if dependent upon some more powerful feeling untouched by sadness. With the Bishop, pity is entirely sad, and his most radiant goodwill suggests something acquired, not there by nature, acquired, laboriously, through obedience to accepted doctrines and disciplines.

She is wrong about our laughter. Whenever we were together laughter enfolded us, coming from her to me, from somewhere to both of us. Sometimes I deliberately drove it away, desiring, for one of my elucidations, a surrounding gravity. And gravely she would listen. But in her response there was always laughter, in her quietest responsive smile a dancing laughter.

CHAPTER II

'SAY something funny, Auntie.'

William's confident grin broadened as she smiled back at him, revealed all his white teeth and brought to his eyes the conspiratorial gleam that was at once his silent salute to their good understanding, a tribute to past performances and an invitation to immediate jollity. But her heart, that so recently had missed a beat in imagining Jean, and Jean's love that was her own passport to eternity, abolished from the universe, now contracted before the spectacle of William so precariously launched therein. There, unconscious of risk, he sat, squarely and incongruously upon the fragile chair salvaged by Bennett from the Henderson crash and seeming to summarize, even while it brought, together with the little inlaid table and the Italian landscapes, into Sally's crowded sitting-room a touch of the vanished graciousness of the drawing-room at Barnes, the hazardous circumstances wherein the decisive events of his boyhood were swiftly telling themselves off.

Bennett's son, steady and sturdy and honest to the core, he was the son also of the Bennett who now, with entertainment her immediate preoccupation, entered her mind coming hot-foot down the gangway of the parish hall to join for a moment herself and Sally sitting in frozen astonishment while the vicar-led audience eagerly and dutifully applauded a bald young man's impersonation of a suffragist as a shrieker of the incoherent vituperations he delivered, arm-waving, upon the top notes of his shrillest falsetto. Bennett, arriving radiant, with tears of joy in his eyes, cheeks almost as red as his steward's rosette, had stood for a moment applauding and then had turned to say, between husky chuckles betraying him as having laughed, during the exhibition, to coughing point: '*Wasn't* that good! Clever chap, isn't he?' So much in his element in helping a good cause and at the same time reaping first-class entertainment, so confident of sharing the delight that had driven him to desert his post, that he either did not notice the reservations in Sally's response, or had taken the half-surprised, half-judicially meditative tone of the agreement given at the bidding of her sense of the amiability-at-all-costs due to the occasion, for a confession of an imperfect appreciation now become, under the guidance of a superior judge, retrospectively perfect.

But Sally's son, too. Having so full a share of her sensibility that already, in social intercourse, his eyelids had often to serve as shutters for his swift perceptions.

Across the room whose atmosphere still carried the chill of fireless days, he radiated a warmth that left Marian untouched. Alone.

'Nothing there. *Butterfly*.' Alone as she had been when Sally heard these words, clear and meditative, coming from the nursery where for a moment Marian had been left unattended, and had found her squatted in an empty corner, facing the blank wall, intent. But, now, in no dream-world. Already seeing everyone about her, family, neighbours, friends, with ironic clarity. Yet, socially, kindlier than Sally, whose judgments were apt to leak through.

Experienced for the first time as sole hostess, this child, Sally's amused, adoring confidante and Bennett's only tyrant, so aloof and so helplessly observant, was giving to the little party the character of a public gathering to whose unknown elements one must feel one's way. For the moment the bright lens of Marian's spirit was dimmed by her preoccupation with correct behaviour. Seated farthest from the struggling fire, upright upon the sofa, her chilblained hands clasped in her lap, her face raised, exposed and available as should be, she knew, that of a hostess receiving company, she held out against the embarrassment of finding her eyes, the moment William's words were on the way, glancing desperately from point to point about the room. No retreat, for her, behind dropped eyelids. Her struggle for serenity lifted her finely marked eyebrows and compressed her almost tremulous lips, while

within the intelligently reflective eyes always, on social occasions prepared, if fully met, disarmingly to smile, the battle was
visible between vexation with William and her own embarrassment, leading her to seek some stately piece of drawing-room
furniture as sole confidante of her awareness of the unsuitability,
for the entertainment of a convalescent aunt, of the attack
launched by William the moment Sally, abandoning her
presidency of the reunion, had gone back to the kitchen.

'I suppose you don't feel strong enough to give a concert,'
pursued William, his voice breaking on a well-controlled chuckle.

'Poor Auntie!'

An echo of Sally, one of Sally's presidential comments
punctually thwarting every attempt at direct contact with the
children's minds, but free from Sally's meditative tone that was
always a plea for reconsideration rather than a reproach, leaping
into the arena as lively as the blush risen to Marian's cheek
while, to create an opportunity for turning upon William the
whole of her gathered resentment, she raised a hand to the knot
of ribbon nowadays confining, at the nape of her slender neck,
the barley-gold hair so delicately, in profile, clasping the outline
of her head. (Mozart. The profile of the young Mozart
seated playing. The resemblance, so eagerly sought a few days
ago at first sight of Marian, grown almost beyond recognition,
and now discovered, only to remain, lest it add doubtful fuel to
the fire of Sally's devout wondering observation, an incommunicable mental note.) Scorn? But not so much for
William as for an enormity Marian hoped, though now beneath
his dropped eyelids William's cheeks were redder than her own,
to see recanted to the accompaniment of a general hilarity under
whose cover she might retire, unobserved, to her coign of
vantage.

'Well,' Miriam said, hurrying into speech while still Marian
was within the party and lending it her warmth, 'what about a
trio; or is it too late to hunt for combs and paper?'

Speaking across the room towards William's shuttered isolation, she read in the eyes now raised and turned, after a shy,
swift, grateful glance in her own direction, in anxious watchfulness upon Marian, his recent progress from disappointment to

disappointment. For even *The Gipsy Rondo*, performed at competing speeds, would be a poor substitute for the improvisations so delighting him in a life that held so few delights and above which hung, for onlookers, already the shadow of a swiftly advancing destiny, saddening at this moment to garden light flowing freely in through the french window behind him, outlining his solid sturdy shape, gilding the obstinate flaxen hair of all the Brodies. Changeless and unremitting for as long as his strength should hold, some stereotyped toil would close down, within a few years, upon his restricted existence. Was he already aware? And craving, therefore, as throughout their confined lives within the world's accumulating machinery do so many men, thus earning part of their reputation for selfishness, only for effortless diversion, entertainment, forgetfulness?

'Yes, I think it's nearly lunch time, Auntie.'

In spite of his pathetic disarray, William's mere presence in the room, representing manhood, a comforting blind cliff, bringing freshly to mind, in illustrating its truth at the irreducible minimum, Mag's fervent preference, seemed at first both mysterious and revolting, for the society of men on account of their securely dependable inability to recognize necessary deceptions, made endurable the experience of being bathed, at the hands of this small relative, in a feminine clairvoyance that was trying to hide its own inevitable embarrassments not, in Amabel's revealing way, by a clenched, almost stuttering recoil from speech, prelude to an abrupt change of topic, during which she would glance about as though seeking an invulnerable receptacle for a cascade of incommunicable emotion, or, in her more uplifted moments, as though desperately endeavouring to escape into forgetfulness, but beneath dropped lids and behind childish lips uneasily moving under pressure of a courteous desire to avoid revealing, by their compression, the holding in leash of an implacable disapproval, or, by their twisted disdain, a challenge to defence.

Yet however welcome was William's blindness to one's longing to feel these enclosed, interminable moments end in escape to the shelter of distributed family activities, and his acceptance of a rarely seen relative as an enlivening visitor from a world in regard to which his imagination remained incurious, it made upon the weariness of convalescence a more exacting demand than Marian's intuitive perception of that world as occupying, even at this moment, more of the aunt's attention than the one where illness had temporarily stranded her. A perception so clear and so deep that for an instant at whose end their eyes met and Marian's, obedient to her firm little will, produced their social smile, she could believe the child actually discerning, where it lay sharply engraved upon the aunt's consciousness, the experience of those final moments upstairs, the finding and hurried reading of the letters that Jean's had driven from her mind, and the ending of the sense of being stranded in a vacuum whose sole light was the certainty of Jean's immortal love. She could believe the child aware of the meeting, in one post, of the letter embodying Rachel Mary's incredible suggestion, and the one enclosing the astonishing bestowal of the means of carrying it out.

But it was William, receiving no unspoken communications, making no demands beyond those brought by opportunity beneath his kindly little nose, who struck most deeply at her conscience, reproached her for having failed in the past to see as much of these children as so easily would have been possible at the price of refusing to spend every one of her disengaged week-ends in hanging about within London's magic circle.

'Perhaps,' she said, and saw hope glimmer again in William's watchful eyes, 'there is just time to tune up an orchestra.'

Almost barring the way as she squeezed past it to reach her conductor's post behind the piano, the elaborate upright chiffonier, self-satisfied, unquestioning, dominating its surroundings, taking the full light of the french window and reflecting in its gleaming central mirror and in the smaller ones above its pillared brackets, the room's brief perspectives and those of the little garden beyond it, broken only by the images of its own knicknacks, brought to her mind the Brodie relatives who had selected it as a wedding present for Bennett. Here they stood, powerfully represented. Unanimous in being for ever alert upon the social front, ready to risk life and limb in the performance of social duties, knowing nothing of singleness and solitude, they were ranged permanently upon the borders of Sally's consciousness, an everlasting challenge. Their warm, rallying voices sounded musically in the room duplicated by that of Sally, their half-convinced recruit, as it was when she used the tone taken over from them as a prop to sustain her in her dealings with grouped humanity; even when the occasion was nothing more formidable than the summoning of her family to a meal.

And this, she reflected, disengaging a floating sleeve from a protruding angle, this application of an alien technique, was amongst the things that had kept one away. And here, safe, in this unused, uninfluenced corner between the slanted piano and the wall, the joy overarching her preoccupations came down and closed with her, clamouring for an instant's tribute.

Remaining crouched, 'I think,' she intoned in a warbling falsetto, an instalment for the audience, and a screen, 'I'd better have a hassock.'

Following William's crow of delight came Marian's quiet voice, judicial, but with judgment for the moment suspended: 'I expect it's in the dining-room,' and the room was empty and she stood upright and watched, in the distances substituting themselves for the sheltering wall, the little figure of Rachel Mary going busily about, using every small journey towards or away from her fellow creatures as an opportunity to return to the centre whence she drew life and strength; Rachel Mary presiding at table, bending her head in the midst of a discussion that threatened to become fruitless dissipation of force and pretending, with downcast and apparently investigating eye, to rearrange her fichu while she turned with her whole being towards the source of unity and peace, to come back with some little sally that at once distributed the tension. Rachel Mary writing of her mother's death, tenderly and soberly, reminding one of the Quakeress who 'gently closed the eyes of her dead and came down to tea'; and, adding, when all was told: 'Your word-pictures make us all feel we have been in Switzerland.' Rachel Mary, only last week, initiating and presiding over the family discussion that must have been the prelude to this morning's letter, written, on a corner of some crowded table and, as ever, only just in time for post, the little note that serenely hastened to its still incredible conclusion: 'And if you have no other plans, you might like to come to us again. We'd all be glad to see you.'

A few more days of gathering strength within this enclosed circle no effort of mine can open towards the lights that fill my sky, the promised week-end with Michael and Amabel and then —*home*. The place I found and where I belong, amongst those who regard even the loveliness now increasing all about them and calling to me with claims as powerful as their own, as being merely 'pleasant.' Who rob the world of its power.

Yet without Mrs Harcourt, perfectly at home in the world and living according to its values, there could be no going back. What a strange interweaving; Jean, listening to the tangled story, would say, at the end of a moment's meditation: 'I see what you mean, Dick, but somehow for you it is different.' But Mrs Harcourt, admitting no such difference, would regard my proposed use of her determined gift as a base treachery. And perhaps it is, and I cannot care if it is.

Though away in her hotel, ski-ing every day and seeing me so rarely, she felt, just as she had done at the Oberland *Alpenstock*, that she had me under her wing. Witness her abortive efforts to bring about a romance between me and her German professor and, towards the end, her meditative inquiries as to my circumstances and plans. And when, in response to my ghastly suggestion of qualifying for an orthodox secretarial job complete with shorthand, that out there amongst the mountains whose summits at the moment shone madder-rose, did not seem so ghastly, she said nothing, it was not only because she knew I should take her approval for granted, but also because even then she must have been planning to forward my laudable scheme.

But I *knew*, in advance, when she began questioning me. And because I knew, I improvised a plan that would appeal to her, and half knew, all the time, that nothing on earth would persuade me to carry it out. Jean, what do you think of that?

But still smiling, Jean answered, with one of her rare hand pressures: 'Dick, with you it is different.'

Knowing little of the inside life of the *Lauriers*, Mrs Harcourt imagined herself the nearest friend I had in Vaud, and was no more prepared for the quality of Jean's presence at the station than was Miss Pelham, who came to see me off only to ascertain whether Jean, ill as she was, would yet be there. But Mrs Harcourt, self-controlled and relatively selfless, instantly taking in the situation, abdicated to the role of indulgent onlooker, sitting opposite to me near the door and dividing her attention between the unexpected little drama and the bustle on the platform; while Miss Pelham, bunched in the corner opposite Jean, her secret fury breathing from her very garments, kept repeating her frantic appeal for Jean's retreat to the house, not so much because she feared for her as because only with the help of these outcries could she endure what she saw and remain seated, paying no attention to the departing traveller who still, on the outskirts of a consciousness centred on the inevitable parting, was feeling gratitude for her hints, given in that disconcertingly English-villa chalet, on the playing of Chopin, and was sorry as well as glad that she should be compelled to witness what she so bitterly resented: Jean, muffled to the eyes and hardly able to speak, herself became an amused spectator, almost flaunting, as she sat defiantly tucked into my side, her gay sadness of farewell; lifted, for these final moments beyond the control of her determination not to hurt feelings, not able to care who saw and suffered in the seeing.

'*Well*, dear people?'

Sally's voice, in perfect reproduction of the Brodie intonation, at the half-open door.

'Here's the rest of the dear people.' Marian's, half-mocking herself and everyone else, from the door of the dining-room.

The lights and shadows of the passage were full of secret perspectives. And from the kitchen window, as she squeezed herself into her place between it and the table, a glimpse of the ancient rain-barrel bearing upon its battered lid a sun-gilt pool patterned by twig shadows; of the shady angle between the trellised fence shutting off the back garden and the low ivied wall only partly screening the neighbouring back door; of the little gate in the fence, invitingly open towards the hidden back garden, a world apart, its high trees already preparing summer shelter for that refuge from household tensions, giving upon the slope to the river and the towering elms that lined its bank.

And when she was in her place, instead of the dining-room furniture awkwardly crowding the available space, and the huge Henderson portraits looking on from the small walls, looking forth from their old world of unquestioned ease and stability upon the family's present disarray, the ample doors, flanking the kitchener, of Sally's store-cupboards, the clear, busy glow of the kitchener, the unhurrying wooden tick-tock of the clock on the mantelshelf in the middle of Sally's row of canisters, all battered, but each one offering a dimmed picture or decorative design.

This chequered kitchen tablecloth, too, rather than reinforcing, as always and everywhere does the usual cold spread of white napery, the bleakness of the midday light, softens it with a suggestion of morning and evening colour.

'. . . because the dining-room fire takes so long to warm the room.'

Even at Dimple Hill, she reflected as she roused herself to respond to Sally's remark, bleakness, thrown up from a white tablecloth, hovered above the gathering beneath the summit of the day's light. But only for a moment, only during the settling down of the party separated for the morning and still engrossed, each in his own concerns. After the silence, the dropping of preoccupations and the turning towards the everlasting source within and without, the bleakness was gone. But here, without even the grace whose hurried murmuring by one of the children made, whenever Bennett was present, the unvarying prelude to either of the substantial meals, there was merely the sense of the family gathered together, its natural sympathies and animosities firmly in place, to still the pangs of hunger in a crude light whose dominion could be shattered only by the precarious expedients of human talent; turns, staged to fill the void.

'Yes,' she said weightily, suddenly hopeful of initiating, by transforming Sally's apology into a topic, at least the semblance of a unified contemplation, and paused before adding, in perfect imitation of the Roscorla manner: 'I suppose it *does* that.'

And was translated, while she spoke with her mind truly set upon the image of the small fire slowly struggling towards mastery of the cold, to her place at the Dimple Hill table, to possession of her prentice share of the medium wherein the Roscorlas met and communicated with each other and that gave to every seated figure an inalienable dignity; and was aware, the moment her words were sped, of the incompatibility of the two atmospheres: the one enabling the speakers to address each other indirectly, impersonally, from a distance, so that even the simplest words became jewels set in a spacious light; and the one wherein each speaker, competitive, represented only himself, the quality of his production dependent upon his single ability.

For here was William grinning delightedly, from across the way, his assumption of some concealed hilarious intention; and Marian, before assuming her air of courteous attention, had darted an inquiring glance.

Yet in Oberland, where there was neither grace nor Quakerly silence, where communication flowed at once, there was at least an approach to the desirable atmosphere. Created by those in whom the Oberland quality went right through. By people like Harry Vereker and Mrs Harcourt. Its source was the same? For whence did England acquire her code of universal urbanity, its social method? No exhibitions, no prize-fighting. Smiling retirement, the moment conflict raised its head, backwards, bowing, as from the presence of royalty. But also, no thought. Only tastes and prejudices.

'It gen'ly takes ovra-naah to have any effect.'

In spite of the casual word-clipping and Sally's obvious pre-occupation, mental hands set, ever since the dismissal of the burdened and burdensome Emmaline, even in leisure moments upon the intricate machinery of house-running, here was a remark, an impersonal statement that could be handled, provided no one broke in during the necessary brief Quakerly pause, in the Quaker manner, given, together with the one who had spoken it, its full due of dignity and consequence.

Keeping herself at home in her place at the Dimple Hill table, she imagined the remark falling amidst the leisurely to and fro distribution of necessaries that, there, seemed not so much preparations to feed as means of conveying, from one to another, a quiet delight in this fresh meeting, in sharing a moment, as were the moments of all true Quakers, new and unique in human history, and sought, in the minds of those seated at the long table, a development of the theme.

Almost anyone at the Roscorla table might have produced her response to Sally's first remark. But the one she now had in mind would have come either from Richard securely home from the farm at tea time, haggard and weary, distributing the largesses of his inexhaustible good-nature, or from Alfred who was at least Richard's equal in the family game of caricaturing a tussle with a practical difficulty. And it was in the person of Alfred that she said, 'And it's got to have its hand held to accomplish that much,' and was at once aware of the loss the borrowed words sustained in being divorced from Alfred's way of dropping them sideways, as if into the ear of an invisible neighbour, rather in the manner of a stage 'aside,' but with the difference created by Alfred's experience of being so frequently the self-made butt of friendly family laughter that even when the victim was not himself he would retreat from his sally with a small crow of apprehension and the head-ducking movement of one dodging an expected blow.

William's adoring grin spilled over into a giggle. Putting forth a hand and swiftly withdrawing it, as from a flame, '*Whee*,' he squealed, but very gently, and returned busily to his food with downcast, disclaiming eyelids, with the air of one saying it's no affair of mine, almost of one saying *now* you've done it. Caught speculatively glancing, Marian smiled, the hesitant faint smile expressing at once her all-embracing amusement and her apology for being amused. Sally too produced a smile, a belated recognition of family mirth, with reservations, as if saying yes it's all very well, we may smile but it's neither here nor there and doesn't alter anything.

The situation was hopelessly astray. Intending a gravely respectful continuation, a sympathetic following up of Sally's

apology for a kitchen meal, she had launched, in her preoccupation with another environment, a remark Sally would consider
mannish and not, perhaps, in the best taste. And if now she
were to disown it, explain its origin and elaborate in simple
statements the idea now beckoning her with a genuinely smiling
radiance, Sally would respectfully attend until, growing weary,
she would intimate, tempering the wind of her impatience to the
reduced strength of a convalescent, her disapproval of 'going
too deeply into things.' Sally knew, had known all her life,
Mim's tiresome insistence on thought and now, at this date, if
one were to produce what one had in mind, she would think to
herself: 'That's the sort of thing that keeps you without a
home.'

Conversation at a standstill. All three waiting upon her
next move, suppressing, to leave the way clear for her, their
customary interchange. A turning-point, the perfect opportunity for a test. Here and now she would abandon for good
and all the role of entertainer sustained here at every meeting
during the years that had made her increasingly a stranger.
They must learn, if she were to represent Quakerism, to
tolerate her silence. Sally, dreading group silences on account
of her large share of Henderson self-consciousness and lack of
spontaneous volubility, would not immediately learn to distinguish between a steady Quaker stillness and one's old sullen
silences, alternating with the non-stop verbosity born, at home,
of perpetual disagreement and a desire to restate everything
that was said: even now not always kept in check by regret for
the hostility aroused by perpetual restatement. And during
one's withdrawal, since the hardest, the preliminary work of
attaining to Quakerly stillness cannot be achieved to the
accompaniment of sociable attention to whatever may be going
forward, Sally would imagine criticism volubly at work; unless
the sheer intensity of concentration required to attain inward
serenity in the presence of others, should reveal to her its
goodwill, should presently, ah, if it were possible, attain her and
reveal to her its power of blossoming, unaided by a tiresome,
conscious, watchful determination to be amiable, into friendly
and fruitful exchange, or, what sometimes was even better,

a recognition of the more than sufficiency of just being together.

The sharp jar, against a plate, of William's knife with power behind it, and a fragment of crust flew over the table edge.

Marian's bird-like 'Wheep!' collided with '*Oh*-dear-me' from Sally, conversational, allowing her to draw herself up, to look sprightly, glad of her smile arrived of its own volition, the girlish smile she never herself saw and that, once seen, would forever transform her in her own eyes.

'That's the worst of *pie*.' William's voice, rising from under the table, followed by his scarlet face.

Caught thus, half way to her bourne, she imagined, in response to William's swift investigating glance, revealing him, in the midst of his disarray, uncertain of the aunt's sympathetic approval of the flying leap, Richard remarking, her voice warm with the desire to rescue, and wide with the Mephistophelian smile it only partly belied: 'That bit wanted a run in the open.'

But Richard was not quite the model here to be represented: not quite the authentic Quaker brand (disliking entirely silent Meetings because 'you've nothing to do but sit and *think*,' explaining that 'it wouldn't be much good for Elphick to pit himself against *me*,' and, when asked why not, fingering his moustache and saying with a laugh: 'You see I'm the bigger man'; bracing himself against those boys racing round the refreshment tent at the flower show so that they cannoned into him and fell); an illustration, standing somewhere between the world, even the *beau monde* eternally jesting, and the gentle tradition that was his birthright, justifying those Quakers who just now are making a pother about birthright membership of the society.

'That bit,' nevertheless she began, for Richard refused to budge from the forefront of her consciousness, but Sally's voice, colliding with her own, won the day. 'It's a *lovely* beefsteak pie,' she said. Not a defence, but a proclamation sung out across the room for all whom it might concern. One for me and my mannish oblivion of all that goes to the production of savoury food. And Sally leaned towards William, murmuring, as if under cover of a lively conversation: 'You should put the

fork into the crust and press it *gently* down till it comes in two.'
and remained thus leaning, watching him as with downcast lids,
isolated, he squirmed his loathing and resentment of this public
instruction, until, realizing that her pressure was useless, she
turned again towards the centre with the air of one apologizing
for absence and eager to take part in whatever was going on.
And met only a wave of disapproval, resentment of a technique
that had shattered all links. Always Sally had isolated the
criminal and driven the crime home and waited, oblivious of all
else, for acknowledgment.

What would a Quaker, other than Richard, be doing in this
spiky atmosphere, with Sally now across the room dishing up
the second course with brisk energy, part of whose source was
resentment of one's resentment, and Marian, with thoughts no
one could fathom, secretly contemplating a familiar scene, and
William, still crestfallen, glancing across, when one was not
looking, awaiting a diversion.

But to come to his aid, after having failed him at a crisis,
would be to add, to the crime of one's own departure into wrath,
the offence of making common cause with him against Sally; a
meanness wherein he, too, would be involved.

Rachel Mary?

With a mighty effort, against which her very limbs seemed in
league, she joined her hands, rubbing them round each other in
Rachel Mary's way, looking down at them the while, to escape,
be lifted away from conflict, and return, perhaps, with a
healing contribution.

Widespread, blocking the way, the garden grounds of Dimple
Hill shone clear amidst their vast surroundings, coming so near
that she could almost hear, rising from the gardens, the daily
chorus of sounds blended by the wide distances and lost in the
heights of the summer sky. Another effort, a closing of her
inward eye, and she found herself thrown back, farther than
ever from that far region of the spirit whence she might truly
have joined those about her, alone in a void, dizzy with the
weakness of convalescence, and turned to cling again to the
loveliness that was to be hers without price. April, whose face
in Sussex she had not yet seen, was even now making beauty for

the familiar figures scattered in the beloved enclosure. Somewhere within each consciousness, lightly or deeply engraved, together with the sense of on-coming summer, was the expectation of her arrival.

If now, from the depths of her profanity, she were to speak, her very voice would betray her to Sally as merely putting in time, handing out easy animation while waiting to be elsewhere.

'Wish we had some *cream*.'

William, recovered, taking a small revenge.

'*Do*-you.' Mock-angry emphasis, carrying off Sally's satisfaction in having a witness of this restoration. '*Nothing* goes better with prunes than rice—if it's properly cooked.'

'*Just* caught on the top.'

Instructed by Sally, William will never be indifferent to the finer shades. Never will his wife hear Bennett's anything'll do for me, my dear, that yet so often must be a blessed lightener of Sally's ceaseless labour.

The neighbouring back door burst open for the resounding crackle of a shaken tablecloth.

'*La*-dee*dah*dy, *la*-dee*dah*dy . . .'

'Dear me,' murmured Marian, glancing round to collect reactions, 'lunch early today for a change.'

'Tom's feeling cheerful,' said William, also *sotto voce*, but warily, eyelids down.

Like her own, William's heart had responded to the sound of gaiety. Her smile waited to greet him. Was observed by Sally who, having in a lightning-swift glance fathomed its meaning, dropped her eyes to seem not to have noticed and said briskly, again as if dropping an irrelevant remark into an engrossing conversation: '*Noisy* people.'

Muted by the slammed door, the cadences of the waltz-song were still audible, and the startling, living glow, spontaneous, needing for its production no complex preparatory controls, that had gone forth to meet them, now rose heavenwards from the depths of her being. Within the tones of the lad's voice sounded the common qualities of British philistia, of the thoughtless, musical-comedy-loving English worldlings: profanity, pluck, confidence; incredible density, kindly humanity.

And while, yielding to self-revelation, and to the joy of inspiration, a warm and comfortable blush, she remarked upon the day's increasing mildness and welcomed the summer, their riverside summer, now on its way, 'garden teas, picnic lunches on the river, summer clothes, summer evenings . . . all those things that spread all over the year, really . . .' and saw them all awake and glow and begin chirruping one against the other, she saw within her mind, evoked in all its first clarity and revealed as immortal, the hitherto unpondered vision of that last, late afternoon on the Vaud rink whence Jean had been driven by the rising mist. Leaving one, forlorn yet glad, to wait, empty, blind and deaf, for solitude again to yield, as on that one lonely afternoon on the balcony, clearer depths of perception than the united contemplations that left, even while bringing reassurance, so many vistas to vanish unexplored.

The little group of players at the corner of the rink, festally illuminated on behalf of the lingering skaters who on that day ignored the message of the growing twilight, had become, the moment Jean's little figure, plodding along the hard-beaten snow to the roadway, vanished behind the brushed-up rinkside drift, the very moment of crossing the chill barrier between companionship and solitude, magicians, cunningly, tootling out, into the thin, bitter Alpine mist, for the English already fused into fellowship by the sense of the season accomplished behind them and now at its end, and by the common risk of missing, for the harvesting of these last, precious moments, time to dress for dinner, the English waltz of the moment, the *Merry Widow* waltz to whose familiar swinging rhythm, supporting and enlivening their movements, they skimmed, within eternity, enchantedly about, a few couples even, after a fashion, waltzing on the ice; a triumph setting them apart from the rest, unenvious in this pre-separation unity, unity of harvesters that on that afternoon seemed to include even E. F. Benson still, to the last possible moment lost-souling about, depositing within himself layers of indestructible experience.

CHAPTER III

A MOMENT'S silence, the first. Amabel meditative, perhaps holding in leash some freshly arrived irrelevant emotion. Michael, still alight and expansive, gazing now across the common centre to where the open window gave access to a world showing always a single face: his summary.

The small room reasserts itself, stating Amabel's quality. But to look about now, to be caught investigating detail, will be to break the spell of this first reunion, emerge into the oppressive sense, hanging so heavily over this sprawl of outer suburbia, of the shallows of life hurrying heedlessly along. Yet already, in this brief pause, lies nothing but the assertive presence of the little room, rapidly telling its own story as the successor, for Amabel, of the acceptably elegant, sophisticated club, her dingy room at Tansley Street, mitigated by books and the Empire coffee-set, and the battered Flaxman attic brought to life by geraniums.

Imagined empty as the builders left it, it becomes a small characterless square akin to millions of its fellows destined to grow smaller with the introduction of cheap, pretentious suites, and anecdotal pictures drawing the walls together with their teasing lack of distances. Rooms wherein the eye finds neither food nor rest. Keeping the centre clear and the walls a pale, soft shade, Amabel has created space and perspectives by her treatment of the corners. Deep, rich tones, rose, and gold, and, somewhere, for it had greeted one on entering, an angle bearing vertical strips of that rare, indefinitely retreating eastern blue, making a far distance there, enhanced by the bulge beneath it of a gently assertive pouffe, silky-crimson, gold-patterned. No graven images.

Here, in this little room, with its riot of rich colour held in check by severe economy of line, she has created for her own

596

beauty and for Michael's, hitherto each seen in surroundings throwing it up by sheer contrast, a perfect setting. Here, where most people would look incongruous, they glow like jewels.

Yet though this successful room already, during their brief residence, by the two of them so richly magnetized, offers itself as a worthy topic and one might well inquire, by way of expressing willingness to prolong this knitting together of past and present, whether they are not glad to have escaped the bob-fringed art-serge lodgings sheltering their first six months, one finds oneself, as soon as the little room has said its say, once more out in the unfinished roadway, gazing into the brilliant, live varnish of the stray celandine encountered on the way to the house; again feeling, as just now, while Amabel waited, controlling her always so readily provoked impatience lest its outbreak mar the triumphal entry, the unconfessable relief of escape from suburbia, from the raw, unfinished road and the crudity of the small, uniform houses, into the Roscorla's life-fashioned, richly girt homestead so soon to pour into one's being, where dwell already the scenes of the rest of its year, the unknown loveliness of its spring time. Spoken from that far distance, the question would lack even the semblance of sincerity.

'The light is going, Babutschka. Will you not immediately show Miriam her room?'

Rescue. Suddenly weary, as of old, Michael desires cessation. For the best part of an hour, fresh from the ceremonial tubbing (whose final cascade, reverberating through the house as proudly she opened its door, had yielded Amabel the joy of a witnessed rejoicing in her achievement for Michael of a life wherein at last he could conform to the pattern of his beloved ritual), in sabbath frock-coat topped by a deep crimson tie visible, when he raised his head, beneath the beard no longer trimmed to a worldly point and already on the way to becoming an oblong bush, rabbinical, the massed fine strands of his grandfather's pale gold watch-chain garlanding his breast, and the antique ring in place whose pimple of seed pearls rising from its bed of blue enamel set in graven gold, together with his air of leisure and availability, so vividly recalls those first, far-off evenings at Tansley Street, he had glowed responsive while she and Amabel revived their common past, moving, with each of his gusts of incredulous laughter, to and fro between their hazardous makeshift world and his still incredible little home re-created by the presence, not realized as unenvious, of one in whom all his English years and the whole of Amabel's London life are stored up.

The remembered Russian in him, wandering into irrelevancies sounding like fragments of a conversation going on elsewhere, and the middle-European intellectual, Emil Reich's aggressive continental luminary, coldly convinced and, for an unhappy while, convincing, and always in the end turning out to be *lucus a non lucendo*, are either in abeyance or, with his new growth towards his own roots, being gradually shed. At last, child and man, he is at home.

And Amabel?

Recalled from what might have been one of her sudden, determined retreats into realization, dependent for its depth upon the presence of others whose evocative speech should make no demand upon her direct attention, Amabel has leaped up, whirled, raised an arm to a switch. Light floods the room, the brilliant light whose instantaneous appearance Miriam has never failed secretly to applaud ever since in London and in the newer country houses she visited, it had begun to drive into a benighted past all other forms of illumination. Now, for the first time, it seems too abrupt, too easily, unceremoniously attained. Triumphant, indeed, as is also Amabel's face on which it shines. But while she contemplates the miracle, the sudden banishing of the shallow suburban twilight, whose relative it nevertheless seems to be, just as it is the relative of the dense, sacred twilight of central London, and the way it gives to the now brilliantly gleaming interior the semblance of a richly surrounded centre of town life, her truant inward eye turns gladly to the dim, dumpy little figure of Rachel Mary, her short arms outstretched, her serene, pleased anticipation revealed by the small glimmer of a flickering match as carefully she creates the evening's friendly glow in a room whose shadowy distances will recall, after the lamp is alight, the rich depths of the country twilight.

But even the present violent, unmitigated translation to evening demands some form of recognition. The clear, diffuse brilliance, like the sudden arrival of a host, enlivens the waiting guests who indeed should now drop the fragment of interchange languishing on their hands when he appeared, yet, rather than disperse, leaving him to himself without even a moment's tribute to his presence, should properly, under his benign influence, make some fresh departure. But Amabel, beckoning, and still silent, is leading the way, compelling abandonment and swift enterprise, into the windowless little passage dimmed almost to darkness as the door closes behind them.

Opening another door, she turns and, for a moment, prelude to standing aside to allow one to enter, stands framed in the doorway, in the soft light of the room's west window, finger to lower lip; her call either for solicitude or for a speechlessly shared contemplation.

A small strip of a room. New. Intimately familiar. Familiar sideway-falling radiance of a fading sky upon the pathway from door to window of polished green linoleum, pools of its light upon moss-green crockery, clear reflections in the oblong lake of a black-framed mirror fixed to a wall the colour of sack-cloth.

How to respond? How cross the chasm standing between today, already itself flooded by the rapidly approaching morrow, and the far past Amabel had here so charmingly recreated and that for her, still living within the framework of the London that was its background, seems only yesterday?

'It's adorable, Babinka,' she breathes, hoping against hope that Amabel, whose head is now pressed against her arm, will fail to be aware of the incompleteness of one's presence within the little shrine.

'It's your room,' whispers Amabel, releasing her and tiptoeing to the window, 'your Flaxman room. I made it for you.'

She is disappointed? Has gone off, alone, to seek in the open sky the rewarding response anticipated while she assembled the furnishings of her little spare room? But the lingering sound

of their two voices, hushed as in the past they had been hushed
whenever, reaching, by their so widely different routes, awareness of a shared inward life, they are aware also of challenging
perspectives opening ahead to put that life to the test, and feel,
in that same moment, the stirring of its growth as it feeds upon
the strength of a united recognition, together with the sight of
her, so much more richly attractive than that of Jean, standing,
as of old, absorbed, contemplative, gracefully outlined against
the frame of an open window, has worked the miracle the room
alone had been unable to achieve. Their old world, unrivalled,
incorruptible, is all about them and for a moment it seems as
though the little room must open and let them through into the
past. Easy now to move, to drift, thoughtless, along the
gleaming linoleum pathway to her side. To let her see,
arrived there, making no polite guest's comment on what
doubtless will be a little garden plot not quite robbed by
surroundedness of its power to send fragrance into the air
streaming down the room, how fully one perceives the return
of their common life.

Emerged from an instant's unconsciousness of all but the
breath-taking loveliness of the blossom whose little cups out-
shine the newly opened leaves against which they cluster, that
yet, pure new green, not only state their own perfection but
serve as foils for the densely white, rose-striped petals, Miriam
cries out in protest to an Amabel become a thief whose
plunder grieves the world.

'I know,' she murmured out into her garden, solicitously,
'but wasn't it worth it?'

The final, perfect touch of her welcome. Had anyone, ever
before, gathered apple-blossom to decorate a room? Amabel's
perfect gift, yet leaving one bereft. For the rapturous first
sight of it, in its place against blue sky amidst the spread of a
spring-green countryside, could bring no fuller pang of the joy
of return than did the unexpected presence here of this little
snapped branch paying with its life for a delight one would
gladly have foregone. During that instant of breathing in the
inexhaustible joy of its just perceptible colour, perceiving the
miracle of its form, revealed more powerfully here in the

darkling light than in the sunlit open, one has been transported, unprepared, unequipped, into the heart of the world that still stands two days away.

'You're going *back*, Mira.' Speaking dreamily out into the barely visible little garden, deliberately averted while laying gentle, privileged hands upon the immaculate future, seeing it as something to be dealt with; still believing one prepared, as behind her air of easy spontaneous improvisation she herself is always prepared to deal with situations, to calculate and plan. Asking, therefore, for confidences. Leaning on arms propped upon the window-sill, so far out that one must lean, too, to hear.

'I *love* your Miss Roscorla.' Rachel Mary, the first, save only Michael, of one's human belongings she had unreservedly approved. 'And Richard,' she breathed, almost inaudibly, 'an *utter* darling.' Here it is, her interpretation, inviting confirmation, of the two communicated items; the removal of the old lady and Rachel Mary's little *ballon d'essai*.

'Indeed he is. Everybody's darling.'

This swift hand-pressure upon one's arm might mean either sympathy or a reproof for sacrilege. Let her speak again since she is set, or she would have swung gaily round to carry one off to the rest of the house, upon continuation. Let her make a fresh departure or ask, unmistakably, her unanswerable question.

'You're going *back*,' she repeated, with a catch in her voice.

'Yes, but I don't know what *to*.' To the old house, beloved to its every musty cranny; to its spreading gardens, huge, yet lost in their vast surroundings; to the silent eloquent company of light, present even during the hours of what townsfolk call darkness. Enough, at almost any price that will enable one just to survive. And, thrown in with all this, the strange intimations of unpredictable growth. 'I believe I'd go more gladly if he were not to be there.'

'I *know*.' Passion, this time, in her voice. Nostalgia, awaiting opportunity to confess, for the perspectives she has sacrificed to matrimony? Or a restatement of her oft-expressed doctrine in regard to things eagerly grasped: that they invariably reach one's hands *broken*.

Drawing abruptly back into the room, 'Come and see the kitchen,' she says without enthusiasm, automatically, her mind elsewhere.

As if greeting their entrance, a clock begins to strike.

'Holy Moses!   I must get supper!'

Sweeping impatiently from point to point she fills the room with movement that leaves no pathway free, aimless movement expressing, as well as resentment of momentarily forgotten, inexorable demands, a longing to be left alone to deal with them that keeps one rooted in the doorway reduced to the status of a man, a useless alien.   Everything in the brightly lit little interior, save only its inevitable kitchener, is pleasant to contemplate, each object exactly in place and bearing itself with an air of coquettish elegance; all unsightly detail contained, like the windows, with crisply starched cotton patterned with a small blue and white chequer.

Small, compact and brightly burnished, the little kitchener, the heart and meaning of the room, prevailing over its decorative surroundings, draws one's eyes with its mystery, acquaintance wherewith places Amabel amongst the household women, shows her caught, for life, in a continuously revolving machinery, unable to give, to anything else, more than a permanently preoccupied attention.   Impatiently, now, she is poking, rootling about behind the bars, defiant of her material, uncertain of its behaviour, destroying, in treating it as an enemy to be outwitted, its air of sturdy benevolence, driving one yet again into truancy.   At this moment in the roomy Dimple Hill kitchen, quiet, and dark save where at its far end the practical harsh light of the unshaded oil lamp falls upon the serene figure of Rachel Mary bent over the shabby ancient range, the fire's rosy glow stands out against the blackness of the great flue starting on its journey up through the house into the open whose fading twilight is the promise of dawn.

How express to Amabel, remembering her meditatively murmuring, when faced with the loveliest of the Dimple Hill vistas: '*How* does anyone endure country life without servants and a motor?'   (If she *had* meant to be crushing, I ought promptly to have told her that motors are now called *cars*), what it is to look out, in solitude, from some remote doorway, upon that dawn-promising evening twilight? How make her see the inexhaustible wealth of life down there apart from, and success-fully competing with, any form of human association?

'You know, Amabel, it's queer. Quakers are full of plant lore and natural history. They're what Michael calls "facta-tive." Never, even in their own quiet way, are they beside themselves out of doors. "Pleasant" is their extremist tribute even to the loveliest scene. The Puritan tradition, perhaps, from which most of their forbears came forth to join Fox. From which Fox himself came forth. They place the more negative ethics of Puritan living side by side with their own fundamental beliefs and never see their incompatibility. Yet their alphabet, their way of handling life, I mean the business of minute to minute living in the spirit which gives them their perspective and their poise and serenity, is the best I've met. But the thought of the missing letters makes the idea of a Quakerized world intolerable. And the thought of a world without Quakers is equally intolerable.'

'Mira.'

Something is coming. The low-pitched tone, meditative, revealing her unarmed and wholly present, means an appeal in the name of the fullest of their past inter-change. Some question that will strike to the centre of one's being. Not in regard to Richard. Considering that episode closed, Amabel would experience, if told how the thought of his share in Rachel Mary's invitation reinforced the other inducements to return, the pull of Quakerism, the equal pull of the earth and the light only a contemptuous amazement.

'Will you become a missionary?'

In advance, as ever, of one's own thoughts, she has put the obvious question waiting ahead of a full acceptance of Quaker doctrine.

'Your friends will miss you.'

Unanswered, she is taking silence for consent, and has moved forward into a future seen by her as in some measure bereft. Believing that I hold, in my consciousness, so much of the drama of her life, an investment that no longer, once I am removed, will yield any return? If now she knew that Jean, unquestioning, trustful of all I may do, stood central in my being, she would rejoice with me? Rejoice that the day of her full power, recalled by the present retrospective radiance, is over?

This is no acting. With her head bowed on my knees, for the first time neither in irrepressible mirth over my stupidity nor in half-amused adoration, Amabel is not being audience for her own performance. Her whispered words held despair touched by real fear, leaving one isolated with the misery she has so quietly described. Michael, across the way, still hunched forward in his comfortless kitchen chair, his clasped hands between his knees, though a silently consenting witness of Amabel's recital will be by this time far away within the cage of his own fixed ideas. Absent from the bitter climax. To and fro his mind will be swinging, suspended between phrases, recalled from his restricted 'novelistic readings,' phrases embodying 'the disillusionments of marriage, depicted, for example in most-wonderful small touches by Tolstoi, who is always a most masterly speechologue.' Amabel has doubtless heard all of these, has given her deeply dredged reasons for finding them inadequate.

Having believed and stated himself to be forewarned, having always been ready to admit masculine shortcomings, never weary of repeating his repulsive little tag about the difference between a fiancé and a man taking his ease at home, *en pantoufles*, he is now fatalistically accepting the proof of the findings of his European luminaries. In a moment he will be cracking his finger-joints and following up the detonations with his depressing 'ach-ma.'

Echoing forlornly in the bright spaces of the discredited little kitchen, Amabel's 'What are we to *do*?' brings back her first warning note, sounded just before she and Michael left their furnished lodgings: 'Marriage is awful. I mean just what I say. It may be, I'm free to confess, helped to be awful by these lodgings and the weird people who run the house. When Mike is out, life is far from gay. But when we're shut up here together: my God! And it's not Mike's fault, nor mine. Believe me, Mira, it is just *marriage* that is so impossible.' And then, later: 'We're moving, thank the Lord. Next week. To a maisonette. Do you see me? In an own house I'll be all right.'

To either, alone, one could plead that people, and especially those who expect each other to be the sole source of rapture, cannot *go on* feeling consciously rapturous. Admitted. What then? What of the worst loss of all: the loss of unthreatened solitude? Useless, cruel, to mention that. Like saying: I told you so. And the state of these two is the worst of all. Far worse than the normal incompatibility of man and woman is the absence in their daily life of a common heritage, stating itself at every turn. Amabel, freer than most, more genuinely catholic, could not foresee this and now pays the price. In misery.

'I don't know.'

'Well, I *must* say, you are a *goode* friend.'

Michael's deepest bass. More than reproachful. For the first time, to me sarcastic; the measure of his hurt. Not cynically aloof, he has been listening, following, countenancing. Perhaps, counting on my help, had even suggested this outpouring.

Unanswered, unanswerable, his words stand upon the fevered air. Not the rejoicings, the happy reconstructions of yesterday, seeming then so sure a foundation for whatever of the future the three of us are to share, but this piteous scene will accompany us tomorrow, stand between me and the threefold joy of Dimple Hill.

No remedy. Nothing to be said or done. Cajolery, or even reason, with Michael silently supporting, would drive Amabel to excess.

Risen to her feet, she strolls about the room as if seeking, hopeless of human aid, refuge amongst things inanimate.

'Be glad, Mira,' her gravest tone from the farthest distance allowed by the small room, 'that you can go *away*.'

CHAPTER IV

THE TRAIN moved off, carrying her forward within the deep peace welling up the moment she had uttered, at the pigeon-hole, the name of the little station. Unintentionally she had adopted the Roscorla pronunciation, the gently shortened vowel and slightly lingual 'l' transforming Hayleham to Heyl'm, seeming courteously to salute the place, and suggesting unlimited courtesies in reserve. Last year this station had meant just the end of the journey towards an unknown refuge. Today it is the gateway to Paradise.

Meadows, forlorn, London-dimmed, their green silvered by the night's rain. But any moment now skied orchard-bloom will suddenly appear, sail by, vanish, leaving no regret. Then the little woods of Surrey, their too many conifers ousting the sense of spring. Then Sussex.

On last year's journey, though the coming six months' free-dom seemed an eternity, the Sussex woods, heavy with summer leafage, demanded breathless watching. Today, for the first time, even when the woods bring close alongside the doings of light and shade within their depths, there will be no longing for the train to go more slowly, but only gratitude for these instal-ments of wealth waiting ahead to be enjoyed for a period extending unenclosed. Perhaps for life. Perhaps, this time, there need be no return? Upon Mrs Harcourt's gift of six months' living, I can hold out at Dimple Hill for at least a year. Writing. Becoming increasingly what Hypo calls turnip-minded. No more argumentative articles. No more short-circuiting humanistic socialism. ('I've thrown science and socialism overboard.' 'Right, reckless Miriam. But don't get drowned when you plunge to retrieve them.' 'If I ever do, submergence will have changed them.' 'Everything's changing all the time. That's one of the things humanity has to learn.' 'Und ob alles in ewigen Wirbel kreist, es ruhet im Wirbel ein stiller Geist.' '*Geist*, my dear Miriam, is a very questionable term.' Spirit, at the centre. His obsession with evolution makes him see theosophy as alone sane and reasonable amongst the creeds. An endless spiral. Nightmare. Wrong metaphor. Spirit is central.)

I must remember to tell Jean about thought. About the way its nature depends upon the source of one's metaphors. We all live under a Metaphorocrasy. Tell her I'm giving up thinking in words. She will understand. Will agree that thought is cessation, cutting one off from the central essence, bearing an element of calculation. 'Ye must become as little children.' Meaning, as those who do not *calculate*. But children are heedless. When elders say 'you did not think,' they really mean 'did not reflect.' Did not reflect any actuality but your own. Most people don't. I don't. I've been reflective only in my own interest, and heedless. Laying up a past that one day will smite unendurably.

Will begin at once to smite if I pursue the pathway so suddenly opened last night. Towards the past. Inexhaustible wealth. Inexhaustible remorse. Why do they say distance *lends* enchantment? Distance in time or space does not *lend*. It reveals. Takes one into heaven, or into hell. From hell, heaven is inaccessible until one has forgiven oneself. So much, much more difficult than accepting forgiveness. Not God, but we ourselves, facing the perspective of reality, judge and condemn. Unforgiven, we scuttle away into illusions. But, all the time, we know. We are perambulating Judgment Days. That will make Jean, the permanent forgiver, laugh till she weeps. But it is the truth. If one could fully forgive oneself, the energy it takes to screen off the memory of the past would be set free.

Perhaps the sudden return of past reality is the result of temporarily losing freedom to move, of being compelled to concentrate, for a whole evening, upon affairs other than my own; to endure, in that workaday kitchen, the background deliberately chosen by Amabel to emphasize her translation of a Christian Sunday into a Jewish weekday, the revelation of suffering I could not hope to relieve.

For when at last I escaped to my little green room it enclosed no longer the past I had shared with Amabel. Inhabited only by the April night and the apple-blossom, it let my being expand, touch the borders of a destination that she, entangled, could not reach. As soon as I was at peace within the darkness where still the young green leaves and crimson-striped buds of the apple-blossom seemed visible, and on-coming sleep just a swift passage towards today's journey, I suddenly saw, substituting itself for the boundless mind-view of Dimple Hill towards which I was drowsily drifting, the gabled porch at Barnes, the shallow, wide steps leading down from it, the tubbed yukkas. Unchanged. Yet subtly changed. No longer quite the secret, sacred portal, the sight of which always hurried my footsteps as I came up the drive, and always brought me as I passed through it, no matter what my mood, or the circumstances awaiting me inside the house, a moment in eternity, but just the well-known porch seen for the first time impersonally. And I knew at once that it was bringing a message. And while sleepily I wondered what revelation was about to come, I discovered a figure seated there in the dim light. Harriett. Sitting there alone, in possession, gracefully ensconced where the stone balustrade meets the upright of the porch. And for the first time I realized that my porch was Harriett's also.

Only now does it occur to me to wonder where, on that evening, I could have been. For during the summer of the dress Harriett was wearing I was at home, and we were always together. But to reach the depth of contemplation in which now I found her she must have sat, not for a few chance moments of my absence, but for a long time, alone. There she was, gazing, in solitude, into her own life, realizing it as it slipped, with the approach of marriage, away into the past, realizing that soon it would be inaccessible.

Within the depths of that moment I seemed to gaze into her being. Aware of it as if it were my own. For the first time I realized the unique, solitary person behind the series of appearances that so far had represented in my mind the sister called Harriett. And as the scene vanished, its curious darkling light spread, fading, across the world, showing me, as it moved, dim unknown figures as real as she.

Returned to the heart of the darkness, I begged myself to remember, every day, this sudden glimpse of reality. But shall I? Amidst the daily call of things that come between me and the sense of any human presence?

A year secure. Given by a kindly philistine for a purpose I mean to ignore. Three hundred and sixty-five days. Each with a morning, an afternoon, an evening. Three eternities. Yet they are not three eternities but one eternity. The ever-changing light, one light. Unbroken. Every day a choice of experiences, any one of them presently returning of itself with power to move me to put it into words, to spread hours in oblivion from which I awake to find a piece of life gone by unheeded.

To write is to forsake life. Every time I know this, in advance. Yet whenever something comes that sets the tips of my fingers tingling to record it, I forget the price; eagerly face the strange journey down and down to the centre of being. And the scene of labour, when again I am back in it, alone, has become a sacred place. Just one evening's oblivion gave me everlasting possession of the little white table standing under the brilliant light of my Vaud bedroom.

If Jean had not gone out to squander her evening upon the unhappy Cattermoles, it would not have occurred to the Bishop to lend me, by way of compensation, *The Friday Review*. If I had not been curious as to the nature of his chosen periodical, I should have spent my evening writing letters instead of venturing back into the world of conflicting ideas. Dreary it seemed, irrelevant. Each party drawing different conclusions from the same data, unaware of any common ground. Soon weary, I looked up. Found my little room stripped of its magic. Played with the idea of going downstairs to spend, unsupported by Jean, the rest of the evening in Lhassa, where, if it should occur to the Bishop to ask how I liked his review, I might expiate my backsliding by a small sparring-match ending in a smiling draw. Glancing again through the paper, I came upon that shapely single column I had somehow overlooked: *The Threshold of Spring*. One of those things Hypo calls 'middles' and urges me to try my hand at: 'Anyone can do 'em. Any old theme. Worth two guineas.' Though annoyed by the super-fluous words cluttering up the title, I read and presently was watching a seedy little man walking along a lane; *observing*. Carefully, right and left. Could hear his voice, a little raised as though addressing students, and having the colourlessly clear enunciation common to so many London universitarians, giving to each syllable a uniform emphasis and making, between each, a just perceptible pause ('*see, this, pop, lar*') so that his phrases were a series of hammer-blows neatly striking dead everything to which he called attention. Yet here he was, full of specialized nature-lore, welcomed by the editor to supply the weekly oasis, read by countless people who heard no voice, found refreshment, instruction, interest?

In vain this knowledge-burdened naturalist deplored my ignorance. There I stuck, outcast by all standards of intelli-gence and kindliness, with no comfort but the certainty of Jean's forgiving laughter for my foamings.

Putting down the paper, I craned round to ask the face of my clock how long I must wait for Jean's return. But my eyes never reached it.

One after another the scenes passed before me, each with its unique claim. Impossible to choose. Impossible without special knowledge to convey. Flesh without bones, as Hewar's sketch was bones without flesh; a tour through a museum, he the curator, cataloguing its specimens.

With the return of scorn, the Dimple Hill scenes disappeared.

It was while I was recalling what Susan told me about that man who wrote, every week, about something he had seen: 'Any old fing. Someone buying a bunch of flowers, or board-ing a bus,' that the auction in the thirty-acre shot into my mind and got me to my feet. But on the way to the table, freshly aware of the presence, outside my shuttered room, of the Swiss night and its promise for tomorrow, there came that moment of warning, of regret for having involved myself, unwillingness to spend of my diminishing store of evenings in oblivion.

And when near midnight the sheaf of filled pages lay before me, and confidently I saw it arriving, unsolicited, under the eye of the editor, saw him held forgetful of all else, as I, while writing had been held, heard him tell himself how much better it was than Hewar's, I still could have wished it away and my evening restored. There it lay, part of me, yet now independent. And then came that knock at the door, gathering me back to listen into the house I had deserted; and to speculate. And then the door ajar, and Jean's tired voice murmuring that she was not coming in, murmuring good night. Did she notice how startled and over-emphatic was my response, how it proclaimed my forgetfulness of her very existence? Her light footsteps died away down the corridor, leaving me alone with the realization of a bond, closer than any other, between myself and what I had written.

Which room will they have given me to forget them in?

For a while, whenever Rachel Mary, disappointed of a sister-in-law, and Richard, at once regretful and relieved, are alone with me, any silence will bring them embarrassment. But this evening will be filled with speech, and during the next few days while still the sight of me recalls their vicarious experience of Vaud, Rachel Mary will be able, at need, to grasp at something described in one of my letters. I must be prepared if, sensing a clamorous void, she should reproduce her written comment upon my 'word-pictures,' not to squirm. If I should squirm, they will imagine me scuttling about to avoid encirclement by the circumstances leading to my retreat to Vaud. I must devise a generalization that will at once leave Vaud intact and provide a point of departure.

Vaud will disappear. The past, all our pasts, falling back into their places, will vanish from our midst, and our life together will be as it was in the beginning, a moment to moment building up of shared experience. Current existence, the ultimate astonisher. Whose testimony will be the ease and depth of our silences. But Richard still fears, at table, any silences beyond those prescribed by Quakerly technique. The leisurely Sunday dinner-hour will still give him opportunities to relate, upon the remotest pretext, his dreadful anecdotes, never failing to delight all the others and to bring home to me the difference in our sense of humour.

Henceforth, whenever some local happening serves him to recall, with kindly malice, a kindred incident in the far past, withholding his own laughter until, prompted by the turning upon me of his patient mephistophelian smile, my slow intelligence shall have grasped, unwillingly, the pictured situation, I shall remain upon my own ground; refuse to pretend to find food for mirth in the described spectacle of acute embarrassments and yield him, from beneath lowered eyelids, only Amabel's meditative half-smile that so clearly indicates 'we are not amused.' *That* may learn him. In any case it is high time for a gap in his career of immunity from feminine criticism.

Vaud and Jean, have vanished. Not a word, even to Rachel Mary, about Jean.

If I were less than I am, I should talk about her until my friends would grow to dread her name. If I were more than I am, I should follow her path, the path to freedom. But I forget. Again and again, until something pulls me out into remorse. If only I could remain always in possession of my whole self, something of Jean-in-me would operate.

Good that she is gone. How right are the Catholics in separating within their orders those who grow too happy in each other. To give oneself, fully, to God-in-others, one must belong to no one. Careful though she was, and in the end taught me to be, to avoid, in public, any revelation of partiality, we yet aroused jealousies. As those last weeks slid away, the glow we created in each other could not be concealed.

Jean. Jean. Jean. My clue to the nature of reality. To know that you exist, is enough. Those final days fulfilled the whole of our winter. Whenever, with the date of my departure drawing near, I was on the point of making moan, something held me back. Every day in that last week brought a richer depth of happiness. Did Jean know, all the time, that in the depths of reality there is no room for lamentation? Was she waiting for me to discover this? Or was our experience, to her too, a revelation? Leading, as for me it led, to the sudden discovery coming when on that last grey afternoon while side by side we sat gazing in silence at the thawing remains of winter:

that in separation we should not be parted? Perhaps she felt me realizing this when simultaneously we turned to each other, laughing, and returned, without a word, to the landscape.

With Jean, for me, friendship reaches its centre. All future friendships will group themselves round that occupied place, drawing thence their sustenance.

What room will they have given me? Today, being washing-day, Eliza will not have begun on it until this afternoon. At this moment, within a dense cloud of dust, she is busily sweeping. Rachel Mary, at the last moment, will put finishing touches. Will scatter petal-dust in every drawer. Hearing the carrier's bus climb the hill, she will trot briskly downstairs, removing her apron as she goes. Will be in the porch. The others, their day's work finished, may be about. Greetings and handclasps, and I shall be at home. In no time, the first tea-party. Lively interchange, but no spilling over. After supper, when Richard lifts the great brown Bible on to the table, we shall all feel ourselves quietly together again, free of space and time. It will be as though I had never left.

But before I can feel fully at home, Mrs Harcourt must know I'm not carrying out her plan. Then I need think no more; for ever. My letter to her will be what Hypo calls 'a version.' But she will know. Will understand that I never meant to qualify for a job in an office. I don't, can't care. I'll tell her I've come to stay where I can live on almost nothing, and am going to write. What does Mr Godge mean? Would he agree with Michael that in England writing is becoming a base trade? He asks for more sketches, tells me to write only when strongly moved to do so, and then warns me that there is not a living to be made from sketches like *Auction* 'because they take too much thought.' What does he mean by thought? Imagination? Not in the sense of *making up*. Imagination means holding an image in your mind. When it comes up of itself, or is summoned by something. Then it is not outside, but within you. And if you hold it, steadily, for long enough, you could write about it for ever.

'If you can describe people as well as you describe scenes, you should be able to write a novel.' But it is just that stopping, by the author, to describe people, that spoils so many novels?

A copse sails by, bringing escape, absence within its glimmering depths.

Now open country. Sweet air, elastic; perceptible even within the London-impregnated carriage. Lowering the half-opened window, she sits down to attend to a hovering statement now come into the open to answer this man's evident belief in the importance of novels.

Novels are irrelevant.

Irrelevant to what?

To follow his advice would mean spending enormous pieces of life away from life. Perhaps novels are important. Whenever anyone sneers at them, I am moved to defend. Anyway to smack long-nosed people who sit in the seat of the scornful.

Green meadows, low-lying. Red-brown Herefords, with ghost-white masks, all seated, serenely chewing. Every line of their confident great shapes rebuking contempt for anything or anybody.

It's true. Scorners nearly always have long noses, with clean-cut nostrils that can curl and twitch. Cogitative, reflective people are mostly snub-nosed. Dr Stenhouse is betwixt and between. A kindly, investigating, doctorial eye, blinkered. 'Odd, the way we synchronize.' Or a shape of some kind? Whether I reached Lyons' early or late, he had always just arrived for his lunch, or came in almost at once. If he had merely expressed speculative wonder over the general love of novels and neglect of history, we might have put our heads together. But his bitter contempt for those who read novels and know next to nothing about history, put my back up and spoiled my prunes and cream. And while I was deciding to suggest that he should read, as Anglo-American history, first *Little Lord Fauntleroy* and then *The Ambassadors*, he trotted out, to bring me back and secure my attention, his stock remark upon the excellence of Lyons' coffee, his call, whenever I became incommunicative, for a unifying duet. And it was only after he discovered that I had done three middles for the *Friday* and was waiting for a third to suggest itself, that the underlying strange *shape* came out into the open; as it *always* does if you leave things alone. I'd spent the morning reading Erdmann's *History of Philosophy* at the Museum, and was feeling very remote while he told me of his years at Cambridge and presently reintroduced his theme of History versus the Novel and suddenly slapped down at the side of my plate, with an air of triumphant finality, a folded manuscript. 'Perhaps,' he said, hiding his very slight embarrassment behind an assumed indifference, 'your editor might be interested in that.' Important, I felt, a writer to whom this Harley Street doctor was humbly appealing. Yet sorry, too. For I knew he would have described what he disliked by its defects and what he approved of by its qualities, and both very tamely, so that inevitably the editor would 'regret.' And at the same time I merely relished his certain discomfiture. Never dreaming by what a strange route this was to arrive.

In the afternoon, my seat in the library under the shelf holding the Erdmanns was empty, and that young man who for weeks had been my engrossed, congenial neighbour, still in his place, but not, as usual, sitting bent in an attitude of studious concentration over a single volume. There he sat, with all my Erdmanns piled on his section, looking through one of the volumes with a dreamily interested smile on his good-looking face. For how long did I stand indignantly staring before I sat down to think out the wording of a disdainfully courteous request to be allowed the use of any volumes he might have finished with? But while I sat thinking, appearing to be tranquilly engaged with my note-books, I observed out of the corner of an eye that he was not only scanning the summaries at the heads of the chapters, the menus of my incomparable feast, but also taking notes. With that realization he became myself, eagerly tracing the development of Greek thought. Not for anything would I have interrupted him. And then into my emptied mind came suddenly, standing out among the room's subdued rustlings, that sound like the popping of a cork, calling the odd forgotten name of that man who had 'written so illuminatingly about the Arian controversy; that decisive turning-point in the history of Christianity,' and I wanted only to leave Greek thought to itself and get hold of his book while I remembered the author's odd name.

And when it came, the slender little volume brought me the two gifts which I might have missed but for the stealing of my Erdmanns. First the discovery of this 'Gwatkin' as a professor in Stenhouse's time at Cambridge at Stenhouse's own College; then, incredibly, that passage about the novelist's advantage over the historian on account of his freedom to isolate and illuminate the interplay of human passions; and then, after I had triumphantly copied the passage for Stenhouse the journey to the end of Gwatkin's little book, happiness in Athanasius' salvation of truth, together with realization of the need for dogma and the tragic limitations of verbal statement.

Irrelevant to what?

There is something to find out. Something fundamental that applies to the whole mass of what Michael calls novelistic writing.

CHAPTER V

THE SHAPE of the spade-flattened hard-frozen face of the snow-drift outside the woodcutter's chalet, and the outlines of one or two of the figures chiselled thereon with such reckless prodigality of craftsmanship, grown at last clear in her mind's eye, demand now, if words are to be summoned that will express anything of their quality, a further immeasurable withdrawal from the beatitude so richly overflowing, on this first morning, from everything within sight.

The first effort had aroused the almost vocal protests of the beloved shabby furnishings of this little room, as if they knew that her return to them from even a momentary absence will find her, and themselves, and the relationship between them, already a little changed.

As yet, not much damage done. The things in the room have retired a little: not sure whether they have been affronted or merely momentarily forgotten. If one rejects the demand for a second departure they will at once fully return, bringing their treasures; evocative.

· Daily, however varying, this light, subdued on one side by the dense branches of the evergreen oak, pours through the window upon everything in the room. Light-absorbing, light-reflecting individuals, pathetic and proud. Claiming acknowledgment and interest. Wilting under neglect. But beneath the high morning sky, the just visible distant marshes, the near green meadows and the piled downlands away to the right, though ignored and forgotten during the moments of withdrawal, hold now a livelier glow than when, sitting down at the table, she had first greeted them. Seem to promise, if she should face the second journey, a further increase of their inexhaustible response. The garden, partly tamed, domesticated, turned in on itself, expresses only a tolerant neutrality.

And now, exactly at this moment of wavering, interruption.
The door coming cautiously open.   Rachel Mary, still radiating
welcome, sparing a moment of her busy morning to inquire as
to one's welfare.   Passing through the doorway from bustling
kitchen to silent dining-room, scene of the triumphant fulfilment of kitchen labour, along which she will have trotted on
holiday, on a pleasant journey, taking in as she passed, without
looking towards it, the loveliness beyond the window, the little
high-walled enclosure now all fruit bloom and early flowers;
aware, as she approached the farther door, of the glass-misted
green light of the peach-house; aware, the next moment, as she
turned into the passage, of the larch-darkened light coming
through the open door of the gun-room, and then of the full
light of the front hall across which she trotted to this door;
cautiously grasping its loose handle to avoid rattling, gently
pushing the door open, prepared, if all is well, immediately to
retire.

Incredibly, Richard.

And not by mistake.   Not only not withdrawing at sight of
her in possession, but actually acknowledging his awareness by
closing the door as slowly, as quietly, as he had opened it.
And while thus silently he tells her of his intention not to
disturb, even of his willingness to be regarded as not present,
he announces at the same time, in stentorian tones ringing out
amongst the spheres, a planned, deliberate intrusion.

Blessedly her pen has remained, during her meditations,
poised ready for writing.   No need for any movement that
might suggest a settling down after an acknowledged
disturbance.

Now to retain concentration and its accompanying capacity
to see, without looking, everything within her range of vision,
and thus present to Richard a meditative mask behind which,
while apparently engrossed in an exacting task, she can plumb
at leisure the depths of this amazing departure.

Meanwhile to be writing something, anything; to empty the
room of any sense of her presence as hitherto known to him.

Meaningless words would serve better?   For, already, in
setting down '*A thing of beauty*,' decoyed by its never-failing

charm, she has fallen behind, failed to remain on the alert, missed the immediate impact of his refusal to notice the far chair set so conveniently near the window's direct light. Yet at all costs the writing must go on. '*Is a joy for ever*'—the carefully decorative script demanded by the words, so often traced out at crises as to flow from her pen almost of themselves, make easier the preservation of the meditative mask. Richard has come deliberately to meet her in her own world? Curious enough, interested enough to risk a misreading of his motive?

'*Its loveliness increases, it will never*'—now to discover what lies at the heart of the radiation enclosing her while he sets himself hugely, gently down into the chair at right angles to her own, noiselessly, save for the light scraping, as he settles himself, of clumsy boots against the bare boards beneath the table.

Papers. A neat sheaf of loose leaves, almost as incongruous as his presence.

Has he come in, on the pretext of business to attend to, counting on my believing he does not know that this room has been set apart for me? Driven by sheer curiosity, the naïve desire to see a writer writing.

'*Pass into nothingness, but always keep*'—evade thought. Travel, while I write, down to that centre where everything is seen in perspective; serenely.

Rugged, weather-stained hands, quiet now, resting one on each side of the arranged papers. The right hand taking up a freshly-sharpened pencil. Where, now, with the scene set and a gap of less than two inches between the nearest paper and the top of my manuscript, is his mind? Mine retires and retires. I am as calm, as steady, as if I were alone. I am myself, my own. Can go on writing, or stop writing, concentrate my attention upon discovery and still appear to be far away. As indeed I am. Spared the need for speech, I can think at leisure. While slowly his huge fingers push the pencil across the page.

In allotting this room instead of the large upstairs sitting-room I had last year and that now and again has to serve for social gatherings, Rachel Mary said: 'You'll be able to work there undisturbed.' The whole household has certainly been told. Richard, with a letter to write, goes always to the little gun-room, sits at the clear table there, the peach-packing and grape-packing table, the open door leaving him visible and visibly available, sociable; only too pleased to explain to a passer-by the exact nature of his exceptional employment, if the passer should linger, to talk and talk.

No. He has come, upon an invented errand, with some perfectly clear purpose.

Not called upon to furnish a social façade, I have all my world about me. Closer than his huge form is the rival who came to my rescue while we talked across his bicycle in the lane. Who kept me at ease and inaccessible while silently, with his eyes never leaving mine that saw only the local scenes assembled in my mind, Richard asked me to believe he regretted, even while abiding by it, his mother's decision, reminded me that she had gone, that now there was no barrier, only to meet, while wistfully breathing as though instead of coasting down the steep hill he had been hurriedly climbing it, he produced his lame remarks, merely a politely listening stranger. The rival who in London, during the midnight talk with Amabel before her wedding, kept offering a suggestion: apart from his surroundings, Richard is, for me, almost nothing.

Nearer to him than I am, than I could ever be, is his inseparable companion: the ceaseless challenge of his labour. Beset, in all his solitary comings and goings, by secret joys. Joy in hill and valley, in meadow and wood, in air and sea and sky. It is of these alone that he never speaks lightly, never with a jest, never at all save in the company of a fellow worshipper. When, together with his coming and going, these joys are removed, his end will be swift.

Silent, devoid of words that in their mere sounding bring all humanity into the room, we share a piteous smallness, seem alone in the universe, threatened, vulnerable. Yet drawing strength from each other. Strength that remains; making a link that perhaps, between two people who have ever met in silence, is never broken. Words are separators, acknowledgment of separateness. The strength drawn when several people talk together in a room comes from one person, is paid out by him from some definite level of advantage, and disappears at the moment of separation. Spirits meet and converse and understand each other only in silence. Hence the strength available in a vitally silent Friends' Meeting. In Meeting, people live together, grow aware of each other's uniqueness. And consequence. Each silent figure is miraculous. Self-sufficiency dies and the meaning grows clear between perfection, which nobody really wants, and completeness, which can be reached only with the help of others. Certainties state themselves, with or without words, within the mind of everyone in the gathering.

Is it something of this kind that Richard wishes silently to demonstrate? Is this incredible situation intended to be a Quaker Meeting in miniature? Has he come, voluntarily abandoning his social armour, to disclose, in silence, the true nature of our relationship? To welcome personally, lose no time in assuring me that I am again one of themselves and everything is once more as it was at the beginning? That we are Friends together, sharing a common vision, rather than man and woman?

But if this is the explanation and justification of his extraordinary enterprise, what of the rest of the household? Not even to Rachel Mary can he have explained what he was about to do. This morning, for some reason, he is at home instead of at his Windmill Farm. Whenever he is at home, things centre round him. Everyone knows, at any given time, where he is or, not happening to know, asks. Rachel Mary knows, at every moment, exactly where her darling is to be found and what he is doing. His time is punctuated by visits to the kitchen for chats with her about this and that; easy, sociable, Irish hanging around, whence, usually belatedly, and usually under the stimulus of a veiled hint, he departs with his *Well,* I'll be doing' this or that. Anyone wanting him in a hurry and not at the moment able to locate him, goes to Rachel Mary.

He is capable, of course, sly Richard, Dimple Hill's champion diplomat, of watching his opportunity to get in here without being seen. What then? For he has also to escape. The chance of his visit remaining unknown is nil. And, according to the traditions of his class and the manner of his upbringing, to say nothing of the ideas of all his associates, such a visit is decisive. In breaking into a young lady's sitting-room and remaining shut up alone with her there, he commits himself beyond recall. He waits, therefore, for some encouraging acknowledgment of his manœuvre? When he crept in, carefully preventing the door handle from making its usual din, he expected me to look up and *smile*, hand out the invitation without which, according to Hypo, the doughtiest male is paralysed.

But you *know*. Philanderer though you be, always on the alert, in regard to any young woman newly met, for one or other of the signals meaning philandering welcomed, deep down in your being you know as well as I. Within your consciousness, vivid in your memory, as in mine, is the eternal vast interior of last summer's revealing moments. A destination never to be lost. Neither of these moments was contrived. Without prelude, they opened before us. Surprising. New. For me, their quality was your certificate. You passed the test, Richard, more fully than I would have believed.

Then came cunning interference, calculation, and a wise retreat. Then my long absence. Now, immediately on my return, you come, crashing through all the conventions of your circle. Sitting incredibly there, at my elbow, you believe that you give me the opportunity of giving you an opportunity? If that is the truth, even now, with the whole of our past electric about us, enclosing and separating us from all the world, nothing on earth shall persuade me to step forth and help you in the way you expect; and also dread and despise.

You contrived this situation. It is for you to use it. Time is suspended, but moments are ticking themselves away. Here I am, more fully here, than you have ever known me to be, and so much at peace that I could smile. Not the smile you expect, but the one that contemplates, weighs and approves. As you see, I can barely repress a smile in taking, unexpectedly to myself, this long deep breath. The deep inspiration automatically arriving when one relaxes from the effort of getting something into words. How will you take it, you who so astonishingly know everything?

Laughter rings within her as this tremendous silent intaking is duplicated, at her side, by a gusty sigh. This, then, is a conversation. Having inadvertently opened it, and received response, she is now responsible for its continuance? No, Richard, that won't do. You cannot, or is it indeed possible that you can, to such a degree, be the yokel-swain? Must I, even at this moment, reconsider you, decide whether or no shall be precipitated a future that for ever would contain this lamentable prelude?

Almost before she realizes the opening of the door, Rachel Mary stands in the doorway. It is upon Richard, and Richard alone, that her eyes are turned as she says:

'Ah, there you are, Richard. They've been looking for you. Mr Swanson's been here some time; down in Jubilee.'

'Ah. I guess I'll go right down and talk to him.'

Addressing, as he rises to his feet and gathers up his papers, not Rachel Mary but the opposite wall, he swings hugely, grace-fully away down the room and through the door left clear by her departure, closing it as soundlessly as when he entered so long, long ago.

Gone in disgrace. Disgrace for keeping the great Mr Swanson waiting? For being, without her knowledge, where Rachel Mary has at last found him?

Presently I'll go along to the kitchen and ask Rachel Mary if she realizes how many expressions today considered as originating in America, went there from Ireland.

CHAPTER VI

IF I launch that remark, she will turn her head, halting for an instant her sturdy little march, and say: 'Y'know, you're a *Friend*.'

Did she, did they all, after taking counsel, decide to suggest my coming down here again on the chance of my finally deciding to join the Society? Was that, after all, Richard's imaginary justification for his amazing intrusion?

She is waiting for me to begin. Remembers how, whenever we are alone together, I always talk. Yet half suspects that most of my talk is improvisation. Does she realize while I wind it out, relate anecdotes, describe people, air points of view, that I am holding off the sense of being together that presently, if I remained silent, would bear, in speech, unpredictable fruit; bring me nearer to life as she sees and lives it, nearer to being involved in ceaseless *doings*.

She is waiting.

But, today, with a difference. Hidden within her anticipation of an excursion into my world, stands a preoccupation, waiting to be expressed. Something she intends, 'when the way opens,' to communicate.

I don't want it. Want nothing that will affect even what is lying all about us: the little show we are passing without a word, yet aware, both of us, of the way the April sunlight sharpens the grain of the tree-trunks and makes transparent the pure green of new leaves misting the upper branches. No. I won't draw out what is on her mind. Must say something to keep us where we are. The election.

'Don't you think it a pity that women should go into Parliament as members of *parties*?'

'Well, perhaps.'

'Oughtn't they all to be independents, holding the balance

between different points of view? Belonging, in a sense, to all parties. Imaginatively. Just as they ought to belong, imaginatively, to all creeds. Enter all the churches, at the very least all the churches in Christendom. Look at the churches as they are! Look at the endless damage done to their own cause by these enclosed academies of males—in the case of Rome, by enclosed academies of celibate males—by their definitions of God. True, Basil Wilberforce used to call God the father-mother spirit of the universe, but for most of them the statement that God is Love is coupled with descriptions of a being whose love will operate only at the price of endless abject petitions and non-stop serenadings. Not even a gentleman.'

Defying her little chuckle, a bright blush proclaims shock.

'Now it's odd you should mention *Rome*.' Here it comes, the topic awaiting the opening of the way, introduced in the slightly raised tone she employs in the family circle when attention needs rallying. Tingling into the air, flouting the peaceful landscape, comes the something I am to be told.

'I've been exercised in my mind the last few days by a letter from Friends in Birmingham Meeting. They have just now on their hands a Catholic, a Frenchman, until a few months ago a monk in a monastery abroad. Somehow he has been led to Friends. He is very unhappy and suffering from a nervous breakdown. They think he needs country air, and ask us to take him in. In September, if we can see our way.'

Incredible. Uncertain. Perhaps to vanish, driven off by some small practical difficulty. Standing alone once more in the corner of the little musty white-washed room opening out of that little side chapel of the Hoddenheim cathedral, feeling, while the priest displayed to Fräulein and the English and German girls the jewelled treasures from the oaken cupboard and French-Protestant mademoiselle stood aside scared and disapproving, Miriam felt again that longing, stronger than any she had ever experienced, to remain for ever within this small, dim extension of the sanctified premises. And now, at last, she was to meet one who had come forth from the very midst of the life it represented. He must come. *Must* come.

Controlling her rapid breath, she casually inquired: 'Do you think you could manage it?'

'Well—*yes*. We've *room* for him. But that's not quite the whole matter. I've a stop in my mind about it. I can't think why.'

Quietly she had spoken, looking away into the distance as if to find approaching thence the reason for the strange arrest, communicating itself from the depths of her spirit and reaching one like a blow upon one's whole being.

No genuine Friend can ignore a stop in the mind. Some, perhaps, may reason it away. But to Rachel Mary its warning is absolute, above and beyond reason.

The silent moments pass. Gradually the enclosing scene expands. The months ahead, no longer a mere bridge towards a strange felicity, lie outstretched at their full length, a vast expanse of days, each day to offer, as did all the days down here, its sudden moment in eternity. Yet still September, though returned to its distant place, reflects the glow that for a moment had so deeply enhanced the month's natural gold.

And why, with the matter so surely settled for her, does she take me into her confidence? To talk it over, hoping perhaps to discover the cause of the warning, to devise some means of averting a possible danger? Unlike her brothers, she does not regard Catholics with a blend of fear and contempt. Does not, when the subject crops up, enquire why nuns wear such horrible-queer clothes. Also she will be feeling it her duty to give the unhappy young man, already living with Friends, the chance of recovering his health in the shelter of her quiet home. This must have been her first impulse, so strangely checked by the stop; my enemy. Yet I do not dare challenge it. It must take its chance against her warm impulse, her selfless consideration for others that may, by its own strength, presently move the barrier.

'There's something else I must tell thee.'

Left alone, while Rachel Mary hurried to the side entrance to reach her quarters by the swiftest route, Miriam went slowly up the sweep, aware of herself for the first time since newly arrived she had rung its echoing bell, as an outsider. In place of the interior, whose well-known rooms, sanctuaries she had taken for granted as everlastingly available, had been swept away while Rachel Mary outlined her own plan for the coming summer, she saw only the blank face of the house, shutting her out, seemed to gaze, with studied indifference, away across the distant marshes waiting, in April sunlight, for their summer. For the summer whose months, only just now, she had transformed into a brief enchanted bridge towards the strange promise of September. Meanwhile, the time still in hand, the few weeks before Rachel Mary left for her long visit to the distant brother, stood bereft, empty and hurried, each day shorter than the last.

Gathered at the dinner-table, the Roscorlas present themselves for the first time as isolated individuals, each one at the mercy of circumstance. Rooted as they seem in their inviolable home, life prepares for them as for everyone unpredictable change. From moment to moment, beneath the to and fro of pleasant voices, life is stealthily at work bringing not only the familiar circling of the seasons to which they gladly move, engrossed as in the figures of a dance, but also *change*.

The coming disruption will bring self-consciousness. Even though at first they may relish the sense of freedom brought by the removal of the gentle overseer, before they have been long in the hands of this hired housekeeper, this Mrs Somebody from Somewhere, not even a Friend, they will be losing the savour of each day and each moment in looking impatiently forward to the return of the preserver of their unity.

Where to go, until her return allows me too to come back?

Where to go, where, until September, to hide? Where to find both the solitude provided by this family of workers and the enlivening background of shared convictions?

Where, where in the world to go? The words echoed monotonously in her mind as she went upstairs towards the solitude of her own room. In a moment she would be within it, a passing occupant, confronted, if the window should be pushed up, by the clear view of the Downs-flanked, sunlit meadows and the distant marshes, sea-rimmed, the whole scene averted, disowning her, as had, this morning, the many-windowed housefront.

The door, ajar. Coming open with a prolonged squeak whose exact tone, for the first time and as if from far away, she was now attentively noting. It passed into her being, claiming immortality, joining company with the never-to-be-forgotten voices of doors from the past: those of every kind of interior door, from the metallic rattling of glazed doors with loose handles, to the smooth soft slurring of stately portals pushed open across thick carpets, and standing out above them all, the sharply echoing paint crackle, breaking the wide, high Sunday morning stillness, of Tansley Street front doors opened to the strident cries of the paper-boy.

Driven into her lonely self she moved, an alien presence, into the centre of the disowning room that only an hour ago had been the inviolable reservoir of the securely inflowing future. Where to *go*?

Arrested, she gazed incredulously at the spectacle arisen within her mind and projected thence so clearly that the surrounding room vanished. From the narrow, mean street, hitherto unknown, just off the centre of the West End, its dingy, high confronting buildings shutting out the summer, she went forward into the dark house; into that gloomy back room to interview, on Eve's behalf, the stern-faced woman who answered questions with an unwavering air of dictatorial benevolence. Was escorted by her into that extraordinary sleeping-room, divided into cubicles by thin, faded curtains washed nearly colourless. Its midday was a twilight. Its two globeless gas-burners stood high, enclosed in circular wire cages.

There it stands, this central London branch of the Young Women's Bible Association, transformed. No longer part of an institution the mere idea of whose existence used to make me squirm. Not even a temporary refuge, but a place where I can belong. Whose atmosphere of shared convictions, redeeming the lifeless surroundings, will sustain me while I get on with my sketches for the Friday Review.

Absurd to have imagined the door would be ready to open as

soon as I wished. Unattractive, chill, this vacancy they offer, far away in a suburban branch. St John's Wood. That vague cricket-ground region on the way to Mr Hancock's place in Hampstead. Far from the sheltering depths of London proper.

CHAPTER VII

'AND LIGHTS out at ten o'clock. Well, I think that is all you need to know *tonight*. The rising-bell sounds at half past seven. Breakfast at eight-fifteen. Prayers in the large room at eight o'clock.'

With a final friendly smile, little Miss Bigg closed the door of the incredible bedroom and departed on the long journey down through the house, leaving Miriam exultantly aglow with speculations as to the rules and regulations presently to be found securely enhedging her four months of life as an un-qualified guest of a kind of lay convent. Again she came upon it standing substantial in its high-walled garden, again was welcomed by the friendly, controlledly bustling little woman, was given a glimpse of a large-windowed room running the whole length of the house and furnished with a stately high-backed harmonium and rows of cane-seated chairs. 'Our concert-room,' smiled Miss Bigg. Then up the wide staircase whose half-landing window gave upon a garden, a large square, mostly lawn, trees at the far end and high walls all round; then up the next staircase on to that wide landing with its few dignified doors through the nearest of which came the strains of a popular waltz played by four hands on a resonant well-tuned piano. 'Our common-room,' smiled Miss Bigg. Up again on to a similar landing, one of whose open doors displayed gaily curtained cubicles, and at last this vast free landing, generously sky-lit, broken by no staircase and showing, right and left, a number of small closed doors, all doubtless leading into little bedrooms similar to this. The elegant little suite of furniture, well polished and so arranged as to give an air of spaciousness to the small interior, together with the pure, fresh air entering the open window, make the room seem like a small guest-room in a country house. But one is not a guest. A boarder, free, within whatever may turn out to be the rules and regulations, to come and go without palaver. High above the street with the sky for company and a large house available to wander in, but not encroaching. Again the good fortune, as in Wimpole Street and Tansley Street, of large characterful surroundings. All as if planned, down to the absence, exactly until September, of the student to whom this room belongs.

Until September. Golden month now glowing, while I experience this new world, infinitely far away.

All the gardens, every side road I passed, held trees. Large. Old. St John's *Wood*. Remainders, they must be, distinguishing it from other suburbs. Making it perhaps unique. As indeed must be this branch of The Young Women's Bible Association to which I have made my way. Several Bedford College girls, said Miss Bigg impressively, various Council School teachers, an Indian medical student, a Russian girl and, strangest of all, one of Pelissier's Follies.

Here they all are, nearly filling the rows of chairs. Here am I, after that deeply peaceful sleeping, launched, in the morning light, in the life of the house. Five minutes past eight. Yet Miss Bigg, at her little table with the opened Bible in front of her, seems to be waiting. In a stillness broken only by the light tapping of a tree-branch against one of the huge windows.

'Make a noise! Make a noise!'

Following the breathless voice, from perhaps half way up the staircase, comes the sound of hurriedly stamping feet upon the lower flight. Miss Bigg waits. In come a few girls, soon followed by two tall breathless young women, clearly from the top floor, who make their way, still panting, to two empty seats in the front row. The taller generously built, radiating amused friendliness, reveals, as she sits down, the back of a dress many of whose fastenings gape unattached. Glancing at the head of her companion she suffers, at the sight of a small turret of hair tilted perilously sideways from its base, a convulsion ending in an irrepressible squeak that joins company with the gentle voice of Miss Bigg: 'Let not your heart be troubled.'

Just a short passage, read simply, with no trace of unctuous devotion. Joy, rather, over-fresh, within the meditative tone. Then movement of the whole roomful round on to knees, elbows on chairs, faces cupped in hands. And again little Miss Bigg's quietly confident voice: 'Our father.' What a pity! All the voices will now mutter the strangely combined phrases. . . . No. On goes the quiet voice, alone: 'always with us, with each one of us, ready to guide us through the difficulties of this new day.'

'So I come to your country to find what is the secret of your many-many religions and to find why so many-many peoples from my country come *heere* instead of to elsewhere for a refuge.'

Here, once more, is Russia. But not quite the Russia brought by the Lintoffs. This girl in the beautifully moulded black dress, its sleeves perfectly modelling her slender arms and coming down in points nearly to the knuckles, her black hair flatly framing the pale indoor face, reporting Russian winter, is here as an interested investigator.

'Have you discovered?'

'Some things already I see.' The sad, meditative voice chimes perfectly with the sadness of the face. Young well-to-do, free to move about, she yet has the hopeless look emphasized by the droop of the full lips, of one ceaselessly watching tragedy. 'I see first that the English are *healthy*. I see that they question *nothing*. Also I see, and this I find most-strandge, that they never think of *deadth*.'

'Yes, I suppose in general that is true. It never occurred to me.'

'No? Yet you are not-English as well as English. That at once I see.'

'You've been about amongst people over here?'

'So wonderfully heere in St John's Wood. A little. Enough

to see quite much.   And Kropotkin, who allows that I visit him for talking, tells me much, living now in your High-gate.'

'Then you're a revolutionary?'

'To this I cannot answer you no or yes.   Each way of belief brings to me much thoughts.   And I read now your H. G. Vells.   The best I like is this writer's *Sea Lady* . . . (perhaps there are better dreams).   Ah.   That for me is most-wonderful. For this I take to him to leave on his door-step an Easter egg.'

'Charming of you!   You know where he lives?'

'Kropotkin have say me it is Hampstead, and I find his house in the directoire.'

'Did you leave a message?'

'Just I write with gratefulness from Olga Feodorova.   Ah, this man is most-wonderful.   Also he is most-English.   Ah, I think I will remain heere in England and marry an Englishman and have many-many happy childeren.'

Healthy?   Neither questioning life nor thinking of death? Is that as good as saying we never grow up?   A result of the freedom, unknown in Russia, that Michael when first he came, was perpetually remarking?   Yet also he used to agree with Spinoza that he who has never known illness knows nothing of health.   Yet revolutionary Lintoff, watching the masses in Hyde Park, sternly declared: 'These people are not free.' Lintoff, with eyes inturned upon a far distance, sees everywhere 'the people': exploited, forgotten.

'Yet perhaps even in this house there are girls not quite so wildly unconscious . . .'

'Yet think?   It is perhaps so.   One thing I clearly see: that all are jealous against each other in respect of you.   They make competition.   You did not know this?   Strandge.'

Basis Olga has, as outsider, for observation.   But sees only in terms of her own values: mental, aesthetic.   Accepts with unenvious indulgence the merely good.   Does not realize them as far above me.   Sets them aside as very simple.   Very English.   The few who appear to be drawn to me have full lives outside this house.   Find me, in their leisure hours, a tonic for their weariness.   Someone new in their experience. Mysterious therefore.   Unoccupied, apparently, the whole day long. As also is Olga. Yet to her they are not drawn. Are jocularly critical, objecting to her continual prolonged occupations of the bathroom, whence invariably she emerges with wet hair; to her evening monopoly, when they come home tired out, of the most comfortable chair in the common-room. For them she is just a 'foreigner,' queer, as are all foreigners.

To me they are drawn, unconsciously, by my deep delight in all the common doings of our life here? In which I am onlooker as well as participant; the common possession of the large house, wherein we are all guests, the shared night, the fresh blossoming each day, friendly prayers in the morning light pouring east and west through the large windows; the shared breakfast usually consumed in a preoccupied silence broken only by an occasional jocular outburst from huge Tiny; tinklings of pennies into the fine-box by those arriving late; hailings and farewells for another day; certainty of meeting again for the evening meal; leisure in the common-room for display of superficial fluctuating preferences; for the gathering, by the few close friendships, of wealth from surroundedness, that each rare time of being alone together is the renewal of an everlasting moment; renewal kindred to that bestowed upon our enclosed Association by our monthly tea-party for the old almshouse women, by our Sunday afternoon at-homes for all and sundry, our jubilant part-singing of cheery hymns and 'Crossing the Bar'; and those secret suddenly arranged small prayer meetings in one or other of the little top rooms: a moment's silence, then a young voice, usually Tiny's, opening a wide sky above our enclosure with a plea, murmured through face-covering fingers, for guidance in all our doings; a few husky amens and all of us on our feet again in a dancing gaiety.

Tiny. The largest, fleetest, most light-footed of all the Young Women. At work upon herself. Keeping herself perpetually available to the inflowing spirit. Truthful. Yet able unscrupulously to misrepresent, as seem so many good women, in defence of others. Sometimes even in self-defence against permanently suspicious Authority.

The formal basis of our joy, like the social joy of schooldays, is togetherness on neutral territory, keeping us independent in unity. Something of this there must be in lives monastic and conventual? With the difference that these girls are neither cowed nor mindless as appear to be the rank and file of monks showing in ceremonial photographs.

Are they aware of all they have here? Does its strong appeal for me rest upon my freedom to leave? Yet were it not for the strange magnet pulling at me from September, I believe I could stay on indefinitely. As suddenly I realized when that coldly serene, detachedly critical female visitor privately on her last day protested to me against 'the come-day go-day way most of the girls here seem to be living, planless, never think of the future.' Bewildered I was, standing for a moment within her point of view, wondering whether my sin, if indeed it were a sin, might not be worse than theirs. Only after her aloof departure did I realize that I should have told her that even the simplest of these young women live, even if unknown to themselves, in the Now, the eternal moment, fully; that their sense of Being, whatever their discontents and longings, outdoes for most of them, the desire to Become. Will triumph, throughout their lives.

Is this conviction of the wonder of mere existence, the amazingness of there being anything anywhere, the secret of my feeling, wherever I go, upon my native heath and wishing to stay there? Belgium; Holland, though seen only in passing through; Oberland; Dimple Hill; and now this half-nunnery? Only from Flaxman's did I fly, from enclosure in squalor I was powerless to mitigate; ready to agree with.

CHAPTER VIII

RICHLY enclosed we feel when, at our large parties in house or in garden, we are distributed, dressed in our festive best, among our visitors; onlookers, enhancing our awareness of each other, heightening our sense, more or less dormant in daily life, of individual capacities brought attractively to light in the interest of making the occasion a success.

Olga alone stands aside, a silently preoccupied witness of all we have devised for the entertainment of our guests. Sternly she over-rates my contributions to what others have initiated. When at the end of the festival I come upon her isolated in some corner, conforming only by sitting unoccupied, deprived of her usual resource of slowly inscribing, in almost microscopic handwriting, letters, on postcards, to people in Russia, she murmurs: 'You waste yourself. Pairls before Swine.'

What does she find in me? Why, among all my sketches for the *Friday*, did she single out the one about the wind heard murmuring far off along the shore, gradually approaching, with varying voice, across the marshes, reaching the near meadows to hum within their dense hedgerows on its way to thunder at last upon the walls of the house, squeal through every crevice, roar down the chimney, reach the unsleeping listener, who greets it with laughter as 'the best lover.'

'Ah, *that* I like. Pure decadence.'

Then her appeal, when for a few days I was with Michael and Amabel, 'Come soon back. This house has lost for me all life. No one is here with whom to speak,' on a postcard bearing that haunting Russian picture of a girl whose features, their expression remotely hopeless, recalled her own. Disturbing it was to be challenged by this outcry in the midst of the new happiness of Michael and Amabel. 'All of bliss to Mike and me' she had written in sending her invitation from the two of them 'and from our son now beginning his journey into the world.'

Hopeful, at first, seemed her meeting with them, giving her the opportunity of speaking Russian, but nearly ruined for me by Amabel's wild enthusiasm, a concentrated version of her invariable treatment of a newcomer, lasting until she has taken the measure of their possibilities, but redeemed by the sound of an endless Russian dialogue, whereof so little could be learned by questioning Michael. 'Yes, yes, interesting she is,' he granted, with sceptically pursed lips, and then, being pressed: 'She belongs quite clearly to the upper-class Russian intelligentsia. But revolutionary, no. Lost, rather, in abstractive insolubilities.'

Dark in the background of all I have gathered here lies this strange Russian *sadness*. Seeming, in Olga as in Lintoff, though in her it includes a personal wistfulness, sorrow equally for oppressor and oppressed, sorrow for all humanity. Sounding in the tone of her voice, even in her rare laughter. Leaving one, if silence follows, arrested. The only other sound heard during these months that casts a shadow over the house is the gravely indignant voice of that woman complaining to me at the end of her visit: 'All these girls live come-day, go-day; without *plans*.' Not being a plan-maker, I had no answer. But am still arrested by her thought.

Are we English, on the whole, static? Living in the Now because we have a relatively good Now to live in? A Lhassa, exclusive? Lintoff, like Olga's friends Kropotkin and Stepniak are aware of the whole world; spokesmen, without distinction of class or race, for everyone for whom they desire a more generous share of the Now. But Olga's sole comfort resides in individuals. Her enemy is life itself rather than social injustice. Finding no ease of mind in her luxurious Russian home, she came to England in the hope of discovering the secret of English optimism.

Is the English consciousness static? While carrying our sporting sense of justice and fair play to the ends of the earth, we regard all un-English humanity, all 'foreigners,' as in some way inferior. At the same time, all the other races, however differing from each other, are united in perception of our oddity.

Are we motionless? Is that what Michael's friend, that

German-born Russian ethnologist, meant when he told me in 1900, 'the Russians are the strongest kinetic force in Europe. Watch Russia.'

From the moment I realized, hearing the distant rumblings come nearer, that my arrival at the Brooms for my promised week-end visit could pardonably be evening instead of afternoon, the occasion became immortal. Though none of the girls happening to be at home and caught like myself by the storm would be leaving London on Monday after spending with old friends a week-end lit by the glow of all that lay ahead, yet I felt they were sharing my recognition of the quality of those hours handed to us by the elements.

Competing with the growing darkness we improvised a concert. Someone defiantly raised the lid of the piano for my fling at the thunderous last movement of the Pathétique. Then all who could sing, no matter how, were called upon to contribute. Playing accompaniments, I felt all about me an awareness, conscious in the few, shared, like an infection, to some extent by all, of the strangeness of the adventure of *being*, of the fact of the existence, anywhere, of anything at all. No need, I felt, in this foreign country created by the storm, to inquire of these girls, as so often I had been tempted to do in strange surroundings shared with people who seem to take life for granted: 'Do you *realize*.'

When the occasion came to an end with the departure of the storm that had given to my time in St John's Wood an end so richly confirming my sense of having always available there a congenial shelter, I wondered, setting off for Dimple Hill via my two days with the Brooms, whether, had Olga been with us, our sense of unity-in-difference would have survived the challenge of her unswerving aloofness. Wondered, thinking of her as I set out, what she would have told me returning from her first meeting, at Kropotkins, with those Russians newly arrived from Moscow. Wondered whether, if indeed, as she declared, life in the hostel was now to become for her 'a livink deadth,' she would follow my suggestion of coming down for a while to Dimple Hill. Wondered what she would make of the serene friendliness of Quakerdom.

CHAPTER IX

ARRIVING late last night, I learned only that he was in the house. Since when? How, and when, did Rachel Mary get over the stop in her mind sufficiently to allow him to come? Here he sits, at my side. On Rachel Mary's left hand, opposite to Richard, kept always on her right no matter who may come to stay. My place, first on her left, is now given up to this stranger, making me secondary. For him, I am a lodger, having the use of an upstairs sitting-room, joining the Roscorlas for meals. For me, he is Rome in flight from Rome.

'This is Mr Charles Dekorry, Miss Henderson.' 'Ducorroy?' Charles Ducorroy. Frère Charles, reduced to secularity. Tall. Dark, black-haired. Neatly round-headed. Dressed in a close-fitting black alpaca jacket above knickers of some woollen material. No trace in the well-cut features of the cowed, mindless expression of monks shown grouped in ceremonial photographs. French, urban, courteously playing his part in the meal-time business of handing things about; speaking, when necessary, a few words of broken English. At any moment my opportunity may come. Temptation to show off? To surprise and please this wandering fragment of that world so powerfully drawing me as I stood aside from the others in the hush of that little cell-like room just off the side chapel of that ancient church in Hodderheim. 'Plizz?'

Someone spoke to him. I missed it, being elsewhere.

'Pass them here, Ernest.' Rachel Mary, holding out her hand for a vegetable dish, Ducorroy still turned towards Ernest. Are those eyes really *grey*? So rare. Here is my chance. 'Encore de légumes, monsieur?' Only just in time, with Rachel Mary already lifting the lid.

'Vous parlez français, mademoiselle?'

Grey they were, transparent, but a shock, utterly belying his

639

manner in turning to me; swift, eager. Relieved, I thought he was. But meeting those eyes was a plunge, as if one were falling from the side of a cliff, into an abyss of sorrow. There he dwells, aware of nothing else. Nothing comes to him from the sight of the garden glowing just beyond the open window in ripe September sunlight. Nothing from the Roscorlas, so far, for him, no more than kindly strangers granting him wayside rest on his hopeless journey to nowhere.

No more of this, isolating us within a cloud of reactions. Even while answering his few inquiries, put to discover the circumstances of my presence in the house rather than to express interest in that presence, I could feel, coming across the table from Richard—once my patient tutor in what had seemed to me, until I realized it to be the armoury of one still defying the ravages of a humiliation inflicted long ago, the unquakerly art of perpetual jocularity—resentment, fruit of the enforced silence of one accustomed to be the household referee, the perpetual guide and centre of meal-time talk, now, in the presence of a stranger, dethroned. Even Rachel Mary, something more than a hostess, a woman interested, albeit unaware of the nature of her interest, in this strange, attractive-looking young man, was feeling, side by side with satisfaction in supplying him with an unexpected rescue, something akin to jealousy of the rescuer. Vying with these two streams, came, from both Ernest and the pupil, a warm tide of admiration, for each of whom the displacement of Richard was not, as it was for Rachel Mary, a source of uneasiness.

No more, then. But when, apart from meal times and occasional general gatherings, shall we be able to meet and talk?

Cunning I felt when, the next morning, on my way to the garden for a few flowers for my room, I left *Modern Thought* in a prominent place on the hall table.

But the discomfort, that had come between me and the out-door loveliness vanished when, on my return, I found him hanging about in the hall and knew that he must have seen me, through the open door of the little back room and, having heard from the Roscorlas that I spend my morning at work in my upstairs sitting-room, had come through, with a cunning equal to my own, to catch me on my way back.

'C'est à vous, ce livre, mademoiselle?'

Long ago now seems yesterday's morning's meeting in the hall. There he stands in my life, there he stood, throughout my afternoon walk, courteously marvelling over my possession of such a book; begging to be allowed to borrow it; still surveying me, while he spoke his gratitude for my permission, with the puzzled air of one facing a phenomenon; going away down the hall with a lit face and the light easy tread of a slender Frenchman, the precious volume clasped to his breast.

Leaving me wondering whether, in handing him this guide to the enchanting intricacies of metaphysic, I may be distracting his attention from the clear pathway he has so painfully reached.

And now, for good or ill, he is in my hands. Amazement still transfigures the moment of finding him, that same evening, waiting for me in my sitting-room. Uninvited. Making no apology. Making, before we sat lost in talk, the surrounding room aloof and strange, as when I had first seen it.

Not yet has it occurred to him to wonder what the Roscorlas, with whom his small command of spoken English keeps him nearly silent, will make of this spending of evenings with me. So far in their minds is knowledge only of his breakdown, his need for rest, for sleep; and the hope that presently he will begin life anew as a member of their Society, a prisoner rescued from an institution that for them is a revolting mystery. They are not experiencing the warm gaiety of his home in east France, do not see two of his sisters joyously departing, at the end of their schooldays, into convents, his own departure, from College, to the Paris Séminaire des Missions Étrangers. Do not share his meeting there with rumours of Loisy and the Modernists, who may yet turn out to be neither fish, flesh, fowl, nor good red herring, but who, when he was settled as he thought, for life, at work on the printing-press of that monastery in China, began to appear, to him, like lights in a coal-mine.

'Imaginez, mademoiselle, mes sentiments, moi, béni depuis

mon enfance, de l'amour d'une mère adorable, ayant aussi deux
sœurs consacrées à la service de Dieu, en étant obligé d'imprimer
ceci: "La femme, c'est un tas d'ordures".'

They do not see him lying sleepless in his cell night after
night besieged by thoughts his confessor condemned as devil-
sent temptations. Do not see him grope his way along the dark
corridor to this confessor's cell, there to fling himself face
downwards across the end of his narrow bed, imploring permission to read and to think. In vain.

And now, after reading my Maeterlinck, he glories in the
belief that a man who has never rested his head upon a woman's
breast can become truly illuminated. And I am aware, within
the depths of his uncontrollable weeping, of a manly strength
waiting to emerge. As also is he: 'Un de ces jours vous
sentirez *un homme* près de vous.' A man already stating himself in French and in Catholic fashion, the fashion that exalts to
Heaven the Mother of God because with their reverence for
motherhood they *must* have her there. So that his concept of
womanhood is a combination of deep respect with amusement
over what he believes to be its untraversable limitations.
Revealing his outcry when he found me trimming that hat:
'Ah! Voilà! Ce qu'elles ont pas dans la tête, elles ont dans
les mains.' Stranger, too, it was, when with my hurt foot I was
limping home from Meeting side by side with Rachel Mary,
just in front of him and Richard, to hear him exclaim in broken
tones: 'Poor littul thingue!' And when in our talk I state
ideas that for long have stood central in my consciousness, he
looks at me as if I were incredible: 'Non, vraiment c'est
étonnant!'

Yet my oddity has not altered his view of marriage as
dependent, for success, upon the husband's unquestioned
leadership, illustrated by the conclusion of his account of his
married sister's unhappiness during the year while her young
mind was being 'rudement balayé' by her husband: 'Main-
tenant ils sont *une âme*.' Immediately he proceeded to recount,
and punctuate with delighted laughter, the incident of that
winter's morning when the husband, to prevent her going, with
a heavy cold, to early Mass, locked the wardrobe containing all

her hats, only to see her, a little later, sailing down the road with her small head supporting his large bowler, draped elegantly with a white veil.

Here, then, is the explanation of the investigating glances Rachel Mary sent my way during breakfast. Speculative, I thought them, in regard to Charles and myself, until she turned, the moment the others had left the room, to the corner cupboard, bent down, produced the card in an extended hand and announced, without looking at me: 'This came for you by the post.' And it was with her eyes that I saw, and with her consciousness that I swiftly hid from the rest of the household, the picture of Rodin's *Le Baiser*, a disturbing revelation, for her, of an unsuspected angle of my being.

And even now that she knows the outline of Olga's tragedy she still feels differently towards me.

'My friend in Paris has now made full investigations. It appears that Miss Feodorova went there with a Russian she had met, for the first time, only the evening before, at Prince Kropotkin's, and had been there with him for only a few weeks when she took her life. The date upon the card sent to you indicates that it was posted during her last day. She came to her lodgings in the evening with a beautiful bunch of hothouse flowers for her landlady, will then have gone upstairs, locked her door, dragged the settee out on to the balcony, undressed, drunk the whole of the bottle of veronal and lain down in her nightgown on the settee, very soon, the doctors say, to become unconscious. She was not found until towards ten o'clock the next morning. The measures taken at the hospital might have saved her life but for the night's exposure which produced pneumonia, of which she died, without regaining consciousness, at the end of a few days, during which the young man remained at her bedside. It is a tragic affair, both for her friends and the young man she had hoped to marry her.'

'This picture by Rodin shall show you where I have been. In a world so beautiful that I can no more return to the world-life as before. To you alone I say goodbye, with the words of your so wonderfoll Mr Wells: "Perhaps there are better dreams".'

The Sea Lady.

Impossible to make Rachel Mary understand, to remove the barrier that has changed me in her eyes. Yet she has moved a little since we first met. Reading Wells's *Anticipations*, though here and there it puzzled her, enlarged her consciousness, already prepared, by her residence in Quakerdom, calmly to face, whatever might be its findings, the results of scientific investigation. But the personal findings and conclusions of *First and Last Things* made her weep as she watched him make, again and again, a close-shave past the point of departure towards the reality no science can enclose.

When I told him of her grief it moved him to suggest coming down to 'have a look' at my Quakers. Furiously he called me a fool to declare that he, with his spy-glass focused in advance would be unable to see them. Would he, bringing his wealthy poverty to confront their poverty-stricken wealth, have grasped anything beyond their aesthetic and cultural deficiencies?

Suppose Olga had come, as lately she had thought of doing? She sought life. Believed for a while that in England she had found it, found a vigorous sanity untroubled by speculative questionings. But soon began, perhaps with Kropotkin's help, to doubt, as did Lintoff, the freedom of our people, to see the amazing blindness of our prosperous classes. Love carried her into a temporary eldorado. But sex-love dies unless it grows, for both partners, towards universal love. Meanwhile, it is comedy for onlookers, who yet share and rejoice in its beginnings, whether or no they have themselves experienced them. So various in their similarities.

Still upon my left cheek burns the scar made by that first kiss, horribly dropped there, between dances, by that empty-headed little philanderer on the very evening of my first rapturous certainty that one day Ted would kiss me, shyly, out into life with him until the end of time. *Was* it our sudden descent in poverty that drew him away? I shall never know. But knew, soon after Sally and Harriett were married, that the routine life of enclosed suburban housewives is not for me.

Just as I must dimly have recognized, in that decisive moment with Densley, my unsuitability to manage the background of a Harley Street practice. Yet that surprising moment brought revelation. Down from behind me as I sat idly at home and at ease in his consulting-room—scene of our endless discussions—came his arms surrounding me while they held before my eyes that picture of the Grand Canal. Then his deepest tone, a little shaken: 'Isn't that where people go for their honeymoon?' For what may have been a whole minute I was alone in the universe, all my garnered experience swept away as I moved forward in a mist of light. No temple this, but bringing later to my mind the meaning, for him, of one of his quiet generalizations: in marriage, women enter a temple where no man can follow. Certain it is that in that long moment I was aware only of myself as traveller. Sorry I was, disappointed, when I returned to my surroundings, big book vanished and his arms withdrawn, to find that my silent unresponsiveness had driven him to stand, an offended stranger, elbow on mantelpiece in the neighbourhood of one of those dreadful framed photographs of soul's awakening young women displaying long hair draped carefully waistwards down the fronts of their shoulders. Even then I could have recalled him. Was it because I knew myself not only beloved but, henceforth, free from the inconveniences of living, as Hypo had remarked long ago, only just above the poverty line, that I had stepped out alone, in blissful silence? Or because I suddenly realized that speech and emotional display in face of a lifelong contract were out of place. Sacred that moment had been, undisturbed by my knowledge of our incompatibilities. For I knew that in one way or another all men and women are incompatible, their first eager enthusiasms comparable to those of revivalist meetings and inevitably as transient. Only in silence, in complete self-possession, possession of the inwardness

of being, can lovers fully meet.   An enthusiastic vocal engagement is a farewell.   Marriage usually a separation, life-long?

  Life-long unless resting upon the foundation of shared belief.
For me, hitherto, all along the line, transfiguration had always
been of the universe rather than of its inhabitants as I knew
when telling Amabel in London that I believed Richard, apart
from his surroundings, would be nothing to me.   But now, for
the first time Charles and I were separated, I found myself in
the London train actually living the life described to me by that
unhappy woman sharing my compartment.

  Back here, sailing blindly after breakfast on my first morning
into my bedroom, astonishing myself by tripping over the large
water-jug prominent on my pathway to the window, sending
its contents awash across the carpet, I met further surprise in
the amused chucklings of Rachel Mary and the maid obliged to
lift, roll and carry it down into the garden.   But when the next
morning I repeated my exploit, Rachel Mary's laughter, the
heartiest I had ever heard from her, told me my secret was hers,
was probably known to the whole household.

  'But I feel, Rachel Mary, that he ought, when he goes out
into the world, to be quite *free*.'

  'I'm not so sure about that.   It might be best for him to be
engaged when he goes out amongst people.'

  She approves, heartily.   Sees Charles and me as acquisitions
to the Society.   For her, our future stands clear: the social
concerns and activities of whatever Meeting we join.   Into that
life, divorced from the past, I should disappear.   Into what for
the most part, though every Meeting has its leaven of genuine
mystics, is a Protestant, biblicist, ethical society.   Aesthetic and
cultural starvation.   Charles, too, is fully awake to one aspect
of this limitation.

  'I have deserted my mother.   Each time I enter the Friends'
Meeting, the loveliness of her churches is before my eyes, their
music in my ears, reproaching me.   Still, I can live in the
memory.'

  Did he not see, in proposing to spend his life under the

perpetual shadow of regretful memories, the impossibility of becoming a whole-hearted Quaker?

Intently he listened while I told him of the local flower show's competition for table decoration, of how, when I borrowed, for my table, Rachel Mary's long-stemmed, wide-topped fruit-dish, Alfred, who never spends a penny upon anything but necessities, horrified me by bringing home a huge bunch of maidenhair fern plus a few speckled tiger-lilies, to brighten up my already arranged mass of love-in-a-mist, its gentle blue shining clear through its cloud of green, with trailers of smilax spreading thence to each corner of the table, the whole, in Roscorla eyes, inconspicuous beside the greenhouse opulencies of the tables to right and left. And when I told him of their astonishment over the winning, by my table, minus these expensive offerings, of the first prize, he cried, after a moment's meditative silence, '*Ah!* Je comprends,' and then, returning at once to his lamentations over the beauty of his deserted mother, left me uncertain as to whether he approved the Roscorla offerings or my refusal to use them.

Looking ahead, I see him built into Quakerdom, into one or other of its generous enterprises at home or abroad, into an outlook as truly Catholic as that of his beloved Church, yet walled up within the irreverent puritanisms brought to it by the sects whence most of the early followers of Fox came forth.

Can I face such a life, become in its background, a kind of Rachel Mary, ceaselessly busy, my share in his life that of recipient of the record of his daily doings? Can I even promise myself to him without confessing the past? This I must soon decide. Think it out at Brighton, if indeed I join Pauline in her little escapade. Write to him from there.

Hurrying almost the length of the long platform in search of corner seats, finding in every carriage just four men screened by opened newspapers, we meekly took windowless middle places and sat, unnoticed, in hilarious silence; interlopers in this six o'clock preserve of middle-aged City men sufficiently well-to-do to be living in Brighton and evidently enjoying this hour on neutral territory, remote from office and from home.

The deprecating smile of the head of the stately Y.W.B.A. branch at once revealed its every room occupied. Despair. Until, perceiving our dismay, she hesitantly revealed another branch, small, never crowded, but run chiefly for women of the servant class temporarily out of work. Brighton was ours, reborn; the long gay sunlit, high-skyed front, the sea-girt piers, the distant way over the downs of Rottingdean on the edge of nowhere.

While still the gold of slanting sunlight lay upon the town's seaward face, we were out again, adream amongst holiday-making visitors, none, we felt, experiencing the extremity of bliss wherein we wondered silent, planless, our known lives curtained by oblivion, the coming night securely strange in the shelter of those small cubicles in the bedroom of the dingy house in the remote back-street.

Enrichment, this sharing of the night with strangers. Perhaps only for so long as they remain unknown? Yet even then darkness might bring a kind of unity. As does even a deep twilight as it enters, late on a summer's evening, a roomful of contestants. Host and guest in one, it can be felt at work reconciling differences, transforming each sitter into an almost invisible fellow-traveller within the mystery of space and producing, as it deepens, first a lowering of voices and presently a silence so nearly complete as to impel the arrival of the blindingly brilliant indoor light. Restoring at once the sense of enclosure in a walled room and reducing the gathered company to sharply separated exponents of different points of view. Yet, even then, the healing touch of the vanished twilight may be felt. Argument will not recur, or, if it does, will be softened by cordiality.

Shared night-darkness abolishes, even indoors, the division between night and day, though not there so fully as in never-quite-complete-darkness of the open. But to be aware of this absence of division, whether indoors or out, one must remain for a while awake. Will Pauline confirm this, or just agree, as always, with anything I suggest? Is she awake there behind her cubicle curtains? Or at once asleep as she was on those nights beneath the high trees giving us shelter from the slight breeze swaying their distant tops to and fro against the visible night sky; a gentle movement extending incredibly to their very roots perceptibly stirring in the earth beneath me. Dawn roused her, roused us both to bird-song, to the thunder of hoofs scampering in a distant field, presently to multitudinous small thuddings coming up through the earth, discovered, when we were on our feet, to be the patterings of chickens cooped along the floor of the deep valley on whose edge we had lain.

CHAPTER X

'DEAREST MIRETTA:

By all means tell your man about me, if you feel you ought to. Tell him also that if I were compelled to settle, for life, with just one woman, it would have to be you.　My confident blessings on you both.

Hypo.'

Can this be true?　It confirms things he said from time to time all along the way.　Ah no.　He says these things to every woman in turn.　No.　It is a kind, cleverly thought-out message, for Charles, a first-class 'reference.'　But even if I could bring myself to show it to him, it would not mitigate the shock I must give him in answering his appeal for my return, his question as to why, with my London friend departed, I linger on in Brighton.

Distance, and the daily companionship of that remarkable old woman, bitter judge of all the earth, had mitigated the week's suspense.　But during the short homeward journey its place was taken by certainty increasing with every mile through the callously averted landscape.　Reaching at last the familiar lane, her own territory, she felt hope return, become, as she passed the little shaw where she and Charles, silenced by the trans-figuration of everything about them, had walked hand in hand, hope became certainty.　Here was the house.　Confidently she unlatched the evocative gate.　In a moment the open porch would receive her, then the hall, then the room where Charles awaited her.

But the porch was not open.　Strangely, at this early hour of a fine, warm evening, its outer door stood closed. Consulting its face, she read there a challenge to her right of entry so clear as to seem spoken aloud. Pushing wide the door, feeling as she did so the vanity of the movement that left her still alone in the open, she heard, sounding from behind the half-open inner door, the voice of Charles, an unknown voice, confidently raised:

'Alfrède! Ara you reddie?'

Alfrède. No longer Monsieur Alfrède. Thursday. *Lodge* evening. To which, inconceivably, Charles was going.

Here was the answer to her letter. Here too, the history of the past week. Charles was now fully at home with the Roscorlas. One of the family.

The door came open. There he stood. Unrecognizable. Unrecognizing.

'Ah, bonsoir, mademoiselle.' The words reached her from far away within the deeps of his sorrow.

Murmuring response as he moved aside to let her pass, she went forward into the hall. To be met almost at once by Rachel Mary come out to greet her with the smiling cordiality due to a paying guest. A moment later came Richard, overdoing the same manner.

At supper, no Charles, no Alfred. Throughout the meal Rachel Mary and Richard kept up their excessive attentiveness. Kept going, with endless questions, the topic of her time in Brighton, avoiding any kind of behaviour that would restore the sense of shared life that hitherto on her return from temporary absence had immediately made her feel she had not been away. Noticing the cold she had developed during the last few days, Rachel Mary suggested the wisdom of breakfast in bed.

Upstairs, she found that life had left her familiar room. Left all that its window looked out upon. Beckoned no longer from behind the curtain of the unknown future.

'You had much talk with him during this past week?'

'We had.' Can this hard-faced woman be Rachel Mary?

'He confided in us. Of course we could only tell him we knew *nothing* about you. Only that you came here from London with a nervous breakdown.'

'I see.'

'Now that we've come to know him, we all like him. He seems like one of my own brothers.' That break in her voice upon the last word tells a tale of which she is unaware. Consciously, she only knows that somewhere within the present tangle is the origin of the stop in her mind that should have prevented him coming here. Blaming herself, she now does her best to protect him: keeping me away from the breakfast table, sending him to Richard's farm for the day.

'I must tell you we cannot keep you here beyond the end of this week. We're having things done in the house, painting and decorating.'

The end of these planned speeches leaves her scanning my face, across which, if Amabel is right, will have passed the expression of all I feel, she will have seen my incredulous despair. Her face changes. Softens. We are back in our old relationship.

'You might, if you like, find quarters somewhere near at hand. Charles loves you. He has told me so. He said: "I love this woman. I cannot not love her."'

Dear, puzzled Rachel Mary. Once more, a compromise. If he wishes, we are to go on meeting. But not under her roof.

Sudden gay laughter, her irrepressible contribution to the Sunday dinner-time exchange, sweeps her into complete despair, though now more faintly than ever before. Again, as ever, the curtained future called to her to push forward through unbearable pain for what felt like the end of life.

Reaching her sitting-room, she heard his footsteps on the stairs. In a moment he was with her, weeping, with clasped hands.

'Miriam, Miriam, j'ai péché. J'ai péché contre l'amour.'

In silence she gazed at him. Everything now was in his hands; and he in the hands of the Roscarlos. Impossible to respond, to attempt in any way to influence the movement of his thought.

Sitting at his side on the alien settee she heard his voice, already, now that it had steadied, the voice of a stranger, quietly remark that the confession in her letter had given him pain; then saw his hands move as if to brush away a merely incidental obstruction. This pain then, he had accepted and disposed of. What more could there be? A pause. Then his voice, deep and trembling: 'Is your health goode? You have had, like myself, a nervous breakdown?'

Here then was the single, simple explanation: Gallic practicality? Aroused in him by the talk of the Roscorlas, combined to display all they could find in her disfavour: unsuitability for Quakerdom plus poor health the latter, for him, the more important? In either case, with his mind made up, impossible either to remind him of their mutual reservations in regard to certain aspects of Quakerism, or to explain, by way of self-recommendation, her carelessness, on first coming to D. H. to recover from the natural results of overwork plus recklessly late hours, of the technical term 'nervous breakdown' so applicable to his own condition of depression, persistent sleeplessness, inability to consume any but small quantities of carefully selected plain food, or to walk more than short distances. Impossible even to speak. Even through the very sound of her voice, wherein he had found whatever had made him say 'j'ai eu ton âme. Dans la voix je l'ai entendu' might cause him, even now to return to her from the journey taken during the last few days.

About to murmur a goodbye, she became aware of footsteps in the passage, of the door opening, of Richard, importantly genial, speaking from the doorway:

'Ah, there you are, Charles. M'sister has just asked me to remind you adult school meeting'll be a half-hour earlier this afternoon for the convenience of the friends due back at Groombridge by tea time.'

Entering her bedroom on that last evening, she stood for an

instant arrested, lost, while behind her the door shut gently to,
in the unexpected.   Joy flashed through her with the realization
that for a moment everything had been forgotten, nothing had
existed but the glad shock of the spectacle that had held her
eyes; the sight, along the lower edge of the window the servant
had carelessly left uncurtained, of the ivy leaves, outlined by
moonlight that drew their dark pattern more clearly than ever
she had seen it in colour-revealing daylight.

With incredulous gratitude she recognized as again and again
in the past she had done the power of light, seen signalling from
untold distance, to obliterate all but itself.   Banish all sense of
current misery and call her forward into the unknown lying ahead.

Only when she was nearly ready for bed, her preparations
made slowly by the light of the moon, her spirit cut away across
the meadows, across the moonlit pools of the marshes, did she
remember her door, still unlatched.   Reaching it she barely
resisted the impulse to hold it wide and sing out through the
passion-fevered darkness: 'Isn't this moonlight heavenly?'

'Mirry!'   The voice a smack; of friendly anger.   'That
Bedford College girl'll be back in this room next week.   You've
got to find another somewhere.   Where do you think of going?'

'*Anywhere*.   Don't care.'

'Shall I find you one?   Somewhere near by?'

'If you like.   So long as it's an attic at not more than seven-
and-six the week, and no other lodgers in the house.'

The next day she was telling me I must at least see, before
moving in, the room she had taken.

'Why?'

'Because you *must*.   Come along, I'll show you where it is.'

Off the main road.   Sequestered short terrace of narrow
little four-storeyed stone houses, Regency; entered by a dividing
passage where hollyhocks look up above grey stone walls.
Somewhere the sound, through an open window, of a piano:
firm hands skilfully pounding out the final complete crescendo
of the Chopin ballade that welcomed me in Oberland.

Knocking on the blistered front door produced no result.

Yet voices sounded from the open basement window. Laughter, led by the voice of a young man, curiously *smoothed* voice, neither weak nor strong, urbanely mirthful—satirical. A second hammering brings to the door a man, hurried being who gives one glance and vanishes. The next moment the owner of the voice stands there, the host of the basement party, tall skeleton in tattered garments compelled to elegance by his bearing, regretting in courteously thoughtful voice, while dark hazel-brown eyes look through me into space, the absence of the landlady, and offering to give a message. Clearly a lodger, unconfessed by Mrs Gay.

Yet at the very moment of reproaching Mrs Gay for conceal-ing the presence of another lodger in the house, there stole over me, as I stood by the wide window of this sunlit top-back room and saw for the first time, just beyond the leafage of the house-high lime tree, easeful carelessness in regard to the rest of the house. Far away, invisible, inaudible, on first floor and base-ment are the Gays and their family. In the very room where she allowed that weird artist to entertain his guests, I am blessedly to have a solitary breakfast for only half a crown added to my rent.

Affection there was, within the sound of her hearty laughter as she disposed of him: ''*Im?* You needn't count '*im*. Couldn't have a nicer man in the house. A gentleman, Mr Noble is, if ever there was one. And quiet, well you'd never know he was in the house. Out, he is, too, most of the time. Comes in late; or early you might call it. Shuts the front door without a sound, turns out the gas in the passage and goes upstairs as light as a feather.' To that second-floor front room, the prize room of Regency houses, with long windows lace-curtained right across.

No one in the other room of this top floor. The garden, its washing lines, ash-heap and dustbins invisible from where I sit alone with the sky, the lime tree and the tops of those poplars pointing up in the next garden.

Solitude. Secure. Filled each morning with treasure

undamaged by compulsory interchange. Every distance a
clear perspective. Why say distance *lends* enchantment?
Each vista demands, for portrayal, absence from current life,
contemplation, a long journey. Slower this morning, more
difficult, because of that meeting with Mrs Gay. Only for a
minute or two, but conserving much more than time. Yet I
had to hand over that crumpled pawn ticket.

'Oh, my goodness! *Isn't* it a pity? That was a lovely pair
of boots they sent him from home. He's been flapping about
in an old pair of evening slippers with one sole loose.'

She likes that weird young man. Is genuinely sorry for him.

Pawn ticket just inside the front door. Dropped there last
night, or in the small hours of this morning. Breakfast tray,
everything quite cold, on the table outside his door. An
undisturbing presence. Easy to avoid. Existing for me only
as the sound of that strange voice, not strong, not weak,
unassertive, yet confidently vibrant with a kind of awareness
unknown to me, yet already associating itself with this corner
of St John's Wood that inexplicably begins to offer itself as my
native heath. Yet every place I have stayed in, at home and
abroad, has sooner or later so offered itself, but none with just
this indefinable quality. Here, the very sunlight, compared
with the sunlight along the main roads, seems more mellow and
leisurely. In the brief local roadways and odd passages people
go about as if at home, at ease. Like that man farther down the
terrace coming out unconcernedly in a plaster-smirched overall
from the little door in that tumble-down bit of fencing backed
by untrimmed shrubberies hiding all but the battered roofing of
what must be a studio. Above the passageway alongside the
sculptor's studio, some large room whence daily the tremendous
last movement of Chopin's last sonata encompasses me. Joining
forces with my silent lime tree it sets aside all personal problems.
Abolishes, so long as one is alone, as completely did the sudden
spectacle of those moonlit ivy leaves when I entered my bedroom on that last night at D. H. two years ago, even tragedy.

Only when I am with others does my sense of isolation return.
To last, if they are right who declare that the state of being
deeply in love endures for exactly five years, for exactly another

three. Until this autumn of 1915, I shall still be alone with Charles. Still feel sure when I am writing, a loneliness that now may encircle the rest of my life.

While I write, everything vanishes but what I contemplate. The whole of what is called 'the past' is with me, seen anew, vividly. No, Schiller, the past does not stand 'being still.' It moves, growing with one's growth. Contemplation is adventure into discovery; reality. What is called 'creation' imaginative transformation, fantasy, invention, is only based upon reality. Poetic description a half-truth? Can anything produced by man be called 'creation'? The incense-burners do not seem to know that in acclaiming what they call 'a work of genius' they are recognizing what is potentially within themselves. If it were not, they would not recognize it. Fully to recognize, one must be alone. Away in the farthest reaches of one's being. As one can richly be, even with others, provided they have no claims. Provided one is neither guest nor host. With others on neutral territory, where one can forget one is there, and be everywhere. Hence, for me, the charm of that Eustace Miles place. Unique amongst cheap restaurants, most of whose customers don't seem to be fully present, seem, even in the evening, just food consumers. All day the place awaits me. Gives me the long ramble from suburb to centre, sure of the welcome of a spacious interior well filled but never crowded. Sure of a seat in some corner where, after the queer, well-balanced meal comfortingly independent of slaughter-houses, I can sit within the differently nourishing variations of the assembled company, reading as receptively as if I were alone, yet feeling one even with that woman who sat at my table last night eye downcast in meditation, breathing out now and again her Buddhistic O—m. Then, at closing time wandering home by a different route, circuitous, to sleep my way into the dawn of tomorrow.

Available, not too weary, not too far off, Jan, glad to be helped with her translation of Strindberg. Still wanting me to meet that journalist who only wants to meet me because he admires Hypo more than any present-day writer. Further off, but still accessible, Amabel.

Haunting each thought of her as Mrs Michael Shatov, a variety of moments, some of them adding up to what seems to be alienation, one, bringing to me an immortal desolation together with insight into her current development. Foremost between the two of us is that talk on the first morning of my visit after the arrival of Paul whose promised birth had brought 'all of bliss to Mike and me.' Talk that soon showed itself to be, for Amabel, a more than welcome opportunity for throwing out, casually, with eyes turned away to glance inquiringly through the window as if attracted thither by something of immediate interest, statements intended to show me myself as Michael now saw me, or as she would like me to believe he saw me: a deluded female who admired Emerson and supported the suffrage movement. Her 'Mike has done with Emerson. We both find him trite' soon led, perhaps because my face will have betrayed a blend of incredulity and consternation, to 'Marriage, and Paul, have swept away all my interest in votes for women,' and, before I could frame my reminder of the large proportion of wives and mothers amongst the active suffrage workers, she was on her feet bringing the sitting to an end in the manner of a busy, responsible housewife disposing of an amiably cherished young visitor saying: '*Well*, my poppet,' and going on to suggest the disposal of my morning.

Yet all such moments, since she knew how thankfully I had given Michael into her hands, surprise me with their continuous suggestion of successful rivalry; while still the essence of our relationship remains untouched. Still we remain what we were to each other when first we met. Something of the inexpressible quality of our relationship revealed itself in that moment she did not share, the moment of finding the baby Paul lying asleep in his long robe in the sitting-room, gathering him up, and being astonished to feel, as soon as he lay folded, still asleep, against my body, the complete stilling of every one of my competing urgencies. Freedom. Often I had held babes in my arms: Harriett's, Sally's, and many others. But never with that sense of perfect serenity. If Jean's marriage with Joe Davenport brought her a child, should I feel, in holding it, that same sense of fulfilment?